THE SAPPHIRE HEART

THREE SCRIBES

First Edition: October 2025

ISBNs:
979-8-9988241-0-4 (hardcover)
979-8-9988241-1-1 (trade paperback)
979-8-9988241-2-8 (ebook)

WHAT OTHERS ARE SAYING

"Intricate worldbuilding and complicated heroes make for a deliciously satisfying fantasy epic." —*Kirkus Reviews*

"This book is a stunning piece of epic fantasy... The world-building is incredible... full of history and magic... I couldn't stop reading. It's the kind of book that stays with you even after you finish the last page. I cannot wait for the second..." — Jude (Crafty Goblin), *Out & About* blog

"The Sapphire Heart is a(n) incredible epic fantasy read. If you love The Fellowship of the Ring or even Frieren, I think you will enjoy this story... There's lots of world building and lore ... lots of [lovable] and interesting characters... the plot/story is compelling... I can't wait to see what happens in the next book."
— Rachel, Netgalley Reviewer

"I was hooked pretty much by the first page... The authors have packed so many details into this world that I know I can close my eyes and ... see absolutely every single thing. The planning... must have taken ages. The same can be said about the characters, there was a spectacular mix of

them... This is a must for all fantasy lovers... (and) is going to be one of my books of 2025. I just hope there isn't a long wait for the second book."
— Sarah, *Sarah Reads* blog

"I could not put this one down from start to finish. I wouldn't want to spoil anything but if you love a good epic fantasy than this is one you won't want to miss... Told with an amazing narrative voice, with a diverse and varied cast of characters and believable world and storyline, this is a must read."
–Siobhan, *What You Tolkien About* blog

For those who dream the future and thereby change the world.

Six Dragons Make a World

The first gave his heart for he was kind.
The second gave his will for he was fierce.
The third gave her tears for she was just.
The fourth gave her breath for she was pure.
The fifth gave his thought for he was wise.
The sixth gave her soul for she was love.

Old Mother's Tales —(Traditional)

And So It Begins...

...a new eryn of renewal, with all the promise and hope that attends the entry of a fated Erynvor into the Eolemaran realm. Will this be the one true Uniter? The All pray it is so.

Eolemar, herself an Entity, though not often thought of as such except by her disciples, trumpeted the arrival to the farthest hills, a clarion cry to the seers and the seekers and the sages who can interpret her blustering leaves and thrumming stones—Hear and rejoice all who live upon my breast. A new Erynvor has arrived to lead us from Destruction to Revival.

Even so, we who participated with the One Above All in the founding of the worlds, fear that the corrupting avarice of the Souls of Noble Beginning will arise again. Yea, the remnants of those dark days can yet be seen in the blights and banes of this present time.

Thus, we weep for this Erynvor, as we did for those souls who came before, each assuming the crushing mantle of Restoration. Who better than we who have seen everything could understand the peril this Erynvor faces? Resurrecting a perfected world from imperfect shards is the journey of a thousand dangers and a million snares. Indeed, it has been the undoing of ten previous aspirants.

Hence, we watch with narrowed eyes and shielded hearts, fully aware of the commitment required to accomplish this singular feat. It is not for us to say whether this eleventh Erynvor will succeed or fail. It is only for us to wait and preserve the Way.

We, the Elect, have spoken.

CHAPTER ONE
ORU FEN

Why do the thoughts that come in the darkest hours weigh heaviest upon the heart?

The Wycche had been here before, of course. Many times. The thoughts had come before too, like pernicious birds swooping down from the shadowy corners of her mind, reminding her that failure would be the end of everything. She shooed the bird-thoughts back to their hiding places and prepared to cast her soul once again into the hidden realm of thought and dream, that other world called Oru Fen.

She settled back against the upholstered chaise, the soft sigh of crisp satin pressing worn velvet a momentary distraction as her arms folded across her midsection, her thoughts ticking through the meditative routine that would unlock her mortal flesh and allow her essence to ascend into the unseen. Her lungs filled with the stale air of the lightless chamber even as her soul separated from her body, walking forth down an unfurling starshine pathway leading into a world as ancient as Eolemar itself.

It was a realm the Wycche knew well. She, like all her fellow Shadowen, regularly walked its twilight corridors. A place of neither day nor night, time nor memory, this adjunct plane to the physical world was accessible to all but understood by few, a fourth dimension where the Wycche was a master and her wraithwolf was a king.

Her gaze fastened on the fogged horizon, determination honing her thoughts to daggers. She had to get it right this time.

A shadow-dark wolf materialized from the haze and issued a low growl, his lips curling back to expose his ancient teeth. The Wycche spun toward him, not in fear but in welcome for this was her ally, the wraithwolf called Venge.

A flick of the wrist and Venge lowered his brutish head then bent his right foreleg. A second flick and the wolf stood, his ravening eyes locking onto hers. A roiling cloud of darkness descended upon the wraithwolf's lanky frame before coalescing into a set of deadblack armor that rendered him nearly invisible. Only his head, tail, and feet were left exposed. His midnight eyes began to heat with the glow of war lust. A battle would soon be at hand, and he was ready.

The Wycche was also eager. Her vor—the transformative force inherent in every soul—was the strongest it had ever been, augmented by the Arcana of Vorie Supin. Night after night, with the assistance of Venge and other Malvisse wraithwolves like him, she had siphoned away countless dreamers' soul energies, melding their animating forces into her own. It had taken effort for her to harness the disparate vibrations, but the task had proven worthwhile, for she now wielded enough power to turn this present Erynvor away from the hated Elect and toward a future free of their interference and constructions.

She had thwarted similar pairs in the past, each time thinking she'd broken the Founding Dragons' hold, only to have yet another Erynvor come storming into the realm to start the cycle anew. This time would be different. Cold fire braced her will, invigorating her for what lay ahead. She must enter the sleeping Uniter's dreamsphere.

The Wycche had tried to enter this dreamer's sphere before but never with as much power as she held this night. Never with as much inner conviction or sense of rightness. But first, she and Venge would have to subdue the white wraithwolf, and that would not be easy. The Vorien was no fool, nor was he without his own sense of conviction. It would take cunning, craft, and determination to prevail. And an overwhelming amount of vor.

A thrill raced through her as she thrust her searching vorik—the manifestation of her vor energy—into the orusphere.

Venge stirred, his eyes fever bright, his desire ramping up her own heart rate. She sent him the mindwords he was waiting for.

Take me to her.

Essiant could feel it. A shift in the wind. A changing of shadows. A hint of song drifting from afar, faint but true. It was time for his night-ward to enter Oru Fen.

As a truth bearer, the white wraithwolf understood that no soul held more importance than another in the heart of Primeryn Vor, but for this cycle, his night-ward had undertaken a magnificent responsibility, and it was vital she become proficient in this realm where Shadowen walked and wraithwolves warred. He had prepared himself for the challenge, knowing he would be called upon many times during her formative period until she gained sufficient competence. He had pledged to make the necessary sacrifices—as had she—for the greater good. He intended to fulfill those vows.

Their pact with the Elect had been forged before descending from Inverna, she to take bodily form on Eolemar, he to take ethereal form in the dreamworld enjoining the two. She, an Erynvor by birthright but not yet by merit, was the eleventh soul to attempt the Great Restoration. He, her bonded wraithwolf, had pledged to guide and shape her dreams as she navigated that journey while also guarding her dreamdoor against those wishing to derange her course.

It was he who kept care of their collective memories, gathered through their many lives, beginning with the forming of the worlds by the Elect using their Great Wisdom and Gladsome Xha, to the Age of All Knowledge when men could fly powered solely by divine parambek and noble purpose, to the Great Destruction when corruption, greed, and selfish desire nearly destroyed the All. The memories, every emotion still attached, were seared into his and his night-ward's shared soul. Only the constraints of incarnation prevented her from being overwhelmed by the memories they carried within. He did not have that shield.

Instead, he had the advantage of Absolute Mind, the ability to view memory without the burden of emotion. A gift from Primeryn Vor for which he was grateful.

The wraithwolf readied himself, his white coat dazzling in the purple-gray twilight. Every muscle quivered in anticipation and his ears pricked high upon his head as he tuned into the vibrating orusphere of soulsongs flowing past. A shaft of starshine broke through the haze, striking his forehead and highlighting the crescent moon centered there, an outward symbol of the soul pact he had made long ago.

He sent a surge of vorik into the gloaming, an echolocation to find his night-ward's soulsong amongst the chirring buzz that filled his ears. The faint strains of her familiar song floated back. He immediately recognized the high soprano tone and bright timbre, its notes of longing and wanderlust a perfect match to his own. All other vibrations faded as he tuned into the one true song of his heart.

Before his night-ward could join him, he would have to time his soulsong perfectly. Too soon and she would not be able to quiet her tumultuous thoughts enough to get beyond the dreamless sleep of the uneasy mind. Too long and sleep would evade her entirely.

Essiant closed his eyes and breathed deep the misty coolness of Oru Fen, focusing on their connection until he could feel all that his ward was feeling, could think all that she was thinking. He waited for the moment when her waking mind released its hold to howl his soulsong into the dusky sky and call her into his realm.

Her soulsong answered with a crescendo of lilting notes. Essiant widened his stance and howled again, in unison with her this time, his tone matching hers beat for beat, their synchronic vibrato echoing across the misty fen.

In an instant she was there before him, resplendent in her ethereal form, her luminous eyes full of love. Their soulbond formed instantly, as it had done innumerable times in the past. His radiant fur brightened with Saska vorik, the special soul-level energy shared between a wraithwolf and its night-ward. The invisible barrier that separated them while his night-ward was awake had yielded to the force of their combined Saska.

Her dreamdoor assembled—an enormous construction of

crystalwood, chalumbra vine, and brunnestone—and he scanned it briefly. Tonight, she would be dreaming of the parambeks again, those power centers lost during the Great Destruction. It was good for her to do so. Soon she would begin her journey to resurrect the first of those ancient ruins and restore it to its original purpose as a vor attunement center. Meanwhile, Essiant would guard her sacred dreamdoor until she awakened, placing himself between it and those who would try to dissipate her lifeforce while she slept. It was a duty, but it was also his greatest joy.

Still, it was never easy. There were the Shadowen dreamwalkers to consider. Most were harmless, but there were those that practiced the wicked Arcana of Vorie Supin, using Malvisse wraithwolves to steal etheriant from unguarded souls. The Malvisse had lost their way long ago. To Essiant and all the wraithwolves of the Vorien League, the Malvisse were the bane of this otherwise peaceful plane, and he had been forced to battle them many times since this latest sojourn had begun.

Chief among these essence stealers was the one called the Wycche who, in tandem with her fearsome wraithwolf, were the strongest of the Shadowen lifeforce thieves. And well they should be, having existed in Oru Fen for time beyond time. Even now he could feel the cold chaos of the Wycche's energy in the orucon beneath his feet and with it, the dark swirl of her wolf's insatiable greed. She and her wraithwolf were already searching the realm for his night-ward's dreamsphere, each attempting to discern his ward's unique energy signature from the murk. So far, Essiant had deflected the duo, but those were only temporary evasions. The pair would not stop until his night-ward had either fulfilled her destiny or been driven back to Inverna in defeat.

Essiant grounded himself, his vorik emanating through his paws into the nebulous substrate until his night-ward's soul-key materialized, a golden glint hovering in the space between himself and his ward.

She patted his forehead and smiled before turning toward her dreamdoor. Essiant knew she would not remember this exchange in the waking world, but he cherished the moment no less. That touch said that she recalled their many sojourns together. That she felt their eternal bond and understood he had been created for her from the wholeness of her own soul. He longed for the time he could guide her through this mystical environ. When he could show her its marvelous secrets and terrifying shadows. Soon, that time would come, but not yet. Not this night.

The door closed and the stardust key inserted itself then turned, locking his ward's venerable soul inside the dreamsphere of her creation before removing itself and transmuting into a pendant Essiant would wear until his ward was ready to reunite with her slumbering body. He turned to keep watch, preparing for what he feared would come next.

Night after night his vigil had been disturbed by the Wycche and her Malvisse attempting to enter his night-ward's dreamsphere. And each night the vorik required to keep them at bay had increased. Essiant lowered his head, and breathed deep from the mists encircling him, drawing strength for the task ahead.

Beneath his paws, thought energy pinged through the orucon, an endless web he used to locate his adversary. It was a skill only the most adept wraithwolves possessed, this ability to divine individual energy strands within the interconnected weave of collective thought underpinning the realm. Another gift from Primeryn Vor for which he was grateful. Locating the Wycche and her wraithwolf would give him time to strategically strengthen his ward's dreamshield where it was needed rather than wasting vorik fortifying the entire sphere.

A return of his searching vorik indicated a dark presence looming to the east, but as soon as Essiant strengthened the dreamsphere's proximal shield, the orucon indicated the presence had shifted, then shifted again, its location drifting from place to place like smoke.

Within the presence Essiant sensed the two entities for whom he had prepared, splitting apart then reuniting then splitting apart again. He felt his energy draining as he countered their ever-shifting approach by moving vorik from one part of the dreamshield to another.

The pair charged, their combined forces slamming into the rear of the sphere where it was weakest. The shield gave way, a tear splitting up from its base. Essiant wove his vorik into the void, knitting it back together. Another tear opened and he directed his vorik into a plastering repair. His hackles rose. The pair were trying to deplete him before they made their final assault, dividing his attention to conquer their quarry.

Let them try.

Essiant flattened the shield, disguising his ward's dreamdoor behind a fog of astral gloom. To complete the illusion, he projected a dozen perfect replicas of the portal onto the surrounding plane, imbuing each with a spark of his night-ward's etheriant. Only he knew which of the doors was authentic and only he held its key.

He felt the pair converge once again, the wicked dreamwalker and her corrupt wraithwolf. Each footfall rattled his paws as they picked their way to the closest door, their suspicion a bristling carpet of pent energy beneath him. They stopped and turned in place, parsing the ethers. Essiant projected a wolf-shaped silhouette onto the nearby fog.

The deadblack-clad wraithwolf bared its teeth and sprang at the shadow-wolf while the Wycche shoved her hand through the miraged door. Both illusions disintegrated into wisping stardust. The wraithwolf keened while the Wycche's form twisted into furious cloud.

More doors sprang up, surrounding the Wycche and her wolf in a spiral of possibilities. Enraged, she launched a firebolt of vorik through the orucon but Essiant anticipated her, blasting a wave of counter-vorik through the same web to blunt her assault, his mind leaping ahead to what he must do. It was time to copy from their book and become like smoke.

He refocused, projecting wraithwolf-shaped thoughtforms upon the thresholds of the counterfeit doors. A swirl of mist here, a footfall there, a growl in the dark.

The pair's anger mounted as they tried again and again to fight wolves made of shadow, to enter dreamdoors made of shine. At last, they stilled, their rage a sharpening tension beneath Essiant's paws.

A sudden explosion—*BOOM*—and Essiant's carefully crafted illusion shattered.

Instinctively he spun then, leaping onto his hind legs, threw himself against his night-ward's dreamdoor, spreading himself as widely as possible to absorb the shock. His body vibrated violently as the vorik slammed into him, his thoughts blurring for an instant. How had the Wycche accumulated such a vast amount of vor? But he had little time to ponder as he materialized a set of stardust armor, preparing for the battle he knew must come.

The starshine armor settled upon Essiant's imposing physique, its brilliant light repelling all shadows while his opponent's dense armor condensed until it was almost beyond detection, a void of darkness consuming every scrap of energy around it. Essiant wasn't daunted. He knew that deadblack was strong but also thin, making it vulnerable to puncture by toothfang or claw. He also knew that deadblack maintained its power by siphoning etheriant from an opposing wraithwolf's armor.

He wouldn't let that happen.

Stardust was not without its advantages. Its pulsating light blinded those who spent their time in the dark and it radiated at a frequency that could reverse the power draw of deadblack if the wearer's vorik wasn't strong enough to maintain the void.

The two fully armored wolves circled, each waiting for the other to make the first move. Essiant recognized his opponent whose eyes glowed hot as new stars. He had felt the wraithwolf growing stronger with each nighttime encounter and knew it meant the Wycche's vor was also increasing. This night, the wraithwolf's deadblack was especially stout, a resolute vacuum that would be difficult to pierce.

The Malvisse went on the offensive, his mindwords accusing Essiant of cowardice and dereliction. It was a worthy trick, but Essiant didn't fall for it. He knew his sense of duty and desire to protect his night-ward would never waver. Taunting words from a Malvisse would not change that. His accuser was quite the opposite—a reprobate whose moral compass had been overridden long ago by its own debased ambition. Perhaps it was because this wraithwolf had spent so much time in this in-between plane, with its gray margins and foggy bogs. It had been an unnaturally long tenure that must surely have had its effects. Essiant doubted this wolf could even remember its noble beginnings, so far had it fallen since, but when faced with a wolf newly arrived from that golden realm of spirit, the self-loathing must come and with that, rage. Or perhaps it was pain that came writhing to the surface. Either way, this Malvisse seemed more committed to defeating Essiant's ward than even its wicked partner.

Essiant's mind shifted. Where was the Wycche? He knew to remain wary of her. Too many wolves had succumbed to her devious tricks, losing their night-ward's soul-key through either their own or their ward's foolishness. Once relieved of their sacred key, the hapless guardian was doomed to binding with the silver cords of Dysetheria, remaining so until released by their night-ward's enlightenment. It was a purgatory that often lasted a lifetime, and Essiant knew of far too many corded wraithwolves who were powerless to prevent the Wycche from entering their night-ward's dreamsphere and siphoning away their vital energy.

Then there were the ones that fell into a stupor, narcotized by some potion their night-ward had consumed. These wolves were in bondage of a different sort, and though it only lasted for one dream cycle, in that brief time, their night-ward was vulnerable to the Wycche's insatiable lust for etheriant. He suspected the Wycche was stealing energy from the night-wards of these compromised wraithwolves—a thought that revulsed him—and that, unless she was stopped, there would be no end to her insidious predations.

Essiant felt a rise in the dark wolf's fiery mood, equal parts anger and eagerness, but the Wycche's desperate desire to enter his night-ward's dreamsphere was his greater concern. He could feel a trap being set and knew it could be his undoing if he wasn't careful. He must rebuff the Malvisse while nullifying the Wycche's threat or risk the vitality of his night-ward's soul.

Essiant knew outright physicality would not win this fight. The deadblack was too strong. Instead, he would need to outwit his opponents. His night-ward's Spyrtt vor would provide the power to blunt the dark pair, while conserving his vor for future encounters. He formulated a plan, one he knew his ward would not approve. She abhorred manipulation in all its forms. His only comfort was the knowledge that the All would not be so judgmental of him using the tools at his disposal. The thought of her disapproval pained him, but he could see no other option.

In a white-hot thrust, he sent Spyrrt vorik out into the tangled web holding Oru Fen together, this time laying aside his innate soul defenses and opening himself up to his opponents' thoughts and desires. A foreign wantonness flooded his mind, and he sagged back, sickened. He could feel the Wycche's burning desire to control his night-ward along with an overwhelming rage that her chance was slipping away. Beyond lay eryns of self-aggrandizement and the bone-deep ache of a grief not spoken, all driving her to relentlessly destroy in the name of preservation. The revelation startled Essiant, nearly breaking the psychic bond. He forced his thoughts away from the snare of reason and concentrated on the task at hand.

Her wraithwolf lunged forward with a guttural snarl, its eyes narrowing to slits. It slashed its fangs toward Essiant in a bid to snatch energy from his stardust armor. Essiant dodged while simultaneously implanting an illusion in each of their minds. But not an illusion of his own creation. He knew not where it came from, but full force, he brought forth the borrowed memories in images that transferred from his soul into the minds to which he was connected. It was a channeling of something more profound than any previous thought or memory of his own. To the wolf, a recollection of its own glorious beginning as a newly created wraithwolf in a world of light and peace. To the Wycche, a vision of a wounded soul with mistaken intent, a shattered gray orb in pieces at her feet, a blinded Founding Dragon of the Realm intoning "We see you."

Instantly, the Wycche and her accomplice were gone, disappearing into the ethers. For this night, his ward was safe.

Exhausted and heartsick, Essiant felt a rumble beneath his paws as an ancient voice from somewhere far away yet deep inside pronounced, "It is time."

Warnings of a
Wraithwolf
(Excerpt One)

Only while the DREAMER sleeps, have I VOICE... Ggrrff... Their MINDwords ... ggrrff... these strange THOUGHT sounds... gggrrff... more WRONG than right... gggrrfff... but enough MAYBE... gggrrrfff... to bend your SMALL ideas... ggrrrff... toward TRUTH.

HARK!

KNOW that you see LITTLE... ggrrfff... and UNDERSTAND LESS... ggrrf... while WE see every THOUGHT thing... Ggrrff... TIME flees... ggrrrff... to RESTORE THERRA... gggrrff... FYRRE... ggrrf... AQUILLA... ggrrf... ATMOS... grrfff... SHADOWE... ggrrfff... SPYRTT.

HEED these words BEFORE it is too LATE.

–Collected and interpreted for the Most Exalted Monarch, Geldizian Rennesseau, by a scribe

CHAPTER TWO
AT AN END

Elorah Niav bai Calliaigh's gasp pierced the silence of her bedchamber as she shuddered awake. She reached into the satchel hanging from the corner post of her bed to pull out her Journal Imagini before the dream's details vanished from her mind.

Pushing back her chestnut curls to swipe away the sweat sheening her forehead, she gathered her Spyrrt vorik and channeled it through her outstretched palm, sending golden light onto the journal's cover until the black leather transformed into a nightscape of glittering stars. An aching nostalgia for something vast and wonderful swept over her as she opened the book and flipped through blank pages until she came to the one she wanted. Another shine of Spyrrt light, and the otherwise invisible writing darkened into black script. She scanned her notes, gleaned from a book she'd found hidden in the Academie Vorik's Libroir detailing the vorestone bedrocks of Eolemar. It seemed a vital detail if she was to make anything of her latest dream.

The richest store of brunnestone, the complement-stone of Therran vorik, lay beneath the fertile soils of Valenvia and the surrounding Basin. Other vorestones had their concentrations in more distant places, but it was brunnestone that underlaid the deep-brown soils of her homeland. She came again to the question she had asked herself so many times.

Why, with so much Therran vorestone beneath and so much fertile loam above, were the crops dwindling year upon year? All seven districts, including her family's, the District Calliaigh, had felt the effects. No longer were Therran voricians able to imbue the barleycorn and spelt and trickle-rye fields with the vitality of plenty they'd bestowed in generations past, and the harvests were suffering greatly because of it.

The perplexing decline had been the source of much unrest within the Valenvian Council. Though Elorah took little interest in the goings-on of that collection of busybodies, she did take a keen interest in the welfare of the Caeldish people as a whole and it was clear most were suffering from the steady losses to their livelihoods.

She turned to a page near the back and, using the tip of one glowing finger, recorded her recollection of last night's dream:

Physio: Perspiring, heart racing, foreboding

Memories: Gathering plants in the forest, looking for one with the face of a wolf. A fantastic tree of light, more colorful than a rainbow and brighter than the sun, sprang up from the forest floor, growing until it was larger than a mountain. A wind blew in a black fog, dulling the tree's shine. A branch broke free and I caught it. It glowed in my hands until I could see nothing but its light while somewhere, wolves growled and snapped their teeth. Next, I was standing on the same flat-topped mountain as always, near the same enormous structure pulsing with blue light. Then I heard a voice shout Restore the five to revive the one!

Analysis: Another call to action, but to do what? Still unclear...

Elorah read what she'd written, the imagery from the dream returning to her mind. *What did it mean?* The magnificent tree felt familiar, as if she had seen it many times, although she had no waking recollection of it. Was it one of the parambeks? She felt sure the flat-topped mountain with the pulsing blue-light structure she'd dreamed of countless times was one. Was the tree another?

She'd heard of parambeks—the synergistic energy centers the

Ancients had used to enable emvors and even commoners to elevate and enhance their innate vorik—but always in the context that the stories were myth, old mother's tales told to wide-eyed children with no basis in fact. And yet, her heart told her differently. She'd dreamed of other such places, of other wondrous structures that vibrated with vorik energy, from the time she was small, and every time, she'd felt as if she were being called to search for the fabled monoliths. But why? The answers always seemed just beyond her grasp.

The sounds of wolves had become more common too, leaving her unsettled when she awoke. She traced a finger over the riddle, pondering its meaning. The voice had been insistent. Commanding.

Restore the five to revive the one.

What did it mean? A clatter from the hallway interrupted her thoughts.

She withdrew her vor and shoved the journal back into the satchel amongst the rest of her most precious things—elemental vorestones, a box of luminae needles, a tenderwood shilk, a forlian earbob, a black hallett scrying stone, packets of healing herbs, and her vergrize, the personal lorebook she'd begun when she first arrived at the Academie Vorik at the age of ten. She'd since compiled a hand's width of pages containing careful notations and sketches during the ten annums she'd spent under the tutelage of highly skilled Therran emvors, including the Academie's own headmistress, Kearyn Malenvie. Tomorrow, if her testing went well, Elorah would go from Apogent to colleague, with a coveted Master Emvor pin to show for her efforts.

As she looked back, her time at the Academie had been both long and short, in that strange way that time can unfold and then fold back upon itself when the mind retrieves its memories. At times it felt as though it would never end and yet now, with practicums and graduation fast approaching, it seemed as if the annums had gone by in a blink.

She'd felt a kinship with all her instructors, but her fondest memories were not of time spent in the classroom but rather of the quiet moments spent with the Academie's chief gardener, Silvi, a wizened woman with long, silver-white braids that framed a creased face as brown as a spent leaf and a toothy smile that flashed bright when something amused her.

Elorah suspected that Silvi was not the gardener's given name, for Wandering Silvi was a nondescript ground-rambling vine with potent healing properties. It would be like Silvi to take on the name of a humble plant with hidden power. Elorah was sure there was a lesson in that, as there was in nearly everything the gardener did.

It was Silvi who'd shown Elorah the art of Viexha, lessons that had captivated her imagination. Viexha, as she understood it, was the creation of vorik wholly out of one's own self-belief in unity with the perfect energy of the All, without the use of tools or tradeskill. Silvi had once called it the gift of the Ancients, but when Elorah pressed her to elaborate, the gardener had simply smiled and looked to the sky. Elorah longed to command Veixha as effortlessly as Silvi. In fact, the idea was nearly an obsession, so often did she dwell upon it. That and her desire to search for the parambeks occupied most of her free time, although she admitted this to no one.

She never asked about Silvi's past, and Silvi never volunteered anything in that regard. Elorah wasn't concerned with such matters anyway. It was Silvi's incredible knack for innovation and Veixha that Elorah admired because it was so opposite to the static, tightly controlled vorecraft she had learned at the Academie. Yes, the Academie had taught her how to efficiently harness vorik and perfectly modulate its deployment, but she found its precision incredibly boring. Academie vorik was powerful, but it was also predictable, especially to other Academie-trained emvors. Elorah couldn't help feeling she'd spent half her life learning party tricks rather than real-world skills.

Things were different with Silvi. With her, Elorah was free to try new things, to embellish and invent, because Silvi accepted her without preconception or prejudice. She encouraged originality, expected it even. The only rule was that Elorah could not use Viexha to create or destroy. It could only be used to transform.

Elorah cared not that Silvi had led an "interesting" life. The rumors that she was a Shadowen in hiding, rather than repelling Elorah as it did most of the Academie's students and staff, only intrigued her more. Here was someone who lived life without bending the knee to societal pressures. Elorah could only aspire to be so strong. Silvi's mind was another marvel, as were her knobbly, calloused hands at once gentle and strong, the tools of an artist and a sage whom Elorah admired enormously.

She reached back into her satchel, her fingers feeling for the tin of soothesalve she'd prepared. With the stress of studying for exams as well as preparing to return home for the annual Festival of the Urslan Sisters —an event more important than ever with the poor harvests—she'd nearly forgotten to deliver the gift to her mentor. It was a small token in comparison to all that Silvi had given her, but she felt a happy satisfaction knowing she could bring some comfort to the older woman, if only for a little while.

It was still early, and Elorah guessed she would find Silvi in one of the examination gardens, making last-minute preparations for the testing tomorrow.

Elorah wasn't looking forward to the practicums, not because of the testing but because she knew Aikin would be there, showing off in his usual ham-fisted manner. In all the time she'd known him, Aikin Froihg dai Bairrtraigh had never missed a chance to show off his prodigious Therran talents, and tomorrow, with the whole Therran section of the Academie watching, she knew he wouldn't be able to resist the opportunity to impress.

Elorah wondered if Silvi would attend. She hoped the gardener would but knew it was unlikely. Elorah had never seen Silvi at any of the previous examinations. Then again, perhaps that was best. Elorah would feel even more nervous if Silvi was there.

Her musings were cut short by a knock on her door.

"Elorah? Are you there?"

She recognized the lyrical southland accent of her closest friend, Mierrle Jazh. She stashed her satchel before opening the door.

Mierrle looked a shadow of her usual self, her wavy, deep-brunette hair sitting like a mop atop her oval face, her fire-gold complexion dull as old brass. She bit her lower lip, her long fingers worrying creases into the blue silk of her tunic.

"Is something wrong?" Elorah asked, ushering her inside.

"I don't think I can do it." Mierrle's sea-green eyes brimmed as she slumped into a side chair and put her head in her hands.

"You can do anything you put your mind to," Elorah said, embracing her friend's hunched shoulders.

"No, I can't. I've tried, but it's no use. I'm going to fail tomorrow. I know it. My family has such high hopes, and it's all going to be ruined. How can I tell my father that after ten annums at the most esteemed school of vorik in all the world, I can only manage the most basic water manipulations. My whole family is depending on me, and I'm going to let them down."

"It can't be as bad as all that. What are you having trouble with? Maybe I can help."

Mierrle shook her head, dismissing the idea. "I'm supposed to go home after the testing tomorrow, but how can I? My family has so many expectations and plans. Water is everything to us. It's our livelihood. It's our history. It's our destiny. We've been water merchants since the day the Great One created it." Mierrle stood and waved a cupped hand toward the ceiling. *'Viesh alco Jazh evlea alco emlea'...'* Her voice trailed away, and Elorah gave her a quizzical look. "It means 'Water follows the Jazh as night follows the day'. How many times did I hear that when I was young? Everyone said it was so. But not for me..." She paused, her eyebrows drawing together. "It isn't only my family I'm letting down. All the Wahzim people depend on the Jazh to find them water. It's our trade, but it's also our duty." She picked at a raveling on the sleeve of her tunic. "It wasn't always so difficult. When my grandparents were young, the water flowed in underground rivers as wide as a village. My noni and popi told me the stories, how the water would leap from the ground into the jugs. But something happened when my parents were young. The water began to disappear. Where there had been rivers, there were only streams and where there had been streams there were only trickles. So, they sent me here to learn the ways of water, to find where it's gone and how to bring it back. If I show up without a pin, they'll know I've failed. That all they'd hoped for is gone. I couldn't stand the shame of it."

Family expectation was something Elorah understood well. Her mother made no secret of what she expected from Elorah—to become a Therran emvor of the highest order, marry into a Caeldish family of prominence and large fortune, become a respected Eldra on the Valenvian Council, preserve and enhance the Niav name, produce robust, exceptional children, honor and serve the Urslan Sisters... The list seemed endless, and Elorah was often torn between feeling she would never measure up and feeling that if she did, she could never stand it. The idea of settling down to a quiet Caeldish life of monotony felt like a betrayal of all her youthful dreams, a turning away from the very thing that made her who she was.

A thought struck.

"What if you came home with me for the Festival of the Urslan Sisters? My family is hosting, and we'll have to arrange for water, along with about a thousand other details. You and I can practice, and I can keep my mother happy at the same time."

"But you're Therran. How can you help me learn Aquillan vorik?"

"I have an idea," Elorah replied, her mind shifting to what Silvi had taught her of Viexha.

"What will I tell my family?"

"Tell them you're helping a friend. Surely, they wouldn't object to that. It will only be for a few days, and then we can arrange for you to return home."

Mierrle's teary eyes shifted from Elorah to the window then back again. "But I still would not have a pin."

"You would have something better."

"What is better than a pin?"

"Belief."

Mierrle considered this for a moment before asking, "What is this Urslan Sisters Festival?"

"It's the time we Caeldish come together to honor our protectors and ask them to bless our crops."

"Who are these Sisters?"

"Twin bears who live amongst the stars and keep watch over Valenvia." Elorah could see her explanation wasn't helping. She didn't know why she felt compelled to go on—she didn't believe most of it herself—but the words continued to flow. "It's Caeldish legend. Some say it's nonsense, but no one wants to take the chance of not honoring the Urslan and dooming their crops, so every New Spring, we come together, all the clans and the bards and the faldings, to celebrate the past gifts of the Sisters and pledge our faith to them once again."

Mierrle looked doubtful. "Wouldn't I be out of place? I don't exactly look like..." She brushed a hand toward her arm.

Elorah shook her head, spreading her bronzy arms wide. "I don't look like everyone either. Besides, marans from all over come to the festival to sell at the marketplace." She lowered her voice. "Even a few Shadowen fortunetellers."

Mierrle perked up. "Maybe they could tell me what my future holds."

Elorah shrugged. "If you believe in that sort of thing."

"You don't?"

"I'm not saying that but wolflore, eternal night, dreamwalking, it's all a bit, I don't know–"

A male voice interrupted, "Weird."

Aikin Froigh dai Bairrtraigh stood in the open doorway, his handsome, chiseled features hardened into an expression of disgust. Nicknamed the golden son, he looked every bit the part with his bright-copper hair, statuesque build, and deep brown eyes.

Elorah's set jaw and narrowed eyes betrayed her annoyance. "Is there something you wanted?"

He turned to Mierrle, ignoring the question. "Have we met?"

Mierrle's cheeks pinked as she ducked her head. "Yes," she mumbled. "Several times."

"Forgive me for not recalling." He turned back toward Elorah. "I've taken the liberty of asking Fyndd to bring you a horse when he brings mine."

"That's very kind but entirely unnecessary. I've already made arrangements. Why is Fyndd coming here, anyway? Isn't he still with the Bards?"

"Apparently, the Most Exalted Blasphemer has hired his troupe to spread the word about our festival. As if she has any right. Fyndd is none too happy, I can tell you. If I had my way, outsiders wouldn't be allowed anywhere near the sacred grounds. My father says all this mixing and mingling will be our ruination."

"Yes, well, your father isn't known for being progressive. Maybe we can set an example. Surely that would be a good thing."

"Your piety is admirable, but you speak of what you do not understand. Without my father and men like him, the Ways would be lost forever. These past ten annums, Her Most Exhausting has done nothing to help and plenty to harm our people. Give her another ten, and she'll have erased what's left of our traditions and have them replaced with her Iellian monarchist nonsense."

"Men like your father are too stuck in the past to see what the future could be."

"And you think Zephyrria Rennesseau from her palace in the airy peaks is creating a future for *us*? She needs our farms, our labor, and our loyalty. We're nothing but tools in the grand design of her Iellian revival. She won't be satisfied until she's declared monarch of the entire Basin, including Valenvia. That's why we must fight, with everything we have, or all that we know, and love will be lost.

"You make too much of things," Elorah countered. "Are we not better able to conduct our lives than we were before she offered her protection? Did she not push the Drasgor back to their northern homeland when they invaded?"

"One skirmish on the northern border with a renegade band of barbarians," he said. "It's hardly the great victory certain clans make it out to be. And if those savages had reached the Basin, we could have turned them back ourselves. We didn't need any of her most exalted meddling."

"But you can't know that," Elorah said. "And what of the maraneaters to the south? Do you think we are in no danger from them?"

"Old wives tales made up to scare children into their beds at night," Aikin scoffed. "I'm talking about something real, an invasion happening right before our eyes, while we stand around like bullied sheep letting everything that matters, everything that says we're Caeldish, get taken away. We're sliding tail-first into servitude, and not lifting a finger to stop it. Do you think we'll continue as before once Her Most Egregious seizes permanent control? She has ambitions and plans for our lands, and the means to put those plans into action. I have it on good authority she's reviving the Arcana of Vorie Atmos, and has offered a chest of gold to the first scholar who can find and translate the ancient texts on the secrets of flight. They say she even has a stable of trained gryphons for use by the High Hells. The High Iellian Order of Enforcement," he added for Mierrle's benefit.

Elorah cut her piercing amber-and-blue flecked eyes from Mierrle to Aikin before shaking her head. "Trained gryphons? Now I know you're not being serious."

"Oh, but I am. Deadly serious. Can you imagine how the High Hells could terrorize our people with those?" he said, his baritone voice rising an octave.

Elorah shuddered. She'd never seen a gryphon, but she'd read about the fearsome beasts that lived on the craggy ridges of the Blackshales, the mountains bordering Valenvia along its eastern and northern borders. Her grandmama, Aleea Chrysolan, had once confided that her father, Rylan, had escaped an encounter with one bearing a jagged scar upon his thigh and a hair-raising story. Grandmama had said it proudly, for he was her son after all and not many lived to tell such tales but for Elorah it was like hearing about a stranger.

She'd never met her father. By the time she was born, he was three moons gone on a crystalwood gather to the wildlands of Whitemond. And although Elorah wished it were not so, she knew that despite her mother praying daily to the Urslan Sisters and tending his elaborate shrine, he was never coming back. She'd seen him in his golden home beyond the clouds when she was three. Her mother's reaction to the news had been swift and severe. Novah Niav bai Calliaigh had rebuked Elorah in the strongest terms and forbade her from ever speaking of such things again, deeply impressing upon her to keep her unwelcome visions to herself.

"I hope you're not planning on traveling back alone. Fynnd says the High Hells are edgier than usual because of all the rabble coming into the Basin for the festival. They've set up checkpoints on the high roads," Aikin said.

"Then we'll take one of the low roads," Elorah said.

"That will take twice as long, and there's all manner of bears and wolves in those woods, not to mention sneakthieves trying to avoid the checkpoints."

"We must go home some way," Elorah said, exasperated.

"Then use my horse. She's fleet of foot and a good jumper. Or better yet, allow me to escort you."

Elorah paused, searching for an answer. She was touched by his concern, but she didn't want to give him the idea she needed a guardian.

"Could I borrow your horse?" Mierrle asked, her voice soft.

Aikin pivoted toward her. "Sorry?"

"Could I borrow your horse?" she repeated, her voice only slightly louder. "My father can pay you."

Aikin frowned. "I'd hoped... What I mean to say is, this mare's a bit of a handful. She's not suitable for an inexperienced rider."

Elorah tried to warn Mierrle off with a look, but her friend's attention was only on Aikin.

"Do you know of any horses that would be suitable?" Mierrle murmured.

"We're taking Samm," Elorah said. "He's a gentle old plodder with a strong back. We can ride double since it's not too far."

"Why would you want to ride that old plow horse when you could ride one of the finest mares my family's stable has ever produced?"

"I like riding Samm and anyway, he's needed back home for planting."

"And you're taking... I'm sorry, what was your name again?"

"Mierrle Jazh."

"You're taking Maiss Jazh where exactly?"

"To the Festival. With me. As my guest."

"Your clan knows this?" Aikin asked, his eyebrows arching in surprise.

"I'm sure they'll welcome the help." Elorah nodded emphatically at Mierrle.

"What do you need? I can get you help." Aikin stepped forward, his expression earnest.

"Water," Mierrle chirped.

Elorah sighed and rolled her eyes. *Don't tell him that.*

Aikin furrowed his brow. "Let me see what I can do," he said, turning on his heel.

"That's really not necessary," Elorah replied.

But it was too late. He was already gone.

CHAPTER THREE
FLIGHT OR FIGHT

Brynz Alleu pressed her tongue against the roof of her mouth and whistled.

A screeching cry followed by the clatter of talons scraping stone echoed back from the depths of a massive enclosure constructed from stout iron bars and woven-iron mesh. It was a cage built for a beast. A beast running straight at her.

She stood a few steps inside the keeper's door, her black leather boots planted on the graystone floor, her back ramrod straight beneath her sky-blue training leathers and dark blue undertunic. She reached into a wooden bucket next to her boot and pulled a dead hare out by its oversized ears, holding it so the gryphling galumphing toward her could see it dangling from her fist.

The gryphling flapped his molting wings, the emerging silver-blue feathers swishing in the thin, mountain air. His black-scute front legs lifted slightly before his taloned feet settled again.

Brynz used the training rod clutched in her other hand to tap the ridge of each wing, whistling two short blasts. "Settle," she said in a low, even tone. "Settle, Zell."

The gryphling shook his head and folded his wings against his body, the down clinging between his half-grown feathers fluffing out for a moment. Soon, the Cyrulean Blue gryphling would gain his adult plumage and look every bit the part of the majestic Iellian mascot but while he went through his juvenal molt, he looked as ragged and rotten as molded bread. His dark gray skin glowered like a malignancy beneath his bedraggled hatchling down and juvenal plumage. His hindquarters were also changing, the blue-gray dapples of his hatchling fur sloughing away in patches to make way for the sleek silver fur of adulthood.

Unlike the common Tawny Gryphon found throughout the highlands, this gryphling was of a distinctive breed found primarily on the northern face of Cyrulian Kalt, a craggy spire at the northern tip of the Blackshale Mountains. Soon the gryphon would glisten and shine, his body and wings a bright silver-blue; his hind paws, ear tufts, and tail a slaty gray; his front legs and beak a shiny black. Already he had the azurite stare said to pierce the heart if one wasn't careful. At this moment, however, it was hard to see beyond the scruffy awkwardness to the fierce beauty sure to come.

Brynz gave a sharp, high whistle and tossed the hare. The gryphling caught it with the talons of one banded front foot, tore it in half with his black hooked beak, then gulped it down in two swallows.

The gryphling had received his first set of leg bands as soon as he'd clawed his way out of his leathery egg. She'd done it herself, clicking the bands into place before the hatchling wobbled to his feet. *You are like me, and I am like you. We are together, one and the same.* Over and over, she'd repeated the words as she'd stared into the hatchling's blue-gray eyes—so like her own—while he blinked and squawked and stretched wings matted down with wet fuzz. She would be his leader, and he would be her charge. She would be his mentor, and he would be her friend. They would be one together. She would make sure of it this time.

Brynz rubbed a hand against her forearm, rough with itchy, red skin beneath the stiff leather armguard she wore. The bane of her existence, these scaly red patches that erupted on her arms and her legs, and, during the windy season, her neck and forehead and cheeks. This chapping that marked her out as different had been her constant companion for as long as she could remember and had made life a hard road full of self-loathing and loneliness. It was only when she was with the falcons, or the horses, or the gryphons that she could be herself, far away from the pitying stares and low-breathed jeers that inevitably came when she mixed with her own kind.

"Careful, Brynz," said a deep male voice behind her. "His eye's on the bucket."

She nodded and swept the training rod in front to draw away the gryphling's attention.

The voice belonged to Garrod Daell, the head of Special Forces in Service to the Imperial Guard of the Most Exalted Monarch. A high-sounding title for what he did which was attend to whatever the monarch, Zephyrria Rennesseau, demanded. Her current obsession revolved around using gryphons as flying beasts of war, and she'd appointed Garrod over all her other counselors to oversee the project.

In turn, Garrod had plucked Brynz from the herd of scrubbed-up orphans at the charity home to assist him, ostensibly because she was good with animals. She'd certainly spent most of her time in the barns, preferring the animals' company to any other. More likely the carers had grown tired of smelling her reeking boots and fouled clothing and knew a child with the manners of a goat had little hope of ever finding a respectable family. Then again, it could have been her peculiar ability to harness wind that had singled her out. Or more to the point, the windstorms that followed her like a shadow. Whatever the reason, she'd been the one chosen that unseasonably warm spring day to accompany Garrod back to the royal grounds, twelve annums and a-half-a-lifetime ago.

Garrod stood outside the keeper's door, his hand resting on the iron latch. A tall, broad-shouldered man of forty-odd, all wiry grace and hard muscle beneath his fitted black leathers, he was the kind of man that impressed without ever trying. Brynz had learned much about him and from him since she'd come under his tutelage. Things like how he'd ended up at the royal grounds after a stint in the Special Forces. How he could move air with the slightest brush of a hand. How he could perceive vibrations the way a hound perceives scent. How he always knew which way his quarry would go. She looked sideways and saw he was pointing toward her foot.

"He's still eyeing the bucket," Garrod warned.

"I'm watching," she said, her training rod rapping against the floor —*THRAP THRAP THRAP*—as she stared into the gryphling's eyes. He blinked and clacked his beak twice before shifting his gaze away from the bucket and toward her face.

"There he goes," murmured Garrod. "You've got him listening now."

The gryphling shook his head again and scraped his beak against one of the leg bands.

"Give him some wind," said Garrod. "Then we'll see what he's about."

Using her will, Brynz pushed up a sharp breeze then whistled a long note with a chirrup at the end. When the gryphling breached his wings she reached into the bucket and tossed another hare into Zell's open beak who bolted it down in one go.

"And now without wind," Garrod said.

Brynz turned her will against the wind and the air stilled. She whistled a chirping blast and the gryphling refolded his wings. She tossed a third hare, landing it on the graystone next to a front leg. The gryphling eyed the hare for a moment before lowering his head to pick at the carcass.

"Good," Garrod said. "Very good. That's enough for today." He opened the keeper's door and Brynz exited, bucket and training rod in hand.

She watched as he locked the door behind her, using a brass key on a ring crowded full. After refastening the keyring to his belt, Garrod reached out and patted her on the shoulder. Always tall for her age, she stood nearly eye level with him.

"Her Most Exalted will be most pleased with your progress," he said, his tone warm and familiar. "He'll soon be under saddle at this rate."

Brynz blanched. "You said we wouldn't rush him. He's nowhere near ready for saddling."

Garrod looked away, his eyes scanning the peaks on the northern horizon. "Her Most Exalted expects he'll be ready sooner than anticipated."

"You mean, Her Most Exalted has demanded he be saddled before he's ready," Brynz spat.

"We live by Her Most Exalted's pleasure, you and I. Never forget that."

Brynz squeezed her eyes against the burning tears, reminding herself that if she hadn't been singled out by Garrod, she would still be training the charity home's pigs and ducks and chickens. She certainly wouldn't have seen, let alone trained an animal as wondrous as a gryphon. Still, the image of Totz came flooding into her mind. His swayed back and crippled hindquarters made useless from carrying too much weight at too early an age. His blank, staring eyes after being put down to make way for a new gryphling when it became apparent his utility was at an end. Regret punched her in the stomach, and she swallowed hard to force down the bitterness rising into her throat. She'd sworn things would be different with Zell. That the lesson had been learned.

"But anyone can see he's not ready," she said, turning to watch the gawky gryphling as he minced around his massive cage, his wings cocked away from his molting body. She turned back to face Garrod, the tears she'd tried to hold back streaming down her face. "You know it could kill him. Is there no way to persuade Her Most Exalted to wait?"

Garrod's face remained inscrutable. "It is not for us to decide. We are but servants. It would do well for you to be mindful of that."

Brynz clenched her jaw and bit her lip. "Couldn't we at least try?" she asked miserably.

"Her Most Exalted is quite decided on the matter. One must choose one's battles carefully. This is not a battle you can win."

"A saddle perhaps but no weight," Brynz pleaded. "Surely Her Most Exalted does not wish to put weight on him."

Garrod's jaw tightened, and his storm-gray eyes sparked with anger. Brynz flinched, expecting a cuff to the head, though Garrod had never raised a hand to her in the past. Others had, and those reflexes remained. After a moment, she opened her eyes. Garrod was looking at the gryphling, his expression both angry and sad. "It's one festival," he said, as if trying to convince himself. "Only one festival and then we can resume our training program with no further interference." He turned his gaze toward Brynz. "Her Most Exalted is not so very heavy, you know."

Brynz swiped at her eyes. "She's not so very light either," she ground out, thinking again of Totz. She took a deep breath to steady herself. "When is this event? Or should I ask, what is it?"

"Three moons hence. A celebration hosted by the Caeldish." Garrod paused, then added, "In Valenvia."

Brynz shook her head. "He'll barely have his plumage by then."

"A spiff of silver dust, and he'll shine like a newborn sun. That will do the trick for this crowd. He's only meant to evoke a certain reaction. It shouldn't take much to give the desired impression."

Brynz chewed her lip, her pale cheeks hotly pink.

"I will make sure no harm comes to Zell," Garrod said in a tone meant to be reassuring, his expression softening into a sympathetic smile that did nothing to allay Brynz's fear.

"I gave him my word I would protect him," she said, fresh tears scalding her cheeks.

"And you have done. As much as you are able. You have not let him down."

Not yet perhaps. But soon, that will not be the case.

She realized what she must do. She'd given her word, and she meant to keep it, no matter the consequences. It wouldn't be easy, but then, nothing in her life ever was.

CHAPTER FOUR
WHEN CAVING

Rachmyn Umbrae set the firewood he'd gathered on a pile near the cave opening then turned to stare at what had become a familiar landscape of jagged rock and scrubby brush. A deep-seated yearning was tugging at his thoughts, an internal plea to escape the drab splendor before him for the starry mists and shifting shadows of his soul's true home—Oru Fen.

As nightfall neared, he readied himself, a slight smile playing on his lips as he anticipated the quiet comfort of walking glowing paths in that peaceful, in-between realm. No idle conversation to be had, no one to answer to. Nothing but stars and twilight as far as his mind could think.

Never one for companionship, he'd nevertheless spent most of his life in that role. He'd learned early on that choices often decided themselves, and though he wouldn't change his path, he sometimes grew weary of the responsibilities and worries thrust upon him at the age of thirteen.

He recalled the first time he'd seen his bosom friend, Haedyn Khin, as if it were yesterday. He'd been five annums at the time, Haedyn a baby of just six moons. Returning from a wolfken gather to the stronghouse of the family's employer, the Umbraes had been confronted with a gruesome scene. During their absence, unknown invaders had overcome the guards and killed the entire household, noblemen and servants alike, slitting their throats then casting their bodies aside like garbage, blackening stains blotting out the shiny tiled floor beneath their lifeless forms. Only later did Rachmyn realize the stains had been drying blood. Ringing out above it all had been the sirening cry of an infant. To their credit, rather than turning tail, his parents had run toward the sound, and he had followed, his widespread hands clapped across his eyes and nose to block out the worst of the sights and smells.

In a back bedchamber they'd found the fat-cheeked infant, his red face caked with snot, his gummy mouth pink and wailing, a thin fuzz of blond hair haloing his head. A lone survivor with no idea he'd already lost everything. That his parents and kinsmen were no more. It was a miracle Haedyn hadn't been killed, a miracle the Umbraes had been gone harvesting wolfken at the time. That week-long trip away had likely saved the Shadowen family's lives.

Later, how Haedyn had survived what should have been a certain death had been the subject of much speculation. Arwyn, Rachmyn's mother, would always mention the feathery scorch marks upon the cradle, the blistered paint upon the walls. Luchmyn, Rachmyn's father, would always talk of flames licking out from the stronghouse chimney on a warm day when no fire was lit. But they all agreed they'd returned to a house full of death and rot with a bawling infant, a square of wemble cloth, and a maroon-bladed knife at its core.

While his parents discussed what to do in hushed tones, Rachmyn had stared at Haedyn, the knowledge that the squalling baby was all alone piercing his heart and sealing their bond forever. Arwyn had settled the argument by plucking Haedyn and his bundle up and, hugging both to her breast, murmuring a line that had been repeated around campfires and in caravans by Shadowen since the beginning of time—*to my heart you are family*. Without another word, the Umbraes had piled into their caravan and galloped their black-and-white splotched horses north toward the Lawless Mountains.

Eight annums later, his own parents had met as bitter an end as any that could be imagined, their throats cut, their eyes burned out, their tongues removed and laid across their chests, their left hands stuffed into their gaping mouths. That was another sight Rachmyn would never forget. He and Haedyn, fresh from a day of exploring and excited to show off the gray-brown wolf that had appeared from the brush, coming home to find his parents dead, flies buzzing around their cooling corpses. Later, he would find out that the left hand in the mouth was a tell-tale message from the brutal Zenzae—*better to swallow your own fist than to say too much.* Whatever his parents had done, the Zenzae had ensured they would never do it again. Rachmyn and Haedyn, clinging together like moss on rock, had fled into the night, the wolf trailing behind them.

The next eleven annums had been spent grubbing and scratching and getting by, surviving on the animals they trapped, the fish they caught, and the roots they dug. They lived wherever they could, constructing makeshift shelters from deadfall or flotsam left behind at abandoned campsites. The best memories were of the time spent in the caves hidden beneath the Lawless Mountains, their cooling damp a balm to Rachmyn's worries and fears.

He forced his thoughts to the present. Focusing on the past wouldn't help ground him, and he needed his mind rooted to this plane before he thrust his consciousness into another. Otherwise, he could lose his connection to both worlds and spin off into the nevernever. It had happened to others. He'd heard the stories of dreamwalkers turned to stone, their eyes glassy, their breaths slowing to nothing as their hearts gave out.

He walked into the cave he and Haedyn had been calling home of late, his wolf, Elgre, close at his heels. He barely noticed the wolf now, so accustomed was he to Elgre's devotion. While Rachmyn's body slept, the wolf would curl into a ball at his feet until he awakened. Rachmyn knew not why the wolf had chosen him, for it was not a usual thing, even amongst the Shadowen, but he was glad of it. All these annums later, the wolf was as he had ever been, though he should be grizzled and arthritic by now. Rachmyn sometimes wondered at that but then remembered another Shadowen saying—*marans make the music but Mystery calls the dance.* Some things couldn't be explained.

He glanced at Haedyn on his way to the back of the cave. The younger man was seated by the fire in a chair chiseled from a punky log, his head bent forward as he struck his knife against a chunk of avobanc stone, shaping out an arrowhead. Rachmyn marveled at his companion's knife. Its blade was a lustrous burgundy red, the handle formed from the burled wood of a blackheart oak. The entire knife—both blade and handle—was overlaid by gold-thread pictographs that moved when lit by flame. The fluttery glyphs had provided much entertainment when they were younger. There was something else about the knife. The blade never dulled, even after repeatedly striking stone. Haedyn accepted this as normal, but Rachmyn knew it wasn't natural for a knife to retain its edge when used in such a manner. It was truly a wonderment.

Elgre growled at the fist-sized grynt perched on Haedyn's shoulder. The tiny raptor chittered—*chirrt-chirrt-chirrt*—then puffed out its deeply black plumage and shook its scarlet head crest to make itself appear fierce, a defiant glint in its shining black eyes.

"Easy, Fryk," Haedyn soothed, his crooked finger tugging back the edge of his leather vest to reveal the pocket inside. The bird chittered again before crawling into its pocket nest. Haedyn straightened his finger and the vest flapped back against his chest. He didn't bother to ask Rachmyn where he was going. "This is my fifth arrowhead today," he said instead, holding up the triangular white stone, his hair like molten gold in the firelight. "How much do you think I can get for it?"

"Avobanc holds its edge better than most. I'd think you could get at least a hektra, maybe even an auriel if you find the right maran," Rachmyn replied. "That is if we decide to go trading."

"I thought we already decided that."

"No, we decided we'd *talk* about it."

"And when will we be doing that? Anytime soon?" Rachmyn's expression soured. Haedyn bulled ahead. "Don't you ever get bored? Don't you ever wish you could go on a real adventure?"

"No."

"Well, I suppose you wouldn't, having a whole other world to explore any time you want." Haedyn motioned toward the darkening sky outside the mouth of the cave. "If I could close my eyes and go wherever I wanted, I wouldn't be bored either. But some of us aren't so lucky. All I have is this cave and this mountainside and the view, and let me tell you, none of it ever changes. The closest I've come to adventure is trying not to get snakebit having a wee."

Rachmyn smiled despite himself. "I see you haven't lost your gift for exaggeration."

"And I see you haven't lost your knack for avoiding conversations you'd rather not have." Haedyn clapped his knife against the avobanc, a white chip flying off into the gloom.

Rachmyn sighed. Oru Fen would have to wait.

He sat on a tree stump opposite Haedyn and interlaced his fingers across one knee. Elgre folded onto the sandy ground and laid his muzzle between his paws. "Okay, let's talk," Rachmyn said evenly.

Haedyn's char-gold eyes brightened. "Are we going to be reasonable? Because I have reasons. Plenty of them."

"We're always reasonable," Rachmyn replied, his hand reaching up to push his moonbeam-pale hair behind his shoulders before reaching down to scratch Elgre's head.

Haedyn dropped the unfinished arrowhead into his lap then laid his wonderment knife on top to free his hands. He stuck his index finger into the air. "Reason one, we need money." Rachmyn opened his mouth to speak. Haedyn shook his head and waggled his finger. "Let me lay out all my reasons before you tell me I'm wrong." He stuck up a second finger. "Number two, we need a change of scenery. You know we shouldn't stay in one place too long, and we've been in this cave for nearly seven moons. Number three." Another finger went up. "We're almost out of food." Rachmyn opened his mouth again. "Nuh uh," Haedyn shushed him. Rachmyn gritted his teeth. "Number four." Another finger. "Spring rains are coming, and this place will probably flood. Remember the last time we stayed in a cave during the spring melt?"

Rachmyn's stony expression softened as he acknowledged that point as a good one. They'd nearly lost their entire cache of tools, including their wemble cloaks made from the cloth in Haedyn's cradle, when a flashflood of meltwater filled the cave they'd been staying in. Even he had to admit that had nearly been a disaster.

"Number five." Haedyn's thumb popped up. "I'm bored out of my mind. I've chiseled so many arrowheads, I could do it in my sleep. And what's the point if we're never going to trade or do anything with them." Rachmyn cut his gaze toward Haedyn's bow as an argument against that point. Haedyn cleared his throat. Rachmyn returned his attention as his friend brought his index finger to his lips and blew. A flame appeared at the tip as if he'd lit a candle. He blew on his remaining fingers and thumb then flourished his flaming hand at Rachmyn with a proud grin.

Rachmyn pursed his lips. Wasteful.

"What do you think?" Haedyn enthused.

"Boredom never hurt anyone," Rachmyn said, ignoring the theatrics. Haedyn flopped his head backward and let out an anguished groan, his fingertip flames fizzling out as his hand dropped to his lap.

"You do make some good points though. Our rations are running low."

Haedyn picked up his head, his face showing a faint glimmer of hope.

"And the spring melt is a concern," Rachmyn allowed.

Haedyn began to smile.

Rachmyn remained stoic as he considered the options. He knew his young companion was right. They had stayed in this cave on Dragontail for too long. Three or four moons was their usual limit before moving on. Trouble was, he had a fondness for caves, and always found it difficult to leave a suitable one. And this one had been exceedingly suitable. Dry and roomy, with a sandy floor and a wonderful view of Deadman's Peak which, contrary to its name, was one of the most beautiful summits in the Lawless Mountains. Not to mention the large number of wolfshead orchids growing near the cave's opening providing a ready supply of seed for wolfken speck, the green-black powder that facilitated a Shadowen's dreamcrafting ability. It was the kind of place where Rachmyn would have stayed forever, if such a thing was possible. But it wasn't possible. His parents had made that mistake, forgetting or ignoring that they'd put themselves in danger when they took in baby Haedyn. Not heeding that danger had cost them their lives. Rachmyn vowed never to let that happen to him or Haedyn.

"And what about all that speck you've got?" Haedyn interjected. "What are you planning to do with it?"

"Let me worry about that. But, to your point, we should be moving on. We could head toward Deadman's Peak and perhaps, visit one of the trading posts along the way."

Haedyn's smile stretched back toward his ears.

"That doesn't mean if we stop, we're going to stay," Rachmyn said. "We'll sell what we can, buy what we need, and then we're gone. None of that idle chit chat you're so prone to."

"You really are a sourpuss, you know that? What do you have against people, anyway?"

"What do you have for them? They're nothing but trouble. We're fine by ourselves."

"Maybe you are but I like meeting new marans and hearing their stories."

"And singing their songs and drinking their sweetsweet," Rachmyn added with a rueful shake of the head.

"I only did that once," Haedyn protested. Rachmyn gave him an admonishing look. "Okay, more than once. But that was a long time ago. I'm more mature now."

"I hadn't noticed," Rachmyn deadpanned.

Haedyn snorted. "I'll pack while you're off doing whatever it is you do when you're passed out in the corner." He was already shoving his knife into the leather sheath at his hip. "We can leave tonight if you make it snappy."

Rachmyn bit back a cutting remark about who was more prone to passing out in corners, instead heaving himself to his feet. If they were going to leave tonight, he needed to get the lay of the land sorted.

Elgre arose, stretched, then padded behind Rachmyn to a far recess in the cave's interior. There was a lot to do before the moon met the horizon and the sooner he got started, the better.

Rachmyn breathed in the familiar mist, allowing it to fill his being. How he missed this place when he wasn't here. How long had it been? How long since he'd left that other life that seemed so far away and unreal? It felt as if he'd been here for an eternity. But no, that wasn't right. Timelessness was one of the pitfalls he needed to avoid if he was going to accomplish the task bubbling up in his mind like a half-forgotten dream. Fortunately, his Shadowen vor would keep him focused.

His silvery-black wraithwolf materialized beside him, her brilliant shine pushing back the misty gray. A name flashed into his mind—Spectra. The one that had been with him since the beginning, and was here now, to assist and protect him. His heart swelled with love. Her kind blue eyes returned his emotion as their Saska vorik brightened. Spectra's mindwords inquired whether he wished to dream or walk.

"Walk," his mind answered.

With that the scene came sharply into focus, the dusky rendering of the cave's spired interior making it look both fearsome and lonely.

It was up to Rachmyn to choose his path. He watched as a starry pathway unfurled toward the horizon, a distant light on Deadman's Peak its endpoint. Energy sprites split away from the main path then split away again, and yet again, whizzing off in every direction until the entire landscape was overlaid by a sparkling web stretching to infinity. This would provide his navigation system as well as his route back to his sleeping form, now tucked inside the cave, Elgre at its feet. He looked down at his body and was startled, as he always was, by how frail it looked. Like a husk that could be blown away by the slightest breeze. Elgre looked up, his intelligent gray-green eyes seeming to perceive Rachmyn's hovering form, the wolf's lips drawing back to show his teeth, a wolfish grin Rachmyn had seen many times.

Rachmyn set off, out of the cave and down the mountainside, his etheric-self racing over treetops toward the valley below, Spectra at his side. As he went, each nuance of the topography registered in his mind as a glowing contour map of ridges and swales, rises and drop-offs, an etching that would remain after he awoke in the form of intuition, strong and perceptive, but still requiring discernment and self-belief.

Other Shadowen were also about, their energies a buzz that waxed and waned as he went. Not all were of good intent, but Spectra was adept at steering him clear when necessary. He remembered one that was always avoided, a Shadowen wycche that was both powerful and ferocious with a wraithwolf to match. He'd felt the fiendish pair's dark energy a time or two when he was young, but his guardian had always intervened, grabbing him by the scruff of the neck and running him far away.

He whooshed across the valley at the foot of Dragontail, noting the placid river wending its way across the bottomland. He continued on, looking for two things. A cave on Deadman's and the best route between it and the cave on Dragontail.

Different skills were required for each task. As he approached Deadman's, his vor probed for the honeycombed airiness that distinguished the mountain's caves from surrounding rock. He, like most Shadowen, had a gift for finding even the most well-hidden caverns.

He hurtled up the mountain's windward side, all jutting rock and scraggly trees, summitting at astounding speed. He was halfway down the leeward side when Spectra veered him toward the ground, bringing him to a stop above an overgrown roadway. He turned to the wolf, a question forming.

The answer flashed into his mind: *Inverna Pass.*

Rachmyn had heard of it, the legendary trade route of the Ancients, although it looked as if it hadn't seen use since the time of the Great Destruction.

Spectra widened his view, shooting him up until he could see the entirety of the pass from the high peak where it began to its switchbacks to where it leveled out and headed east toward the fertile lowlands of a distant green plain.

What is this place?

The reply was swift. *Everything begins and ends here.*

With that, he plummeted to the abandoned road.

Remember.

Spectra was prompting him to create a specific memory of this place which would remain in the glowing gridmap his mind was creating, a touchpoint he could recall later. He had other touchpoints already stored away from previous dreamwalks. It was always his choice whether to accept Spectra's gentle suggestions, but he rarely ignored her nudges, and he did not ignore it this time. He turned in place, allowing his mind to record the panoramic vista. That done, he used his Shadowen vor to superimpose an energy imprint of the thoughtform upon the contour gridmap. It was a psychic signpost that would help him navigate the vast realm of Oru Fen. With it, he could move at the speed of thought from touchpoint to touchpoint, a useful shortcut that facilitated nearly instantaneous movement when properly applied.

His wraithwolf nodded her approval and they were off again, heading away from Deadman's Peak toward a distant green-spanned plain, passing over villages and smallholdings as they followed the pass until the topography leveled out, the avobanc cliffs giving way to sloping shalestone.

Rachmyn detected a divot—the characteristic warp he had been searching for—his vorik indicating a bottle-shaped cave running parallel to a formidable stone wall blocking off the mountain's foothills from the Valenvian Basin.

Rachmyn returned his attention to the cave, assessing its size and depth. Satisfied, he sent Spectra his mindwords—*this will do*—and her blue eyes sparkled.

He called up the memory of the Inverna Pass touchpoint and was back on the flat spot, Spectra already at his side. They did not linger, launching across the glittering grid, following their vivid astral trail to Deadman's Peak, across the cut-grass valley and silvery river then zinging up the leeward side of Dragontail, into the cave's mouth and back to the nook where his sleeping body lay. Rachmyn bid Spectra farewell before sliding his etheric-self inside his sleeping husk as if slipping on a well-worn coat.

Rachmyn awakened and shoved his hand into his pocket, his fingers searching for the crystalline gray rock-shard that had been his lucky talisman since he was a boy. Yes, there it was.

Elgre's head went up and his tail wagged.

Rachmyn got to his feet and walked to the front of the cave, the wolf following.

Haedyn had mustered their gear into a pair of rucksacks sitting beside two walking staffs that were leaned against the fluted wall. A handful of coals smoldered inside the fire ring. Beyond lay Haedyn, stretched out and snoring, his wemble cloak crumpled at his feet, his sleeping grynt perched on a t-shaped branch stuck into the sand near his head.

So much for leaving tonight, Rachmyn thought with a chuckle.

He pulled the cloak up over Haedyn. Even though his companion was grown, Rachmyn still felt the need to protect him. The grynt's eyes flicked open then blinked shut again.

Rachmyn rummaged his cloak from his rucksack, wrapped it around his shoulders and sat in the log chair, staring at the ash-red coals until the wemble began to warm him. Elgre stretched out and closed his eyes. It wasn't long before they were both asleep.

CHAPTER FIVE

VISIONS AND DREAMS

It took Elorah nearly an hour to locate Silvi. Even a vor search through the plant roots hadn't revealed the older woman's presence. Elorah knew Silvi was adept at blending into the landscape, and she wondered if her mentor really was a Shadowen who could make herself invisible using some trick of the mind.

She finally found the gardener in the herbary after her third search.

Silvi had been busy; her willow basket frothed high with greenery Elorah recognized, their uses immediately springing into her mind—Bishop's Seal for digestive upset, Chippytip for throat catarrh, and Eyebright whose name said it all.

"Ah, Elorah," Silvi trilled. "What brings you to the gardens today?"

Elorah reached into the pocket of her dark green amlyn—the silken Academie-issue gown she wore over her tunic and leggings—and pulled out the small tin of soothesalve.

Silvi's wrinkled face broke into a wide smile. "What is this?" she asked, taking the tin into her hands and cracking it open before bringing it to her nose. "It smells of threadleaf and birdnettle..." She sniffed again. "...and blisterbane if I'm not mistaken."

"A little..." Elorah said, pinching her forefinger and thumb together.

"...to warm the joints. Your hands have done so much for me, I wanted to do something for them."

Silvi's gnarled index finger scooped out a dollop of salve then massaged it onto the knuckles of her other hand. "Ah, yes, that's nice," she said, replacing the tin's lid. "You've become a fine healer, dear heart. As I always knew you would do." The older woman grasped Elorah's arm and gave it a little shake.

"It seems strange this might be the last time we see one another," Elorah said, a lump forming in her throat.

"We have been friends since the beginning, and shall remain so until the end, even when we are far apart. You have learned all the lessons this place can teach. It is time for you to take the next step."

I don't want the future everyone has planned for me. I want to do something more.

"And you shall," Silvi said.

Elorah was caught short. Had the older woman read her thoughts?

The gardener reached into the pocket of her apron and brought out a stone pendant suspended from a fine silver chain. She pressed it into Elorah's hands. "Remember, we write our own destinies. It is up to us to make sure the journeys we take are the journeys we desire. And always it is intention that determines the outcome. Without intention, we are rudderless ships, in constant motion but going nowhere."

Elorah stared at the pendant as Silvi explained that, rather than a single gemstone, the vorestone was an intricate layering of the six elemental affinity stones—golden-brown brunnestone for Therran, orange-red flamite for Fyrre, blue-green aquirria for Aquilla, glitter-white arocol for Atmos, purple-gray gryszliek for Shadowe, and lavender-blush luminae for Spyrrt—in a spiraling pattern that had no beginning and no end. A marvel of color and light, the pendant was a masterpiece of craftsmanship far beyond the ability of any ordinary vorestone shaper.

Overcome, Elorah looked from the necklace to Silvi, realizing with a start that the gardener's eyes swirled with the same iridescent colors as the mysterious stone. How had she never noticed that before? "It's so beautiful," she stammered, her voice strange inside her head.

"A rare gift from Eolemar herself," Silvi said, pointing a sharp fingernail at the stone. "Notice the order of the stonestrands, each a force unto itself, yet also dependent upon the greater whole. Understand, for it is this truth that rules all things. Where one is great, the All is greater. Remember this and all will turn out well." The gardener's ineffable eyes went distant with some unspoken thought.

"Will you be at the testing tomorrow?" Elorah asked, reaching back to fasten the chain around her neck before tucking the stone inside her tunic. The pendant nestled against her breastbone, its presence instantly calming her racing heart.

Silvi shook her head, her silvery braids swaying against her shoulders. "What could I see there that I haven't already seen? That is a show for others who do not know you. But we have no secrets, you and I. You are already here." She pointed toward her heart and smiled. "And that will always be so."

Elorah swallowed hard. "I will miss you," she said, tears welling up.

Silvi patted Elorah's arm. "That will pass. The hatchling only misses its nest until it finds its own wings. The time has come for you to fly, little bird. Be strong and know that when you do, nothing can stop you except yourself."

Elorah wrapped her arms around Silvi's bony shoulders, and the gardener pulled her in with a surprising strength. "Go and do all the wonderful things you are meant to do," she murmured into Elorah's ear.

After a few moments, Elorah broke away, her eyes leaking hot tears, her heart a cold weight beneath the warmth of the pendant.

"You should go back, dear heart," Silvi prompted. "There are some who are already missing you." She gave Elorah's arm another pat. "See true in all you do, and the world will change." A final squeeze and Silvi let go to retrieve her snips. Without another word, she returned to clipping Bishop's Seal fronds and dropping them into her basket.

Elorah took her leave, following the river-stone path leading from the herbary to the Academie dormitories. It was the longest, hardest walk she'd ever had to make. Even leaving her mother and grandmama on her first day at the Academie had not been this difficult. No tears had flowed on that day, no strange catching in her throat, no squeezing pressure in her chest.

She took a detour, heading toward the Academie's Contemplative. Perhaps some quiet reflection within the darkened meditation room would help calm the emotions roiling her stomach.

What's wrong with me? she thought as she shambled along. *What is this feeling? Grief? Loss? Is this the way mother has felt all these annums?*

It had turned into a fine spring day, but Elorah drew no pleasure from it. The heating sun felt like an insult, the freshening breeze like an assault, the loamy smell of unfurling leaves like an accusation. She broke into a run, desperate to slip into the windless peace of the sanctuary.

The weathered green door of the Contemplative beckoned to her like a lantern in a storm. She ran to it, seized its brass handle, and heaved it open.

Her cheeks burned against the stone-damp chill as she entered the familiar six-sided room. Various depictions of faceless emvors employing elemental vorik decorated four of the sidewalls. The remaining two were plain graystone. Elorah had often wondered why those walls had been left blank, knowing that every detail at the Academie held hidden importance.

The room, always unlocked, was rarely used. Elorah could count on one hand the number of times she'd met anyone else when she'd been inside.

Normally, she would light one of the candles sitting upon the bronze stands in each half-corner of the room. The tradition was to light the candles on either side of the wall dedicated to a particular Affinity, but Elorah never bothered with that. Any candle would do as far as she was concerned.

As her eyes adjusted, she saw that a candle was already burning in the half-corner between Atmos and one of the blank walls, its guttering light casting wavering shadows upon a tall, uniformed figure wearing a bulbous black hat and sitting in a chair drawn close to the unadorned graystone. The man jumped up and whirled around in one smooth movement as she closed the door. He bowed, the silver goatee beneath his manicured mustache brushing the light blue wool of his brass-buttoned coat, his hand clamping the hat onto his head, a smoke-brass wolf's head ring on the third finger glinting red pinpricks from its jeweled eyes. Noting her interest the man straightened and swept the hand behind his back, his long face cracking into the thinnest of smiles.

"Excuse me," she said. "I didn't mean to interrupt..."

"Please come in," he said, his accent sounding Iellian and overly formal. He strode toward her. "I was just on my way out."

Elorah watched the man's approach, the ringed hand knuckled firmly into the small of his back. She took a step sideways as she grasped the door handle. At the same moment, the man reached forward, his left hand landing atop hers. An intense jolt of not-quite pain shot through her and she inhaled sharply, the pendant going cold against her breast as a horrifying scene of shadowy figures wearing hooded robes seized hold of her mind.

Like penitents, the figures stood in a semi-circle around a luminant gray orb bound by a netting of silver cords to a fitted black-glass pedestal. Streaks of light shot away from the radiant orb at random intervals, their piercing brightness dissipating quickly in the dusk. With its dark center and lighter edge, the orb reminded Elorah of an unblinking eye, and she found herself searching its depths for something she couldn't name. A scattering of small voids came into focus, interrupting jags that marred the orb's otherwise glowing surface. Pity washed through her as she thought of the orb peering for all eternity through its broken mosaic of darkness and light. If only she could gather up its missing bits and mend the orb into a vibrant whole. An impossible task, and yet, she yearned to do exactly that.

A strange rippling began inside, a merging of energies as if she and the orb had become one entity together. A hammer blow of nausea struck her midsection and a chaos of emotions—betrayal, revulsion, rage—clawed her throat. Her breathing shallowed and her insides twisted tight. She shut her eyes and braced, convinced she would implode at any moment. As quickly as it had begun, the internal squeezing released, giving way to airy lightness.

She opened her eyes to find she was now floating high above the scene, separate from the orb yet unable to tear her gaze away from its tormented stare.

As one, the hooded figures clutched thin cords wound round their necks and lifted them away so that the attached gray-shard pendant dangled like a bell clapper from hands bearing smoke-brass wolf's head rings. The figures all took a step forward and the shards, as if magnetized, swung toward the orb, pulled in by some invisible force. The cultists turned their cowled heads toward a small figure wearing a twilight-colored cloak, standing at the apex of the semi-circle.

The small figure held up a manicured hand with its own distinctive wolf's head ring, its corona of sparkling gemstone stars catching the last of the dying light. The delicate hand gestured toward first one black-robed figure and then another, inviting each to scrape their shard against the surface of the orb, their pendants taking on an eerie glow that brightened with every strike. As she watched, sharp pains needled Elorah's own eyes, bringing tears. She blinked hard to drive them away and the scene evaporated, her attention returning to the icy glare of the uniformed man as he jerked her shaking hand free and exited.

Elorah swiped at her watering eyes and made for the nearest chair, her breathing a series of gasps. Her stomach lurched, forcing her heart into her throat and for an awful moment, she thought she would be sick.

She collapsed onto the chair's wooden seat and, pushing her trembling hands under her thighs, forced herself to take several deep breaths until a thought sent her scrambling toward the Contemplative's door. She must warn the Headmistress before something terrible happened.

Headmistress Kearyn Malenvie's office and living quarters occupied the entire east wing of the Academie. Elorah ran from the Contemplative to the main entrance, covering the distance in half the usual time. Elorah knew she was taking a chance on finding the Head in her office given that she often walked the grounds or retired to her private quarters when classes were adjourned, and she said a silent prayer as she pulled open one of the Academie's huge wooden entry doors.

The Head's office was on the second floor, at the top of a circular stone staircase, its steps carved to look as though they wound their way up an enormous tree trunk, the wooden handrail and balusters shaped into stylized branches. Elorah had climbed these stairs countless times but never with the urgency or fear she felt now.

The Headmistress had taken a special interest in her from the time she was small, and had overseen Elorah's course of study, challenging her to reach heights in the Arcana of Therran that were far above what most students achieved. After their many annums together, Elorah felt certain the Head would be as disturbed as she by her vision and would know what should be done.

At the top of the stairs Elorah made a left, and then another, which found her standing in front of a hand-carved door displaying amlyn-clad figures engaged in the four basic affinities. In the center was the Academie's crest overlaid by its motto *Help All, Harm None* in gilt lettering.

Elorah raised her hand to knock then let it drop to her side after hearing the low murmur of indistinct voices from within. Protocol dictated she wait until the Headmistress was free. Despite her overwhelming sense of urgency, Elorah crossed the dimly-lit corridor— every nerve jangling—to an upholstered chair and sat, her amlyn scuffing against the slub-wool cushion.

She couldn't decide what to do with her hands while she waited, clasping and unclasping them in her lap. When at last the door opened, she sprang to her feet. A figure emerged wearing a bulbous black hat and a light blue uniform. She sagged back against the chair, her mind reeling. The man from the Contemplative. Was she too late? Had something already happened?

The man seemed not to see her, instead turning and walking in the direction of the stairway. A moment after he turned the corner, another figure came out into the hallway.

"Emvorite Calliaigh?" the Headmistress asked in a voice both quiet and compelling.

"Yes, Headmistress." Elorah's voice sounded tinny and faraway to her ears. She stepped out of the shadows, relieved that the Headmistress was unharmed.

"Is there something I can help you with?" The Headmistress glided forward, the deep purple amlyn signifying her station skimming the plush green carpeting.

Elorah's voice deserted her as her eyes searched the Headmistress's face for any sign of distress. From the black hair coiled atop her head, to the bladed cheeks and dark green eyes, the straight nose and full lips tipping downward with concern, there was nothing about the Head that seemed amiss. She was as she always was, dignified and composed, her expression exuding kindness and compassion.

"Your face is flushed. Are you unwell?" the Head asked, stepping forward and placing the back of her hand against Elorah's forehead.

The horrific scene from the Contemplative began again but this time from a different perspective. She was now at the apex of the semi-circle, facing the black-robed devotees, who stood expectantly around the gray orb, their dangling pendants and wolf's head rings clearly visible. She raised a twilight-cloaked arm, a wolf's-head with a corona of stars glinting on one manicured finger, then signaled the nearest figure to strike their pendant against the orb. Elorah's breath caught in her throat, and her head went hot, overwhelmed by the sudden knowledge that the leader in her vision was the Headmistress whom she had loved and trusted for all these years. A buzzy ringing filled her ears, and the hallway went swimmy. Her knees buckled and it took all her concentration to keep from passing out. She sucked in air, trying to steady herself, Silvi's stone a frozen lump against her chest.

"I feel heat. Perhaps you are coming down with ague. Come. I have something that will help." The Headmistress drew her hand back then beckoned, a softly drawn smile on her lips.

Elorah's first thought was to run, but the kindness in the Headmistress's eyes filled her with doubt. Maybe she *was* coming down with some mind-affecting illness. She desperately wanted that to be the cause of her malaise. Otherwise, she would have to accept that the oath she'd recited for the past ten annums and believed in with every fiber was being flouted by the one person she'd trusted most to uphold it. That *Help All, Harm None*—emblazoned on every lecture hall door— was a lie. Her bleak hope that she was wrong about everything dragged her reluctant feet into the Head's office.

Once inside, Elorah looked around the familiar space. The leatherbound books on the shelves, the ornately carved furniture, the colorful vorestone pendulums hanging in rows from the smokewood peg rack, all looked as new and strange as they had ten annums earlier when she'd made her first visit to this room. This time though, instead of seeing the wonder and beauty of the items, she saw the potential for destruction in each. It was something she'd never considered before. Silvi's words rushed back to her—*always it is intention that determines the outcome.*

The Headmistress motioned her to a nearby chair and Elorah folded onto the wooden seat like a spring being compressed. "Headmistress," she began.

"We needn't be so formal," the Headmistress said, making her way to an embossed-brass tea trolley in the corner. "Once you've graduated tomorrow, we will be colleagues, and I hope, friends. From today, let us begin as we wish to go on. I shall call you Elorah, and you shall call me Kearyn."

"Kearyn," Elorah began again, her throat strangling on the name as she watched the Headmistress remove the lid from a wooden canister, and, using a small silver spoon, dip out four measures into a foil packet, sealing it with a bead of wax before replacing the lid and walking the curative to Elorah. Their fingers brushed in the exchange, and the horrific scene flashed again into Elorah's mind, every detail unchanged. Her heart hammered as she thrust the packet into her pocket and mumbled a thank you before vaulting to her feet, a bitter taste in her mouth.

"A brew thrice today and once tomorrow should put you right. Now, can I be of any other assistance?"

"I wouldn't want to impose myself further," Elorah said, her eyes darting toward the door. Closed.

The Head approached, her piercing eyes flashing above a simpering smile. Elorah's ears began to roar; Silvi's stone went colder. "You have an extraordinary gift, you know. I've not had another student who has shown the level of proficiency you've attained in the Arcana of Therran. To have played some small part in your progress is... well, I very much hope we can continue on together."

Elorah took a step sideways, her chin on her chest, her gaze fixed on the closed door. "Yes, well..." Each word fell like a stone. If she could get to the door, maybe...

Kearyn stepped in front, her lips falling into a faint frown. "I have some influence in certain circles, with people who can effect real change. Let me help you find a position where your talents would not only be welcomed but celebrated. Your family surely understands that an emvor of your ability shouldn't be held back by society or tradition. You were born to do great things. Wonderful things. To make important and lasting contributions not only to the district of your birth but to the wider world as well."

"Your confidence flatters me," Elorah said, each word feeling like a betrayal. She took another step sideways, eyeing the door. She could almost touch it.

"My confidence is always well placed," Kearyn said. "I know your heart and your dreams, you see. I know you've seen the world faltering and that you're bursting to do something about it. I also know you can do much, given the right circumstances. There was a man here today inquiring after a graduate suitable for a place in the Iellian court. I could think of no one more suited and took the liberty of giving him your name. I've invited him to tomorrow's examinations so he can see for himself your immense capabilities. I've no doubt he will be more than impressed. A position in the Royal Court would put you well on your way to doing all that you've ever desired."

Elorah startled backward.

"Is something wrong?" the Headmistress asked, her hands moving to brace Elorah's shoulders.

Elorah dodged sideways, her hand diving for the doorknob, her mind praying it wouldn't be locked. The brass sphere jiggled, then stuck. She gave it a nudge, her heart sinking when it held fast. Rising panic drove the air from her lungs, her mind screaming *Run! Now!*

"It would be the perfect opportunity," the Headmistress pressed as she moved toward the door, the simpering smile returning. "Think of all you could do with the support of Her Most Exalted. Nothing would be impossible. He's asked for your answer after the examinations. I imagine you could begin as early as the day after if you wish."

"Thank you. I'll consider it," Elorah said, steadying her quavering voice. "I should get back to my studies." She pulled the jammed handle again, the terror inside becoming nearly unbearable.

"Yes, of course," the Headmistress demurred, reaching for the door. Elorah jerked back and the Head's shapely eyebrows peaked as she grasped the handle and gave it a twist. Her sharp gaze cut toward Elorah's shaking hands, and she shoved them into her pockets, her fingertips recoiling from the foil packet. "Until tomorrow, then, " the Head murmured, her lips a thin line as the door swung open.

Elorah bobbed her head and scuttled through the opening.

She heard the soft tread of feet as the Headmistress stepped out into the hallway behind her, the heat of her green-eyed stare searing Elorah's back. She inhaled and forced herself to calmly stride away despite everything inside urging her to run.

CHAPTER SIX
ALWAYS THE HARD WAY

Thane Arlot had always been a grifter. A swindler. A deceiver. A thief. A rogue amongst rogues, wasn't that how the old saying went? He was all of that and more. Along the way, he'd made his share of enemies and lost his share of friends, but he didn't mind, was proud of it even because it was all part and parcel of the maran he'd become—someone canny enough to spot an opportunity and hard-nosed enough to seize it.

His knack for turning untapped potential into tangible reward came from a deep understanding of marans and their desires. For him, reading dupes was easy, the result of a childhood spent gauging the mood of the room, and he had no qualms about using that ability to exploit the weak-minded and the foolish. It was another point of pride he'd never come out on the wrong side of a deal. That alone had gotten him farther than anything.

Of course, he'd gotten into the odd scrape. Been beaten more times than he could count. Stabbed a few times, too. Once, he'd found himself on the wrong end of an axe, and it had taken every bit of guile he possessed to come away with his limbs and life intact. He'd learned many painful lessons along the wandering goat-path comprising his twenty-six annums, each one making him tougher and wiser than he'd been before. And if that wasn't exactly his history, it was the one he'd chosen, because it explained the scars and the squint and the attitude in a way that helped him forget that it was his own father who'd inflicted most of the damage.

It hadn't been easy, spending his childhood dodging a derelict who drank too much, worked too little, and enforced the peculiarities of his will with his fists or his belt or the gimlet he carried in his pocket. After one particularly violent beating, Thane had run away, fleeing to the rocky Elequian coast without money or hope, seized by the idea he should hurl himself into the arms of Maarathia—the sea-dragon that lived at the bottom of Belaquis Bay—as a penance for being such a monumental disappointment. If not for a crew of mercenaries about to put to sea in their double-masted rabbout, that would have been his end. But one lithe brown youth had noticed the whip-thin lad with the battered face commanding white-capped waves to rise and fall at the whim of his hand and, sensing something useful, exhorted the ragtag band of Rabboutiers to have him join what he later learned was an illicit expedition to harvest brakken kelp, gilded pearls, and other treasures of the seas where his skill at moving water had proven most useful. Those had been interesting times.

Now, his father was dead and so was his past. All of it. It was time to look forward.

Thane tried to ignore the fact that he was riding toward his future on a wheezing, spotted ox. Instead, he focused on his destination, the Calliaigh district of Valenvia. He was on his way to the Festival of the Urslan Sisters, the pack on his back filled with oddities and trinkets he'd acquired—a few legally, the rest not so much—to barter and sell. That wasn't his primary interest, however. Bartering was only a gateway, an opening to bigger and better things. What really interested him was finding his next mark, and the festival was sure to be rife with slow-witted clodbusters and cloud-brained fools ready to hand over their valuables to a glib stranger with a gift for telling them what they hoped to hear.

Thane had allowed himself plenty of time to make the journey and inveigle his way into the best spot for his brand of business, intending to set up shop wherever he could entice the greatest number of marans to buy his gimcracks or play a game of Find the Pea, or if he got lucky, take him into their confidence. If all else failed, his ability to find and move water would surely be of interest to someone with the means to pay for it.

Thane had no understanding whatever of the convoluted bear cult the backward Caeldish celebrated at their annual festival. Nor did he wish to understand it. His only concern was whether he could turn a profit and secure a position. If all went to plan, by the final day he would have ingratiated himself with some rich landowner who, in exchange for one or more of his many skills, would provide him with a comfortable living for the foreseeable future.

The ox stumbled—nearly pitching Thane over its head—and let out a rancid belch. Thane had lost count of how many times he'd huffed ox blow during his ride, but it wasn't until he realized he could walk faster than his eructing mount that he began to think about trading it off.

He ended up ditching the spotted calamity at the next village in exchange for a bag of meal, a joint of smoked meat, and seven auriels. Considering he'd only paid five to begin with, he was happy to leave the ox behind and walk the remaining distance, telling himself he still had plenty of time to reach the festival grounds.

He wasn't the only one on the Valenvian High Road. Others were also making the trip to the Calliaigh district. Most were Caeldish, their clunky oxcarts, homespun clothing, and bovine expressions giving them away. There were also a fair number of musicians, voricians, and bards, judging by the stringed instruments, finger chimes, and tim-tam drums they carried. Thane recognized a few from past encounters in alehouses and district thiefkeeps, but he was discreet and so were they. The less said about that, the better.

One surly-looking humpbacked fellow trundled a specialized handcart featuring naive drawings of desert krychles seated in miniature chairs and wearing formalwear complete with hats. Fist-sized coops—each containing a single krychle—thunked rhythmically against the cart's wooden frame as it bumped along, the tiny lizards flapping their wings and chirring in a lilting chorus that sounded as if it were being produced by a single instrument.

An old nursery rhyme popped into Thane's mind. *Krychle sing high, Solimar shine, Krychle sing low, rain will soon flow.*

Thane had handled a few krychles in his day, but he found the creatures annoyingly loud and restless. He couldn't understand why anyone would want one for a pet, but these dimwitted farmfolk seemed to love them.

Then there were the Shadowen, their gaudy caravans—decorated with mystical-looking moons and stars and wolves—hooked to black-and-white Plenderre horses with tinkling bells on their shiny black harnesses. The Shadowen always traveled in groups, banding together for protection and companionship. No self-respecting citizen wanted to be seen associating with them, except under the narrowest of circumstances. Most towns only allowed the showmen in once per annum when the rules were relaxed for a celebration. After the barleycorn festival or apple pitch or flea circus was over, the Shadowen were forced to move along, taking with them their fortune telling, their dreamcrafting, and their charm draughts promising cures for the lovelorn and the desperate.

Thane had long experience with the charms, having used several over the annums, and he was particularly fond of the dreamcrafting, finding it a pleasurable alternative to the ugly world his waking mind inhabited. The cruelty came when the dream faded, stealing back his happiness as quickly as it had been lent. Yet that never stopped him from wanting more. Seeing the Shadowen wagons and hearing their jingling harness bells tickled up a familiar longing for another pull of joy-juice from the bottles the showmen provided for a fee.

He spotted trouble ahead.

The High Hells had set up a checkpoint on the border of the Calliaigh district to inspect traveling papers and survey the influx of celebrants and vendors. Thane knew he didn't have the required documents. If he wanted to get in, he was going to have to find an alternative way. He wasn't surprised. He'd expected there to be some kind of trouble. There always was.

His opportunity arrived in the form of a hay wagon piled high. The driver plodding beside the four-oxen team was an oafish-looking lad with a pimply face whose attention was fixed on the flashy mural painted on the side of a nearby caravan. Thane saw his chance, walking over and casually hoisting himself aboard before burrowing into the scratchy hay.

"Hoy!" shouted a child's voice. "D'ya see that? There's a fella wallering into that hay!"

"What are you talking?" came a gruff man's voice.

"I seen it!"

Thane held his breath, expecting to be hauled out at any moment.

"Get back to yer mam, stripling. And say a prayer the Urslan never heared ya." Then lower, "Always spoutin' nonsense, that one."

When nothing happened, Thane let out his breath and nestled down into the hay, pulling a hollow bone-colored tube from a front pocket on his pack. It was a hoewler, the silent whistle the Shadowen used in their dreamcrafting. He'd won it in a game of cards with a handsome rogue whose brilliant smile had almost made up for his appalling sweetsweet habit.

Thane poked the hoewler up through the hay, clenched it between his teeth and laid back, sucking in a lungful of fresh air. It was the first time he'd found a use for the thing. The rogue he'd gotten it from, despite his good looks and charming smile, had turned out to be utterly useless.

He settled back and tried to relax, his attention focused on inhaling and exhaling in long, measured breaths. The High Hells were legendary for their ability to detect anomalies in air currents. His time with the Rabboutiers had taught him that, and he knew that his breathing, if not controlled, could be perceived by a trained Iellian guard. He hoped he wouldn't have to resort to using the one talent he'd been born with, the ability to coax water from the ground, because that could get messy, not to mention tiring. It would be much better if he could slip into the district in the back of a wagon with no one the wiser.

The wagon ground to a halt and Thane heard the approach of two guards, one lighter of foot than the other.

"Produce your papers," a raspy voice demanded.

Next came sounds of shuffling and murmured assent, followed by a lengthy silence. Thane strained his ears and further slowed his breathing.

PFLAM

A wooden rod plunged into the hay beside him, nearly impaling his shoulder before striking hard against the wagon's wooden bed. Thane bit his bottom lip to stifle the shriek that jumped into his throat.

PFLAM   WOAAM

The rod impaled the hay on his other side, once, twice. He gritted his teeth and willed himself not to scream. His heart hammered in his ears as he waited through another interminable lull until a deep voice called, "All clear."

"On your way then," droned the raspy voice. "Enjoy your visit to the United Valenvian Territory by the grace of Her Most Exalted, Queen Zephyrria Rennesseau."

The ox-wagon's wheels juddered into motion.

Thane monitored his breathing for several beats before allowing his body to collapse with relief. He'd made it. He was in. He sucked in a huge breath then blew it out through the hoewler. It was the closest he could come to shouting. Soon he would be able to wash away the gamey smell of ox, tidy up his shaggy hair, don the embroidered jerkin in his pack, and present himself in his new role of respectable merchant. Valenvia had changed since the last time he'd visited and so had he. The better life he'd dreamt about since childhood—when being different had earned him nothing but scorn and beatings—was closer now than ever. He could feel it.

CHAPTER SEVEN
NIGHT OF THE XETILI

The drums pounded out a terrible warning, one that had haunted Xyleea from her earliest memory.

AH-BAH-BAH AH-BAH-BAH AH-BAH-BAH
All will die All will die All will die

Night after night, the unrelenting sound assaulted the Ushoku—the People—as they sat in their wasakas grinding goru root for stew, chewing faka leaf for courage, and waiting for the next attack.

The Xetili—People of the Blue Mud—dark-skinned and fierce, had the entire wasakagee surrounded. By the light of a hunter's moon, an uncountable number of warriors had attacked, their bodies and faces smeared with the blue mud that *glooped* and *blopped* in mud pots near the foot of the grogakee's mountain. Many Ushoku had been wounded, some had died, still others had fallen into a twilight state, the light gone from their eyes, their bodies like fallen trees.

The Ushoku didn't have warriors; they had grandfathers and fathers and boys who grabbed whatever their hands could find—wooden shovels, stone axes, reed blowpipes—and ran off into the tangled green of the keleekeluk to avenge their fallen family members.

But that had been three days ago, and still the men had not

returned. As another night loomed, the remaining people huddled inside their wasakas, praying to the sky and listening to the drums.

It was the blue mud that made the Xetili act as if they had no chuulzu, no force of spirit. The Ushoku said it was the fiery breath of the grogakee that made the mud boil. And it was the grogakee's chuulzu trapped inside the mud that made the Xetili *beeka*. Crazy.

Xyleea stroked her galeesha's hand and tried not to listen to the incessant drums. Her grandmother was the wasakagee's only chuulzu deeta—spirit healer—but it was Cree Shee who was in need of healing after a dart from a Xetili blowpipe had found its way into her thigh. For two days, Cree Shee's chuulzu had walked in the land of the dead, fighting the poison's evilness while her rigid body lay on a bed of comfort-weed floss, her eyes staring blindly at the grass mats that served as a roof.

Xyleea wasn't sure what to do for her galeesha. Already she had tried the crystalwood staff and the gimchee but still, her grandmother remained like stone. She tried to imagine what Cree Shee would tell her if she could talk, but it was like trying to conjure a dream while still awake. Thoughts of healing chants and forest songs floated into her mind only to float back out again, leaving behind a crushing emptiness and feeling of doom.

Xyleea was afraid to fall asleep, afraid to even move, fearing that if she didn't keep her attention on her galeesha's face, she would miss some little sign that Cree Shee's soul could be retrieved, that her life force wasn't forever trapped in the in-between. The few times she'd left her galeesha's side to make water, she'd been terrified she would return to a corpse.

"Come back," she'd whispered over and over into Cree Shee's ear, searching her galeesha's face for a flicker of recognition. But there was nothing.

Xyleea heard distant thunder. The voice of the grogakee her galeesha had called it.

Listen to the dragon with your whole heart, and you will hear his truth.

Xyleea closed her eyes and concentrated, hoping to hear the answers she so desperately wanted. Another rumble, closer this time. She strained her ears, parsing the noise for vibrations that often passed unheard. Sounds that were deeper than the grumble of clashing clouds and falling rain, sounds that were mythic and true.

But she was disappointed. She could hear nothing hidden in the wind that began to whistle through the reed walls of the wasaka, wrinkling the floss beneath her galeesha's prone form. No whispered wisdoms telling her what to do. Only the wind and the drums.

The air cooled as the storm rolled in, and Xyleea pulled a large bajee fleece out from a pile in the corner and used it to cover Cree Shee. She wrapped herself in a second fleece, the soft, reddish-gold wool driving back the damp chill already settling in like an unwelcome guest.

Outside, the storm's darkness had overtaken the wasakagee, and many villagers lit their pitch torches, the defiant flames marking them as either foolish or brave. Too much faka leaf, perhaps. It made people foolhardy. Xyleea considered lighting the torch that stood next to the fire ring, reasoning it might help her galeesha's spirit find its way back but in the end, decided against it. She did not want to make it easy for the Xetili to pick her wasaka out, should they decide to attack again. Better to sit in the dark and wait. And pray.

The storm was ferocious, tearing at the wasaka's roof and shaking its walls for most of the night, the furious wind chasing away the sound of the drums.

Xyleea sat near her galeesha, her mind snagging upon memories like a river tumbling over jagged rock. Cree Shee had taken her in after her parents were killed in a Xetili raid. She had been only seven at the time, and the thought of living with the white-haired deeta with the milky, staring left eye, and bark-brown skin had terrified her. She called her galeesha, but it was a title of respect. Cree Shee had no children of her own. A true chuulzu deeta always chose their calling over having a family. To try and have both was said to divide a deeta's power. The fact that Cree Shee had taken her in anyway filled her with gratitude, once she was old enough to understand.

A new deeta was chosen after the wasakagee's current deeta had seen the vision that foretold their passing to the spirit world. It was assumed that Xyleea would succeed Cree Shee, and indeed, her galeesha had spent the last twelve season-cycles instructing Xyleea in the ways of chuulzu, but until the healer chose their successor, it was never certain who would receive the chuulzu kereet, the sacred headdress handed down from deeta to deeta.

Cree Shee's kereet was exceptional, sporting the golden feathers of the deleemelee, the carrion bird of the mountains; the spiked black horns of the bajee, the rock-climbing mountain sheep; and the gold-spotted paw of a chassa, the large hunting cat that roamed the keleekeluk. The headdress was meant to impart courage, wisdom, sure-footedness, and huul waal, the internal strength to face life's joys and hardships with equal vigor. Xyleea doubted she would ever be worthy of wearing it.

Near daybreak, the storm moved on, leaving behind the rich smell of greening plants stretching rain-soaked leaves toward the rising sun. Not long after, the men returned, boasting of their battle-fresh scars. The rain had driven the Xetili across the Meneemeena River, the beeka mud dripping onto the ground as they ran. The wasakagee had been saved.

Xyleea heard the shouts when the men arrived singing their victory songs. She smelled the smoke from the fires that were lit, heard the bleating of the goat that was snared from the communal herd for the people to eat. From everywhere outside the wasaka came the sounds of celebration—the chatter of happy voices, the rattle of reed sticks, the stamp of dancing feet.

Xyleea gripped Cree Shee's hand and whispered, "Galeesha, come back. The men have returned. The wasakagee is safe."

A smile flitted across Cree Shee's face. Xyleea blinked, her heartbeat in her ears. Could it be? Was her galeesha returning?

Cree Shee's hardened features lost their rigor, her eyelids drifting down over her staring eyes, her features reshaping into the face Xyleea loved. The poison abated further and the gripped muscles of Cree Shee's body loosened. She flumped against the flossy bed, the bajee fleece slipping to the floor. Xyleea removed the fleece from her own shoulders and covered her galeesha. Saying a prayer to the ancestors, she lit a fire using a flint rock, the fuzzy seed head of a fireweed, and several sticks of dry gumwood.

When the flames took hold, and the gumwood began to char, she pulled a pinch of gimchee powder from the small goat-hide bag she wore around her neck and tossed it into the fire. The gimchee sizzled and sparked, filling the wasaka with its spicy-sweet smell. She ladled water from the cistern by the door into the boil-pot, intending to make a tonic tea.

"Xyleea," Cree Shee croaked.

Xyleea set the pot on the floor and rushed to her galeesha's side. "I am here," she murmured, taking hold of Cree Shee's hand who turned her head to accommodate her good eye.

"Bring the kemeekemee."

Xyleea retrieved the sacred bajee-skin bag and laid it across her galeesha's chest, asking the ancestors to forgive her unworthy hands.

Cree Shee flopped her hand onto the bag, her brown fingers clawing at its clasp.

"The daala..." Cree Shee's voice faded out.

Xyleea did not know what she meant. Cree Shee closed her eyes for long moments before reopening them. "The daala," she said again, her voice stronger, her fingers more insistent.

Xyleea reached under her galeesha's hand and released the bone-and-thong clasp.

Cree Shee crawled her hand inside, pulling out a dark-brown nut and placing it carefully in the extended palm of her other hand.

"It is time for the daala to return to its rightful place," Cree Shee said, the color returning to her cheeks. She looked younger than she had during Xyleea's youth. Even her milky eye was a brighter white. "He who once gave it has need of it now, and it is your destiny to deliver it into the hands of the One who has pledged to restore it. For this you were born." Her voice resonated within the wasaka. "As the Uniter was born to restore the daala and revive the parambak for all." Cree Shee used her other hand to pull apart the nut, revealing an orb glowing with otherworldly brilliance.

Xyleea bent forward, awestruck by the shimmering orb. She tried to understand what it was made from, for it looked both watery and solid, airy and dense, and seemed to contain every color of the keleekeluk—the browns and reds, the greens and blues, the purples and oranges—each blending into the whole yet luminous in its own right. It was as if her galeesha held a rainbow in her hand, a rainbow plucked from the heart of the keleekeluk.

Cree Shee smiled at Xyleea as she extended the orb toward her. "Protect it with all your strength, as I have done all these many season-cycles." Xyleea's throat went tight, and tears flooded her eyes as she took the brown sphere into her hands, even as her conscious mind tried to blunt her body's visceral reaction. Never had she felt as if her body was separate from her thoughts, with its own reactions beyond her control, but it must be so.

A burst of energy rolled through Xyleea, expanding her until she thought she would explode with joy. The orb surged and ebbed, pulsing with a force far beyond her ability to comprehend. It felt as if she had been reunited with a bigger and better version of herself, with an infinite chuulzu that understood her completely. In that moment, her body was a burden, a barrier between her truth and her reality, and she desperately wanted to be free of it.

Cree Shee reached out and replaced the nut's cover, the indescribable feelings dissipating. Xyleea looked down at the object in her hands, and realized it wasn't a nut at all but instead, a sphere of brunnestone. She handed the daala back and watched as her galeesha put it away then pushed the kemeekemee toward Xyleea.

"My time is soon," Cree Shee murmured, her new-found vitality already ebbing.

"No, galee–" Xyleea started to interrupt.

"Listen, Xyleea. This bag of bones..." Cree Shee patted her thigh, "...will soon be of no use. When I have gone, it must be returned to the keleekeluk from which it came. Only when that is done, can I reunite with the supreme chuulzu."

Xyleea knew what her galeesha meant. She was speaking of the bone ceremony, the practice of putting the dead on a ceremonial platform and allowing the deleemelee to feast upon the remains. Cree Shee was asking Xyleea to observe the ancient custom once her heart had stopped beating.

"When I am one with the supreme chuulzu and can walk with the ancestors, that is the time you must walk with the kemeekemee and follow where it leads. It knows the winding path you must take. Keep the daala always inside its protection stone, to shield it and you from the Evil One Who Never Left who hungers for it as a chassa hungers for bajee. The Uniter will soon begin her journey to find you. She will recognize you by your kereet. Keep it and the daala with you always."

With that, Cree Shee closed her eyes and began to chant a monotonous tune. Xyleea leaned close, her ear brushing against her galeesha's fluttering lips.

Come for me ancestors; take me to the farworld.

Cree Shee was calling for the ancestors to escort her into the Weeleekeela, the golden land of eternal spirit that lay beyond the land of the dead.

"Come back," Xyleea whispered. Even as she said it, she knew it was in vain.

Cree Shee's lips stilled, and her jaw went slack, her good eye rolling up to stare at the green reed ceiling.

The ancestors had heard her song. She was gone.

Strangling grief grabbed Xyleea's throat, choking her with emotions she hadn't felt since her parents died. But unlike then, her tears held the entirety of her sadness as they streamed down her face, allowing her mind to clear. She closed Cree Shee's eyelids, crossed her shrunken hands across her concave chest, then bid her galeesha a silent goodbye.

After a time, she took the chuulzu kereet down from its honored spot, feeling the full weight of the sacred headdress. Someday, she would honor her galeesha by wearing it, but first she would honor her by obeying her words. She would wash and prepare Cree Shee's body, tending it with the same loving care her galeesha had always shown her. Only after the delemeelee returned her galeesha's form to the keleekeeluk would Xyleea put on the chuulzu kereet and begin her journey to the Uniter.

WARNINGS OF A WRAITHWOLF (EXCERPT TWO)

To the ONE who LINGERS... ggrrff... and DESECRATES... ggrrrf... that which was SHATTERED... ggrrff... the Elect SEE your PERVERSIONS... ggrfff... and KNOW your great WICKEDNESS... Ggggrrfff... REMEMBER what was lost... Gggrrfff... It is not too LATE. REPENT!

ATONE for your great FOLLY... Ggrrfff... RETURN that which WEEPS... gggrrff... before the RECKONING BEGINS.

–Collected and interpreted for the Most Exalted Monarch, Geldizian Rennesseau, by a scribe

CHAPTER EIGHT
GOING HOME

Elorah reined the skittish Felderre mare back onto the narrow path winding its way through the woodlands of her home district of Calliaigh. The path had featured in many of her youthful adventures, but she hadn't time for happy memories, not with Headmistress Malenvie to consider. After tomorrow, the Head would be free to travel, and Elorah feared she would come straight to the festival to speak with her mother. The thought was almost as terrifying as telling her mother she wasn't going back to the Academie, that she would never be pinned as a Master Emvor of Therran. The horrific visions flashed into her mind and though she didn't understand what she was seeing, she knew it was an abomination. Her stomach roiled as she pushed the thoughts away.

She looked back to ensure Mierrle was still behind her and was heartened by her friend's bright smile.

Elorah hadn't intended on bringing Mierrle with her. It was only when her friend showed up at her room to see if Elorah would help her practice one last time that she remembered her promise. When she'd confessed she wasn't staying for the examinations, Mierrle had assumed Elorah's escape was for her benefit, running to her room, throwing her belongings into a rucksack, and returning before Elorah could finish her own packing.

Aikin, true to his word, had had a mare waiting for her at the Academie's stable.

"Maister Bairrtraigh was quite clear that this mare was for your use, Maiss Elorah," the stable hand had shouted over the mare's deafening whinny. "She's a bit of a character, but I warrant she'll give you a cracking ride."

In the end, Elorah had decided to make use of the hot-tempered mare. Samm was as honest as a horse could be, and she didn't want to sway his back with the weight of two riders and their baggage. She knew the gray-dapple horse would have walked on his knees if she'd asked. She also knew he wasn't the sour sort that took advantage of inexperienced riders. Mierrle only had to point the broad-backed Grenderre in the right direction, flap the reins, and the gelding would walk to the end of the world unless she stopped him first.

"Is it much farther?" asked Mierrle. Her thin leggings weren't suited for riding, and Elorah feared she would be saddle-sore tomorrow.

"Another few hills and we'll be there," Elorah promised. The familiar pangs of homesickness stirred as she caught sight of her family's witterang in the distance, the two-story round stone structure with its sturdy batten-and-thatch roof standing tall on the highest hill in the district. She loved this place so much, it hurt. And yet, she also had an unexplainable desire to leave it far behind. She didn't understand how it was possible to have both feelings at the same time, and she wondered if she was going mad.

"Is that it?" Mierrle asked, her eyes locked on the witterang.

"Yes," Elorah answered.

"It's beautiful," Mierrle breathed.

"Yes," Elorah said, as if seeing it for the first time. "It is."

After stabling the horses, Elorah and Mierrle entered the witterang's great room. Two stories high with a long stone hearth in the center, the great room was the heart of the dwelling. Within the massive hearth three separate fires chased the chill from the room. Enormous oak pillars supported the roof and the daub walls. Quarter-rooms surrounded the central great-room, four on the first level, and four on the second, each with a small, round window of green-flashed glass etched with the symbol of the Calliaigh clan—clasped hands holding a barleycorn sprig.

While Mierrle gazed open-mouthed at the vaulted ceiling overhead, Elorah charged into one of the quarter-rooms on the main level. After a quick search, she returned to the great-room and gave Mierrle a reassuring smile before bounding up the curlywood staircase to the second level, only to return a few moments later.

"I was looking for the apothecary chest," she explained as she rummaged through her satchel, not mentioning she'd also been looking for her father's crystalwood staff. "You'll need liniment for your legs, but maybe I can do something to help," she said, indicating toward a chair. Mierrle gratefully sat. Elorah hummed the five-note inspiriting tune she'd learned at the Academie while directing healing vorik into a green oblate crystal until it took on a soft glow.

She knelt before Mierrle and passed the crystal up and down each leg, sensing the dull ache throughout the muscles along with a sharper sting near the knees. She increased her vorik on those points then passed the crystal a second time. Satisfied, she brought the stone close and hummed the five-note neutralizing tune upon it.

"There, that should help," she said, putting the stone away.

Mierrle stood and ran her hand down each leg, a look of wonder on her face. "It feels much better. Thank you."

"My family must have already put up our garol. The hosting family always sets up early before raising extra garols for those unable to bring their own. Come, and I'll show you where we'll be staying." Elorah hefted her rucksack and her satchel. "Bring your things."

The festival grounds were a short walk from the witterang and Elorah was pleased to see Mierrle's gait improving as they made their way forward. It wasn't long before colorful clan flags came into view, waving gaily in the brisk breeze. Soon, the entire festival grounds were laid out before them.

Festival hosting duties rotated to a different Caeldish clan every annum, the event held at grounds located in the most picturesque area within a district. This annum was Clan Calliaigh's turn. Elorah knew her mother and grandmama were likely frantic, trying to get every detail right, not for themselves but for the sake of the crop. Every year of poor harvests placed additional pressure on the hosting clan the following New Spring. Five annums of disastrous yields had made the weight of expectation on the Clan Calliaigh heavy indeed.

If that wasn't enough, the Iellian monarch—the protectorate ruler of the United Valenvian Territory—had opened the festival to outsiders, creating even more details in need of attention. Traveling bard troupes had been singing rhymes for weeks, ginning up interest in villages and farmsteads from the highlands of the Whinden Wood to the grassy expanse of the Dallovian plains, directional signs appearing in the berms alongside every high road throughout the territory. The crowds could be enormous.

The decision to admit outsiders to what was supposed to be a sacred event was anathema to the conservatives on the Council, and there had been talk of revoking the Iellian monarch's proxy, but Elorah knew her family would put the clan's best foot forward, despite any misgivings they had regarding the Iellian monarch's impositions, providing a well-ordered venue for the week-long festival, while also accommodating the motley assortment of peddlers, merchants, and opportunists whose only interests were the auriels they stood to collect.

Then there were the invited guests to account for—Iellian citizens of means who came to gawk and stare and cluck their tongues at Caeldish traditions. Though Elorah wasn't a conservative, even she could see how the Iellian monarch's decision to exploit Valenvia was destroying Caeldish culture and making a mockery of their sacred rituals. On that point, she and Aikin agreed. Where they disagreed was how to react. Aikin favored militancy and revolution, while she favored a more inward approach.

"Prayers won't stop a tyrant, Elorah," Aikin had said during one of their more heated discussions. "You can't change the hearts of the unwilling without the use of force."

"Peaceful resistance is the way to true revolution," she'd responded. "Trading one tyrant for another solves nothing. Cooperation is the only path to a better world."

It was so like Aikin to think that the way forward always meant wielding a sword in one hand and a scythe in the other. She wanted to win over the hearts and minds of those who disagreed with her while he preferred to winnow them out.

Elorah and Mierrle had reached the edge of the festival's marketplace when a young girl of about thirteen came running up.

"Elorah, you're back," the girl singsonged, her wavy, ginger hair bouncing against her shoulders.

"Ghielle!" Elorah greeted Aikin's younger sister. "It's so good to see you."

"Have you seen the pageant grounds? Oh, it's so beautiful. Even my mother says so. There's a huge picture of the Urslan Sisters made from moss and bark where you walk in, and then near the main stage, a collage of flowers with all the clan symbols, which looks grand, and oh, you should see the stand for the berres. It's divided up by a lattice of toadstools. It's so clever. There's pink ones and purple ones and maroon ones with yellow spots and little bright green ones and oh, all sorts of colors I don't even know the name for."

"It sounds–"

"Amazing," Mierrle burbled.

"Oh, hello," Ghielle said. "My name's Ghielle, what's yours?"

"Mierrle."

"Are you Gorsh?"

"Mierrle isn't from a clan. She's my friend from the Academie," Elorah said.

Ghielle grinned, her eyes full of mischief. "Do you know my brother, Aikin?" she asked. "He goes to the Academie too. He's the best vorician there. After he gets his Master Emvor pin tomorrow, he'll be back for the pageant. He's sure to get picked as Solimar because everybody says he's the handsomest maran in the basin. Don't you think he is, Elorah?"

Elorah was caught by surprise. She'd been focusing on how much Ghielle's blustering resembled her elder brother's. "I've often heard that," she replied. Mierrle blushed.

"Did you already get your pin?" Ghielle asked, her expression going serious. "Was it as hard as my brother says it is?"

"We didn't–" Mierrle began.

Elorah cut her off. "Have you seen my mother, Ghielle?"

"I think I saw her by the garols."

"Would you care to sit while I retrieve the liniment?" Elorah asked Mierrle, pointing to a nearby bench.

"Oh, I'm fine. I should keep walking. The exercise will help."

Mierrle sounded distracted, her attention already on the marketplace and its vendor stalls arranged in neat rows. Each overflowed with a variety of wares—spices and fruits, breads and beers, whiskeys and weavings—while long curls of smoke heavy with the scents of roasted meat, crusty loaves, and sticky treacles drifted by on the breeze. A few offered livestock whose squawks and bleats and grunts counterpointed the musical tapestry of strumming lutes, wheedling pipes, and trinkling chimes hovering overhead like an invisible cloud. Everywhere was the motion of industry as shopkeeps stoked their fires, measured their barleycorn, spun their yarns, stirred their pots, bagged their herbs, jugged their ciders, kneaded their doughs, poured their candles, and scolded their children.

Elorah could see Mierrle was both fascinated and enthralled, her step quickening with the excitement of discovering an exotic new world. She did not share her friend's allurement but then again, she'd seen it all before. Many times. Over the past ten annums, the number of outsiders had steadily increased until now, it seemed there were more Iellians, Shadowen, and Inirians at the festival than Caeldish.

"Oh, there's your mother." Ghielle pointed toward an approaching figure wearing a brown cloak over a cream-colored dress embroidered with wildflowers. "I'd better get back before my mother starts looking for me. We're about to start assembling the herbals for our berre. I was supposed to be looking for bristlebane," Ghielle giggled then gave a little wave before scurrying off.

"Elorah?" the figure called as it got nearer. "Is that you?"

"Yes," Elorah answered, her palms going clammy. If only she could find some way to deliver her news without disappointing her mother. "Give me a moment," she said to Mierrle before trotting over, leaving her friend out of earshot.

Elorah embraced Novah and gave her the customary kiss near her right ear to signify respect, her lips brushing the cocklewood comb holding back her mother's silver-streaked blonde hair.

"I didn't know you would be back today," Novah said, joy lighting her face. Elorah felt another sharp scratch of guilt. "Have you gotten done early with your examinations? Have you your pin?" She glanced down at Elorah's tunic then back up again, the lines between her eyebrows deepening.

Elorah blinked and swallowed, but still the tears welled up. Novah's mouth ohed in surprise, then fell into a frown as she realized this wasn't the happy reunion she'd thought. She cocked her head to one side, and Elorah took a deep breath, her stomach falling to her shoes.

"Maissel Calliaigh, I'm so honored to meet you," Mierrle chirped. Elorah swiveled her head to see her friend was now standing nearby, her eyes shining with excitement. "It would be my greatest pleasure to assist you in any way possible with the hosting of your spectacular undertaking," Mierrle continued, her gaze taking in the marketplace before returning to Novah. Elorah swiped her forearm across her brimming eyes.

Novah pivoted stiffly toward Mierrle. "That is very kind," she said evenly. As the head of the Clan Calliaigh, Novah had long years of practice at keeping her tone from betraying her thoughts, but Elorah knew it was a bad sign that her mother was using her official voice. She might have escaped for the moment but there would be a reckoning.

"I'm not as skilled as Elorah, of course. Nobody is," Mierrle gushed, "but perhaps I can make some small contribution."

"I don't believe we've met," Novah said, her face tightening into a stretched smile. Another bad sign. The official face was in place as well.

"This is Mierrle Jazh, my friend from the Academie," Elorah said.

"I see. And you've both come here. Early," Novah said. "That's a novelty I wasn't expecting."

Just then a squat Inirian, barrel-chested from a life in the higher

72

climes, stomped past on a pair of bowed, pipe-cleaner legs, an empty leather sack that was more patches than bag slung over one shoulder. His unwashed odor was enough to announce his arrival, without the smoke puffing from the stone pipe clenched between his browned teeth smelling like burnt goat dung.

Novah turned to watch as he clomped along, unmindful of the impression he was making, his beady eyes taking in the marketplace the way a weasel studies a henhouse. Elorah also watched the man pass, noting his dust-covered shoes split and flapping, his tattered breeches the color of rot, and his flat cap so full of holes it was a mere suggestion rather than an actual head covering. Only his shapeless cloak, made from a pelt of brass-colored fur, wasn't a complete ruination.

"Gryphon hide," Novah said in a low voice. Her sky-blue eyes narrowed.

The man veered, heading toward a brackish pool intended for livestock. He pulled back the front of his cloak and rumpled up the edge of a grease-grimed shirt, exposing a sliver of fishbelly-white skin. A flick of the wrist and he'd unclipped a metal cup dangling from a braided twine belt buckled together by a horseshoe nail and a washer. A quick bend of the knees and he'd filled his cup. Straightening, he pulled the pipe away from his lips with one hand and jammed the vessel against them with the other. Two guzzling slurps and the cup and pipe traded places, the peddler's eyes squinting against the smoke wafting into his eyes as he resecured the cup and continued forward.

"Who is that?" Mierrle asked.

"An Inirian peddler," Novah answered, her eyes following the man as he stomped into a tent with the words *Herbals - Teas - Fine Smokes - Sold Here* painted in brown letters on its canvas roof. A moment later, a stout woman wearing traditional Caeldish homespun and a green kerchief, chased the peddler out with a willow stick broom. As the man stomped away, the woman shook the broom and spit on the ground before going back into her tent.

Novah turned toward Elorah. "We'll speak later," she said pointedly. "Mierrle, it's been a pleasure. I hope you enjoy your time here in the District Calliaigh. Forgive me, but I must get back to my duties."

"Yes, Maissel, thank you. I'm so grateful you've allowed me to come here today. I never expected Elorah to postpone her own exams to help me with mine, but she knows how much my family is counting on me to pass. She's always so kind to me. Truth be told, it wasn't looking good, but I think if I can practice a little more, and with Elorah's help, I might be able to get my pin after all. It would make my family so proud if I could."

Novah raised her eyebrows. "I see. Well," she said, looking at Elorah. "I suppose we could use some help in the vendor area. I was thinking of installing a fountain in the center with an herbal border but with my other duties, I've yet to see to it. A group of Iellian delegates will be here later to inspect the grounds in anticipation of the Iellian queen's arrival tomorrow. Perhaps a fountain with a nod to Her Most Exalted might help with that."

Novah bustled away looking worried. Elorah knew she was the cause of her mother's distress, and she felt terrible about it. If she could help with the preparations, perhaps she could alleviate some of her mother's anxiety.

"Let's stow our things, Mierrle, and then we'll see about that fountain," she said, heading toward an adjacent field where dozens of round canvas tents had been set up, some large and grand, others small and cramped, the unifying features being the flags hooked to the tents' center poles—each displaying the colors and symbols of the seven Caeldish clans—and the planting by each entrance serving as a tribute to tradition and a locator for Therran emvors.

As they approached the encampment, Elorah sent a surge of vorik through the rootweave, searching for her family's signature planting—meadowmint from their back garden. A menthol ting returned, creating a pathway between herself and the Calliaigh garol.

"This way," she said, setting off.

CHAPTER NINE
GAMES OF CHANCE

Finding the cave had been easy; the journey beforehand anything but.

They'd left at dawn, Rachmyn leading the way using his Shadowen intuition. First down a series of steep switchbacks, the wind whipsawing their rucksacks as they went. Next, across a silvery river cold enough to numb their feet and muddy enough to suck off their boots had they been wearing them. A brief rest next to a sputtering fire before—boots on—thrashing their way across a valley of ankle-high cutgrass that snagged burrs into their leggings. Up another set of switchbacks, their bodies bent forward to keep the relentless wind from tossing them off the mountainside until the small victory of Inverna Pass, then down once again, following a third set of switchbacks, slippery with stones that scuffed beneath their scrabbling feet before falling away—*clunka-clunka-clunk*—into the chasm below.

The nights were equally treacherous—brief snatches of uneasy sleep interrupted by long stretches of staring into the unquiet dark, ears straining for the growl of a bear or the clatter of sliding rocks.

At last, they'd come to a trading post where a barter with the proprietor had left them with a pocketful of coins, a bundle of dried sweetcane, and two strips of jerky with a peppery aftertaste. Haedyn had been quite proud when his avobanc arrowhead brought three auriels on its own.

"Ha!" he'd crowed afterward. "Three auriels for the avobanc. You said I'd only get one."

"I underestimated how many fools there are in this world," Rachmyn had replied, peering off into the distance to plan their route.

Another ten leagues and they were able to hitch rides with a succession of shepherds and farmers until they reached the cave. All told, it had taken nearly a half-moon to make the journey, but they were finally here.

Rachmyn had hoped they'd be able to stay for at least three moons, but a blabbering farmer had put an end to that with his long-winded stories about some celebration in a place called "the basin". The idea sounded horrific, purposely seeking out a crowd of noisy marans and stinking farm animals. It was all Haedyn could talk about.

"If I got three auriels for the avobanc from that shopkeep, think how much I can get at a festival where everyone walks around with empty heads and full purses. You heard what that farmer said. They're all rich and throw their money at anything shiny."

Haedyn had chiseled out another ten avobanc arrowheads since they'd made camp and was working on his eleventh, cutting the white rock with his wonderment knife as easily as carving butter, while his bird preened on its branch-turned-perch, its crop full of crickets.

Rachmyn closed his eyes, trying to draw strength from the ethers for yet another rebuttal. He'd lost count of how many times he'd made this same argument over the last two days. Elgre let out a sigh, giving voice to Rachmyn's exhaustion.

"Your arrowheads aren't shiny."

"They're white, which is basically the same thing."

"No. White and shiny are very different. And anyway, we aren't traders. We're..." Rachmyn paused, searching for a comparison that would stick this time. "Lone wolves. We aren't meant to mix with society."

"You keep saying that, but how can you be so sure? We might be perfectly suited to a life in society, but we'll never know because you're too afraid to find out. And anyway, wolves don't live alone. They live in packs. With other wolves." Haedyn arrowed a look at Elgre who yawned and closed his eyes. "Can't we do this one thing? If it doesn't work out, I promise I'll let it go. I'll accept we're misfits, or lone wolves, or whatever you want to call us, and that I'm doomed to spend the rest of my life whittling rocks and watching fire shadows inside some miserable old cave while you're lumped up in a corner, that daft smile on your face, your mind off in some faraway place no one else can reach."

Rachmyn sighed. "You've no idea what you're asking for," he said, images from those long-ago days of terror arising like ghosts in his mind.

"We can't hide forever," Haedyn said. "Even you have to admit, this isn't a life. It's barely an existence."

"Death has knocked on your door once already. Do not tempt fate by inviting him in."

"I know you think you know what's best, but we're all going to die. When it happens, wouldn't you rather be doing something worthwhile, instead of withering away in a gloomy hole doing nothing at all? What's the point of that?"

Rachmyn ran his hand through his hair, settled back against his rucksack, and crossed his arms across his chest. Nearby, Elgre chewed the leg off the dead hare he held between his paws, one of three they'd managed to snare. The other two were roasting on a spit over the fire. "What about that wall? That wall is meant to keep out people like us. More to the point, the Iellian guards on that wall are there to keep out people like us. We'll probably end up in some third-rate thiefkeep because you've a misplaced urge to do something spectacular."

"Not spectacular. Normal. I just want to be normal."

Rachmyn's brow furrowed. Being normal was never going to be on the cards for either of them, but did he have the right to stifle his friend's hopes and dreams? His own parents had lost their lives trying to be normal, instead of staying true to their Shadowen sensibilities. But Haedyn wasn't Shadowen. He was Fyrre, with all the heated passion that affinity conferred. Rachmyn couldn't count the number of times he'd plucked his young friend out of some predicament that portended disaster. And yet...

He picked up a handful of pebbles from the cave floor and started tossing them from one hand to the other, back and forth, back and forth, *click clack, click clack, click clack,* as he weighed the options. Haedyn sighed, his face looking as if he'd already lost the argument.

Rachmyn flipped one of the pebbles at the fire, striking the burning wood and sending a plume of sizzling sparks into the air. Elgre's ears pricked, and he cocked his head. Haedyn brightened.

"I know. We'll flip for it," Haedyn said, digging into his pocket. He placed an auriel on his palm, the embossed portrait of the Iellian queen glinting in the firelight. "Heads, we go." He turned the coin over to show the Valenvian seal. "Tails, we stay. That's the only fair way."

Rachmyn dropped the remaining pebbles and snatched the coin from Haedyn's hand, checking to see that the two sides were indeed different. Satisfied, he placed the coin on his thumbnail. "Alright," he said, "But I'll do the flipping."

Haedyn feigned indignation but he couldn't suppress a smile.

Rachmyn stood and cleared his throat, his thumb sending the coin high into the air. It flipped end over end in a graceful arc before hitting the cave floor with a muffled thud. He bent to look, but Haedyn was already out of his seat and crowding his head in the way. The younger man let out a whoop and punched the air before leaping into an impromptu jig, Fryk launching into a looping orbit around his head as he danced around. Elgre eyed the pair with disdain, then looked at Rachmyn, his eyes full of sympathy.

"Spunk," Rachmyn said, staring at the coin. The sodding queen of Iellia. Heads.

In the end, the wall had been no hindrance; the bottle-shaped cave providing a tunnel that let them bypass it completely. The hidden opening at the narrow end of the cavern had been another matter. They'd had to dig their way out, a whole day on their knees chipping and chopping and chucking dirt by the light of a flickering candle before they could wriggle through the narrow cleft in the rock wall, sweat clinging their shirts to their backs and dampening their leggings.

Haedyn maintained his humor as he scratched and scraped at the hardened dirt with his knife, humming to himself and even whistling a time or two until Rachmyn silenced him with a look. Rachmyn's mood was far darker, his mind full of swear words for his weak will and rotten luck. Only when the job was done did he manage to speak.

"Spunk," he muttered, his mood darker than ever as he pushed first his staff then his rucksack then himself through the excavated hole and into the gathering dusk. Elgre crawled out last, shaking debris from his coat before gazing down the sloping hillside of cutgrass and rock.

Haedyn kneeled beside his rucksack, his grynt perched on his leather-clad forearm. The bird's black talons, though small, were sharp enough to easily shred unprotected flesh. Its black eyes were also sharp as they surveyed the landscape. A nearby scurry swiveled the bird's head. It let out a piercing *chirrt-chirrt-chirrt*, and cocked its wings in preparation for flight.

Rachmyn signaled for silence, and Haedyn quickly hooded the raptor before tucking it into his vest pocket.

Rachmyn crept out from behind the rock formation and glanced toward the huge stone wall separating them from the foothills of Deadman's Peak. Only two guards were visible, both standing behind the wall's parapet, their silver helmets drawn together. The taller one passed a pipe to the shorter one who took a tug, a pinpoint of orange light glowing bright before dulling again. The short one passed the pipe back, his head wreathed in white smoke. The taller one ground his gloved thumb into the pipe's bowl before jerking his head to look out across the sloping ground leading toward the eastern horizon.

Rachmyn sagged down and ducked his head, his heartbeat in his ears, his neck beginning to welt from the scratching grass. The last thing he needed was a broadhead embedded in his temple courtesy of an Iellian crossbow. He allowed several moments to pass before he raised his head and looked toward the guards again.

This time, the tall one was holding a wooden pole with a metal ovaloid connected to the end. The guard swept the device in an arc, his attention fixed on it. The short one had a spyglass crammed against his eye surveying the landscape.

Rachmyn heard a rustle. Haedyn had crept from the rock formation and was crouching beside him.

"What's that thing?" he whispered.

Rachmyn put a finger to his lips then grasped Haedyn's shoulder, pushing it toward the grass while walking two fingers of his other hand across the ground then pointing toward the rock formation. Haedyn nodded his understanding.

The two forearm-crawled their way back to where their rucksacks and staffs were, Haedyn taking care not to injure his pocketed grynt as he dragged himself along.

Elgre stood and wagged his tail, his eyes bright, before plotzing to the ground and stretching out his hind legs in imitation of his packmates. Haedyn jerked his thumb toward the wolf and smiled.

"D'ya–" he began.

Rachmyn clapped one hand over Haedyn's mouth and used the other to signal for silence. Haedyn nodded his understanding, and Rachmyn let his hand drop. The thought had come to him that the Iellian guard was using some sort of listening device. He couldn't be sure. He'd never seen one before, but he remembered a conversation with his father about the Iellian gift for vibrations and didn't want to take any chances. He etched a message into the dirt.

We wait till dark then move.

Rachmyn underlined the words to make his point. Haedyn peered at the scratchings then, pressing his lips together, pushed himself into a cross-legged sit, his chin propped in his hands, a look of wistful excitement in his eyes. Elgre pulled his hindlegs under his body and put his head between his paws.

Rachmyn settled next to a boulder to wait, misgivings looming large in his mind. What were they doing out here? They should climb back inside the cave, follow it to the other end, hoist themselves out and set a path north. He cursed himself again for getting sucked into another game of chance. When would he learn? Wasn't that how that sodding, eye-plucking bird had ended up in his friend's pocket? He should have remembered that, but he'd thought surely this time, *this time,* good fortune would be on his side. That it would be his turn to win. But no...

His hand went to his pocket for his shard. Yes, there it was. He ran his thumb over the stone's smooth surface, taking comfort from its familiar shape and the way it nestled into the contour between his index and middle finger. There was something ancient and true about the stone, something that made it seem almost alive, as if it could hear his thoughts and understand his heart. When he had doubts or fears, the feeling of the shard in his hand was enough to drive them back to the far recesses of his mind, giving him the clarity he needed to face any situation.

Haedyn opened his vest and brought his hooded grynt out onto his arm. He stroked the bird's keel, and the grynt stretched its neck in pleasure. Rachmyn watched, the ice of his misgivings beginning to melt.

Haedyn looked up then balled up his fist, shook it twice, and grinned. Their secret signal that all would turn out right. The look of pure happiness on his friend's face put a smile on Rachmyn's. As much as he hated what they were doing, his love for Haedyn was strong. It was the one constant in his life he couldn't imagine living without. Rachmyn shook his fist twice in return.

The gloom would soon thicken into darkness, and they would be able to continue toward their destination. Perhaps this festival wouldn't be as bad as he'd imagined. Perhaps he'd at least get lucky with that.

Once night had settled, Rachmyn judged it safe to venture forth. If he and Haedyn could get across the open ground undetected, the tree line on the horizon would provide sufficient cover until morning.

Rachmyn gauged the distance between the rock formation and the trees at about four hundred paces, a long span to be out in the open. With the moon casting a silvery glow, they needed some way of disguising themselves. Often, they would attach greenery to their clothing then creep forward on their bellies but in this case, the only thing available was cutgrass, and it did not lend itself to camouflage or crawling. Their only option was to break up their silhouettes by strapping their rucksacks to their chests, tying their walking staffs to their waists and, after linking arms, hunching over and waddling like a bear in the hope that darkness would do the rest.

Through a series of hand signals and pantomime, Rachmyn communicated the plan to Haedyn who nodded his understanding. It was a trick they'd used before, and they both knew how to proceed. The man in front would walk with his head near his knees to get the proportions right. Haedyn, being shorter by a hand, was the natural choice. The last time they'd done it, Haedyn had been younger and smaller and less burdened with things to carry, but Rachmyn still thought they had a reasonable chance at success. Dragging their walking staffs was a bother, but he didn't want to leave them behind, a decision he hoped wouldn't prove to be a mistake.

If all else failed, he could create a mindshield, using his Shadowen vor, to project an image of their surroundings into the space between the guards and themselves. He would use that skill if it came to it, but the vorik output would be immense, leaving him drained due to the size and complexity of the image required in an expanse this large. In more confined spaces, he could preserve some of his vor but in this case, he knew he would be severely depleted by the time they reached the tree line, putting them at risk later. He hoped the bear-walk illusion would be enough to get them through so he could preserve his powers.

They began preparing. Haedyn stowed Fryk then removed his vest, laying it on the ground before rummaging out his cloak. Taking care that the bird was safely positioned, he secured the vest to the rucksack, strapped the bundle to his chest then tied his staff to his waist using a snare string.

Rachmyn, already finished, watched Haedyn as he worked, wondering again why they had to be burdened with the sodding bird. Elgre never needed the coddling Haedyn's companion required. It was exhausting watching him fuss and fret over the bothersome creature.

Rachmyn put on his cloak and checked the compass tied to his wrist while he waited. He would need it to keep their path true.

Haedyn gave his pack one last check then bumped his fist twice to indicate his readiness. Rachmyn glanced at the wall then nodded. Time to go.

Haedyn put on his cloak, shoved his fists into his pockets, and stooped his shoulders low. Rachmyn slid his upper body under his friend's cloak before turning his head toward the compass then lowering it near Haedyn's hips. It was an uncomfortable contortion for them both and four hundred paces would be an eternity, but this way, he could guide their progress and prevent Haedyn from rushing. He knew his friend well enough to know he would soon become impatient with their slow progress and try to speed things along.

He prodded Haedyn who started into a leisurely galumph, Rachmyn following suit. Several paces in, Rachmyn squinted at his wrist to check their heading. The compass was difficult to read in the low light, and he looked at it for several blinks before making a slight adjustment by tugging on Haedyn's waist as they toddled along.

It was hard, sweaty work, and they paused several times, Rachmyn checking his compass to reconfirm their course. The wemble helped shift the heat of their exertions away from their bodies but did nothing for the cramping in their backs and legs and arms and necks.

When they finally entered the tree line after what felt like an age, they broke apart and shed their disguise before slumping against the stout trunks of two sourwood trees. Rachmyn unhooked a waterskin from his bandolier and passed it to Haedyn, who took a drink then passed it back. Rachmyn took a long draught then capped it.

The pair settled back and covered up with their cloaks.

"I'll take the first shift," Rachmyn murmured, his eyes scanning their periphery. Haedyn nodded, his eyes already closed, his hooded bird perched on his shoulder.

Rachmyn reached into his pocket for his shard. Yes, there it was. He slipped it into the groove between his two fingers and ran his thumb across its smoothness as he listened to the soft drone of his friend's snoring. Overhead, thin clouds framed the iridescent corona surrounding the full moon, a rare phenomenon he'd seen only a handful of times. *Not a bad way to spend an evening,* he thought as he admired the view. *Not a bad way at all.*

Elgre circled twice then curled himself into the leaf litter at Rachmyn's feet.

Tomorrow they would make their way to a festival that promised nothing but chaos, but tonight, they would sleep beneath the stars and a haloed moon, in the peace of a sourwood forest that cared not who they were or where they were from. It would suit.

CHAPTER TEN
THWARTED

The Wycche awoke in her chamber seething with rage. She keened through gritted teeth and pounded her fists against the tufted velvet of the chaise, anger clamping her throat and threatening to choke her.

She opened her eyes to the blackness enveloping the hexagon-shaped room. Windowless and accessible only through two thick wooden doors, each with four separately keyed brass locks, the womb-like chamber remained as blankly dark as a scrying stone, making her feel as if she were floating in a void. She stretched her thoughts back to Oru Fen.

The white wraithwolf had forced her to use nearly all her vorik before causing her to fail. The dreamdoor she'd searched for night after night had been tantalizingly close this time, the etheriant on the other side pure and full of power. But it had all slipped through her grasp.

The cursed Vorien had woven a spell more cunning than she had managed, a memory trap, breaking her concentration and spinning her out of the realm. Who was he to judge her? She who had walked those starry pathways for time beyond time. It was she who did the judging. It was she who decided the fates.

How had he conjured up that long ago scene and planted it in her mind, distracting her from attaining what she most desired? It had been clever, using her own memories against her. She rarely found herself outwitted, but the white wolf's night-ward had Spyrrt forces, and that had given him leverage.

She should have been more cautious, but she'd forgotten. She distantly remembered being able to pull from that source, but that ability had faded long ago. Now her weapons were the treachery of sharpened thought and the treason of amoral ambition. It wasn't often these daggers of the mind proved insufficient.

Her wraithwolf had suffered the same fate. He had also been driven back by the white wolf's mind trick, his deadblack vanishing into the ethers. Without the force of her vor, he was nought but another fallen Malvisse prowling Oru Fen like a wandering ghost.

It would take time to rebuild their supply using the harvested energies of the unguarded. The Arcana of Vorie Supin would help, but until she was fully recharged, she would be unable to dreamwalk with any great ability. Her wolf would likewise be unable to assemble enough deadblack to form up his armor until she was restored. They would have to be cautious during this time of lean.

The white wolf would almost certainly know their weakness. His vor was strong, because his night-ward's was strong. Until they had reassembled their own powers, both she and Venge would need to avoid confrontation. It galled her to think of it, for she was used to having the upper hand, but she was also practical. She could see no way around it.

She swung herself upright then stood, smoothing her dress, and running her fingers through her flattened hair, her mind closing the door on Oru Fen. She would soon have to reenter the waking world, and she needed to focus on that. There would be other opportunities, other chances to actuate her plans, but until then, she would rebuild, gathering strength for the time when she could enter Oru Fen with enough power and purpose to finish what she had started.

CHAPTER ELEVEN
DANCING BEARS AND A TRAVELING MAN

It wasn't hard to find the spot Novah had intended for the fountain. A ring of rose-quartz boulders in the center of the marketplace separated an area the size of a quarter-room from the rows of tent stalls and carts and caravans. A layer of green-slate shingle was already laid. All that was left was to install the statuary and water.

A large, white canvas tent stood beyond the circle, an indigo flag emblazoned with the Iellian mascot—a silver-and-slate gryphon on its hind paws, beak gapped wide, three zig-zagged bolts in one taloned front foot—bracketed to its center pole. Dark blue and silver pennants fluttered above a walkway of narrow dark-blue carpets bordered by sky-blue flowered shrubs connecting the stone circle to the tent's entrance.

Elorah had been working on the fountain for nearly an hour.

She'd already used her Therran vorik to grow and shape bushes from the walkway into topiaries depicting two bears gracefully balanced on their hind legs, their near-side forelegs extended in the half-embrace of a dance, their far-side paws holding a large leaf over their heads as an umbrella. Elorah was happy with her approximation of the Urslan Sisters, but the water that was meant to be fountaining up between the dancing bears and pattering down upon the leaf umbrella was not coming together at all.

Mierrle was despondent. She'd been trying to use her vorik to locate and transpose a vein of water for the fountain's spray, to no avail.

"I'm hopeless," she said, exhausted from her efforts. "I thought I felt something moving and it seemed like water, but..." She flapped her palms out in exasperation.

"Oh, dear," Elorah murmured, looking at her spent friend as she sat on one of the boulders, her shoulders slumping, her dark hair curtaining her deep frown. The fat, golden disc of the late afternoon sun had settled onto the horizon. Soon it would be dark.

Elorah closed her eyes and concentrated, searching for the emanating pulse of Eolemar beneath her feet. After a few moments she could feel it, an infrasonic thump something like the beat of a heart. She formed a question, a request to the All, to hear her small voice in the shouting wilderness, then sent it forth from the soles of her feet past the rootweave—the infinite tangle of rootlets connecting every plant with every other—down and down toward the insistent thrum. She slowed her breathing and cleared her thoughts of anything other than the *bohhmmm, bohhmmm, bohhmmm* of an ancient vibration that had existed since the beginning of time. She focused on immersing her vorik within the vibration's immense flow, until she and it were one.

She visualized a stream of water flowing through a sand seam below, channeling the vision into a summoning, her heart asking for the water's cooperation. In her mind's eye, the stream changed course, pulling upward toward her beckoning call. Accomplishment shot through her, breaking her concentration. She opened her eyes.

Mierrle sprang up. "I felt it!" she exclaimed. "The water. Coming up from below."

Elorah nodded, then took a deep breath, checking for the fatigue of vor depletion. She felt none and another thrill ran through her, despite her best efforts to stay focused.

Silvi had warned her of the tendency for self-congratulation and cautioned her to work hard to overcome this thought pattern. "*One cannot meld with the All while retaining the consciousness of the individual. To be one with the energy that animates, one must see past the illusion of the animation. One can only surrender to the All when one is free from the limitation of thoughts that are but incomplete echoes of that which is true."*

Elorah understood the importance of mental discipline, but she still struggled to control her thoughts. Silvi had assured her this was normal, telling her it would take much practice before Elorah would master her errant mind, but she was still annoyed that her connection with the All had been broken almost as soon as it had begun.

She checked her surroundings to reorient herself.

Four Iellian guards caught her attention as they swaggered by. The guards, attired in the blue uniform of the High Iellian Order of Enforcement, gamboled from stand to stand, checking official vendor stamps and helping themselves to the beers and fruits and baked goods on display. A yellow-haired baker of the Clan Thrast came charging out of his tent after two of his piffle buns went into the gullets of two guards.

"Hey, what's this, then? That'll be a fennig each, if you please," the Thrastian said, clapping the back of one hand against the palm of the other.

"Back to your ovens, you straw-haired burntfinger, and be quick about it, or you'll find yourself in the thiefkeep for disorderly conduct," barked a whiskey-nosed guard. "We've the right to ensure the purity of any and all goods in this marketplace, as a condition of your stamp privilege." The guard pushed his flattened hand forward, producing a gust of wind strong enough to force the baker back a step. The baker readjusted his skullcap and glared at the guard before retreating into his tent, muttering oaths as yeasty as the baked goods on offer.

The High Hells laughed and moved on to the next stand, an orchardist's cart stacked high with crates of fruit. One picked up an apfel and bit into it, clear juice running to his chin before his blue-cuffed wrist swiped it away. Another picked up a peir and bit off half before holding it out and nodding his approval to the red-cheeked orchardist watching, his close-set eyes sullen, his jaw flexing tight.

A whip-thin young man occupying the narrow space separating the orchardist's cart from a tobacconist's conveyance hustled his wares into a leather rucksack then trotted toward Elorah and Mierrle, his shifting eyes appraising the High Hells as he approached.

"Gentle ladies, may I be of assistance?" the dark-headed young man with a pointed goatee asked in a tenor voice both melodious and resonant. He swung round to catch sight of the High Hells, who had moved on to the tobacconist before turning back, his brilliant green eyes taking in the topiary bears. "Is it meant to be a statue, or..."

"A fountain, actually," Elorah said.

"Ahh, I see." The young man set his rucksack down and hitched up his knit leggings. "The name's Thane Arlot, by the way." He bent forward, giving Elorah and Mierrle each a courtesy bow. "Forgive me, but don't fountains involve a quantity of water?" A smile ticked up the corners of his mouth. If not for the wide scar jagging down his right cheek and the crooked nose that looked as if it had met more than its fair share of blunt instruments, he might have passed for handsome. His voice was his most attractive feature, although it was the voice of an innocent, and there was nothing about his appearance that fit with that.

"Well, yes," Elorah allowed. "We were just getting to that part."

Thane glanced at the High Hells who had crossed the aisleway to harass a round-bellied herbalist and his rounder wife. He crowded his thin frame close.

Elorah took a step back, as did Mierrle.

"May I propose, if it suits, to assist you with your project? You see, water is something of a specialty for me, and this..." he gestured toward the topiary bears, "...masterpiece is deserving of only the best." He finished with a smooth smile.

Mierrle nodded, but Elorah caught the insincere edge in Thane's words. "Do you really think it is a masterpiece?" she asked archly.

"But, of course," he replied, his smile broadening. "Anyone would. Although it is missing that finishing touch that would make it truly special."

"Your papers, sir. We're told you've been selling trinkets without a license." Whiskey Nose strode over to bawl the words into Thane's ear. Behind, the herbalist crossed his arms, resting them upon the shelf of his bulging stomach, his chin jerking forward, his rotund wife planting her fists on her hammy hips.

Thane stood stock still, his eyes widening before tracking sideways toward the guard's voice. "I wouldn't dream of selling without a license," he began, his face imploring Elorah to confirm his words. "I am here as a participant only."

"You're one of these Caeldish? Which clan?" the guard sneered, his hand dropping toward the cudgel on his hip.

"Clan..." Thane's voice trailed off.

"He's in the employ of Clan Calliaigh," Elorah supplied. "I am Elorah Niav bai Calliaigh and I am the one who has employed him."

The guard gave Elorah a doubtful look. "Employed, you say. Employed for what purpose? He looks a common grifter to me."

"That's where you'd be wrong, gentle sir. I have a way with water," Thane said, his voice cracking. "A command of it, if you will."

"Let's see it then," the guard challenged.

"Certainly. We were about to begin." Thane stepped toward the topiaries, rubbed his hands together then raised them to the level of his shoulders before closing his eyes and deepening his breathing. After a moment, his hands began to theatrically gesture, slowly at first, then faster and faster, as if he were conducting an invisible orchestra toward a crescendo.

"Get on with it, grifter," the guard warned, his gloved fingers tightening around the cudgel's stock.

"Gentle sir, a moment please," Thane murmured, his eyes still closed, his hands still circling toward the topiary bears. Elorah and Mierrle exchanged worried looks.

The gravel beneath the topiaries darkened. Mierrle grabbed Elorah's arm and pointed. "Look," she whispered. Elorah nodded as the dampness spread.

Thane made a series of coaxing motions until silty water burbled beneath the bears' feet. After a moment, Thane thrust his hands skyward, and a clear jet of water spurted high above the leaf umbrella before settling into a fanning descent.

Thane opened his eyes. "Is that what you had in mind?"

"You've captured it perfectly." Elorah clapped her hands together and turned toward the guard. "A masterpiece, wouldn't you say?"

The guard snorted, and Thane cast an ironic pursed-lip frown at the back of his head before it whipped round to face him. "What are you staring at?"

90

Thane shrugged innocently, and the guard stepped back, his hand moving away from the cudgel. "See that we don't catch you selling without a license." He turned to his squad. "Come on," he blared. "We can't stand around here all day."

Thane ducked his chin and brought his hands together in a prayer-like pose near his chest.

The High Hells strode toward a flashy caravan, Whiskey Nose throwing a scowl over his shoulder before turning his attention to rousting the caravan's inhabitants, most of whom were already scurrying off in several directions. "Produce your papers," he shouted as he approached the gaudy wagon.

"That was wonderful," Mierrle enthused. "Now it looks like the bears are dancing in the rain. How did you do it?"

Thane shrugged. "Water has been my friend since I was small," he said.

"Have you accommodations?" Elorah asked.

"I'm fixed well enough." Thane tapped his rucksack and hoisted it onto his shoulder. "I've had it worse." He eyed the guards who were now harassing an Inirian wood carver selling keraswood smoke pipes.

"I would be remiss if I didn't offer a garol for all that you've done," Elorah said.

"A garol?"

Elorah gestured toward the tent for the dignitaries. "It wouldn't be as grand as this, but we've plenty for travelers. My mother prides herself on our clan's provisions for those who haven't garols of their own." She didn't add that her mother held the belief that her dead father was still alive, and that her treatment of strangers would influence how strangers treated him. The law of similars, she called it. Elorah's stomach pinched.

Thane shook his head. "I've a few irons in the fire that need tending. But I thank you, maiss."

"You must at least allow me to see that you're fed." Elorah eyed his slim physique with a mixture of concern and pity. "We were about to eat. Would you join us?"

Thane started to protest, then, after shooting another look at the High Hells, thought better of it. "I would be delighted," he said.

91

Elorah pointed out the various clan flags as the trio made their way to her family's garol. The barleycorn growing from stone of the Bairrtraigh clan flew from many of the center poles. "The Clan Bairrtraigh are Caeldish to the roots of their boots," she explained. "One of the founding families of Valenvia and not shy to tell it."

"Is that Aikin's clan?" Mierrle asked.

Elorah nodded. "It is." She pointed to a flag with a shock of bound farina. "That's the banner of the Clan Fola. The fields there are as wide as the sky. Barleycorn, farina, and tubers but mostly farina."

Mierrle pointed to a flag with a six-teated milking gelft and a bucket. "What's that?"

"That's a milchgelft. The Clan Rairrsaigh are famous for their gelft herds. And their cheeses."

"Famous for something else, too," Thane added. "There's truth to the old joke that if you don't have a pocketful of coins or six milking teats, you'd better find somewhere else to lay your head. No one stays for free in the District Rairrsaigh."

They passed a tent whose flag depicted loaves of bread arranged in a three-lobed barleycorn leaf. "The Clan Thrast," Elorah said, "Famous for their breads and their brews."

"And their tempers," Thane added, arching his eyebrows at Mierrle and rubbing the scar on his cheek, a rueful smile on his lips.

Elorah pointed to another flag, this one of a four-horned Plynton bull's head. "And that's the bull's head of the Clan Gorsh. And there's the mint-wreathed apfel of the Clan Hiegh."

"The Hiegh lad who spent his rent on cider, ale, and merriment," Thane said, quoting a well-worn line from *The Hiegh Lad*.

At last, they came to the Calliaigh family garol. Elorah motioned toward their flag of clasped hands and barleycorn. "And of course, the flag of the Clan Calliaigh," she said as she ushered her guests through the garol's opening.

The interior was crowded with appointments from the family witterang. Wooden chairs with padded seats sat opposite three willow-wood frames topped by canvas bedsacks puffed fat with roving wool.

Woven mats had been laid for the floor while the ancestral tapestries depicting emvors, barleycorn, and spirit bears from the witterang's hallways were suspended between the garol's side poles, creating a colorful mural of Caeldish tradition stories. Rylan's shrine was in place beside one of the bed frames, along with the tall brass-plated apothecary chest that had likely taken three men to move. It made for a cozy room that almost felt like home.

Between the three of them, they put away two Thrastian loaves, three-fifths of a Rairrsaigh cheese wheel, three apfels, two peirs, and a pitcher of Hiegh sweet cider. Thane polished off an entire loaf, two-fifths of the cheese, two peirs, an apfel, and two tankards of cider, wolfing it all down as if he were afraid it might disappear. When he'd finished, he sat back, pulled a silver toothpick from his pocket and employed it.

"Where will you go after the festival?" Mierrle inquired, nibbling at a piece of cheese.

"I haven't secured a position, but I'm hopeful," Thane replied, returning the toothpick to his pocket.

"I'll speak with my father. I'm sure he would employ you."

Thane's eyebrows lifted, his expression quizzical.

"We're water merchants. We sell to most of the Wahzim and even to the Heddrians on occasion. He would pay you well."

Thane's eyes lit with interest. "Is that so," he said, his voice evenly modulated.

The entrance flap flew open, and Elorah jumped up from her chair as Aikin came striding in, his face racked with worry. A dark-haired young man followed, a four-string lute strapped to one shoulder, the smudge of a new mustache shading the gap between his pointed nose and upper lip.

"Aikin? Fyndd!" Elorah exclaimed. "It's been an age!"

"It has indeed." Fyndd replied.

"A bard's mustache. My, how stylish."

Fyndd smoothed his fuzzed upper lip, a self-deprecating smile springing onto his face.

Aikin broke in. "What's happened? Are you well? Why did you leave the Academie?"

Fyndd ducked his head and stared at the ground as Elorah turned.

"I was needed here." Even to her own ears, the words sounded less than truthful.

"But you've missed the examinations and the pinning," Aikin said, his arms lifting into a posture of bewilderment.

"It seems you've missed as well," she said, her face falling. "I hope not because of me."

"Of course, it's because of you. How could I stay after finding out you'd left without so much as a goodbye? I've never seen the Head so upset."

Elorah sighed. "It couldn't be helped."

"It was because of me." Mierrle's chin began to tremble. "Elorah promised to help me learn the ways of water."

Thane quirked an eyebrow at that.

"Is this true?" Aikin asked.

"I did make that promise," Elorah said, choosing not to elaborate.

"But why?" Aikin cried. "You were so close. And now, it's all gone. All that time and effort wasted."

"Are you speaking of me or yourself?" Elorah asked. "I never intended for you to leave early."

Thane leaned back in his chair, his eyes dancing as he watched the exchange.

"And who is this? Another one of your charity cases?" Aikin turned toward Thane. "What's she giving up for you?"

"We have a business arrangement, gentle sir. Nothing more," Thane replied with a crooked grin. "But indeed, I should be going. I thank you, maiss, for the excellent meal. It was most appreciated." He rose from his chair and hoisted his rucksack onto his thin shoulder.

"I believe I know you," Fyndd said, his finger pointing toward Thane, his brow knitting above his lively brown eyes.

"I can't see how," Thane answered. "I've only just arrived."

Fyndd pursed his lips. "No, I've seen you somewhere," he said, his expression tight, his eyes far away, as he searched for some forgotten memory.

"Perhaps," Thane allowed. "A traveler I am and always will be, across rugged lands and o'er rough seas," he sang, his high tenor ringing

94

throughout the garol. Fyndd cocked his head at the well-known lyric. "I believe that's how it goes," Thane said with a smile that held no warmth.

"Lock up your maisses, lock up your gold, lock up your sweetsweet, or forfeit them all," Fyndd bleated, striking a chord on his lute. "Yes, we all know that one." He exchanged a look with Aikin, whose glare hardened.

"I don't think this is the time or place for drinking songs," he spat.

The entrance flap opened and Vaytah Niav bai Calliaigh entered, her blue eyes bright above a mischievous smile. Her pearl-gray hair, gathered at the nape of her neck, tumbled down her green-cloaked back. She looked around and clapped her hands.

"Are we singing?" she chortled.

"Grandmama!" Elorah cried, running toward the older woman. Vaytah opened her arms, and Elorah fell into an embrace, her face burying into the green-on-gray pattern of her grandmama's ceremonial gown. She inhaled the familiar scents of sweet herbs and smoke before breaking free.

"Good evening, Maissel Calliaigh," Aikin said. "We were–"

"I've seen wonders, I've seen sights, I've seen marvels, too, but I've ne'er seen anything half so fair as the maiss with the eyes of blue," Vaytah sang in her quavery alto. "She's round above, she's round below, her cheeks are rosy rare, and when she shakes her roundy bits, oh don't the young men stare."

"Grandmama," Elorah admonished.

"Oh, there's no harm," Vaytah chuckled as color rose to Elorah's cheeks. "Aikin, no need to tell your mother. Just a bit of fun, eh? Fyndd, your father either."

Aikin harrumphed, his disapproval evident from his stiff posture and stony expression. Fyndd burst into laughter despite his friend's icy glare. Thane also laughed, while Mierrle smiled, happy the mood had lightened.

Vaytah looked at Thane. "I don't believe we've met."

"Thane Arlot." He took a step toward the exit. "I was just on my way out."

"Arlot... Is that Inirian?"

"Elequian, maissel. Quelp, to be precise."

"My, but you're a long way from home. Have you come all this way for our little festival?"

"Not exactly. A combination of happy accident and mysterious coincidence has brought me to your charming district."

"Charming?" Vaytah laughed. "Well, I suppose it can be. We certainly try to put on a good face, but it hasn't the seaside views or emerald pools or blacksand beaches you're used to."

"You're familiar with Elequia?" Thane asked, genuinely surprised.

"A bit. Now, how about tea." Vaytah bustled to the apothecary chest and opened a drawer. "Sit." She directed Thane to a chair. "Please." She pointed Aikin toward a different chair. "Yes," she said to Fyndd, already folding into a third chair. "Have a seat, maiss." She indicated Mierrle to a nearby bed, then turned, "Elorah, some help please?"

Elorah went to her grandmama and whispered, "But we've no fire." Individual fires were frowned upon during the festival, an effort to foster communal gathering amongst the clans. Instead, families were expected to use one of the many iron-grated firestands scattered throughout the garol area to warm their stews and their teapots and their backsides while wood-fired ovens huffed alongside, their interiors lumped full of loaves and biscuits and buns.

"And why would we require a fire?" Vaytah clucked, pulling a copper teapot with a fitted brazier and trivet from a basket beside the chest. She met Elorah's look of surprise with a mirthful smile as she set up the self-contained unit on the brass top of the chest. "It's rather marvelous, isn't it?" she said, filling the brazier's reservoir using an oil can with a long, thin spout. "Iellian. From the marketplace," she confirmed as she inserted a thready wick, then used a specialized iron striker to spark it until the wick glowed orange. "No flame at all," Vaytah called for the benefit of Aikin. "Perfectly proper."

She set the brazier lid in place and turned her attention to the teapot, spooning in brown leaves from a wooden canister. Elorah was reminded of the foil packet the Head had given her. She'd chucked it into the Academie's latrine before she left, fearing the Head might use it as a finder's mark.

Vaytah poured water from a jug into the teapot then set it upon the brazier.

"Now, we wait," she said. "A story, perhaps, to fill the time."

"I have one," Fyndd said, stating the obvious. A bard always has a story.

Aikin groaned.

Vaytah settled beside Mierrle and motioned for Elorah to sit beside her.

Fyndd unstrapped the lute and set it on the floor before leaning forward, his arms draping across his knees.

"Long ago, when the moon was young, a traveling man was on his way to a certain village. He carried very little usually, but this night he carried almost nothing, having only the clothes on his back, a twist of tobacco, and a candle. The night was soon upon him, and a cold night it was, so he stopped at a farm and asked if he could spend the night in the farmer's barn. The farmer, a hard character, asked the traveling man how he proposed to pay, for he wasn't one who believed in charity for charity's sake."

"Must have been in Rairrsaigh," Vaytah whispered with a puckish grin. Elorah laughed. Mierrle also laughed, though her face said she didn't understand what was funny.

"The traveling man produced the twist of tobacco from his cloak and asked if that would be sufficient. The farmer shook his head. 'Nay, I've no need of another man's tobacco when I can smoke my own. What else do you have?' The traveling man produced his candle and asked if that would be sufficient. The farmer shook his head. 'Nay, I've no need of another man's candle when I have my own to keep out the night. What else do you have?' The traveling man took off his cloak and held it out. 'Would this be sufficient?" he asked, already shivering from the cold. The farmer shook his head. 'Nay, I've no need of another man's covering when I have my own thick cloak to keep me warm. What else do you have?' The traveling man thought for a minute, then stooped down and slid off his leather boots. He held them out and asked if they would be sufficient. The farmer shook his head. 'Nay, I've no need of another man's boots, when I have my own matched pair. What else do you have?'"

Mierrle leaned forward, captivated. Aikin rolled his eyes. He wasn't one for stories when he had other pressing concerns. Thane stroked his bearded chin and eyed the entrance flap. Fyndd rose and began to pantomime.

"The traveling man replaced his boots, threw on his cloak, then put away his tobacco and his candle. 'I've nothing left for man nor beast,' the traveling man said, 'and so I'll be on my way.' The farmer shook his head. 'Nay, lad. You've forgotten the most valuable thing a man can offer. The honest sweat of his labor. Promise me that, and we can yet strike a bargain.'"

"I don't trust that farmer," Vaytah whispered to Elorah.

"Now the traveling man knew that the farmer was shrewd and that he should be wary, but the night was cold, and the barn was near, and it seemed a harmless enough trade. Still, he asked the question. 'And what labor would you ask in exchange for a night in yon barn?' 'Just a bit of digging,' answered the farmer. 'A lad as strong as yourself, with an early start would be done before the morning dew dries.' The traveling man thought about this, for he did have a strong back and a stout heart, and it sounded an easy enough task, but he had dealt with dishonest men before, and so he asked one more question. 'And would I be digging up or digging down, for I am a man who must know where he's going before he can begin.'"

"That's not even a sensible question," Aikin muttered.

Fyndd snapped his fingers, then pointed at his old friend. "Ah, but it was just the question that needed asking, for this wasn't a sensible situation." Fynd cracked his knuckles before continuing.

"Now, the farmer pondered the traveling man's question but could find no ready answer as he turned it over in his mind. The traveling man then made his own offer. 'Let us agree that you can have until morning to decide which it shall be. Come the first cockcrow you will give me your answer. Until then, I will make use of yon barn.' The farmer agreed to this, for he was a man accustomed to knowing the answer to every question and having the last word. With that, the traveling man tapped his finger aside of his nose and gave a smart nod which was the custom in those parts when an agreement was reached. The farmer did the same. And so they parted, the farmer to his house and his ponderings and the traveling man to the barn for a night's rest."

Fyndd sat, his gaze resting on each listener for a moment before moving on.

"All that night, the farmer tossed in his bed, his mind chewing on the traveling man's question until the black-before-blush when he fell into a deep sleep. Meanwhile, the traveling man slept well beneath his woolen cloak in the farmer's barn, arising when the first faint glow pinked the eastern sky. He donned his cloak, checked his pocket for his tobacco and candle, then stepped out to greet the new morn. He looked toward the farmer's house and saw it was as dark and quiet as the grave."

Fyndd jumped back up, his contorted hands slashing the air like a striking owl. Mierrle jumped, her eyes wide. Elorah and Vaytah looked at each other, their eyes full of merriment while Thane's and Aikin's thread-thin smiles flattened. Fyndd beamed a broad smile at them both, his eyes flashing bright beneath peaked eyebrows.

"The traveling man leaned against the barn and waited, for he was a man of his word. Soon came the scratch and cluck of the farmer's hens as one golden ray and then another crept between the slats in their coop. But the house lay silent with no sign of the farmer. The traveling man stubbed his feet against the ground to knock the dust from his boots as the cock crowed its first salute to the dawning day. Again, he looked to the house, but still there was no sign of the farmer. The traveling man hitched his cloak tighter and watched the sun crawl higher above the horizon while the hens clucked and fluffed their feathers. A second crow split the air. With that, the traveling man set off. Just then, the farmer shambled out of his lightless house, one crooked finger raised, shouting 'And what of the digging? Would you leave and not fulfill your oath?' The traveling man stopped and turned, his eyes gone dark as char. 'There'll be no digging from me this day, fair friend, for the cock has crowed twice and our bargain is no more.' The traveling man tapped his finger against the side of his nose and shook his head, which in those parts was the custom when an agreement was fulfilled. The farmer shook his fist and stamped his foot, but it was no use. He knew the truth of the traveling man's words. At last, he tapped his own finger against the side of his own nose and shook his own head, though it pained him sorely to do so. The traveling man turned and walked away, whistling a happy tune. Behind him, the farmer spit upon the ground and cursed his rotten luck, as the cock crowed a third time. Muttering all manner of foulness, the farmer stomped back to his house, his digging and his pride both left undone by the wit and guile of a traveling man."

Fyndd clapped his right arm across his waist, his left arm across his back then gave a bow, as was customary when a bard finished a tale.

Mierrle, Vaytah, and Elorah applauded while Aikin and Thane threw sidelong glances at each other before clapping two slow beats.

"Well, that's the second time today I've heard an ending I didn't expect," Vaytah said, placing a hand on Elorah's knee and giving her a meaningful look. "But those are often the best kind, eh?"

The teapot whistled out a ribbon of steam. Vaytah bustled over and poured a golden brew into six demitasse cups. Elorah delivered one to each guest, the dainty half-cup disappearing in Aikin's huge hands. Thane discreetly sniffed at his, disappointment drawing down his lips.

Vaytah held up her cup. "Family's bread and friends are butter, don't have one without the other," she recited.

"To friends!" Fyndd cried, raising his cup, everyone echoing his words as they raised their own.

Sailing Men
(A Song of the Rabboutiers)

Oh, we love them men who sails the seas and stops at every port,
They brings us jugs of fine sweetsweet and beers of every sort,
We gives them all our money, yes, we gives them every cent,
Without them bloody pirates, we'd have nothing to repent.

CHORUS:

Yo ho, shiver me bones, I'm drunk as drunk can be,
 I owe my state of inebriate to them men who sails the seas.
(Repeat)

I drink yer health with the finest brews that ever filled a mug,
And when I finds the bottom, I breaks out another jug,
Oh, let's hear it for them sailing men, so daring and so bold,
Let's drink to all them Rabboutiers, who brings us liquid gold.
(Repeat chorus twice)

—Excerpted from *Traditional Shanties of the Rabboutiers*
   for the Ascended Regent, Kallizia Rennesseau, by a scribe

CHAPTER TWELVE
THE BONE CEREMONY

Xyleea had helped Cree Shee pray over many bodies destined for burial under stone pilings in the valley of the dead, but only once had she helped her galeesha prepare a body to return to the keleekeluk. When she'd asked Cree Shee why the old man wanted the bone ceremony, her galeesha had explained he'd been a woodcutter with no wife or children, his love devoted instead to the juulko and gumwood trees that provided his living.

Xyleea had been with Cree Shee one moon at the time and little help except with the easiest tasks—fetching gumwood and fireweed for the fires that burned to keep away the chassa and bears, stripping curly green leaves from white-barked juulko branches for the chuulzu sticks, and collecting the golden feathers the deleemelee left behind.

Cree Shee had explained each step as she'd prepared the old man's body. First, the ceremonial washing. "Washing removes the impurities of living," Cree Shee had said as she methodically swabbed the old man's body with a watery mixture of gimchee seed, plimroot, and feelaa leaf. "Gimchee gives the soul huul waal," Cree Shee had continued, making a fist and rapping it twice against her chest. "Feelaa relieves it of guilt, so nothing holds it to this world of pain and sorrow while plimroot gives it wings to fly through the nearworld, past the grogakee and the soul stealers into the farworld where the ancestors wait. Now run and fetch the men."

Xyleea didn't remember where she'd found the three men waiting—in her mind they had appeared from the shadows when she'd stepped out of the wasaka and followed her inside. With their help, Cree Shee had laid the old man's body face up on a bed of juulko leaves, his loin covering of tanned bajee hide still in place.

Cree Shee had then directed Xyleea to a basket in the corner to find a small clay bottle of amberstone dust, a larger clay jar of *puuko* oil, and a leaf packet wadded with gum paste. While Xyleea pawed through the basket, she'd heard muffled movement behind her. When she'd turned around, the old man's body was lying face down, his loin covering removed. The same three men, their faces stiff as masks, had shuffled to the doorway then out into the night.

"Come closer, Xyleea," Cree Shee had said, beckoning to her. "It is only an empty vessel now." She'd patted the old man's back. "See. Nothing to fear. Shree Duu's chuulzu isn't here. It's up there, watching." She pointed at the ceiling, then smiled. Xyleea had looked up, expecting to see the woodcutter floating like smoke, but there were only the woven dark green of the wasaka's roof.

She'd handed Cree Shee the amberstone dust, gum paste, and puuko oil. "Fetch me the stonewood bowl and the stir paddle," her galeesha had murmured.

Xyleea had retrieved the items and handed them to Cree Shee who set to work, her wrinkled hands measuring and pinching and stirring gum paste and puuko oil and amberstone dust into a thin, gold paint.

Cree Shee then bent to the task of applying the mixture, her goat-hair brush working its way around the old man's back, then onto the back of both hands.

Once finished, she'd pointed to the golden symbols. "Birth, youth, vigor, wisdom, death. The never-ending wheel we all endure," she'd said, her finger tracing the marks forming a circle that reached from the old man's shoulders to the small of his back. Next, she'd pointed out the symbols on the back of the man's left hand. "This is the nearworld. His chuulzu must fight from here..." she'd pointed to the old man's wrist, "...to there..." her index finger moving to the tip of the old man's middle finger, "...and from there to here," she'd finished, her finger drawing back down to the wrist. She'd then pointed to the markings on the back of the right hand. "That is the farworld where the ancestors live. The place of golden light where we start and end." She'd nodded at Xyleea, her good eye twinkling. "That is our true home," she'd said, reaching out to tousle Xyleea's golden brown curls.

Cree Shee had retrieved the chuulzu kereet from its place on the corner shelf. Underneath was a creamy white bajee hide inscribed with a spiraling pattern of symbols similar to the ones on the old man's back and hands.

Xyleea had watched Cree Shee's lips move in a silent prayer as she'd placed the kereet upon her head then picked up the circular hide and begun to chant, her good eye trained on the silvery leather as she'd turned it round in her hands. Later, she'd explained that the prayers would direct the old man's chuulzu through the dangers of the nearworld and into the golden farworld of the ancestors.

When Cree She had finished, the same three men had appeared again, as if summoned by an unheard voice, this time toting a carrying sling. They'd set the sling beside the woodcutter and in one movement, transferred his lifeless body onto it. Cree Shee had taken hold of her staff and walked to the door, singing an ancient dirge, the men carrying the woodcutter out behind her.

Xyleea had walked behind the men, watching the old man's pale-bottomed feet bob and sway as he was toted to where he would make his final offering to the keleekeluk. Her child's mind had tried to grasp it was only his husk on the carrying sling, not the essence that had been the woodcutter, but it had been difficult for Xyleea to maintain her certainty as she'd stared at the man's bouncing feet.

Now it was her turn to prepare her galeesha for the bone ceremony, a process she felt wholly unprepared to undertake. But there was no one else to do it, and so she mixed the gimchee seed and the plimroot and the feelaa leaf into the clay vessel of water and used it to wash Cree Shee's body, first one side and then, after the men came in and turned her galeesha over, the other.

Next, she measured and pinched and stirred the gum paste, puuko oil, and amberstone dust using the stonewood bowl and the stir paddle until it formed a thin, gold paint. The color wasn't an exact match to her memory of the paint Cree Shee had made for the old man, and she was still fussing over it when the leader of the men chosen to build the greeja came into the wasaka to inform her all was ready.

The greeja—the high platform that would hold her galeesha's body until the deleemeelee completed her transformation—had been constructed from a pile of juulko trees hacked down in the keleekeluk and dragged to the appointed clearing. There, the men had stripped off their leaves and limbs, driven the four largest into the ground to serve as corner posts, then bound the rest together with twining red vines to form the platform. The chuulzu sticks were then driven into the ground in a circle around the greeja. Crystalwood would have been preferred, but it was difficult to obtain now that the Xetili roamed the surrounding forest.

Xyleea mouthed another prayer of forgiveness to the ancestors for her clumsiness and her errors. She wished her recollections were clearer of that long ago time when Cree Shee had prepared the old man, but she had only been a child and her memories came in snatches, like bright beads on a necklace, strung together on the thinnest of threads—the aromatic smell of the gumpaste tickling her nose, the bone-white of the juulko bark, the blood red of the winding vines, her galeesha's brown, wrinkled hands as they worked, the old man's bobbing pink feet, and the lamenting notes of the songs as the woodcutter was carried to his greeja.

The symbols had been the most daunting to remember, and she lingered long before applying the amberstone paint with the tapered end of a goat-hair brush. She stopped several times and closed her eyes, studying her mind's picture of the old man's back before continuing, her lips mouthing her prayers.

She surveyed her work, not entirely satisfied she'd recreated the sacred wheel as well as she should have done. She started to ask her galeesha what she should do, then shook her head, blinking to clear her eyes of the water in them. She took a deep breath, her mind forcing down the doubts pushing their way into her thoughts then closed her eyes, concentrating until she could visualize the symbols on the old man's hands. With slow, careful strokes, she painted the nearworld symbols on the back of Cree Shee's left hand, trying her best to replicate her memory. She rolled her shoulders a few times to loosen the muscles, then circled her head around until her neck cracked before dipping the brush into the paint and bending over her galeesha's right hand to apply the most important symbols of all, the dots and whorls and lines that would guide her into the farworld.

When at last she was done, Xyleea walked to the corner shelf where the chuulzu kereet sat and picked it up. Beneath lay the round bajee skin inscribed with the sacred prayers. A chilling fear swept through her. What if she didn't say the proper words in the proper order? Would her galeesha be trapped forever in the nearworld? Would her inexperience doom Cree Shee to remain forever separated from the ancestors? Xyleea swallowed hard, trying to calm her racing heart.

She heard a voice chanting as her eyes followed the spiraling symbols on the bajee pelt in her outstretched hands. The words were soft and deep, the tone a mixture of joy and sorrow. She could feel a gentle heat begin in her midsection, spreading until her entire body felt warm. It was only when the sound died away and her hands dropped that she realized the voice had been hers. The words had come from somewhere else, somewhere outside of herself. She thanked the ancestors, her heart full of love for them and her galeesha and the Ushoku and the keleekeluk.

As if summoned, two men walked into the wasaka, carrying the sling. Xyleea placed the chuulzu kereet on her head and began to sing as the men placed Cree Shee's body face down onto the stretcher. Xyleea picked up her galeesha's staff, cool to the touch, and walked toward the door, the pain and joy in her heart leaking out through the melancholy sound of her song.

The men stood at each end of the sling and lifted before following Xyleea out the door into the fitful rain of an afternoon shower.

Despite the drizzle, every member of the wasakagee was gathered outside Cree Shee's wasaka to pay their respects to their departed deeta. Many of the women held large baka leaves which they waved in a solemn salute when the men carried Cree Shee toward her greeja. The children shook small juulko branches in intermittent bursts, their curly, golden-brown hair flattened like mushroom caps by the rain. The men stood ramrod straight with their arms crossed, their stiff hands stuck into their armpits, their thumbs hooked against their upper arms, their thoughts unreadable behind their clouded eyes.

The loss of their chuulzu deeta was a blow to all the Ushoku, and the uncertainty and fear of what came next was engraved upon every face old enough to understand. To not have a deeta to guide and protect them put every member of the wasakagee in danger. Because Xyleea had not been chosen by Cree Shee to succeed her in a ceremony before the people, she would have to prove her huul waal before she could be the people's deeta. And though she'd never felt worthy of becoming the spiritual leader of her wasakagee, she was overcome with a deep desire to do exactly that. Perhaps there was some unseen power in the staff she held in her hand, pulling her chuulzu in a new direction. Perhaps it was the power of the kereet upon her head, guiding her thoughts and setting her path. Perhaps it was the unseen hands of the ancestors, pushing her toward a future she never foresaw. Something inside was changing, whether from the forest songs she sang, the kereet she wore, or the bajee skin she held. She was transforming as she led her galeesha toward the greeja, her own thoughts and desires being replaced by the thoughts and desires of the supreme chuulzu.

The people fell into procession behind Xyleea and the men bearing Cree Shee's sling, carrying their baka leaves, their juulko branches, and their unspoken doubts deeper and deeper into the keleekeluk, past the goats huddled miserably beneath a cluster of kava trees and the big-eared tuskees tethered to gnarly posts with too-thin ropes, their trunks sweeping dried leaves up into their chewing mouths as they watched the people pass.

The men's eyes jerked back and forth as they walked, searching for blue-painted Xetili behind every tree. The women's eyes swept the sky above, searching for a break in the weeping gray clouds, some sign that all would be well. The children's eyes stared into the worried faces of their elders, searching for some understanding of what was happening.

Far into the keleekeluk, a bone-colored scaffolding as tall as a wasaka dominated a small clearing. Juulko branches as thick as a man's arm—

the chuulzu sticks—encircled the greeja, excepting a section left open for the sling-bearers. Several stripped branches were piled nearby, ready to fill in the gap once Cree Shee was placed on the platform. Only after that was accomplished would the prayers to the ancestors be said, the remaining branches pounded in, and the fires lit.

Xyleea walked to the greeja then turned and faced the people. She shifted the bajee skin to her left hand which held the staff, then raised her right hand into the air and waited while the men climbed the ladders and gently placed Cree Shee face down on the platform. Xyleea knew the deleemeelee would not leave their perches high in the canopy until the clouds lifted and the rain stopped. As the men shifted Cree Shee onto the platform, Xyleea closed her eyes and imagined her hands sweeping aside the clouds. When she opened them again, she was startled to see the clouds had broken apart, allowing through a few rays of light.

Her heart lifting, Xyleea sang the song of the ancestors.

Come to our aid from the land of spirit

As the last note faded, Xyleea stepped away from the greeja and walked through the opening toward the people, her right hand raised to the sky. The men sprang into action, pounding the remaining chuulzu sticks into place. Once that was done, Xyleea motioned toward the fire-carrier, a man of wisdom age holding a long-handled stone hod full of glowing coals. He stepped toward the first of five firewood mounds built at regular intervals around the chuulzu sticks. The fire-carrier thrust the smoking hod into the center of the mound.

"Birth!" Xyleea said, her right hand dropping to signal the fire-carrier. He tipped the hod, sending coals tumbling onto a fuzzy knot of fireweed. Despite the rain, the weed caught flame as the fire carrier withdrew the hod. He carried it to the next mound and waited. Xyleea raised her right arm again.

"Youth!" she said, her right hand dropping. Another handful of coals tumbled out of the hod and onto a knot of fireweed. Another flame lit. The fire-carrier walked to the third mound.

"Vigor!" Her raised arm dropped again. The fire-carrier lit the third fire and walked to the fourth.

"Wisdom!" She brought her hand down yet again. The fire-carrier lit the fourth fire and walked to the fifth mound. Xyleea inhaled, steeling herself before raising her right hand.

"Death!" she cried, her voice cracking. She signaled and the fire carrier dumped the hod's remaining coals onto the fireweed, setting it ablaze.

"Behold, the never-ending wheel of life!" Xyleea called. The people murmured, their heads nodding.

Xyleea began the final prayer.

Come deleemeelee, take our deeta to the ancestors.

The baka leaves and the juulko branches began to sway as the people joined in, their combined voices adding into the keleekeluk's creaking and sighing and soughing.

When the last voice died out, Xyleea began the long walk back to the wasakagee, the kereet heavy upon her head, the staff and bajee pelt heavy in her hands, her heart heavy within her chest.

The sling-bearers followed, toting their empty stretcher, while the rest of the people fell in line behind them, their eyes searching the keleekeluk for blue-skinned trouble, their hearts lamenting their lost deeta.

HEAR THESE WORDS...

...all ye who are sentient, for the time has come to speak of things long buried, and to bury things long spoken.

We speak today of traditions, those customs and beliefs that sprang up after the Great Truths were deliberately obscured when the Souls of Noble Beginning lost their way. In the time and eryns since, we have seen how the grasping mind has invented and venerated its own creations, having nothing better to moor itself to, and thus, how spurious myths have grown and flourished in the chaotic aftermath of the last destruction. Beware these shadows of Truth. Beware these sham talismans. Beware the illusion of hope and delusion of division they create. See them instead for what they are—endangerments to your very souls.

Soon the wisdom of the Ancients will again be made manifest in the hearts and minds of those unfettered by invented rites and rituals. Prepare ye now for that marvelous Advancement. Set your feet rightly upon the path that leads to Truth by turning away from the falsities of this present age. Throw off the shackles of custom and creed and prepare for the glorious awakening that will change all that is and all that will be. Choose ye well, for the time of reckoning is near upon your doorstep.

We, the Elect, have spoken.

CHAPTER THIRTEEN
THE CHARMS THAT BIND

Rachmyn had never seen such a conflation of colors and sounds in all his life. If a headache could be brought to life, it would look like this wretched, crowded festival. He shifted his rucksack higher onto his shoulders.

Haedyn, two steps ahead, gawped like a dying fish, his eyes goggling at the carts and tents of the shopkeeps peddling their wares at the Festival of the Urslan Sisters.

"You're doing it again," Rachmyn said.

Haedyn spun around. "What?"

Rachmyn gave him a slack-jawed stare then sobered. "We're supposed to be blending in, remember?"

Haedyn motioned toward Elgre as he trotted at Rachmyn's side, the pair unmindful of the frightened stares and cowering retreats around them. "You call that blending in? At least my companion isn't scaring everyone." He patted his vest, his face smug.

"Haven't these marans ever seen a wolf before?" Rachmyn groused, his eyebrows bunching into a scowl.

"I doubt it." Haedyn pointed at a distiller's tent with a large sign—*SWEETSWEET - WHISKEY - CIDER - FREE SAMPLES - BEST PRICES*—then wiggled his eyebrows.

"Don't even think about it," Rachmyn warned.

Haedyn shrugged and flashed a toothy grin.

"What are we doing here? All these marans, all this noise." Rachmyn's scowl deepened.

"You're such a misery guts sometimes. Look, there's some of your people." Haedyn pointed at a Shadowen caravan. "Since you're so against the drink, maybe we can get a charm draught to fix your mood."

Rachmyn shook his head, his pale hair falling forward. "My mood is just fine."

"If you say so." Haedyn turned toward a fanciful handcart with an abundance of small cages attached, each emanating a sonorous hum. He stepped up to look into one of the tiny coops. "It's a little lizard with wings!" he exclaimed. He bent closer. "It's singing!"

The humpbacked krychlekeep took his opportunity.

"Are you looking for a krychle?" he asked, pasting an insincere smile on his craggy face. "Ho ho ho. I see you have an eye, sir. That's a rare one. Very rare, indeed. A shimmer-skin female. You won't find many of those. No no no. Not many at all. Hey hey hey, what's that?"

Fryk's head emerged from Haedyn's vest, its keen stare fixed on the krychle. Sensing danger, the lizard flattened its wings, lowered its body, and ceased its noisemaking as did every other krychle on the cart. Haedyn tried to thumb down the bird's head, but it was having none of it, slashing forward in a blur of wings, its talons raking open the reed coop's side. Haedyn clawed desperately at the attacking bird, throttling it a moment before it snatched the cowering krychle. The bird let out a shrill *chirrt-chirrt-chirrt,* setting off an explosion of squeeing from the krychlekeep's cargo. Haedyn clapped his hand over the grynt's eyes as the shimmer-skin slithered through the hole and skyed away, its translucent wings a dazzle of movement.

"Fryk! Out of it! Ooooff!"

Rachmyn jerked Haedyn's shoulder. "Let's go," he gritted.

Elgre trotted off—tongue lolling, fangs gleaming—festival goers fleeing like terror-struck rabbits before his imperious stare. Rachmyn started after the wolf, his hand clamped round Haedyn's arm, dragging him along.

"Hey! Hey! Hey! You'll have to pay for that shimmer-skin!" the krychlekeep shouted, shaking his fist. "She were the best of the lot!"

Haedyn dug a handful of coins from his pocket and threw them at the keeper's feet. "That's all I've got!" he cried, clapping his hand over his screeching bird's eyes and scrambling after his friend.

Rachmyn sighted four guards hurrying toward them. *Where had they come from?*

"Hey! Hey! Hey! Them three are a menace to all us folk!" the krychlekeep bellowed for the guards' benefit before stooping to pick up the coins.

"Elgre! Left!" Rachmyn shouted. The wolf veered, and the friends followed, all three pelting for a nearby verge. They plunged in, fighting their way through a thick knot of wiry whipcanes before bursting out into the tent area on the other side, their sudden appearance startling a hawk-nosed woman carrying a stewpot by its bail. She screamed and heaved the pot toward them, its contents spilling out in a steaming splay.

"Sodding bird!" Rachmyn growled, skipping sideways to avoid the hot debris.

They sprinted through the maze of tents, dodging guy lines as they went, until they reached a wooded area on the far side. Several paces in the friends pulled up, their sides heaving. Rachmyn peered over his shoulder.

"I don't think we've been followed," he panted.

"You've put us right in the soup, Fryk," Haedyn huffed, his gaze shifting to Rachmyn. "Still, it could have been worse." A cajoling smile crept onto his face as he forced the grynt into his vest pocket.

Rachmyn pressed his lips into a thin line. "I hardly see how." He looked around. There was something odd about these woods. He couldn't put his finger on it, but it made him uneasy. He nodded toward a clearing ahead. "I wonder what's over there."

"Let's go see," Haedyn said, taking a step forward.

Rachmyn blocked his path. "Let's not. We've caused enough ruckus for one day. Better we lay low until nightfall," he said, looking around. No scrub. No brambles. No underbrush. Only trees sticking up through clipped grass like giant posts. The unnatural tidiness set his nerves on edge. A noise caught his attention, and he cocked his head then pointed to his ear as he turned toward the sound.

Two women—one older, one younger—ambled along a path a few strides away. Haedyn strained forward and Rachmyn felt a prick of worry at his friend's sudden calf-eyed interest. This was no time for muzzy thinking.

The young woman stood a head taller than her companion, her long neck prodding toward a bear-shaped form in her hand. She tucked a coil of chestnut curls behind her ear, her expression pensive. Suddenly her chin lifted, her eyes cutting toward them.

Rachmyn motioned toward a nearby tree but to no effect. Haedyn's attention remained fixed upon the young woman.

Grief's teeth! He's completely addled!

Rachmyn's worry grew as Haedyn continued to stare, and he tugged again on his friend's arm, a strange buzzing starting at the top of his leg. His hand went to his shard, now pulsing inside his pocket.

Shifting stars! What manner of bewycchment is this?

"Come on," he growled, giving his friend's arm a stronger pull.

Haedyn shrugged him off. "Do you feel that?" he murmured, one hand drifting to the hilt of his knife. "That's never happened before."

Rachmyn's buzzy leg slid forward of its own accord, and it took all he had to drag it back. "This place is wycched," he hissed, his gaze finding Elgre. The wolf yawned and settled to the ground. Rachmyn's brow furrowed. Elgre had never led him into danger, but what was this if not danger? His perplexion deepened. "Let's go," he muttered, his hand pulling at the front of his leggings to separate the shard inside the pocket from his leg. The buzzing instantly transferred to his fingers and arm. "We can't stay here," he whisper-shouted, letting loose of the shard to yank Haedyn toward him, nerve stingers prickling through his leg. He clenched his jaw then spun round and began stumping back the way they'd come, dragging Haedyn along. Elgre sighed and sprung into motion.

Soon they were back amongst the round tents, making their way toward the marketplace.

"Where are we going?" Haedyn asked when Rachmyn stopped.

In truth, Rachmyn had no idea. He wanted away from all of this, but here he was. Here they were. Where would they go anyway? Back to the Lawless Mountains?

He glanced toward the western horizon. The wall complicated things, and he didn't like their chances of escaping that way undetected. A better idea might be to wait until the festival ended, then catch a ride inside a Shadowen caravan. His fellow Shadowen could always be counted on to trade easy favors for profitable gain, and his wolfken speck would be highly desired. Inside a caravan, he could conjure a mirrorshield to get them past the guards. In the meantime, they would have to keep their heads down and wait it out. At least the jolting in his leg had gone. Thank the stars for that.

Elgre wandered off as a ginger-haired girl carrying a basket of cakes rounded the curve of a nearby tent then stopped short, her brown eyes wide in her freckled face.

"Are you lost?" she asked.

"No." Rachmyn glared, hoping to scare her away.

"Actually, you might say that we are," Haedyn stepped in, sending a sideways glance at Rachmyn before flashing a smile. "This is our first time at the festival."

"Your first time? My, isn't it grand? This is my twelfth time," she bragged. "That's our garol over there." She pointed at the largest tent on the grounds, its huge flag depicting a sprig of green growing from a rock. "Which clan are you?"

Rachmyn bent forward. "We haven't a—"

Haedyn smashed his heel into Rachmyn's foot.

"Aahh! Sodding—"

"Sorry!" Haedyn cut in, giving Rachmyn an apologetic look before turning his attention back to the girl. "We're from that one." He pointed up at the nearest flag.

"Oh, the Clan Hiegh. I hear you lot love the drink!" She giggled.

"We do not—" Haedyn stomped Rachmyn's foot again. "Mind your sodding feet!" Rachmyn blasted, his eyes narrowing to slits.

"What my friend meant to say is, yes, we do. We certainly do love the drink."

Rachmyn let out an exasperated snort as he rubbed his trodden foot.

"We love a good cake, too." Haedyn winked at the little girl's basket. She cocked her head again. "My name's Ghielle, what's yours?"

"I'm Haedyn."

She wrinkled her spreckled nose. "That's a funny name. It sounds like one of those binding charms the Shadowen sell. Course I'm not supposed to know about those, but I do." She giggled again. "Well, I suppose you can't help what you're named. Even my mother says so. Are you going to the pageant?"

Rachmyn shook his head.

"That's why we're here," Haedyn confirmed with a nod before arching his eyebrows, his head bobbing at Rachmyn. "My friend loves pageants."

"He does?" One eyebrow peaked as she sized up the scowling, pale-haired man.

Haedyn cupped his hand to his lips and leaned forward. "He doesn't let on because he's afraid people will think less of him," he whispered.

Rachmyn rolled his eyes. Haedyn chuckled, enjoying his friend's exasperation.

"Oh, he shouldn't worry. Even my brother loves them, and everyone thinks he's grand. If you come to the pageant, you'll see him. He's nominated to be Solimar, and I'm sure he'll get the vote because he's the handsomest one."

"I bet he is," Haedyn agreed. Fryk popped its red-crested head out of Haedyn's vest.

"Oh, hello!" Ghielle exclaimed, craning her neck forward. "May I pet him?"

"No, Fryk," Haedyn said, pushing the bird down before buttoning his vest. "Better not. He's been terribly naughty, I'm afraid."

"Oh, poor little Fryk." Ghielle reached into her basket of cakes, plucked one out, and handed it to Haedyn. "Maybe a cake would help. It always helps me. When my mother says, 'Ghielle, don't do this or you can't have cake', or she says 'Ghielle do that, and then you can have cake', you know what? I don't do it, or I do do it, whichever she wants, because cake is the best. Do you know what I mean?"

"I do, and it is," Haedyn agreed with a knowing nod before taking a large bite, his smile wobbling up and down as he chewed.

"I've no idea what she means," Rachmyn muttered. "Load of nonsense–watch it!" He swerved his foot a moment before Haedyn's heel smashed down a third time.

Haedyn contritely offered the bitten cake to Rachmyn. "This will help." He turned to Ghielle. "It's a very good cake."

Stone-faced, Rachmyn reached over his shoulder and shoved the cake into his rucksack.

"Where is this pageant?" Haedyn asked.

"Oh, the other side of the Bonny Wood." Ghielle pointed toward the unnatural grove. "There's a big picture of the Urslan where you walk in, and up by the stage, a flower collage of clan symbols, so everyone knows where to sit. And there's toadstools. They're just the loveliest, dearest little things all set into this lattice pattern..." She trailed off, her face shining.

Rachmyn mouthed "Toadstool?" at Haedyn who shrugged and shook his head.

"The pageant's tonight, right?" he prompted.

"No, silly. Tomorrow night. The festival hasn't even started yet!" Ghielle laughed.

"Grief's teeth! That's what I meant. Tomorrow night. Like I told you." He shot a superior look at Rachmyn who met it with a tight nod and an over-wide, teeth-baring grin.

"Right," Rachmyn replied, drawing the word out.

"Have you a garol?" Ghielle asked.

"A garol..." Haedyn crinkled his brow. "I'm afraid not. Is that a problem?"

"Oh, no. Elorah's family always has extras. Find one without a flag, and you can use it."

"You don't say. Well, isn't that something," Haedyn grinned at Rachmyn as if he'd expected Ghielle's answer.

"You brought your flag, didn't you?" she asked.

Rachmyn started to shake his head until Haedyn shoved an elbow into his side.

"Of course," Haedyn replied.

Rachmyn groaned again and turned toward the Bonny Wood, looking for an escape from this interminable conversation. His leg had begun to tingle again.

Elgre wandered into view. Rachmyn whistled, and the wolf trotted over, leaning companionably against his affected leg when Rachmyn scratched the hump between his ears.

"Oh, my goodness. Is that a wolf?"

"No," Haedyn tutted. "That's our sheepdog."

Ghielle looked at Elgre, doubt linking her eyebrows into a single line. "Your sheepdog looks an awful lot like a wolf."

"I know, but don't tell him," Haedyn said, hitching his thumb toward Rachmyn. "He gets grumpy when people say that."

"Pardon?" Rachmyn asked, glaring at his friend.

"Nothing," Haedyn chortled, giving Ghielle a conspiratorial wink.

"We should be getting on," Rachmyn grumbled.

"Yes, of course." Haedyn turned toward Ghielle and bowed. "You've been most kind."

"Oh, there's Elorah!" Ghielle shouted, her pointing finger jamming into Haedyn's eye.

"Aahh!" Haedyn smacked his palm against his eye, tears streaming as he doubled over.

Rachmyn sighed. *Just what we need. Another sodding disaster. Speaking of...* The tingling feeling was strengthening, and he shook his leg to dispel the sensation.

"Oh, my goodness! I've blinded him. Elorah!" Ghielle windmilled her arms toward two women approaching from the direction of the Bonny Wood. Rachmyn recognized them as the young woman and her older companion from earlier.

"I'm fine," Haedyn protested, one hand waving as he braced his knees, tears dripping off his nose and onto the ground. "Give me a moment."

"I'm sure he'll be alright," Rachmyn said, rubbing at his thigh to alleviate what were now icy-hot splits of pain. He got hold of the shard only to drop it when the nerve-pinching once again transferred to his arm. Better the leg than the arm.

"Oh, I've ruined everything. What will my mother say?" Ghielle wailed.

"What's happened?"

Haedyn raised his head at the sound of the young woman's voice, the corners of his lips lifting into a crooked grin. Rachmyn cursed under his breath—definitely addled—then cursed again when Haedyn's hand went from his face to his knee revealing the extent of his injury. The eye was darkening and swelling at a rapid rate.

"You've got the start of a pretty good shiner," he said with genuine concern, his fist pounding at his thigh.

The young woman watched Rachmyn for a moment before kneeling to the level of Haedyn's hanging head. "Let me get my bag," she said.

"This is awful," Ghielle blubbered. "Elorah, please say you can help."

The young woman patted Haedyn's knee. "Don't worry. It's only a scratch."

Haedyn's face lit like a lantern as she spoke, his golden eyes going hugely round and sparkly. Rachmyn's stomach sank, the injury now the least of his concerns. Getting away from this wretched festival had just become infinitely harder than it had been a moment earlier.

WARNINGS OF A WRAITHWOLF (EXCERPT THREE)

GUARD your THOUGHTS... ggrrr... for a MIND UNTENDED is easily... ggrrff... DISTRACTED by vagary... gggrf... and DIVERTED by caprice... Gggrrff... CONCENTRATE... gggrrff... on TRUTH... ggggrrffff... rather than COUNTERFEIT DREAMS... ggrrrff... and addictive DRAUGHTS.

TAKE HEED!

AVOID those who seek CONTROL... ggrrfff... like a WOLF at the door... ggrrff... COVETING your birthright... gggrrff... and CRAVING your ESSENCE... Ggrrrff... Do not be FOOLED... Gggrrff... Remain VIGILANT... Ggrrf... GIRD your RESOLVE... ggrrf... for it is only through LACK of WILL... grrff... that these VILLAINS can ENTER... ggrrfff... the SEAT of your POWER... gggrrr... and the HOME of your SOUL.

BEWARE!

These THIEVES in the NIGHT... gggrrrff... for they will not HESITATE... ggrrf... to STEAL your VITAL SPARK... ggrrfff...and leave you BEREFT of SPIRIT... Gggrrr... WE have SEEN the DAMAGE... ggrrff... the terrible LOSS inflicted... ggrrff ... when this WARNING is IGNORED... Gggrrfff... Do so at your PERIL.

–Collected and interpreted for the Most Exalted Monarch,
Geldizian Rennesseau, by a scribe

CLOUD ALOFT

Oh, to float, as cloud aloft,
Shrouding peaks, and gowning trees,
In silvered mist and whited tuft,
that drifts upon the breeze.

Oh, to float, as cloud aloft,
Of this is what I dream.

–Epigent Zephyrria Rennesseau, aged 14
Volume 3234, Page 308
Essentia Libre, Academie Vorik

CHAPTER FOURTEEN
SECRETS OF A WILD HEART

Brynz crossed her legs, bent forward at the waist then swept her hands behind, her forehead brushing her knees as she executed a monarch's curtsy. Zell flumped his hindquarters onto the enclosure floor, his tufted tail thumping the graystone, his piercing blue eyes glittering in the moonlight. Brynz straightened and pulled a sausagebit from the pocket of her night tunic, tossing the reward into the gryphling's open beak.

She'd chosen the sausagebits because they were easy to hide, easy to transport, and one of Zell's favorite rewards. The greasy stains they left on her dark blue tunic's pockets were of little importance. Details of appearance had never concerned her, much to her superiors' chagrin.

Brynz was pleased. The night lessons were going well. After two moons of steady work, she'd managed to shape Zell's behavior into a series of missteps she hoped would delay saddling long enough for his bones to strengthen. She'd come up with the idea after a long night spent crying and worrying over Her Most Exalted's foolish plan to rush her charge's training. Its simplicity was matched only by its audacity. If the subtle sabotage was discovered, the punishment would be severe but a promise was a promise, and Brynz had promised Zell on the day of his hatch she would protect him. She was prepared to accept the consequences, whatever they might be, for making good on her vow.

Zell retook his feet, his attention keen. Brynz curtsied again. The gryphling sat and opened his beak. Brynz straightened and tossed another sausagebit. After gulping down the treat, the gryphling clambered to his feet.

Brynz picked up the saddle pad she'd brought and took a step forward. Attached to the underside were two sets of metal combs designed to rub against Zell's back, causing enough irritation to induce a reaction. Whether it be a strike of the beak, a shudder, or a rippling roll of the back muscles, Brynz would shape the behavior into what she wanted. She was careful to show Zell the pad before strapping it on, so the gryphling would associate the irritation with it.

She held up the pad as she approached, clucking softly. Zell bobbed his head as she slung the pad onto his back then snugged the surcingle. The reaction was immediate, the gryphling striking the pad with the hook of his beak and ripping a gash into the fleece, Brynz leaping away just in time.

Too strong.

She loosened the surcingle then snugged it again, taking care not to make it as tight. The reaction was less destructive but just as quick, Zell bumping the pad with his beak.

That should do.

Brynz tapped the top of the gryphling's beak, mimicking a gryphonmare's feeding prompt, a trick she'd learned from the Inirian peddler who'd brought the leathery, slate-colored egg to the royal stable thirteen moons ago, arriving when the winter snows were melting under the warming breath of a new spring. Zell's beak gaped and Brynz tossed in another sausagebit, before loosening the surcingle, removing the pad, and stepping back.

She showed the fleece pad to her charge again, and Zell pranced, anticipating. Brynz set it in place and snugged the surcingle. The gryphling bumped the pad with his beak. Brynz tapped Zell's beak, and it opened wide for another sausagebit. She repeated the process thrice more, rewarding her charge each time.

Brynz looked toward the horizon where the first pink strands were weaving their way into the purple-black sky. Soon the day would begin. She removed the surcingle and pad, then gave Zell's shoulder a pat before rolling the two into a loose tube she finagled under her tunic, tightening her belt to hold them in place. Hiding the gear would prevent awkward explanations.

She locked the keeper's door using the key she'd stolen from the spares in Garrod's office then hurried toward her sleeping room, taking care to avoid the rectangles of light streaming from the back of the palace. She hoped she hadn't been missed, but if she was, she had a story at the ready. The day before, one of the Imperial Guard's geldings had colicked, and she would say she'd been checking on the recovering horse. Lying was becoming more and more a part of her life, and although she wasn't happy, she couldn't see any way around it. She told herself she was serving a higher cause, but that did little to make her feel better. Anger flared at the monarch. Why must she be so selfish? Why must she always insist on having things her own way? She supposed all monarchs were the same. Her Most Exalted's husband, some variety of minor ruler from Elequia, was another example, with his constant drinking, sloppy manners, and general lassitude. Everything about him repulsed Brynz— his gray hair formed into sausage-roll curls, his flabby jowls that shook when he spoke, his veiny red nose beneath piggish green eyes, his prodigious stomach sagging across his vast thighs. No wonder Her Most Exalted spent so little time with him, preferring instead to ride her stallions, fly her falcons, or hunt her lurchers while being attended by Garod Daell and the rest of her Imperial Guard. A stint in the royal pigsty would have been preferable, Brynz supposed.

The rosy glow of dawn was giving way to the gilded shine of morning. A stable hand hurried by, giving her a sideways glance of curiosity.

"Morning, maiss," he said as he passed, his long strides taking him toward the compound where the staff's sleeping rooms and dining hall were located.

"Morning," she replied, her arms crossing in front of her night tunic. As if it mattered with him already past and seeing everything. She picked up her pace, hoping Garrod hadn't sent for her. Today Her Most Exalted was inspecting the foals, and Brynz was expected to assist with rounding up the mares from the steep hill pastures.

She made it to her room without further incident. After stowing the riding gear under her bed, she splashed her face and arms with water from a milk-white ivortine pitcher sitting atop a small table in the corner, then scrubbed herself with mint-scented soap to erase the lingering smell of gryphon. After donning her stable clothes, she pulled a comb through her unruly hair and plaited it into two braids she twisted high onto her head before securing them with hair pins. She finished by tying a kerchief over top and dashing out the door.

Garrod was pouring a cup of macca tea when she took her place at the table. The austere room was empty save for the two of them. His eyes appraised her over the top of his cup as he took a sip. She felt color rising into her cheeks as she picked two rounds of toasted bread from a platter. She dropped them onto her plate then, using a spoon, scraped a red dollop of jam onto each.

"You've missed out on the sausage," Garrod said. He raised his eyebrows and shrugged.

Brynz shoved a toast round into her mouth and chewed, her mind alive with worry. Was it an idle jibe or did he know what she'd been up to? She swallowed, forcing the dry bread down her closing throat.

"And the eggs," he continued, taking another drink.

"I overslept," she mumbled.

His eyebrows shot up. "Hardly the way to start the day, when we have so much to do."

"I'm sorry." She tried to sound contrite.

"Perhaps a little less nighttime activity, hmmm?" he said, taking another sip.

Brynz snapped to attention.

"Of course, your personal time is your own but in future, try not to make a public spectacle of shifting yourself from place to place in the early dark of morning. We've a standard to uphold. Might I remind you, Her Most Exalted has a distinct dislike for any whisper of scandal as it pertains to her household."

Brynz inwardly groaned. The stable hand. Of course, he would have told the entire staff about seeing her in her night tunic. She opened her mouth to protest, then thought better of it. Let them think what they wanted. What did she care for their opinions?

"And I hardly need mention, in a place such as this, a person's reputation carries far more weight than it should, more even than the things they do. Take care in the keeping of yours."

Brynz swallowed the last of her toast as she nodded, her ears and cheeks aflame.

Garrod drained his cup and set it down with a decisive clink. "Yes, well, that's that then. Time to get to work. Twenty-five mares and foals to gather, and the monarch expecting a grand tour of them all before luncheon."

He rose from his chair, leaned over, and brushed a crumb from his starched blue jodhpurs. Brynz was already out the door by the time he looked up.

The mare gathering had gone as well as expected, which is to say, it was twice as hard and took twice as long as it should have done. By the time it was finished, Brynz was covered in dirt and manure, with a few bruises and scratches thrown in for good measure, a purpling shadow on her left cheekbone the most noticeable. Her hair had escaped when a low branch tore the kerchief from her head, the plaiting and pins giving up not long after, leaving her looking like some deranged animal had built a nest atop her head.

By contrast, Garrod looked unruffled by the day's proceedings. His clothes were still crisp, his black paddock boots polished to a high sheen. Even his black-felt riding hat had remained dust free. Brynz couldn't understand how he managed to keep above the fray, but he always did. She, on the other hand, spent most of her time looking as if she'd been dragged behind a horse.

If it had been an ordinary day, she wouldn't have bothered about her appearance, but she was expected to look presentable in the presence of Her Most Exalted, so she ran back to her room, took off her stable clothes, and scrubbed off the dirt. She only had two red patches on her skin at present—one on the back of her knee, the other on the hinge of her elbow—and she took care not to irritate them. When she finished, she put on a fresh undertunic then her training leathers and boots before tackling the mess that was her hair.

After combing it through several times and pulling out a handful of snarls, she braided what was left, coiled it atop her head and pinned it in place. She glanced at her reflection in the looking glass tacked above the ivortine pitcher. She couldn't hide the bruise and her braids weren't aligned, making her head appear lopsided. Hardly the look expected. She sighed. It would have to do. She headed out the door.

The parade of mares was set to begin, and Brynz tried not to focus on the anxiety clawing at her stomach. She shouldn't be nervous; this was the fifth time she'd helped with the annual event, but the thought of so many people staring at her always made her queasy.

Her Most Exalted, clothed in a splendid white riding habit accented by gold braid and gold buttons, sat astride her favorite stallion, a dappled silver Felderre named Corrius. Her ice-blue eyes surveyed the mares and foals with lively interest as they passed. Her long, golden hair was woven into a herringbone pattern accented with crystal hairstuds. The hairstyle framed her face before flowing over her shoulders and onto her back. Instead of a crown, a pyrolean crystal diadem dazzled forth like rime ice in the bright light of near-noon.

Though she was entering middle age, the monarch was the handsomest woman Brynz had ever seen. To look at her was akin to staring at the sun. How such a wondrous beauty could have married such a toad was beyond Brynz's comprehension. She felt fortunate her station in life precluded her from having to marry someone so abhorrent. From having to marry at all.

All ten stable hands had been called into service for the inspection, and they each strutted past with their mare and foal pairs, their chins high, their eyes searching for some sign of favor from Her Most Exalted. Brynz was the opposite, her slumped shoulders, downcast eyes, and solemn demeanor aimed at getting her through the day without raising any interest whatever. When her turn came, she locked her gaze forward as she led an aging, black-pointed dun mare and her frisky cream-colored colt past the monarch and her entourage, including Garrod, who always seemed to be at Her Most Exalted's side during events such as this.

"He has the stamp of Corrius upon him," the monarch purred, giving her stallion a congratulatory pat.

"That he does, my queen," Garrod responded from his seat atop a magnificent black Plenderre stallion named Juulle. "Pleasing conformation and an agreeable temperament. I shall be keeping a close eye on him."

"I always find it's the father's line that casts the die," the monarch stated as if it were indisputable fact.

"But it's the mare that carries the larger burden of development," Garrod observed.

"Perhaps," the monarch allowed.

"I don't think he looks well at all," whined a girl of about sixteen to the monarch's left. "He's all legs, and his coat is the color of curdled milk." The girl sat astride a blue-roan gelding who looked asleep. She wore a small diadem of ice-blue arocols in her dark, upswept hair to proclaim her royal heritage, but she had none of the beauty of her mother, the monarch. Her features had more of the Elequian toad than the Iellian swan about them, but as the only child from that union, she would no doubt have her pick of the handsomest, most prosperous marans in the land. Indeed, in all the world, for as heir apparent to the Iellian empire she had much to recommend her. Even now, the unattached members of the royal guard sat a little straighter in their saddles when she spoke and jutted their lantern jaws that tiniest bit further forward. To their great dismay, Deanndria Rennesseau remained oblivious to their subtle posturing. Instead, she folded her gloved hands across her saddle's pommel, stared off into the distance, and yawned.

The mare Brynz was leading let out an ear-splitting whinny and her dawdling colt broke into a gawky gallop to catch up. The roan startled awake, jostling his royal rider who had to grasp the saddle to keep her seat. The monarch slid her gaze toward her daughter, faint displeasure creasing her mouth. Deanndria shot a hot look toward Brynz.

"She did that on purpose," she huffed, pointing an accusatory finger.

"Perhaps you should keep better control of your mount," the monarch quipped.

Deanndria's eyebrows arched, her mouth rounding with surprise before falling into a disgusted frown. She arrowed another searing look at Brynz.

Brynz's face flushed as she fixed her eyes on the rocky ground, her long legs striding toward a large holding pen beside the stables, her mind already inside the cool building. How she wished she were mucking out stalls right now rather than parading past a line of upturned noses and judging eyes.

After turning loose the mare and foal, she watched the swaybacked Felderre trot toward the far corner, her colt galloping beside her. A black mare with a chestnut colt whinnied a greeting. Brynz smiled as she tripped the gate's latch.

"You going to stand there all day?" said a churlish voice. It was the stable hand from earlier.

"I might do," she replied. "What's it to you?"

"There's some of us has to work for our keep. Not that you'd know about that," he replied as he brushed past toward the still-to-be-inspected mares.

"What do you mean by that?" Brynz bristled at the stable hand's insinuating tone. "I put in my time, same as you."

"Everybody knows you're the special pet, though," he said as he opened the gate then closed it. He pulled a sweet from his pocket and held it out to make the mares easier to catch. Two came trotting toward him. "It's not quite the same for the rest of us."

"Have you been drinking?" she asked, her face incredulous. She couldn't fathom any other reason for the hand's outrageous opinion.

"Course not," he spat as he slid a rope halter onto the head of a smoky gold mare who was nuzzling at his fist. "You think I'd jeopardize my position for something as stupid as a tug on the bottle? I've worked too hard to get here, maiss. Not all of us start at the top, you know. Most of us had to work our way up." He fastened the halter, then opened his hand, waiting for the mare to lip the sweet into her mouth before patting her neck.

"You don't know anything about me," Brynz spat.

"Can you get the gate, maiss?" the hand asked, ignoring her outrage.

She snorted as she unlatched the gate and opened it.

"That's where you're wrong," he said, leading the mare through, her dapple-gold filly scampering to keep up. Brynz slammed the gate behind them once they were through, tripping the latch. "I know a lot about you. You, on the other hand, know nothing about me, or anyone else around here. I'd wager you don't even know my name."

Brynz was taken aback. It was true. She had no idea what his name was.

"Tolleck," he supplied.

She looked at him.

"My name," he said. "It's Kodston Tolleck." He took a step then stopped. "Didn't you wonder why the rest of us always steer clear when you're around?"

It had never crossed her mind. The dapple-gold filly rubbed its starred forehead against Brynz's side, scratching its shedding coat on her leathers. Brynz took no notice.

"We were all warned off you," Tolleck said as he clucked and started walking.

"Warned off me? By whom?"

"Who do you think?" he asked, his tone sarcastic.

"I have no idea!"

"Your benefactor." He tossed the words over his shoulder as he continued walking.

"The monarch?"

Tolleck stopped, then turned to give her a withering look. "You think the monarch has conversations with the likes of me? Don't be daft."

Brynz lifted her shoulders and held out her hands. "Then who?"

"Daell." Tolleck shook his head as he led the mare toward the parade ground.

Brynz watched him go, her mind trying to dismiss his words as nonsense while resisting a desire to gust him with dust for his impertinence. It was only because of the horses she turned away without raising the wind into a force that would put Kodston Tolleck back into his place.

CHAPTER FIFTEEN
SHADOWEN RISE

The knowing came upon Essiant the way all such knowings did—as a sudden thought flashing through his entire being. Tonight, he would usher his night-ward into the next stage of her development as an adept in Oru Fen, introducing her to the starry pathways that would allow her to master this realm.

The orusphere hummed with the songs of souls zinging toward their wraithwolves. Essiant listened intently to the hum surrounding him. There it was, clear and bright, the song he had been waiting for. He howled into the dusky sky, calling his night-ward into his keeping.

Instantly she was there before him. He thrilled when he saw her, as he always did, glorying as their Saska vorik joined. She turned toward where her dreamdoor should have been, then turned back, her hands held out in an unspoken question. He sent his mindwords to her.

Tonight, you have come into your power. Let us walk.

His night-ward smiled and embraced his powerful neck, her joy matched only by his own. After a moment, or maybe a lifetime, she straightened, her eyes shining with delight.

Where do you wish to go? his mindwords asked.

Flickering images from her previous dreams surrounded them, a kaleidoscope of remembered thought-images. She struggled to choose one idea to focus on. It was common with new walkers. Knowing the task ahead, he put forth a suggestion, seizing one image and holding it in focus. It was of a flat-topped mountain made white by crystalwood trees with a large brunnestone megalith in the shape of a bear. The construction crackled with vorik energy as dedicants from throughout the known world crowded within and without, drawing strength from its emanating vibrations. It was a glorious sight, and she instantly latched onto it.

What is that? her mindwords asked, the kaleidoscope gone as she focused on the image.

The reason you came into the realm all those annums ago.

Do I know this place?

Your heart knows this place, your soul knows this place, but your mind has only just begun to search for it.

Is it a place only here?

Like all things, it exists on many planes, but do not concern yourself with that. What is important is its manifest form which has lain dormant for many eryns, awaiting restoration by a Uniter of pure intent. You are that Uniter if you choose it to be so.

A message from his night-ward's memory blazoned into both of their minds.

Restore the five to revive the one!

His night-ward took a step back, as if she'd been blown by a mighty wind.

I do not understand, her mind said, the words fading away.

All will be made clear in the fullness of time. Understanding is not required, only a willingness to remember things wrought and writ in times past. This will prepare you for what is to come. I will keep care of our memories until they can best serve.

She paused, assimilating what he had said then nodded as the words found a home inside her heart.

I trust you, my old friend. Take me where you will.

It was the words he had been waiting to hear. With a thought, he materialized the energy pathway they would follow, unfurling its starry light toward the glooming mist on the far horizon. Around them, the realm came into sharp focus, putting them inside a gray-purple version of the garol in which his night-ward slept. Her mind startled as she saw her sleeping form on the willow-wood bed beneath them.

Am I dead? A ripple of sorrow washed over them both.

Essiant shook his head. *Merely asleep,* he replied as he brushed away her melancholy with a sweep of his lucent tail. She smiled, and he could feel her exhilarated relief, a bursting energy that made her feel as if she might explode.

Her eager mind leaped forward, following the starshine he had laid out before them. He went beside her, ensuring she kept to the prescribed pathway. She had no experience with the consequences of wandering off, no understanding of how the mind could get distracted from its intended course and stumble into oblivion. Maintaining her focus while walking was a skill she needed to develop, one of the many required. But he would always be there to help, to nudge her mind back should that become necessary. He had pledged long ago to guard her steps and guide her way.

It was a good night to dreamwalk. The Wycche and her Malvisse, in their current weakened state, should pose no threat. It was the perfect time to put his night-ward's feet firmly beneath her and get her accustomed to navigating this realm of light and thought, for the day had come when she would need to be as agile and expert here as on the manifest plane.

In a blink, they were beyond the limits of her waking adventures, past the District Calliaigh and the Academie Vorik, past the flatlands of the Basin, and the rolling hillsides of the Whindon Wood. Essiant brought her searching mind to a halt at the foothills of the Blackshale Mountains, the dark-gray shadow of Cyrulian Kalt looming tall in the purpling dusk. There was something here he wanted her to remember. She would need to use her Shadowen vorik to create a touchpoint, a skill she had never attempted or even known existed until this moment. Essiant was counting on her innate ability to carry them through. Though it was a force still naive and untested, it was also powerful and pure.

See true, his mind reminded, and he brought her focus back to the map of light she had been creating as they went, putting his own vorik into it so she could see the wonder of it. She looked around, wide-eyed, at the gridded energy patterns spooling out around them.

I never knew, her mind whispered in awe.

See true, for all that is to be is reliant on this. He felt her mind falter, doubting the truth of her perceptions.

Never doubt, always trust, for you are mightier than the moon, and more powerful than the stars. Here, they bow to you because it is your mind that creates their destiny. Do you feel the force rising within you?

His night-ward nodded, her mind pulling into itself to acknowledge the ancient power rising within. With it came a feeling of heightened acuity, focused reasoning, and unfettered freedom, sensations she found both thrilling and frightening.

Do not get lost, Essiant warned. *Grasp your power. Control it. Use it. Do not let it use you.* His words cut through her overwhelmed mind, helping her rein in her thoughts. When she had them under control, he continued. *Remember.*

She looked at the wraithwolf, not comprehending what he was asking her to do.

He went on. *Center yourself, grasp the power within, and see true all that is about you. Do that and you will create a touchpoint in your soul memory of this place, a spot of remembrance you can return to again and again.*

She paused, gauging her internal fount of power. Essiant felt her marshal it, her mind compressing and shaping the vor into a concentrated ball, the way a child rolls diaphanous spiderweb into tangible shape between their fingertips.

He pushed his head underneath her hand then marched in a circle, his mindwords urging her to *see, see, see* until they had completed a full rotation.

Remember, remember, remember he repeated until he could feel the thought-form she'd recorded in her mind being etched upon the gridded light map by her Shadowen force.

She smiled. *I've done it,* her mindwords marveled.

It is good. There is much here you will need.

Recognition rolled over her, and she clapped her hands together with glee. *This is my grandfather's house! I remember this place! It was so long ago.*

Yes, you were barely weaned when last you were here.

It was all so big and new, and the crystalwood staff... Is this where I got the crystalwood staff?

Yes, the crystalwood staff. Keep it close for it holds secrets and power.

But my father... how was his staff not with him when he left on his journey?

It was left for you. Your mother knows this although she will claim not to remember. Do not allow her fears to alter your course.

But he left before I was born. How could he have known?

The plans of the All do not always make themselves apparent to those who wish for easy answers. Look within yourself, and you will see it was all necessary for your development. The path was laid when first you pledged to take on this task, but it is up to you to find and follow its way. It has not been easy, nor will it ever be easy. It is not for the faint of heart, or the faint of spirit. Search your own soul, and you will know the truth of these words. Even now, your vow to the All rings like a bell within you, calling you toward your true destiny. Do not be afraid to answer that call. Know that you already have all that you need, but it will take discernment, faith, and courage to accomplish the noble triumph you have undertaken.

His night-ward's face turned serious as she contemplated the enormity of his words.

He went on. *There are forces already opposing you. Powerful forces locked into a nightmare of their own creation, for they have become drunk on stolen power and seduced by perfidious greed. They are many, both here, and on the manifest plane. Do not be discouraged by their perceived power and might. They are as nothing in the face of that one true power that comes from the All. I will shield your essence here, but you will need to once again gather protectors on the manifest plane from that eternal alliance you have known for as long as your soul has existed. They who have given their pledge to the All to assist you in your sojourn are near about and ready to serve if you but ask.*

How will I know them? his night-ward asked, and he could feel the doubt creeping in again.

Believe and they will appear. There is one near, even now, searching, though he does not know for whom he looks.

A second wraithwolf appeared, its radiant silver-black coat a bright counterpoint in the gathered gray fog obscuring the distance.

Who is that? his night-ward asked as she stared at the guardian.

As soon as her mind asked the question, a tall figure appeared at the side of the wraithwolf. With a thought, Essiant and his night-ward stood nearby.

The figure beside the wraithwolf seemed not to see her, his attention fixed on some faraway point, his pale, shoulder-length hair catching and reflecting the stray shine of stars. His face was both stern and soft at the same time. Worried, perhaps.

I have seen this maran! Essiant's night-ward exclaimed.

Yes, he confirmed. *He is waiting to hear you. Listen to your soul and speak its words.*

His night-ward paused, her thoughts turning inward. *To my heart you are family,* her mindwords murmured. The pale-haired man's attention riveted onto her, his mouth dropping open in surprise, his silver-floss eyebrows arching.

To my heart you are family, her mindwords repeated, more forcefully this time, the weight of conviction behind them.

The pale-haired man stepped back, a look of shock on his face. He looked down at his wraithwolf in bewilderment. His guardian thrust its head against the back of the man's leg, pushing him forward.

Essiant took a step toward the pair, a shaft of starshine illuminating the crescent moon on his forehead. The silvery wraithwolf lowered its head then bowed to the massive white wraithwolf. The pale-haired man watched in amazement.

Essiant dipped his head, an acknowledgement of the honor paid, and the wraithwolf straightened. Like smoke in the wind, the pair were gone.

Come, Essiant's mindwords urged. *We have further to go.* He directed his night-ward's attention to the starry path stretching toward a pulsing light on the smudged line of the horizon.

His night-ward's mind leaped forward again, flying high above the Blackshale Mountains, their craggy backbone a guideline beneath their feet then onward across a vast flat of frozen gray, the sawtoothed profile of a distant mountain range a shadow to their south.

A lone, flat-topped mountain rose in front of them, sparkling white in the dusky dark.

Crystalwood, his night-ward breathed.

Yes, Essiant confirmed.

Where are we?

Where you've wished to be for all these many annums.

The mountain shone brightly in the gloom and his night-ward's mind bounded toward it, attracted like a moth to a flame. In an instant they were hovering above the ruins of a stone structure.

His night-ward's attention fixed upon the brunnestone megalith, cracked and covered in grime. He could feel her intense sadness at all that had been lost. He allowed the feeling to remain.

Remember, Essiant prompted.

This time, his night-ward knew what to do. She gathered up her Shadowen vor, compressed it, then set her gaze upon their surroundings and turned in a circle, the touchpoint etching itself onto her internal grid map. When she was finished, she smiled at her wraithwolf.

It is good. Look now, for you remember little of the Elect, while they remember all of you.

A crevasse opened and the megalith's brunnestone panels subsided into it. Another shape began to form, drawing itself together from the dirt and stones and herbage of the mountain. A giant, reptilian head shook its way free, lifting high into the sky. Its entirety was covered in a layer of sparkling crystalwood, tangled shrubbery, and twining vine, and set upon a neck as thick as a small mountain, yet long and supple and lithe. Essiant's night-ward sagged back, her mind struggling to comprehend.

You must know this, Essiant urged, throwing his considerable size against the back of her legs to move her forward.

The ground shook, a mighty quake opening a cavernous rent in the rocky ground. A huge body assembled from the stones and vines and trees, its massive tail sliding up and out of the crater before unfurling down the side of the transforming mountain. The body lurched upward, supported by stout legs set upon clawed feet sabering into the shale from whence the creature had emerged, its massive, moss-covered wings lifting before spreading across the sky.

A dragon. His night-ward's staggered mind barely managed to think the words.

The dragon's eyes remained closed as it assembled to its full height, and Essiant's night-ward quailed at the thought of them opening and seeing her standing so close. As soon as the thought came the lids opened, revealing iridescent orbs as depthless as an infinite sun, shining with a fierceness that cut straight through all that they gazed upon. There was nothing unseen beneath the great one's penetrating glare, nothing hidden from its omniscience.

Fear not, Essiant urged as his night-ward drew back, a shiver running through her. *This is the great good Grogauk, founder and keeper of Therrania.*

Recognition shot through Essiant's night-ward. *I have read about Therrania. Many times. But never about a keeper. Never about a dragon.*

Some truths are only revealed to those who seek to know.

The dragon brought its head low to stare at the quaking girl. *See true,* its mindwords intoned in a kind voice that came from everywhere. *And all will be well.*

Essiant bowed low to the Founder and his night-ward did as well, although in the case of the latter, it was more of a collapse than a curtsy.

The lids closed, the massive wings drew tight against the gargantuan body, and the Founder sank into the ground, disassembling as it went until it was once again a mountain covered in trees and vines and shrubbery, looking as it had before the great guardian's appearance, the plateau on top as flat and empty as an abandoned dream.

Essiant nudged his night-ward's hand. *And now, rest.*

With that, they raced back the way they had come, over mountains and valleys and fields, until they were back inside the garol.

His night-ward gave Essiant a pat on the head. *Thank you,* her mindwords murmured as her etheric form slipped inside her slumbering body, breaking their Saska bond.

Sleep well, Essiant thought before ascending into the realm of their dreams.

Grogakee, Grogakee

Grogakee, Grogakee
(Dragon of the mountain, Dragon of the mountain)
Callaska Hee
(Come quickly)
Grogakee, Grogakee
(Dragon of the mountain, Dragon of the mountain)
Chuulzu Palleea
(My spirit wishes to speak)

Grogakee, Grogakee
(Dragon of the mountain, Dragon of the mountain)
 Oolla-ka Wasakagee
(Watch over this village)

Grogakee, Grogakee
(Dragon of the mountain, Dragon of the mountain)
Daala Ushoku La
(With the Eye of The People)

—Excerpted from *The Ceremonial Songs of Sree Kaa,*
and interpreted for the Most Exalted Monarch,
Geldizian Rennesseau, by a scribe

CHAPTER SIXTEEN
ALLIES AND FRIENDS

Rachmyn awoke early and checked his pocket for his shard. Yes, there it was. He thumbed its cool surface to calm his thoughts. In all his time in Oru Fen, he'd never encountered another dreamwalker. Spectra had never allowed it. Until last night.

He'd been scouting an escape route from this infernal district and its wretched festival when the chestnut-haired healer appeared out of the gloom, a magnificent white wraithwolf at her side, speaking words that pierced his soul—*to my heart you are family*. Was it a message? A sign? The image remained clear in his mind, as did the certainty that this young woman had been his ally for as long as he had existed. Even now, after coming fully awake, he couldn't shake the unquiet feeling the encounter had provoked.

He glanced at Haedyn, stretched out on his cloak, his head on one crooked arm, his hand tucked up under his chin. Still asleep. His friend's serene face showed no sign of the black eye.

Rachmyn felt a surge of nostalgia, remembering all the times he'd watched over Haedyn during the annums they'd been on their own. His friend had grown up right before his eyes into the handsome, golden-haired maran stretched out before him. Rachmyn felt a pride of accomplishment that he'd gotten them this far, tempered by a longing to return to that simpler time when his parents were still alive. He sighed. That happiness was gone forever.

The use of the garol had been fortuitous, but Rachmyn didn't intend they should stay more than one night, despite Haedyn's efforts to claim it by drawing up a crude Hiegh flag using a discarded apron and a lump of charcoal. His friend had tacked the misbegotten creation, smudgy fingerprints and all, onto the garol's center pole as proudly as any Caeldish farmer, one eye squinting into the golden light of the setting sun. Rachmyn smiled, recalling Haedyn's rakish grin when he'd finished, his menace of a bird glaring balefully from his shoulder.

Rachmyn stood, and Elgre sprang up, the wolf sinking into a front-leg stretch as Rachmyn hoisted his rucksack onto his back. The pair padded out of the garol. Rachmyn had an errand, the kind best pursued under cover of darkness.

Once outside, Rachmyn looked up at the predawn sky twinkling with the muted shine of distant stars, then set off toward the marketplace. This wasn't a meeting he wanted, but he saw no other choice. What he had to sell would only be desired by Shadowen dreamcrafters. After the death of his parents, he'd sworn to never ally himself with another Shadowen but in present circumstances, there weren't many alternatives. It galled him, but he and Haedyn needed auriels and a way out of this trap they'd put themselves in. This meeting could provide both.

Soon he was heading toward a black caravan with painted sides depicting a snarling wolf materializing from a swirling mist. In the dark, the wolf's eyes glowed like purple jewels beneath large silver letters touting bold promises.

THE GREAT ALLIARI
GRAND MASTER OF THE ARCANE MYSTERIES!
SEE YOUR DESTINY! FIND TRUE LOVE!
HEAL ANY DISEASE! ATTAIN FORTUNE AND FAME!
ADVENTURES FOR ONE AND ALL!
ONLY 25 AURIELS!

Rachmyn rolled his eyes. Alliari Stulko had been the dullest of his childhood playmates when the Umbraes had thrown in with the Kalto band after the slaughter of Haedyn's family. Rachmyn knew it was only the liberal use of wolfken that enabled Alliari to eke out a living as a dreamcrafter. It wasn't his skills, which were appalling, or his mood charms, which were nothing more than flavored powders in silver-foil packets. He was the barest form of charlatan, the kind of Shadowen who more than earned the scorn he received. His main attribute, if it could even be called that, was his siring by the legendary dreamwalker, Challyn Stulko, now deceased. Then there were his large brown eyes which some found appealing, their expressiveness evoking the piteous stare of a dying deer or begging dog. All of which made him the perfect buyer for what Rachmyn had to sell. Someone with plenty of coins and few questions. The kind whose lack of skill would make him unable to misuse the speck as so many Shadowen did. It was the best Rachmyn could do.

He scratched his fingernails against the caravan's side then listened for stirrings within. When none were forthcoming, he scratched again, harder this time. Elgre pricked his ears and cocked his head.

"Who comes scratching in the dark of the night?" creaked a voice.

"An ally from the past, come with a bargain and a proposition," Rachmyn answered.

The front door squeaked open, and a slight man, still wrapping a silky dressing gown about his hirsute torso, stuck out his head. "No," the man said, his voice heavy with disbelief. "Can't be. Rachmyn Umbrae, is that you?"

Rachmyn stepped away from the caravan. "It is."

"Come, come." Alliari waved him forward, his dressing gown flapping open to expose his hairy chest. "Come inside."

Rachmyn climbed the caravan's steps and entered as Elgre lay down to wait.

Alliari lit an oil lantern, and it swung from the wagon's center bow, casting a swaying oval of flickering light that flattered the shabby interior.

It had been a long time since Rachmyn had been inside a caravan. The air smelled of smoke and spice, just as he remembered. A thread-worn purple curtain separated the front from the sleeping bunk at the back. Rachmyn noted more than one hole in the divider's tatty material.

Alliari scurried around, picking up scattered papers and cast-off garments, clearing a path to an ornate chair set beneath a banner proclaiming it, *THE SEAT OF ALL KNOWLEDGE*. "Please." The showman swept a hand toward the ostentatious chair. "Sit, my old friend."

Rachmyn shrugged off his rucksack, setting it on the floor before folding onto the chair's silver-and-purple upholstery.

Alliari hitched the dressing gown about himself, drew the sashing belt tight then sat in a carved wooden chair opposite, his smeary, charcoal-outlined eyes fixing on Rachmyn with an expression of bemused astonishment. He clapped his hands, rubbed them together, then laughed and shook his head. "I never thought I would see you again. Especially not in a place such as this." He laughed again, a creaking rumble that grated the ear.

Rachmyn's face remained hard as he reached into his pack and pulled out a small wooden box. He removed the leather cord around his neck and, using the attached key, unlocked the box and flipped back its lid. Alliari sobered and leaned forward, his greedy eyes scanning the four rows of thin glass vials packed inside, each filled with a greenish-black powder and sealed with a bead of wax.

"Is that all speck?" Alliari asked, his doe-eyes widening.

Rachmyn nodded.

"Great good night. How did you come by such a store?"

"Are you interested?" Rachmyn asked.

Alliari looked up from the vials to Rachmyn's face. "That's more speck than I could use in ten annums." Rachmyn grimaced and started to close the lid. Alliari grabbed his hand. "No need to be hasty. What aspect?"

"Ascending," Rachmyn answered. "Hand cast," he added, his eyes locked on the showman's overly familiar grip.

Alliari loosed his grip and rocked back, one hand reaching up to sharpen the points of his waxed mustache before dropping to stroke his wavy, black beard, the silver beads woven into it making a faint clicking noise. "Yes, I would have guessed that. Umbrae speck was always of the highest quality. How much?"

"Five thousand," Rachmyn said, knowing it was a ransom.

A thump sounded behind the curtain, and Rachmyn's head swiveled toward it. He side-eyed Alliari.

"Auriels?" Alliari asked, his unflinching gaze firmly on the speck.

Rachmyn nodded, giving the curtain another hard look. The showman's eyebrows shot up as he exhaled sharply. Rachmyn forced his attention back. "Each," he added.

Alliari's eyebrows rose higher, two black crescents approaching his hairline. It was a fantastic sum for something that could be held in the palm of one's hand. More money than Rachmyn had seen in all his life.

"Not enough," Alliari murmured.

It was Rachmyn's turn to be surprised.

"Not that I have that, understand. You've caught me on the wrong side of prosperity, I'm afraid. Not to mention I spent a spunking fortune stocking up for this festival on speck not half so fine as this, and I've yet to sell a single grain."

Rachmyn nodded, shutting the lid and locking the box. He slipped the cord around his neck, the key settling against his chest. "I appreciate your time," he said, sliding the box into his rucksack.

"There's only one who could afford such a sum," Alliari mused. "And would have need of it all. Yes..." He stroked his beard again, his charcoaled eyes scanning the canvas roof. Rachmyn's gaze remained steady. Alliari came to a decision. "But not here. It would have to be done very discreet you understand. Very discreet. It would take me some time but yes, I could get you a meeting. I'm sure I could. You've come to the right maran, my friend." His face broke into a wide smile.

Rachmyn gave Alliari a skeptical look. "I think I'll take my chances finding a buyer," he said. "I'm not looking for a partner."

"Partner?" Alliari laughed. "I propose nothing of the sort. This would just be one friend helping another, one hand washing the other because they find themselves in the same basin."

Rachmyn's skeptical frown deepened.

"I can see you still aren't convinced." Alliari stretched his splayed hands forward in a posture of persuasion. "Let me say it like this. I know the value of what you have, and I know who will pay that value. Gladly pay it. Can you say the same?"

Rachmyn shook his head.

"Let me bridge that divide, then." Alliari brought his hands together, interlacing his fingers to make his point. He nodded down at them then at Rachmyn, his eyebrows waggling.

"What would I have to do?"

"Not a thing. All I need is enough time to get things sorted." Alliari unclasped his hands and slapped them onto his knees.

"And what payment would you require?" No self-respecting Shadowen ever worked for free.

"The skim off the cream," Alliari purred. "A mere shaving from the plank. Rest assured, you'll get your price and more besides."

"How long would you need?"

"One day. Maybe two."

Rachmyn despised the idea of staying at this festival another moment, and yet, he couldn't shake the feeling he needed to find the chestnut-haired healer. Two days would allow for that.

"Have we an understanding?" Alliari leaned forward in his chair, a wheedling smile curling his lips, his eyes famously huge.

Rachmyn gritted his teeth, fighting back the urge to tell the old phony he was fooling no one. Instead, he placed his forefinger aside of his nose and gave a curt nod.

Alliari returned the gesture, his smile widening. "You've made a wise decision, my friend."

Rachmyn flattened his lips.

"I think it's best we keep this between us, understand? There's some here that aren't as trustworthy as yours truly." Alliari gave his chest a stiff-fingered pat, a grin plastered to his grease-painted face.

"I'll not be spreading any news," Rachmyn growled.

"Nor I," Alliari said, his tone thick with false sincerity.

Rachmyn cleared his throat and rose to his feet, slinging his rucksack onto one shoulder. "I'll be in touch," he muttered, making for the exit.

Alliari sprang up and laid an ushering hand on Rachmyn's back. He gave a shuddering jerk, and the showman desisted, disappointment deepening the lines bracketing his frown.

Rachmyn opened the door, trying to ignore the sinking feeling this meeting had been a terrible mistake, then stepped out onto the stoop. He hitched the straps of his rucksack tight and descended the three-step ladder. Elgre rose and stretched. Rachmyn shook his head at the wolf.

Alliari's head poked through the doorway. "Meet me at The Running Fox tonight when the moon is high," he said, then seeing Rachmyn's confusion, added, "You'll find it by way of the High Road, on the bank of the Wydderhalle near Duntin Town. I'll have your buyer there."

Elgre gazed at the disheveled man as he fumbled with his dressing gown before looking to Rachmyn, who returned the wolf's austere stare.

"I'll be there." Rachmyn turned and strode away, Elgre leading the way.

A shaft of sunlight fell through the garol's gapped opening, striking Haedyn's face as he lay on his cloak. He squinted awake, threw a hand up to block the glare, and got to his feet. He stretched a leather glove onto his right hand.

Rachmyn and his wolf were gone, a fact he barely registered as he nudged a knuckle against Fryk's grasping feet then felt the familiar click of talons wrapping on. He lifted the bird toward his chest, tilted his finger downward, and tucked Fryk away into his pocket.

Haedyn exited, his mind alive with new and wonderful thoughts. She was out there, somewhere, on this bright, clear morning, maybe watching the same golden-jewel sun rise above the horizon. He patted his ungloved fingertips against his eye, marveling at how ordinary it felt. How had she healed him? He closed his eyes, reliving the cooling touch of her fingertips against his hot, bruising flesh, remembering how the pain faded, replaced by a pleasurable sensation emanating from his chest and spreading in a warming tide throughout his body. Even now, the feeling lingered, flaring up in his midsection as he directed his attention toward it. He'd never felt anything like it before, this yearning to be as close as possible to another maran. In some ways, it was like the feelings he had for Rachmyn but then again, wholly different. For one thing, he'd known Rachmyn forever while he didn't know this beguiling young woman at all. But then again, was that right? Deep inside, he felt he'd also known her forever while at the same time understanding that wasn't possible since they'd only just met.

He surveyed the festival grounds, setting his course. He would find her today and when he did, he would... well, he didn't know what he would do but right now, that didn't matter. All that mattered was that she was out there somewhere with no idea about these feelings he had inside. By sunset, with any luck at all, that would no longer be the case.

Rachmyn had talked himself out of trying to find the girl by the time he got back to the garol. Haedyn was outside, his countenance glowing as he gazed at the rising sun.

"Morning is upon us," Rachmyn observed.

"So it is," Haedyn agreed, his voice as distant as his gaze.

"I've found a buyer for the speck."

"Do you suppose she's thinking about me right now?"

"Did you hear what I said?"

"What did you say?"

"We've a meeting set for tonight," Rachmyn said, his tone irritated.

"Did you see her eyes? The most beautiful blend of amber and blue... Like a sunrise..." Haedyn's voice trailed off.

"At the Running Fox, by way of the High Road," Rachmyn persisted.

"What do you call that color—"

"We'll have to set out this evening—"

"—the glow of a sunrise—"

"—and stay clear of the guards—"

"—the mixture of flame and sky together—"

"—so rest up, because it's going to be a long night of walking—"

"—flame and sky and night, all in one. Is there a name for a color like that?"

"Are you listening to me?" Rachmyn complained.

"Are you listening to me?" Haedyn countered.

The friends looked at each other, as if seeing one another for the first time.

"No, there's no name for that—" Rachmyn growled.

"Why do we have to leave tonight—" Haedyn grumbled.

"—bunch of fanciful nonsense—"

"—Can't we at least wait—"

"—and what does it matter anyway—"

"—until we've seen the pageant—"

"—whether you know the color of her eyes. What good will that do—"

"—She'll be there, you know. She has to be."

Rachmyn looked at his friend, all eagerness and hope, and a pang of love struck his heart. Haedyn turned toward the brightening horizon. "She'll be there," he marveled.

Rachmyn took a deep breath. "Yes, I know," he allowed.

"I want to stay." Haedyn shifted his gaze, his golden eyes pleading.

Rachmyn took another deep breath. "Yes, I know."

Haedyn's stare hardened, until his friend's longing became Rachmyn's own.

"We have to stay," Haedyn whispered hoarsely.

Rachmyn sighed. "Yes, I know."

CHAPTER SEVENTEEN
SPECTACLE OF EVERY KIND

Elorah held the berre in her hands, her mind parsing possibilities. She could use sweet-smelling roots, intricately lobed herbals, and jewel-toned berries to embellish the bear-shaped talisman for the Blessing of the Berres. Or the delicate fluff of moss and lichen to effect a realistic depiction of the Urslan. A rash idea invaded her thoughts. Her Therran vorik could grow something fantastical, a living sculpture perhaps, transforming the thille form her grandmama handed her earlier.

Grandmama Vaytah had emphasized the importance of the Blessing Berre during their walk in the Bonny Wood. Previous poor harvests meant this year's crop needed to be exceptional or many would suffer. Her grandmama also confided that Novah felt a great burden to make this year's festival especially pleasing to the Urslan Sisters to secure a bountiful blessing for this year's crops.

It occurred to Elorah that this might be the last time she completed this task. The last time she would be responsible for creating the talisman believed by every Caeldish to bring an annum of good fortune. It was a bittersweet thought, for she'd always enjoyed creating her family's berre using gatherings from her district's fields and forests.

Until this moment, she'd never considered the larger implications so focused had she been on the task at hand but now, it all seemed meaningless, like so many other things about this festival. The more she thought about it, the more she realized none of it mattered. Not the Blessing of the Berres, or the Grand Pageant, or the Calling of the Clans or the Council of Emvors. It was all hollow tradition. Minutia dreamed up to placate unthinking minds.

She supposed she owed her current mood to her dream from the night before, if it could even be called a dream, for even now her recall of it was as clear as any waking memory. It had created a powerful desire within her to find the mysterious megalith and restore it to its original state. Even as she thought the thought, she felt wholly inadequate to it despite an overwhelming urgency to do exactly that.

It was a parambek she'd seen, of this she was certain, although in all her reading about these vor attunement centers, she'd never imagined how much transformative power a parambek held. How such a quantity of vor could be concentrated in a singular place was beyond fathoming, and yet, she now knew it to be true. Parambeks weren't some myth or fable, as she'd been taught. Nor were they old mother's tales fashioned from fanciful wishes. They were real places used by real marans for real vorikal advancement. Or at least they had been once. Even in the books she'd read, the idea that parambeks were physical places had been refuted, and yet, she'd always wondered, what if such places did exist? And if they did, how much benefit would it be to her fellow marans? She'd spent long hours daydreaming about them, but nothing she'd read or dreamed had prepared her for the magnificence of the real thing. Even now, she felt awestruck by it.

She'd recorded the vision in her journal as soon as she'd awakened, feeling all the while her words were poor substitutes for the actual experience.

Physio: Feelings of excitement, sorrow, wonder. I did not feel asleep.

Memories: The pale haired man appeared. I think we've known each other forever. *To my heart you are family* He and his

*companion feel like old friends. Next, the same bear-shaped edifice
Therrania on a mountain covered in crystalwood. The fabled
Whitemond? The walls were buried in mud. I felt much sorrow
seeing them. Then, a voice said "uniter." Uniting who or what?
Unclear. In a thunderclap the mountain transformed into a
dragon *GROGOK* as tall as the sun, with mossy wings that
blotted out the sky. Such terror until I looked into his eyes, every
color imaginable in an endless swirl. He spoke with the kindest
voice I've ever heard. *See true and all will be well* (Silvi's words!)
I bowed to him, for he was the most majestic being I've ever beheld.
He sank into the ground, the trees and rocks from which he'd
formed settling back to their usual places. I believe he may be the
mountain itself...*

Analysis: A call to action I can no longer ignore.

The gray orb came into her mind, its brokenness and sorrow so like
the brokenness of Therrania and the sorrow she felt upon seeing it. She
wondered if there was some connection between the two.

"Have you finished?"

Novah's voice cut through her thoughts. Elorah looked down at the
thille berre and decided what she would do. She summoned her Therran
vorik and sent it zinging into the blank. Tiny leaflets sprouted then grew
into a plush covering of green. Near the top of the head, threadlike
stems pushed up between the miniature leaves, lifting delicate white and
blue flowers around two oak twig horns spiking upward. Another zing
of vorik and four black seed pods approximating two eyes, a nose, and a
mouth appeared. The seed pods serving as eyes transformed into
cotyledons marked with black dots, while the seedpod serving as a nose
butterflied into two halves, each indenting to form a nostril. Another
nudge of vorik and the flowers near the horns wove themselves into a
miniature wreath. A perfect likeness completed in the blink of an eye.

"Oh," Novah said as she approached. "Isn't that lovely."

Elorah looked down at her creation, but rather than feeling pride,
she was stricken with remorse. Her mother took the berre into her

hands, turning it to see the detail. The tiny silverthorn claws, the textured leaves resembling fur, the blinking, seedpod eyes and flaring nose making it appear the creation was breathing.

Novah's eyes narrowed. "You've used vorik on this," she said, arrowing a look at Elorah. "You know that's against Council rules."

Elorah ducked her head, ashamed. "I'll make another," she mumbled as she started to step away. Novah reached out and grasped her arm.

"Look at me, Elorah."

Elorah raised her eyes.

"Are you in trouble?" Novah asked, her eyes going wet. She pinched the bridge of her nose then scraped the tears aside with her thumb and forefinger. "You've been so different lately."

"I'm sorry," Elorah said, her stomach tumbling. How could she explain her thoughts and feelings from these last two days? Truthfully, she *was* different, but seeing the pain and sadness in her mother's eyes made her wish it wasn't so.

"Has something happened? Something I need to know about?"

Elorah swallowed hard and shook her head. "No, mother," she replied, ignoring the voice inside telling her to speak the truth.

"Whatever it is, we can work it out." Novah's voice cracked on the last word. She took a deep breath then let go of Elorah's arm and handed back the berre. "I'll leave it up to you what to do with that," she said, her gaze dropping onto the blinking talisman. She took another deep breath then drew herself up and squared her shoulders, her expression forming into her official face. "I'm sure you'll make the right decision." She walked away, heading toward the sacred grounds.

Elorah sighed then carried the berre to the nearest fire pit and tossed it in.

Time to start over.

"So how do you know which ones are the dream tellers?" Mierrle asked, her eyes roving as she walked. The marketplace was in full flow and full voice as vendors heckled customers into their stalls and tents and caravans.

"Dreamcrafters," Thane corrected with a smile. "You've really never had one done?"

Mierrle shook her head.

"I envy you. The first time is always the best."

"Are you sure you don't mind? Paying, I mean. Just until I see my father."

"Consider it an investment in our partnership."

Mierrle giggled. "Partnership. I like that."

"We're going to do great things, you and I," Thane replied, flourishing his hands in the air. They passed a tobacconist's cart and a sausager's stall before approaching a black-and-silver caravan. "Here we are."

Mierrle's eyes grew large as she stared at the caravan's side. "The Great Al-ee-air-ee," she pronounced. "Are you sure this is the one?"

"Quite sure," Thane said, bounding up the steps and knocking.

The door swung open and a voice crooned, "Back so soon? You couldn't get enough of the Great Alliari, you had to come back for more?" The showman emerged wearing a purple coat with black lapels, a silver-and-black pointy-peaked hat, a pair of round-framed spectacles, and the smile of a cat that's got the cream. He reached out for an embrace.

Thane stepped back and cleared his throat. "I've brought you a customer, Maister Alliari. Allow me to introduce Maiss Mierrle Jazh."

Alliari's eyes slanted away from Thane toward Mierrle, his arms wilting to his sides. He planted his heel and pivoted. Mierrle smiled up at him then bit her lower lip and curtseyed. "Pleased to meet you, Maister All-ee-air-ee."

"The pleasure is all mine," Alliari boomed as he gave her a bow. "How may I be of service, Maiss Jazh?"

"I, uh..." Mierrle faltered.

"Maiss Jazh has a profound desire to experience her first dreamcraft adventure," Thane said, winking at her.

"Has she indeed?" Alliari exclaimed. "And what type of dream does she desire? A love adventure, perhaps? Those are always exceedingly satisfactory."

"I, uh..."

"Or perhaps a hero's journey where you save a kingdom?" Alliari continued, searching Mierrle's face for her reaction.

"Well, uh..."

"Or maybe something quieter. A relaxing stroll through a peaceful forest or a soothing ride down a slow-moving stream?"

"What do you think, Mierrle?" Thane asked.

"What's a love adventure?" she murmured.

"Pardon?" Alliari crowed.

"Love adventure. What's that?" she asked, her voice slightly louder.

"Always a good choice." Alliari gave Thane a knowing look.

"Always a mistake," Thane laughed.

Alliari's eyes narrowed, his jovial mask slipping. "Always a good choice," he repeated, biting off each word.

Thane cleared his throat, his eyebrows rising, his lips pursed. "You're the expert."

"Yes," Alliari said. "I am." He pinioned Thane for an uncomfortable beat before returning his gaze to Mierrle, a broad showman's smile back on his face. "You won't be disappointed, maiss. A love adventure always lifts the spirits. Now, there's just the simple matter of payment."

"You can put it on my tab." Thane's tone was casual.

"Your tab..." Alliari adjusted the plain-glass spectacles he wore for effect, his head theatrically cocking to the side, his expression quizzical. "I don't recall–"

"The one I started last night. You remember," Thane said.

Tart annoyance pinched Alliari's cheeks a bright red. He lifted his chin. "Ah, yes," he replied, his flattened eyebrows sinking toward his narrowed eyes. "Now, I do." The two exchanged hard stares before Alliari stepped down and held out his hand. "Right this way, maiss."

Mierrle giggled and placed her hand atop his, allowing herself to be led up the stairs. Thane remained at the bottom. Mierrle turned to look at him.

"Aren't you coming?" she squeaked.

"Might be best if I stayed here." Thane's gaze cut toward Alliari.

"But we're partners, remember? He can come, can't he?" she asked Alliari who wore a grim, pasted-on smile.

"Of course," he said. "Whatever you wish, maiss. It's your adventure." His mirthless eyes bore down on Thane. "Come up, my friend, and join your partner." He expectorated the last word like a wad of phlegm.

Thane bounded up the stairs, ignoring Alliari's cold glare. "As you wish," he said, taking Mierrle's arm.

"A bent arrow never shoots straight," Alliari harrumphed as Thane led Mierrle past him and into the caravan.

Elorah returned to the garol only long enough to retrieve a few coins from the apothecary chest. The blessing ceremony was set to begin at near-noon. With the sun halfway into its rise, she knew she hadn't a moment to lose if she hoped to recreate her family's berre before the ceremony began.

She hurried to the marketplace, bustling from shop to stall to cart in search of supplies. The best forms and finishes had already been purchased, leaving her to sort through the scraps rejected by everyone before her. Desperation drove her forward. How would she ever finish in time? Had her foolishness doomed her family to another annum of poor harvests and bad luck? She brushed aside the thought and focused on the job at hand.

She purchased the last items at the sixth herbalist's stall she visited. After handing over her remaining coins and clutching her finds to her chest, she scurried out, the scent of meadowsweet in her nose, the shopkeep's gravel-voiced admonishment—"You've left it mighty late, maiss. I'd say a little too late"—scouring her ears.

Her mind was already assembling the berre as she rushed through the crowded marketplace, going through the steps she would follow as soon as she returned to her family's garol. When the collision happened, it took her a moment to realize she was lying flat on her back and not still running.

"Maiss? Maiss?" a deep voice called. "Are you okay?"

"I'm fine," she mumbled as her circumstance registered. She pushed herself into a sit.

"You ran right into Georgy," the stout-bodied man accused as he patted the cresty neck of the bay horse at his side. The horse bent its head low to sniff at her. "Lucky he's as solid as they come, unlike some." The man squinted down at her.

"My apologies," Elorah groaned as she got to her feet, her eyes searching for the supplies that had been in her grasp a moment earlier. The flowers and leaves were now a drifting disaster, green- and gray- and rose-colored scraps whirling away in the breeze. She started chasing after them, trying to snatch the scatterings from the air, but it was no use. The moment she'd grab for one, the wind would twirl it away.

"No sense running about like a spring rabbit. You'll never catch them now," the man observed, shaking his head. "You be careful, maiss," he said as he led the horse away.

She soon gave up on salvaging any of her purchases and looked back to where she'd fallen. The thille berre was still there, laying on its side, one leg and one ear broken off. She walked over and picked up the pieces, cradling them against her chest as a feeling of hopelessness washed over her. She squeezed her eyes tight, forcing back the tears burning hot at the corners before sniffing twice. After a moment, the despair eased. She looked down at the three pieces in her hands. She would have to do the best she could with what she had.

That decided, she hurried toward the garols taking care to watch where she was going.

Thane watched Alliari closely as he offered the silver cup to Mierrle, even taking it from the dreamcrafter's grasp and sniffing it before handing it to Mierrle. She giggled and took a sip.

"Drink up, maiss. Soon you'll be walking amongst the stars with the maran of your dreams." Alliari turned toward Thane and rolled his eyes before giving him a ridiculously swoony gaze.

Poor sod. He thinks himself the soul of wit. If only he knew how foolish his feeble attempts at humor make him look.

Thane pointedly looked past the showman's facial gymnastics to beam a smile at Mierrle. "Get ready," he whispered, grasping her hand, "for the ride of your life." He squeezed twice before letting go.

Mierrle's eyes went wide, a gormless smile on her face. She tipped the cup and gulped the remainder.

Thane laughed. "Yes!" he cried, clapping once as he rocked backward then forward again on the rickety stool Alliari had assigned him.

Alliari flipped the lever on a silver-plated timer sitting on a table near his elbow. The device was a clever construction depicting two wolves, one white, the other black, their slavering mouths touching at the pinch point between the timer's phials. Once the lever was pushed, the wolf at the bottom rotated to the top, enabling a thin stream of sand to flow from its mouth into its opposite's. Alliari took little notice, his lips a downturned crescent beneath his pointy mustache. "Sit back, maiss, relax, and allow the Great Alliari to lead you to your destiny," he said in a voice that sounded both peeved and bored.

Thane nodded encouragement as Mierrle relaxed against the purple-and-silver sateen of the Seat of All Knowledge, her heavy eyes drifting shut.

"Yes, that's it," Alliari droned. He picked up the hoewler sitting near the timer and put it to his lips, blowing through the bone-colored instrument twice.

In all the times he'd experienced a dreamcraft, Thane had never once heard a noise come from a Shadowen's hoewler. When he'd asked what the hoewler's purpose was, he'd been told that if he had to ask, he wasn't ready for the answer, which had made him angry enough to turn the dreamcraft—for which he'd paid a goodly sum—into a nightmare of running from an endless series of slavering wolves.

Alliari closed his eyes and lowed, "Tell me, what do you see?"

"I'm in my father's house." Mierrle shifted, a shadow crossing her face.

Thane looked at Alliari. Beneath his closed eyes, a draconic smile propped up the showman's painted cheeks.

"This is where you feel most happy?" Alliari snorted, the smile dismantling into a captious grimace.

"No!" Mierrle shook her head. "Wait." She paused for a long moment. Thane leaned forward trying to imagine what she was seeing. "There's a storm outside." She sounded frightened, her eyes jerking back and forth beneath her closed lids.

"Do you see the door?" Alliari asked.

"Yes," Mierrle said, her quavering voice rising.

"On the other side of that door is the maran you have waited for. I want you to walk to that door and open it. Can you do that?"

Mierrle nodded, her hands moving in her lap. A broad smile split her face. "He's here," she cried. "He's come to rescue me."

Alliari's charcoaled eyebrows drew together then flew upward, his eyelids stretching taut, his breathing coming in gasping riffs. Thane's brow knitted. Something wasn't right.

Mierrle sagged back, her expression serene. Thane wondered what she could be seeing that would give her such a look of otherworldly calm. His first dreamcraft had been a jaw-dropping adventure that had left him breathless and exhilarated. That wasn't happening here. Thane changed his focus. Alliari's hands gripped his chair as if trying to squeeze water from a dry sponge, his face a rictus of astonishment. Fear began to nibble at Thane's composure.

Alliari slumped sideways, his elbow bumping the ornate timer. Thane craned forward, his hands cupping to catch the device. But it didn't fall. Instead, it teetered twice, then resettled and resumed its steady flow. Thane sat back, nervous energy ripping through him.

What is happening?

Alliari's face softened, and his hands relaxed as he drooped against his chair. His eyes flew open, staring wildly for a moment, before he came to himself. He cleared his throat, lifted the hoewler, and inhaled a shaky breath through it before setting the instrument aside.

"Maiss, it is time to return to the present," he said, his throat garbling his voice.

Mierrle sighed as she straightened her back.

Alliari clapped his trembling hands and announced, "Awaken, maiss," before looking at Thane with a mixture of bewilderment and terror that hardened into a resentful scowl.

Mierrle's eyes fluttered open. Her gaze found Thane, the hint of a smile on her lips. "That was wonderful," she said in a faraway voice.

"The first time always is," Thane said.

She got to her feet, and Thane leaped up to take hold of her arm.

"Steady. You'll have to be careful till the effect wears off," he advised, helping her toward the door.

"I trust we're square." Alliari's tone was acidic, his charcoal-lined gaze a warning.

"For now," Thane replied, giving him a flirty smile. Alliari's expression softened slightly. Thane winked, and Alliari begrudged him a small smile before opening the door. Thane's gaze lingered on the showman as he ushered Mierrle out then helped her down the stairs.

That should smooth things over.

Alliari always had been an easy one to charm, which was fortunate because with another deal on the cuff, the last thing Thane wanted was to burn any bridges.

Elorah's plan was simple. Embed the end of a luminae needle into the separated leg then shove the other end into the body to join the pieces together. As for the broken ear, there wasn't much to be done if she couldn't use vorik. She would have to glue it with pitch and hope it stayed.

She quickly made the repairs and was soon running from her garol to the sacred grounds. The only decoration she'd had time to add was a sprig of mountain mint from the garol's planting, which she wound around the berre's neck in a makeshift garland.

By the time she arrived, the ceremony was set to begin. Every seat was filled, with many spectators standing at the back of the outdoor theater. A large collection of ornate berres, each facing the raised stage, crowded the toadstool-laced dais directly in front. Looking around, it was evident that much thought and work had gone into each of the talismans, save the one in her own hands. She set the pitiful excuse at the back of the Calliaigh section as her mother took the stage.

Novah's eyes caught Elorah's, then drifted down to the lumpish berre, her face crumpling into a disappointed frown. The glued-on ear slid forward, skidding down the eyeless face to rest at the tip of the noseless snout. Avoiding her mother's look of dismay, Elorah plucked the useless ear away and dropped it into her tunic pocket, a miserable shrug the only answer to her mother's unasked questions. A familiar voice called out.

"Elorah!"

Her head swiveled toward the sound.

Aikin waved from his seat in the middle of the Clan Bairrtraigh's section. "You can sit here," he called, his elbow nudging Ghielle who stood and flounced away, emptying the seat next to him.

Heads turned, directing stares of either expectancy or annoyance her way as Fyndd, seated on Aikin's other side, gave her a wry smile and a speculative shrug. Not knowing what else to do, Elorah made her way toward them.

"Welcome to the District Calliaigh," Novah's voice projected to those in the back, "as we pay tribute to our beloved Urslan. We shall begin with the Blessing of the Berres." Novah swept her hand toward the berres, and the crowd applauded. She waited before continuing. "It is my great honor to invite Eldra Clairn Malla bai Fola to the stage to conduct the sacred ritual of blessing."

Novah gestured toward an ancient-looking woman already clomping to the stairs, a curlywood staff topped by two carved bear heads clutched in one bird-talon hand. Once on stage, the old emvor tottered toward Novah, her wrinkly face alive with fervent enthusiasm. Novah escorted the Eldra center stage then glided away, taking a seat next to Vaytah at the front of the Clan Calliaigh's section.

Elorah kept her attention on the stage, even as Aikin leaned in close and asked, "Can I speak to you after the pageant? It's a matter of some importance."

She turned, an excuse already on her lips.

"Please," he whispered, his handsome face earnest.

She sighed. "I'll try."

Aikin smiled and looked at Fyndd who pretended he wasn't listening.

On stage, Eldra Malla closed her eyes and, in a whistling voice, recited the Urslan supplication verses from memory. Many in the crowd had their eyes closed and their hands raised, their lips miming along. When she finished, the crowd held its breath, waiting for confirmation that the Urslan Sisters had accepted their prayers and would bestow a blessing for the coming twelve moons.

A long moment passed before the emvor's eyes popped open, her misted gaze skimming across the audience as she exclaimed, "The Beloved Sisters have accepted our prayers and pledge their blessing." Eldra Malla's weathered face split into a concave grin that lacked most of its teeth. She clutched the staff and lifted it chest high before dipping the twin-bear-heads forward and sweeping them in a slow arc toward the decorated berres.

Elorah glanced at her mother. Novah was staring at the broken-eared berre, a deep sadness tugging down the corners of her mouth. Vaytah put her arm around Novah's shoulders and leaned in close to whisper into her ear. Novah nodded, her gaze still fixed, melancholy wrapped about her like a funeral mantle. Vaytah spoke again, and Novah snapped her attention onto Eldra Malla. The emvor reoriented her staff then leaned against it, preparing for the slow plod to her seat.

Novah forced a smile, stood, then hurried on stage to help the doddering Eldra back to her seat at the front of the Clan Fola's section.

Once the elder was settled, Novah retook the stage wearing her official face. "That concludes the Blessing of the Berres. Please rejoin us at sunset for the Grand Pageant of Inverna. Those of you chosen to participate, we request you come early for final instructions and costuming. At the conclusion of the Pageant, designated Clan representatives are asked to remain behind for a brief Council meeting. Thank you for coming, and enjoy your stay in the District Calliaigh." Novah bowed her head and waited for the crowd to begin dispersing before making her way off stage, throwing another look at her family's berre, sitting like a brown carbuncle at the rear of their Clan's assemblage.

Elorah's head dropped, and she sank further into her seat, her mother's disappointment a weight upon her chest that made it hard to breathe.

Aikin leaned toward her. "We should speak before the Clan Council," he murmured, oblivious to her distress.

"What?"

"So, we can get things settled beforehand."

"What are you talking about?"

Fyndd leaned past Aikin to give her a sympathetic look.

Aikin lowered his voice. "This isn't the place," he said, his eyes scanning the crowd. He stood and turned toward Fyndd who was already on his feet and giving him a nod. He turned back to face her. "Until later," he said with a bow before heading toward a cluster of Bairrtraigh elders congregating where the faldings—the Caeldish without a clan connection—had been seated. Elorah watched him go, her mood a mixture of relief and irritation.

Fyndd proffered his hand to help her to her feet. "He means well, you know," he said, his face apologetic. "But he has much on his mind just now."

Don't we all? Elorah thought, but she held her tongue.

"It's important," Fyndd continued, "you speak with him before the Council meeting. Please say you will."

She was about to retort that there was nothing under Solimar's glare that could entice her to do so until she saw the hope on Fyndd's face.

"I will," she relented, "for your sake."

Fyndd smiled. "I thank you, maiss." He started to walk away then turned back. "That was impressive," he said. Seeing her confusion, he added, "Your berre." He nodded toward the stage. "Isn't it the broken that are most in need of blessing? You've reminded us all of that."

She stared at him, looking for any sign he was jesting but saw only sincerity in his eyes.

"When it comes down to it, I suppose we're all broken in some way, only most of us aren't brave enough to reveal our scars. You've shown that it isn't our defects that matter. That we're all deserving of a place. There's not many who would dare make such a bold statement in such a public way. You do your clan great honor, maiss." He tapped his outstretched finger against his forehead before turning and walking away, giving Aikin a sideways glance as he strode past him and his group.

Aikin, hammering home some point to the seven men crowded around him, paused to watch Fyndd pass before resuming his speechifying.

Elorah shook her head. Some things would never change.

She checked the sun's position. Mierrle, who had spent the morning touring the marketplace with Thane, should be back by now. She set off for her family's garol, ignoring Aikin and his gaggle, intent only on finding her friend.

CHAPTER EIGHTEEN
FIRE IN THE BLOOD

Haedyn gave up after circling the marketplace and the garols and the Bonny Wood more times than he could count. Rachmyn, who'd retired for a nap, would soon be awake, and he had nothing to show for his morning. He'd been so certain he'd see her, his disappointment a pit in his stomach.

"Elorah, where are you?" he whispered, the name lingering on his tongue and setting fire to his blood.

He leaned against one of the fountain's pink boulders, watching the water surge high then patter down onto the bears' leaf-shaped umbrella. He'd seen his share of waterfalls, but never water spouting toward the sky. It fascinated him.

He wasn't the only one. The fountain was ringed by onlookers. One well-dressed man tossed a shiny coin, laughing when it plinked against the green slate between the shrubby bears.

Haedyn furrowed his brow. *Why would anyone throw hard-earned money away?* He resolved to return later and collect the discards.

Another man used his thumb to launch a coin, then handed a second to a boy of about eight standing beside him. The boy squinched his eyes and let fly, his coin striking one of the bears in the leg. Haedyn shook his head then used his stiffened fingers to push himself upright. City people had strange ways.

A commotion drew his attention. He turned to see six guards double-timing toward him. Nothing for it but to blend in. Running would only draw attention.

He casually turned and regarded the fountain, sending furtive glances over his shoulder. It appeared the guards were clearing a path for an official-looking processional. Haedyn realized with relief that he was not the subject of the guards' attention. Rather, they seemed to be the vanguard for a parade.

Most of the spectators drifted away from the fountain to join the crowd assembling near a flag-embellished tent. Haedyn moved with them, ducking his head when the guards took up positions along the wide opening at the front. Next came eight white-uniformed cavaliers riding silver-dappled horses, their brassy buttons and epaulet bars shining like tiny suns. The riders split by pairs, forming a line along each side of the aisleway then parking their horses to face their opposite.

Six officers riding three across on black-dappled horses appeared, their dark-blue uniforms sporting brass buttons, epaulet bars, and gold-corded aiglets that coiled around their right shoulders. They proceeded through the gauntlet of white-uniformed cavaliers before splitting and parking in the same fashion.

Then, a lone figure dressed in the same dark blue uniform, with a gryphon-shaped brass medal on his left breast trotted forward on a gleaming black horse. Haedyn watched the officer's sharp eyes scan the crowd as his horse approached the tent, stopped, then executed a collected pivot to face in the direction they'd come.

Four chair bearers came next riding shining white mounts and wearing white uniforms complete with white gloves. Jutting out from the pommels of their saddles were flat, brass bars, one side supporting a corner of a smokewood platform by dint of a suspending brass pole, the other side sporting a brass counterweight in the shape of a gryphon.

The platform bore a magnificent chair encrusted with gemstones apart from the seat, which was padded with plushy, blue velvet. The chair's armrests, shaped to resemble a gryphon's taloned front limbs, and its legs, carved into round-toed paws, were covered by a layer of Pyrolean crystals. The headrest—a carved gryphon head—bore feather-shaped arocols, a black hallett beak, and a deeply-blue azurite eye. Under the dazzle of the afternoon sun, the chair sparkled with eye-watering brilliance.

Who could sit in such a thing?

The chair bearers halted and, at a command from the hawk-eyed officer, performed an acrobatic dismount, each swinging their straightened outside leg across their mount's neck to line up with their inside leg before leaping to the ground.

As one, the bearers went to a corner of the chair where, upon a second command, they lifted and walked it onto a dais inside the tent and, upon a third command, set it down. A fourth command stepped them back to their horses where they remounted. A fifth command, and the chair bearers guided the empty platform next to the tent. They paused, waiting for a cluster of High Hells to roust spectators out of the way before backing the platform into the vacated space.

Only then did the crystal-clad carriage appear, the glare blinding as it rounded the corner at the end of the aisleway. It was pulled by a foursome of dappled Felderres, their coats gleaming like polished silver. Many in the crowd gasped. But not everyone was impressed. One man behind Haedyn bleated "grief's teeth, what a blinking waste" while another muttered "sodding Iellians" and a third croaked "mind yer eyes, boys, she'll blind ya if you let her." Haedyn chuckled to himself.

The metallic-looking horses trotted in unison, their feathered legs lifting high as they drew the carriage nearer. The coachman—liveried in a smart-looking deep-blue coat overlaid with swirling gold braid, dark blue breeches, and a black top hat—gripped four sets of reins in one blue-gloved hand while steadying the perpendicular stance of a golden ceremonial whip in the other.

The carriage drew up to the tent, and the crowd inhaled, a collective intake of anticipation and awe. The coachman set the brake, disembarked, then strode to the carriage door. A quick turn of the brass handle and the door was open, the coachman offering his gloved hand to the occupant. A slim hand sporting an arocol the size of a hen's egg grasped on before a figure in a glass-beaded gown of silvery-blue stepped a slippered foot out.

Everything about the queen of Iellia, from the glittering diadem in her sculpted blonde hair to the tips of her shiny silver shoes, radiated light. She turned her ice-blue eyes toward the gathered crowd, a joyless smile on her face.

"Who is that?" Haedyn whispered to the man standing next to him.

"Did you just crawl out of a cave? The Most Exalted Monarch, Queen Zephyrria Rennesseau," came the gruff reply.

"I thought so," Haedyn said, affecting a knowing look.

"Bit overdone, if you ask me," said another, "She better watch she don't step in a pile of horse donk with them fancy footclaps." Several snickered.

"I hear these Caeldish are none too happy she's here," said a third man dressed in Inirian wool and leather. "There's talk they're planning a bootsman's sendoff for her."

"What's a bootsman's sendoff?" Haedyn asked.

The man drew his straightened finger across his throat and issued a gurgle, nodding for emphasis.

Haedyn's eyes widened, and he turned back toward the queen, trying to see why she deserved such a fate.

A light-blue uniformed man with a silver-shot goatee and a bulbous black hat walked up and took the monarch's elbow, leading her to the radiant chair. She gave a small wave before settling onto the tufted seat. The goateed man clasped his hands behind his waist and took a deferential step back.

The queen surveyed the crowd, her expression blank, her demeanor detached. A hush settled.

"Is she just going to stare at us?" soughed a red-haired man, his freckle-tanned cheeks going pink, his plump hands tugging down the wide leather belt buckled around his homespun tunic to better accommodate his bulging waist.

Haedyn shrugged. "That's queens for you," he said, looking around. As far as he could tell, there was nothing remarkable about the crowd. Still, the queen continued her measured surveyance, her face betraying nothing.

"This is nonsense. I've got better places to be," blared a rough-faced man with sloping shoulders and an overbite, his meaty forearms clearing a path through the crowd.

The goateed man leaned forward to speak into the queen's ear. Her eyes rolled toward him, and her eyebrows lifted, though her head never moved as she blazed a sharpened stare across the heads of the crowd.

A buzz erupted at the back, the crowd parting for a dark-haired woman sweeping forward in a dusk-purple academic gown. She stopped at the front and gave a slight bow, pleasure flitting across the monarch's face at the gesture. The goateed man looked away, his face a studied blank. Haedyn frowned. He'd spent enough time with gamblers to know a bluff stare when he saw one.

"Who's that man standing behind the queen?" he murmured to the red-haired man.

"How should I spunking know?" The man spat a wad at his boot.

"Sebazgh Andyrria," supplied a voice behind him. Haedyn spun around to face a slim young man dressed in a fitted Iellian suit. The man continued to look toward the monarch, his words sliding from the corner of his tightly held lips as he added, "Chief Councilor to Her Most Exalted, and a real bastard. Take my advice and steer well clear."

Haedyn turned back toward the tent, his interest piqued. His gaze drifted to the hawk-eyed officer whose fierce attention was locked onto the woman in purple. The officer's forehead creased, and his jaw flexed as his formidable glare hardened.

The woman in purple paid no attention to the officer, her focus only on the monarch.

Haedyn stroked his chin. He'd spent enough time with sore losers to know a killing stare when he saw one. That look should raise the hackles, yet the green-eyed woman seemed oblivious. His gut told him something was amiss.

"Grief's teeth, she's gonna speak. Sodding Iellians," gritted the red-haired man.

The queen held up her bejeweled hand, and the crowd quieted.

"Citizens, countrymen, and friends," she began, her voice bell-like in its clarity. "It is my great pleasure to greet you on this most felicitous of days. For ten annums, through the vast goodwill of both of our peoples, we have forged a mutually beneficent partnership. A partnership that has withstood many challenges and changes, emerging stronger and better for it. On this day of celebration, I, along with my council, offer our highest congratulations to the Districts of Valenvia on their great achievement and extend our sincerest and best wishes for a successful festival."

A smattering of polite applause broke out, and she waited for it to dissipate before continuing.

"The citizens of Iellia remain steadfast in our commitment to do all within our power to ensure the vitality and prosperity of all marans within the United Valenvian Territory. Now more than ever, it is imperative that we lean upon our historical cooperation to carry us forward into an even more glorious future. Together we can accomplish great things. Together we *will* accomplish great things. I, as your sovereign, give you my pledge that I shall never waver in my fidelity to the principles of our common purpose. May the blessings of the Urslan remain upon us, one and all, now and forever."

The Iellians in the crowd responded with another round of applause while the Caeldish directed disgusted looks at one another and issued low-breathed jeers. Many stalked away, their faces grim. Haedyn watched them go—jutted jaws, dark scowls, balled-up fists—and wondered what the monarch had said to incite such a reaction. He turned toward the sharp-eyed officer, noting the man's gaze had softened now that it rested upon his queen. Haedyn realized there was something to that look too, some hidden current connecting the two.

It all happened in an instant. A rumble beneath the feet, an upheaving of ground, and the magnificent chair toppled forward, dumping the queen face-first onto the carpeted dais in an inelegant heap. The goateed man shot a hot look into the crowd as he hurried to help his monarch.

"That's where you belong, you blaspheming wycche!" shouted a brawny man wearing a green homespun tunic and a wide leather belt. The man's face was red, his eyes as dark as his night-gray beard.

"Ahhh, that was foolhardy, Eamen Dol," murmured the Iellian. Haedyn turned to look at him. "An emvor from the Clan Thrast.

Always been strong-tempered, as are most in that clan," he explained as he penciled a note on a scrap of vellum and tucked it away inside his suit jacket. "He'll pay for that, I'm afraid."

By the time Haedyn looked back, the hawk-eyed officer was off his steed, his saber drawn, his eyes two burning coals in a thundercloud of a face. With an outward push of his free hand, the officer directed a gale-force blast of air at the shouting emvor, knocking him to the ground and pinning him there until two guards got him into wrist irons.

"You're not wanted here!" Eamen Dol shouted as the guards jerked him to his feet by his handcuffed wrists and dragged him away.

The red-haired man elbowed Haedyn. "She had that coming," he said with a small, satisfied smile.

On the dais, a pair of blue-clad officers helped the queen to her feet while a second pair stood facing the crowd, their hands on the hilts of their sabers, a current of warning wind buffeting wherever they looked. Sebazgh Andyrria stood to the side, his arms rigid next to his body. He dropped his turgid gaze toward the purple-clad woman then looked up and away.

Haedyn was tracing Andyrria's sightline when he saw her. *Elorah.* All else faded from view.

She was standing behind an officer's horse, her eyes fixed on the milling crowd, her face dismayed. He felt a sudden stab near his heart. Why was she distressed? His hand flew to his knife, his fingers wrapping around its familiar grip, his feet already moving toward her.

She stepped back, then scurried away before disappearing from view. Haedyn quickened his pace, dodging spectators as he hurried forward, his mind conjuring up ploys to charm and impress her.

He caught sight of her as she ducked around the backside of an herbalist's tent, and he ran to catch up, rounding the corner at a furious clip.

"Ooof," he grunted, pulling up just short of knocking her down. Her eyes went wide, but she made no sound. Recognition lit her face. Haedyn laughed self-consciously, stuck his hands in his pockets and took a step back. "I bet you weren't expecting to see me again," he said, his cheeks burning.

"No," she said with a smile.

Ah, that smile, he thought, his blood pounding in his ears. She bent her head to the side, an amused expression on her face, and he realized he was staring at her. He took a deep breath and set his jaw, hoping he looked more together than he felt.

"Was there something else?" she asked in a voice that made his heart flutter anew.

"No... I mean, yes." He paused, screwing up his nerve. "I wanted to thank you again for..." He pointed toward his eye.

"No thanks needed," she said. "I'm delighted it's looking so well though." She leaned closer to get a better look, and he thought his knees might give way. His hands flew out of his pockets and into the air as he recovered his balance.

She reached out. "Are you okay?" she asked, sounding concerned.

He laughed again, his head and neck on fire. "Never better!" he blustered.

"Good," she said, her expression quizzical as he continued to stare. She looked past him toward the aisleway.

"That was exciting, wasn't it?" he said, following her gaze, his expression puckish.

"That kind of excitement I can do without," she said, her brow scrunching.

Haedyn shifted his feet and stuck out his hand. "Haedyn Khin."

"Elorah Niav." She clasped his hand, a faraway look in her eyes.

After a moment, she pulled back, and he reluctantly let loose. She turned to leave. "There is one more thing," he said, holding up a finger. Her indescribable eyes found his. He cleared his throat and looked away afraid he might drown in their limitless depths. "I couldn't help noticing you seemed bothered back there." He jerked his thumb over his shoulder. Her eyes dimmed, and she bit her lip. "It's none of my business, but from what I saw, I think you'd be wise to stay away from all of that."

"All of what?" she asked absently.

"Well, that woman in purple for one thing," he said. She refocused, her expression questioning. "She's a room setter."

"What does that mean, a room setter?"

"I take it you're not a gambler."

She shook her head.

"A room setter is someone who can set the mood of a room when they enter it. Sometimes, they bring the mood up, but more often, they bring it down. That woman can do both at once."

"Yes, I think that's true," Elorah said, her tone full of wonder.

"For a gambler, a room setter is both a gift and a curse. Trouble is, you never know which until the end of the night when you're either scraping a pile of coins into your purse or selling your boots to pay your tab. I always found it best to walk away when one showed up."

"I see," she said. "And what would you advise someone do if they can't walk away?"

"I'd say, they better find a good dummy."

"A dummy?"

"A dummy is a silent partner that runs interference with the house and the other bettors to shift attention away from the sharp. A good dummy is a sharp's best friend."

"And which are you? A dummy or a sharp?" A mischievous smile quirked up one side of her mouth.

"Depends on the night," he said.

She laughed, a tiny dimple indenting the bottom of one cheek. "I see."

"Rachmyn says I'm a better dummy. Not that he would know. He always loses at games of chance."

"Rachmyn... Is that who was with you yesterday?" He nodded. "How long have you two known each other?" There was a poignant quality to her voice that squeezed at his throat. He swallowed hard.

"Forever," he managed to croak.

She looked as if she wanted to say more, then thought better of it. Instead, she asked, "How does one go about finding a good dummy?"

"Sometimes you have to look, but sometimes..." He indicated toward himself, a grin on his face, "...the perfect dummy just shows up."

She laughed. "This must be my lucky day."

"No, it's mine," he said, suddenly serious.

"Are you offering to be my dummy?" she asked, one eyebrow a bemused arch.

"Whatever you need, that's what I'm offering to be."

This was the last thing Thane needed. Mierrle grinned up at him as he walked, his arm clamped around her shoulders to guide her.

"What's the matter?" she singsonged. "You look upset." Her gaze rambled across his face as he dragged her along.

"Not at all," he lied, wishing she would pick up her feet. "Only a little further."

She stumbled then giggled. "I feel so strange," she said, one hand going to her forehead.

"Let's get you to your garol," Thane puffed. His arm was killing him. What foul elixir had Alliari concocted? This hadn't been part of the plan—his new patroness getting blotted out of her mind. He cursed himself for a fool. Alliari had a vindictive streak and was known to spike a charm, but Thane hadn't thought the showman would be so cruel as to inflict his petulance on a helpless girl. Clearly, he'd underestimated the jealous nightjolly.

He counted the tents between the Calliaigh garol and himself. Five. Surely his arm could make it that far. Mierrle suddenly went limp, slipping out of his grasp and onto the ground. He fell to his knees, panic seizing his chest.

Alliari, what have you done?

Thane leaned nearer Mierrle's face and was grateful to hear her breathing. She let out a heavy sigh, and her eyes rolled back, her slack body stiffening into a spasmodic fit of jerking and writhing. "Mierrle? Can you hear me?" he cried, wrapping his arms around her shuddering form and pulling her to him. She stared up blankly, her face frozen into a soundless scream. Desperation gripped him as he held on, his thoughts a chaos of fear and guilt.

Moments later, the shaking ceased, and her eyes closed, her body relaxing.

Thane eased her to the ground and felt her forehead. Clammy. He looked around, deciding whether to go for help, or stay and hope someone heard his shouts.

"Over here!" he yelled. "Please, someone!" The words came out in a strangled shriek.

Mierrle's eyes fluttered open, her brow puckering. "Where am I?" she wheezed.

"I've got you," Thane said, the stricture in his chest easing. "You're going to be fine," he added, hoping it was true.

Without thinking, his free hand curled into the Quelpian luck sign, the thumb resting on the nail of the fourth finger, the remaining three held straight. He wasn't superstitious, but he needed every scrap of good luck he could muster.

Mierrle wasn't watching his hand; she was staring at the sky. "I'm so tired," she said, her dozy eyes closing.

"Can you move?" Thane asked, rubbing her hands to drive heat into them.

She startled awake and rolled her eyes toward him as she nodded slowly. Her heavy lids closed again.

"Mierrle! Stay with me!"

Her eyes flew open then blinked several times.

"Can you move?"

"I think so," she said, squinting at her arm as she raised it. She wiggled her fingers, looking pleased. "See?"

Thane maneuvered his arm around her and braced her shoulders. Mierrle leaned in, giving him a grateful smile. With a heave, he raised them both to their feet and started the long, lumping walk to the garol.

Elorah had noticed him first, though he hadn't known it at the time. His attention had been on Eamen Dol's display along with everyone else in the crowd. But not hers. She had been riveted by Kearyn Malenvie, an icy dread paralyzing her like a mouse in a circling hawk's sights. Then she'd seen him, his blazing eyes cutting keen, his demeanor calm and assured in the ensuing clamor and felt her own courage refire. How had he done that, without so much as a word? What secret power did he hold? She felt the pulse of Sylvi's stone as she mulled the internal fire his gaze ignited, convinced they shared a destiny. The thought made her unexplainably giddy. While he'd tried to impress her with his boyish charm and winsome smile, she'd been struck by the feeling she'd seen it all before—the sideways head tilt, the lowering of the eyes to look up through the golden lashes, the nervous flare of the nostrils, even the self-deprecating chuckle accompanied by the small backward step—all were as familiar to her as the back of her hand.

Had she always known him? Her heart told her it was so. His pale-haired companion, too, felt as familiar as any friend. But how could that be when they'd only just met? What made her think they'd all been together many times?

When he'd offered his hand, though she knew she shouldn't, she'd concentrated her Spyrrt vorik on their shared touch, feeling a sharp zing as they'd connected. Then she was back in time watching a scene from his past.

He was clad in leather armor, astride a blood-red horse—its neck and flanks lathered white—galloping up a hillside under the burnished glow of a setting sun. Though she knew it was him, he looked different, older, his hair darker and his eyes deeper set beneath the pot-shaped helmet he wore like a crown. She could feel his determination and his willfulness. His confidence that he knew best as he dug his heels into his horse's sides, spurring the stallion to go faster and faster while tree limbs clutched and tore at them. There was something ahead, something both terrifying and exhilarating. Another dig into his horse's sides. Faster. Faster. He never saw the burrow hole hidden behind a tussock of grass, its opening just wide enough to catch the stallion's hoof. First came the startled scream as his mount's head dove toward the ground. Then came the muffled crack of the horse's front leg fracturing as its body tumbled over, throwing the man to the ground before cartwheeling end over end and crushing him. The pale-haired man, riding some ways back, looked different too, his skin tone darker, his wavy hair the color of evening clouds. He screamed an oath and spurred his chestnut mount. Ashen faced, he leapt from the saddle before the horse was stopped and ran to his stricken friend, cradling the man's bleeding head in his arms. She could feel the pain of the man's injuries, but more than that, the crushing regret that he'd failed at something important, something for which he'd prepared his entire life. As his friend sobbed, the man felt nothing but devastating disappointment at the waste of it all. So much promise destroyed in the space of a breath. *I've suffered a fool's death*, his final thought as his spirit floated up and away into the beckoning sky.

Shaken, she'd almost blurted out what she'd seen, only stopping herself after remembering her mother's admonition that such things were not to be spoken.

By the time he'd offered to help her find Mierrle, she'd recovered enough to accept, which is how he came to be escorting her through the marketplace.

Before they'd set out, he'd taken his bird from his vest and tethered it to his leather armguard. The bird now rode his shoulder, its glassy eyes taking in every movement, its wings akimbo as its body bobbed and swayed.

The High Hells were out in force, patrolling with extra vigilance. Many of the Shadowen were packing up their caravans. They always knew when the wind blew chill.

Where could Mierrle be?

She looked in yet another vendor's stall.

"Maybe she's gone back to your garol," Haedyn suggested, his wary gaze on the patrolling guards.

"Perhaps," she allowed, changing course. She glanced at the sky, noting the low set of the sun. The Grand Pageant would be starting soon. Her heart sank. She had to go, though it was the last thing she wanted to do. What she wanted was to find her friend and hear more about her escort and his companion. But that would have to wait until the Pageant was over. It was then she remembered her promise to speak with Aikin and her heart sank lower. She was already dreading whatever patronizing lecture he had in store. She set her jaw, the memories of his previous moralizing unwelcome guests in her mind. To distract herself, she focused on the feel of the grass beneath her feet, sensing each blade's soothing energy through the thin leather soles of her shoes. It was like walking on a tingling green-velvet cloud. Before she knew it, they were back with the garols.

Haedyn was lost in his own thoughts, a slight frown on his face, and she wondered what he was thinking.

"Here it is," she said.

Haedyn looked up at the embroidered flag posted to the center pole. "Good flag," he said with genuine admiration.

Elorah glanced up. She'd never thought about it before, but it *was* a good flag with its message of Therran cooperation and friendship. She felt a tiny surge of pride for her clan as she pushed through the canvas door. Her eyes took a moment to adjust to the dark interior.

Mierrle slouched in one of the padded chairs, her arms dangling at her sides. The relief Elorah felt instantly changed to concern. Thane was perched on a nearby chair, his scarred face taut with worry. It was then she noticed her friend's vacant smile. Her stomach twisted.

Haedyn stepped through the opening. "I should get going before Rachmyn..." He tilted his head and peered at Mierrle. "Are you alright?" he asked, taking another step inside, Fryk hunkered low on his shoulder.

"Yes," Mierrle singsonged. Haedyn's eyes cut toward Elorah, his eyebrows raising.

Elorah looked at Thane for an answer to her friend's condition.

Thane's lips tightened. "Mierrle and I had quite the adventure this morning," he began. He swallowed hard. "She wanted to experience a dreamcraft and–"

"It was wonderful," Mierrle interrupted. Her attention landed on Fryk. "Oooooh, can I hold your bird?" she trilled. Before Haedyn could respond, she catapulted from her seat and fell forward in one arcing move, her reaching hand a lever pulling her down. Haedyn leaped and grabbed her mid-fall, startling Fryk. The bird let out a loud *chirrt-chirrt-chirrt* and launched at Mierrle's face, the jesses snapping tight before it could complete its strike. Instead, the raptor ricocheted onto Haedyn's forearm, its razor-sharp talons puncturing the leather armguard. A thin trickle of blood ran out and dripped onto the floor.

Haedyn groaned as he guided Mierrle into her chair then plucked the embedded bird out of his forearm. "Fryk, why are you such a monster sometimes?" he growled, his free hand retrieving the toe end of a green sock from his pocket before popping it over the bird's head. He set the hooded bird on his shoulder then swiped his bleeding arm on his leggings.

Elorah went to Mierrle and put a hand to her forehead, feeling only the barest glimmer of subtle energy, as if her friend's soul force had been drained. She ran to the apothecary chest and searched up the blue-glass vial of starseed. A decoction of the nervine along with a circulatum with the balancing shilk was her only hope for restoring Mierrle's foundering vor. She fumbled out the tea brazier, the oil can, and a wick, setting them on top of the apothecary chest. She filled the brazier's oil reservoir and inserted the wick. But where was the striker? She searched the basket again, but it was nowhere to be found. She bit her lip and let out a worried sigh.

"Can I help?" Haedyn asked.

"I've no way to strike a fire," she whispered, her gaze indicating the wick.

His face broadened into a smile as he held up his index finger. A whiff of smoke and a tiny flame burst forth from the finger's tip. Elorah's eyes widened. He held the finger flame against the wick's end until it glowed bright orange then pursed his lips and blew, extinguishing the flame with another smile. She forgot herself for a moment as she stared into his golden eyes.

How had he done that?

Thane cleared his throat and bounced up from his chair. "Is there something I can do?"

Color pinked Elorah's cheeks as she forced her attention away from Haedyn. She held out the teapot. "I need this filled with water. There's a spring at the edge of the Bonny Wood."

"I know the spot," Thane said, taking the teapot and exiting.

Elorah looked at Haedyn's injured arm. "Do you need me to tend to that?"

He shook his head. "Fryk gets feisty when he's startled. I should have known better." He used a finger to stroke the raptor's chest. "Don't judge him too harshly. He's a good character most of the time. Aren't you?" he murmured. He looked up at Elorah through his lashes, and her heart raced.

What is happening to me?

She turned back to her friend. "Don't worry," she said, dismayed at the tremble in her voice. She took Mierrle's hands into her own. "We'll soon have you back to your old self." She tried to sound reassuring, to not show her worry that her friend's condition might not be reversible. Subtle energy was difficult to affect, and she wondered what could have happened that would have left her friend in such a depleted state.

Mierrle raised her head and beamed a smile. "You're the best friend I've ever had."

Elorah felt a stab of guilt. A good friend would never have allowed this to happen.

"You'll soon be right," Haedyn assured Mierrle with a smile that brightened when he turned to Elorah. Her pulse quickened, and her head went hot. She pinched her wrist to distract herself, wishing she could control her body's unpredictable whims.

The door-flap slapped open, and Thane barged in, the teapot dangling from his outstretched hand like a lantern. "Here," he panted, shoving it toward Elorah.

She rushed it to the brazier and plonked it down, her tapping toe betraying her impatience.

Haedyn moved to her side then placed his hands on the device and closed his eyes. Within moments, steam chuffed from the teapot's spout. "There," he said, his breath tickling her neck.

Is there anything this maran can't do with fire?

Her hand shook as she spooned starseed into the boiling water then drizzled honey from a glass jar into a demitasse cup.

Why am I shaking for pity's sake? What is wrong with me?

She tried to ignore the unnerving sensations Haedyn's nearness was provoking as she waited for the starseed to brew. It took real effort for her to strain the teapot's dark brown contents through a square of cheesecloth into the cup without spilling it.

"Can I help?" Thane asked, coming up to stand beside her. She handed him the cup. "Have her drink this. The honey should help, but it will still be bitter." Thane signaled his understanding.

Haedyn retreated to a chair, his bird a small black lump on his shoulder.

Elorah went and unhooked her satchel from a bedpost then rummaged out her tenderwood shilk, a slender rod the length of her forearm with a belled knob at one end. The shilk would help her balance Mierrle's energy once the starseed innervated her subtle force.

She turned in time to see Thane tip the last of the cup's contents into Mierrle's mouth.

"That's done it," he crowed as Mierrle gagged.

"That tasted terrible," she accused, her eyes squinting tight, a grimace emphasizing her disgust.

Thane shrugged. "Sorry," he said, his contrite tone unconvincing.

Mierrle shook her head and wrinkled her nose.

Elorah focused on the shilk, imbuing it with healing vorik until she could feel a slight pulse.

Starting at Mierrle's midsection, she circled the belled end above her friend's torso, the vorik in the shilk gathering the subtle force the starseed was creating the way a magnet gathers iron filings. Once the shilk was loaded, Elorah drew the bell end up to the crown of Mierrle's head and began the tedious work of evenly dissipating the soul energy, sweeping the shilk back and forth in a tight pattern while drawing it downward in increments.

She reloaded the shilk several times then repeated the careful dissipation until a balanced cocoon of subtle energy surrounded her friend.

As Elorah worked, Mierrle's eyes closed, her expression serene. Thane and Haedyn watched in quiet wonder.

At last, Elorah drew back, exhausted. Never had she invested so much of her own vor into a healing, and she felt woozy from the effort.

She tucked the shilk back into her bag then laid a hand on Mierrle's forehead to reassure herself that her friend's subtle force had been restored. Yes, she could feel it now. Relief washed through her, along with a wave of gratitude. After a moment she turned toward Thane. "What happened?" she asked, steadying her voice.

"I don't know," he said, his gaze raking the matted floor, his bottom lip sucking behind his front teeth. "I trusted the wrong person, I guess." His shoulders sagged then lifted in apologetic resignation. "I meant no harm, maiss, I swear."

Elorah frowned. A shaft of low-angle sunlight fell through the garol's door opening, interrupting her thoughts. The Pageant would be starting soon. She leveled a frank look at Thane. After a moment of careful consideration, she said, "I believe you."

His features relaxed, and he let out a rasping sigh. "Is she going to be alright?"

"I have every hope, but only time will tell." She glanced at Mierrle.

"She will," Haedyn stated as if it were fact. "No doubt about it." Elorah shot him a querulous look. "She will," he proclaimed, "because she had you."

THE TELLER, THE HEARER, AND THE TRUTH

The teller spins the story, the hearer weaves the tale, but neither knows the truth.

Old Mother's Tales— (Traditional)

Warnings of a Wraithwolf
(Excerpt Four)

A TRUTH that must be RECKONED... ggrrr... by every CREATED SOUL... gggrrr... AS ABOVE... ggrrr... SO BELOW... Gggrrrfff... FORCES for ILL... gggrrrff... and for GOOD ... ggrrff... ALWAYS seek to UNITE... gggrrff... with THOSE of corresponding INTENT... gggrrffff... for a ROPE... gggrrffff... is made STRONG... ggrrff... when it is FORMED... gggrrrf... of many STRANDS.

HEAR THIS!

These FORCES... gggrrr... are REFLECTIVE of a larger TRUTH... ggrrrfff... for they derive POWER... gggrrr... from INDIVIDUAL INTENTION... Ggrrff.... WITHOUT the INDIVIDUAL... ggrrr... and their CHOICES... ggrrrffff... there can be no POWER of FORCE.

KNOW THIS!

Ye are SURROUNDED... gggrrrff... by these INFLUENCES ALWAYS... ggrrf... and must DECIDE your INTENTION... ggrrfff... AGAIN and AGAIN... Gggrrfff... The FUTURE DEPENDS WHOLLY... gggrrfff... upon these DECISIONS... gggrrr...JUST as the PRESENT... gggrrr... was BUILT from SAME... Gggrrfff... This is the BLESSING... gggrrfff... and the CURSE... ggrrrff... of MANIFEST CHOICE.

–Collected and Interpreted for the Most Exalted Monarch,
   Geldizian Rennesseau, by a scribe

CHAPTER NINETEEN
RAMPAGE

A long night lay ahead, of this the Wycche was certain.

It had been many an annum since she had been forced to scavenge and scour like a neophyte for the power that was rightfully hers. So long ago, she could scarce remember the circumstances. Yet here she was, depleted and desperate and on the prowl for naifs and nodders and ne'er do-wells. It made her blood boil.

Venge was similarly desperate. He too had used up most of his vor in the confrontation with the white wolf, and now the burden fell to him and his Malvisse cohorts to find as many softheads as possible before the night came to an end.

The wraithwolf had already gathered a pack brimming with experience including sharp-fanged Flaye and keen-eyed Mouk, his two loyal lieutenants. Others too, Syba and Kruszk, Gnar and Tenze—all skilled at stealing essence from the unsuspecting. Together the miscreant pack would sniff out the weakest of the wraithwolves in this vast twilight and separate them from their night-ward's dreamdoor using the deceitful Arcana of Vorie Supin. The easiest would be the ones whose night-wards' waking choices corded their dreamworld guardians. Nearly as easy were those whose night-wards had taken wolfken to facilitate Shadowen dreamcrafting, especially if the crafter was of low ability. The Malvisse always knew when these tin-horn charlatans were in the realm. So too, they knew which ones relied upon spiked charms, leaving their dreamers exposed to Malvisse deviancy without even realizing the dangers at hand. Easy pickings.

For their troubles, the packmates would receive a portion of the harvested etheriant once the Wycche had completed the extractions. Over the course of a hunt, if several dreamers were found, those portions added up to a sufficiency worth having. As for Venge and the Wycche, they would keep the larger portion for themselves, using the siphoned power of the many to feed their dark ambitions. There was one dreamer whose very existence threatened every tenet the pair held dear, and once this tedium of essence gathering was done, their search would resume for that elusive confounder and her white wraithwolf. But this night, while the orusphere hummed with soulsongs, and the Malvisse slavered for etheriant, the Wycche and her wraithwolf would put that aside.

The Wycche leaned low and murmured into Venge's ear.

Find that which we desire.

With that, the charcoal-colored wraithwolf and his ghastly pack were off, bounding across the purple-gray veld, their fanged mouths flashing nova-bright, their heated eyes gleaming like fearsome stars. In mere moments, they had their first victim in sight. The Wycche followed behind at the speed of thought, her shadow-gray raiment a tempest of cruel storm-cloud and merciless wind trailing behind her in a furious huff.

Soon they were at a dreamer's door, a piteous construction of silty brown and slaggy gray. To call it a door would be overly generous, so poorly did it stand. In front of the slumping portal lay the dreamer's guardian, a thin wraithwolf pale as timid smoke and missing the tip of one ear, its body trussed by silvery cords. This dreamer, through the grievous choice of committing to those forces actively opposing the Elect, had doomed their wraithwolf to the perpetual misery of impotent bystanding in the face of relentless Malvisse draining.

Forlorn, the pale wolf wept as Venge swaggered forward and slashed at the pitiful door with a front paw, once, twice, until a gap crumbled open. The Wycche slid through the gash with practiced ease, transforming herself as she went into a wind that blew through the sphere's colorless dream and back out again without trace, picking up etheriant as easily as a gale gathers dust. In a blink the transfer was done —the dreamer none the wiser, the wraithwolf infinitely sadder, the Wycche's vor that little bit stronger. She retook her accustomed form and was away, following Venge and the Malvisse as they tracked toward the threshold of the next hapless dreamer, the mudheap of a door reforming into a sludgy lump behind them.

So it went, doorway after doorway, on and on, the Wycche staring into the gloaming for yet another door and urging the Malvisse onward, her raiment a twirling rage of nimbus.

And then it appeared, a pristine portal ripe with possibilities.

Venge loped toward the whited door, shimmering like an oasis in the graylight, Mouk and Flaye at his heels. Further back, Tenze and Gnar kept pace at the center, while Kruszk and Syba formed up the rearguard. The pack moved as one, gliding across the starry plain in a fluid constellation of purpose. The Wycche urged them on, sensing there was much to be gained behind this last door.

Soon they were upon it. As the Wycche suspected, its guardian lay in front of the door's threshold curled into a tight circle, fast asleep. The Wycche sniffed toward the slumbering wolf. The sweet scent of wolfken lay heavy upon it. She sniffed again and caught the acrid bite of yellow wort. She wrinkled her nose and snorted to rid herself of the smell, delight crackling inside. Yellow wort enhanced wolfken's sway. She looked for the crafter, knowing yellow wort was a Shadowen trick of long standing but saw no one. The crackle surged into excitement. Till now, the night had been a disappointment, with little to show for her efforts, but it seemed her luck was turning.

Venge sniffed at the insensate wolf, a cruel snarl exposing his primordial teeth. Flaye poked a paw into the soft puddle of its underbelly but even this failed to rouse it. Mouk fastened his sallow stare on the Wycche. She pointed a delicate finger, and Venge hurled himself against the door, stumbling as it gave way without hindrance. This crafter was of low skill indeed to leave such a door unlocked and unguarded. Venge recovered his feet as the Wycche took a cautious step forward. The plump, rich smell of etheriant wafted to her from inside the sphere, and her hunger for it became like a living thing.

It was then she saw the fleeting glint of spectacles and the shadow of a pointed hat. A ghoulish smile settled as she recognized the Shadowen showman lounging inside this dreamer's sphere. She knew him as both a fop and a fool with no small ego and a fraud to boot, a flash huckster whose dreamcraft skills were questionable at best. She need only assume a guise that would distract both him and his gullible dreamer and all that lovely etheriant would be hers.

She opened her mind to the thoughts within the sphere, sifting and sorting until she hit upon her scheme. It would be a dual presentation, which would require some of the soul-energy she had so painstakingly gathered, but this did not deter her for this sphere promised an exceedingly rich reward. She transformed into a brawny youth of noble stature, with copper-bright hair, a well-chiseled jaw, and a familiar oaken name. It was thus that she stepped through the door, upon the invitation of the dreamer and indeed, the crafter, who fell into an open-mouthed swoon. The dreamer, too, stared in awestruck silence as she swanked about like a gilded prince and murmured sweet nothings.

It was far easier than it should have been, and it was all the Wycche could do not to laugh out loud at the dumbfounded pair when she diffused into a colorless wind before their saucer eyes, sweeping around the sphere and gathering all that luscious etheriant into herself while the two gawped like stunned sheep.

It was a heady amount, easily ten times as much as her previous gatherings that night, so that by the time she flew out the door, she felt something akin to her old self again, the whited door closing behind her with a shuddering bang. Even then, the dreamer's wraithwolf failed to wake. She could hear the muffled drone of the crafter's voice as she skyed away, fat with stolen power.

The Wycche hied herself far from the last dreamer's door before reassembling into her preferred form. The pack gathered about her, eager for their shares. She pushed the tip of her pointed finger into the forehead of each, transferring an allotment of etheriant, saving the greater portion for Venge, whose black eyes lit with greedy pleasure.

Sated, the Malvisse each gave a bow before sallying off into the gloom, Venge giving each a nod as they trotted away.

The Wycche whipped her tempestuous raiment about herself, satisfied that she and her wraithwolf had made a good start. There would be many more nights such as this needed before they would wield the power they'd possessed prior to the white wolf, but tonight's accomplishment helped blunt that hollowing thought.

As she prepared to enter the waking realm, she sent a final thought to her wraithwolf.

Well done, my steadfast liege.

CHAPTER TWENTY
THE HUNGER OF WANT

A fat moon hung low in the char-black sky, the shadowy leaves of gumwood trees tickling at its sagging edge. Xyleea stared up at it, her mind filled with pleading for her people.

In the time since her galeesha had returned to the keleekeluk, the sky over her wasakagee had hardened, becoming the shell of a great blue egg that kept away the clouds with rain.

She ran a toe along the edge of a crack, one of the many spiderwebbing the roasted ground. Sere grass rasped in the breeze, gone so dry the goats, before they'd left, had begun stripping bark and digging roots to survive. Her larder box was empty, as were most in the wasakagee, all sitting like silent accusations in the back corners of the people's wasakas.

Many times, after the sky sealed shut, the hunting parties had screwed up their nerve and slipped into the keleekeluk, their faces hopeful as they slung their game bags over their shoulders, stuck their blowpipes into their belts, ran their fingers along the taut strings of their bows and sharpened edges of their arrowheads, only to straggle home later, empty-handed and empty-hearted.

Xyleea shifted her gaze to the posts that had once tethered the tuskees, the moon's spilling silver accenting their loneliness. Their carer had released the tuskees some time ago when the hay had dwindled to nothing, amidst the sniffling bawls of the children and the silent tears of the elders. There was no living memory of the wasakagee without tuskees, and though they still haunted the surrounding forest like old friends, they were as good as gone.

The last of the goats had released themselves, a wily few escaping the relentless slaughter of a people with nothing else to eat, fleeing into the crisped tangle of the keleekeluk with their tails high, their bleating a trailing lament. Xyleea wanted to follow them to a happier place, though where that might be she couldn't say.

When bellies grumble, so do people her galeesha had told her after hearing the complaints of a woman who, after losing her mate to a snakebite, hadn't eaten for uncounted days. Cree Shee had given the woman two handfuls of goru root and a huul dree—a heart blessing— afterward telling Xyleea the huul dree would help the woman far more than the goru root. Right now, with her own belly pinched tight and her mind flying apart, Xyleea would have welcomed either.

Xyree Muul had been the first to speak up, coming to Xyleea's wasaka, a look of doubt on his gaunt brown face, his gaze scratching the dirt floor as he'd asked her to speak to the ancestors. *The food,* he'd said, his basso voice the low rumble of distant thunder. *Perhaps the ancestors know where it hides.* He'd held out his pink palms in mute obeisance, his liquid brown eyes locking onto hers, fear drawing his face tight. She felt her insides seize as she realized the enormous responsibility that lay upon her. She gripped his hands and squeezed, more for her own sake than his, her heart crying out to the ancestors to grant them both a huul dree.

Others had come too, their faces imploring, each one certain she could stave off the disaster befalling them. Afterward, she'd gone to her knees, her mind begging Cree Shee to tell her what to do. But like the rains, the blue-egg sky had dried up her prayers.

Water was also scarce, and it was that, more than the food, that worried Xyleea. Though she did not have the wisdom of a deeta, she understood her wasakagee would not survive long once the water was gone. But just as finding food was becoming more difficult, so too, was finding water. The scouts were forced to venture further and further, always coming back with too few filled jugs and too many fearful words.

She gave a final look at the moon before pushing away from the rock she'd been leaning against and walking back to the emptiness of her wasaka, a decision forming in her mind. The time for fear was past. Tonight, she would sleep so that tomorrow she could keep her promise to the people.

First light found Xyleea on her way, the chuulzu kereet pulled low onto her head to keep it from falling off. Why she'd decided to wear it she couldn't say, except she'd gotten the notion that the wisdom of its previous wearers might still linger in its feathers and horns and pelt.

She held the kemeekemee close as she followed the goat's path into the keleekeluk, her hand reaching inside to curl around the daala. She startled at the hoot of a maandaba, the large black-and-green bird the Ushoku called the watchman of the forest, and her racing heart jumped into her throat. She braced herself for the inevitable riot, the canopy exploding with maandaba hoots. She cupped her hand to her mouth and hooted, a chesty sound that rattled her ribs. The canopy exploded again, maandabas hooting loud and long in reply to her mimicry. She smiled and waited for the hoots to die out before cupping her hand to her mouth and issuing a spongy roar from her tightened throat. The sound of the chassa, the fearsome hunting cat that prowled the keleekeluk. Maandabas from every tree took flight amidst a cacophony of hooting. She grinned as the frenetic black cloud wheeled away, before setting forth again on the goat path.

The thought of the chassa sent her hand to the blowpipe stuck into her woven reed belt then to the darts poking from a quiver attached to her chest strap. Below dangled a small bone bowl—carved from a goat pelvis—with a thin slit in the top. The bowl held weela, the poison dust derived from the ground-up remains of a certain caterpillar. Further down was a thumb-sized turtle shell, a blop of ballast clay stuck to its ridged interior. She hoped she wouldn't need the blowpipe, but there were many dangers in the keleekeluk, including Xetili war parties. Having her pipe at least gave her a chance.

She'd poured the last of her stored water into a goat bladder and strung it to her belt, the gentle *thwap-thwap-thwap* as it hit her thigh providing a rhythmic comfort as she walked.

Her thoughts kept clanging back to a single question. *Would her plan even work?*

A snuffling sound cut her thoughts short. She peered past a thicket of thorns to the shadow beyond. She blinked and held her hand out toward the tuskee staring back at her, its tranquil river-green eyes the only light in the brake's darkened depths.

Xyleea issued a series of soft grumbles, imitating the sound a young tuskee makes when calling its family group. "Come, my sweet," she murmured, her hand reaching toward the tuskee's long face, balanced on each side by a short white tusk. The tuskee snorted through its swaying brown trunk, blowing a layer of dried leaves upward in a rustling cloud. The tuskee swayed for a moment before taking a step toward her. Heekaba branches with spikes the length of little fingers tore at its furred brown sides and cream-striped legs as it blundered from the thicket to stand before Xyleea.

She recognized the notch in the tuskee's far ear and knew this was Kaambree, the matriarch of her wasakagee's tuskee herd.

Xyleea walked up and patted the bottom of the tuskee's thick brown neck. Kaambree lowered into a kneeling position and turned to look at Xyleea, an unmistakable invitation to climb aboard its broad back before shifting its weight and throwing its near leg forward into a right-angled step.

Xyleea stared into the tuskee's gentle eyes, asking permission from the old mother. Kaambree blinked and flapped its large, drum-top ears. Xyleea patted the tuskee's wooly jaw, grasped the suedey leather of its earflap, and stepped onto its bent leg. She threw a leg over the tuskee's neck and levered herself into an upright position, waiting until the tuskee regained its feet before scooting forward to sit behind the jutting occiput overlaid by a topknot of flowing, brown hair. She snugged her knees into the folds of Kaambree's thick neck and smiled at the familiar scent of tuskee musk. It was a good smell, full of memories of when she was young.

"It's good to see you, old mother," she said, scratching the high spot between Kaambree's ears.

The tuskee serpentined its trunk, touching the backside of the upper curve against its forehead before swinging its head and letting out a deep rumble that shook its entire body.

Xyleea answered with her own rumble then squeezed her legs tight until she felt the old matriarch lumber forward. She pressed a knee against Kaambree's neck, and the tuskee turned onto the goat path. Xyleea squeezed both legs, and Kaambree rambled forward, its trunk swaying as it went.

Soon, they came to a dry creek bed dulled gray with hardened sludge. The tuskee plodded on, its tree-stump feet sidestepping the sharper stones. Xyleea leaned forward, her fingers entangling in Kaambree's topknot to steady herself as it picked its way across.

On the other side was a small clearing, the grass trampled flat in pathways spoking away from a rock circle in the center. As they got closer, Xyleea could see the ashy remains of a long-dead fire inside the stone ring, along with fragments of what had once been a clay pot. She tugged on the tuskee's ears to bring it to a halt before dismounting.

Xetili, she concluded after examining the blue fingerprints on the potshards. She lifted her head and nervously looked around. Her fingers stroked the reedy ends of her darts, ready. The clearing was quiet save the brushy sighs of the waving grass. She wondered how the rocks had gotten here, for they were large, and she knew the Xetili had no tuskees to do their heavy lifting. The stone ring was a mystery.

Xyleea followed the spoked pathways with her eyes, unsure which one she should follow. Something told her to head across the clearing toward the mountains in the distance. Cree Shee had often told her all water flowed from there. Once she'd found a steady supply of water, and enough food, she would have to convince her people to move the wasakagee. It was the only way she could see for them to survive. But first, she had to find enough water.

She remounted then squeezed her legs against Kaambree's neck. The tuskee plodded forward.

By the time the sun sank below the dark-edged horizon, they had traveled far, finding themselves in a shadowed grove of kava trees. Xyleea tugged the tuskee's ears, deciding the grove would be as good a place as any to spend the night.

A light tap on the neck and the tuskee kneeled, allowing Xyleea to dismount. Another tap and the tuskee got to its feet. Xyleea patted Kaambree's jaw, and the tuskee shook its head before trundling to the nearest tree where, using its long trunk, it began stripping off leaves and sweeping them into its triangular mouth.

Xyleea unsealed the bladder and took a pull, the tepid water a balm to her aching throat. She scanned the squat trees looking for one isolated enough to discourage prowling chassa. The tuskee would be her best deterrent. It was a rare chassa that would take on a fully grown tuskee. She only hoped she wouldn't have to contend with any of the tree-loving snakes that made the keleekeluk their home. Her mind shooed them all back to the grogakee.

She resealed the bladder, fastened it to her belt then thanked the ancestors as she clambered up a kava tree, settling into a high crotch that afforded a good view of her surroundings. She knew Kaambree would spend most of the night pulling down leaves, tuskees having the remarkable ability to forgo sleep for days at a time. Xyleea also knew kava was a favorite which was one reason she'd chosen this place. She considered tethering Kaambree, then decided she would rely on the ancestors and the kava to keep the tuskee close. It occurred to her that the ancestors had heard her prayers after all, sending her a huul dree in the form of a gentle brown mother.

Finding the matriarch had been a gift she hadn't expected, and she knew she'd been able to cover twice as much ground with the tuskee. The thought made her glad, a feeling of hope sparking within. Perhaps tomorrow she would find a new place for her wasakagee. She closed her eyes, trying to picture how such a move could be accomplished, drifting off to sleep imagining nutbrown men and their nutbrown wives packing up and carrying their lives toward a brighter future, their nutbrown children with their bouncy, golden curls waving juulko branches and singing happy songs as they went.

Terse voices forced Xyleea awake. For a moment, she thought she was back in her wasaka until she opened her eyes and remembered. She rubbed her bleary eyes with her fingers, focusing on the kava leaves fluttering like moth's wings around her before looking beyond at the surrounding landscape. The light was thin, only just beginning to push back the black shadows of night, and she had to squint to see the black-brown men clustered under one of the kava trees, murmuring to each other and pointing.

Where is Kaambree?

The question struck like a dart, her startled intake of breath loud in her ears as she looked in the direction the men were pointing. One was taller than the rest and the shorter men surrounded him like wolf pups around a sire. Xyleea counted six, all with fierce-looking scar-tattoos on their faces and arms and chests. Their black hair was pulled up into woven mounds that hugged the tops of their heads. Each carried a blowpipe, a short spear, and a hatchet. The only thing missing was the blue beeka mud, meaning they were Xetili hunters, not warriors.

One of the shorter men gibbered to the taller man, his voice rising by increments as the tall man looked over him and blinked, his scarified face somber. Xyleea craned her neck, looking for Kaambree. The tuskee was nowhere to be seen. Xyleea's stomach dropped.

She turned her eyes back to the men. The light was improving, accentuating their hollowed-out cheeks. They all had the same desperate stare of her own wasakagee's hunters, the same hungered look of want etched deeply into their drawn faces. Underneath their loose woven-fiber shirts and skirts, she could see they were all corners and angles as if their bones were bundled together juulko poles holding up a sagging hide. She was glad Kaambree was gone. The tuskee would have surely been killed by these slack-skinned hunters. The thought brought a lump to her throat she couldn't swallow away.

She pulled six darts from her quiver, dipped the sharp end of each into the weela bowl then stuck their blunt ends into the ballast clay, leaving them there while she pulled out her blowpipe and held it against her body. It would only take a moment for her to load the pipe if the men moved toward her.

A high voice floated to her ears. It was the tall man, speaking in slow, measured syllables, his tongue clicking against his teeth. The shorter man scowled but fell into line as the men retook the path, the tall man leading the way. Xyleea watched them until they disappeared into the undergrowth, their voices fading to nothing.

She slipped the blowpipe back into her belt, her muscles relaxing.

The wind was picking up, exciting the kava leaves into a dance. A chill ran down her back, and she wished she had a bajee pelt as she rubbed her upper arms and considered what to do. She had two choices. Follow in the footsteps of ravenous men with starving eyes or retreat to her wasakagee in failure. What would her galeesha think of her foolishness, heading into the keleekeluk with no preparation and no plan? She could see now she'd been rash. A true deeta would have waited for the ancestors to show the way. Inside her heart, where yesterday there had been so much hope and conviction, there was only doubt and creeping fear.

She felt for the sphere inside the kemeekemee, remembering the feelings the orb had inspired when her galeesha had shown it to her. Even now, her heart beat a little faster. Then it struck her. Not only did she have a responsibility to her people; she had a responsibility to the daala. If something should happen to her out here in the forest, she would have failed both.

She leaned her head back, resting it against scaly bark, and looked up at the brightening sky, her mind ticking between going forward and going back. She closed her eyes and breathed deep the dried-crisp scent of the grove while the kava tree hummed its secret song, a faint ripple against Xyleea's skin. She deepened her concentration until she could hear the many forest songs surrounding her, could feel the hope with which the keleekeluk greeted the rising morning.

A tickle ran along her leg, and her eyes flew open, one hand already pulling the blowpipe toward her lips. The fingers of her free hand were fumbling for a readied dart when she saw the tuskee trunk lift away and wrap around a cluster of leaves.

Kaambree.

She nearly shouted, clapping her hand against her mouth, a small squeak still escaping. Where had the tuskee come from? How had it slipped past the hunters? A wordless thought invaded her mind. She could see the Xetili hunters from the dense tumble of a brushy copse, her nose recoiling from their bloody stink as they traipsed past. Their crunching footfalls pained her ears while their killing thoughts stabbed cold darts into the soles of her feet. Xyleea's body tensed, holding itself without breath until the men passed, a formless blot in a thicket of shadows.

As quickly as it had flown into her mind, the thought fled, leaving her changed. All this time, she had been as hardened and unreachable as the sky above, when the answers were all around her if she would open her mind to them. She felt hope rise. She only needed to ask the right questions, and listen to the wisdom that surrounded her, for the answers were there, in the whispering leaves and the wandering beasts and the wasting sky.

She climbed down from the tree and patted Kaambree on the neck. The matriarch gave her a sage look then kneeled and stuck out a leg.

Xyleea hoisted herself aboard, her mind visualizing water until she could hear it, smell it, feel it, taste it. She put the force of her heart into the question as she asked the old mother to guide her toward her vision, her mind opened wide for the answer.

The tuskee rumbled and began to walk, setting the path forward.

CHAPTER TWENTY-ONE
IN PIECES

Brynz tugged at the strap securing her chest protector over her dark blue undertunic. The light blue leather was stamped with the Iellian crest, a Thunderbolt Gryphon beneath the words *Brecceu Aro Neus*—Without Air Nothing. The stiff strap chafed a newly erupted red patch on her side, and it was all she could do not to unbuckle it and throw it aside.

The trip had been long, five days spent in the company of the Imperial Guard and the Special Forces. Zell had been hooded to keep him calm while he bumped along in a rolling wagon built to accommodate two horses. A jacket of strong netting pinioned his silver wings, its edges hooked together with brass snap-locks while his banded front legs were chained to a set of thick iron rings screwed into the wagon's floor. A gryphon's first instinct was to slash forward with its talons if it felt endangered. The chains prevented inadvertent injury to Zell or his keepers. As a further precaution, a set of hobbles tethered each hindleg to a leather surcingle encircling the gryphon's keel. The tortuous-looking device forced Zell into a seated position, stabilizing his bulk during the juddering trip down the mountainside.

Brynz hated Zell's bindings as much as she hated this trip, but she kept her voice calm as she reassured the gryphon that all was well. It had taken a week to convince Garrod to let her travel with her charge. She'd won him over by reminding him her voice would settle Zell as well as any sedative, with none of the side effects.

She went over her plan as she watched Zell sway. She would walk him as soon as they arrived to work out the kinks caused by the restraints, as she'd done the previous four nights.

Weeks of nighttime sessions had instilled a set of behaviors aimed at preventing the monarch from sitting astride the silver-blue gryphon, now fully fledged in his adult plumage and pelt. A curtsy, a raising of one foot, a tilt of the head, a nod, all were tied to evasive behaviors the gryphon had learned, picking up the cues so quickly Brynz would have to take care not to move without intention. An absentminded scratching of the nose could lead to catastrophe if she wasn't mindful. Her red patches wouldn't make that easy.

The caravan halted in a newly-mown field behind what looked like a celebration in full swing. Brynz pressed her face against the bars and looked toward the collection of tents and caravans. The air smelled of smoke and food and animals, the Iellian flag flying high above it all.

As she understood it, there would first be a parade to seat the monarch. Her and Zell's part would come later, at an evening event called the Grand Pageant. It was still morning, giving her most of the day to feed, water, exercise, and groom her charge, already gouging at the wooden floor with his restless talons. She would need every bit of that time.

Stable hands unhooked the four horses harnessed to the rig and led them away. Meanwhile, a crew of workmen erected a canvas-walled enclosure around the horse wagon before pounding two enormous stakes into the ground at the center of the circular pen. No one was to see her charge until the monarch's speech, and the canvas walls would ensure the gryphon stayed out of sight. Brynz reached up and unbuckled the leather hood from the gryphon's head.

Zell clacked his beak and issued a grumbling noise in response to the loud screech of ungreased metal fighting metal. The back wall cracked open along the top, and two burly men eased it down until it rested against the ground, forming a ramp.

Both men clomped up the slope toward the gryphon. Zell flung a front leg forward, then screeched when the brass band bit into his shiny black scuta.

"No!" Brynz cried.

The larger man shot a sideways glance at his partner who shrugged. "Suit yourself," the partner said as the two made their exit.

"Settle," she soothed. "You're all right."

Once the gryphon quieted, Brynz unbuckled and pulled away the hobbles. Zell got to his feet then sank into a stretch of first his front and then his hind legs. His wings lifted a fraction before meeting the resistance of the netting, and the gryphon swished his tufted tail, the pupils in his bright blue eyes constricting.

"Not yet," Brynz admonished, pushing against the closest wing until it reposed. She slid the blinkered halter over Zell's blunted beak, the sharp point ground away the previous moon at the same time his pin feathers were lopped and his talons squared. Garrod had performed the maiming after Brynz confessed she couldn't bring herself to do it. He'd nodded, his face stoic. It was already done the following morning when Brynz arrived at the enclosure.

Garrod appeared outside the cage.

"How did he travel?" he asked, his gaze piercing.

"As well as could be expected," she replied, casting a look around the cramped wagon.

"Certainly not ideal," he allowed, his eyes tracing the cage before returning to her. "I've no doubt you've done him a world of good. I imagine things would've gone much worse without your attentive care."

The note of gratitude in his voice caught Brynz up short. "I made a promise," she said, stroking the gryphon's feathered neck.

"Yes, well..." He turned toward the Iellian flag, visible above the canvas sides of the enclosure. "We're both in service to promises made."

Brynz wondered what promises Garrod had made that now weighed upon him.

"I'll leave you to it. If you need assistance, find Tolleck. He's a dab hand with the stock. He'll see you right."

She nodded, unable to prevent her upper lip from lifting into a faint sneer. Kodston Tolleck was the last maran she would ever ask for help. Garrod strode away.

She turned back to her work, adjusting the halter's interwoven cap to sit atop Zell's poll before buckling it tight, making sure the chain stringing through the brass rings at the back wasn't twisted. She threaded a smaller chain through two rings at the bottom of the halter encircling the sensitive skin around the gryphon's beak, then, after pulling on her gloves, attached two leather-wrapped lead chains, one to the throat chain and a second to the beak chain. The final steps were unchaining the gryphon's front legs and adjusting the halter's blinders.

She gave a soft cluck and tugged on the two lead chains. The gryphon followed her down the ramp and out into the enclosure, his blue eyes blinking in the bright morning glare, his long tail undulating, the tufted tip thwipping against his netted wings.

"Steady," she crooned, holding the lead chains in one hand while reaching beneath and unfastening the snap-locks. She pulled the netting away and tossed it through the open door into the cage. Zell stretched his wings high, unfolding them as they rose, until they towered like silver sails. The canvas walls weren't high enough to obscure the wings, and Brynz signaled Zell to bring them down. The gryphon complied, giving himself a final shake to settle his feathers.

"Walk on," she commanded, pulling the lead chains and stepping out. The gryphon followed, his sinewy muscles rippling beneath his silvery pelt, his talons denting the ankle-high grass.

She planned to walk the gryphon long enough to loosen his muscles and take off the edge before his first meal. The feedings had been carefully planned, the largest scheduled for evening. She would add a supplemental feeding at mid-afternoon before the heavier evening meal so that by the time of the event, the gryphon would be as docile as possible. Three sheep carcasses butchered into quarters had made the journey in a separate wagon along with a box full of dead mountain hares and a bag of sausagebits.

She left the surcingle in place, knowing she would need to remove it before the actual saddling. An involuntary shudder went through her. If her plan didn't work, it was likely Zell would be injured, and if her plan did work, it was likely she would lose her position. Either way, life as she'd known it was about to change. By this time tomorrow, it would be done, for good or for ill, and as much as she tried not to think about it, that knowledge hung over her like a dismal cloud as she walked her charge around his pen.

Thane looked at Mierrle, trying to determine if she had any idea what they were watching. Her eyes were wide, her lips curved into a smile.

Of course she's delighted. She's easy to please.

By contrast, Thane felt every moment spent here was a loss to him personally. He was itching to jimmy himself into Alliari's speck deal and the tick-tick-tick of his internal clock screamed that his chance was passing him by. The nightjolly was no doubt already on his way to The Running Fox, and Thane could think of nothing other than rushing off to the ramshackle alehouse. Yet here he sat watching men and women dressed as stars and bears cavort their way through a story that was as boring now as when it was first written, while his seatmate sat enthralled, staring at the proceedings as if she were newly hatched. At least she seemed in good vigor after her earlier setback. Thane would have a pointed word with Alliari about that near-tragedy.

He and Mierrle were in the falding section at the back, along with every other unaffiliated laborer who worked a shovel for a Caeldish clan. Both were dressed in scratchy homespun tunics cinched at the middle by wide leather belts, rummaged from a trunk in Elorah's garol. The tunics were huge, and Thane reckoned he looked like a toothpick rolled up in a carpet. Mierrle's didn't do her any favors either, ballooning above and below her belt. The plan was for Mierrle to return to Elorah's garol when the pageant concluded, at which time Thane would take his leave. He'd have a hard ride to make it to The Running Fox before the pale-haired man and his speck arrived, but he'd already made a deal with a horse sharp and had a mount lined up that could cover the distance with enough speed to get him there in time.

The golden-haired man with the bastard bird stood behind them. Thane stole a glance over his shoulder. The man's tunic fit far better than his or Mierrle's, which irritated Thane no end. Why did they have to wear the wretched things anyway? But Elorah had insisted, and so here they all were, looking like lumpy turnips. Thane didn't know the man's name, but he did like the look of him—the strong jaw, high forehead, and striking gold eyes. He'd always had a soft spot for hero types, which had gotten him into far more trouble than they were ever worth. Still, it didn't hurt to look. The golden-eyed man shifted his gaze downward, his eyes questioning. Caught, Thane held up a hand and shrugged as he turned around and gazed toward the stage where a copper-haired man dressed as an amber sun offered a hand to Elorah who was dressed as a horned bear—an Urslan, Thane presumed. The sun man escorted Elorah in a circle around a youth portraying a blue star.

A hum began, the vibration so low it was barely detectable, almost as if the ground was singing. Thane swept his gaze around the rapt audience. Many had krychle cages pinned to their tunics, and the creatures' thrumming added a monotonous counter-drone to the vibration beneath his feet. No one else seemed bothered, which only made him more determined to get away from this place. It was regrettable, having to leave Mierrle behind, but that had always been a slim hope, while the speck was a sure thing. He knew he could turn that for a profit. He'd been hoping to work both angles, but that plan hadn't fallen together. Like any grifter, he knew a sure thing beat a slim hope, and that had made his decision.

The Running Fox was a place Thane knew well. It had been a favorite of his Rabboutier crew whenever they'd had goods with murky provenance in need of a broker. The proprietors, Hebediah Jimpkins and his wife Wrynne, were both as salty as sailor's rations and about as appealing. Both had run with Rabboutier crews in their youth and had connections with shopkeeps and brokermen from here to Elequia. Wrynne was a sharp-tongued scold whose prickly manners and permanent scowl rendered her disagreeable to all but her clowder of seven-toed cats. Hebediah, on the other hand, was an avuncular liar with the red nose of a chronic inebriate and the slippery morals of a bribed judge. Thane quite liked him. Both were savvy enough to know dealmaking was what kept the alepots flowing in their disreputable establishment, and so they turned a blind eye and a deaf ear to all but the most egregious of conduct. Thane appreciated that kind of deliberate obtuseness in an establishment.

The speck was an interesting prospect. He'd have to find buyers, but that shouldn't be a problem. His time with the Rabboutiers had introduced him to Shadowen bands all over the basin and up into the Lawless Mountains. His own predilection for dreamcrafts hadn't done him any harm, at least in terms of meeting those most helpful to his cause. Amongst that secretive society, hand-cast speck would sell itself, and he could make a tidy profit so long as the Zenzae stayed out of it. It was risky business, but he'd done it before.

Convincing the pale-haired man to prefer him over Alliari was a different proposition. Of course, he'd spied when the pale-haired man made his offer. Alliari should have expected him to do at least that. The nightjolly's assertion that he had a single buyer did not carry the ring of truth, which Thane would be sure to mention if he got the chance. There had always been rumors of a large speck buyer from the north, but when pressed, no one knew who the buyer was. The Shadowen of his acquaintance spent little time in the north, preferring either the anonymity of the Lawless range's caves or the ease and pleasure of Valenvia's fertile basin. He reckoned Alliari was angling to take all the speck in one go and then part it out to his connections. Thane had that exact scheme in mind as well but with the added benefit of a wider network of contacts. And he planned to offer better collateral. Brakken cloth to be precise, two large squares which he carried at the bottom of his rucksack. Brakken was both a vorik enhancer and vorik shield. There was no more valuable cloth in all the world, and he'd lost much in getting the little he had. He hoped to use some of his profit from the speck to purchase more, but in the meantime, he was willing to part with what he had to grease the wheels of a deal that could make him as wealthy as any Rennesseau in Iellia.

Light applause broke out as the sun man and Elorah stepped toward a black backdrop spattered with painted stars. Thane looked to where the Iellian queen and her retinue were seated and wondered what they were thinking. Surely this low fare wasn't of any interest to them either. A scribe sat near the queen, scribbling in a bounded book. Thane had a great respect for Iellians, mainly because they held most of the wealth in the world. Dressed in shining white and wearing a treasury's worth of jewels, the queen's face retained its serene composure as she watched.

He envied her. He could only dream of wearing such finery. He envied her imperturbable demeanor as well. He could gain much by studying only that. Even the bizarre assembly of bear effigies stared in awe at the sparkling monarch in her glittering chair. *How could anyone take such a strange religion seriously?* He shifted in his seat, the scratchy homespun irritating his backside.

When the monarch had swept in with her retinue, they'd received a hostile reception from the crowd. A bellicose few had been rousted by the Imperial Guard. Others had turned their backs in a show of mute repudiation. Even now, Thane could feel a seething undercurrent of hatred from the farmers and herdsman comprising most of the audience. It made the queen's composure even more fascinating. In his estimation, remaining unsullied by hot emotion was a quality to be emulated.

On stage, the sun man was presiding over an array of barleycorn-dressed youths, men dressed as four-horned cattle, women dressed as milchgelfts, and children dressed as flowers, all swirling about in an intricate dance. Elorah filtered through the whirling participants, touching each on the crown of the head as she passed. The audience began to hum, their voices joining with the hum beneath Thane's feet. The krychles changed pitch, providing an overtone and creating a diaphony Thane could feel inside. Beside him, Mierrle hummed along, swept up by the music.

He stole another glance behind. The golden-haired man and his bird were gone.

The humming was having an effect. The rancor had faded, the crowd seeming to focus on the droning sound. There was something soothing about the tonality of voices both blending and resonating that smoothed the edges of his ragged impatience. Despite himself, Thane was intrigued by this manipulation of the voice to evoke emotion. It was a trick he'd like to use if he ever got away from this pageant, which was looking less likely with every passing moment.

Rachmyn scraped his knuckles against his eyes, clearing away the lingering stupor. How long had he been asleep? He looked around to get his bearings. The sun had surrendered to the shadows of night. A whole day gone and he'd missed it. Where had he been?

He'd intended to go into Oru Fen and walk the path between here and The Running Fox, but he couldn't manage to unravel from his body's chrysalis. He remembered Spectra standing in the distance, watching him claw at the denseness clinging like glue. She did not come to him, nor did she howl his soulsong or send her vorik to greet him. And yet, her love was protecting him against... what exactly? His mindwords asked the question, but no answers came, his beloved guardian only shaking her head before turning away. Next, a cottony fog filled his head and though he'd fought it, he'd fallen into a dreamless sleep.

Now, all this time later, he'd resurfaced. His hand slipped into his pocket for his shard. Yes, there it was. He stroked his thumb across the familiar smoothness to steady his nerves.

Elgre sat near the garol's opening, staring out at the gathering gloom.

"Are you finally awake?" came a familiar voice.

Rachmyn stood and stretched as Haedyn walked in, a grin on his face.

"As you can see," Rachmyn replied. "Where have you been?"

"Seeing the sights," Haedyn said with a cheeky smile. "But that's a story for another time. How long do we have?"

"What?"

"Before we leave."

Rachmyn glanced at the waning light. "We should get going—"

"—I wanted to say goodbye to someone first—"

"—while the guards are distracted—"

"—it won't take long—"

"—and the high road is fairly quiet." Rachmyn tensed his chin. "I don't think we should wait. We'll be walking most of the night as it is."

Haedyn's face fell.

"I hope you got some sleep," Rachmyn said as he pawed through his rucksack to check its contents.

"Sleeping was the last thing on my mind."

Rachmyn stood, his packing forgotten.

Haedyn swallowed hard and shook his head. He reached into his pack, pulled out an apfel, and lobbed it toward Rachmyn who caught it mid-air. Next out was a piffle bun. Haedyn tossed it onto his friend's rucksack. "I knew you'd be hungry," he said with a morose shrug.

Rachmyn's heart lurched. He fist-bumped twice to show his gratitude. Haedyn returned the gesture. Rachmyn smiled bleakly before turning his attention to the bun, his expression going serious. "Some cheese would have been nice," he deadpanned.

Haedyn launched a second piffle bun at Rachmyn's head who grinned as he flinched sideways, the bun sailing past and landing on the floor. Elgre trotted over and sniffed it before snorting and walking away.

Rachmyn stuck the first bun into his pack then bit into the apfel. He clapped Haedyn on the back. "Time to make our fortune," he garbled, mouth still chewing, his tone trying for a levity he didn't feel.

The wolf trotted out of the garol. Haedyn checked his bird then shouldered his pack and exited.

Rachmyn stowed away the second piffle bun before following him out.

He really believes all this, Elorah thought as Aikin led her center stage for the final time. His shining skin, enhanced by amberstone and the setting sun, glowed like molten bronze. But there was more to it than that. He'd somehow transmuted his anger at the Iellian monarch into an inflamed arrogance that burned as hotly as any sun. Even now, as he stepped forward to accept the hammering applause of the audience, he looked as if he were afire, his proud face radiating a heat born of righteous indignation.

He swept his hand toward Elorah, and she bowed, feeling a fraud as she had throughout the entire pageant, despite the crowd's applause. She had none of Aikin's fervor, none of his pride of culture. She scanned the crowd as she straightened, then the Calliaigh section's berres. Her broken talisman was not there.

She looked out at the throng of assembled Caeldish, their eyes burning bright, their faces flushed with belief, their zealous chests puffed out, their calloused hands clapping. Her pendant lay warm against her chest, pulsing in rhythm with the crowd's enthused response. The missing berre slipped from her mind.

The nearest guards got to their feet and hustled forward to take up positions in front of the dais. The monarch rose, looking regal in her sparkling white. Four blue-uniformed men surrounded her as she moved to take the stage.

Elorah turned toward her mother. Novah's shocked disbelief smoothed into sober resolve as she stood—jaw set, back ramrod straight —and strode toward the stairs. A guard stopped her progress midstride with a gust of wind from his hand then proceeded to blow her backward step by step until she was pinned against her chair.

Alarmed, Elorah started to run forward until a strong hand hooked onto her shoulder and dragged her back. She whirled around, her protesting cry dying on her lips as she found herself staring into the scowling face of a High Hell.

"Stop right there," he warned. An unnatural coldness emanated from Elorah's pendant. It wasn't a sensation upon her skin but rather, a freezing feeling deep inside.

The crowd's applause petered out, replaced by the low rumble of bitter muttering. A few shook their fists while the rest cowed obediently as the guards along the front pushed forward a wall of air that forced the stunned crowd against their seats.

Elorah looked for Aikin, but he was gone.

A guard shoved her, and she stumbled toward the other participants already clustered near the midnight-sky backdrop. Next, a group of High Hells herded the stunned pageanteers down the stairs before forming a corralling perimeter around them.

The monarch made her way center stage then turned toward the audience, her shining face like carved ice.

"Citizens and countrymen," she began, her voice ringing above the guards' whistling wind dam. "Tonight marks the start of a great and glorious future for the United Valenvian nation. Generations will look back and herald this day when two peoples of noble tradition conjoined into one, a union fostering the best in both, a grand advancement for the good of all. In these uncertain times when enemies gather at every border, rest assured this newly formed nation will secure the safety of all peoples within our glorious basin--"

KEEEEEAAAAAARRRRRRRR

The monarch's words were cut short by an ear-splitting shriek. She pivoted toward the noise and motioned. An awed hush fell over the crowd as a majestic silver-and-blue Cyrulian gryphon was led on stage by two handlers.

The one closest to the monarch was a man attired in a dark blue uniform, a gryphon-shaped medal pinned to his jacket. On the far side stood a young woman outfitted in dark blue overlaid with light blue leathers.

The gryphon's blinkered head jerked sideways then up as it took stock of its surroundings, its handlers watching its every move. Half-hidden by its folded wings sat a gilded saddle, held in place by a golden breast strap and a polished black girth. Elorah had never seen such a ferociously beautiful creature in all her life. Its piercing azurite eyes fixed upon her in a predatory stare, and she clutched the pendant as if it could somehow protect her.

The gryphon lowered its head and pawed at the floor with a front foot, spits of dirt flinging onto its hind paws. Elorah looked to the gryphon's handlers. Both were quite tall. The man had a strong countenance and muscular build despite being in his middle years. Young and lithe, the woman's face drew tight beneath the dark windings of her wavy hair, her blue-gray eyes focused on her charge.

The gryphon stood behind the monarch, the two looking like an illustration from a history book. As if to prove the point, the monarch raised her arms, affecting a pose of heroic grace beneath the darkening sky.

"It is only through strength above and below that our newly united nation will find true peace." She motioned toward the uniformed man. He stepped away from the gryphon to lend his hand. At the same moment, the young woman executed a formal curtsy.

It all happened in an instant. The gryphon's hindquarters dropped into a sitting position as the monarch attempted to hoist herself aboard the golden saddle, throwing her in a backward splay. The uniformed man, endeavoring to catch the queen, yanked the chain around the gryphon's neck, tightening it to a near-strangle. With a loud shriek, the gryphon reared, its forelimbs springing up then slashing forward with frightening speed, its wings unfolding in a mighty stroke. The monarch landed against the uniformed man's shoulder, who struggled to keep them both upright as the gryphon's wings sailed over their heads, its beaked head flinging side to side to dislodge the biting chain.

"Brynz! Don't let go!" the man shouted, the lead ripping from his hand.

Blue-clad guards surrounded the monarch who was somehow still on her feet. The uniformed man sprang forward, grabbing for the lead whipping past.

"I can't hold him!" the tall girl shouted. "Zell! Settle!"

"Leave me," the queen commanded, her face as darkly cold as a midwinter night. The guards stepped back, and the monarch drew herself up. With an arcing sweep of both hands, she sent a volley of wind toward the thrashing gryphon.

The wind only emboldened the gryphon's attempt at flight, its battering wings stripping the lead out of the young woman's hands as it reared up and slashed its taloned feet.

KEEEEEEAAAAAAARRRRRRR

The queen stepped back, hot anger cracking through her glacial demeanor. Guards bustled her to the far side of the stage.

The young woman sprang into action. Pulling up to her full height and spreading her arms wide, she somehow gathered the monarch's wind volley into a swirling tumult she threw toward the crowd.

The unnatural windstorm sucked up the berres, banging them against each other until they chinked apart like unstrawed brick. The ball of wind whirled on, riding over the guards' air dam, before blasting out into the open space beyond the amphitheater, leaving a rubble heap where the berres had been moments before.

Elorah gasped, along with every other Caeldish, a rising, choking outcry from a people staring into an unfathomable abyss. Elorah ached inside for her mother as Novah stared at the disaster, her face whittled out by shock. Never before had such a thing happened, every berre destroyed in the blink of an eye. Any favor they'd gained with the Urslan was gone; any bestowed blessing withdrawn. The crops would have no intercessor to ensure success. It would be the ruination of them all.

The pendant pulsed, reminding her of its presence as a vision of Therrania sprang into Elorah's mind. *Restore the five to revive the one!* Was that the answer? She felt it was so. Hadn't her dream told her exactly that? That she needed to restore the seat of Therran power? Another screech from the gryphon interrupted her thoughts.

The lead flipped by the uniformed man again, but this time he snatched it into his grasp then sat back on his haunches, dragging it down with all his might to bring the gryphon's forequarters to ground. Blood stained the feathers where the throat chain was, red drops falling onto the stage floor.

"Garrod, you've cut him!" The tall girl hurled herself toward the uniformed man only to be pushed back by a gust of wind from his hand. Elorah could see the desperation on the young woman's face as she tried to get to the gryphon, but the man's wind kept her at bay as he pulled the gryphon's head round with the other. The gryphon pinwheeled away from its bent head, its hindquarters cantering sideways.

Elorah focused her Spyrrt vorik on the young woman, but she could only feel her panic and fear without any context. The pendant pulsed hard against her breast, and she felt herself running toward the stage, breaking past the guards and warding off their controlling airstreams with countering gusts of wind. *How did I do that?*

She cleared the stairs in a stride, heading straight for the gryphon.

"Stay back," the uniformed man warned as he ran to keep up with the gryphon's spinning body, cranking its blinkered head still further to tighten its circling. The gryphon screeched in pain as it crashed onto its side, its legs flailing. He was dodging the gryphon's lashing front feet when the tall girl launched onto his back and smashed her fist against his neck.

"Let. Him. Go!" she screamed, landing three heavy blows before the uniformed man shucked his shoulders backward, dislodging her. She fell to the ground then scrambled into a crouch.

"Get back!" he bellowed.

The girl sent him a furious glare as she darted past and unbuckled the girth and breast strap. She was reaching for the headpiece when the gryphon's thrashing feet found purchase in the packed dirt floor. She leaped aside as it clawed its way upright and with a mighty head thrust, ripped the lead chain out of the uniformed man's hands. The golden saddle wrenched sideways and off as the gryphon danced away, the lead chains flipping around like weapons. The uniformed man ran forward, his hands grasping for the beak chain and missing. The throat chain slammed against the back of his head, knocking him to the ground.

"Seize her!" the monarch cried.

Two guards drew their sabers and ran toward the girl, before pulling up short when the gryphon let out a blood-curdling screech and cocked its giant silver wings in a menacing posture. Its head dove toward the guards, its black beak clacking, the lead chains scissoring beneath its neck. The guards scuttled backward, their blades awkward appendages.

"Seize her I say!" the monarch screamed.

The guards righted their sabers and advanced. The girl ran behind the gryphon as the uniformed man got to his feet and made another grab for the chains. The sudden movement sent the gryphon onto its hindlegs, the leads flying out of the man's reach once again.

The guards split in a flanking move, their sabers thrusting toward the gryphon as they edged toward the girl.

The guards' control of the crowd was also faltering, many of the stunned audience members breaking through the wind barrier and rushing to their rubbled berres, wailing as they went, their krychles keening on their chests. Most stood over the heaps of thille and flowers and herbals shaking their heads and crying. A few were on their hands and knees, picking through the shards for their family's effigy.

Elorah took in the scene, her mind searching for a way to mend the chaos. She looked toward her mother watching the collapse of her festival with the horrified stare of someone seeing their own death. She looked toward the despairing crowd as they wailed over their ruined berres. She looked toward the gryphon as it prowled the stage, its fraught wings akimbo, one front leg pawing dirt, its bleeding, blinkered head parrying forward while the tall girl huddled against its keel. *Start here*, she thought.

Elorah brought together her hands, concentrating her healing vorik into them before holding her palms out toward the wounded beast, her only thought to relieve its suffering and restore it to wholeness. A moment later, its wings dropped, and its head lowered. Through her hands, she could feel the gryphon's pain points. Around its beak and poll were the worst of it, and she directed her vorik there first. Next, she sent vorik to the vague pains in each of its wings as well as the tip of its beak and its talons. The pendant pulsed like a second heartbeat as she worked. Something within her was also changing. Aligning. Where she should have felt depleted, she felt invigorated. Empowered by a force outside of herself.

Viexha.

This time, when the realization came, she observed it as another experience, the same as seeing her mother and the crowd and the gryphon. It carried no more or less weight than any of the rest. Without thinking, she'd somehow tapped into the abundant vor flowing through every particle that existed.

She turned her attention to the berres, her mind visualizing the broken pieces joining together into an unbreakable unity. The despondent onlookers hovering over the shard heap moved back, the sorrow on their faces changing to astonishment as mismatched pieces drew together and fused into kaleidoscopic patterns that defied reasoning. Separateness unifying into a whole. As more and more joined together, Elorah felt the power of Viexha coursing through her. An image popped into her mind of a towering Urslan, its body formed from the melding pieces and gatherings. Even as she thought it, the unifying berre-shards formed up into a shape.

Guards drew their sabers then hacked at the rising bear-shaped mound but it was as if they were wielding dull spoons. The honed blades left no mark as the Urslan assembled, drawing up material from the broken berres as it went.

"It's the Urslan," whispered first one then another in the crowd.

Elorah paid no attention as she used her mind to shape the effigy.

Relieved of its pain and fear, the gryphon allowed the man to get hold of the throat chain, but as soon as he pulled, the gryphon shied, and the halter slid away, freeing its head. The girl smiled triumphantly as she snatched it from where it fell and unhooked the two lead chains.

Sensing its newfound freedom, the gryphon flapped its powerful wings lifting first its forequarters then its hindquarters into the air. Both handlers' mouths dropped open as the gryphon took flight, rising higher until it was soaring above the throng.

The monarch, her eyes darting between the rising Urslan and the escaping gryphon, cried, "Stop them!" as she pushed past her guards. The uniformed man drew his blade and reared back as if to launch it skyward but let his arm drop when the gryphon veered north, disappearing into the gathered darkness.

The monarch heaved her own desperate wind volley into the sky, but it was no use. The gryphon was gone.

"Seize her!" the monarch screamed, her composure devolving into abject fury, but the girl was already running, her long stride putting distance between herself and the stage as she sprinted toward the Bonny Wood, the halter clutched in one hand, two guards giving chase. She spun around and hurled the headpiece with furious strength, striking one in the face. He stumbled to a stop, blood gushing from his mouth. She crashed into the wood, the other guard close behind.

The Urslan effigy, having subsumed the berres, now towered at the front of the stage, a hodgepodge of materials transformed into a unified whole. Around it stood a crowd of wide-eyed spectators whispering, "is it real?" to one another. A few poked tentative fingers against it for confirmation. Elorah's mother and grandmama, still in their seats, whispered to each other as they stared at the creation.

With a terrific noise, a huge crack opened behind the Iellian queen and her guards, the dirt floor splitting wide as if to swallow the group whole. The monarch teetered back, forcing a guard to break protocol and seize her by the waist to keep her from falling into the crevice opening like a set of jaws.

The guards ushered the monarch away, guiding her past the splits opening beneath their feet. The queen paused at the edge of the stage. Her eyes narrowed, and her chin lifted as she blared at the stupefied crowd. "Make no mistake. It is already done. That which was a territory is now a sovereign nation. For good and for all. Those who endeavor to sway us from our course will meet with swift and strong consequence. They shall not prosper or prevail." She gave the crowd a final, heated stare before allowing herself to be escorted away, her retinue following behind with her fanciful chair. When they were gone the ominous shaking ceased.

Only then did Elorah see Aikin at the back at the Amphitheater, his bronzed face constricted, his brow furrowed, his eyes two slits. Beside him stood ten additional emvors of the Bairrtraigh clan, each with the same concentrated stare. Fyndd sidled up to Aikin and whispered into his ear. Aikin's gaze cut sideways towards his friend. He gave a slight nod then stalked away, heading toward the garols, Fyndd at his side. Elorah watched them go, a sudden thought clanging. *Where is Mierrle?* She strained to see her friend but neither she nor Thane were anywhere to be seen. Worry pricked her stomach as both her mother and her grandmama came onstage. Vaytah walked straight to her while Novah turned to address the audience.

"The Council will convene in the communal area near the Calliaigh garol!" Novah shouted, her arms raised to gain attention. "All clan emvors and council members are asked to attend!"

"Go," her grandmama urged in a low voice, her hands grasping Elorah's shoulders. "If you leave now, you won't be missed until you're well away." Elorah looked into her grandmama's reassuring eyes. "Take your father's crystalwood staff," Vaytah continued. "It's hidden beneath my bedsack."

"How did you–"

Vaytah cut her off. "The Urslan have spoken. Through you." Her gaze flicked toward the towering effigy. "This..." she nodded toward the crowd, "...will all be here when you get back." She looked toward the Bonny Wood and gave Elorah's shoulders a push.

Elorah swallowed hard and nodded. Vaytah went to stand by Novah, while Elorah made her way off stage, her mind whirling, her heart leaping, her feet running toward a new horizon.

CHAPTER TWENTY-TWO
UNCERTAIN PLACES

The decision to go to The Running Fox had been arrived at quickly. Thane had planned on going alone, but after speaking with Elorah, he'd realized keeping Mierrle as a patron might still be on the cards. He'd volunteered to arrange their mounts and escort them to the alehouse, well situated on the Wydderhalle, the wide river that flowed from the Blackshales to the Dallovian Plains.

Procuring three horses had taken work, but Thane and his pack of trinkets had managed it, a finger-sack of gilded pearls convincing the horsesharp to part with half of his string.

They'd made good time, the cloak of night getting them past the Iellian guards who'd waved them by with hardly a glance. Strange that, but he'd had little time to think about it, his attention focused instead on staying upright as his gelding raced along the High Road.

He glanced at Elorah standing in her stirrups, her head leaned low over her horse's neck. She'd clearly ridden at speed before. He looked toward Mierrle. Even in the dark, he could see her white-rimmed eyes, clamped legs, and clutching hands, her body jerking with each pounding step. It was a wonder she was still topside and not trampled beneath the horse's flying feet. No horseman himself, he'd at least found his stride and was maintaining his seat despite his fatigue.

Thane galloped ahead then veered his horse onto a lesser road. Elorah and Mierrle followed, their mounts rounding the curve at breakneck speed. This road was narrower, only wide enough for two abreast. Thane took the lead, his mind worrying whether they were ahead or behind the pale-haired man. He gigged his mount at the thought they might be behind.

His horse burst forward, and he grabbed a fistful of mane to keep from falling off. Behind came the thunderous tattoo of the other two horses, and he turned his head, nearly losing his balance before facing forward again.

"Slow down!" Elorah shouted.

"Can't!" He gave his horse's sides another dig, his mind already in the alehouse.

All three horses were lathered, their breathing coming in sharp-edged snorts by the time the trio rounded the final turn, and the roadhouse appeared, its laneway puddled with the sallow light of a lone oil lantern.

Moonlight improved the alehouse's appearance, lending it a dissolute charm Thane knew would fade with the rising sun.

The moss-riddled front consisting of two cracked windows, a peeling red door, and a chalkstone stoop channeled out by countless boots, squatted beneath a moppy thatched roof. All in all, an unimpressive-looking place for the money flowing through it on any given day, Hebediah Jimpkins overseeing it all with a wily grin. A running fox, indeed.

Thane steered his mount onto the laneway, Elorah and Mierrle following behind.

Elorah barely had time to catch her breath, let alone gather her thoughts as her horse galloped pell-mell behind Thane's, the leather case containing the crystalwood staff bouncing against her leg. She could feel Mierrle's terror, and she split her concentration between keeping her own seat and steadying her friend. What had she gotten them into? Her friend's collapse, and now this. What kind of friend was she turning out to be? If they made it to The Running Fox in one piece, no one would be more surprised than she.

Mierrle had reluctantly agreed to return to her family after Thane assured them passage could be secured on one of the skiffs plying the Wydderhalle. He'd see to it tomorrow after they'd had a chance to rest. She couldn't expect Mierrle to follow her to the wilds of Whitemond in search of a place that might not even exist. Elorah had no proof that it did and much proof it did not, if books could be counted as proof. It was only her dreams and intuition that persuaded her differently. But even her dreams hadn't shown her how to resurrect a destroyed parambek once she'd found it. She had no idea what she would do then.

She'd resolved to go to her grandfather's and speak with the legendary crystalwood harvester about his many trips to Whitemond. If anyone knew how to reach that place of legend, it was Pfolan Chrysolan. He would set her on the proper path, and he would understand her reasons for going.

She needed help. Of this she was convinced. Her thoughts turned to Haedyn and his friend, and she wondered how she would find them again. Her vision of the horrific death he'd suffered along with his charging stallion came back with sobering clarity as her own horse careened down a dark road lit only by moonlight. She felt the pair were important to her journey. Hadn't she been told help would come if she asked? Why else would she have seen them? She dwelt upon that for a moment, her heart filling with purpose. Once she saw Mierrle home— she wasn't about to leave that to anyone else—she could begin her trip in earnest. Perhaps by then, she'd have found the two who had featured in her visions and dreams.

She shouted at Thane to slow down which only made him go faster. Annoyance creased her brow. She glanced at Mierrle. Her friend was clinging to her galloping horse, tears streaming from her eyes, her legs and hands contorted into desperate claws. Elorah sent a surge of heart vorik to her friend to give her courage. The pendant pulsed against her chest.

At last, a lone lantern appeared, its flame casting fitful shadows upon a sign depicting a red fox bounding over a green beneath a faded black banner advertising *The Running Fox* in faded gold lettering.

The alehouse sat several paces off the road, a dull-white building looking as if it had been dragged up from the sod, gathering a few grimy windows and a grubby door as it went.

Thane reined his horse onto the laneway at speed—Elorah's and Mierrle's mounts galloping behind—before heading toward a sagging construction of piecemealed boards, faded metal, and blackened thatch. A line of horses hitched to a half-rotten pinekin rail along the backwall sent up a shiver of whinnies.

Thane and Elorah pulled up, while Mierrle's horse stuttered to a halt. They all dismounted—Mierrle's more of a falling away than a planned move—and tied up their mounts. Thane was already starting for the alehouse when Elorah reminded him to untack and water his exhausted mount.

"He'll seize up with colic," Thane protested.

"Not if you take your time," she countered.

He huffed but did as she asked.

That done, the group shouldered their gear and gimped toward the alehouse, Thane hurrying ahead to open the front door then fanning away a gout of smoke as he held it wide.

A fug of spilled ale, stale sweat, and smoke hung heavy in the air as they made their way to a table at the back, threading past rough-looking characters laughing, arguing, drinking, and gambling. Mierrle plopped down into a chair, and Elorah gave her hand a squeeze as she sat beside her.

A voice boomed out, "Thane, my boy!"

Thane shaded his eyes and peered toward the sound. "Hebediah Jimpkins! You old sod!"

Jimpkins set down the tankard he'd been polishing and squeezed his sizeable girth out from behind the soot-stained bar. The big man made his way toward them, a gap-toothed smile tucking into the whiskery, dimpled cheeks either side of his red-veined nose. He extended a meaty paw, and Thane slapped his hand into it before lurching forward as the barkeep jerked him against his broad front, his free hand banging twice at Thane's back before letting loose.

"It's been too long," Jimpkins cried. "Wrynne! Look what the cat's drug in!"

A blowsy, red-faced woman behind the bar shook her head dismissively, her carroty strawstack of hair bobbing as she dispensed ale into a tankard from a large cask. Two cats sat either side, their petaloid feet planted on the black-oak countertop, their haughty eyes oblivious.

Thane quirked an eyebrow at Jimpkins.

"I see your maissel's as happy as ever to see me," he said with a laugh.

"Oh, she's delighted. She threw nothing. That's how you know." He gave Thane a wink. "So, what's on the wind this fine day?"

Thane shrugged, and Jimpkins' smile broadened, the tip of his tongue poking out like a pink berry between his brown-edged teeth.

"Just three travelers stopping in for a rest." Thane indicated toward Elorah and Mierrle, his eyes tracking Wrynne's heavy-footed approach.

"A gildy good evening to you both," Jimpkins said with a bow. "It's not often we're graced with two lovely ladies on the self-same day."

"Ah, you old fool, I'm here ain't I," Wrynne squawked, plonking a tankard in front of a raw-boned Rabboutier wearing a leather eyepatch and a lopsided sneer. "You'd think I weren't from the way you're goin' on." The Rabboutier's eye squinted as froth spumed down the tankard's sides. "And none of your vit'rol Raffa Breck. Foam ain't ale, ere it." She held out her hand, and the Rabboutier begrudgingly gave his coin.

"No one's more aware of your charms than I, my sweet," Jimpkins crooned, his lips drawn back in an ingratiating smile. "No need to remind me." Wrynne harrumphed and planted her hands on her hips, her pebble eyes hardening, her sizeable prow heaving with wounded outrage. Jimpkins widened his toothy smile until she snorted then turned and made for the bar. "That tongue's sharper'n a card cheat's knife," he muttered as he grabbed a tankard from a neighboring table and guzzled its contents.

"Hey, I were drinkin' that!" whinged a lank-haired man, his Adam's apple bobbing like a buoy. The man's hand dropped to the knife strapped to his thigh.

"Never fear, friend. There's more," Jimpkins said, motioning Wrynne to bring a fresh tankard. Her scowl hardened as she drew another ale, then tromped over and clunked it down, a goodly amount splashing onto the table. "On the house," Jimpkins said, his gaze following his maissel's floor-pounding retreat. The offended man eyeballed Jimpkins before lifting his hand from the knife to the tankard and latching on, his adam's apple bobbing furiously as he slugged down a throatful.

Jimpkins turned to Thane. "So, what'll it be? Black ale? Ah, wait. I know." He snapped his fingers. "Sweetsweet, am I right?"

Thane shook his head. "Do you have tea?"

"Tea!" Jimpkins roared, his face reddening before settling into a chiding smile. He wagged his finger. "Ah, you almost had me. Tea," he scoffed.

Thane smiled thinly, his gaze indicating his companions. "Something without legs, then."

Jimpkins sobered. "I've some sweet cider, newly arrived from the Hiegh district. No legs but a strong bite."

"Bring three."

The front door banged open and in walked a tall, handsome dark-skinned man, his sea-chapped black hair wound into a multitude of thin cords bound together by golden rings, a horsetail that fell to his waist. His beard was deeply black and shaped to enhance his strong jawline. He wore a loose white-linen shirt and dark breeches, separated by a brown leather belt, knife handles visible on both hips. Small golden rings pierced his left nostril and the high curve of his left ear, a fine gold chain connecting the two. More gold chains encircled his neck, one suspending a coin-shaped medallion.

Thane poured himself into the chair next to Elorah and slumped down, his gaze darting toward the man then away.

Jimpkins sallied off, his beefy hand waving a greeting. After a word, he clapped the man on the back and gestured toward the bar, the two walking together as if well acquainted, all gum-showing smiles and hearty laughs.

"Who is that?" Mierrle asked. "He looks important."

"He's not."

Elorah turned toward Thane. "How do you know?"

He shrugged and sank lower in his chair.

As Jimpkins and the man approached, Wrynne's face softened, a small laugh escaping when the cord-haired man leaned forward and bussed her cheek. He flashed a smile, his teeth brilliantly white, his dark brown eyes dancing with merriment.

"He seems to know your friends," Elorah observed.

"He knows a good many barkeeps. It's his living. Don't be too impressed." Thane mimed as if drinking and raised his eyebrows. "He's the Rabboutier that brings it," he added.

"Do you know him?" Mierrle asked.

"We're acquainted," Thane said, stealing another glance.

The front door banged open again and in walked Aikin and Fyndd.

"Aikin!" Mierrle cried, her arm raising.

Elorah tugged her arm down, then placed her straightened finger against her lips and shook her head. Mierrle caught her meaning, her green eyes questioning.

Aikin's head turned toward them then turned back as he fell in behind Fyndd already making his way to the dark-skinned man at the bar.

What are they doing here?

As a bard, Fyndd had perhaps some reason to be acquainted with this place but Aikin? He looked as ill at ease as a rooster whose strutted into a wolf's den only to realize he isn't the guest, he's the dinner. She watched as Fyndd leaned into the space next to the Rabboutier, who turned from his conversation with Wrynne, recognition lighting his face. He and Fyndd shook hands like old friends. Fyndd motioned toward Aikin and the man shook his hand as well, his enthusiasm more tempered. Thane seemed transfixed by the exchange.

"What do you think that's about?" Elorah whispered.

Thane cocked his head. "I couldn't say, except..." His brow wrinkled. "Rodric Perrent dips his hand in many pots though which one he's dipping into just now is anyone's guess."

Elorah sat back and chewed her bottom lip. For Aikin to leave the festival and show up here was not only unexpected, it was perplexing. At first, she'd been afraid he'd followed her in another misguided attempt to act as her guardian, but she discarded that idea when she realized he couldn't have known she was coming here. She moved on to a darker thought. She was certain he, along with his fellow Bairrtraigh emvors, had been the ones opening the chasm in the stage when the monarch made her speech. It was likely he was also involved in trying to push the queen into the massive hole using his vorik, although Therran was ill-suited to such a task. Still, they'd almost managed it, which said something about their commitment. She suspected she was witnessing the next step in his clan's plan to rid the Caeldish of Zephyrria Rennesseau and her influence. Of course, Elorah had been as shocked as anyone when the queen made her announcement, but there'd been so many other things to think about, she hadn't given it another thought. But for Aikin and his clan, there would be no other focus for it marked the culmination of all their suspicions and fears.

She stood.

"Where are you going?" Thane blurted.

"To get some answers." Mierrle rose to follow, determination tightening her pallid face. "Stay here," Elorah murmured. Mierrle's dark eyebrows drew together, her eyes clouding with dismay. Elorah picked up her staff case. "Would you watch this for me?" Mierrle glanced wistfully toward Aikin for a moment then tightened her chin and nodded. She took the case and hugged it to her chest before sinking into her chair. Elorah felt a pang. Mierrle was always so willing to help. She would be sad to see her go home.

She did her best to ignore the hard stares training on her as she made her way past table after table on her way to the bar.

Aikin's back was to her when she approached, and Fyndd tugged his sleeve, his head bobbing sideways. Aikin spun round then jutted his chin and raised one eyebrow.

"What are you doing here?" he spluttered.

"I should ask you the same thing," she replied.

The dark-skinned man smiled, his brown eyes kindly and warm. "Rodric Perrent," he offered in a luxuriant baritone.

"Elorah Niav," she said, allowing him to buss the back of her hand.

"A pleasure," he said.

"Does your family know you're here?" Aikin asked.

"Does yours?" she retorted.

"It's not the same," he sniffed.

Elorah caught herself. They always circled this same path, going round and round with neither hearing the other. Her pendant pulsed as she changed tack. "I'm sorry I left before we could speak. With everything happening..."

"It's fine. I had other matters to attend to."

"I saw," she said, her gaze intensifying. "Is this more of the same?"

"If you're asking whether we're planning to take back our sovereignty, the answer is yes."

"There's a better way," she said. He puffed up, his cheeks coloring. Her pendant pulsed, pushing her past her discomfort. "But I need your help." She studied his face, willing him to hear her this time. After a moment, his shoulders dropped.

"What do you need?"

She pointed toward an empty area near a back corner. Aikin nodded.

"My apologies," he said to Rodric.

"None needed, my friend. We'll be here when you return." Rodric took a sip from his whiskey glass. Fyndd swallowed a smile as he stuck his hands in his pockets and stubbed his boot toe against the wooden floor.

She could feel Aikin's consternation grow as they wound past tablesful of sour faces and surly looks until they reached the appointed spot. She turned to face him, her hand going to her pendant, her stomach tying into a knot. His face went wide with unasked questions, and she steeled her nerve, her dream rushing back to her—*believe and they will appear.* "I saw what you did to the stage," she said in a low voice. "Not many could have done that. What I have in mind will require someone with your talent and stamina." The unexpected compliment knocked him back, his expression softening. "Have you heard of Therrania?"

"In old mother's tales when I was too young to know better."

His derision stung, but she pushed on. "I know you think it's a myth, but it isn't." She lowered her voice further, a note of fervor creeping in. "I've seen it."

"That's not possible."

She ignored his flippant dismissal. "Therrania is the answer. Once it's revived, the full measure of our Therran power will be restored. We're out of balance. In here." She pointed at her midsection. "We've lost our way because our spirits have lost touch with what grounds us. Until Therrania is restored, we will never thrive. I know you think we can fight our way to freedom and prosperity, but we can't. Until we restore the power within, we'll never be free."

"Therrania doesn't exist," he stated, bald certainty amplifying his disbelief.

"It does!" she cried, then remembered herself. She dropped her voice. "It does exist. On Whitemond. It's buried, but it's there. It will be a long, hard trip, with no guarantees, but once we uncover it, the world will change for the better, I promise you."

He studied her, considering. "How can you be so sure?"

She took a deep breath. She'd been dreading this part, explaining that her plans rested on dreams and visions. "I know how this will sound, but I've been dreaming about Therrania since I was a child." She paused, searching for the right words. "But not only that. I've seen it, right in front of me, as real as you are now. I've seen how it was before the Great Destruction and how it is now and how it can be again."

"The Great Destruction! That was eryns ago!" He went silent, his gaze sweeping the dusty floor. "Only a Spyrrt wycche could have seen that," he hissed, his worried eyes finding hers.

Her lips formed a grim line as she nodded. He inhaled sharply, his face folding in on itself as if he'd been punched. The air went thick, and time slowed. Her stomach roiled at the knowledge her greatest secret was secret no more. There was no going back now. The pendant pulsed harder, pushing her to finish what she'd started. "I'm going," she stated flatly. "With or without you," Even as she said it, she felt a nameless panic. She paused, pushing down the crippling fear making her want to run and hide, to do anything other than say these things to someone she knew would never believe her. "But I'd rather you came," she croaked, amazed to be speaking the words. It was as if an outside force was using her as a mouthpiece. "You would be helping not only me but everyone who calls the Basin home."

To her surprise, the words had the desired effect, his shocked face becoming concerned. "I can't let you go on such a journey alone." He laid his hand on her shoulder. It didn't feel out of place, an unexpected surge of friendship flowing through her. "When do you plan to leave?"

"Tomorrow."

"That soon?" he asked, surprised.

She nodded, though she wasn't nearly as decided as she'd sounded.

"Let me speak with Fyndd. There are loose ends in need of tying up. If he agrees, you have my pledge."

She thanked him, the pendant's warmth infusing her with peaceful calm. The mysterious stone seemed to be a guide, letting her know when she was on the right path. Silvi had given her a marvelous gift, and she silently thanked her beloved mentor.

She felt an unexplainable lightness as she and Aikin walked back to the table. No longer would she have to hide who she was. She'd crossed that bridge and could leave it behind.

Night made things easier, but Rachmyn remained cautious. The moon was bright enough to be a betrayer of shadows, and he made sure they stayed off the roads others traveled.

They'd been lucky getting past the High Hell checkpoint, their escape courtesy of a drunken Inirian diverting attention by brandishing a hatchet and charging the guards. They'd been luckier still escaping the gryphon who'd flown out of nowhere to skim above their heads. At the sound of its piercing cry, they'd fallen facedown to the ground, Haedyn cupping a hand to his breast to keep from squashing his bird, laying that way—faces shoved into a bent arm, eyes straining upward—for long moments until their ragged breathing slowed, and their heartbeats faded from their ears.

Because Rachmyn hadn't walked their course in Oru Fen, he was forced to rely on his compass and his instincts to get them to The Running Fox. He still hadn't worked out why he'd been unable to dreamwalk, and it nettled him every time he squinted at the dial on his wrist. He couldn't recall it ever happening before, even when he was young and learning the craft.

The High Road ambled north, and they followed the same general course, keeping to the nearby brush and thickets. It made for tough going, forging through brambles and stranglevines in the dark. Elgre took the point, and it was the wolf that turned onto the lesser road followed by the friends, Rachmyn noting the fresh churn of hoofprints and crisp dents of wagon wheels.

Another half-league of fighting underbrush and the alehouse came into view, a gray smear on the black horizon. Rachmyn was glad to see it. Soon he'd be done with Alliari, and they could be on their way. With any luck they would be out of this wretched basin before daybreak.

As they approached the wattle-and-daub establishment, Rachmyn wondered what sort of place The Running Fox would turn out to be. He wasn't one to seek out alehouses, and he felt uneasy as he surveyed its moss-riddled exterior. Haedyn had gotten his bird out and perched it on his arm, its cowled head swiveling toward each new noise. Elgre zig-zagged in front, his nose held high to inhale scent. The shrill cry of panicked horses split the air. They'd caught wind of the wolf. Elgre shot a disdainful glare toward the stable. Rachmyn smiled. How many times had he seen that contemptuous look when the wolf was faced with herd animals reacting as one? Elgre despised mob mentality.

"Whoa, Fryk!" Haedyn barked as the startled bird shot up to its full height, its wings a blur, its razor-talons chinking into the armguard.

chirrt chirrt chirrt.

Rachmyn elbowed Haedyn. For the life of him, he couldn't understand why his friend put up with the little gobsmite. Haedyn laid a hand on the grynt's back until its wings refolded.

Rachmyn looked around. They needed a place to wait but without money, a room was out of the question. He spotted the moon-silvered fingers of a dock jutting out into the wide river running behind the alehouse. It wasn't a cave, but it would suit.

They made their way to it—Elgre swinging wide around the stable —then poked their staffs into the shadow-black crevice beneath its long approach. A brown rat scurried out, its naked feet paddling until Elgre pounced upon it, shook it twice, then scarfed it down. Rachmyn swept his staff a second time before crawling underneath the weathered boards into the darkness. Elgre flopped down on the shore nearby with a satisfied groan.

Rachmyn crabbed his way to a support piling then flipped onto his backside and leaned against the splintery wood. He checked for his shard—yes, there it was—then stretched his legs and crossed them at the ankles, his ears lulling to the gentle *wap-wap-wap* of the Wydderhalle rubbing soft against a shingle shore.

Haedyn kicked his rucksack and staff under, then eased Fryk into his vest pocket. As the dummy, his job was to scout the alehouse before Rachmyn made his entry.

"No sweetsweet," Rachmyn warned, stowing Haedyn's gear with his own.

"See you inside," Haedyn laughed.

Seeing Rodric had been a shock, and Thane didn't quite know what to do with himself. Part of him wanted to run away but the other part, the one that got him into trouble, wanted to run to Rodric as he'd done so many times before in their shared past. But no, that wouldn't be right. Hadn't he been the one who'd turned their life together on its head and lighted out in the middle of the night, his pack bulging with stolen brakken cloth and jewels and coins? Hadn't he been the one who'd thrown happiness away with both hands in favor of a life with no strings attached? Rodric, so handsome and kind, hadn't deserved any of it, but Thane had been too young and brash and full of misbegotten pride to allow himself to fall for anyone, even if they were one of the finest men that ever breathed. It was only afterward, when his stringless life turned out to be anything but, that he'd begun to see how foolish he'd been.

The jewels and the coins were long gone, thrown away on a dizzying spiral of charm draughts, dreamcrafts, and inebriants, none of which had made him even remotely happy. Indeed, he felt as hollow and used up as an empty sweetsweet cask.

Ahh, the bitter taste of past mistakes, he thought, a familiar need boiling up.

Though Jimpkins had brought the cider, it held little appeal when the smell of strong drink was all around, his tongue aching for its soothing caress. He let out a sigh and drew his head into the cleft of his hunched shoulders. So he remained until Elorah returned. She gave him a quizzical look.

"Are you unwell?" she asked.

"Only in ways that cannot be mended," he replied. She sat, a troubled look on her face. Mierrle laid a hand on his arm, her dark green eyes full of empathy. He let it stay for a moment before sliding his arm away.

He still had the brakken cloth, so that was something, despite it being a liability given present company. He would have to be even more careful when he spoke to the pale-haired man, if he was afforded the opportunity. First things first, though. His companions needed rest. Once he had them tucked away in a room, he would book their passage to Ghysszim, the southernmost port on the Wydderhalle, using trinkets from his pack, on the promise of a handsome reward from Mierrle's family. It was chancy, putting up his own collateral, but his instincts were usually good, and the girl seemed genuine. It wasn't how he liked conducting business, but he needed away, and a trip down the Wydderhalle wouldn't be the worst thing.

He gained Jimpkins' attention and whispered an inquiry about a room. Jimpkins winked, his shoulders lifting as he held up one finger then two. Thane held up a single finger—one room required. Jimpkins nodded and bustled away.

Thane turned to Elorah. "Maiss, may I see you and Mierrle to a room before I make my way to Duntin Town to book our passage?"

Elorah shook her head. "I can't let you do that without first resting yourself."

"I've only arranged for the one room," he said. "It wouldn't be seemly."

She gave the alehouse a cursory glance. "This crowd doesn't seem too judging of such things." She turned to Mierrle, who'd grown morose at the mention of Ghysszim, and gave her a sympathetic smile. "Soon you'll be back with your family."

"Yes," Mierrle said, sounding miserable. She dropped her gaze to her lap where her hands fiddled with a fold in her tunic. "It's for the best I suppose."

Elorah frowned, and she sat for a long moment looking undecided. "It would, I suppose, bring your family great joy to see you again after being apart all these moons."

Mierrle shifted, her bottom lip quivering. "No, not joy. There is no joy in the return of a daughter who has failed."

Elorah sat back and drew a deep breath. "Failure only comes to those who try. Would your family be terribly sad if you didn't come home right away?" Her face was pensive as she clutched something near her collarbone.

Thane took her measure, skepticism drawing his eyebrows together. *What's this then?*

Mierrle looked up, hope sparking in her eyes. "My family would be sadder if I returned with nothing to show for my time away."

Elorah nodded as if she'd come to a decision. "Would you consider staying with me?" She turned to look at Thane. "Both of you?"

Thane hadn't expected that. *What is she even talking about?* He had plans, none of which included her. He opened his mouth to tell her thus when she continued.

"I've come to realize the stumbling blocks of the past do not haunt those who can turn them into stepping-stones." She looked at him as if she could see all the ugly wounds festering inside, and a prickle went up his spine. Thane's eyes cut toward Rodric—his smile a lost sun shining upon the copper-haired man—before shifting back to focus on her. How had she known the one thing that would shatter his brittle demeanor, exposing the emptiness he tried so hard to hide. He felt once again like that skinny boy standing on the shore of Belequis Bay, his bare feet numb, his flayed skin burning, his weepy eyes staring at the unknowable as he wished with all his might he were someone different. "I know what I'm asking is a terrible sacrifice for you both," she continued. "I don't take that lightly." Her hand tightened around the thing she held near her throat. "But I also know I need both of you if I'm to have any chance at success."

Thane cocked his head. "I can't say I know what we're discussing."

She lifted her chin and took a deep breath. "Of course..." She set her jaw and inhaled as if preparing for a fight. "What would you say if I told you there's an ancient center that was destroyed long ago but once it's restored, would save marankind from themselves?"

"I'd say you've been reading too many old mother's tales."

Mierrle looked at Thane, her eyes reproachful.

"I can't blame you for thinking that," Elorah said. "But say there is such a place. Would you be willing to put aside your plans, and your doubts, for a chance to fill that emptiness inside with something bigger and more magnificent than anything you could do on your own?"

Thane looked at her, his good sense tamping down a sudden, wild urge to throw in with her on this misadventure she was proposing. "Charming words, maiss, but I learned long ago not to rely on things I can't hold in my hand. This world doesn't run on promises and pretty speeches."

Elorah nodded. "I see," she said, sounding disappointed.

"I'd wager you've never had to sleep face-down in a ditch or go hungry for so long your navel rubs your backbone or run until your legs give out to escape the whip or the blade or the fist that wants to send you to the next world."

"No," she allowed. "I have lived a fortunate life, that is true."

"I've done all those things and more that don't bear speaking. I don't recommend it." He took a sip from his mug and grimaced at the bitterness underlying the cider's cloying sweetness. "All best avoided, if possible," he added.

"And this reasoning, it brings you happiness?"

He pursed his lips, a small *pffft* escaping. "It brings me to another day. That is all. Happiness is not required."

"Perhaps not but neither is unhappiness."

"I'm not unhappy, maiss. But I am practical, and what you're proposing is a fool's errand."

"Elorah is not a fool," Mierrle bleated. Thane shrugged.

"I may be a fool," Elorah said without rancor, "but isn't it the fools who dare to do what practical men only dream of? And by so doing, change forever that which is considered practical? Surely even a man such as yourself would allow that to be true."

"As you say, maiss," he said, unwilling to pursue the point further.

At the mention of fools, Alliari's doe-eyed visage sprang unbidden to his mind. *Where is that old fool? He should have been here by now.* Something about the nightjolly's glaring absence did not set well. He looked at the hatch hidden under a neighboring table. He knew every route out of this place including the nearby trapdoor and the one behind the bar, both of which led to a set of tunnels dug out beneath the alehouse, one emptying near the dock, the other surfacing in the woods across the road. He'd had to use the trapdoors a few times, and hoped never to repeat the experience, remembering the seeping mud, sticking spiderwebs, and scurrying rats from his previous crawling escapes. He glanced first toward the front, then toward the back, his mind counting the steps between himself and the doors. He appraised the windows, wondering if he could still fit through one. He'd done that before too, though he'd been younger and thinner at the time.

Thane's gaze drifted to where Rodric had been seated, but the Rabboutier was gone. The bard he'd been talking with had disappeared as well. Questions crowded his mind so that when Aikin approached, Thane hardly noticed.

"May I join you?"

Thane shrugged and leaned to look past him.

"Please do," Mierrle breathed.

Thane rolled his eyes as Aikin drew up a chair. "Where's your friend?" he asked with forced nonchalance.

Aikin arrowed a sharp look at him before shifting his gaze to Elorah. "What are you drinking?" he asked.

"Cider," Thane supplied, taking a drink and grimacing.

"Can't abide the stuff." Aikin took a slug from the tankard he'd brought with him. "Thank the Urslan I'm not from Hiegh."

"It's not very good," Mierrle agreed, then looked at Thane. "Sorry."

"So, it's all settled with Fyndd?" Elorah asked.

Aikin nodded. "It is. I'm at your disposal."

Thane was curious despite himself. "Are you joining maiss's excursion?" he asked, his tone more cutting than he'd intended.

"So it would seem. You?" Aikin asked.

"No," Thane replied. "I've other plans I'm afraid."

Aikin's expression lightened. "Good."

Thane gave him a bemused smile. *Wouldn't it nettle you no end if I did go.* He was almost tempted by that alone.

"I've been trying to convince him, but so far, he's remained unmoved," Elorah said. "I'm not giving up, though." She smiled at Thane, her eyes dancing.

"As you wish, maiss," he said with a dismissive shrug.

"You don't know what you're up against," Aikin said. "She can be quite persuasive."

"Spoken by one who seems to have already abandoned his better judgment," Thane said, his expression pitying.

Aikin flushed as he chugged his remaining ale, clanking the empty tankard onto the scarred tabletop when he'd finished.

It seems I've found the red-haired dolt's tender spot.

Aikin raised his hand, and Jimpkins scudded over with a full tankard. Aikin slid the barkeep a coin, and Jimpkins grinned, palming it with one hand while whisking the empty away with the other. "Much appreciated, I'm sure," he said as he clipped away.

Thane eyed the frothy ale. It wasn't sweetsweet, but a sip would do much to quell the longing in his throat. Aikin's gaze slid sideways as he wrapped his hand around the tankard, pulling it closer. Thane sighed. *Ahh, well. Only disappointment to be had there.* Then sighed again. Nothing was going to plan. Nothing whatever.

Haedyn ensured Fryk was in his pocket before pushing open the peeling red door. He knew what he was about, his focus on drawing attention so that Rachmyn could run his deal without interference. *Shouldn't be too hard,* he thought as he stepped into the alehouse.

The room was smoky, and he worried a little for his bird. His gaze jumped to the source, a fitful flame sulking inside a stone hearth at the far side of the room. That would serve. He walked to it and, summoning his will, stoked the sputtering flame into a roaring blaze. Those nearest paused their conversations to scowl at him. Surprising. Folk usually preferred a blaze sending smoke up a chimney to a smolder sending it out into the room.

He was still puzzling over it when a rotund man of considerable height bundled up.

"I see you've a way with fire," the man allowed. "Very good, very good. It's just that..." He leaned in and pointed toward a large sign above the bar—*No Vorik Allowed In This Establishment. No Exceptions!* Beneath the sign glowered a hard-faced, red-haired woman, the two cats flanking her regarding him with sullen contempt.

Haedyn held up his hands. "It's my first time here," he said, thinking the fire might be the perfect attention-getter if he didn't get himself put out the door.

"Can't say I mind, but the maissel, she's a stickler for rules," the man apologized. "Hebediah Jimpkins." He thrust his hand toward Haedyn.

"Haedyn Khin." The two shook, Jimpkins' grip lingering longer than necessary. *Sizing me up, eh?* Haedyn thought, doing the same.

"What's your pleasure?" Jimpkins asked, waving a hand toward the bar.

"Have you any sweetsweet?" Haedyn replied, banishing Rachmyn's disapproval from his thoughts.

"Prinkin, Balkie, or Gulsetta?"

"Sweeeetsweeeet," Haedyn repeated slower and louder, assuming the big man had misheard him.

"Right. As I say, Prinkin, Balkie, or Gulsetta? We have them all, my friend."

Haedyn, realizing his error, shrugged. "Surprise me. I'm in the mood for an adventure."

"And you shall have one!" Jimpkins cried, winking as he barged off.

Haedyn surveyed the noisy crowd. Rachmyn had told him to look for a Shadowen with the eyes of a dying deer. He couldn't feature what that meant, but he studied the crowd anyway, hoping it would become apparent. None of the rowdy-robs on display seemed to fit. Perhaps the Shadowen hadn't yet arrived. Haedyn strode to the bar, stationing himself to gain a good view of both the doors and the crowd.

He felt a vibration coming from his knife and his heart leaped even as his mind dismissed the sensation as imagination. Still, his eyes scanned the room, crowded with all manner of scoundrels and thieves, his blood thumping. *Surely not*, he thought as he searched, his knife urging him on.

He saw her, and everything stopped.

She was sitting at the back, a sparkling jewel in a sea of gloom. *Elorah.* He whispered her name to prove he wasn't dreaming. He'd been certain when they left the festival he would never see her again yet here she was, looking lovelier than even his memory. He couldn't believe his luck. What was she doing in a place such as this amidst a crowd of roughnecks and rogues? Beside her was her dark-haired friend looking wan and scar-faced Thane about whom Haedyn hadn't made up his mind. There was another maran at the table as well, but all he could see of him was the back of his copper-haired head, his muscular neck, and broad shoulders.

Elorah was deep in conversation with her tablemates, and Haedyn found himself once again captivated by the flash of her mesmerizing eyes as she leaned forward to make some point, her shiny brown curls slipping past the ridge of her shoulders to curtain the front of her tunic. His delight grew, replacing all thought of looking for the doe-eyed man.

His reverie was cut short when Jimpkins plunked a short tumbler in front of him, filled to the brim with reddish-brown liquid.

"A stout vintage of Prinkin, with legs enough for any adventurer." Jimpkins' urging eyes probed Haedyn's face until he dug a hektra from his pocket and handed it over.

"Two hektras," Jimpkins prompted.

"I've only the one," Haedyn said.

Jimpkins considered this for a moment, then lifted the tumbler and poured half its contents down his throat before setting it in front of Haedyn and pocketing the coin. "Half an adventure is better than none, eh?" he said, placing a hand upon his chest, his gaze soft and far away. "Indeed, adventure is the true desire of every heart."

"I've always believed that," Haedyn agreed, taking a sip from the tumbler. He was unprepared for the Prinkin's effects, first inside his mouth, where a bracing wind chilled his teeth, his tongue taking refuge in the smoke-nuanced warmth of the fire igniting at the back of his throat. His cheeks seemed to stretch up and out with all the powerful fullness of a fearsome animal, a bear perhaps, or maybe a wolf. The sweetsweet slid down his throat and a new set of feelings took hold—a lingering heat as the liquor flumed downward, plummeting through his airy chest to land in the expanding radiance bubbling bright against his ribs as if he'd swallowed a sun. Haedyn eyed the cup with admiration, his hand checking whether the fire within could be felt without.

Jimpkins gave him a sotted grin.

Haedyn took another sip and then another, each time marveling at the panoply of feelings the liquor produced. It was only after he'd emptied the tumbler that he thought again about Rachmyn waiting for him in the dark. Should he make himself known to Elorah or step outside and confer with his friend? In the end, the decision was made when Thane picked him out, his eyes going wide as he leaned toward Elorah's ear. She looked startled, her gaze searching back and forth before finding Haedyn, a slow smile spreading across her face. The heat inside ramped up to an alarming degree, migrating up his neck and jaw and into his cheeks and further still, up his forehead and into his dampening hairline.

A familiar figure stepped into his sightline. Rachmyn. His friend's frosty gaze moved from the tumbler to Haedyn's eyes. He casually elbowed the empty aside and pretended to scan the room. Rachmyn cleared his throat, his jaw jutting forward as he walked away, his moonbeam hair a beacon in the dim interior.

Haedyn leaned back against his bent arms propped atop the bar's counter. It was a rougher crowd than he'd first thought, the whiff of danger all around. He was watching a game of dice and picks unravel when Rachmyn returned.

"Good evening, friend," he said, his gaze remaining on the game where a curly-haired bruiser traded toothpicks for a handful of coins amidst grumbling sour faces.

Rachmyn did his own study of the hubbub around them, his expression purposely blank. Haedyn knew this game. Strangers just met. Easy enough. "Nothing good about it, friend," Rachmyn replied.

Jimpkins sidled up and stuck out his hand. "I don't believe we've met. Hebediah Jimpkins."

Rachmyn regarded the barkeep's hand as if it were a lump of rancid meat. The hand dropped to Jimpkins' side. "Can I get you a drink?"

"No," Rachmyn replied.

Jimpkins' expression tightened. "We've only room for paying customers. Quite crowded, you see." The barkeep's smile was unreasonably apologetic.

"Understood," Rachmyn replied, looking around again. He clapped his palm twice against the bar then turned to find Thane standing next to his shoulder, his expression speculative. Rachmyn eased back a step, his spine stiffening as the scarred man motioned Jimpkins to set up a drink.

"Friend of yours?" Jimpkins asked.

"Not quite," Thane said, his eyes appraising Rachmyn's reaction. "But I'd wager we'll be good friends indeed before this night is done." Rachmyn drew his chin back and narrowed his eyes. Haedyn knew that look, had seen it many times. It always preceded Shadowen trickery. Thane leaned past Rachmyn to look at Haedyn.

"Are you two together?" he asked, his finger wagging between the friends. Haedyn shook his head. Thane smiled solicitously. "As you say," he allowed, then winked at Jimpkins who'd returned with a tankard.

"A pint of the pink," the barkeep blared, setting the tankard down near Rachmyn.

"Hiegh hard cider. Very choice," Thane said with an appreciative nod, sliding the tankard closer. Rachmyn's gaze flicked down then away, his hand slipping off the bar and into his pocket. He walked off without comment. Thane drew his head back, his mouth collapsing into a frown. He looked at Haedyn. "Is he always like that?"

Haedyn caught himself before he blurted out an answer. Instead, he shifted the bulge of his bird and sauntered off in the opposite direction, intent on working his way back to where Elorah was seated. Thane sprang after him and grasped his shoulder.

"Listen," he said. "I've a proposal for your pale-haired friend, but I need your help." Haedyn started to protest. "Don't bother," Thane interrupted. "We both know you're together. I felt it from the first. I also know he has something of great value he's looking to sell. But it's better we don't speak of such things here." Thane pointed to his ear, then circled his index finger to indicate the number of sharp ears listening, his eyes cutting left then right.

Haedyn changed the subject. "How'd you get that?" he said, his finger tracing down his own cheek to approximate Thane's scar.

The question seemed to catch Thane off guard, but he recovered quickly. "Boring story, bad ending. Not worth the telling really," he said, a shadow crossing his face. He gripped Haedyn's shoulder tighter. "Have a word with your friend, eh?" He released his hold and walked back to where Elorah sat.

Haedyn ran a hand through his hair then pulled it back from his heated forehead before following Thane to the table.

His arrival was met with a mixture of reactions—Elorah and Mierrle looking well pleased; the copper-haired man regarding him with chary surprise; Thane smirking before leaping up and dragging a chair over from a neighboring table. He indicated for Haedyn to take a seat before retaking his own.

The Prinkin was having its effect, a pleasant sense of bonhomie fuzzing Haedyn's thoughts and overriding his reason. "Ahh, sun man," he said to Aikin. "Still glowing, I see."

"What?"

"You've some sparkle right...." Haedyn pointed a finger at Aikin's ear, then brought it back behind his own. "...here."

"Do I know you?" Aikin asked, his hand reaching up to swipe at the spot.

Haedyn shook his head and smiled.

"Won't you sit with us?" asked Elorah, her voice bright. She looked across the table and motioned. "Aikin, make room."

"Do you know him?" Aikin griped, jostling his chair sideways.

"We're acquainted," she said, shooting a look at Thane.

"As I thought," Thane said, his gaze fixed behind Haedyn's shoulder.

"What?" Haedyn asked, bending over to lean his forearms on the back of the chair.

"Let's go," a familiar voice growled into his ear. Haedyn glanced over his shoulder in time to see Rachmyn straighten, his jaw flexing.

"What?" Haedyn asked again.

Thane was already pulling another chair over to the table. "No need to rush off, friend," he said to Rachmyn as he bumped the chair into the narrow space between his own and Haedyn's. Aikin harrumphed, moving closer to Elorah. Rachmyn's gaze never wavered, drilling into the side of Haedyn's head.

A ruckus broke out at a nearby table where a game of Rabbit Run had run aground. Two drunken Rabboutiers threw down their cards and went for their steels. The red-haired man was quicker, stabbing his dagger down into the patched leather coat of the mustachioed man sitting opposite, missing the man's arm but pinning the coat's sleeve to the tabletop. The mustachioed man, one hand still fumbling at his belt, let out a roar of indignation while Red Hair pulled a second blade from his boot and held it at Mustachio's tremorous throat. "By the Wrath, you'll not have even one more," he shouted. "I'll see you hanged fer a thief first."

A third Rabboutier with patinated copper chains knifing through his thick black hair leaped up and smashed his fist into Red Hair's shouting gob. "Put yer blades away, ya fleeking softhead," he roared.

Red Hair staggered back, his blade swinging wildly as he regained his balance. He drew back his free fist and rounded on Copper Chains, landing a solid blow to his opponent's gristly ear followed by a second to his windpipe. Meanwhile, Mustachio had managed to jerk the blade out of his sleeve, and he brandished it at Red Hair.

"No blades!" shouted Jimpkins, rushing over to flail his way into the fray. He seized Mustachio's wrist, squeezing until the man's face flushed crimson, and the knife clattered to the floor. Two burleys from a nearby table jumped in fists first, scything swings crashing into Copper Chains and Red Hair at the same time two Rabboutiers from a different table waded in, fists flying. A third raised a chair above his head before smashing it against Copper Chain's back, laying him flat.

Jimpkins pushed the chair-wielding man back with one arm while ripping the chair away with the other. "Spare the fitments!" he shouted, his knee smashing into Mustachio's face who was rooting under the table for the dropped knife.

Thane was on his feet as soon as the brawl began.

"Get your things," he urged. Mierrle, saucer-eyed, stared at the fight until Thane shook her shoulder. "Quick," he barked. She blinked and turned toward him. Elorah's attention was also on the fight, her hand clutched near her collarbone. Thane reached across and thumped her shoulder. "You, too." Her head swiveled toward him, and she nodded, grabbing her pack, satchel, and staff case. Mierrle's attention came unstuck from the commotion, and she grabbed her rucksack. Thane turned to Haedyn. "Get your friend out of here. Use the back door." He jerked a thumb over his shoulder. "Or that." He pointed toward the trap door. "It leads either to the woods across the road or back to the river. I'd choose the woods." He looked at Aikin and gestured until Aikin hurried to Elorah's side, relieving her of her satchel and rucksack despite her protests.

The group were almost through the rear door, Thane leading the way, by the time Haedyn, still foggy from the drink, looked at Rachmyn. Anger flashed in his friend's eyes, as he jerked his chin toward the back door. They ran to it.

The door opened into a dim hallway. Thane sprinted to a door at the far end and flung it open, the rest following him out.

Once outside, the group scrambled toward the stable before pulling up short.

Every horse had been cut loose from the hitching pole. A pair of bucket-hoofed Venderres cropped at the grass in sway-backed leisure, but the rest, including the three Thane had procured, were gone.

"Looks like someone's trying to keep us here," Thane said, surveying the scene.

"Why would someone do this?" asked Elorah.

They didn't have to wait long for the answer. Behind them, five mounted men, dressed in black and wearing twisted headwraps, came thundering around the corner. They pulled up their horses in a semi-circle facing the back door and drew their swords.

"Zenzae," Thane murmured, turning wide-eyed toward Haedyn and Rachmyn.

"Spunk." Rachmyn spat. The Zenzae always meant trouble. Haedyn reached for his knife, preparing for whatever was about to happen. Rachmyn grabbed his arm and squeezed. "Not the time," he gritted. Haedyn desisted.

Thane signaled for the group to follow as he bent low, clutching his rucksack to his chest, and rollicked toward a clump of sand willow.

Behind the shrub yawned an opening into the bankside, and they all burrowed into it like feral creatures going to ground.

It was a tunnel, not much wider than a man's span, smelling of dank earth and river rot. As he crawled inside, Haedyn felt a tickle against his chest, and he pressed until his grynt's wings went still.

"We'll have to hope no one else uses this," Thane whispered as he eased his head past the entrance for a look. A passing shadow sent him scrambling backward, and he crashed into Aikin.

"Get off me," Aikin rumbled, shoving Thane away.

"Wolf," Thane hissed. Both men backpedaled, Thane squeezing up tight against Aikin.

Haedyn hiccupped a laugh, and Rachmyn walloped his arm before leveling his gaze at the two. "The wolf's with me."

Thane's head swiveled. "Pardon?"

"The wolf's with me." The words hung in the air before Rachmyn spoke again. "He'll do you no harm, but I can't say the same for anyone else who happens near."

Thane's gaze flicked between the wolf standing like a sentry beyond the opening and the echoing darkness leading back to the alehouse.

Aikin shoved Thane again, setting him on his rear with a muffled thump then squinted into the tunnel's blackness, his legs folding, his arms bracing his upper half away from the mud-slicked floor. He stayed in the half-crouch for a long moment as if debating his options before crawling toward the alehouse, putting distance between himself and the rest. He plunked onto his backside and scooted against the wall, shooting a wary glare at the scar-faced man.

Elorah reached out and clasped Mierrle's hands, giving them a little shake as she nodded at her friend.

Warmth ran through Haedyn, a wide smile bursting onto his face. He glanced toward Rachmyn, staring hard past his wolf into the gray-black night, as if by sheer force of will, he could make the shadows reveal their secrets. It was a look Haedyn had seen too many times. His smile vanished. *If only Rachmyn could enjoy life a little,* he thought, leaning back against the cool damp of the tunnel wall. He thought about the Zenzae and their sudden appearance. He still had enough about him to know the Zenzae were always to be avoided, and he reckoned this was as good a spot as any to lay low. His gaze went to Elorah, his heart a sudden lump blocking his throat. Even in the dark, she seemed to glow with some ineffable light. All other thoughts fled as he dwelt on that curiosity. She looked over and a thrill ran through him. He'd hidden in plenty of stinking holes but never with such charming company.

This will suit, he thought, a smile returning to his face.

BY ORDER OF—

—His Most Exalted, Geldizian Rennesseau, let it hereby be known that any maran adjudged to have aided, abetted, or participated with the Zenzae or their affiliates in acts of murder, mayhem, or malicious mischief shall be subject to imprisonment and/or death, as determined by a magistrate of the High Court in service to the Crown. Furthermore, let it be known that such punishment as is deemed appropriate shall be carried out with all due speed and vigor as a means for preserving the peace.

—*Canon of Magisterial Law,* Volume Ten, Section 14, Page 132

LET US SPEAK NOW

...of that time before the breaking up of the powers, when the Souls of Noble Beginning existed wholly within the All by virtue of concordant vibration, that perfect balance which is aptly deemed the Original State. During this time, known and recorded as the Age of All Knowledge, those deeds and creations which are now accorded as myth were common experience. It is only when disharmony arose, and souls moved away from that perfect state, that imbalances leading inevitably to disease, to discord, to disaster, separated them from their divine beginnings.

Thus, it was that vibrational centers—the so-called parambeks—were created to correct these imbalances within and without the mortal forms of incarnate souls. Moreover, as individual souls became increasingly unbalanced, so too did Eolemar, through an accumulation of dissonant energies, as can be seen in the disruptions to those patterns of weather, of wind, of water, and the like, upon which manifest entities depend. We, as founders of the realm, through a desire to create a more perfect union between souls and the ambient influences in which they move, did create these centers, one for each subtle energy force, to correct the increasing vibrational discord within individuals as well as within their surrounding spheres.

For a time, these centers did much good, fortifying and perfecting the vibrations of souls by removing that which is best described as dross. Alack, there remained a resistant faction that persistently endeavored to misappropriate the concentrative aspects of these purification centers for selfish gain, a perversion which threatened the stability of the whole, and so, all but one were obscured until such time when souls had matured to a better understanding of that which empowers them. Accordingly, knowledge regarding these gateways was purposely hidden from common consciousness, while the physical constructions were shrouded in the form of that which are called ruins.

These centers, and the energies which they perfect, comprise the Way, that etheric pathway toward Oneness inscribed in the ancient tomes. Profound understanding of the underlying principles of harmonic vibration in conjunction with purposeful implementation of the corresponding parambek, is integral to the rejuvenation of a misaligned soul, and more widely, a misaligned world.

Accordingly, until such time as the Way is at last made manifest, we remain ever vigilant, bound to these esoteric dismantlements until that day when the last Erynvor, through belief and unity, has found and returned each of the five ensnared Founders' Infinite Eyes, those missing connectors that, when rightly placed, will unlock the long-closed doors shuttering these arcane gateways. We pray for that great and glorious Restoration, when every soul, and indeed, every created thing is returned to their Original State. Until that time, we remain steadfast in our commitment to protect and preserve the Way.

We, the Elect, have spoken.

CHAPTER TWENTY-THREE
THE CLOUDS OF DOUBT

Brynz ran and ran, her ears attuned to the whiss of displacing air as she hurtled forward, her feet skimming light across the ground. The guard had stayed with her for three rods before the pound of his footsteps slowed and slowed again then faded entirely, leaving only the sound of the wind and her breath and her own flying feet. Still, she ran on, driven forward by blinded love—and blinded fear—for Zell. Around her, the wind shifted and shoved, pushing her on when her own limbs tired.

It wasn't enough. Zell was nowhere to be seen.

How had he flown? It was impossible. Her mind churned the word as she ran.

Impossible Impossible Impossible.

Impossible.

But he had.

The festival grounds were far behind by the time she came to a halt, hot tears streaming down her wind-rouged cheeks, her nose dripping snot onto her upper lip. She dragged her forearm across her face, her tunic sleeve coming away smeared with wet. She'd unmoored herself from her life in the most conspicuous way possible with no idea what came next. Despair gripped her chest, squeezing her breath out in wracking gasps.

Where was Zell? Where had he gone?

Questions flew inside her head like storm-scattered birds, and it was several long moments before she was able to focus on her current situation. She was a fugitive. If she went back, she would lose her position. More likely, she would be placed in a thiefkeep for sedition, or even put to death as an enemy of the Monarch. If she ran but ended up caught, her punishment would be even more severe than if she turned herself in. None of the choices appealed; running seemed the best of a bad lot.

She looked down at her clothes. The hated chest piece was the first to go, flung off into the brush. The rest would have to go too, as soon as she found something else to wear. She ran a hand through the snaggy tumble of her hair. It also needed shed. She wanted rid of everything from her previous life because she knew she could never go back, a thought both terrifying and surreal.

She'd thought often about setting Zell free over the past three moons, spending most of her waking time entertaining dreamy thoughts of returning the gryphon to the austere rock ledges of Cyrulian Kalt. Always the idea of defying the monarch and liberating her charge had brought a subversive thrill. Never once had she envisioned the disaster that unfolded. Now Zell was injured and worse, set loose in an unfamiliar and potentially dangerous area. In trying to protect him, she'd put her charge squarely in harm's way. Her culpability in his current predicament was a devastating blow, but the only thing she could do was to move forward and try to fix the terrible mess she'd made.

She was in a wooded glen, surrounded by unfamiliar sounds and smells. Pinekin trees towered over her, their needles a crunching carpet beneath her feet. She craned her neck, trying to get her bearings.

"Kark!" boomed a deep voice. She jumped, a scream leaping into her throat, but before it could be set free, she was smashed from behind with overwhelming strength.

Unnnnnph

She fell forward, her face embedding in the thick underlayment, sharp needles ramming up her nose and into her eyes.

Spluttering, she lifted her head, her fingers clawing away stiff prickles when a metallic glint sliced forward, followed by the icy feel of a blade against her throat.

"Kark," the voice said again, with a rumbling laugh. The blade moved back as a huge hand grasped the nape of her neck and lifted, forcing her to scramble to her feet.

Brynz strained her eyes backward, trying to see her attacker without moving her head. She flicked her gaze forward, her heart hammering in her chest, as a hulking form approached.

It was a man, taller than she by at least three hands, with limbs as stout as tree trunks. The grip on her neck pushed her forward, out of the shadows and into the moonlight. She brought her hand to her forehead and squinted into the gloom.

"What do you want with me?" she asked, her voice surprisingly strong. 'Who are you?"

The blade swung round to hover near her throat.

Around her, guttural voices barked unfamiliar words from some unknown language. The blade shifted and a warm tickle traced down her neck.

The figure bellowed, "FOONK! HOWLK! Mraf flep KWRARG!"

The knife pulled back slightly, allowing Brynz to brush at the stinging line across her throat, her fingertips lingering over the slow seep at one end. The giant man stepped into the moonlight, his hand holding the chest piece she'd discarded.

"Yours?" he asked in Iellian, his accent flattening the word into an accusation.

She nodded, staring at his dirt-caked face. He had a heavy brow, a crooked nose, and deep-set eyes glittering like jewels in the dim light. Odd braids dangled from both his drab-yellow beard and long, drab-yellow hair, a few augmented with jagged teeth and hooked claws. The giant looked about her age but carried an authority that made him seem far older. He shoved the chest piece toward her and motioned for her to put it on. The knife drifted back again but remained close enough to prevent escape. Once she had the chest piece strapped into place, the man grabbed her arm and spun her around.

She was surrounded by six of these huge men, all of them fiercely countenanced. They all wore leather and had long hair adorned with braids and teeth and claws. They all smelled of dark forests, musky meat, and smoke. The leader looked younger than all but one of his band.

"Darnk," he said, and the men surrounded her. "Kwulf lel," he barked, and the men moved forward as one, marching her along as they went, their strides long, their footfalls unnaturally quiet.

She had no idea where they were headed or what the men's intentions were; she only knew she needed to find some way to escape. Wind was the only defense she could muster, and she concentrated on whipping up a turbulence. A spear thrust into her chest piece, piercing the leather and the thin tunic underneath, its tip raising a welt on the tender flesh covering her breastbone. Moonlight reflected off four hooked barbs attached in offsetting pairs at the top of the wooden shaft beneath the spearhead.

"No," the leader warned in his accented Iellian, his eyes hard. She tamped down the rounding wind, the swirling column of pinekin needles and dirt settling back to ground. He pulled the spear point away and swung it forward, his face a warning.

Her mind raced. She'd heard of these barbed spears. The Drasgor were named for them—*dras* for the weapon, *gor* for their use. Even she, with her limited knowledge of the wider world beyond the cages and stalls of the Royal Stables knew of the dras and the scars they left behind. Garrod's left foot had been deformed by one, a souvenir of his time with the Special Forces. He'd told her, when she'd asked, the dras had gone through his foot and into the barrel of his mount, gutting the poor horse as it ran, bringing them both down with a single shot. Garrod had managed to hack himself free and hobble away, dragging his damaged foot. His horse had not been as fortunate.

Drasgor. The word sent a chill through her. Blood-thirsty barbarians of the north. How had she gotten herself captured by a band of the notorious warriors? She didn't know where she was, but she was sure she was far south of their usual border, accepted to be the northern slopes of the Blackshale Mountains. How had they gotten past the Iellian guards stationed at every pass leading into the Basin? What were they doing here? And why were they interested in her?

She struggled to keep pace as the men broke into a ground-eating trot, their arms swinging in scything strokes. The muscles in her legs and arms burned, and she stumbled several times, her tired mind railing at her leaden feet. After what seemed like hours, they entered a clearing. The leader stopped and held up his hand. The party halted around her. Brynz bent over, clutching her side. She'd never run as far as she had this night, and her legs felt as if they were melting. It took all she had not to collapse as she sucked in air that burned like fire.

Around her, the Drasgor checked their multitude of weapons— short-handled knives in sheaths tied to thighs and lower legs, longer-handled knives in scabbards tied to belts, leather-pouched stone slings, and single-edged axes dangling from hips. All the men toted tubular carriers angling from hip to shoulder across their backs, the wooden shaft of a dras sticking high enough for easy access. The whispered *swith* of metal being removed from leather then reinserted raised the hairs on Brynz's neck, tightening her nerves until her teeth were on edge. Around her, an oppressive calm had settled, as if even the trees stood in frightened awe of these monstrous fighting men.

Once done, the men formed up around Brynz and set out across the clearing at a brisk walk, a man-knot of gargantuan might bundling forward with Brynz at its core. The men kept watch as they moved along, their legs like great hammers striking the ground with soundless power. By contrast, Brynz's footsteps sounded thunderous, crunching creaks piercing the quiet as she clubbed forward on her faltering legs.

The group continued for what seemed an eternity until the first notes of birdsong caromed off the trees, signaling that morning, still a meager promise hovering grimly at the horizon, would soon be upon them. Brynz's feet and legs, long since numb, shook like a new colt's by the time they stopped. It was a wonder they held her upright.

They stood in a copse of snaggled trees on a high bluff overlooking a wide river. Brynz believed they'd been following a northeasterly heading throughout the night, putting them on course for the Inirian highlands and the Blackshale Mountains. She wondered whether Zell was following a similar course, but her thoughts were cut short when the leader gave a nod, and one of the men grabbed her hands and pulled them behind her back.

A second man drew his knife and pointed it at her chest. She winced as her wrists were tied together, the rope biting into her flesh. A sudden jerk sent her scrambling backwards. The first man pulled her toward a nearby tree where a third man heaved a rope up and over a high limb. The first man held her tight while the third tied her bound wrists to the rope then pulled back to crank her arms upward. Meanwhile, the second man secured the rope's other end to a large stone set some ways behind her. She was well and truly trussed with no way to move or even sit without pulling her arms out of socket. Her only choice was to remain upright and pray her wobbling legs held out.

"Stay," the leader said, as if she had any choice.

Five of the men, including the leader, drew their weapons and disappeared into the surrounding woods. One stayed behind to keep watch. He leaned against a tree and folded his arms across his chest, his brutal features shadowed by the shifting light. Brynz felt the cold traction of his dark eyes as he stared at her, his lips drawn back in a half-sneer.

She looked skyward, gauging the rope. It was two fingers wide and coiled thrice around the limb. There was no escaping its torsional grip.

Over and above the ache of the rest of her muscles, her shoulders and upper arms knifed pain up her neck and into her head from their pose. Her throat was dry, her lips stiff and cracked. Her red patches burned and itched at the same time, especially the one on her side while the sweat along her back chilled beneath her tunic, sending a shiver through her already shaking body. Her entirety was a complexion of burning, itching, freezing, and aching, and she closed her eyes against the misery.

"Hrul," the large man said. She opened her eyes. He was pointing a meaty finger at himself before pointing it toward her. When she didn't react, he banged his thumb against his chest and repeated, "Hrul," before leaning forward and pointing at her again.

"My name? Is that what you're asking?"

He thrust the pointing finger closer.

"Brynz," she breathed, hoping it would satisfy him.

"Brinzzz. Brinzzz. Brinzzz," he droned, his grumbling voice turning her name into an odd buzzing noise. He nodded then leaned back against the tree, folding his bulging arms across his chest, his bark-colored hair shagging forward to cover the fronts of his shoulders.

Brynz closed her eyes again. If only she hadn't gone against the monarch. Against Garrod, come to it. But that would have meant abandoning Zell to his fate, and that was also untenable. Despite how things had turned out, knowing Zell was now free sparked a tiny flame of comfort inside, and she clung onto it for all she was worth.

The next time Brynz opened her eyes, she was being freed from the pinioning rope and wrist shackles. She sank to the ground in utter exhaustion and rubbed her dented skin to restore the circulation.

The leader knelt and shook her shoulder then pushed a waterskin against her lips and tipped it up. She gulped down three mouthfuls before he pulled the waterskin back and shoved a chunk of pith into the top.

"Enough," he said, then after a moment, "Brinzzz."

"Brynz," she corrected, shortening the ending consonant to the barest tick against the back of her teeth. The leader seemed not to notice.

"Brinzzz," he said again, then clapped a closed fist to his chest. "Uhnkre."

"Unn-kraw," she repeated.

He shook his head. "Uhnkre."

"Oon-kre," she said. He nodded, satisfied.

"What do you want with me?" The words tumbled out in a rush.

Uhnkre cocked his head, his eyes a curious mixture of violet and gold in the morning light. He pointed at her chest. "This."

She looked down at the stamped leather. "This?"

He picked up a nearby branch, pointed it at her chest piece then broke it across his knee.

"You want to break this?" She thumbed the leather protector forward. He nodded. "You can have it," she said, moving to unstrap it.

He grabbed her hands and shook his head, forcing her to stop, then let loose and stood. He raised his arms and spun a half turn. "Break all..." He pointed at the Iellian crest. "...this."

"You mean Iellia?"

"Yes. Iellia."

"You want to break Iellia?" Her voice betrayed her disbelief.

He nodded. "Break Iellia."

"What does that have to do with me?"

He pointed at the gryphon in the crest then at the eastern sky. "High Iellia."

"Me?" she squeaked. "I'm a servant." His gaze remained level. "I'm not high Iellian. I am only in service there. You understand?" He continued to stare. She made a few hand movements to pantomime being a servant then gave up. "Not High," she said, raising her hand and shaking her head. "Low." She dropped her hand to the forest floor. "Very low."

"You..." He held out his two hands, one forward, one back, then shifted them to the opposite pose. "...trade."

"What?"

"You..." He made the motion again. "...trade."

"You want to trade me?"

"Yes."

"You think you can break Iellia by trading me?" She laughed at the absurdity of the idea.

"Foonk!" he bellowed, stunning her into silence. "No trade..." He sliced his thumb across his neck, his eyes like daggers. Brynz apprehended his meaning.

"Trade, yes." she babbled, one hand reaching up to her abraded neck.

"Trade Brynz. Break Iellia."

"Break Iellia," she agreed, trying to sound as if she believed it could happen.

"Yes." He unstopped the waterskin and handed it to her. She took two swallows before he reclaimed it.

He signaled to one of the men, who brought over two dead hares, handing one to Uhnkre and dropping the other into her lap. Uhnkre motioned for her to eat, but she could only stare down at the jelly shine of the hare's unseeing eye.

She startled as he reached out and twisted the hare onto its back, exposing its gutted underside before flopping it onto its side. He motioned again for her to eat. She lifted the hare, trying not to gag. He snorted then seized the carcass, stripping off its pelt before dropping it back into her lap. He peeled his own and took a large bite from its hind. She closed her eyes and forced herself to take a half-hearted nibble, imagining she was Zell and not herself. It almost worked until her stomach heaved.

Uhnkre snatched the hare from her grasp, a look of scorn on his face as if she'd failed some test and strode away. He grunted at Hrul, who heaved himself up from the log he was using as a seat. Uhnkre jerked his thumb toward Brynz and Hrul, his face shiny with grease, wandered over to take up his watch position against the tree. Any thoughts she had of escaping vanished when he pulled a knife from a scabbard at his waist and began to whittle at his horn-like fingernails. Instead, she crumpled to the forest floor, hugged her knees, and tried not to cry.

CHAPTER TWENTY-FOUR

CRYSTALWOOD SEEKS ITS OWN

Rachmyn checked his pocket for his shard. Yes, there it was. He thumbed its familiar smoothness as he stared out at the brightening day.

It hadn't taken long for the others to fall asleep including Elgre and the spunking bird. Only Rachmyn had remained awake, ready should trouble arise.

Haedyn slumped against the opposite wall, his eyes half-closed, his mouth half-open. It amazed Rachmyn how easily his friend found sleep no matter the circumstance. Rachmyn required a settled mind first, and right now his thoughts were far from settled. They had a decision to make, and it weighed heavily upon him. He already knew Haedyn's feelings, but ultimately it rested on Rachmyn to decide whether to throw in with Elorah or go their separate ways. The idea of leaving Haedyn was not even a thought to be explored, akin to contemplating hacking off his own leg. Unthinkable.

He was inclined to say no, his instincts telling him there would only be trouble, but then there was his shard, which even now quivered beneath his thumb when he thought about what to do. Was that reason enough to swerve from doing what was prudent, namely returning to the Lawless Mountains? His gut told him it was not.

Then there was the matter of who was leading this adventure. Since the death of his parents, Rachmyn had always made the decisions and set the course for Haedyn and himself. What did this Elorah know about surviving when you had only your wits and your mettle to rely on? Precious little, he would guess. Then again, there was something about her and her quest he couldn't easily dismiss. His mind drifted back to Oru Fen. How had she found him there? How had she known his mother's words—*to my heart you are family.* But he couldn't allow that to make his decision.

Even in the tunnel's dim light, it was easy to see the naivete of most of his companions. It lay fresh upon them like morning dew. The scar-faced man had perhaps a bit more guile than the rest but was still worryingly soft where it counted. Hardly the group one would pick to take into the wildlands unless one planned not to return. Only Haedyn, despite appearances at present, was someone he knew was tough as hammered iron. With him Rachmyn could face anything but the rest? The rest were like clay. As apt to crack as to cure under the heat of adversity.

No. That would be his answer. It was the only answer he could give under the circumstances. The warmth inside disappeared, replaced by cold resolve. He would tell her as soon as she awakened. No sense waiting.

Elorah's eyes opened, and she gave him a small smile. "Thank you," she murmured.

"For what?" he asked. Her smile widened, as if she knew something about him he didn't know himself. She turned to look out the opening.

"Does he have a name?" she asked, gazing at the recumbent wolf.

"Elgre," he said.

"Guardian."

Rachmyn looked at her in surprise. *Elgre* in Gaen did translate as guardian, but more accurately, it was the word for a lifetime pledge of unselfish protection to another. Only a Shadowen would know that. Or someone familiar with the ancient language spoken by Shadowen peoples around their campfires and in their caravans. Gaen was handed down from generation to generation as a birthright, as much a part of Shadowen life as dreamcrafting and charms.

The no that had seemed so certain a moment before began to waver, a haze of fascination clouding his thoughts.

"He is devoted to you," she said, nodding as if she understood the complex meaning of the wolf's name. Her eyes shifted toward Haedyn. "As you are to each other."

The odd vibration beneath Rachmyn's thumb gained momentum as his mind swayed away from logic and toward her cause.

"I admire that," she said.

Haedyn stirred as his bird crawled out of his pocket. Rachmyn shoulder-nudged his friend, and he awakened with a groan.

"Whaa?" he mumbled, straightening his back.

"Mind your bird," Rachmyn prompted, his head bobbing toward Haedyn's chest.

"Don't I always?" Rachmyn's lips flattened as Haedyn beamed a smile at Elorah. He turned back. "We're going, right?"

Rachmyn flexed his jaw, his mind working through the choices, his lips nearly invisible.

"Right?" Haedyn pressed, his voice rising.

Rachmyn glanced at Thane. His eyebrows arched above his closed lids. Feigning sleep. That maran was one to watch. "All right," Rachmyn agreed, removing his hand from his pocket.

"Yes," Haedyn whisper-shouted, balling up his fist and shaking it twice.

"Wonderful," Elorah said.

"That took long enough." Thane opened an eye, then smiled at Rachmyn's annoyed scowl.

"What say you, Thane?" Haedyn leaned forward. "Still planning your escape?"

Thane stretched. "I suppose going north wouldn't be the worst choice. There's opportunities everywhere for someone who knows where to look." His gaze locked on Rachmyn's face as he gave a knowing nod. Rachmyn narrowed his eyes. He got the distinct impression this fellow was referring to his speck, and he was glad Thane was here and not poking around by the dock. Alliari's moony face popped into Rachmyn's mind. *It's best we keep this between us.* Anger flared at the shiftless fraud. If this opportunist knew, how many others also knew?

Even more reason he and Haedyn needed away from this wretched basin.

The copper-haired man stretched and blearily looked around. "What happened?" he said, his voice craggy with sleep. The dark-haired girl opened her eyes.

The grynt drew itself up and bobbed its blinded head. Rachmyn gave Haedyn a warning look, and he pressed the top of the bird's head to settle it.

"Now that we're all awake, I say we crawl out of this bowel and find something to eat," Thane said. "Duntin Town's only a stone's throw from here."

"What about the—" Elorah began.

Thane cut her off. "Long gone, I'm sure."

"How do you know?"

"Because the Zenzae always arrive in a rush and leave in a hurry."

"Elbows for toes," Rachmyn muttered to Haedyn.

"Pardon?" Thane leaned forward, his head cocking.

"Elbows for toes," Rachmyn repeated without further explanation. Confusion creased Thane's face.

Haedyn smiled. "He thinks you're talking rubbish."

Thane's eyes narrowed into a calculated stare.

"I'll have a look," Elorah said, propping herself forward onto her hands. "Provided Elgre approves of course." She smiled at Rachmyn who gave her a nod.

The copper-haired man got onto his hands and knees. "No, let me," he huffed, crawling past Elorah toward the opening. She harrumphed as his bulk forced her onto her heels.

Elgre raised his head, his hackles rising, his upper lip lifting to reveal his teeth.

Aikin paused. "He won't attack, will he?"

"One way to find out," Rachmyn replied, his gaze level.

"Aikin," Elorah said. "Please. This isn't some contest."

"Rachmyn can see without going anywhere," Haedyn said, his golden eyes twinkling.

Rachmyn inwardly groaned. A peering did seem a good idea, but he neither needed nor wanted an audience.

Haedyn motioned toward Aikin. "Have a seat. This might take a while."

Aikin dropped onto his haunches as Rachmyn closed his eyes and with a thought, was away from his form and into Oru Fen, Spectra beside him, The Running Fox beneath his feet. A quick scan showed no sign of the Zenzae. Another thought and he was inside the alehouse. Aside from the fight's wreckage and Jimpkins wandering around with one hand clamped atop his head, there was little of interest.

Spectra rammed her forehead against the back of his leg, propelling him out of the alehouse, high enough to give a wide view of the countryside.

The High Road ribboned off to the north, and he followed it for several leagues before wheeling away, making a wide circle above a patchworked landscape of fields and trees and winding brooks. Other than a single patrol of guards, he saw nothing to hinder them. Satisfied, he retraced his astral trail and slipped inside his reclining body.

He opened his eyes.

"That was fast!" Haedyn clapped Rachmyn on the shoulder.

Rachmyn got to his feet. "There's a patrol to the north. We can avoid them if we stay off the High Road."

"How do you know that?" Aikin asked.

"He's done the peering," Thane replied. "Shadowen have a way of seeing what the rest of us can't."

Aikin looked queasy as he swallowed hard.

Rachmyn crouch-walked out of the tunnel, heading for the dock, Elgre at his heels. Haedyn caught up while the rest strung along behind. After dragging out their hidden gear, Rachmyn turned to Elorah. "I assume you know where we're going?" he asked, patting his rucksack to ensure the speck box was at the bottom before shrugging the straps onto his shoulders. He picked up his walking staff.

"All the books say Therrania lies on Whitemond. That's where we must go," she said, her expression fervent.

"Books with maps I assume," Thane said.

"No maps." Elorah said as if maps were of no consequence.

"But you do have a book," Thane persisted.

Elorah shook her head. "No books either." She leveled a steely stare at him.

"You mean, we're relying on a memory of an interpretation of books you don't possess?"

Despite his lingering distrust, Rachmyn couldn't disagree with Thane's skepticism.

"Not just a memory. This," she said, pulling the crystalwood staff out of its case and thrusting it toward the sky. Even in the pale morning light, it shone brightly. Aikin blanched, and Elorah shot him a defiant look. "This staff belonged to my father, and to his father before him, both renowned crystalwood craftsmen who journeyed to Whitemond, and brought back much of the crystalwood in use today." She lifted the staff above her head and spun in a slow circle. "Crystalwood always seeks its own. If we listen, it will lead us to its homeland."

"You mean, that has a memory like a person has?" Aikin asked.

Elorah looked at him. "Of course."

"But—"

"How else could it hold such a magnificent store of vorik for such a long period of time?" she asked. "If it had no memory, it would be like any other artifact."

"But the Council banned—"

"In the wrong hands, yes, a staff such as this can be dangerous. But in the right hands, it is a powerful tool for good. The loudest voices aren't always the wisest."

Aikin's eyes shifted sideways, his lips bending toward his clefted chin. "In the right hands..." he said to himself.

"After you." Rachmyn swept his hand forward.

Elorah held the staff in both hands, closed her eyes for a moment then nodded. She put it back into its case and started off, her step quick and sure, Mierrle beside her. Aikin followed close behind, his expression thoughtful. Rachmyn exchanged a look with Haedyn before they fell in behind leaving Thane to bring up the rear.

"I still don't think this is a good idea," Thane muttered. Rachmyn turned as the scarred man's gaze bounced across the chop of the gray-green Wydderhalle.

"No one said you had to come," he reminded.

Thane turned from the river, his broad smile never reaching his eyes. "Let's resolve to be friends. I believe you'll find we have much in common."

"I assure you we do not," Rachmyn ground out.

Haedyn snorted a laugh as he transferred Fryk to his shoulder, the fist-sized raptor bobbing in time with its master's jaunty walk. Thane shot him a look. "Elbows for toes never goes far with him. Might as well know that now," Haedyn said before laughing again.

Elorah and the group had been walking for several hours, making a wide loop around Duntin Town and the villages of Florian and Haddle. It occurred to her how little she knew about her own district. She'd never been to the town or the villages. She'd only ever been to Berrets Town, an easy distance from her family's witterang and to Cragermore where the harvest crops were sold. Beyond that, the Calliaigh district was as much a mystery to her as the Northern Passage. Ten years at the Academie had given her a deep understanding of Therran vor but had also left her woefully ignorant of her own birthplace.

After Rachmyn's peering, they'd avoided the High Road as they continued north, skirting stone-fenced pastures and plowed fields. As Elorah listened to the twittering of unseen birds and the scampering of unseen animals, Therrania and Grogauk returned to her mind, the vorestone pulsing like a second heartbeat, the crystalwood staff humming against her back.

Rachmyn and Haedyn had gravitated to the front, flanking her as the group moved forward. Mierrle and Thane traipsed behind with Aikin acting as the rearguard.

As they approached woods, a sudden jolt beneath her feet snapped Elorah out of her reverie. She looked down but saw nothing other than dry leaves and fallen branches. A second unnerving vibration traced through the ground, and the staff's humming silenced while her pendant cooled. She stopped, her nerves tingling.

"What's wrong?" Haedyn asked, scanning their surroundings as he fumbled Fryk into his vest pocket.

"I don't know... Something's happening..." A third jolt blasted beneath her feet.

ffffwwwwwoooooosh fwoosh fwop Fwop FWOP FWOP

A mass of thorny green branches exploded from the rosebush in front of her, barbed canes whipping up and out in every direction. She scrabbled back, barely keeping her feet. The rest retreated in a ragged line, gaping as rugose brambles knitted into a towering hedgerow that stretched to the horizons, its canes erupting with razored thorns and rapier leaves, its swollen buds exploding into blood-red blooms the size of platters.

Elorah forced her attention to the unnatural vibrations beneath her feet. Vorik, a great deal of it, was pumping through the rootweave beneath the leaf-strewn ground. Her mind burrowed into the loamy dirt until she was surrounded by flowing energy. There was a familiarity about it that stretched her mind to its corners, searching for what or who it could be. She felt the crispness of the energy's flow, the precision of its modulation, the tight concentration of its deployment. This was the work of a supremely skilled vorician. A master whose vorecraft was without error or waste, so focused that the vor used would have minimal consequences for its creator. Over the last several moons, Headmistress Malenvie had been tutoring her on how to channel her own vor into a powerbeam such as this, but she had never come anywhere close to this level of proficiency. She paused. There was something else, a dark thread coiling around the vorik beam like a stranglevine, pushing its own black intention into the mix. The shattered orb burst into her thoughts like a warning.

A shocking realization sucked the air from Elorah's chest. The Head must be the originator of this superlative vorik display. But not just the Headmistress. As she parsed the energy, she could feel the desperate tendrils of her own mother's Therran vor undergirding the Head's amplifying force. It seemed impossible the two would be working together against her, trying to force her to turn back, but her senses told her that was the case. Her mother's pained face flashed into Elorah's mind and her vision went misty, remorse constricting her throat. But what had the Head used to find her? Then Elorah remembered. She stuck her hand into her tunic pocket and retrieved the berre ear.

"Watch out," Haedyn cried, pulling her back a blink before a thorny cane slashed past, barely missing her face. The ear dropped from her hand as she scuttled backward.

"Elorah!" Mierrle screamed as she took off toward her friend. Thane grabbed her arm. "Let me go!" she cried, struggling against his restraining grip.

Aikin leaped forward and assumed the Correan Vee handshape. He pointed his tented fingers at the hedgerow, his eyes grimly focused until a sizzling void began to form. Writhing canes blackened then fell away, spitting off crumbling red petals as they collapsed. Like a wounded beast the hedge clawed out, its long, spiked branches flinging toward Aikin over and over until one managed to strike a foot. With vicious precision, the canes homed in, coiling themselves around an ankle and yanking him off his feet. He gave a loud cry as he fell flat onto his back, his head striking hard against the ground. More canes snaked out, wrapping first around his legs and then around his torso, his struggling efforts doing little to halt their trussing capture. Widening circles of red blossomed beneath the thorns' cruel bite as they daggered through his woolen pants and into his flesh, pulling him toward the slashing churn of frenzied canes.

"Aikin!" Elorah cried, starting toward him.

Haedyn jumped in front. "No! Go back!" he commanded, his hands shepherding her toward the others as green growth erased the void Aikin had created.

"Shifting stars, what manner of bewycchement is this?" Rachmyn breathed.

"Don't move!" Haedyn pulled out his red-bladed knife and plunged forward, hacking at the writhing foliage, bilious smoke spiraling into the air.

Aikin grappled and tore at the imprisoning canes, groaning as the thorns dug deeper. Only after several more swings from Haedyn's blade was he able to free himself and dog-crawl away. Haedyn sheathed his knife and thrust out his hand, giving a mighty pull when Aikin grabbed on to lever himself upright. The pair sprinted several paces to where the rest were standing, their mouths dropped open in horrified disbelief.

Elorah clutched her vorestone as her mind cried out to the Urslan

Sisters for help. A terrific roar filled the air, and the ground gave a mighty quake, the group wobbling like jackpegs.

It all happened in the blink of an eye. Two hillocks rose from the flat of a nearby pasture, the stones of a fence noisily tumbling away down their lengthening sides. A weathered stock-gate splintered from the strain, ragged pieces of board scattering like matchsticks. The sod split into a tortoiseshell mosaic of damp brown and ocher-tipped green as the hillocks continued skyward.

Atop one, a huge, half-dead tree buckled, the herd of Plynton cattle beneath making a bawling run down the steepening slope a moment before the snag crashed to ground.

On the second hillock, the long branchlets of a jewelberry patch swayed upon its burgeoning front, forming a cascade of shiny green.

With another thundering *BOOOOM*, eight stout legs pulled up from the substrate, one at each corner, wrenching the hillocks out of the soil and thrusting them still higher. At the same time, the rounded head of a bear pushed its way out from the top of each.

"Sodding hell..." Rachmyn's mouth dropped open, and he looked down at Elgre pinned against his leg. The wolf took off, loping toward the seething hedge, his lips curled back in a snarl. Rachmyn's gaze followed the wolf's run for a moment before turning back to watch the spectacle of heaving dirt.

"Woooaaaah!" Haedyn exclaimed, his voice getting louder as the hillocks took shape.

"The Urslan!" Aikin shouted above the din, his eyes wide with terrified wonder.

"Fleek me, there's two!" Thane cried, his scar bleaching white as the color drained from his face.

Mierrle's mouth moved, but no sound came out as she gaped at the emerging behemoths.

The snouts of both bear heads opened revealing jagged rocks arrayed like teeth, while packed-dirt antlers pushed up and out from between the rounding ears. The bears roared in tandem, an ear-splitting sound that sent the group to the ground, flattened by a wind that smelled of freshly-turned loam. The hedgerow bent beneath the bears' tremendous breath before springing high again.

The gargantuan legs broke free, and the behemoths charged, running straight at the thrashing hedge. The group vaulted to their feet, fleeing like ants before the lumbering bear-hills, their arms flailing in a vain attempt to stay upright as the Urslan pounded past, the *kerPOW kerPOW kerPOW* of their giant paws shaking the ground with every stride. The undulations threw the group onto their knees and faces and backsides as the mighty pair slammed into the hedge, its tightly laced brambles no match for their overwhelming bulk. Writhing canes ripped free, snarling into the sedgegrass blanketing the Urslans' sides. The massive bears rambled on, long streamers of bramblecane flapping from their huge bodies as they went. Behind them, a pair of massive openings marked their passage through the hedge even as a furious flush of bright green growth began pushing its way into the holes.

As soon as the openings appeared, Elorah sprang up and ran toward them, her gear slapping against her back. "Come on!" she shouted. "That's our way through!" The rest scrambled upright and followed her lead.

Elgre was already there, looking at the gaps as if he'd always expected them. The wolf darted through the closest one, the group sprinting hard to follow him.

They hit the holes at a dead run, their heads ducked down, their hands paddling to knock back the canes already stringing their way across the openings. It only helped a little. Briars slapped and snagged and sliced as the group fought their way through, tearing their clothing and leaving long bleeding lines on their arms and necks and legs and faces.

On the other side, the Urslan were mangling their way forward, a swath of destruction trailing behind them like a wide, ugly tail, the sounds of crashing and splintering and roaring louder than thunder. The group followed in the giant bears' wake, picking their way around broken trees, uprooted shrubs, and deep ruts for the better part of a league before reaching the edge of a large clearing where the wreckage gave way to a meadow. In the center sat two peaceful-looking knolls, separated by a narrow swale of tender grass, a formation of rocks something like a crown, topping each. There was no sign of the rioting

Urslan. It was as if the enormous twins had vanished into the sun-bright air.

"Where'd they go?" asked Mierrle.

Elorah looked behind and marveled. Where there had been destruction, there was now green meadow and colorful wildflowers, all looking as if they'd always been there. She looked at the group around her, agog at what they'd witnessed, their faces and arms and legs striped by drying crimson. She was struck by a sudden surge of love. They were bleeding, they were bruised, but they had made it through, together. She felt more admiration for the five around her than she had ever felt for anyone, a quiet belief taking hold. Whatever lay ahead, they would face it. They would face it, and they would prevail.

Haedyn trotted up the nearest slope then came to an abrupt stop. He bent to snatch something from the grass before straightening and holding up his fist, a length of wilted bramblecane dangling from it like a tattered green ribbon. He grinned as his bird climbed out of its pocket and onto his shoulder. "I think I've found your Urslan," he said, spreading his arms out to indicate the two knolls. "It looks like they've gone to ground."

Warnings of a Wraithwolf (Excerpt Five)

CONFLICT is the ENEMY... gggrrrr... and the ALLY of CHANGE... Ggrrrff... That these TWO TRUTHS can exist at once... gggrrr... speaks to the DUALITY... ggrrr... existent WITHIN every MIND... ggrrrff... and every SPHERE... Gggrrrff... An ADEPT sees through... gggrrrrfff... this apparent DICHOTOMY... gggrrrfff... to the UNDERLYING PRINCIPLE... gggrrff... that OPPOSITE STATES... ggggrrffff... are merely DIFFERING EXPRESSIONS...   gggrrrff... of a singular CAUSE.

HEAR THIS!

It is only by DEGREES... gggrrr... that these DIFFERENCES exist... ggrrrfff... and only by APPLICATION of WILL... grrff... upon these VARIATIONS... gggrrrr... that CHANGE can be ACHIEVED.

FURTHERMORE!

It is ONLY within the MENTAL SPHERE... grrff... that one CAN and SHOULD... grrff... seek to effect CHANGE... ggrrfff... for without a preceding THOUGHT... ggrrf... there can be no MANIFESTATION... ggrrfff... in the PHYSICAL SPHERE... Gggrrff... ONLY by CHANGING the MIND ... ggrrfff... can one CHANGE the WORLD.

–Collected and Interpreted for the Most Exalted Monarch,
Geldizian Rennesseau, by a scribe

CHAPTER TWENTY-FIVE
THE GATHERING

Essiant had been anticipating this gathering for a lifetime, longer if he factored in all the previous sojourns leading to this moment. Just as it was finally time for their night-wards to join together, so too was it time for their wraithwolf guardians to form a pack.

All had made a pledge to assist this eleventh Erynvor before descending into their respective realms, though the incarnates had no waking memory of such; it would be a hindrance for them to carry that knowledge around as a constant companion. Every guardian had a crescent moon on their forehead as a sign of their promise to the Elect, and the time had come for these Voriens to make good upon that promise.

Overhead, the purpling sky glittered with a never-ending tapestry of crystalline stars, more points of light than could be counted in a thousand lifetimes. Essiant surveyed the five wraithwolves who had answered his summoning howl as they stood before him in resolute solidarity. He had known them all before, and it was with joy he'd greeted each as they'd appeared like a bright memory out of the nebulous fog occluding the horizon.

It had been the responsibility of each guardian to ensure their night-ward had gathered the necessary knowledge and experiences over their short lives to fulfill their pledge, and all had taken those duties seriously. Of course, the job was far from done, but it was well begun, and Essiant congratulated each on their tutelage thus far.

Spectra had been especially diligent in the preparation of her night-ward, knowing much would be required of him in the days and moons and annums to come. Even now, the silver-frosted wolf remained keenly alert to the dangers he faced. She still grieved the mistakes of the past, those lives that had started so promisingly only to end in calamity, and her mindwords were never far from the cautionary warnings of those blighted sojourns.

Likewise, red-gold Embren had been assiduous in the guidance of her fiery charge though he remained unaware of her influence, an intentional choice on her part. She and Spectra had crossed paths innumerable times during this latest incarnation owing to the fact their night-wards were inextricably linked, and they greeted each other with tail-wagging cheer.

Sand-colored Ajai, slender and strong, his large, pointed ears set high atop his head, stood back a little from the rest, as was his nature. Always a thoughtful observer, he was aware his timorous night-ward had yet to face the challenges that would build her courage into an unstoppable force. This too was deliberate. All packs had a hierarchy, and though it might not be apparent, every member was important, both the leaders and the followers. One could not exist without the other, and both needed the influence provided by their opposite.

Much like her night-ward, stocky, dun-brown Raya was an implacable force, unwavering in her determination to push forward no matter the circumstance. Essiant appreciated this quality far more than his night-ward did at present, for he knew more of what lay ahead. It was true Raya's charge had made his share of blunders through the eryns, but none were from a lack of conviction. Both the precision pick and the blunt instrument had their uses, and Essiant believed it wise to always have both available.

Night-black Ieeva, tall and elegantly slim, seemed the least approachable of the guardians, though Essiant knew this was far from the truth. Her mercurial night-ward's trajectory had been perhaps the most difficult to navigate, and what could be construed as cool indifference to certain tragedies had been a carefully considered allowance for self-correction. Essiant admired Ieeva's unending patience with her charge's willful mistakes. Hers was the long game and, in Essiant's view, she was playing it with consummate skill. The old adage *the past does not predict the future* was never more true than in the case of Ieeva's night-ward.

Essiant knew there were other guardians out there, working toward their common cause though they weren't gathered with him at this moment. Their time would come. For now, these Vorien League dedicants would be equal to the task at hand. The wraithwolves knew their charges faced a long stretch of challenges, any of which could prove their undoing. They'd already seen the first. The cording of the mother's wraithwolf, an unfortunate but necessary sacrifice, had preceded a mayhem of malicious Therran vorecraft. A necessary reminder that powerful forces were aligning against both the Uniter and the Vorien League. As they grew stronger in their combined efforts, so too, would their opposition.

Spectra was the first to speak, her mindwords flinging out like a gauntlet. "The time has come to shutter the griefs of the past and look forward to what lies before us. The dreams that brought us to this moment are gone as well. The future is yet to be counted, but in the now, where we exist, let us focus on the goal to which we all made our vow."

"We will be ready," Raya growled, her mindwords full of blockish assurance.

"What of the mother and her guardian?" asked Ajai, his soft brown eyes full of pity.

"The cording will remain until the mother renounces her alliance with those opposing this Erynvor. It is unfortunate for Beledal, but there is always hope for reversal," Essiant said.

Ajai blinked before nodding. A pall settled as the guardians thought about their brethren wolf and the anathema of his plight.

"It is not a failure," Essiant continued, as much to convince himself as his fellow Voriens. "We will make sure of that."

Ieeva's green-silver eyes glittered beneath the fringe of her night-black lashes. "Still, the pain of it wounds us all," she said.

"Indeed," Essiant agreed.

Embren walked over and placed a front paw atop Spectra's to signify their deep bond, but her mindwords were for the group. "We all wish it wasn't so, but it is a thing we cannot change. It is always the night-ward who decides their wraithwolf's path."

"And what of Venge and the Malvisse?" asked Ajai.

"Weakened at present but always a threat," Essiant replied.

"The Wycche still prowls," Spectra added. "And has many a Malvisse trick up her sleeve. Do not let down your guard for even a moment."

"Spectra is right. Ten times before, a Uniter has come this far only to be defeated by her cunning. Though she is weak at present, she will regain her strength soon enough. We must be prepared for that." Essiant's gaze swept across the group.

"We will be ready," Raya growled again.

Essiant allowed the dun-brown wraithwolf a small nod. The blunt instrument was already proving useful. "Most assuredly we will," he said, his confidence a visible boon to the rest.

They all straightened their stances, knowing their moment was upon them then lifted their heads and howled, long and loud, an announcement to one and all that the foretold uniting had at last begun.

Chapter Twenty-Six
Signs in the Keleekeluk

Chassa scat.

Xyleea swiped a stick at the brownish mound, scraping off the grass and leaves scuffed on top by the big cat's hind paws. She bent for a closer look.

A bone shard poked from one ashy turd like a misplaced tooth. She flipped the pile over. Six days old. Maybe seven. She looked up, searching for a fierce green stare, finding instead the round yellow eyes of a golden minkee troop camped in the upward spread of a baka tree. The minkees chattered and chiffed, their pale, old-man faces turning this way and that, their fluffy tails swishing, their old-man hands prying open brown-shelled fruits they scraped across their bottom teeth. Chattering minkees were a good sign no chassa lurked nearby. Xyleea relaxed.

She propped a hand against her shrunken waist. Water had been scarce, food even scarcer. Days earlier, she'd found a nest with four small eggs. Two had gone into her mouth, shell and all, her mind thinking about anything other than their gummy texture and foul taste as she crunched them up and swallowed. She'd left the rest to appease the bird haranguing her from a nearby branch and moved on. Looking back, she should have eaten those too, screaming bird or not. A few days later, a fist-sized clot of grubs had shown up after a glancing blow from Kaambree's front foot split a rotten log in half, revealing their hiding place. Those too had been chewed up and swallowed while her mind focused on other things.

Kaambree used its trunk to aim a hard blast at the chassa dung, grass and leaves twirling up. Xyleea patted the tuskee's soft brown neck. As time lost its grip on her, one constant had remained. Kaambree. Since the night when the tuskee used its trunk to snug Xyleea's shivering body against its great chest, the matriarch had been her comfort and strength. *Why didn't I at least bring a bajee fleece?* she chided herself. But what had started out as a whim had turned into a long slog of searching interrupted by tense moments of hiding from the Xetili warriors who seemed to lurk around every corner.

Her water bladder hung like a spent teat at her side, the last mouthful having gone down her throat earlier. She tried not to panic. Though they hadn't found enough water for her wasakagee, Kaambree had found enough to keep them going. Doubt niggled at her. *What if there isn't enough water anywhere for my people?* Thoughts of failure were becoming more frequent the deeper she went into the keleekeluk making it that much harder to keep going forward.

A flurrying whoosh followed by an ominous lull focused her attention overhead. The minkees had vanished.

Kaambree coiled its trunk around Xyleea, tugging her close before stepping them backward into a stand of threadleaf. It was then Xyleea heard it, the unmistakable throaty rumble. Fear raced up her back and tightened her scalp. Her legs began to quake though she felt nothing, her body having gone numb. Kaambree's trunk wrapped tighter, cramming Xyleea's blowpipe against her midriff. *I should have readied a dart. Too late now.*

A large male chassa melted out of the brush and onto the trail, its yellowish-gray fur broken up by irregular gray-green stripes and splotches providing near invisibility in the keleekeluk's dense undergrowth. Xyleea had heard the call of the chassa many times, but seeing one was another matter. The big cats were rarely found out in the open, making their home instead in the canopy with its crisscrossing pathways of intersecting tree limbs. For this chassa to be on the ground at midday rather than at dawn or dusk spoke to the scarcity of prey. Known to hunt all but the biggest tuskees, the cat was quick and agile despite its squat appearance, owing to its short legs, long tail, and oversized paws which were nearly as large as its head. Those same paws allowed the cat to pad soundlessly through the keleekeluk and inflict its lethal bite before its prey sensed the deadly shadow behind them.

Kaambree stood as still as stone. Xyleea stiffened her own arms and legs, hoping the trembling chuulzu kereet would not give her away.

The cat sauntered forward then grumbled as it stopped to sniff the upended scat. It lifted its tail, and sprayed urine on the pile before yawning, its upper fangs scissoring away long enough to show their terrifying length. The chassa sniffed the air, its large eyes rolling skyward to scan the treetops, its rounded ears switching to and fro. It gave another rumbling growl, its languid gaze shifting to the stand of threadleaf where Kaambree and Xyleea stood, lingering there for several long beats. Xyleea shrank back under the chassa's stare, her heart flopping like a fish, her blood drumming in her ears. She was torn between ripping the blowpipe from her belt or remaining stock-still and hoping the scent of the tuskee would be enough to deter an attack. She knew she had little chance of getting off a dart before the chassa was upon her, and even if she did, the poison would take time to work, especially on an animal of its size. She only had one choice. She tensed her body further, until even her breathing was the barest movement, then said a prayer to the ancestors to spare her life for the sake of her people.

The chassa picked up its head and looked down the trail—alert ears quivering—before disappearing into the underbrush.

Xyleea let out a spongy breath, her muscles going slack. She stretched against the tuskee's hold, but Kaambree's trunk remained resolute, its grip firm around Xyleea's chest. Then she heard it. The scuff of a kicked rock. The crack of a twig. The slap of feet on gravel.

Three Xetilli warriors crow-walked into view, blue mud whorled on their legs and faces, quivers strapped to their chests, blowpipes held in front of weela bowls by blue-dotted hands.

In the bright sun, the blue mud had a turtle-shell shine Xyleea had never noticed before. One of the warriors stopped where the chassa had vanished. He poked his blowpipe into the brown-tinged brush then gave the spot a hard look before turning, his mouth opening to speak.

The chassa burst out in a fury of flashing claws and gnashing teeth, its croaking rumble filling the air as it sprang toward the warrior. The man gave a horrified look over his shoulder and leaped into a sprint, arms wheeling, mouth bawling, blowpipe clattering to the ground. The cat's claws slashed through the warrior's woven-fiber shirt, gashing open his pumping shoulders before coming to a snagging stop on his bow strap. The man jerked sideways, and the chassa reset, its claws digging deep, its fangs gleaming as its snarling mouth dove toward the warrior's lower back. The man fell to his knees, his hands wresting off the chassa's gripping paws before he half-crawled, half-rolled away from the full bite, one fang gouging open his twisting side, bright red spraying onto the ground. A small clay vessel winged away as he pelted for the cover of a nearby bush, the chassa close behind.

AAALLLLAAAALLLLAAA!

The other warriors' ululations stopped the big cat in its tracks; it pivoted toward the sound.

PFFOOOT PFFOOOT

Two darts struck, one in the flank, one in the shoulder. The warriors reloaded their blowpipes.

PFFOOOT PFFOOOT

A third dart hit high on the cat's neck while a fourth flew past, landing on the trail.

The cat yowled and sat on its haunches, its hind paw scratching at its neck and then its shoulder. It turned and bit at its flank, the dart coming away in its mouth before it tongued it off with a shake of the head.

The poison was having its effect. The cat looked around, confusion in its blinking eyes, its mouth opening wide to pant. The front legs slid forward, and the cat slumped down. A low grumble and the head slipped to the ground, the pupils in its listless green eyes constricting, its long, pink tongue slabbing out the side of its tooth-filled mouth. A final groan and the cat's broad chest stilled.

The injured warrior stepped out of the bush wearing a dazed expression. He wrapped his arms around his midsection, his hand jamming into his gashed side. The other warriors trotted to him, the taller throwing an arm around his blood-soaked shoulders. The second pulled a clay vessel from his belt, banged it against his palm, then spit twice. He kneaded the contents into a blue paste he smeared onto the wounds, repeating the process four times before he was through.

The trio moved to the side of the dead chassa. The tall one used his foot to roll the limp body onto its side, one green eye staring at the sky. Laid flat, the spotted pelt couldn't hide the big cat's ribby gauntness. It had been starving. Dying. Seeing that, Xyleea realized how close she'd come to ending up inside the desperate predator. It was only Kaambree's musk and trunk that had saved her. Her heart thumped, and she sagged against the tuskee's steadying hold.

One of the warriors pulled a blade from his belt and set to work separating the chassa's pelt from its carcass while the injured warrior hovered over, clutching his side and cursing. The claws were lopped off and divided up, each warrior draining a fistful into the pouch on their belt.

The tallest warrior dragged over a stout baka limb then, wrapping a thong around the lower jaw, affixed the vacant-eyed head to it, the toothy mouth yawning into a soundless roar. He crossed the mangled front paws atop the limb and tied them in place then repeated the process with the back paws, the cat's hide festooning between like a sling. Finally, the long tail was looped around the limb and the end secured.

The men turned their attention to the carcass. A slice down the underbelly released the slick-pink entrails before the chest was split, and the heart removed. Three squares of deeply red flesh were carved off then stuffed into each warrior's mouth, the remainder going into the taller one's belt pouch.

Next, the cat was separated into thirds. Discarding the ribs, the injured man shouldered the forequarters while the shorter warrior draped the thicker-muscled hindquarters around his neck like a cape. The tallest one bore up the pole with the pelt, his talon-hands hooking around the ends. He had the heaviest load to carry, the injured man the lightest. Without speaking, the men set off in the direction they'd come, the injured man taking the lead, the one with the pelt bringing up the rear, the chassa's gawping head banging against his hip.

Kaambree waited long after the warriors were gone to relax her hold. Xyleea turned and embraced the broad slope above the tuskee's trunk. "Thank you, great mother," she murmured, her throat going tight. She owed the tuskee so much. Everything, really.

The matriarch snuffled, and Xyleea gave the downy jaw a pat before leaning forward for a better view. Satisfied, she stepped out and stretched her cramped muscles as Kaambree bundled past, swerving the gut pile and lumbering to the trail to wait.

Xyleea went to where the clay vessel had disappeared and rummaged until she found it wedged in a clump of dead grass.

The blue-stained container—two thumbs wide and flat-bottomed —was surprisingly heavy. Xyleea unstuck the pith stopper and poked a finger inside. The numbing was immediate. She jerked her finger out then scrubbed it clean on her woven-fiber skirt. A realization dawned.

It was this that allowed the Xetili to endure injury without feeling its effects. Only when the blue mud was washed away did the pain return. That was why the injured warrior could carry on, despite the gash in his side and wounds to his shoulders. The beeka mud had blocked the pain. Xyleea felt a sudden appreciation for the value of such a thing. She replaced the stopper and jammed the vessel into her quiver.

Her gaze went to the discarded ribcage. The curving white bones were clung together by glistening lines of viscera-wrapped meat, more meat than she had seen in weeks. It was tough and rank, but it would get her by, and so she cut away strips, chewed them into balls then choked them down while her mind wandered back to when she'd had an abundance of meat to eat and water to drink without realizing the luxury of either. Would those times ever return?

When she was full, she shaved every pink trace from the ribs before putting away her knife. The shreds went into dreeka leaves she rolled tight then placed into empty baka shells lodged beneath her belt. She cleaned her hands then slipped one inside the kemeekemee, her fingers closing around the daala case, her mind imagining its power flowing through her fingers and up her arm, across her chest and into her heart.

Kaambree gave an impatient snort.

"Yes, old mother, we should be going," Xyleea said, drawing her hand out and getting to her feet. The tuskee knelt and threw out a front leg. Xyleea climbed up, her fingers twining into the tuskee's topknot as her thoughts turned to plentiful water and the bright future it promised.

Kaambree plodded forward, and Xyleea settled into the rolling rhythm of the tuskee's gait, her hope growing stronger with each rollicking step.

CHAPTER TWENTY-SEVEN

THE EDGE OF THE KNOWN WORLD

Pfolan Chrysolan's roundhouse sat like a footstool at the base of a massive hill in the whispering shade of the Whindon Wood. It was clad in weathered bark, the front of it settled forward so that with the sun at its back, it looked like a silver purse spilling golden coins across a petal-flecked meadow. For a woodcutter and adventurer, living at the edge of the known world was a perfect situation, with nearly every kind of tree close to hand.

Now, as Elorah led the way up a long laneway made pink by the shed of countless Ruddylimb blossoms, she felt as if she were stepping back in time. It all looked as she remembered, though she'd been quite young the last time she'd seen it, too young for memories her mother had insisted, but that didn't stop the memories from coming all the same.

It wasn't the cutting of trees in the Whindon Wood that had made the Chrysolan name famous; it was the collection of crystalwood, that rare, glass-like artifact found only in the wildlands of Whitemond, that had made the name legend. Crystalwood, hard as stone yet light as air, retained and amplified not only an emvor's vorik but their intention as well, making it prized by every affinity, including Therrans despite the

Valenvian Council's long-standing ban. It was not an easy wood to obtain, owing to the peculiarities of its harvest. As far as Elorah knew, since the death of her father, the number of marans learned in the ways of crystalwood amounted to exactly one—Pfolan Chrysolan.

"What are we doing again?" Thane puffed. They'd been climbing hills for the better part of a week, and it was taking its toll.

"Preparing for the Northern Passage," Elorah said, her mind leaping to what lay ahead.

"But why must we go all that way?" Thane whined.

"Have you ever been to the north?" Haedyn's tone was bright despite his bird's dark glare from its perch on his shoulder.

"Do I look like someone who enjoys snow and ice and murderous men?"

"I'd wager yes," Aikin spouted.

Haedyn's smile broadened. "Sounds like an adventure to me."

"Your definition of adventure could use some work," Thane snorted.

"The Northern Passage is the fastest way to Whitemond," Elorah said.

"During the warm moons maybe," Rachmyn muttered to Elgre, the wolf a stoic appendage at his side.

"Unless we meet up with a band of Drasgor," Aikin said. "If you believe Her Most Execrable, they stand waiting at the border, ready to attack."

"Do you believe her?" Mierrle chanced a gaze at Aikin before resuming her study of the pathway. Aikin clenched his jaw and shrugged, an angry, jerking movement that forced him to thumb his pack straps back into place.

"My grandfather has made the trip many times. He'll know what we should expect," Elorah said.

"The place looks abandoned." Exasperation sent Thane's voice into its upper register.

It was true. The closer they got, the less inhabited the house seemed. Long strips of bark curled away from its round sides, and its front door hung askew, the sole window imprisoned behind an enormous cobweb.

"Ere you lost?" came a thin, cramped voice.

It sounded like the grandfather Elorah remembered, but the aged man shuffling out from behind the roundhouse looked nothing like her memory of him. His once-straight back had bowed, stooping his shoulders and prodding his head forward. His arms and legs were shrunken and bent, and his face, once plump and full-cheeked, now looked gaunt and wrinkled. If not for the curlywood walking stick clutched in his gnarled hands, Elorah feared he would collapse completely.

Recognition lit his face. "Elorah? Is that you?" he croaked, his eyes kindling with hope.

"Grandfather," she cried, running to him and throwing her arms around his scrawny neck.

"That's the man who's meant to show us how to survive the northlands?" Thane asked no one in particular. "He can barely hold up his own walking stick."

"Show some respect," Aikin growled.

"At last..." Pfolan looked into Elorah's delighted face. "All these years I have waited."

The pendant fluttered like a happy bird as she grinned at him, love wiping away the years in a blink. "So, it has come to you, what you must do. You've already begun it. I never expected such a handsome group, but what do I know? I am only an old man. I trust you've all heard the call and answered it for yourselves." Haedyn and Rachmyn exchanged bemused looks while Thane shook his head. Pfolan's gaze went to him. "Yes, I can see that you have," he said, his bony finger pointing toward a nearly-healed scratch on Thane's nose. Thane frowned.

Pfolan let loose of Elorah and shuffled away, heading toward the wooded hill behind the round house, whistling a reedy tune.

"Where's he going?" Mierrle asked.

"Come, and you shall see," Pfolan chirped. As he shambled forward, his shoulders lost their rounding and his back straightened, so that by the next time he turned, he was transformed into a vigorous version of his former self. "Come, I say. All of you." He held up his walking stick and circled its knobbed end above his head before striding away. Elorah and Mierrle clambered after, followed by the rest, Thane muttering, "What is happening?" as he went.

"Try not to be bothered by things you don't understand," Pfolan advised. "Come, I've much to show you before you leave for Whitemond." His stride lengthened as he began to climb.

"How does he know where we're going?" Mierrle asked.

"He knows a great deal about a great many things," Elorah replied.

The sun had settled behind the hills by the time they arrived at a small stone cottage near the top, the last of the climb up a steep switchback that left everyone blowing like a winded horse except Pfolan who looked as fresh as when he'd begun.

"Here we are," he said, rapping his walking stick against the cottage's oval door. It opened a crack, and he used the stick to push it wide. "Step through, for we have much to discuss and do."

The cottage was quite crowded with gear, and it was a squeeze getting all seven seated around the large table, an overhead lamp painting the room in amber light. Pfolan set about rummaging items from the heaps lining the walls and rounding the corners of the room. As he came to something of interest, he flung it onto the table, which was how there came to be four sets of harness, four packsaddles, six woolen blankets, four oilskin tarps, seven candles, a bag of resin chunks, six water bladders, and a fire striker lumped up in a mound before he paused.

"Load them up," he said, pointing at the packsaddles. "Not too much in each. Even it out or the ponies won't like it."

"Ponies?" Thane scoffed, looking at the others with bemused scorn.

"Yes, ponies," Pfolan exclaimed, slapping his palm against the table. "Bah, you've got a lot to learn, stripling. You can't go to Whitemond without ponies. You'd never make it."

Thane drew his chin back. "Aren't ponies a little small for the likes of us?"

"Bah. You don't ride 'em for pity sake. They're for the gear. And the bravik."

"Bravik?" Elorah stopped her packing to look at her grandfather.

"Monstrous creatures. Half wolf, half bear, with claws as long as this..." Pfolan held his hands out the span of two feet, "...and teeth as long as this..." the hands sprung out to the length of a man's forearm, "...tall as a house and nearly as wide, with snouts like cast iron and fur as thick as ten of those." He pointed at the wool blanket Elorah was folding. "You don't want to meet up with one. But don't worry. The ponies can smell 'em a league away."

Mierrle swallowed hard, her hand finding Elorah's. Haedyn leaned forward, his face alive with interest.

"And where there's bravik, you'll find the mighty men," Pfolan continued.

"You mean the Drasgor?" Aikin asked.

Pfolan nodded. "Roving bands of brutes loyal to nothing except their own appetites. You don't want to meet up with them either." He looked around, letting his words sink in.

"Isn't there another way to get to Whitemond?" Thane grumbled as he wrestled a lumpy blanket into an overstuffed pack.

Pfolan nodded. "There is. Up and through the Lawless Mountains. But you'd never make it there and back before the summer was gone and the snows were setting in, stranding you with no way home." Pfolan resumed his rummaging.

"As choices go, I've seen better," Thane groused.

"You can leave anytime," Rachmyn said, his tone the unexpected cut of an unseen knife.

Thane's lips twisted into a speculative smile. "Seems to me, when you're up to your neck in something, you've already made your choice." Rachmyn's glare hardened.

"Choices are funny things. Some you remember, some you don't," Pfolan said. "Now this..." He pulled out a small wooden box buried deep under a pile. "This is what I've been looking for." He flopped the box onto the table, pulled a key from his pocket and unlocked it. He opened the lid, and removed four neatly folded cloth squares, setting them on the table.

"Wemble cloth," Haedyn said. He glanced at Rachmyn then back at the cloth.

Pfolan, one hand on the stack, looked up at him through his eyebrows. "If you know what it is, then you know what it does."

"I don't know what it is or what it does," Mierrle said, squinting at the yellow-and-red stranded cloth glowing like the embers of a forgotten fire. She turned toward Elorah. "Do you?"

Elorah shook her head.

Haedyn blurted, "It's like having a warm fire and a chill wind in your pocket."

"That's it exactly," Pfolan confirmed. He fixed his gaze on Haedyn then shifted to address Rachmyn. "I only have the four pieces. Not enough for everyone."

"We've—ooof." Haedyn gave Rachmyn a startled look as he clutched his leg.

"Pardon?" Thane asked, his keen eyes challenging.

"We've seen wemble before," Rachmyn replied with stony assurance.

"I don't think that's what he was going to say." Thane looked at Haedyn, his face an open question. "Go on."

"We've seen it before." Haedyn said, forcing a smile as he rubbed his shin.

Thane's scar crinkled into a sardonic leer. "Right," he deadpanned.

"We can surely share," Elorah said. "If need be."

"It doesn't work like that," Pfolan said. "Wemble is a conductor. It moves heat from one source to another." He unfolded one of the cloths. "You see how this side shines? This is the warming side..." He flipped the cloth over to its dull side. "... and this does the cooling. Heat moves away from this side..." He flipped the cloth over again. "...and gathers on this side. But it has no regulator. The person using it does that. Their vor determines how much or how little heat the cloth conducts." Pfolan stretched tall to reach over their heads. "There's one last thing." He pulled down a dust-covered object from the wooden rafters then wiped it clean using the corner of his cloak. It was a crystalwood bow. "Have you your father's staff?" he asked Elorah. She nodded. "Good. Bring it out." Elorah took the staff from its case. With a flourish, Pfolan brought the bow to the staff, touching it against its rounded end. A spark leaped between the two, setting both aglow for a moment. "Now that these have bonded, the bow needs to go with another." He turned toward Haedyn. "Something tells me this is yours to carry." He presented the bow as if it were a priceless treasure.

"Whoa." Haedyn's face split into a grin as he reached out but before he could take the bow into his hands, a second pair of hands was upon it, pulling it away.

Rachmyn held the bow up to the lantern then turned it toward the light, imbuing its recurve with an amber cast. Rachmyn brought it back to his chest and squinted at it.

"If you don't mind," Haedyn said, reaching over and plucking the bow from his friend's hands. Rachmyn set his jaw, his silvery gaze still raking across the weapon as Haedyn turned the bow over several times, a look of awe on his face.

Pfolan watched with an indulgent smile. "Caution is the pathway of the wise, but don't worry. It has no bewycchement upon it." He patted Rachmyn's shoulder before slapping his hands together. "Now that's done, a jarny would hit the spot." He walked over to a cupboard and opened one of the doors. A shank of dried meat came out, and he set to work carving off slices. Next, a rounded loaf of crusty bread was sliced. He placed the meat between two rounds of bread and handed it behind him where it was passed around the table. Pfolan repeated the process five times, made one for himself, then turned to face the group sat stock still, their jarnies in front of them like unopened presents. "Well, go on. Eat," he said, taking a bite.

Mierrle was the first to begin, followed by Elorah. Haedyn picked one of his meat pieces out, squirreling it into his pocket before tucking in. Rachmyn was the last, sniffing then staring at his before taking a testing bite. Pfolan put his down then dipped water from a pail near the door. After taking a drink, he refilled the dipper and handed it to Aikin. "Wash it down with this," he said. Aikin grimaced and took a small sip. "Drink, man," Pfolan cried, forcing Aikin's hand upward, a slug of water pouring into his mouth. He gulped loudly then coughed. "That's it," Pfolan said. "Them jarnies is mighty tight without water."

Once they'd finished, Pfolan slapped his hands together. "We'll see to the ponies at first light." He looked around, his eyes merry. "I wondered if this day would ever come. If I would live long enough to see it." His gaze settled on Elorah. "When you were here last, small as you were, I knew you'd come for a purpose. Does your mother remember that I wonder?"

Memories of her mother's crushing disappointments—Elorah's failure to be pinned, the Grand Pageant's spectacular collapse, the vor-depleting thorn hedge—overtook Elorah's thoughts, and she couldn't help feeling responsible for her mother's unraveling.

"No matter," Pfolan continued. "You're here now, with Whitemond set before you. Follow what I say, and you'll live to tell the tale. Follow it not, and you'll join my Rylan and my Aleea in the golden gloaming of Inverna."

Pfolan went to a metal-clad strongbox beside the cupboard, swept aside a stack of hides sitting on top then, using a second key from his pocket, clicked open the imposing brass lock. The lid sprang up with a puff of dust as he retrieved a worn-looking bolt of cloth. He carried it to the table then waited for it to be cleared before unrolling the stained fabric and carefully smoothing it with his palms.

It was a map. He looked down at it, nostalgia softening his features. "If only my Rylan had taken this," he murmured then shook his head as if trying to cast away painful memories. A flurry of emotions—joy, sadness, worry, exhilaration—played across his face as he gazed at the water-stained, hand-drawn depiction. He tapped his forefinger on a marking to the far left. "Whitemond," he stated. "The peak of legend and dreams. This is where you're going." He pointed at a spot near the bottom right. "This is where you are. The Whindon Wood. And this..." He waggled his finger over a large area between the two. "...is the northlands. You want to follow this..." He traced a broken line running from the Whindon Wood through the northlands, then looping around the northernmost peaks of the Lawless Mountains. Pfolan traced his finger still further, hovering it above a lone peak sitting like an afterthought a fair distance to the west of the mountain range. At various spots along the way were notes written in a cramped hand, the lettering so small, they looked like ant tracks. There were drawings of animals, too, also tiny. He pointed to one, a circle with four stick legs and fangs. "This was where I saw my first bravik. And this..." He pointed to a double-humped shape with stick legs near the upper edge of the Whindon Wood. "...is where I saw my first gryphon."

"We saw a gryphon," Mierrle said.

"Did you now," Pfolan said.

Rachmyn and Haedyn exchanged a look.

"At the festival." Mierrle gave an involuntary shiver. "It was terrible."

"That makes a change from the festival I remember. Mostly bears and such back in my day. Well, if you've seen one then you know how unpredictable those bastardy beasts are. Rylan took a nasty hit once and nearly lost a leg. With the ponies, though, you're more in danger of falling into a bravik pit."

"A bravik pit?" Haedyn burst out.

"Dug out holes as deep as two men and twice as wide, the bottom lined with pinekin poles so sharp and straight, they can punch the heart out of a man before he's done falling. The mighty men use them to hunt bravik. Fall into one and you won't be walking away unless you've a set of wings." He rolled the map up and handed it to Elorah. "Study that. Memorize it. Then set your path and follow it."

He turned his attention to the rest of the group, his gaze drifting to Rachmyn. "From this moment, nothing will be the same. Not here or anywhere." Pfolan's wooly eyebrows went up, his forest-green eyes lingering on the pale-haired man for a long moment. Only when Rachmyn gave the slightest of nods, did Pfolan rock back on his heels and wave his arm toward the backroom. "You're all welcome to bunk up here until tomorrow, though I'd prefer the wolf stays on the other side of the door."

"As you wish," Rachmyn responded. He bobbed his head toward Haedyn. "We've no need for walls or roofs when there's a ceiling of stars to be had."

"That will stand you in good stead where you're going," Pfolan said. "There'll be precious few warm spots between here and there."

"Never has been," Rachmyn shrugged. "We're used to it."

Pfolan nodded. "I don't doubt it," he said. "I'll only say this. It's no weakness to use the gifts allowed you. There'll be plenty of chances to go without."

Rachmyn stood, pushed back his hair then picked his rucksack from the floor and hoisted it onto his shoulders. Haedyn followed suit. "I've always found it's better not to get too comfortable. Come on." Rachmyn headed out the door.

Haedyn gave an apologetic shrug. "See you at first light," he said before following his friend out into the dark.

CHAPTER TWENTY-EIGHT

WHEN SHADOWS HAVE SHADOWS

What a relief, Rachmyn thought once he was outside the cottage. There was never enough fresh air inside buildings, unlike caves where there was always a steady flow. Buildings were like dead things, full of staleness and decay. He filled his lungs with the forest's bracing tang then exhaled. That was more like it. He glanced up at the darkening sky, aglitter with winking stars. Now that was a ceiling worth looking at.

Elgre got up from a pile of leaves, stretched, then picked up a dead hare, his eyes alert. Rachmyn set off toward two trees close enough he could prop his back against one and wedge his feet against the other. It wasn't a cave, but it would suit. The wolf trotted behind, his prize bouncing either side of his jaws. He flumped down near Rachmyn's feet and dropped the hare between his front paws.

Haedyn scoured the shadows beneath a Greenieup tree until he found a suitable limb then, using his knife, fashioned a perch. After transferring his bird, he dug the jarny meat from his pocket and tore it into strips, nodding along as the grynt gorged. That done, he brushed his hands against his leggings, pulled out the sock toe, and popped it onto the bird's head.

"Did you see her smile?" he chirped as he plopped to the ground and leaned back against the Greenieup's trunk. "I think she's taken with me."

Rachmyn pushed his feet and his back against the trees to stretch his spasmed muscles. Too much time sitting. "Doesn't say much for her taste. Course we already know that from the characters she's chosen for this galavant."

Haedyn let the jibe pass as he clasped his hands behind his head and looked off into the deepening dark. "She chose us, didn't she? I think that shows very good taste."

Rachmyn shrugged. "Luck often looks like logic." *Crack.* Elgre put his teeth to work on the hare carcass, his eyes half-closed as his back teeth grated it apart.

Haedyn snorted, his hands flinging wide as he turned to Fryk, hunched on the perch. "He doesn't want to admit my charm is working. You know though, don't you, Fryk. You saw it." The hooded bird sat motionless, an inanimate lump of sock toe, feathers, and talons. Haedyn's hands settled into his lap.

"Looks like your charm's put your bird to sleep," Rachmyn observed, biting his lip to keep from laughing.

Haedyn harrumphed then picked up the crystalwood bow. It glimmered in the low light. "Have you ever seen anything like this?" he asked as he held it up, closed one eye and drew back the taut bowstring. "Now that's a smooth draw. I bet I could knock the ears off a toad with this."

Rachmyn shook his head. "Why would you want to?"

"I don't know. I'm just saying, I could." Haedyn let down the bowstring then set the weapon aside.

"I'll be sure to mark that down on your list of useless skills, right after the drinking and the gambling."

"If I didn't gamble, I wouldn't have fleeced that gold-toothed Rabboutier out of the egg that hatched into my fine friend." He pointed toward his bird.

"Your argument does not persuade me."

"Ah, well. I didn't expect it to. It's nice to know some things never change." Haedyn peered upward, closing first one eye and then the other. He waved a stiff-fingered hand overhead. "Will you be hitting the heights tonight? Setting our course and all that?"

Rachmyn shrugged.

"Well..." Haedyn retrieved his cloak from his pack then threw it over himself, swooping his hand down and forward. "I'll be hitting the depths. Of sleep. First light will be here soon enough."

"Indeed, it will," Rachmyn agreed, his eyes tracing the hills humped along the northern horizon. *What perils lay beyond those?* Pfolan Chrysolan's map had made it clear the Northern Passage was full of terrors, and Rachmyn had little faith in their companions' ability to apprehend danger. Despite his noncommittal response, he'd already decided to scout their path in Oru Fen. His hand slipped into his pocket for his shard. Yes, there it was. He closed his eyes and began the letting go process that allowed him to slip into that other world where dreams lived and paths were made clear. Soon he was away.

It was the Wycche's aim to steal up on the Uniter, quiet as a rising moon, and discover the secrets needed to end this cycle. She'd already gathered a good deal of etheriant and was feeling almost back to her usual self. Venge, too, had regained much of his power, though it was hard to tell, the eryns having eroded the wraithwolf to such an extent that, even in the flattering dusk, he appeared battered and worn. If not for the eyes glittering like daggers, it would be easy to mistake him for a soft touch. Woe to the novice making that mistake, for the old warrior was far from that.

Dreamwalking was not the Wycche's favored approach, but this Erynvor had proven far more elusive than her previous ten counterparts. The Wycche needed only to find a flaw, some little imperfection she could use. Always before, she'd found a way to exploit certain character traits and encourage certain choices, so that failure was achieved. She needed to find this latest Erynvor's weakness to ensure this time was no different.

Dreamwalking afforded her more scope than dreamcrafting, allowing her a means of finding what she needed without contending with her object's wraithwolf, but it was still risky. All Shadowen had the ability to walk these starry paths in the company of their guardian and an Erynvor was, by definition, Shadowen, along with every other affinity. It was still possible for the white wolf to thwart her, but a chance not taken was a chance lost and so, tonight the Wycche would walk.

Venge cut through her musing with a low growl, urging her to say the words.

Take me to her.

With that the wraithwolf was off, the Wycche at his side, fields and forests flying beneath as they focused on their object. Into the Whindon Wood in a flash of thought, to a high hill with a house of wood at its foot and another of stone at its crown. She had been here before, the touchpoint a misted memory retrieved from long ago. She shuddered to a stop, her raiment a curling fume of black. Venge stopped as well, his derelict frame and low-slung head a picture of malintent.

The Wycche sensed a presence, an enormous energy, close at hand. She peered into the sudden gray fog puffing up around her, but it was no use. The fog thickened into a resolute curtain that, try as she might, she could not see past, the countryside that had been so clear a moment before subsuming into the suffocating miasma.

A thundering shout sounded in a voice that was both many and one.

ABANDON THIS TREACHERY!

The Wycche startled, her raiment contracting into a tight shroud. Venge bristled, his deadblack settling in an instant, his sharp teeth and glaring eyes the only things visible in the choking fog.

Anger blazed up inside as the Wycche conjured a firebolt of vorik and launched it into the oppressive gloom.

BOOM!

The firebolt exploded with the force of a world being born, pushing against the stifling grayness laying heavy upon her and making it hard to breathe. The weight of the choking fog intensified as the voice of the many thundered again.

ABANDON THIS TREACHERY, WYCCHE!

Her hands went to her throat, but it was no use. Her chest had become stone.

AAAAAUUUUUUGHHHHH!

Cold shock doused her boiling fury as she fell backward, her hands flailing out in wheeling rounds, everything giving way in a dizzying rush.

The twin flames of Venge's eyes fastened upon her before racing backward into oblivion as she fell down and down, her essence slamming full force into the slumbering form she'd left behind on the chaise.

Pain stabbed her chest as her eyes flung open, the velvet chaise against her back making it clear where she was. Somehow, she was back in the now, an invisible weight compressing her chest, her throat clamping shut. Her hands tightened to fists, her fingernails welting crescents into her palms as she wheezed air into her bouldered lungs. She struggled upright, gasping and coughing, until her sticking throat gave way, allowing in a thin stream of air. She forced in several more shaking breaths before sliding her trembling legs down toward the flagstone floor, one hand reaching up to cradle the curve where her head joined her neck, her mind reaching a terrible conclusion. A different, duller pain settled, bringing with it a feeling she knew all too well and hated— the dark ache of failure.

Rachmyn felt a familiar nudge as he surveyed the land falling away on all sides from the rounded hill below his feet. Spectra was there, as always, pointing him toward a pathway of starlight leading north. Her attention fixed upon a blackness coming fast on the eastern horizon. She growled, her hackles stiffening into spikes.

Use your vorik or all is lost.

He looked into his guardian's eyes, staring hard at him to steel his will. Conviction surged within as the blackness hurtled closer, mesmerizing in the speed of its approach. He forced his attention away from the racing nimbus to the realm's brume margin, his mind capturing its look exactly. He steadied his thoughts, holding the image at the forefront of his mind while summoning up his inner force then joining the two together. With vigorous intent, he pushed the impression out into the ethers. A resolute fog formed around him. He immersed himself in his thought creation, the whole of him becoming one with the fog he was conjuring so that there was no other thought, no other idea except that. In turn, his inner force actualized the thoughtform into a spreading cloud of gray, pushing it out further and further until it obscured everything around him.

When the strike came it knocked him nearly senseless, his mind jolting away from the distortion he was projecting. Spectra sensed his falter and rammed her head against his leg. He refocused, this time adding dimensionality to the imagined fog so that it pressed out with a weight and heft that defied understanding. His focus tightened, shaping its dimensionality into an impenetrable denseness. For what seemed like a lifetime, his mind labored upon the illusion, his power of will funneling every ounce of effort into the thought's attendant form and substance, pushing, pushing, pushing, until he felt he would break from the strain. It was then the words thundered out, coming from somewhere ancient and true.

ABANDON YOUR TREACHERY!

Rachmyn redoubled his efforts, his thought projection sweeping away all before it. Again, the words rang out. Louder. Deeper.

ABANDON YOUR TREACHERY, WYCCHE!

The darkness gave way in a release so great it was like a dam bursting, black particles exploding outward in a corona of negative energy before disappearing. Relief overwhelmed him, and he looked down at his guardian to steady himself, a numbing rush of exhaustion making him weak. Around them, the fog dissipated like stolen breath.

You have done well, came Spectra's mindwords, her eyes full of love. *Remember this, for you will be called upon again, and sooner than you might think. But for now, sleep, for morning is nigh upon you, and you have leagues to go before you will sleep again.*

He nodded, his eyes closing. With a muffled whoosh, his ethereal self plummeted into his slack body, a pebble falling into an open bag. He was asleep by the time he landed.

Six fat jarnies sat on the table, each atop a square of cloth. Elorah encouraged Thane, Mierrle, and Aikin to put theirs into their packs as she tucked her own away. She wrapped up the remaining two and carried them outside.

As promised, her grandfather was up and out of the cottage. Elorah wasn't sure he'd slept at all. He had four ale-colored mountain ponies harnessed, pack-saddled, and tied up, their flaxen tails swishing, their flinty hooves pawing at the leaf mold. Nearby stood six dirt-brown geldings, saddled and chewing hay, their heads pointing north as they awaited their fate.

Elorah delivered the jarnies to Rachmyn. He folded back the cloth corner on one, then mumbled a thank you as Haedyn trotted over. The wolf was nowhere to be seen.

"Most kind," Haedyn said, plucking his bundle from Rachmyn's hand then giving Elorah a small bow. He turned toward Pfolan— forking hay to the ponies from a pushcart—held up his hand and grinned. "Most kind!" he called before sticking the bundle into his pack.

"I always find a good meal sets one on the proper path," Pfolan boomed, spearing the last spit of hay to the largest pony, patting its forehead when it whickered. "Morning!" he called.

Elorah turned to see Aikin, Thane, and Mierrle emerge from the cottage.

"I told you we were meant to eat them," Aikin said, reaching into his pack.

Thane gave him a sharp look. "Eat yours if you wish, but when you find yourself chewing on your own tongue because you've nothing else, remember who made your decision."

Aikin's expression soured. He pulled his empty hand out, hoisted his pack onto his shoulders then strode away, kicking out at a clump of hay and startling one of the geldings as he stomped down the hill. Elorah stifled a smile.

Pfolan motioned her over to where the horses were standing to show her the various girths and straps and buckles and bits. He then led her to one of the ponies and showed her its gear—the halter and sawbuck packsaddle and double-diamond hitches—then braced her shoulders, turning her toward the northern hills and leaning near to speak into her ear. "Remember, the Kalt-Roulk is the easiest and safest of the passes through the Blackshales. That's the way of the High Road. The Glind-Hoak and the Barrish are too high, too steep, and too unpredictable this time of year. Those roads are barely wide enough for a goat in the middle of summer, let alone now when I'd wager they're under ten hands of snow, what with the spring thaw still weeks away. Of course, the High Road means guards and travelers, so you'll have to take care. It'll take a fair bit of cleverness to get you through the High Gate, but I've no doubt you'll do it. If all goes well, you'll reach Whitemond when the Dragon's Moon lights the sky. That'll see you through. Ye've heard of the Dragon's Moon, eren't ya?"

She shook her head.

"Bah, flatlanders'll talk your leg off about barleycorn and bears and never once tell you something worth hearing," he exclaimed. "The Dragon's Moon is rare and red and full of power, the kind of moon what comes once in a lifetime. Twice maybe, if you live as long as me. Now, have you your map?"

Elorah nodded, patting her satchel.

"Good. Study it until it's all up here." He tapped his forefinger against her temple.

"I already have," she said.

His eyebrows peaked in surprise as he smiled. He squeezed her shoulders then stepped away to untie one of the ponies. He half-hitched its lead-rope through a piggin string poking out from the back of its neighbor's packsaddle then hitched the other two ponies together in the same manner, explaining, "I split 'em so in a time of trouble you don't lose all four at once. Take care to remember that, too."

He tied the pairs of line-hitched ponies to the two stoutest-looking geldings. "Put your best riders on these two," he said. "They'll be responsible for all your gear. The rest'll have no trouble with the other four. They're all dead broke and can walk a trail backwards and blindfolded. Once you get to the northlands, stick to the valleys as much as possible but keep a watch on the ponies. They'll let you know if there are bravik nearby. You see 'em trying to bolt upwind, watch out. The gryphons are another danger, but they stay to the highlands. You shouldn't see one if you stick to the valleys. If you do, bunch together, and try to look large. A gryphon won't take on anything it judges to be stronger or bigger, unlike them bastardy bravik that hunt in packs and fear nothing. Your only hope with them is to split up and head upland. They're slow when they're climbing. If all else fails, you can lose the horses, but whatever you do, don't lose the ponies. Them and their packs are your lifelines."

"How far till we get to Whitemond?" Elorah asked.

"It's three moons there and three moons back. You've started early enough the snow might still be a nuisance in the high country. A late storm could put you behind before you even know it. If you haven't made it to Whitemond by the time three moons have passed, you must turn back."

Elorah shook her head. "But—"

"You have everyone's welfare to consider. You can't take the chance of pushing on and not being able to return before bad weather sets in and dooms you all."

Elorah swallowed hard and stared at the horizon. "Then we'll have to make sure we're there in three moons or less."

"That's the proper attitude," Pfolan said. He pointed toward the orange-gold rind of sun hugging the top of a faraway hill. "Today's candle has already been lit. Best you're on your way before it burns any brighter."

"Yes," Elorah said. She whistled a high, sweet note. "It's time we're going," she called. She pointed Aikin toward the two geldings with ponies in tow. "You and I will take those two. Everyone else, find the horse you think suits best. The future awaits. Let us meet it with all good grace and hope."

The group mounted up and, after checking their gear, set out, Pfolan waving them off with a wide smile.

They spent three days working their way northward, up and down hills that got steeper the further they went, which pleased Thane not at all. They were following the general course of the High Road, traveling at night to avoid patrolling High Hells, an idea he understood but didn't admire because it meant the geldings were always trudging along some wretched cowpath in the dark. It was utterly boring.

Things improved on the fourth day when they met up with a band of friendly Shadowen who recognized Rachmyn and greeted him as if he were their long-lost king. For his part, the pale-haired man seemed far less keen to see them than they him, and it had taken strong urging from his golden-eyed friend to convince him that linking up with the band of itinerants was a sound idea. Unlike Rachmyn, Thane was delighted with the company, for he was sure they would bring some much needed excitement to the dull proceedings. The meals might become more regular too, which he wouldn't mind. Who knows? He might even find someone willing to part with a nip of sweetsweet, and that thought made him happiest of all.

The Shadowen also traveled at night and had as many ways of slipping past authorities as there were stars in the sky. It seemed to Thane the High Hells were naive to most of their tricks, which suited him fine. He only worried that once they got to the High Gate, they would meet up with a better-trained set of guards who wouldn't be so guileless.

On the evening of the fifth day, the leader, Flandyn Eccto, called a meeting, and so they were gathered around a smokeless fire, all nine of the Konda band plus the six joiners. The High Gate was still a week's journey away, but much needed to be discussed regarding how they could all get past the Iellian border guards. Thane found it hard to concentrate on Eccto's words, his attention instead on the flame-haired leader's left eye which listed sideways between blinks. What he did gather was that for the Kondas, the other side of the High Gate meant a quantity of lute-spider silk, a crucial component of a potent love charm. Spider-silk gathering was the specialty of this particular band. Thane couldn't say what the other side of the High Gate meant for his group. Likely pain, suffering, and deprivation from what he could tell. He wasn't looking forward to it. If it wasn't for the speck, he'd have been gone long ago.

After a meal of found-meat stew and fried bread, Eccto, who seemed a cheerful sort, solicited ideas for getting through the High Gate should their forged papers not prove sufficient. Thane affected a look of indifference as he employed his silver toothpick, pretending far more interest in his teeth than anything Eccto had to say. Though he did take inordinate pride in his smile, he was in fact hanging on Eccto's every word, hoping mindshields would somehow be involved. He'd heard tales about the confounding mental abilities of certain Shadowen, how they could implant thoughts into the minds of others to gain an advantage or protect their own, and he wished to see if any of those wild tales were true.

His group's many animals added complexity to the situation, as Eccto took great pains to explain. Shadowen used their caravans, not pack animals, to convey their goods. Six horses and four ponies was an enormous number of extra stock to account for without raising suspicion.

A sandy-haired man suggested they pretend to be selling the animals, but that was dismissed when the crooked-nosed man beside him pointed out the guards would expect a sizable kickback for allowing them through for purposes of commerce. A dark-haired woman suggested they say the animals were for bartering with the Drasgor, but again, it was pointed out the guards would expect their pockets filled before the band would be allowed to pass. Other ideas were posited— avoiding the gate by going through the Barrish or the Glind-Hoak, harnessing the animals as a four-in-hand, bribing the guards, overpowering the guards, or killing them, an idea that gained some traction with certain anti-authority zealots—before Eccto held up his hands and called for quiet. The use of wolfken was then suggested, but it would take a quantity they didn't possess of a pure enough grade to quickly disable the guards after being delivered in a manner that wouldn't attract attention. Several turned toward Rachmyn, deferring to him, even as their own leader stood tall. Thane tucked his toothpick into his pack and settled back to hear what the pale-haired man had to say. The solution seemed obvious, but he wanted to hear from an expert.

Rachmyn shifted. "I've not given such an idea much thought," he hedged. "It's not my thinking that counts, anyway. Flandyn has the final say on the matter."

"No, I'd like to hear your thoughts," Eccto said, flipping the back edge of his battered coat out of the way before sitting on a rickety stool. "With your family, I'm sure you have a unique perspective."

Thane noted an edge had crept into the leader's tone.

"Well, erm..." Rachmyn floundered.

"Tell them about the speck," Haedyn prompted. Rachmyn glared at his companion.

"You have speck?" Eccto asked. He along with every other Konda member were at sharp attention.

"A bit," Rachmyn said.

"Oh, it's more than a bit," Haedyn bragged. Rachmyn's glare stiffened into a scowl.

Thane straightened and clasped his hands around his knees. Finally, something interesting was happening.

"Your family was always known for their hand-cast speck. Might you have some of that?" Eccto probed, his eyes searching Rachmyn's hardened expression.

Elorah spoke up. "If our presence will cause you trouble, we'll gladly part ways. We wouldn't want to be a burden."

Eccto narrowed his eyes, all trace of his previous joviality gone. "Trouble follows a Shadowen all his life. That is of no concern. What does concern me is my friend here might have taken me for a fool. If that is true, I find it very grievous. Very. Grievous." A long, tense moment passed.

"I do have some speck." Rachmyn said, his eyes on Elgre who'd gotten up to stand beside his knee. Eccto also watched the wolf's movements. "Maybe enough for what you're suggesting." Eccto's gaze shifted from Elgre to the man he guarded, a slight smile on his lips, his eye drifting left.

Thane saw his opportunity. "The hoewlers. What do they do exactly?"

Eccto jerked his attention toward him. "What does that have to do with it?"

Thane leaned forward so he could use his hands. "Well, I've seen them, but I've never known what they do. It seems to me, in this particular situation, they might prove useful." Thane pantomimed blowing through an imaginary tube.

"You don't put speck into a hoewler..." Eccto began before his voice trailed off. He pursed his lips and frowned.

"It was just an idea." Thane shrugged and sat back. "Not a very good one apparently."

Eccto turned toward Rachmyn. "It could work, you know. If there was enough speck, that is. How much do you have?"

"What are you suggesting?" Rachmyn asked.

"A puff of pure speck into the face of an unsuspecting guard might do the trick. They'd be asleep before they knew what hit them." Eccto clapped his hands together. "Yes," he said, sounding more enthusiastic. "I've never seen it done, but I don't know why it wouldn't work. We'd only have to reverse the hoewler so it doesn't function as intended."

"How would you keep the speck from falling out before you blow?" asked a middle-aged man with large ears, a larger nose, and a lopsided mouth that spit his words out sideways. Beside him, an iron-haired woman with her own set of jug-handle ears nodded along.

Must be his wife, Thane thought. His mind jumped to an absurd scene of the pair staring enthralled at their perfect opposite over an empty packet of lute-spider lovedust. He shook his head to clear the image before he burst out laughing. "Have you some of that foil charm paper?" he asked, not quite managing to keep the chuckle from his voice.

"Yes, but how would that help?" Eccto snapped.

"If you were to seal paper to one end of the hoewler so that when you blew into the other it fell away, I think you'd be on to something."

"Seal it with what?" Eccto asked.

Must I think of everything?

"A dot of honey perhaps?" Thane mused. "A smear of wax?"

Eccto shook his head. "That wouldn't work." He stroked his chin, his eye losing focus. He snapped his fingers. "Egg white would do it."

"I've an egg," volunteered a young girl with brown ringlets and blue eyes. Thane realized with a start the black bump in her lap was a sleeping chicken, its head tucked beneath one wing. She stroked the bird. "Mineena lays one every day."

Eccto smiled. "Then we shall all be in Mineena's debt."

Saved by a chicken. How quaint. Not the stuff of legend or song but a fair children's tale.

"We'll need a distraction," Big Ears put in. "Something to put the guards off."

Elorah turned to Aikin. "I think we can stage something." Aikin nodded, catching her meaning. She looked at Thane. "Don't you?"

Thane nodded. "I think you could," he said with arch enthusiasm.

Elorah cocked her head, her gaze piercing. "I'm sure you want to be part of it."

"Me?" Thane cleared his throat. "I hadn't thought..."

"I knew you would," she said with a finality that cut off further discussion.

"You're missing something important." Rachmyn's voice was low and deliberate, his attention somewhere far away. Elgre laid his head upon the pale-haired man's lap, his eyes rolling upward. "Oru Fen. Success here could very well mean disaster there."

Eccto frowned. "We've no strong walkers or crafters in this band. None like yourself."

"There's one here who knows as much as I," Rachmyn said.

Thane swiveled in time to see him look at Elorah. Mierrle's mouth dropped open as she turned toward her friend. Thane cut his gaze toward the golden-haired man, his bastard bird a glowering lump on his shoulder, his face wide open with surprise. A sudden movement brought Thane's attention nearer. Beside him, the copper-haired man stood and stalked away, retreating to where the horses were tied.

Thane felt a thrill of excitement. *So, a secret only one of us guessed.* He looked at Elorah, a new admiration taking hold. *What else is she about?*

Eccto gave her a half-bow from his seated position. "High praise, maiss."

Rachmyn leaned forward. "There's a storm already brewing in that in-between world. We could tip the balance toward an outcome none of us wants."

"Do you have another idea?" It was Big Ears again. Maissel Big Ears clapped her hands once then threw them out wide and jutted her chin.

"A distraction, yes, but on two levels," Rachmyn said.

"How is that possible?" Eccto asked. "Even the Zenzae can't be in two places at once."

"What do you know of the Zenzae and what they can do?" Rachmyn's gaze was direct, his expression grim. Thane sat up straighter. The only thing he knew of the shadowy Zenzae were fearsome rumors and whispered barroom tales. Strange vorik. Essence stealing. Secret rituals. Bribery schemes. Mysterious deaths. The Rabboutiers he'd run with always accorded them much respect, even as they did everything possible to avoid them. It was said a Zenzae's grudge followed a maran both here and beyond. Even amongst their own, a people known for their secrecy, the Zenzae were little understood and much feared.

Eccto shrank back, his hands pinching creases into his pants. "A figure of speech, only. We know nothing of such things amongst our little group."

Thane wasn't sure he believed the Shadowen leader. His demeanor held an arrogance that belied the words.

"It is well you do not. My friend and I wish we could say the same." The pale-haired man's words were clipped.

The mystery deepens.

"This idea I have, I'm not sure it will work," Rachmyn continued. "But I strongly feel we must try, or the risk of what you propose is too high."

Eccto jerked his quivering chin toward Rachmyn. "By all means, do what you must. Now, are there others who wish to be heard?" He was met with shaking heads and low murmuring. "Let's get to it then," he said amidst a muted chorus of standing and stool folding and shuffling away to prepare for a journey with a High Gate at its end.

Always The Wind

I had a whistle once. It was long and thin and shone of gold, a gift to my father from some foreign visitor. He had no use for such trifles and gave it to me when I was very young. I strung it upon a chain so that it hung from my neck like an exotic instrument, a compendium of sound awaiting a single freeing breath. Though it was beautiful, without my wind, the whistle was but a dead thing, as disappointing as a promise unkept, as moribund as a possibility unfulfilled. But consider, was it the whistle or the wind that created the sound? Which was the more important? I say it was the wind. Always the wind.

–Epigent Zephyrria Rennesseau, aged 16
   Volume 3235, Page 417,
   Essentia Libre, Academie Vorik

CHAPTER TWENTY-NINE

GOING PLACES

Brynz was stronger now, her muscles hard lines that rippled when she moved. Her skin was stronger, too, stretched tight as glass and every bit as clear, the red patches gone. Her hair had hardened as well, sweat and wind felting it into thick cords that hung from her head.

The Drasgor never stayed in one place for long, barely taking time to sleep and eat before moving on, and it was that constant movement that had wrought the changes in her. The days and nights now ran together, a pattern of light, dark, light, dark, sleep, march, sleep, march, that stretched toward eternity. She'd taken to scratching marks into the chest protector, starting under the word *Brecceu* and working her way across, as a way of counting time, although why she couldn't say. Who needed to know how many days had passed when facing a lifetime of the same? What difference did it make? Even so, she made the mark each morning after the nighttime march ended, looking forward to it in an odd sort of way. She also looked forward to counting the marks, the figure sitting in her mind like a victory until sleep stole it away. Twenty-eight. That's how many she'd counted this morning after scratching the latest one into the blue leather. Twenty-eight defiant marks screaming, "I'm still here!"

Much had changed inside as well. She now ate whatever was offered, in whatever form it came. Raw, cooked, peeled, unpeeled, soft, hard, hot, cold, it made no difference. She was long past caring and had learned one could chew and swallow anything once the mind had been convinced it was possible. Sleep had become a swift and welcome respite, a by-product of her perpetual exhaustion. Once she'd given up worrying whether she was going to be killed at any moment, sleep had come much easier. Her tears, on the other hand, had faded to memory, something her mind could recall but her eyes could not. There was no time for tears anyway, and so her eyes had given up on them. It was better this way. It kept her clearer, more focused. Hardened resolve pushed her onward, bringing with it a power that felt both strange and thrilling. Where before the wind had been an outside force requiring her concentration to move, it was now a part of her. Her skills had sharpened, allowing her to nudge the wind's flow with the flick of a finger or the point of a toe, leaves swirling up here, a bird pushed off course there. A few times she'd gotten a fierce look, after a stone hit an ankle, or a branch brushed a neck but for the most part, her diversions went unnoticed.

The scenery was also changing, becoming steeper and colder and rockier the further they went. It wasn't so bad during the day, when golden spires of sunlight warmed the ground between the irregular shadows of interlaced branches, but the nights were long and numbing, the cold turning her toes and fingers and nose into extra baggage she had to drag along as she huffed her way forward.

She'd become accustomed to the raspy bark of Uhnkre's flattened Iellian and to Hrul's cutting stare which no longer made her quake every time it landed on her. She'd learned the other men's names as well, picking them up as they talked amongst themselves in their language of growls and grunts and barks—Ahnkne, who sharpened his dras at every opportunity; Benkre, who could split a moth mid-flight with his axe; Kif, younger even than Uhnkre with blue eyes as cold as a midwinter sky; and Flewd, the stoutest and tallest of them all, the axe on his hip like a child's plaything when compared to his enormous whole.

Though she knew the men's names, she knew nothing more about them. Nor did she know where they were going, how long it would take to get there, or what would happen once they'd arrived. She no longer wondered about it, keeping her thoughts focused instead on the relentless physical requirements of survival, namely putting one foot in front of the other, swallowing water or food when it appeared, and sleeping. With her newfound mindset came an unexpected liberation from the worries that had plagued her throughout her life, opening her up to ideas she might never have discovered had she not been forced to reduce her thoughts to their barest form.

She'd always held much sympathy for Zell and all creatures who toiled under a master's whip, but it wasn't until she found herself in the same situation that she came to a meaningful understanding of how soul-crushing captivity was. She now felt shame at imposing her own limits upon other beings and could only hope she would not be judged too harshly for it. It was small comfort to know her motives, though childish, had been pure and her love unconditional for those under her care, but she had come to believe that just as a monarch should endeavor to lift their subjects toward a benevolent freedom, so too a master should do the same. She couldn't say that had ever been the case for her, no matter how much she wished it were true.

Her anger at the monarch had also changed, simmering down to an unsettling dissonance between understanding the desire for flight and abhorring the methods used to achieve it. Flight would be a wonderful thing, and Brynz also yearned to soar high upon the back of a gryphon as the Iellians of old had once done, but the monarch's ambitions had led to both cruelty and arrogance. That Brynz had been a part of those ambitions made her feel even more conflicted about her past.

A bird cry pierced the stillness. Twice, she'd heard what she thought was the far-off screech of a gryphon. Both times, her heart had tried to fly out of her chest until she realized it was only the call of a shin-hawk or a black-tailed vulpos. Afterward, her mind had spun back through the disaster of the pageant and her worry for Zell before the steady *fwup fwup fwup* of her footfalls brought her back to the present.

She sat in the shade of a squarish tree with her shoe off, picking at a callous on her heel, when Uhnkre dropped half of a split hare into her lap. He leaned against a nearby tree and tore into the other half. The pelt and head were removed, making it easy going. Soon she was done. She flung the bones into a nearby bush then scraped her hands against the dirt-stiffened material of her pants. She slipped what was left of her stocking back on, then her shoe, noting its dark-blue finish had nearly scuffed away.

Uhnkre tossed his leavings, swiped his hands against his tanned leather shirt, then reached down and pulled her to her feet by her upper arm. She had become accustomed to this and offered no resistance. His touch had softened since that first night, a small mercy she barely noticed.

"High Gate," he ground out in his broken Iellian. "Tomorrow trade Brinzzz. Break Iellia."

This again. She tried not to show how little faith she had in his plan. A frisson ran through her. No matter how she pictured it, her future looked grim, yet she still held out hope she would somehow escape her fate.

Uhnkre let loose of her arm and raised his own into the air. The men formed up around them. "Kwulf," he said. *Move.* "Lel." *At the speed I set.* Besides the men's names, Brynz had picked up the meaning of those two words after hearing them night after night. He set off at a strong walk, the blunt handle of his dras swaying like a banner. The rest followed at pace, their footsteps as silent as the fall of a shed leaf. Soon, they were ascending a steep slope. The sun had already dropped behind the hill, allowing darkness to swallow more and more of the light. She turned her thoughts away from what Uhnkre had said, concentrating instead on what had gotten her through so far—putting one foot in front of the other then scratching another line onto her chest piece. Nothing else mattered except for that.

The jingle of bells would announce them far before they came into sight of the High Gate. Still, Rachmyn could see the logic of leaving the bells on the horses' harnesses. To not do so might arouse suspicion. Complacency was what was needed, not additional scrutiny.

He checked his pocket for his shard. Yes, there it was. He would need every bit of its power if this plan was to work.

At first, he'd been angry when Haedyn volunteered him and his speck for this madness. He didn't trust Eccto any more than he trusted any Shadowen. The memory of his parents' end was never far away when he met up with those who shared his heritage and affinity. But he soon realized it mattered little whether he sold the speck to Alliari or used it on the guards, his green-black powder was their only ticket out of this wretched country.

He hoped he hadn't misjudged Elorah or her abilities. That he'd seen her in Oru Fen and heard her words in his mind—*to my heart you are family*—held sway though it didn't seal his decision. She must be Shadowen. How else could they have met in that in-between world? How else could her mindwords have entered his head? And yet, for her he didn't feel his customary mistrust. Instead, there was the start of a grudging respect that defied rational explanation.

His mind went to the giant bears rising from the ground through some mysterious force. The Urslan, Aikin had called them. Who had summoned them? Therran vorik, surely, and yet, Aikin had seemed as overwhelmed and astonished as himself when the bear-shaped hills tore themselves out of the dirt and rammed through the infernal thorn hedge. Hardly how one would act if they'd conjured such a mighty force let alone this prideful maran who would have surely claimed the triumph had it been his to own. Only Elgre, who always seemed to know what was about to happen, and Elorah hadn't appeared unduly awed at their appearance. To have two affinities was unheard of, and it perplexed Rachmyn that she seemed to possess both Therran and Shadowen vorik and could use both with great skill. He'd never come across that before nor heard of such a possibility. It crossed his mind she might be a wycche, but even wycches were only powerful within their native affinity. Her abilities defied everything he thought he knew about vorik and its limits.

He and Haedyn were perched on wooden chairs inside Eccto's caravan as it bumped along, his friend watching their progress through a small, round window in the caravan's front door, his bird a black lump on his shoulder. On the other side, the glow of an oil lantern pushed back the inky dark, its sallow flame smearing orange light across the side of Eccto's head and the croups of his black-and-white horses. Rachmyn had driven caravans enough to know that Eccto would be standing as he drove, his shoulders leaned back against the wooden front wall, his hindparts resting upon a narrow ledge made for that purpose.

Eccto flapped the reins, and one of the Plenderres tossed its head, setting its harness bells ringing. Both horses leaned into their collars to counteract the steepening grade, their hindquarters straining against the load.

Elorah and Mierrle were in the next caravan back; Aikin and Thane in the caravan behind them. The four ponies were tied to the railing at the rear of Eccto's caravan while the six geldings were hitched three-apiece to the other two vans, their saddles and gear stowed under blankets inside each as a precaution.

Elgre had been left to find his own way to keep from spooking the horses. Rachmyn wasn't worried. The wolf had an uncanny knack for disappearing then reappearing as needed.

They went along for better than a league before the terrain leveled out. Eccto pulled up the horses, and the jingling quieted as they lowered their heads to lip at the dew-grayed grass.

Eccto wrapped the reins around a hook on the lantern post and climbed down.

Rachmyn opened the door and looked around. They were on a high plateau, hemmed between two sets of angular peaks. "How much farther?" he asked, descending the stairs to join the red-haired leader.

"Two leagues, maybe three." Eccto scratched the back of his head, his knuckles pushing his flat cap forward. He used both hands to pull it back into place. "Any closer, and they could hear us talk. We mustn't speak of ought but weather and scenery from here on. When we get there, we must be quicker than quick. No time for questions."

"I'll be ready," Rachmyn said.

"Your friend, he knows?" Eccto bobbed his head toward the caravan as Haedyn emerged from the open doorway.

"You good?" Haedyn asked, smiling when Rachmyn shrugged, then adding with studied nonchalance, "I think I'll have a look around..." His words died out as Elorah rounded the corner, heading toward Eccto and Rachmyn. "Oh, hey!" She startled, and he thrust his hands into his pockets. "You good?" he finished awkwardly, his bird staring down from his shoulder, its button eyes glassy in the low light.

Rachmyn sighed. This charm business was becoming tiresome with all its stuttering and smiling and swanning about. He wanted his old friend back, not this new addlepated version.

Eccto frowned and put his hands on his hips.

"Yes," Elorah said, sounding puzzled.

"Good. That's good. Isn't that good?" Haedyn babbled, his moony eyes finding Rachmyn's. Rachmyn snorted, his attention turning to Elorah as she approached, her face serious.

"How will I find you there?" she said. "I'm not as skilled as you seem to think."

"The key is to set your mind upon finding me beforehand and for me to do the same," Rachmyn explained, his eyes flicking toward Eccto. Something about the man's keen expression did not set well. He'd been very careful not to reveal how much speck he possessed, loading all five hoewlers himself while Haedyn kept watch to ensure nobody interrupted him. Each hoewler now held enough speck to knock out a horse. He only had to deliver them to the Shadowen leader before they reached the gate. The eagerness of Eccto's stare sent a prickle down his spine, his credo ringing in his ears. *Never trust another Shadowen.* He didn't worry for himself. Elgre would protect him while he was in Oru Fen, but Elorah had no such guardian while she was there.

He cast a glance toward Haedyn, lounged against the front of the caravan, his expression soft as he watched the exchange. Him, he could trust. Clearly, motivation wouldn't be a problem. Perhaps even that eye-plucking bird would be of some use. It was a thought worth considering. He turned his attention back to the matter at hand. "Shouldn't you warn the others about the talking?" Rachmyn asked, hoping to move Eccto along.

"They know. We've been going to the northern slopes for as long as I can remember. We prefer the Barrish, but this time of year, you can't predict whether it'll be open, so we're forced to use the Kalt-Roulk. Since that wall's been built, it's harder to get past the guards. Mindshields are," Eccto pointed toward his head, "about as easy as carving rock with a piece of soap."

Rachmyn allowed him a grim smile. He knew that feeling too, trying to impress an image upon an active unwillingness, still recalled the draining exhaustion of it. Even now, he could feel the lingering effects.

"What about the Drasgor?" Elorah asked.

"What about them?" Eccto sounded as if he'd never considered them before. "They stay north. We only go as far as the other side of the mountain, and we don't make trouble. We've not been bothered that I can ever recall."

Elorah's brow knitted as she pondered this information.

"Those getting the hoewlers, they know what to do?" Rachmyn asked, looking in the direction of the distant gate and trying to imagine what they would find once they got there.

Eccto nodded. "They'll offer their papers, wait for the distraction, blow for all they're worth—*pfft pfft*—then back aboard, and we're off. We should be well through by the time anyone realizes there's trouble afoot."

"We'll pack the ponies here," Elorah said. "And saddle the horses."

"I don't think that's wise. I thought we were agreed on the best way to proceed." Eccto looked from Elorah to Rachmyn, searching for an ally. Rachmyn tipped his head, his expression stoic. He felt no allegiance to this man and wasn't about to act as if he did.

"If things go wrong, we'll need to split up, and we won't have time for tacking up horses," Elorah said, setting her jaw. "If that doesn't meet with your approval, we'll separate now and wish each other well."

Rachmyn saw the wisdom of her plan. He shifted his gaze back to Eccto, who was pulling at his chin as he considered Elorah's words. Rachmyn spoke up. "It's not up for debate," he said. "The hoewlers and your payment stay with me until I'm satisfied everything is as it should be."

Eccto flung his hands out wide. "You're putting us all at risk," he bleated. "Any hint we're not what we appear and those guards will confiscate our caravans and send us all off to break rocks at Minyoren. Those of us who don't get a blade in the back first, that is."

"As I said, we can split now. We wouldn't want to cause you further trouble." Elorah's tone was steely as she stared hard into the Shadowen's eyes. Rachmyn felt an inching up of his faith in her. Perhaps she had some guile after all.

Eccto rocked back onto his heels, his face tightening. "Better together than apart, I'd say," he ground out. "Do what you must, and we'll do the same."

Elorah gave a curt nod, throwing a look at Rachmyn before turning on her heel and walking away. Haedyn hopped down and trotted after her, his bird taking flight, a dark shadow looping circles through a charcoal sky.

"Where are you going?" Rachmyn called. Haedyn pulled up, his expression all innocent surprise. "You should finish those arrows. I've a feeling there'll be plenty of toads where we're going."

Haedyn started to protest, then thought better of it. He shuffled back to the caravan, his toes scuffing dirt in mute protest. Rachmyn jerked his head toward Elorah. "She seems the type who appreciates a well-made arrow far more than a well-made compliment. Who knows? She might yet find you impressive if you've a bundle or two in your quiver. Besides, a bow without arrows is nothing more than a flimsy club, not much use to anyone in a fight."

"I see your point," Haedyn glummed, holding up a gloved hand and whistling. The circling shadow banked then landed on his fist in a flurry of red and black feathers. He transferred the bird to his shoulder, boarded the caravan, and disappeared inside.

Rachmyn turned back toward Eccto. "I'll see the hoewlers are in the right hands by the time we're at the gate. You worry about getting us there."

Eccto straightened his shoulders. "If all goes well, we'll be there by sunrise."

Rachmyn nodded. In the distance, a familiar pair of moonbright eyes stared out from the filigreed shadow of a bush. Elgre. He hadn't realized how much he'd missed the wolf, and he smiled as he climbed the van's wooden steps.

MAISTER FOX LENDS
a HAND

"The fence is high, the time is late,
The simple path is through the gate."
Fox cupped a paw, three mice climbed inside,
Claws drawn close, they started their ride.
"But what if we're caught?" squeaked one of the mice.
"Don't worry, my dear. You can't be caught twice."

The Collected Tales of Maister Fox— (Traditional)

CHAPTER THIRTY
THE SIMPLE PATH

From his seat inside Eccto's caravan, Haedyn could see the wall was monstrously high, taller even than the one at the base of Deadman's Peak. It was built from enormous brunnestone blocks held together by mortar joints thinner than a feather's edge, its length running east to west from Cyrulian Kalt to Bastlan Roulk.

In the center was the gate, two huge doors grander than anything Haedyn had ever seen, constructed from black-tarred timbers overlaid by an intricate latticework of polished steel. A giant steel gryphon dominated, the emblem split down the middle, one half welded onto each door. Below were three massive black-iron clasps bolting the doors together. There was no breaching such a barricade. The only way forward was through.

Haedyn gripped the crystalwood bow a little tighter, its low hum settling into the bones of his curled hand as he squinted at the fierce glare of the shining gate. His other hand held five hoewlers given to him by Rachmyn for safekeeping. Excitement tempered by worry balled up his stomach, and he felt a sudden urge to have a wee.

Fryk rode the woolen ridge of a rolled-up blanket tied to the caravan's staves, its hooded head bobbing as the wagon jounced forward. Rachmyn craned toward the door's round window, his brow creasing, his eyes shifting as he took in the scene. He turned, one hand splayed wide, the other formed into a circle then pointed toward the window, his expression grim. Fifty. Haedyn forced his attention to the middle ground.

Fifty was an underestimate. Uniformed men were everywhere, blue-coated ants swarming an impregnable cliff. Many clustered in menacing knots, their helmed heads leaned together, their dark-blue scabbards tipping forward from their waists, dragged down by the steel falchions inside. Others strutted about by twos and threes, one arm snugging a crossbow against their sides, a steel-tipped bolt nocked and ready for firing. Many more patrolled from horseback, keeping watch on the proceedings.

A door opened at the base of the wall, and two groups of uniformed men emerged, each foursome toting a pole with the metallic device the guards had used at Deadman's Peak dangling at its far end. As the men walked their appendaged poles forward, Haedyn almost asked what the devices were before remembering there was to be no talking near the gate. Instead, he tapped Rachmyn's upper arm and, when his friend jerked his head round, pointed then gave an exaggerated shrug. Rachmyn shook his head, his stare withering. He indicated the hoewlers then sliced a finger across his neck. Haedyn nodded. Clearly, five would never be enough. He put them into his rucksack.

Various caravans and rigs were lining up to present papers when the gates opened which, according to Eccto, should happen at nine bells. Eccto parked his team behind a heavy dray hooked to a pair of oxen. *Quarrymen*, Haedyn thought as he studied the broad-backed pair sitting on the driver's bench, a rack of sledgehammers bolted underneath.

Eccto twisted round, his face ashen. "Too many," he mouthed with a shake of his head. Rachmyn's lips flattened as his chin jutted. Eccto's head swiveled forward, his left hand snaking out. He dipped his fingers twice, a signal to the other Konda caravans the original plan was off. Each driver would give the same signal to ensure the entire band got the message.

A flare of reflected sunlight split the pale mountain air as the gate began to move, the left door swinging north, the right swinging south.

Arbalists formed up opposite each door as it clanged to a halt, their crossbows tight against their shoulders. Guardsmen approached the first four wagons while additional guards fanned out to patrol, their gaze taking in everything as they sauntered around, one hand resting on their falchion's handle.

The drivers of the first four conveyances disembarked and handed papers to a headguard. Their passengers also disembarked then milled about like stunned sheep. Search-guards lifted covers and lids, poked through cargo, peered at undercarriages, even checked harnesses and seats before signaling an all-clear to the headguard who nodded and handed back the documents.

Meanwhile, the guards with the poles moved from rig to rig, hovering their device over each before moving on. What was it? What did it do? Haedyn turned, questions burning in his mind, but Rachmyn was no longer looking out the window. He was slumped in his seat, head lolled, eyes closed, his near hand stuck into his pocket, the other hanging heavy at his side. Haedyn knew his friend had gone to that unseen place he visited often but spoke of never, and his wadded stomach twisted. He got to his feet and peered out the window.

A gray blur darted from behind the south-facing door, the shape moving at a terrific pace. Elgre. Head low, tail brushing the ground, the wolf charged into the opening, startling the arbalists. Several shot as the wolf careered past, their bolts striking the steel latticework before ricocheting away. Haedyn's knotted stomach climbed into his throat when the wolf disappeared, and he grabbed Rachmyn's arm, the crystalwood bow clattering to the floor.

A shock of crackling energy rolled up Haedyn's arm and into his shoulder, deadening the limb. Rachmyn grimaced then gritted his teeth, his eyelids compressing to puckered slits, wormish veins bulging from the sides of his neck. Haedyn's mind screamed at his hand to let loose, but it was no use; the hand might as well have been a block of wood for all he could do with it. He used his free hand to yank the deadened one away and the feeling blasted into his lifting arm, the numbness running up his arm and into his shoulder, The only way he could feel anything was to lean forward and bang the nerveless limbs against his thighs. After several frantic thumps, a burning tingle replaced the frightening numbness. He searched Rachmyn's face, his ears straining to hear above the roar of his own internals.

Rachmyn sucked in a ragged breath, his body arching forward before he expelled a whistling sigh. He gasped in a second breath, and his rigid muscles went slack, the set of his jaw softening, his neck smoothing down. Relief washed through Haedyn. His friend was alive.

Haedyn leaned over and pawed up the bow. How would they ever get past the guards with Rachmyn like this? How would he ever shoot a bow or wield a knife with these useless hands? The caravan rolled forward then jerked to a stop. Haedyn looked outside, his gaze following Eccto's.

The first four wagons headed toward the gate opening while a second group of four moved forward for inspection.

A commotion broke out around a heavy wagon at the front, and Haedyn pressed his face against the window. Two guards ripped back a canvas tarp, while a third leaped into the bed, crowbar in hand. A pole crew stood nearby, dangling their mysterious device. A poleman chopped pointed fingers toward the wagon, and the guardsman whacked the crowbar's clawed end into the wooden floor. He jerked it free and swung again, bits of wood chunking away. He kept at it until he'd opened a platter-sized hole then threw the tool aside and thrust his arm into the hacked-out void, wallowing it around for several turns before wresting out the twine-cinched end of a sackweave bag. The guard let loose, a sneer on his sweaty face, the sack-end slipping out of sight as he stood.

The headguard signaled, and the sneering guard jumped down, went to the wagon front, and felt under the seat. The driver stared at the ground, his head drooping like a rotting pumpkin, the headguard already clapping a pair of weighty-looking cuffs onto his wrists. The back of the wagon bed flung upward revealing a clutch of sacks nestled like brown grubs.

The headguard drew his falchion and barked into the driver's ear. The rotting pumpkin drooped lower. The guard stabbed a finger toward a block building and the driver began shambling toward it, his cuffed hands brushing against the front of his dusty trousers. The guard swaggered alongside, his falchion blade shining as he held it to the man's side.

The confiscated wagon was led to a hitching pole near the wall, the propped-up floor shimmying with every step. After securing the wagon's team of gray horses, two guards began unloading, dragging out close to thirty bulging sacks by the time they'd finished.

Haedyn kneaded his damaged hands and turned his attention back to the inspection line.

The drivers and passengers of the remaining three wagons had re-embarked and were on their way toward the gate. Four more conveyances rolled forward. Eccto's caravan creaked into motion then juddered to another stop. They were getting close. Only four wagons stood between them and the inspection guards.

Haedyn watched another of the band's caravans pull up to the right, the big-eared Shadowen at the reins, his wife beside him, her hooded eyes taking in the scene. The big-eared man turned toward Eccto, a frown carved into his long face. Eccto waved him on, and the man flapped the reins to move his matched team forward. The band's third caravan pulled up, and Eccto waved it on as well making his caravan the last of the three.

Haedyn looked at Rachmyn. Still off in the nevernever. He rubbed his pins-and-needles hands, panicky fear taking hold. What if his friend was trapped forever? What would he do then?

He reached over his shoulder to his twine-and-willow quiver and yanked out an arrow, noting as he did so that the feeling in his arms had fully returned. *Thank the spunking stars*. He pushed the arrow back in, pleased. He gripped his knife's handle. A tug and it was out of its sheath. He snugged it away then hoisted the bow, cocking the drawstring and reveling in the weapon's silky response. He closed one eye, sighting in on a guard a hundred paces away then leaned back to account for the arc needed and imagined putting an arrow into the man's chest. His old bow would have never made that long of a shot, but this one felt as if he could put an arrow into the heart of the sun if he so desired.

He sighted in on a second guard, his mind whirling ahead. Whatever happened, he wasn't going down easy. He would fight them all. The moment that decision was made, a sudden kinship flowed from the weapon through his arm and into his chest, a pairing up between himself and the bow, the two merging into one entity. It was a feeling like nothing he'd ever felt before, bringing with it a sense of invincibility.

Rachmyn's body spasmed and Haedyn let down the bowstring, fresh hope shooting through him. Had his friend returned?

One look told him he had not.

The caravan lurched, and Haedyn stumbled. A familiar voice warned, "Stay still."

Rachmyn.

Haedyn glanced at his friend slouched in his chair, jaw slack, eyes closed. "Stay. Still," growled the voice again, just as Rachmyn did whenever Haedyn ignored him. He bent closer.

Rachmyn's relaxed face and sprawled body remained motionless yet somehow, his voice overrode the hum of the bow and the *rap-rap-rap* of the caravan's buffeting canvas roof. *How could that be?* He must be imagining things, but no, that wasn't right, because he'd heard his own mindvoice narrating his thoughts at the same moment he'd heard Rachmyn speak. Haedyn mulled this over, his thoughts becoming more and more muddled when the voice bugled, "Your arm is still moving!" The tone was unmistakably Rachmyn's, its razor-edged exasperation as familiar as his own hand. But how was that possible? Haedyn stilled his jiggling arm and looked sideways. How could his friend have seen the arm moving without opening his eyes?

He was still puzzling over it when the wagon stuttered forward. He rolled his eyes toward the window, straining to what was happening outside. "Steady," warned the voice. Haedyn stiffened and shallowed his breathing, his eyes on stalks trying to see the guards. *Why can't I move?* As soon as the thought bubbled up, the answer came. "I've constructed a forgetting mindshield. Any movement will destroy it."

Mindshields were always a last resort. The few times Rachmyn had concocted one, he'd been out of sorts for days afterward. Haedyn couldn't imagine how his friend would be after creating a mindshield of this size. His thoughts turned to Fryk. What if his bird moved?

"Steady," the voice commanded. "Forget the spunking bird. Your mind calls to him as it calls to me."

Haedyn tried to clear his head, but trying *not* to think about something was much harder than trying *to* think about it. Despite every effort, he kept circling back to worrying for Fryk. He was so accustomed to hearing Rachmyn's long sigh when he was failing at something simple that when it came, it was almost a comfort. But he knew the sound was a memory because it had no effect on the rapping of the canvas roof or his own chiding mindwords. At least if he thought about the sigh, he wasn't thinking about... He put his attention back on the sigh.

The caravan rolled forward then ground to another halt. Haedyn remained motionless, despite the movement beneath his feet, all the while wishing he'd been in a better position before being made to stay still. He was standing sideways to the front door, nearly touching Rachmyn with his knees, the bow hanging from his crooked right arm. Grief's teeth. Rachmyn could have at least let him sit down. Holding this stance was getting uncomfortable.

The caravan door whipped open, and a square-jawed guard burst in, planting himself within arm's reach. Haedyn tensed his muscles, his heart rate ramping up. From the corner of his eye, he watched the guard survey the interior, eyes narrowed, hands on hips. One hand went to the falchion. A soft *swith* and the weapon was out.

Steady.

The voice quelled Haedyn's overwhelming urge to reach for his own blade.

The guard thrust the falchion's point under the seat of Haedyn's empty chair, tipping it onto its rear legs. Haedyn held his breath as the guard looked at the carpeted floor where his rucksack lay. The blade withdrew, and the chair thunked back into place. The guard kicked the corner of the rug, his hot breath fluming down Haedyn's neck and making his skin crawl. He stiffened and held his breath. The guard moved past, brushing close enough that Haedyn's arm hair pricked up.

He doesn't see me!

Haedyn's muscles relaxed their grip on his bones. The mindshield was working. The guard squinted up toward the grynt. Haedyn tensed again, his mind pinging between thinking of Fryk and thinking of anything else. The guard stepped forward and reached.

The strike came swiftly, a fluttering whoosh, a blunted thud, a muffled squelch. Haedyn knew what had happened without seeing it. Fryk had gone for the man's eyes.

"GAAAAHHH!"

The guard staggered back, Fryk's sock toe shedding from his hand like a spent leaf. The falchion thudded to the floor as the guard clutched his shredded face, blood squeezing out between his fingers and running down his cheek.

CHIRRT CHIRRT CHIRRT

The grynt's piercing scream came from everywhere.

"Steady!" Rachmyn's voice thundered.

Haedyn gritted his teeth and closed his eyes, the flapping of wings loud in his ears. The whiss of flailing hands preceded a staccato of strikes —*FLUP FLUP FLUP FLUP FLUP*—that ended in another sickening squelch.

"GAAAAHHHH!" the guard wailed.

Haedyn's eyes opened wide, fastening on Fryk swooping into an open cupboard at the back of the caravan, its gelatinous prize gripped in its black talons.

The guard stumbled back a step, his hands clapped over the bleeding hole where his eye had been. He cranked his body sideways and staggered out the door.

"MY EYE!" he bellowed, a thunderscreech of raging terror as he staggered down the steps, the caravan shuddering with every aggrieved footfall. "That sodding bird plucked out my sodding eye!"

Haedyn groaned. *You've done it this time, Fryk.* The bird was too busy slashing apart the eye and putting down the pieces to be bothered.

A pounding of boots preceded the barreling entry of two thick-necked guards, the caravan rocking as they burst in. Both managed to miss Haedyn and Rachmyn as they sighted in on the grynt. A crescendo of shouting announced the entry of a third, this one shorter and thicker than the other two. He elbowed past them, one finger pointing toward the cupboard. Haedyn's hand twitched, the pull of his knife nearly irresistible as the man advanced on his bird.

Steady!

Fryk stared beadily from the dark recess of the cupboard, beak shiny with wet, the plucked eye already down its gullet.

Haedyn's mind went to the hoewlers. If he could get hold of them... His thoughts were cut short.

Steady!

The bird launched at the tallest guard's forehead, its talons peeling flesh from skull and sending a gush of blood into his eyes. The guard swung his drawn falchion, embedding its steel blade into the side of his partner and opening a gash flowing hot with stinking juice. Haedyn wrinkled his nose at the reek of punctured guts. The struck guard dropped to his knees, his forearm jamming into his leaking side, his upper body crumpling forward until his grimacing face met the purled-wool carpet. Fryk flew to a lampstand and latched on, its black eyes tracking every movement.

The squat guard charged, his falchion spearing forward. Fryk bobbed once, then took flight, winging straight for the open door. The guard swung his blade twice at the bird before it flew out of the caravan.

Haedyn turned his attention to the crumpled guard. A spreading stain darkened his blue wool coat, dampness wicking outward despite his clamped arm and bent posture. The guard with the mangled forehead stuffed a handkerchief into his partner's bleeding slash before wrenching him to his feet. The pair leaned together and tottered out while the squat guard took one last look, muttered an oath, and sheathed his blade. He retrieved the fallen guard's falchion and exited, slamming the door. It shuddered against the frame before bouncing open again.

Haedyn let out a sigh. Somehow, he and Rachmyn had escaped detection. He scanned the piece of sky visible through the open door hoping to see a pocket-sized monster flying high, but there were only lacy clouds and peerless blue. His gaze dropped to where Eccto stood. Surrounded by hectoring guards, the hapless Shadowen could only shrug his answers. The squat guard pointed a finger at Eccto's face, his shouting the loudest of all. A set of cuffs were produced while the squat guard pointed his drawn falchion at Eccto's chest. Eccto eyed the caravan as the cuffs locked into place while behind him, the band's other two caravans trundled toward the open space between the gleaming doors.

A guard grabbed hold of the silver-studded bridle of the nearest horse and led the black-and-white Plenderres toward the other confiscated wagon, harness bells jingling as the horses plodded off in one direction, Eccto's cuffs clinking as he shuffled away in the other.

The guard half-hitched a rein to the hitching pole and strode away.

A fit of cramp seized Haedyn's limbs, his knees and elbows locking in place. He stared at Rachmyn, willing his friend to rouse as his contracted muscles tightened into painful knots. When he could no longer take it, he stretched out a leg, expecting a scathing rebuke, but the only sounds were the blow of the wind, the rap of the roof, and the occasional jingle of harness bells. He straightened his back and relaxed his arms, bracing for the verbal tirade sure to come but again, nothing. He looked down. Rachmyn had that crooked grin he always wore when he was goading Haedyn into doing something.

What am I supposed to do?

Haedyn looked out the caravan doorway, hoping to see where his bird had got to and whether the other caravans had made it through the gate, but his view was blocked by the polished backend of a gryphon, gleaming steel lattice, and the bolt side of three massive clasps set against a backdrop of pitch-soaked wood. A thought struck.

Tarred timbers set afire would put out a cloud of smoke as black as night, not to mention flaming doors might prove impossible to shut.

He pulled an arrow from his quiver and directed his fiery will into its sharpened avobanc head, the opaque white taking on a red-orange glow. He nudged the crystalwood bow off his shoulder, smiling a little when its grip nestled into the palm of his hand as if it had always been a part of him. He eased through the open caravan door, nocked the heated arrow, picked his spot, and let fly.

Thwip. Thonk.

It was a solid hit, the arrowhead driving deep into the oiled wood, a thin trail of smoke marking its entry. Haedyn scanned for trouble then, seeing none, drew a second arrow and repeated the process.

Thwip. Thonk.

Another hit. Another wisping trail of smoke. Haedyn went to his quiver ten more times, each *thonk* adding another smoldering shaft to the massive door. He surveyed his work with satisfaction, the faint scent of char confirming what his eyes could not yet see. The timbers were beginning to burn. He noted the stiff breeze buffeting the flags lining the top of the wall and thought again about the arrowheads, sending another heating surge into each before going inside to check on Rachmyn.

One problem always led to another, and this time was no different. The gate had been one thing, his passed-out friend quite another. He still hadn't a clue what to do but with the door beginning to smoke, he'd needed to figure out something pretty sodding quick.

The weaving of a forgetting mindshield was something of a lost art, even amongst highly skilled Shadowen. Rachmyn might never have heard of it at all had his family not joined up with the Kalto band all those years ago.

Challyn Stulko, Alliari's father and a master of the technique, after recognizing Rachmyn's innate talent, had taken him aside to instruct him in the abstruse practice. As Rachmyn recalled, the key was to magnify mundanity to the exclusion of all else, so there remained nothing for the dupe to remember. It took a certain strength of mind to retain a monotonous void at the forefront of one's thinking without ever straying to those distractions that excite. To impress that blankness upon another was an even greater feat. When done well, the only remainder was a vague sense of lost time. It was perhaps the subtlest of mindshield techniques, but by far the most effective. It was one thing to create a shield that obscured its weaver while allowing retention of retrievable memory but something else again to create one that left behind only formless vacancy.

He would never have attempted such a shield had Spectra not pushed him to try. He'd only been a boy when Stulko had explained the process, and his early attempts had been laughably bad, his father deeming the aftereffects of one attempt a 'lingering boredom that festered like a toothache.' Then again, neither his father nor his mother used mindshields and had discouraged him from pursuing what his father called 'Stulko's aberrations', feeling it strayed too closely to the perfidy of mind control. Unlike most Shadowen, his parents held strict scruples when it came to that dark path which was why, when his guardian retrieved the memory of Stulko's instruction, he questioned whether such a shield was proper.

Spectra's reply had been swift and sure. *It is not the mindshield that is good or bad but the intention behind it that leaves its mark.*

As soon as Rachmyn had closed his eyes, he was in Oru Fen, arriving almost before his incarnate shell had relinquished its grip, his thoughts so concentrated on Elorah, that when she appeared with her huge white wolf, it was nothing more than an expectation met. She had preceded him into the realm, her emanating energy a balm to his own disquieting thoughts. In her hands was the ethereal version of her crystalwood staff, aglow with a golden light he had never before seen in this dimension of purples and grays, and he wondered whether it was the staff's energy or its bearer's that he felt.

He reached into his pocket which, until that very moment, had never even been a thought. That he had a hand or a pocket was a revelation, but he had little time to dwell upon it as his fingers found the familiar shape of his shard. He felt a surge in his own internal force, a connecting of the inner him to a power larger than even his most vivid dreams.

The white wolf acknowledged his arrival with a nod, which Spectra returned before producing the memory of Challyn as an encouragement.

Everything seemed so simple with the shard in his hand and the power of the All at his back. Was there anything he couldn't do? Before him appeared the Konda band's three caravans, the details of their interiors coming to mind as easily as any other thought, the only difference being that instead of his mind replicating an existent scene on the physical plane, a task requiring a huge output of vor, he and his shard would weave a forgetting shield to hover like an invisible cloud upon the threshold of each caravan's door, blocking any detail the inspectors' eyes might perceive from registering as memory.

In the first two, the shields had worked a treat, the guards barely giving the interiors a second glance before waving their approval for the caravans to move forward. He suspected Elorah had as much to do with their complacency as his own efforts. Eccto's caravan, on the other hand, hadn't quite gone to plan. Haedyn's fidgeting worry had been some of it. The unexpected contact on his arm had nearly pulled Rachmyn out of the realm and made the weaving that much more difficult. To get it accomplished, he'd had to expend terrific effort to keep Haedyn from ruining everything. He'd never attempted sending mindwords from this realm to the next and though it would have been easier had Haedyn been a better listener, in the end Rachmyn had somehow managed it. Once his friend's mind quit calling his own, he'd been able to weave a third forgetting shield and hover it over Eccto's threshold. And though this guard had been less susceptible than the previous two, the shield had been working until the man somehow perceived the bird. That was when it all fell to bits.

Rachmyn had hoped to get them all through the gate before returning to his mortal shell, but once the eye was plucked, and the gate set afire, he had no choice. Spectra agreed, and it was through her he sent his mindwords to Elorah's guardian.

Forgive me, but I must return sooner than planned.

Her guardian conveyed Elorah's understanding, and before he knew it, he was back inside his slumped body. And none too soon, for the smell of smoke was becoming strong, the gate's huge door studded with licks of flame.

The horses snorted and shook their heads, their eyes rolling upward, the discordant chime of their harness bells ringing out in pealing notes. Haedyn's attention was on the gate door, so that when Rachmyn touched his shoulder, he jumped high enough to brush his head against the caravan's roof. Rachmyn clapped a hand across his friend's mouth, drew a finger to his own, then made a fist, and bumped it twice.

Haedyn's exuberant bearhug nearly knocked him down, and it wasn't until Rachmyn choked out a cough that he loosened his grip. He patted Haedyn's shoulder as he took a strangled gasp then pointed to their gear and twitched two fingers to signal they were going to make a run for it. Only then did he remember the pack ponies tied to the back of the caravan.

They were going to have to figure out what to do with the sodding ponies.

Spunk.

KINDNESS NEVER FAILS

Kindness for the wrong reason is preferable to unkindness for the right one. In truth, kindness is always the better choice for it never fails.

—Excerpted from *The Guide to Proper Etiquette*
    for the Ascended Regent, Kallizia Rennesseau, by a scribe

HARK, FOR THE TIME
NEARS...

...when the follies of the past—of which much has been spoken and written —shall finally be put right, and the first great Founder shall be released from his long sufferance. Let it be as a sign to all, when that day comes, that the long-awaited ascendancy of the realm to its Original State of harmony and balance has begun.

For most, it is far past remembering, that time when peace and beauty reigned, a distant dream recalled only in fits and fragments by pious supplicants and so-called fools. For many, there lingers a nameless fear, a disquieting echo from that time when they counted themselves amongst those who forsook their own birthright to pursue the fleeting pleasures of self. Much have they suffered in the annums and eryns since. Much have they lost to the mists of time. Many truths have they forgotten during their long and steady slipping away from Primeryn Vor.

So too Eolemar has suffered without the unbounded influence of that One whose gladsome Xha and steadfast Kindness once inspired legend and song, cut off, as it were, from the infinite source that served to counterbalance individual tendencies toward self-centeredness and greed.

Yea though, a quickening has already begun amongst the flora and fauna that live upon Eolemar's breast, a keenly felt anticipation that the Restoration of a glorious Founder is near at hand. A quickening, too, has begun amongst those guides charged with the welfare of incarnate souls. Beyond the ken of many, known only to a few, these timeless beings have always wielded much influence upon the fate and future of the realm, for it is through them that the minds of souls are either lost or won in the age-old struggle between the self and the All.

As the time nears, those battles will intensify with all due speed, for once begun, the long awaited Restoration of that One whose sapphire heart still beats with tender affection shall happen in the blinking of an eye. Hark, and ye too may hear the whispered beginnings of that glorious day in the wind and the wild and the wonders that surround you.

We, the Elect, have spoken.

Xetili Drum Song

AH-BAH-BAH   *AH-BAH-BAH* (drum rhythm)
OOR-I-BOS   OOR-I-BOS (vocal chant)
AH-BAH-BAH   *AH-BAH-BAH*
GOD OF ALL   GOD OF ALL
AH-BAH-BAH   *AH-BAH-BAH*
OOR-I-BOS   OOR-I-BOS
AH-BAH-BAH   *AH-BAH-BAH*
NOW ARISE   NOW ARISE

*Translator's note: Chant is repeated for extended periods during ceremonies

Chuulzu Keleekeluk—(Spirit of the Forest)
Transcribed from witness statements collected and translated for the Most Exalted Monarch, Geldizian Rennesseau, by a scribe

CHAPTER THIRTY-ONE
OF NORTHMEN AND MERCY

Brynz snorted to clear the charcoal smell from her nose and wondered what was on fire. Her time with these northmen had taught her that fires were always to be avoided. A rogue breeze must have blown the crisped smell up from the valley.

She'd already scratched another mark onto her chest piece and was strapping it into place when Uhnkre grabbed her arm, pulling her up and marching her away from the others. She kept pace, the chestpiece straps whipping against her sides. They were out of earshot by the time he released her.

Attempting escape came to mind, as it always did, but Uhnkre already had his knife out and pointed at her before she'd even completed the thought.

"Brinzzzzz," he said, his voice the soft buzz of a stinging insect. She raised her eyes to his. "Today you go back."

She thought she detected regret in his voice before her reason returned. "What if I don't want to go back?" His eyebrows raised, the slightest of invitations to continue. "There's nothing there for me." He stared at her. Why was she even trying? Clearly, her thoughts and feelings had no bearing on his decisions.

"Where we go, you do not want," he sighed. A flare of hope sparked.

"How do you know?" she asked, a strange nostalgia tingeing her thoughts. She shook her head. Nostalgia for what? Pain? Fear? Dread? Endless marching? A blade in the back? She must be going mad.

"You High Iellia," he stated.

"I'm not," she countered. How could she explain that if she went back, she would end up dead or worse? The prospect of dying seemed much easier to bear if it were to come in these wide-open spaces, in a place where gryphons flew free rather than in the stifling thiefkeep of a culture that had imprisoned her spirit from the time she was small. "Have you any idea how little I have to go back to?"

"No." His tone was implacable.

She searched his face, her mind parsing his response. Was his "no" an answer to her question or was he refuting everything she was saying? Desperation clawed at her, the thought of returning to her previous life forcing a decision. "No," she answered, staring into his deep-set eyes. "Kill me, set me free, do whatever you want, but I won't go back." Saying the words made her feel stronger, more in control, despite her current circumstance. If it was her time, so be it. Let it be done here and now.

It was his turn to make a decision. "Kill Brinzzz," he said, his free hand reaching up to stroke his claw-and-tooth-studded beard. Brynz eyed the long blade pointed at her chest, wondering how it would feel to be impaled by the gruesome weapon. She steeled her nerve, preparing for the inevitable. "Kill Brinzzz," he said again, his gaze dropping to his knife. She closed her eyes and held her breath. Any moment now, it would be over. Chillbumps broke out on her arms, while desperate half-formed thoughts seized her mind. If she could conjure up a large enough wind, maybe she could knock Uhnkre aside then sprint down the mountain faster than she'd ever run before and—*THWOP*. A thump against her shoulder forced her thoughts to the present. This was it. She was going to die. *Run!* her mind screamed. The muscles in her legs twitched, but her feet remained rooted in the leaf-litter. A second thump rattled her chest followed by a tug and a pulling away. She opened her eyes in time to see Uhnkre fling the chest piece off into the underbrush with the point of the blade. Her eyebrows drew tight, forming a single line across her brow as she locked eyes with him, her body irrelevant.

His jaw jutted. "Kill Iellia, not Brinzzz," he rumbled, his forehead tensing above his deep-set eyes.

Her chest collapsed with relief, hot breath tumbling out in a rush. Her knees turned to water, and she stumbled forward a step, coughing harshly, her forgetting eyes leaking onto her cheeks. Was she laughing or crying? She couldn't tell. Maybe both. Uhnkre looked on with the disdainful glare of a hawk watching a stoat chase its tail, and she thought any moment he would change his mind and run her through.

"Kill Iellia," she babbled as she shambled forward on her uncooperative stems.

He stepped back to sheathe the knife, his eyes trained upon her. "Come," he said, reaching for her arm. She didn't mind the help, her legs gone as crooked and wobbling as a newborn calf's. His grip was gentle, and he took more care than usual guiding her back to the others. It occurred to her that she had passed some unspoken test, had somehow proven herself worthy of Drasgorian respect, whatever that meant. It didn't ensure she would survive, but she might have at least given herself a chance.

The smell of smoke was getting stronger. Haedyn glanced at the numerous white whorls twisting away from the gate door as Rachmyn shoved him forward, out of the caravan and into the sun. Haedyn had his pack and the crystalwood bow, but they'd both left their staffs behind on the caravan floor.

Rachmyn went to untie the pack ponies while Haedyn cut loose the heavy wagon's team of gray Dresners, before untying the snorting Plenderres. He heard a faint noise and cocked his head, leaning toward the sound. A fizzy hiss was coming from the pile of confiscated sacks. He studied them for a moment, looked up at the smoking door then back at the sacks, deciding. He nocked an arrow, his will heating the head.

"Now!" Rachmyn yelled.

Thwip. Thunk.

He stuck the glowing arrowhead into one of the sacks, slung the bow onto his shoulder and hoisted himself aboard the nearest Plenderre. It had been an age since he'd ridden, but it felt as natural as when he was young and rode the Umbrae family's Spots every day.

He pulled the lines to fan the horses away from the hitching pole before nudging his heels. His mount lunged forward, dragging its harness mate for a half-stride before the team synced into a gallop, the caravan rattling behind them. Haedyn clamped his legs, the bow hanging from his shoulder, his hands leveraging the lines for balance.

The Dresners snorted as they jigged away from the hitching pole and stutter-stepped into a gallop, following the spotted team's path. Haedyn heard the crack of hooves striking stone as they gained speed.

"HAAAA!"

Haedyn looked behind. Rachmyn screamed again at the stamping ponies, hauling back on all four lead-lines to get them moving before making a plowman's turn and running toward the gate, the balking ponies breaking into a stiff-legged trot. A sudden movement caught Haedyn's eye. Seven guards, falchions drawn, charged toward Rachmyn.

Haedyn geed the Plenderres straight for them, grit peppering his face as he pulled the horses into a tight turn. The caravan slid, skidding in a sideswiping arc and knocking three guards to the ground, the lantern bouncing free and striking one in the head as he lizard-crawled away. The caravan's iron-shod wheels scudded across the sprawling men, cracking ribs and vertebrae, shoulder blades and legs.

The remaining four guards pounded forward, their blades flashing as they ran. The Dresners cut a sharp left, their heavy wagon swinging wide and scything down the charging guards. The grays plunged forward, the rig's wheels smashing blue-clad bodies and silver-helmeted heads against unforgiving stone.

Haedyn plow-reined the Plenderres into a looping run, the circling caravan providing cover for Rachmyn as he jinked to keep the goose-stepping ponies moving. On his second trip around, Haedyn spotted the Dresners on their own mad scamper, galloping toward a gray-block building where a clot of milling prisoners stood surrounded by guards shoving them one by one into an iron-barred thiever's wagon.

Two guards were manhandling Eccto onto the thiever's step-ups when the grays smashed through, the wagon crunching one guard under a turning wheel while ramming the other in the back with its front corner. Eccto squirmed free and spurted forward, sprinting furiously for the gate, his cuffed hands chopping, his skinny legs pumping.

Haedyn, spotting Eccto's run, pulled the Plenderres out of their loop and sent them toward him, cutting off a contingent of mounted guards chasing down the red-haired man. Haedyn slowed the horses enough for Eccto to leap at the caravan and clamber up the steps, his bound hands acting as a third leg.

Haedyn boosted his legs, and his mount burst forward, catapulting Eccto headfirst into the caravan's interior where he landed with a shuddering clunk. Haedyn grabbed the harness collar to keep upright and trained his eyes ahead, ignoring Eccto's moaning as six mounted guards galloped toward the caravan at a terrific pace. He waited until they were upon him before pulling the outside rein, sending the Plenderres into a hair-pin turn, two of the caravan's wheels going airborne before crashing back to ground when the rig straightened. A loud thump sounded from the caravan's interior followed by a mewling cry. Haedyn straightened and sighted in on Rachmyn. He had to make sure his friend was covered; Eccto could take care of himself.

Meanwhile, the grays had veered south, hurtling through both sets of pole-wielding guards as the men tried to maneuver their devices out of the way, only letting loose when the runaways were almost on top of them. The front-heavy poles pronged forward, the oval devices smashing against the ground with a tinny, cracking noise, crystalline shards spilling out from their imbricate baffles.

Haedyn thundered past Rachmyn and the ponies, cutting off another group of mounted guards. Half of the cavaliers gave chase while the other half wheeled southward to charge down the grays, now stampeding through the inspection line and inciting a melee of fleeing rigs and near-collisions.

The cavaliers came alongside when Haedyn forced the Plenderres into another skidding turn, spinning the rig around in front of the pile of sackweave bags, a series of thuds followed by a blunted moan echoing out from the caravan. The chasing guards set their horses on their haunches, preparing to pivot, when the arrow-stuck sack exploded, brilliant blue flame and black smoke pluming high into the sky, charred bits of sackweave scattering to the wind.

Three of the horses bucked sideways, dumping their riders beneath their slashing hooves before skittering away. The injured riders, limbs at odd angles, struggled to their feet until another flare blew skyward, flattening them again. A fat pillar of black smut and sackweave scrap overtook the blue flame, billowing dark smoke into the sky. Two more cavaliers flew head-first over their spooking mounts' lowered heads. The remaining pair whipsawed their reins and spurred their mounts. One horse reared and flung its head backward with enough force to knock its rider out before trampling him where he fell. The other reared then toppled sideways, crushing its rider before thrashing to its feet and galloping away.

Haedyn wrestled his own spooking team to a halt before sighting in on Rachmyn. The ponies, having cleared the smoking door, were racing for the opening, pulling Rachmyn behind like a forgotten plow. Haedyn's gaze shifted to the arbalists, their attention on the blue fire and rising smoke. He urged the Plenderres into a gallop and reined them toward the opening, shielding Rachmyn as the ponies hit the gap.

The arbalists managed a haphazard volley as the gaudy van shot past. Haedyn ducked low over his mount's neck, his nose filling with the gamey funk of lathered horse and oiled leather. A bolt grazed the forearm of the haw-side Plenderre, and it stumbled a half-step before regaining its stride. Another whiffed over Haedyn's back, striking the door's latticework with a ringing *TONK*. Three bolts tore through the caravan's painted canvas, Eccto yelping twice.

Two more blasts sounded in quick succession, the explosions rippling the eastern section of the wall and the west-facing door as if they were paper in the wind. A series of ominous cracks rang out, and Haedyn cast a glance sideways.

Large fissures gaped across the seemingly impregnable stone wall, revealing its wooden undergirding. He realized with a start the entire wall was a fake and could be taken down if the beams underlying the cracked stone face caught fire. It was a tempting idea.

A second caravan galloped into the opening from the opposite direction, Big Ears braced against the caravan's front wall, hawing the lines to his gold-and-white team, three saddled geldings running behind in a pell-mell parade. The charging, southbound caravan blocked off the arbalists' view as the ponies charged north, towing Rachmyn in their wake.

A series of shouts and the giant doors began to close, pushed along by gusting wind.

A whooshing roar and the smoldering door burst into flame, spewing out tarry smoke that folded itself into the upward sprawl of black coming from the pile of sacks.

Haedyn hawed his team around, and Big Ears did the same, the two shielding Rachmyn and the ponies as they barrelled through the narrowing gap. Once the ponies were clear, Haedyn and Big Ears wheeled their rigs northward, Haedyn's caravan slipping through a moment before the gatedoors banged shut.

Strangely, the arbalists on the northern side of the wall gave nary a blink as the caravans pounded past, instead forming into two separate lines along the stone wall as if nothing untoward were happening, their backs to the unfolding disaster.

Perhaps we'll get out of this alive after all.

Haedyn drove his team in another looping circuit around Rachmyn and his racing charges.

The northlands lay within sighting distance now, and the ponies were determined to go there as quickly as their short-strided galloping could take them. Rachmyn managed to get them stopped near the third caravan, parked some two-hundred paces beyond the wall.

Haedyn pulled up his team, an acrid smell drawing his attention, his panting breaths loud in his ears. He looked back toward the gate. A curtain of swimmy-looking heat distorted the cloud of black smog cloaking the sun, a pushing, southward wind forcing the foul smoke away from the gate and the Konda band's caravans.

He lowered his gaze, his heels poised to send his team into a retreating gallop, but the arbalists, and indeed, all the guards across the wall's northern face, seemed oblivious, their faces staring ahead like slumbering hares. Were they bewycched? Was he? How were they not repelled by the heat upon their backs? By the choking foulness in the air? By the wrecked wall behind them?

Haedyn felt a familiar thud upon his shoulder, and his head turned out of habit. It was Fryk, landing with the grace of a falling nut. His heart leapt, a sudden joy that he hadn't lost his prized bird bursting behind his eyes and bringing tears. Fryk fluffed and preened, unchanged by his escapade.

"You little monster," Haedyn murmured, his throat tight with tender emotion.

"Better come on with it!" Big Ears shouted, galloping his rig past.

Haedyn gigged his heels into his winded mount's side. The Plenderres broke into a half-hearted trot until the caravan reached the others.

Aikin stuck his head out of Big Ears' caravan, a self-congratulatory grin on his face.

What's he done to deserve wearing such a look?

Haedyn put his attention on the flaxen-haired driver of the other caravan as he stared at the sky, his wind-chapped expression rapt, his team's tails switching at flinders descending like swarming flies. He'd hoped to see Elorah, but there was no sign of her.

Haedyn dismounted then stumbled forward as if his legs were made of sand. Fryk's razored talons bit into his shoulder as the bird vised its grip. The crystalwood bow was the only thing on him that didn't feel about to collapse under its own weight.

Eccto peered out from the caravan's doorway. "You'll have to drive till I get these off," he said, holding up his cuffed hands. A nasty cut welted the cheek beneath his drifting eye, a purple knot protruding from his hairline.

"Help me with these ponies first," Rachmyn said as he trudged past, pulling the four along. Haedyn sighed and forced his miserable muscles into motion. "Be quick about it," Rachmyn added. Haedyn did his best to hurry his quivery legs.

Aikin disembarked and jogged over. "I can take it from here," he said. Rachmyn handed him the lines with a cursory nod, and the

Caeldish started away, the ponies falling in behind him like chicks following a hen.

Haedyn chanced another gaze toward Elorah's caravan. Still no sign of her. Rachmyn jabbed his finger into Haedyn's shoulder to get his attention. "We need to hurry. I've no idea what manner of bewycchement this is, but it surely won't last."

"Right," Haedyn said. He grinned and pointed toward his shoulder. "Look who's back."

Rachmyn tsked. "The eye-plucker himself. Still as charming as ever." He indicated toward the third caravan. "Have you seen your heart's other master yet?"

Haedyn's brow crinkled then smoothed as he caught Rachmyn's meaning. "Not yet," he replied, his cheeks heating.

"Leave it to me," Rachmyn said, limping away.

"But..."

"Get yourself ready. We'll be off as soon as possible."

Aikin came around the corner. "I can drive," he said to Eccto, looking as puffed up as a winter goose. "I have some experience—," Eccto closed the caravan door. "—with it..." Aikin finished, his prideful posture slumping as he gathered up the lines and climbed onto the driving platform.

Haedyn turned away to watch Rachmyn ascend the steps to Elorah's caravan, his heart wishing it was him instead.

Essiant greeted his night-ward already aware of what needed done. Around them swirled a chaos of shouting men and stampeding horses, all powered by single-minded stubbornness. It would take a grand effort on the part of his night-ward to ameliorate the strident thoughtforms surrounding them. Peaceability was what was needed in the face of so much hot anger and blinding arrogance, but more than that, a gathering of like-minded guardians investing their spirit and thought into effecting that peaceableness.

The gate was always going to be a difficult prospect, a pinch point where willfulness converged with misguided duty. It was always going to take some doing to overcome all of that, but Essiant felt sure it was not only achievable but worth achieving. He couldn't allow himself to believe anything else, for the onset of doubt was always the beginning of failure.

His night-ward held out her crystalwood staff, and Essiant wagged his tail. She'd somehow managed to bring through the ethereal version of a tangible object, a skill known only to a few, highly advanced souls. That she'd done it without prior instruction or prompting boded well, not only because of the skill required but also because of the innate understanding it showed. That clarity of vision would be vital once the restoration of Therrania was begun.

Summon your intention and place it into the staff.

Essiant need not have even thought the words, for his night-ward was already suffusing the staff with her soul force, its brightly golden light defying the realm's usual murk. He was delighted to realize a shift in their partnership had begun, his night-ward assuming her Erynvor birthright before his eyes. No longer need he worry about curating her experiences, but rather he could now assume his primary role as augmenter of the immense power she wielded by trusting it was hers. Nothing would be impossible so long as she maintained this level of concentration and belief. Together, they would be an invincible force working on behalf of not only the Vorien League but the Elect themselves, those great good Founders who had conceived of their plan for Restoration long eryns before he and his night-ward had given their pledge.

His lusty howl cut through the thrumming orusphere, a call to all those guardians who had vouched support. Spectra's callback came first, her howl blending with his. The brilliant light from his night-ward's staff had beaten back the realm's gray fog, and he could see the silvery guardian with her pale-haired night-ward, her mindwords making clear they were already weaving three forgetting mindshields. An ambitious goal of which Essiant approved.

Embren, Ieeva, Raya, and Ajai's howls soon joined, as they trotted into the staff's golden light. With their howls came an increase in the staff's radiance, the Eolemaran realm coming into sharp focus. Others also appeared, wraithwolves whose intentions were in accord with those already gathered. Many had night-wards involved with the proceedings at hand, and their show of solidarity was not only heartening but necessary. Without them, he and his night-ward's attempts would be akin to shouting into the wind.

He felt his night-ward's growing joy as members of the Vorien League rallied about her, felt the fullness in her heart as she swung her staff in a wide arc, illuminating the vast number of wraithwolf guardians waiting for her to lead them in their common cause. Even Spectra, after her night-ward was forced to abandon the realm, had taken her place amongst the throng.

A ripple ran through the assembly, it's beginning a single thought from the Erynvor.

See true.

The thoughtform gathered strength as it moved through each guardian, their individual energies building and shaping it into a larger and greater whole within the vibrating orucon beneath their paws until it became the irresistible power of a thousand cheerful suns. Pulling from that vast pool of intentional goodwill, the Erynvor, by way of her Spyrrt vorik and ethereal staff, began impressing compassionate light into the minds of those working against her in the waking world. The all-encompassing light would divert their thoughts from opposing her path and ease them toward cooperative grace.

Essiant peered at the gate, gauging the Erynvor's effect. Amongst those charged with enforcement, where before there had been chaos and anger, there was now calm and assent. But for how long? How long could the gathered guardians focus their intention upon the Erynvor's singular cause? How long could the Erynvor maintain her heralding thought? As long as was needed, he decided.

He howled again into the purple sky, overjoyed that the Erynvor had at last assumed the full mantle of her responsibility. This was the beginning of a resurrection that would leave its mark for all of time, and to be a part of it was beyond his highest hope.

CHAPTER THIRTY-TWO
TOO FAR, TOO LATE

Xyleea pinched her shriveled arm to keep from crying. She knew she had precious little water left and couldn't afford to waste it on futile tears.

The chuulzu kereet sat like a stone upon her head, her reedy neck struggling to keep it upright. She thought of all the deetas who had worn the headdress before her, thought about what their eyes had seen —births and deaths, plenty and famine, wartime, peacetime, good times, bad times, happy times, sad times. Through it all, the People had persevered, their deeta and their combined huul waal sufficient to see them through. She felt her own huul waal rise as she contemplated her people's abiding strength.

Kaambree had brought her far upriver, so far Xyleea could no longer recall the path back to her wasakagee. Though they had yet to find plentiful water, she made herself believe they would. She'd come too far, knew it was much too late to think anything else.

That wasn't why she wanted to cry. Her gaze shifted to the swollen carcass laying in the riverbed. About the size of a larder box, the tuskee youngling was bloated near to bursting with the larvae of casking flies, one short tusk pointed at the unforgiving sun, the unbearable stench of death hanging heavy in the air. Without a guardian, the half-grown tuskee had stood little chance. A matriarch would have guided the young one away from the scattered puddles of stagnant water, but this one hadn't had Xyleea's good fortune, and so, alone, driven mad by thirst, it had drunk from the slime-fouled seepage until its guts gave out. She prayed to the ancestors that she and Kaambree would not meet a similar fate.

A maandaba hoot brought her thoughts round. She cupped a hand to her mouth and called back in a voice so dry and scratchy she scarce recognized it as her own. The maandaba didn't recognize it either. Instead, the bird launched into the blue-egg sky, its black wings lifting it high as another bird, massive and gold-feathered, glided down to settle quiet as dust upon the youngling's bulging side. The first deleemelee had arrived.

Kaambree raised its trunk and blew a long, sad note, a lament that shook its entire body. Xyleea wrapped her arms around the hump of the tuskee's domed head, the chuulzu kereet resting against its topknot.

"I'm sorry, Mother," she whispered into Kaambree's notched ear. "May the deleemelee return this young one to the ancestors where it shall never again know pain or fear."

The tuskee abruptly shook its head, its flapping ears cracking against its neck and unsettling Xyleea as it swung its trunk in a wide arc and blew a wet-sounding snort. She wondered if Kaambree was blasting its grief across the dried-out threadleaf and cossiac bushes.

She thought of her galeesha, already gone to Weeleekeela. Perhaps Cree Shee would come back to guide this youngling on its journey from here to there. Her heart wished it to be so.

She righted herself and pulled the headdress down until it touched the tops of her ears, hoping the kereet would help focus her rambling thoughts onto the one that mattered—finding enough water for her wasakagee. Kaambree shook its head again then stepped forward, its brown-furred side brushing a cossiac bush and sending crunchy leaves curling to the ground.

Xyleea reached inside the kemeekemee, her fingers closing around the daala. Part of her wanted to open the case, while the rest of her knew that if she did, she would be lost. She still remembered how she'd felt when Cree Shee had shown her the marvelous orb. Thinking of it whetted her desire. How she longed to be filled with an indescribable hope, to surrender to a kindness beyond words. Even in her reduced state, her body craved that comfort far more than food or water.

She'd brought the daala because Cree Shee had told her she must protect it, but she wondered if, in some strange way, the daala was protecting her. Death was closing in at every turn and yet, here she was, still breathing, still moving forward. Still searching on behalf of her people for that which would save them. She needed to concentrate on that.

Kaambree plodded ahead, its drum-top ears flapping forward and back. What else had her galeesha said? That it was her destiny to deliver the orb to the Uniter who would restore it. That the One who had given it had need of it back. Who or what could have given away such a magnificent part of itself? She couldn't fathom the generosity required for that. Couldn't fathom the majestic infinity of a being larger than the limitless orb.

Her thoughts moved to the Uniter into whose hands she was destined to deliver the daala. The chuulzu kereet felt even heavier upon her head, her neck even less able to support it. She said a prayer to the ancestors to forgive her unworthy neck for its weakness, to forgive her unworthy heart for its doubts. It all seemed so unclear now as she moved past the dead tuskee and the drying riverbed and the dying green. Where was she going? Why was she going there? What was she supposed to be doing? If only Cree Shee were here to help.

Xyleea looked ahead, her eyes sweeping the mountains on the horizon. Were the answers there? Kaambree seemed to think so. It had never hesitated, its flat-bottomed feet ever tracking toward them. Perhaps it was only she who did not know.

The wind shifted, intensifying the sickly-sweet odor of spoilage. Her stomach lurched, her thoughts going to a different decay, the dwindling kind that held her wasakagee in its grip. So much had already been taken from her people. Now their deeta was gone as well. Were they wondering where she was? Were they—like she—wondering what their futures held? Her mind reeled forward to the ending she feared most. It wasn't death, for her galeesha had taught her death was a beginning, not an end. No, it wasn't death she feared. She feared a slow dying far more than its inevitable outcome, for not even the Xetili could steal every thought or destroy every dream from the living. Only the terminal creep of decline did that.

Why had she not at least told Xyree Muul of her plans? But she already knew the answer. He might have talked her out of going, and that would have been disastrous, for despite everything she knew this was where she needed to be. She felt it in her heart as surely as she felt its drumming beat. It was then she realized her decision had been made long ago. Before Cree Shee. Before her parents. Before she was born, even. She had a destiny, and she was on her way to meet it. She only hoped she could summon enough huul waal to survive the journey.

The northlands were far more beautiful than Elorah had ever imagined.

In her mind, she'd envisioned a frozen land of snow and ice, but here in Valley Kalt between the snow-capped peaks, early spring painted a far different picture—a pointillistic landscape of mosscups and noddinheads whose jewellike blooms and belled caps formed brilliant swaths of color as far as the eye could see. Yellows and purples, pinks and reds—plucked to trembling by the breezy fingers of a warming wind—formed a vivid carpet beneath an ice-blue ceiling laced white with frost-thin clouds. The spectacular color-show made it hard to imagine this was also a land of cruel beasts and crueler men.

Eccto and the rest of the Konda band had bid them farewell some leagues back, taking with them their caravans, their spotted horses, and their jingling bells as they headed east toward a hidden dell where lute spiders hummed and spun.

Once they were clear of the gate, Haedyn had cut Eccto free from his shackles using his knife. Afterward, he'd handed Rachmyn the bundled hoewlers, his friend carefully pouring the wolfken back into the vial he'd emptied to fill the devices. Elorah had healed Eccto's wounds as well as his injured Plenderre's while Rachmyn gave him the refilled speck vial for the band's troubles. All in all, both sides went away satisfied, save Thane whose melancholy, Elorah suspected, had more to do with leaving behind the band's sweetsweet rather than the Shadowen themselves.

Her recall of recent events was both exhilarating and strange. She hadn't been sure she could stop the chaos from so far away, but in the end, she, along with Essiant and the other guardian wolves, had managed it. She felt a thrill recalling how they'd gathered in the golden circle of her staff's light and turned aside the anger and fear, replacing it with the calming light of peace. There had been bloodshed, but far less than might have been expected. It gave her hope that she could restore Therrania if she had enough belief. And help. The crystalwood staff hummed and her stone quivered against her chest.

They were riding the geldings on a northwest tack, her grandfather's map emblazoned upon her mind. Aikin, Thane, Haedyn, and herself had one pack pony attached to their saddle while Mierrle and Rachmyn rode solo. The ponies pranced along, their heads held high to better scent the breeze.

Haedyn trotted his gelding alongside hers, his pony squeezing into the gap between them. She looked over and felt an unbidden flutter in her stomach. A bright smile lit her face before she knew enough to prevent it. She straightened her expression, tamping down the unaccountable giddiness tickling her insides. A leader wasn't supposed to behave like a giggling schoolgirl at the glance of a handsome face. She looked toward Aikin, his bright brown gelding a step ahead of the rest, his broad shoulders squared, his back straight, looking about in the manner of a royal surveying his kingdom. His strong jaw and cut-glass physique should have incited those feelings in her. The Urslan knew he'd tried to impress her over the years, and hadn't her mother also tried everything, but never once had she felt interested in him in that way. She imagined every Apogent at the Academie thought her crazy, Mierrle included, as well as every Caeldish with an opinion. Truth be told, she'd never felt that way about anybody. Not until now.

"How long before we get to this place?" Haedyn asked, his golden eyes sparkling.

"Grandfather said three moons. By my calculations, we've two moons to go." She tried to sound self-assured, though she was not.

Haedyn twisted round. Rachmyn sagged atop his dirt-colored gelding like a sack of barleycorn, his face as long as his mount's. Haedyn held up two fingers and grinned. Rachmyn's sullen stare held steady. Haedyn turned forward. "He's delighted," he said, then barked a laugh.

"Perhaps he's missing Elgre," Elorah offered. She hadn't seen the wolf since the gate.

"Oh, he's not gone," Haedyn assured her as he swept a hand toward the horizon. "He's out there somewhere. He'll turn up. He always does." He looked down at the lump at the top of his vest. "Not everyone can have a pet as devoted as mine," he said, and laughed again, a sound that fluttered its way into her chest. She needed to think about something else.

"Is it true he plucked out a guard's eye?" she asked in horrified fascination.

"Don't hold it against him," he protested, giving the lump a pat. "The guard was staring him down. That's like waving a fish in front of a bear and expecting it won't get eaten. He's good most of the time."

"What kind of bird is he?" Elorah asked.

"A Red-Capped Grynt. They're common where I come from." She wrinkled her brow and he added, "South. Near the Scaur."

"Mierrle's people are from the south."

"I'm told my family was prominent there before..." He paused, his eyes getting a faraway look, "...they were killed."

Elorah startled.

Haedyn went on. "I don't remember much. I was a baby when it happened."

"I'm so sorry," she said, her heart squeezing tight. "Did they catch those responsible?"

"I've no idea. Rachmyn's family took me in and moved us far away. I never heard any more, but I think about it sometimes." He looked down at the lump again. "Fryk reminds me that I once had parents of my own. And a homeland. That's why I wanted to win him."

"You won him?" Elorah couldn't keep the disbelief out of her voice.

"In a game of jackpeg with a gold-toothed Rabboutier," he bragged. "I might have skewed the odds in my favor a little." He brought his index finger and thumb together, his tone conspiratorial.

"You cheated to win?"

"I wouldn't call it cheating. I set the game so there could only be one outcome."

"What's the difference?"

Haedyn shrugged. "He didn't know what to do with a grynt egg, anyway."

"And you did?"

"I hatched him and raised him, so I guess so."

"But how?"

"I can't explain it. I suppose it's like how you know about Thurnia—"

"Therrania—"

He chopped his pointed finger at her. "Yes, Therrania. How you know it exists."

"Well, I've seen it," she replied. He gave her an incredulous look. "Seeing things no one else can see is something I've always been able to do. My mother tells me not to talk about it."

Her eyes went dewy. She knew her mother must be depleted after the massive output of vor needed to create the thorn hedge. She also knew the creation was not a singular endeavor, and she thought again of the Head she'd thought she knew so well only to find out she knew nothing at all. She gave herself a mental shake. This wasn't the time for dwelling in the past.

"I don't mind hearing about it," he offered.

"Perhaps another time. If you'll excuse me," she said, nudging her gelding to catch up with Mierrle who was trailing behind Aikin, her gaze drifting between wide-eyed sweeps of the landscape and furtive glances at the man ahead of her. She turned as Elorah drew close.

"I thought it would be all snow and ice. I never expected this," Mierrle said.

Elorah nodded. "It looks like something out of an Old Mother's Tale. I'm expecting to come upon a talking stoat at any moment."

Mierrle giggled. Aikin's head snapped round, and she sobered. "Aikin says we should be on the lookout for Drasgor," she said, her expression earnest.

"Yes, we sodding well better. Her Most Exasperating might have been wrong about them being at the border, but I don't think she was wrong about the dangers of the entire breed."

"They're not animals." Elorah's tone was indignant.

Aikin sniffed. "That remains to be seen," he said, his eyes scanning the horizon. The pony he was trailing stretched its neck forward, opened its mouth wide, and bit the heel of his boot. Aikin kicked backward, but the pony had already reared its head out of reach. "This sodding pony. That's the fourth time the little gobsmite's bitten me." It took all of Elorah's self-control not to laugh.

"Must have a taste for heels," quipped Thane.

"In that case, you better steer clear," Aikin spat.

Thane laughed. "Ah, now there's a truth we can all agree on," he admitted.

Elorah felt the pendant's cold vibration a moment before all four ponies reared, their nostrils flaring, their front hooves scissoring air. Fear seized her, raising chillbumps along her arms. She swept a wary gaze about them.

Thane's pony jerked sideways with enough force to split its lead line. A second jerk and the line snapped. The pony galloped away, the frayed line swinging in wide arcs as it headed toward the western hills. "Mine's come loose!" he shouted as he gigged his gelding into a juddering lope providing little speed.

Rachmyn's mount took off after them, startling its rider as much as anyone. The gelding was surprisingly fleet of foot, and Rachmyn was forced to cling on like a leaf-fly in a windstorm. As it turned out, the horse didn't need its rider to know what to do. It overtook the escaping pony within a few strides then made a directional cut, forcing the escapee to a stiff-legged stop. The pony changed direction in a frantic scramble of side-passing and acceleration, and the horse raced to cut off its path again, almost losing its rider when it forced the pony into another sliding stop. Five more times, the horse outmaneuvered the pony until it came to a splay-legged halt, its head swinging back and forth, its eyes rolling between Rachmyn's horse and the nearby hills. The gelding stared it down until the pony dropped its head. Rachmyn straightened in the saddle and stuck his hand into his pocket, a worried look creasing his brow. His face relaxed, and he moved the hand back to check his pack.

The rest of the party positioned their horses in a circle around the gelding and the pony, providing cover should it choose to run again. Thane dismounted and sprang forward, grabbing the frayed line and leading the pony back to his horse before jig-knotting what was left of the rope to a ring in the saddle's cantle and remounting.

All four ponies had begun stamping their front feet and thrusting their heads.

They must smell Bravik, Elorah thought. The wind shifted, bringing with it a squalling roar that raised every hair. Two roars followed, each more terrifying than the last. The ponies charged, their leads snapping taut as they tried to break for the hills.

"Fleek me, what is that?" Thane cried, one hand gripping his pony's lead to keep it from coming loose again.

"We need to head to higher ground," Elorah yelled, boosting her heels to urge her gelding into a gallop. Mierrle's mount jumped into stride almost dumping her to the ground. Elorah sent a zing of vorik to her friend to help her hold her seat. The rest of the geldings broke into a run, and the group thundered across the valley's colorful floral carpet toward the rolling-up foothills to the west, Thane bringing up the rear.

Elorah glanced behind, fearful of what she might see, but there was no sign of the beasts her grandfather had described. Another roar, fainter this time, turned her head forward. It sounded as if they were going in the right direction.

Soon they were climbing. They slowed their mounts to a brisk trot, the ponies pulling ahead of the geldings as if to hurry their cumbersome partners. A league of climbing and thinner air had all the hoofed animals snorting and blowing by the time they came to a broad shelf. Elorah pulled up for a rest, grateful the ponies had calmed. The bravik, if that was what had issued the terrifying roars, must have gone out of range of their keen noses. She spotted a flash of gray near a brush pile and the sweep of a bushy tail. She looked at Rachmyn, who'd seen it too, judging by the small smile on his face. His guardian was, indeed, still watching over him. She swung around toward Thane.

"Is there water nearby?" she asked. His eyes closed for a moment before he nodded. "We'll follow you," she said.

"Are you sure you want to follow me?" he asked, his eyes going wide.

"Only you know the way," she replied.

He reined his horse toward the barren-looking interior of the shelf, the rest falling in behind as his gelding walked toward an outcropping of rocks. It seemed an unlikely path toward water, but she'd come to believe in his Aquillan power perhaps more than he did himself, and she had no doubt he was leading them where they needed to go.

The northmen had prepared to storm the gate like men possessed, honing the edges of their dras and their blades, plinking stones into their sling pouches, tightening the bindings on their axes. Brynz watched their preparations with dread. What was she to do when the fighting began? None of the options she thought of ended well.

Uhnkre hadn't mentioned trading her since that day in the wood. Instead, he'd taken to brooding and conferring with his men, hardly speaking to her at all. It was as if she no longer existed. Maybe she didn't. When she thought about it, who was she really? Without a home, without a country, without a friend, what was left? Precious little. She'd become someone even she barely knew over the time—who knew how long now that the chest piece was gone—since her capture.

The descent toward the hated gate had been uneventful, apart from the one steep slope that had required skidding down on their backsides to prevent a bone-snapping fall. But once they neared the valley floor it hadn't taken long to realize the impressive construction they'd expected was in actuality a tottering catastrophe.

The remains of the gate's doors hung askew from their giant hinges like the tattered wings of a defeated beast. All that was left were a few blackened chunks of wood clinging to a scaffolding of sooted latticework. The back half of the thunderbolt gryphon was missing. Only the tarnished front end of the Iellian national symbol remained, one dulled eye staring at nothing. It was a wonder the doors still stood given how little was left.

The wall was also a ruin, most of the stone cladding having fallen away from the charred understructure. Several sections canted at untenable angles and looked in imminent danger of collapse. Several more had already given way, the ground strewn with debris.

That wasn't the problem, however. The problem was the number of Iellian guards swarming around the wreckage. Blue-coated men scurried everywhere, guarding a structure one shake away from becoming a pile of rubble. Far more men than the band of six, formidable though they were, would have stood any chance against.

The northmen watched from a bluff overlooking the wall, their breathing the only sound. After long moments, Uhnkre muttered a series of blunted syllables before turning to Brynz.

"We go around," he stated in his flattened Iellian, his thumb slicing toward his men, before curling back toward the mountainside.

"What about me?" she asked, fear grabbing her throat. She'd come too far to turn herself in now. If she wasn't to go with Uhnkre and his men, what was left for her?

"You choose," he said.

She stared at him, her mind warring between leaving or staying. Escape had been her hope from the start, but now that it was an actual choice, she felt a sudden trepidation. She knew more now for one thing. Knew she wasn't prepared to take care of herself. Knew she had little ability to find food or water or shelter. She didn't even have a blade. All she had was an affinity for air and a decent sense of direction, which was better than nothing but only just. She thought of Zell, and her heart lurched. Where was he? Had he survived his ordeal? Was it too late to try and find him? She wanted to whistle, to merge her voice with a carrying wind that might make its way to Zell's ears but knew she could not. Not if she wished to remain among the living.

Zell, by way of a harvested egg, had come from the northern slopes of Cyrulian Kalt, the very mountain she now stood upon. She still remembered the bandy-legged trader bragging he'd plucked the leathery egg right out from under a setting gryphonmare when he'd produced the slate-gray lump from the depths of his gryphon-hide cloak. Had Zell somehow found his way to the craggy cliffs of his forebears? The thought of not ever knowing his fate felt like a punch in the gut. If she could somehow get to the other side, perhaps she could still look for him. It was a daft idea but given the options, no dafter than any other choice on offer.

"I choose to stay," she said with as much confidence as she could muster.

"Stay?" Uhnkre's rumbly voice pitched up in surprise.

"Yes." She nodded at each man in turn—Uhnkre, Ahnkne, Benkre, Flewd, Kif, Hrul. "I stay." The men looked at Uhnkre, waiting for a translation.

"Brynz pok kren fol." The men's focus settled back on her their expressions unreadable. Were they happy? Angry? She had no idea. Uhnkre turned away from the cliff edge. "Kwulf. Lel," he murmured. Without a word, the northmen followed as he led them up and away from the bluff, Brynz falling into step in their midst.

Warnings of a
Wraithwolf
(Excerpt Six)

As THOUGHT precedes that which is MANIFEST... gggrrrr....so too does BELIEF MAGNIFY each THOUGHT thing... ggrrrfff... for GOOD or for ILL... Ggggrrff... An ORIGINATING IDEA only BECOMES... gggrrr... the SUSTAINING FLAME of PASSION... grrrfff... through the APPLICATION of BELIEF... Gggrrrff... WITHOUT THAT... gggrrr...an incepting SPARK will FADE... grrrff... from WHENCE it came.

KNOW THIS!

BELIEF wields a POWER... gggrrr... far BEYOND itself... ggrrrfff... for IT is the underlying FORCE... ggrrrfff... of the COLLECTIVE MIND... ggrrff... whereby the POWER of ONE... ggrrff... becomes the POWER of ALL.

UNDERSTAND!

LACK or LOSS of BELIEF... ggrrf... always precedes FAILURE... Ggrrfff... Just as FIRE... gggrrr... cannot SUSTAIN without FLAME... grrfff... WHERE belief is PLACED... ggggrrf... DETERMINES the FUTURE... ggggrrfff... of the MANIFEST WORLD.

–Collected and Interpreted for the Most Exalted Monarch,
Geldizian Rennesseau, by a scribe

CHAPTER THIRTY-THREE

FAMILY, TOGETHER

Thane gigged his horse into a pokey trot. It hadn't taken long to figure out he'd picked the slowest of the geldings. Even Mierrle's ancient horse had more fire than the dullard he was riding. Ah, well. At least it wasn't a mouth-farting ox.

The pony ambled alongside, giving him hope its recent escapade had taken the steam out of the little gobsmite. Tying the rankest pony to the calmest horse might have seemed a good decision at the time, but he held a different opinion now.

He'd never been to the northlands and was as surprised as anyone by the riot of color surrounding them. But it was the smell that made the biggest impression. It was like nothing he'd ever encountered before—spicy-sweet fragrance hanging heavy in the highland air so that even the pollinating insects were made drowsy by its redolence, every step sending up a cloud of perfumed pollen that gilded the geldings' and ponies' legs.

He'd been morose since the Shadowen band had gone, missing both their sweetsweet and their company. Blond-haired Malwyn in particular had been quite generous, and Thane missed him almost more than his jug of liquor. Almost.

At first, he'd tried to wheedle a dreamcraft from one of the Kondas but abandoned the idea after enduring a diatribe on the long, hard moons spent pinching silk from venomous spiders only to sell it for a fraction of its worth to the showmen and crafters who took all the credit and made all the profit. It was a bleaker version of Shadowen life than he'd imagined, and knowing about it took away much of the allure from the nightjollies who pretended some great mystery about where their silver-foil packets of imagination originated.

Malwyn had been helpful in another way. He was a talker. The emptier his sweetsweet cup, the looser his tongue became. The gutting of his wife, Annakee, had been a frequent topic. "Everyone talks of the bravik," Malwyn had opined, "and the gryphons, but no one ever mentions the sodding tusk-pigs. Those ripsnorts'll kill you quicker'n anything. Done my Annakee straight in. Nothing noble about getting gutted by a filthy pig. No one sings about that."

Thane hadn't mentioned the tusk-pigs mainly because he'd been into his own sweetsweet cup most of the time, and the perpetual pounding in his head had chased the warning away. Only when he saw the cloven-hoofed tracks around the water pool did it venture back in. Could have been deer tracks, his skepticism reminded. But the wallowing slick said something else. Deer didn't wallow. He supposed he should speak up. He cleared his throat.

"Why are you smiling?" Haedyn quirked an eyebrow at Aikin. "You've been smiling since the gate."

"I knew she was false," Aikin replied, his smile broadening.

"Who?"

"Her Most Exaggerative. Zephyrria Rennesseau," Aikin added for Haedyn's benefit.

The fair-haired boy hasn't a mind for politics, I see, Thane thought with a chuckle. *Then again, Caeldish matters weren't of much interest to anyone other than the bumpkins who lived there.* He decided the tusk-pigs could wait. This was getting interesting.

"By the Urslan, don't you know what's going on?" Aikin said.

"Not everyone follows Caeldish affairs as closely as you," Elorah put in.

"Much to our disgrace," Aikin said.

"If you're talking of your queen—" Haedyn started.

"She's not my queen!" Aikin roared. "Nor is she the queen of anyone born of a Caeldish clan. She might reign sovereign over the unfortunates whelped upon her corrupted mountain, but I assure you, she has no power over me or mine. We shall never be ruled by an outsider who cares nothing for our traditions or beliefs. There are many of us who would rather die than bend a knee to an Iellian monarch."

"You might get your chance," Thane observed. "But tell me, with you here and her there, doesn't that make your rebellion somewhat more difficult?"

"You know nothing about it," Aikin sniffed.

"I'm sure I do not," Thane agreed.

"I doubt you've ever done an honorable thing in your entire life. From what I've seen, you're no better than the Shadowen charlatans you spend so much time with."

"That is true. I find conformity utterly tedious and tend toward those who have... what is it called? ...the spark of the wolf about them. Like our friend here." He indicated toward Rachmyn.

"Elbows for toes," Haedyn quipped. "Never works."

Thane grinned. "It's a compliment," he said, turning to better see Rachmyn. "Truly," he added with forced conviction.

Rachmyn's hoarfrost eyes narrowed, his lips compressing. The pale-haired man was having none of his flattery.

Ah well. Moving on.

"I'm curious, though. How do you go about overthrowing a nation that has captured your homeland by invitation? Seems to me you need to convince your own people first." Thane pulled his face into a sympathetic invitation for correction. Aikin snapped at the bait.

"Those on the Council who foisted this grievous interference upon us will soon see the error of their ways when forced to send their harvests to Iellia for whatever compensation Her Most Egregious's duty masters deem fair. The yoke will feel heavy indeed when they can no longer feed their own clan once their annual duty has been paid. Urslan willing, we who have seen the future will turn the tide before it comes to that."

"I imagine you'll be needing weapons of a different sort then, something other than the standard sword and shield, since it is your own countrymen who appear to be your opposition."

"Very prescient of you," Aikin allowed, the severity of his features softening. It was a start, Thane supposed. "It might surprise you to know those plans are being implemented even as we speak."

"Are those the loose ends in need of tying up?" Elorah asked archly.

"Your clan has nothing to fear," Aikin assured. "The Calliaigh have always seen the truth of the situation. But there are others who've been blinded by counterfeit threats and false assurances. The Fola, the Gorsh, and the Rairrsaigh, to name three, have always backed the interference we now endure. Weak districts filled with feeble-minded fools. The Hiegh sit the fence, their loyalty changing with every gust of wind or maybe every jug of cider. Who can tell with those drunkards? It is only the Thrast, the Bairrtraigh, and the Calliaigh that have resisted any abdication of responsibility for our futures."

"Very admirable," Thane cooed. Aikin's scowl returned.

"It is not admiration we seek but survival, and anyone with the ability to think beyond the next filling of their stomach or pipe should be able to see that."

KEEEEEEAAAARRRRR

A piercing shriek shattered the mountain air. The geldings and ponies reacted as one, exploding toward a jut of scrub-pine, their riders grabbing at saddles and manes to keep from being thrown to the ground.

"We need to stay together," Elorah cried, galloping her horse to the front before plunging into the thicket, the others following her lead.

A large gryphon clipped over the top of the nearest hill, its sand-brown body held aloft by black-tipped wings the length of a smallholder's house, the paws of its brown-smutted back legs pulled up tight against its tawny underside, the white boll of some hapless woolen animal clutched in its dusky front talons. The raptor's long, black-tufted tail undulated from side to side while below, a dark smear slid across the mountain's face, marking its flight.

Thane nearly soiled himself, only realizing the shrill screaming in his ears was coming from his own mouth when he paused to take a breath. His mount made for the scrub-pine at half the speed of the other geldings, Thane clutching its neck. It wasn't until he was clubbed off by a limb that his screaming stopped.

He hit the ground with a shuddering thud, his left side taking most of the impact. He scrambled onto his hands and feet despite the fiery crackling in his ribs and spraddle-crawled toward the depths of the scrub, chest throbbing, breath coming in strangled gasps. One scrabbling hand lost purchase, flying out from under him like a bird taking wing, and he crashed face first onto the cloddy dirt, the sound of cracking bone loud in his ears as a familiar pain burst hot behind his eyes.

Ah, fleek me, there's my nose flattened again. This made the fifth time it had been broken.

KEEEEEAAAAARRRRR

He jerked his head upward, forcing his watering eyes to look past the pulpy swelling and scrub-pine limbs to the whitewashed sky where a ferocious predator glided eastward. Only when the creature disappeared did he collapse onto his back and wheeze out a breath.

"Grief's teeth."

He felt a set of hands force themselves into his armpits and pull him to his feet.

"Are you alright?" Haedyn asked, brushing at his back.

"Never better," Thane groaned. He winced as a searing jolt shot through his head. He closed his eyes, convinced his head was splitting in two. A cool touch against his forehead eased the pain. When he opened his eyes, Elorah's concerned face filled his vision.

"Do you think you can retake your mount?" she asked, her hand withdrawing to her side. He reached up to check his nose. It felt no more swollen or crooked than before his ungraceful landing. How could that be? He'd heard the bone break. Felt the gristle give way. Seen the purple-red mound balloon up between his leaking eyes. Perhaps Elorah's touch had done far more than he'd first credited.

"I've got his horse," Aikin called. He was leaned over, his hand clutching the cheek strap of the dullard's bridle, his opposite leg swinging to keep the biting pony at bay.

Thane rubbed his ribs. They too felt intact. Another marvel for which he had no explanation. He shuffled toward his mount, his fingers still poking at his side and nose to ensure his cracks were truly mended, his thoughts filled with amazement. After getting a leg up from Haedyn, he settled into the saddle and checked the pony's tether strap before picking up his stirrups and reins.

Aikin unhanded the bridle, his opposite leg stilling for a moment. The pony snaked out its head and clamped down, giving Aikin's heel a shake before letting loose. "Get off me!" he thundered, kicking backward. The pony threw its head up, a smug look in its white-rimmed eyes when the boot whiffed past. "What are you smiling at?" Aikin brayed, his face reddening.

"Was I smiling?" Thane asked.

"You sodding well know you were."

Thane shrugged. "My apologies, gentle sir." *Gentle sir, bah. Tetchy blowhard more like.* He looked around, first at Mierrle who dashed her chin back, her green eyes frank with reproach, then the others. Only Haedyn's eyes held any trace of mirth.

At least someone has a grasp of the absurd.

Aikin snorted and wheeled his horse around, kicking out again when the pony went in for another bite. "What have I gotten myself into?" he muttered as he moved away.

Misplaced fidelity binds one to curious company, eh? Although that hardly explained his own motives. The speck was becoming less of a reason, owing perhaps to the way the pale-haired man always regarded him with open distrust. He could see it would be a long, hard road getting that to change. His influence with Mierrle was also waning, a fact made clear by every longing look and breathy sigh directed toward the tetchy blowhard. As long as Thane was seen opposing him, she would never be swayed to his cause. More grovel and less gravel might be needed, much as it pained him to think about the abasement required. Then again, he'd done it before and for far less reward. Ah, well. No need to ascribe false righteousness to the situation. Ransoms were never collected without a price.

Thane glanced toward Rachmyn whose attention was fixed upon a stone outcropping some distance away. Thane stared through the brush until the outline of a wolf separated itself from the pile of rockery. He let out a sigh.

So, the pale-haired man's dangerous shadow has returned. Pity. He wasn't keen on the wolf and had hoped they'd seen the last of it. *Another dream dies.*

"We need to head down to the valley floor," Elorah said. She pointed toward a bank of plum-gray clouds scudding in from the west. "We don't want to get caught out in a storm." She pointed her gelding toward a descending trail. "We've not much daylight left, but hopefully, we can get to cover before a storm finds us."

Snowflakes tumbled from the dark velvet sky, settling thick upon the trees and rocks and ground. It had been snowing for hours, fat flakes floating down from the shadowed chasm of a moonless night. Elorah watched with growing despair. Already, they were off-course, and now, they would have to make their way through snow that would slow them further. Her grandfather's words rattled a warning in her mind as she tried to peer through the swirling veil of white. They had so little time to find Therrania as it was, and it felt as if every minute they delayed was an unforgivable waste. She hugged herself, trying to push back the grim thoughts, her grandfather's square of wemble warm against her skin.

Rachmyn had found an approximation of a cave, although it was more of an indentation in the hillside, as if a giant thumb had pressed itself into the stone. Haedyn, in turn, had constructed a fire in a hastily dug hole to keep the storm from affecting the flame. The muffled glow did little to push back the darkness, though its heat did help with the cold.

The geldings and the ponies were tethered to a nearby set of trees, their saddles beginning to disappear beneath a layer of white. Elorah worried for them, but there was nothing she could do now that the full brunt of the storm was upon them. She wished they could have made it to the valley, but they did not manage that before the storm set in.

Though she'd encouraged them to rest, none of her companions had found sleep. Only the bird had managed it. Sleep was the last thing on her own mind, the weight of her responsibility laying like a leaden shroud upon her shoulders. What had she gotten them into? Therrania seemed so far away in so many ways. She closed her eyes and tried to calm her thumping heart, her mind drifting to the memory of her staff's golden glow reflecting from the eyes of a hundred dreamtime wolves. She felt a small comfort at the thought.

"This is a lucky break, don't you think?" Haedyn's voice was full of enthusiasm. Her eyes flew open as she startled back to the present. She turned toward him. His golden eyes brightened, and for a moment she thought she must be dreaming.

"How do you mean?" Her voice sounded strange in her ears.

"Well, tracks for one thing. We'll be able to see tracks." Sensing her confusion, he added, "Makes it less likely we'll get attacked by bravik or gryphons–"

"Or tusk-pigs," Thane interjected.

"Tusk-pigs?" Haedyn and Elorah both turned toward him.

"I should have mentioned it sooner. Malwyn's wife was gutted by one. And I saw some tracks—"

"By the water pool," Haedyn finished. "Yes, we saw those." He cast an uneasy glance at Rachmyn in repose near the front of the talus, his shoulders settled against the dove-colored stone, his arms folded across his chest. The Shadowen nodded once before resuming his study of the eddying snow, his expression thoughtful.

"I think those might have been tusk-pig tracks." Thane said. He went quiet for a moment before adding, "It was a terrible death, to hear Malwyn tell it."

Elorah shivered. Here was one more thing to worry about, along with everything else. Silvi's stone jigged against her breast, as if to distract her from useless defeatism.

"There's something else about the snow," Haedyn went on. "It helps with sound."

Now that he mentioned it, Elorah realized how quiet it had become, as if the entire world had been swallowed up by the relentless white, leaving only herself and her little group. For a moment, the peacefulness almost made her forget her failings.

"Any wind will be a problem," Rachmyn said.

Aikin looked up from his seat upon a boulder, his battered boot in one hand. "As it always is," he put in. He held the boot up and pointed at a spot where the sole was separating from the upper. "This will never hold up to snow."

"Wrap it," Rachmyn said, his gaze still fixed on the falling snow.

"With what?" Aikin groused.

"I've got something," Thane volunteered, searching his pack. He pulled out a length of twine and a leather pouch, handing both to Aikin. "I don't think I'll be doing the Disappearing String trick anytime soon."

Aikin snugged his boot into the pouch then wrapped it with twine, finishing with a tight knot. "I doubt if this works," he grumbled, "but I am indebted all the same."

"When a hand is given, a heart is returned," Thane replied. Aikin cocked his head, brusque exasperation on his face. "An old Quelpian adage," Thane continued. "I never found it held much truth, but perhaps this time will be different." He pasted on what he hoped was a winning smile. Aikin's throat clearing dimmed it substantially.

"Where I'm from, we say 'not at all' and leave it at that."

"Not at all," Thane mimicked with a flourish of the hand. Aikin grunted and shoved the boot onto his foot.

The sky lightened, and the snowfall slowed. Elorah considered what they should do next. Food and water would be needed for the group and the animals both of which would be easier to find in the valley. The snow might not be as deep there, if indeed, any had fallen at all. And the map in her mind made it clear that picking up the Northern Passage would require a descent to the valley floor.

She knew Rachmyn had scouted their path from The Running Fox using his abilities in the in-between realm she'd only begun to discover, and she thought about asking him to do so again, to ensure they set a true course once they were able to move out. She considered whether she should attempt the scouting herself but soon concluded it was foolish for her to try when she had an expert close to hand. The first thing needed, however, was rest. They would have to take turns sleeping and standing guard until everyone was refreshed. Pushing on without doing that would be far more foolhardy than trying to scout their path in Oru Fen. If they had any luck at all, the snow would melt, making the trek to the valley floor easier on them all.

She felt a soft humming against her back as if the staff had been listening to her thoughts and approved her decision. Her 'see-true' stone, as she'd come to think of it, pulsed in time with her heartbeat as it always did when she was at rest. She'd become so accustomed to the feeling she hardly noticed it anymore.

"What would you have us do?" Haedyn asked.

"We should rest," she said. "Then make our way to the valley. Perhaps Rachmyn would consent to using his abilities to scout our path."

"It would do no good for me to do the peering, without some idea where we're going." Rachmyn turned to face her. "And there's only one of us that knows that."

"I suppose that's true," she allowed.

"The peering is no different than what you did at the gate," he went on. "We could do it together, so we both had the knowledge when we came back."

Haedyn's eyes opened wide. "You've never done the peering with anyone before."

"Never needed to before," Rachmyn replied, faint acidity indenting the lines at the corners of his lips.

"But–"

"Your ability with fire, does it have a limit?" Thane cut Haedyn off then glanced at the pit fire awaiting his response.

"I'm not sure," Haedyn said after a moment's thought. "I've never known it not to work."

"Even in the presence of its opposite?" Thane pressed.

"I can boil water, if that's what you mean," Haedyn said smiling toward Mierrle, her face lighting like a candle.

"Yes, I've seen that. But can you boil a sea's worth?"

"Boil a sea? That isn't possible for anyone."

"Nor should it be," Aikin added.

Elorah granted him that. She wondered where Thane was headed.

"Something smaller, then. If not a sea, a mountain. Could you boil a mountain of water?"

"Mountains aren't made of water." Haedyn crossed his arms.

Thane settled his gaze on the snow mounded beyond the front of the cave. "Let me be more specific. Could you boil the water on a mountain?"

"Mountain water is always moving. Water must be contained before it can be heated."

"I see," Thane said. He paused, as if hoping Haedyn would come forth with a solution. When he did not, Thane spoke again. "But what if the water was not moving, and a boil was not required? Could you heat it then?"

"I've never tried," Haedyn said, eagerness sparking. "You're thinking of the snow."

"Not all of it, of course. Not even a Fyrre wycche could do that but a pathway so wide." Thane held out his arms to approximate the width required. "That might not be too much for one such as you."

Rachmyn stepped in. "The internal force required for that would drain him, a dangerous notion by any measure." Elgre walked up to stand by Rachmyn's knee, his gray-green eyes piercing in their intensity. Thane gave the wolf a cursory glance, his distaste evident.

"I think I could do it," Haedyn interjected. "At least let me try."

"This is foolishness," Rachmyn spat. "Only a madman would think that could work."

"Are you saying I'm mad?" Haedyn asked, wounded by his friend's doubt.

"I'm saying this man," a flap of the hand toward Thane, "is mad. He has no idea what he's asking you to do."

"Fair enough," Thane's tone was measured. "But isn't it your friend's decision to make?" He blunted his chin toward Haedyn, encouraging him to fight his corner.

"This is my decision," Haedyn said, realization dawning. "Isn't it?"

Rachmyn stuck his hand in his pocket and pursed his lips, his brow drawing tight. "In the end, of course it is, but," he turned to Thane, "how do you propose to contribute to this adventure? Does your ability with water play some part or do you wish only my friend to take the risk?"

"As you say, I have some ability with water, though less so when it lacks heat. When I was a boy, I could sometimes tickle an icicle into a dance, but that was long ago."

"I wish I could do that," Mierrle sighed.

"I could sluice away the melt, I'm sure of that," Thane continued, his hands gesturing elaborately. "Perhaps help reduce the snow although of that I'm less certain."

Elorah felt a buzzy thump against her back along with a cooling of Silvi's stone, a warning to take care. She spoke up. "We are one, together, and the decisions impacting one impact us all. If we cannot share the risk, then we must find another way. If we cannot forge ahead without using vorik, then we shall discuss options, but for now, we preserve ourselves through rest and prepare to set out at first light tomorrow."

Thane shot her an annoyed look. "The hoewlers would have worked if there hadn't been so many guards. And this will work too, I'm sure of it."

"Just because something will work doesn't make it the best choice. We have many dangers to face and must be sparing of our internal forces whenever possible." Thane's jaw flexed, his jagged scar whitening, and she felt a flicker of indecision. She disliked confrontation, disliked the feelings it wrought. She resisted the urge to smile to diffuse the tension, forcing herself to maintain a serene countenance, picturing the 'official face' her mother had so often worn and doing her best to emulate it. She now understood the effort required to maintain the illusion of stillness when every emotion was fighting to be let out, but she steeled her nerve and continued to stare until Thane looked away. The staff hummed its approval, the see-true stone resuming its warm pulse.

She looked at the faces gathered around her. *To my heart you are family.* Her words to Rachmyn came upon her in a wave, her heart swelling near to bursting with a mixture of love, admiration, and gratitude—this was what family felt like. Rachmyn's quicksilver intellect, Haedyn's golden smile, Aikin's oaken strength, Mierrle's staunch support, Thane's mercurial temper—this was what family looked like. Her family. A sudden calm settled upon her.

They would rest then resume their journey at first light. She and her family, together.

Finding each other was easier this time. Elorah was more practiced, as was Rachmyn, at fixing the mind upon another. Their wraithwolves were also becoming accustomed to working together, and so it was like slipping on the second shoe of a pair to locate the pale-haired Shadowen in the gray gloaming of Oru Fen, his wraithwolf having already brought him near.

Before they began, Essiant reminded Elorah of her ability to create touchpoints.

You will have to rely on these to find your way if you cannot see where to go. She accepted the prompting knowing her guardian understood more than she about what lay ahead.

A gridded light map fanned out beneath their feet, individual energy strands spreading out in all directions. Next, a starry pathway unfurled, running north before curving west. She peered through the light map to the landscape below, noting the narrow funnel of the wrecked gate behind them and the northlands before them. In the distance shone the shining peak marked out on her grandfather's map—Whitemond.

Rachmyn's gaze fixed upon the dazzling mountain. She wished she knew his thoughts.

He sees now what you have seen all along. Essiant's mindwords assured.

He can see the parambek?

Indeed. As it was, and is, and will be again.

Her heart leapt at the thought that someone else would now know what she knew. She smiled and sent him her mindwords.

To my heart you are family. From this day until forever.

I have seen it. His mindwords were full of wonder. She didn't have to ask what he meant, remembering her own visions of the parambek restored, and the great good Founder rising from the dirt.

Let us find our way, then, you and I, together.

Essiant took the lead, Spectra giving way to the white wolf. Her attitude was reflected in her night-ward, who acceded the peering to Elorah despite her inexperience. With a thought they were away, skimming over the northlands, following Essiant's lead. Essiant pulled up and looked into his night-ward's eyes.

This place you must remember. From here, you travel west until you reach Whitemond.

Elorah spun in place while summoning up her inner force, etching the touchpoint onto her soul map. She looked toward Rachmyn, completing his own touchpoint.

It is good. Essiant's mindwords were as much a feeling as a thought, and she delighted in their comforting warmth.

They moved on, passing across the high plains in a blink, the starshine pathway leading straight on to Whitemond, rising like a new promise before them.

A moment later, they were at the base of the mountain. Essiant did not have to nudge Elorah this time. She was already creating a touchpoint, her heart swelling at the sight of the place she had dreamed of for so long. A lifetime of longing stood before her, and it was all she could do to keep her mind focused enough to complete the soulmark. When they had finished, Rachmyn's wraithwolf pushed its head against his leg. Without a word, they were gone, leaving Elorah alone with her guardian.

There are two who have yet to find you though they draw closer every day. One brings the Infinite Eye, the other the forces of air. You will need both before ascending the mountain you see before you.

How will they find me?

The Elect guide their steps, though they do not know this is so. Keep your heart open, and soon they will appear. Be ready, for once they have found you, the Restoration will begin. Come, Essiant howled, and they were off, zinging from touchpoint to touchpoint until they were back where they'd begun.

She bade her wraithwolf farewell, her heart breaking at the thought of leaving him behind, even as she fell down and down into the carapace of her sleeping body.

CHAPTER THIRTY-FOUR
PLOTTING

The Wycche placed her hand atop her wraithwolf's head. The entire realm was buzzing with the latest accomplishments of the white wolf and his night-ward, and she was desperate to learn how they'd managed it. Venge, who loathed the white wolf as much as she, had acquired information from those who had been there, information she needed if she was to depose this presumptuous interferer.

A direct connection was now required before she and her wraithwolf could fully communicate. Long gone were the days when Saska vorik was enough. It dawned on her that she couldn't say when she and her ally had lost that bond, the moment having drifted far beyond memory. No matter. Her hand upon his head worked well enough.

Images poured into her mind of a multitude of wraithwolves concentrating upon a single idea while in the thrall of an intensifying golden light. She could feel the energy the wraithwolves summoned, could feel the power their concentration wrought, but she could not discern the spark from which the conflagration had been built. The inciting thought, whatever it had been, needed snuffing out.

It was the first time an Erynvor had used intentional thought, and the Wycche feared the innovation could carry this Uniter much farther than any of her predecessors, perhaps even as far as the successful restoration of a parambek and the release of a Founder. She refused to consider this for long, knowing such a turn of events would tip the balance of power not only in Oru Fen but on Eolemar as well. It was an outcome she was not prepared to face, and yet, as images flowed in from her ally's vast mindstore, the idea was impossible to ignore.

Judging by the trove he offered, Venge had been relentless in his search, and she wondered what methods he had used to acquire such a vast catalog of thought-threads, each one plucked from a different guardian's experience. It was a stunning collection of impressions, and she congratulated him before removing her hand. Venge bowed low, his ancient muzzle brushing through the violet mist encircling his feet before resuming his normal stance.

Forever at your service, my liege.

The wraithwolf's mindwords were small comfort in light of what had been achieved. The Wycche was unnerved by how many wraithwolves had already been attracted to this Erynvor's cause. Even more unnerving was the number that seemed to be swaying toward it. Every previous Erynvor had labored under the assumption that being chosen by the Elect was all that was required, and this errant thought alone had made them vulnerable. Without seeking support, they had been doomed before they'd begun. This latest Uniter did not seem to hold with that faulty logic.

It was true some Erynvors had advanced farther than others, but in the end, all ten had failed. The tenth Erynvor had gotten the farthest, making it all the way to Whitemond before his steed hooked its leg in a stoat hole and destroyed them both. And though the Wycche couldn't take credit for the horse's fall, she certainly took credit for the errant thinking that had led to it, her mindwords having urged the Erynvor forward in his reckless ascent, his inner self feasting on her whispered promises of unparalleled glories right up until it all came crashing down around his ears. The same was true for the nine previous Erynvors, each one having succumbed to the alluring promises she'd dangled before them, never once seeing it was their own hubris leading them straight into the abyss.

She had expected the same from this latest Uniter, but in that she was also disappointed. This Erynvor had recognized it wasn't a job for one and had gathered others about her. So too, the white wraithwolf had gathered a pack of like-minded guardians, making it impossible to engage him in the dreamtime battles she and Venge had relied upon to keep the Erynvor's wolf weak and ineffective. Once again, she had been outmaneuvered, this time without even realizing her damaged position before the move was accomplished. Anger boiled up, singeing her thoughts. Venge locked his dark eyes on hers.

We must gather our own pack.

The wraithwolf's mindwords cut through the red mist clouding her thinking. Yes, that was what they needed, others to push forward their cause. Ten Erynvors had fallen from stubborn independence, but unlike them, she would not allow herself to fall into that mindless trap. This Erynvor might be cleverer than her predecessors, her white wolf cleverer still, but neither was more clever than she. She would put together a coalition far greater than any these interlopers could muster, for she knew everything about this realm, including the dark Arcana of Vorie Supin. Using that, she and her gathering would become a force far greater than anything seen since the Great Destruction all those eryns ago.

She turned to Venge with renewed vigor, an urgency rising within.

Let us begin.

CHAPTER THIRTY-FIVE
MOVING ON

Brynz kept the feather inside her tunic, the quill end stuck into a tether around her waist.

The tether had come about when her shrinking midsection could no longer hold up her leggings, forcing her to clutch one side or the other to maintain her modesty. The resultant jig had slowed her pace enough that Uhnkre had shaved a strip from his dras carrier strap and handed it to her with a disgusted grunt. The feather had come about when she'd stepped away for a wee and found it lying behind a rock, its silvery-blue color unmistakable. It was from a Cyrulean Blue gryphon. Perhaps from Zell.

She wasn't sure why she kept the feather hidden, except that it had felt like a secret treasure when she'd found it, a reminder of a love she'd lost and longed to find again. Sentimentality seemed a dangerous weakness in present company where survival revolved around a hardness of both thought and spirit, and she supposed that was why she kept the silvery feather out of view.

The quill poked her flesh as she leaned against a boulder to warm herself in the pale gold of the rising sun. The view was spectacular. Below lay Valley Kalt, a paintbox of vibrant color stretching to the dark line of the horizon. She was the only one interested in the scenery. The northmen took no notice at all, each one bent to the tasks of cleaning and sharpening that occupied the majority of their time when they weren't on the move.

fffsssssss

"Foonk." Uhnkre sat atop a flat of striated gray rock, holding what was supposed to be a whistle he'd whittled from a stick. He blew through the whistle again, getting the same slobbery sigh. *fffsssss* "Foonk." He heaved the whistle away.

Hrul, scrubbing his shortblade with a round of oiled doeskin, laughed, "Glab slek."

Uhnkre growled, and the dark-haired northman swallowed his yellow-toothed grin.

"May I try?" Brynz asked, hopping up. Uhnkre shrugged as she picked the whistle out of the prickleburr where it had landed.

She wiped the end against her tunic, put the whistle to her lips, clapped her tongue to the roof of her mouth and blew a long, shrieking note. Uhnkre's head snapped toward her, his lips rounding. The call sounded similar to that of a gryphon.

"Brynz. You do it. How?" Uhnkre sprang up and came to her side.

She demonstrated her tongue position, then brought the whistle to her lips and blew another shrill note. He snatched it from her and brought it to his own lips, blowing a croaking screech. He clapped Brynz on the back, nearly knocking her off her feet.

"Good," he exclaimed, holding up the whistle. "Mral coont grifft."

Was he speaking of gryphons?

A movement down the mountainside caught her attention, and she leaned for a better view. A figure was tracking along a narrow path, a curl of smoke trailing behind the bobbing head. She glanced at Uhnkre, showing Hrul the whistle, before looking down the mountain.

fffsssss

Another slobbery sigh sounded as she watched the figure nimble along. There was something familiar about the mouse-stepping gait and angular posture. She racked her brain, trying to remember. The figure stopped and picked a sprig from the hillside, bringing it up for closer examination. A memory sparked of the bandy-legged peddler who'd brought Zell's egg to the Royal Stables. The figure doffed his rotten-looking hat, stuck the white flower into one of its holes, then replaced it, smoke seeping from a pipe poked into the curve beneath his long nose.

Brynz's heart raced. If it was the peddler, he would know where Zell had come from. If she could talk to him, he could tell her where to look. The figure resumed its progress. She needed to go now if she was to have any chance.

"I need a wee," she said, pointing down the mountainside. Uhnkre gave no sign he'd heard. "I'm going for a wee," she called, her eyes on the peddler. The bent figure stopped and cocked his ear to the wind. Brynz looked at Uhnkre showing the whistle to Flewd and made a decision.

She started down the mountainside, skidding most of the way on her rear, her feet acting as a brake. She avoided the bigger rocks and knuckle-rooted scrub-pines until she came to the trail. She spotted the peddler several paces ahead. He was bent over, his hands on his hips, his beakish nose almost touching the ground. She ruffled up a wind to keep the figure from hearing or smelling her as she moved toward him. She kept one ear out for the northmen, all the while doubting she would hear them. She still had none of their lightness of foot, and even with the wind, her footfalls crumped in her ears.

The peddler startled, his head swiveling. In a flash, he was off, his bandy legs heel-toeing along at a rapid clip. It was all Brynz could do to keep from tumbling down the mountainside as she chased him.

"Getabit," she said, casting a glance up the mountainside. At the mention of the name the peddler stopped and turned around. "Wait."

The peddler put his hands on his hips. "Who comes calling?" His voice was the reedy whistle of a mountain wind. "Who comes looking for Getabit?"

"Brynz Alleu," she said, the space between them now only a few hands.

"Who is Brynz Alleu?"

Brynz was close enough to smell the peddler's gamey musk, strong like that of a boar stoat. He took a step back and sniffed. She realized she smelled no better. "I was a trainer with the Iellian Royal Stables."

He looked her up and down, his brown nose wrinkling. "A trainer? Of what?" His tone was derisive. She noticed the flower in his hat was wilting.

"Gryphons," she replied, pulling up to her full height and squaring her shoulders.

He peered up at her with coally eyes and took a puff from his pipe. "Gryphons," he said. "Surprising." His whistling voice turned the word into a bird call. "A long way from here, the Royal Stables." He took another tug from the pipe, puffing out a ring of smoke that encircled his battered hat. "How is it that you are here and not there?"

"I'm looking for Zell." Not strictly true but close enough.

"Zell?"

"A gryphon that escaped." That was true enough.

Getabit goggled. "I saw this calamnity. And now your queen demands another as if plucking eggs from gryphonmares is easy. But," He held up a gnarled finger, "more easy than catching gryphons." He frowned. "How will you take him? You have no ropes, whips, nets... You have nothing at all."

"I don't need ropes or whips. Zell will come to me because he loves me. And I love him."

"Not true. A gryphon loves nothing." More smoke belched forth to cloud the soured hat. "They only live. That is all."

She wanted to shout that Zell did love her but realized it would do no good. "Where would he go?" she asked instead. "Where should I look?"

"Maybe..." Getabit pointed toward the peaks across the valley. "A gryphon returns to their beginning. He started there."

"I thought he was founded on Cyrulean Kalt," she said.

"Most on Cyrulean Kalt but him, no." Getabit's eyes went wide and quick as breath he scampered away, disappearing into a spinney of scrub-pine.

A moment later, a hulking shadow overtook her as a meaty hand clamped her shoulder. She shrieked, her heart leaping into her mouth, her feet leaping away beneath her. Only the hand prevented her from falling.

"Brinzzzz," Uhnkre growled. How had she not heard him at all?

"I needed a wee," she squeaked.

"We go now." Uhnkre let loose, his violet-gold eyes clouded with unasked questions. He shot a glare at the scrub-pine, before starting back up the mountainside, his large feet skimming at a surprising pace. Brynz cast a look where Getabit had disappeared, but there was no sign of the peddler.

She sighed and began to climb. Two steps in, she was on her hands and knees, crabbing her way up at an angle, convinced she was about to plummet to her death with every slipping step. It wasn't until she pushed up a tailwind that she managed any traction at all, and even then, her climb was slow and treacherous. At last, she reached the plateau where the northmen waited, watching her upward scrabble with sullen eyes. She dragged herself over the edge with a groan then collapsed onto her back, her fingers bruised, her knees raw, her chest heaving air like a ruined horse. After several panting breaths, she grasped Uhnkre's offered hand and allowed him to pull her to her feet. The northmen's faces were impassive as Uhnkre addressed them.

"Ock meng tallik kalt." He pointed toward the valley for Brynz's benefit. She nodded, ignoring the stinging in her knees and fingers, knowing any show of weakness would diminish what little respect she'd built. Instead, she focused on finding a plan for reaching the peak Getabit had pointed out. Uhnkre clapped Flewd on the back as he passed by the big man, adjusting his dras carrier as he went. Flewd sniffed and pushed out his lower lip, his black eyes cutting toward Brynz.

Kif, standing close enough she could see the pin-sized mole near his left eye, hawked up a wad of phlegm and spat it near her feet. Before she could react, Uhnkre had the front of the younger man's stained shirt in his fist, lifting him onto his toes. "Julk!" Uhnkre shouted, his free hand pointing at the glob. Kif's face went red as he snaked out the toe of his boot and stubbed away the spittle. Uhnkre lowered him to the ground, his expression dark. The younger man dropped his gaze. Uhnkre gave him a venomous stare before stalking off. Hrul cuffed the back of Kif's head, the younger man flashing a smile that held no warmth, his gaze sharp beneath his broad forehead.

"Kwulf lel," Uhnkre commanded, starting forward at a swift walk.

Brynz moved to her accustomed position, the rest taking their places around her. Kif spit toward her again, a look of defiance on his face. Brynz stepped past without comment—she had enough trouble as it was—putting her focus on her feet. Only they would get her where she wanted to go. Everything else was irrelevant.

The snow had all but disappeared by the time the group reached the valley, the spring sun melting it into isolated gray-white daubs that dotted the landscape like fallen clouds.

Haedyn should have been glad of it, but he was not. Instead, he was disappointed he hadn't been able to amaze Elorah with his command of Fyrre. He was sure he would have been brilliant and impressive, but she'd put an end to it before he'd even gotten started. There must be something he could do to win her favor. His fevered brain contemplated the dilemma as he ventured another glance in her direction.

A familiar roiling seized his stomach, as if he were about to be sick, but it was an agony he gladly endured for the chance to gaze upon her flawless beauty. From her dazzling amber-blue eyes and aquiline nose to her high cheekbones and long neck, there was not one thing he would change, not even the small ears hugged tight to her head. Her face was perfection. But it wasn't only her countenance he found irresistible. It was her openness and caring that set his heart afire. How she offered acceptance and understanding to all without any hint of prejudice. True, he had little experience with maisses, but even so, he'd seen none so fair or pure. None so self-assured or confident. None so appealing in every way. He could spend every day in her company from now until forever and still not get his fill, so intoxicating did he find her charms.

Of course, Rachmyn thought him a fool. That went without saying. Even now, he could feel his friend's speculative stare upon his back like a dashing of cold water against his heated skin. He sometimes wondered if Rachmyn had any feelings at all, at least about anyone other than the two of them. He never let on if he did. Haedyn wanted in so many ways to be like his friend, to be as composed and cerebral and calm, but then again, he was glad he was not, for what was life without passion?

Without a cheerful enjoyment embracing every opportunity? He couldn't imagine how it would feel to not be thrilled by every new thing. Rachmyn said it was his Fyrre affinity that made him excitable, and perhaps that was true. He was more excitable than anyone he knew but was that a bad thing?

"What are you thinking of?" Elorah had caught him staring.

"I was thinking of where we're headed," he said, shifting his gaze forward.

"Were you?" she asked, a bemused smile on her face.

"Well, partly that," he said, returning her smile. "What were you thinking of?"

"Bravik," she responded. "And gryphons and tusk-pigs."

"Not the Drasgor?"

"Them, too. But men can be reasoned with."

"I'm not sure you can call them men," Aikin said. Elorah shook her head, a perturbed frown drawing down her lips. Haedyn snickered and patted his bird's head. The grynt was perched on his shoulder.

"What would you call them?" Mierrle asked, leaning forward in her saddle.

nnnngggg REEEEE-nnnngggg REEEE-nnnngggg REEEEEEEEEE

A cacophony of grunting squeals pierced the air a blink before the tusk-pigs attacked.

There were three, all as tall as ponies, their bristly coats the sullen rust of forgotten metal, their dark eyes sunken into the sides of their anvil skulls. They charged forward on split-toed black hooves that looked too small for their great size, their ropey, black-tufted tails flagging over their backs. All three raised their wrinkled snouts to better aim the bone-white tusks jutting forward from their screaming mouths.

The first crashed into Thane's pony; the second took aim on Mierrle's gelding, and the third went for the underside of Aikin's horse. It all happened at once, a confusion of rearing and stamping and flashing tusks. Mierrle's old horse went skyward, Aikin's gelding went sideways, and the unfortunate pony tripped, stumbling to its knees for a moment before the tusk-pig's butting snout barrel-rolled it onto its side, its tether giving way.

Mierrle pitched to the ground with a shriek as her horse crow-hopped twice then cantered away, its pony galloping off in a different direction. The chase horse sped after them both, Rachmyn's pale-hair flying into his face, his hand grabbing a fistful of mane to keep him topside. The tether linking the biting pony to Aikin had come loose, and it galloped north.

Haedyn went to his quiver, pulling one of his last three arrows as his horse jinked beneath him, his bird flying up in a startled flurry. He clamped his legs tighter, managing to keep his seat as he nocked the arrow and sent it flying. It was an impossible shot, taken at a precarious angle without enough time to aim and yet the arrow found its mark, driving deeply into one of the tusk-pigs' eyes. It let out a thundering shriek as it cartwheeled onto its side, the sharpened edge of a stone snubbing off the end of its snout in a spray of blood.

Haedyn crooked the bow onto his shoulder and flung his knife at the beast, pegging it in the neck behind the juncture with the head. Blood gouted from the wound as the creature lashed its narrow hooves, vigorously at first, but then, as its lifeblood fountained across the yellow mosscups and grease-gray snow, with decreasing conviction until, at last, they went still.

Haedyn dismounted, clutching his bow, then ran over and pulled his knife free. He wrenched his arrow from the dead pig's eye socket then gave the monstrous head a kick for good measure, wincing when his toes crinkled against unyielding bone. *At least the sodding thing is dead.* He sheathed his knife.

His relief was short-lived.

Thane's pony was back on its feet, a square of bloody hide hanging like a curtain across the deep-red muscle of its flayed shoulder. It stared at its attacker. The tusk-pig charged, and the pony skittered away, the hide flap fluttering like a dirty flag, the packsaddle skewing sideways. The pony wheeled around to face the tusk-pig, and it made another charging thrust. The pony stood firm until the beast was almost upon it before it exploded away in a short-strided canter that took it out of reach, the packsaddle banging against its side for several strides before slipping under its belly and catching a hind leg. The pony tumbled a second time, its head diving between its front legs as it flipped forward, its thrashing back hooves slashing open the capsized pack as they catapulted past its forelegs. The stunned pony lay still for a moment, then lumbered to its feet and gave a shake, the broken packsaddle and its contents falling to the ground in a colorful pile. The pony sighted in on the charging tusk-pig, jumping sideways a split before getting gored then wheeled around. Haedyn could see it was favoring its injured front leg. The tusk-pig circled and raised its snout, taking aim. It charged and the pony juked sideways. The tusk-pig squalled—*nnnngggggREEEEE*—as the pony trotted its backside around to face up its attacker once again, its nostrils flaring.

Haedyn nocked the bloody arrow and let fly, sinking the head —*thwonk*—in the charging pig's brisket. It barely broke stride, dragging a tusk across the pony's flank and opening a bleeding gash. Haedyn pulled a second arrow and buried it—*thwonk*—in the tusk-pig's neck. It squealed—*nnnngggREEEE*—and galloped away, shaking its head.

A scream sounded, and Haedyn swiveled. Mierrle was down, one foot kicking against the third tusk-pig's wriggling snout, the other clamped between its front teeth. Haedyn nocked his last arrow. *Thwonk.* This shot was at an even more impossible angle, but the head hit its target, sinking into the softness beneath the creature's tail before tearing its way down, splitting the pig from bunghole to personals. A shiny loop of slick-looking gut slithered out, but the tusk-pig was too busy savaging Mierrle's leg to notice.

Haedyn looked around, his gaze stopping on a jagged slat stabbing skyward from the broken packsaddle. He ran to it. After wresting it free he sprinted toward the giant pig, wildly whirling the wooden slat above his head and screaming a war cry at the top of his lungs.

The tusk-pig released its hold the moment Haedyn rammed the splintered wood into the snot-slick gap between its quivering nostrils. It let out an ear-piercing squeal—*nnnngggggREEEEEE*—bright red pouring into its frothing mouth. The tusk-pig shook its head, pink spittle flying in all directions as Mierrle crawled away, dragging her mutilated leg.

Haedyn clubbed the tusk-pig's bleeding snout again and again, until, at last, it faltered back a step, then another, one hind foot stamping its trailing gut into the dirt and rupturing it. A spew of feces and blood squirted out. The smell was horrific, and it was all Haedyn could do not to be sick as he pulled his knife from its sheath and charged again, thrusting the red blade into the bristly neck. The tusk-pig let out a gurgling squeal, blood streaming from its mouth. It squealed again, the liquid sound of a creature drowning.

Haedyn jerked his knife free then thrust it again into the globular neck, further up this time. Blood spouted into his eyes, blinding him. He ducked his head toward his sleeve.

WHAM

A tremendous force knocked the air out of him as he flung to the ground, landing in a protective curve around the crystalwood bow. He wiped his eyes on his sleeve, repositioned the bow then scrambled onto his feet. The anvil head swung round, ramming him in the back and sending him into another sprawl. Haedyn bear-crawled his way onto his feet then darted forward. He jerked his knife from the leaking neck and jumped back as the tusk-pig staggered forward. The addled beast stumped ahead several steps then swung its enormous head round—eyes glaring, body swaying—before toppling onto its side in a grunting crash.

Haedyn ran to it and cut its throat. After ensuring the tusk-pig was dead, he yanked his arrow from its backside and stuck the fouled thing into his quiver reminding himself he couldn't afford to waste arrows no matter how badly they smelled. He glanced toward Mierrle then, seeing Elorah was beside her, turned his attention elsewhere.

The wounded pony stood some distance back, head hanging low, sides heaving, blood seeping down two of its legs, the exposed muscle of its shoulder and flank a brave shade of purple. A war had been fought, and it had won but only just.

Haedyn made for the other dead pig and yanked out his other two arrows, pushing them both into his quiver. The pony looked at him, and he noticed its swollen front leg was cocked forward. He bit his bottom lip, wishing he could help, but he knew nothing about healing. He looked around. Where were the rest of the sodding ponies? He cast his gaze further, movement on the horizon catching his attention.

Thane's horse loped due east, golden puffs flying up from its hooves, its rider jerking the reins. The hammer-headed gelding loped on, determined, Aikin chasing three metes behind, the biting pony galloping beside his knee. *At least we have one pony.*

He squinted north. The last he'd seen Rachmyn, he'd been chasing Mierrle's horse and pony. Haedyn now realized he should have kept the pony with him instead of letting Mierrle try her hand at leading it. That was a mistake. He looked in the other direction. Elorah's horse stood a few paces away, its pony tethered to its side. Make that two ponies. Two and a half counting the lame one.

Haedyn now understood the wisdom behind packing each with an identical set of gear, so that no one pony had the whole quantity of a necessary item. He also saw the wisdom of splitting the ponies. Elorah's grandfather had known the dangers they would be facing and planned accordingly. It dawned on him to look for his own horse.

Haedyn spotted his gelding standing ten paces away, head held high, ears pricked, eyes white-rimmed with fear. He held out his hand and approached, murmuring in a low voice then patted it on the neck, grateful he didn't have another chase on his hands. He led it over to Elorah's horse then tied both to a nearby bush.

He looked into the sky and whistled three bright notes. It didn't take long for a black-and-red bird to hurtle down. The grynt landed on the broad expanse of a tusk-pig's side and surveyed its surroundings, looking like a red-hatted bully. Haedyn chuckled to himself. It was so like Fryk to act as though it had brought down the beast itself. The bird hopped to the pig's soft belly and went to work stripping off a meal.

Haedyn's gaze went north again. He could now make out two horses walking toward him, one with a rider, one without. His gaze moved east toward another pair of horses headed in his direction. His relief grew. He turned toward Elorah, bent over and hovering a vorestone above Mierrle's purpling leg. He wiped his hands on his leggings as he approached.

"Can I help?" he asked, kneeling beside her. Being so close made him feel a little dizzy. He put his focus on Mierrle's leg. The worst of it was a crescent-shaped gouge in her thigh, gaped open like a grotesque smile. A second large tear had nearly separated her calf muscle from its mooring.

Elorah shook her head. "I have to draw out the poison," she murmured, moving the stone in a circular pattern. "An open wound is harder to heal than one that is closed," she continued, answering his unspoken question. "Your eye was easy..." Her words were measured as she moved the stone, her voice soothing, and he found himself drawing closer. "Thane's nose, not so easy..." She changed position and brought out a second stone from the bag near her knee, "...but still, not a problem, because the damage was within. This..." She moved the second stone over the largest gash. "...will be trickier. There are forces that must be ameliorated before I can correct the damage."

Haedyn wondered what forces she meant but decided not to interrupt her with his ignorance.

As if she could hear his thoughts, she responded. "Every injury has its counterpart in the energy field that surrounds each one of us. If I do not correct those defects, Mierrle's leg will not heal as it should." She flourished both stones in elaborate spirals. "Her forces remain fragile from her earlier depletion."

He marveled that Mierrle's leg had already lost most of its purple coloring. He'd had his own injuries and knew bruising and swelling took far longer to heal. Mierrle's eyes were closed, and he wondered if she was asleep.

"Not asleep. Only resting," Elorah said in the same soothing voice. She returned both stones to her bag and retrieved a small silver packet. After unfolding the crimped end, she drew out a pinch of bluish-green powder and sprinkled it into each of the wounds, going into the packet twice more before she was finished. Mierrle whimpered, and Elorah laid a hand upon her forehead then began humming with a tonality Haedyn could somehow feel inside, like he'd drunk too much sweetsweet. Mierrle's face smoothed, and he settled onto his backside, allowing the buzzing to flow through him.

Elorah returned the packet to her bag and drew out a small wooden case. She unfastened its two silver clasps and opened it.

Inside were iridescent needles, not much bigger than a thread. She removed one and, holding it in her cupped hands, brought it close to her lips and hummed. The needle took on a light of its own. She continued to hum until the needle was ember bright. She carefully inserted the glowing needle near the top of the gouge in Mierrle's thigh. She picked another needle from the box, hummed it to a glow then inserted it across from the first. She continued in this way until she had inserted ten pairs along the border of the gash.

Elorah returned to her bag and drew out a stone with the same iridescence as the needles. She brought it to her lips and hummed it bright before hovering it above the first pair. Sparks arced from the stone to one needle then the other. Elorah chanted a word that sounded like *vooohhhmmm* and the needles drew together, bonding so that the flesh between closed as if the wound had never happened.

Elorah brought the dimmed stone to her lips and hummed again before hovering it above the next set of needles. As before, the stone's illuminance arced to the needles as she chanted *vooohhhmmm*. The needles drew tight, the flesh becoming whole. Thrice more she repeated the process until the only sign of the wound was a pinkish crescent in the center of the thigh. Elorah lifted the dimmed stone and surveyed her work. Though the skin looked tender, the gash was gone.

Elorah hummed upon the stone, a different tune this time, and set it aside. With as much care as she'd used inserting them, she removed the needles, taking time to hum the second tune upon each before placing them into their case.

She turned her attention to Mierrle's calf, and the process began again. Out came the first stone, and, after careful ministrations, the second. Though Haedyn understood little of what he was seeing, he felt more admiration for Elorah now than before. His heart was like a trapped bird banging against the cage of his chest, and he scarcely noticed Rachmyn kneel beside him.

"The horses are returned," his friend announced, louder than required, one hand corralling his pale hair to keep it out of his eyes. Haedyn gave him a reproachful look, ignoring Rachmyn's annoyed frown as he bobbed his head toward Elorah and touched his index finger to his lips. Rachmyn's eyebrows drew together before he rose and stalked away.

It wasn't until Elorah packed up her bag, and Mierrle gingerly rose to her feet that Haedyn moved at all, a peaceful calm having settled upon him like a blanket.

His sated bird had landed on his shoulder sometime along, so that when he turned to watch Elorah walk away, his view was blocked by a red-capped glutton in need of a nap. Haedyn flapped open his vest, and the dozy grynt crawled inside.

He got up, deciding he better find some task before he also curled up and fell asleep.

CHAPTER THIRTY-SIX
IN A LAND OF MIGHTY MEN

Rachmyn checked his pocket for his shard. Yes, there it was. The reassurance helped only a little. He'd discovered the weather in these northern lands was as unpredictable as it was harsh, and the wind blowing in from the west smelled of snow and danger.

They'd moved north of Valley Kalt to somewhere on the Balliska Plate, a wide-open flat of coarse-leaved shrubs, dark-gray rock, and chill winds.

The loss of the pony and its packsaddle had been a blow. Of the blankets and wemble cloth and waterskins that had gone with it, the waterskins were the biggest miss. If not for Thane, though Rachmyn hated to admit it, they might not have found enough water to keep going. For all its pretty scenery, Valley Kalt was as dry as a bread crust.

They'd gathered what they could from the broken saddle's rubble heap and shoved it into the remaining two packs. Putting extra weight on the ponies wasn't ideal, but it had to be done. As for the injured pony, Elorah had healed it of everything except its tart attitude. Without a packsaddle, there wasn't much the pony could carry, but they'd managed to strap a tusk-pig ham to it. The meat smelled like a dirty foot, and Rachmyn wished they were shut of it. Elgre had refused it outright, preferring his usual diet of rodents. Rachmyn wished he could do the same, but Haedyn had begged him to be agreeable and so, he'd plugged his nose and choked the funked meat down.

The previous evening, Elorah had shown the others where they were and where they were going using her grandfather's map, her finger lingering over the wedge marking their destination, her eyes shining when she spoke its name—Whitemond. His mind shifted back to his time in Oru Fen when he'd seen it for himself.

It wasn't a big mountain—more of a flat-topped hill really—formed from white stone and covered with crystalwood trees, their reflective leaves and branches mirroring back the rays of the sun. Towering above the plateaued top was a construction of stone slabs arranged in a multicursal pattern that, taken as a whole, resembled the head of a bear.

The megalith crackled with energy, each slab pulsing with a penetrative blue light. Marans of every description flowed in and around the structure while many more ascended and descended the mountainside's curving paths. A wider view revealed still more marans pilgrimaging toward or recessing away from the radiant peak.

It seemed like the happiest place in the world, but as soon as the thought struck, a shadow fell, and a terrific roaring filled the air. Next came a rising crescendo of mighty quakes, the entire mountain trembling like a leaf in a maelstrom. The pulsing blue light slowed then winked out entirely as the screeching groan of splitting stone shook the sky. A crevasse yawned open, sundering the plateau into unequal halves. All else faded as Rachmyn focused on the expanding chasm, watching it tear apart, wider then deeper, the mountain stretching open like the maw of a giant serpent swallowing an enormous egg.

With a thunderous clatter, the parambek fell into the massive crater, a huge cloud of dust flinging into the air. In a blink, the crevasse clamped shut, leaving no sign of the monolith that had stood tall only a moment before.

There was something else. A nostalgia had taken hold as he'd watched, as if the mountain held memories he couldn't quite recall. He was sure he'd never been to Whitemond, and yet he felt not only that he had been there, but that he'd failed at something important and was being given another chance. None of it made sense, and he tried to dismiss it from his mind, but the feeling lingered, despite every effort to chase it away.

Of one thing he was certain. Whitemond was nothing like the Lawless Mountains of his youth. Those were proper peaks, rising high enough to poke holes through the clouds, with honeycombed caves every Shadowen held dear. He looked south, his eyes tracing the stair-stepped hills marking the bumpy beginning—or end, depending on how you looked at it—of the mountains he'd loved since he was a boy. A different nostalgia took hold, one much more familiar and comfortable. Those mountains held his heart no matter how far from them he roamed.

Thane, Aikin, and Haedyn had volunteered to fill the waterskins in preparation for the next stretch of their journey. Thane had insisted, and so the three had unloaded the packsaddles save the waterskins and set out, Thane leading the way on Rachmyn's chase horse. Rachmyn, Elorah, and Mierrle were to stay near camp until they returned. Elgre was off on a wander, the wolf keeping his distance to avoid consternation amongst the geldings and ponies.

Elorah and Mierrle, wrapped in wemble and seated on blankets by the fire, spoke quietly. As was his habit, Rachmyn kept his thoughts to himself. To say them would take away their power, and so he left his musings to their flow, observed but unspoken.

Elorah picked up her head. "Do you hear that?" Her eyes searched the horizon.

Rachmyn turned his attention to the sounds of the wind.

"There," she said, inclining her ear and closing her eyes.

Rachmyn concentrated but only heard scraping branches and scratching leaves. He shook his head, a pinprick stinging his nose. He tilted his head upward. An icy bit struck his cheek. Another hit his forehead. Two more hit his chin. As he'd feared, a storm was moving in.

Mierrle stood and held out her hand. She looked up at the sky, one side of her face scrunching when an ice pellet hit her in the eye. "It's snowing," she said with unveiled concern.

Rachmyn took stock of their situation. They'd made camp in an area more open than suited him, but it was the best they could do on this plateau with its flat rocks and lack of trees. They'd set up on the leeward side of a boxytop brake, hoping the waist-high shrubs would provide some cover. He knew the bushes would be of little help in a snowstorm, but they didn't have much choice. They couldn't leave before the others came back.

"I thought I heard a bravik. Far away." Elorah frowned and got to her feet. "I don't hear it now." She looked up at the oppressive sky. "Another storm," she said, her voice full of disappointment. He understood.

"Should we stay here?" Mierrle asked.

Of course not.

He wondered how far out the others were as he squinted at the shrinking horizon. He could make his way to Oru Fen and try to ascertain their whereabouts, but even then, they could only wait. And hope.

Elorah's eyes fastened onto his. "Perhaps someone should look for them," she said, her words ripe with meaning. He shifted his feet and pulled his wemble cloak tighter about his shoulders. How had she known what he was thinking?

"Yes, perhaps," he allowed, his gaze swinging up to the overhanging sky. He shoved his hand into his pocket, his fingers wrapping around his shard, his eyes searching for a suitable place to settle while his mind went elsewhere.

Elgre, answering Rachmyn's unspoken call, came trotting up. He patted the wolf's head.

The wolf set off, stopping once to check that Rachmyn was following before moving on.

This will make things worse.

Brynz brushed snow off the fox pelt wrapped around her shoulders. Uhnkre had handed her the fur without comment, and she wasn't sure where it had come from, although she had her suspicions based on Kif's scowls.

Snowfall was always unwelcome in her opinion, though she'd grown up in a land where it snowed half the time. Even so, she'd never liked it.

Those who called it beautiful often had the luxury of admiring it through a window from a cushioned chair beside a cozy fire, but as someone whose days were spent taking care of animals, she knew better. Mucking stalls, slinging hay, and carrying water was freezing, miserable work when you were tromping through snow to do it.

Uhnkre and the rest of his men were eating cragdogs, agouti-furred rodents that lived in large, underground colonies the northmen called denks. The rodents' inquisitive nature made them easy prey, and the group had eaten several since coming onto the high plains. The northmen talked in terse syllables as they ate, their greasy fingers pointing towards the bone piles. Tusk-pig remains judging by what was left—three swollen heads, two backbones and the bottom halves of a dozen split-toed legs scattered about like fallen branches.

Uhnkre had seemed surprised. "Not Bravik," he'd said. "Bravik kill one. Not..." He'd swept his hand toward the entirety of the remains.

"Gryphons?" she'd asked.

He'd shaken his head.

"Wolves?"

Another headshake, less certain this time, his eyes darting to the singletrack pawprints dimpling the snow near one of the backbones. Too small for a wolf. Likely, a brushy-tailed fox scavenging a meal.

"What killed them then?" she'd asked.

"Men," he'd said as if the answer was obvious. He'd walked away, his shoulders shucking the dras carrier as he went. He'd propped it against a bush near Hrul, busy peeling the fluff off another cragdog. Hrul had handed the carcass to Uhnkre who took it, his teeth tearing into the pale meat with ruthless efficiency.

The northmen seemed unmindful of the snow and Brynz wondered if they even noticed it. It wasn't the reason for their stop, and she expected they would resume their journey once everyone had eaten their fill. From what she could gather they were on their way to some settlement. She tried not to think what that meant for her. Perhaps she would find Zell and—

KEEEEEEAAAAARRRRR

Brynz jerked toward the sound, a sudden fire in her chest.

Zell?

As if in a dream she watched a silver silhouette glide over, its wings and body the color of the snowy sky, its ear tufts and feet the darker gray of storm clouds, a gray-tufted tail trailing behind. In a landscape of snow, there was nothing showy about the gryphon's coloring, the silver and gray allowing it to blend with its surroundings.

She whistled a long note, hoping the gryphon would respond, and thrilled when the huge wings banked, its trajectory swinging toward the ground. She gave another whistle, adding two chirrups at the end, and her excitement grew when the sound seemed to have an effect. The gryphon descended. Uhnkre and the rest of the northmen gaped as the raptor landed near one of the tusk-pig backbones with a muffled thud, its tail thwipping against its silver sides, its azurite stare raking across the carnage.

The gryphon stood near Brynz, and she looked at it the way a starving man looks at a bowl of stew. The gryphon's feathers shone, even in the dull light, the muscles in its hindquarters bulging beneath its slick-looking hide. She peered closer, her hand dropping away from the pelt, allowing it to fall to the ground. One front leg bore a fresh-looking scar, about the level where a leg band might have been. The other front leg had no mark Brynz could detect. Doubt began to set in. This gryphon seemed larger, sturdier, than what Zell had been. Its azurite stare held the cold impertinence of a predator when it swept across her, and she shivered. There was none of Zell's softness of expression, no sign of recognition in the razor-sharp eyes.

"Look away," Uhnkre gritted, his voice a droning buzz inside her ear.

As always, his approach had been silent, but now that she knew he was there, she could feel the firmness of his shadow upon her back. She tried to obey but it was as if her eyes no longer belonged to her; the gryphon's intense blue gaze had captured them completely. The gryphon took a step toward her. And another, its stare intensifying, the tip of its tail twitching. It lowered its feathered head, taking her measure, the talons of its front feet divoting the snow. Still, she could not tear her eyes away; could not move to save herself. It was as if the gryphon's piercing glare had frozen her to the spot.

Uhnkre's huge hand clapped across her eyes, breaking the

connection. Relief flooded her seized muscles. The pelt fell upon her shoulders a moment before Uhnkre's arm hooked her waist and drug her backward, close enough she could feel his breath against her neck. He dropped his hand to her shoulder, his other hand pushing her behind him and out of the gryphon's sights. She blinked to get her bearings, then, clutching the pelt, started away, stumbling past Ahnkne as he rushed forward, holding a loaded dras carrier in front like a staff.

Uhnkre took the weapon then reared back and, with a practiced swing, launched the dras at the gryphon. The dras flew forward in a flattened curve, its head cleaving the gryphon's keel. The raptor reared up, the wooden handle of the dras levering up and down, ratcheting the barbed head further into its feathered breast, an oblong of bright red marking the wound.

KEEEEAAAAARRRR

The gryphon screamed, its huge wings unfolding for flight, but before it could lift away, Hrul launched his dras, burying its head in the gryphon's side where feathers met fur.

The gryphon's front dropped, the dras handles sagging lower. It cranked its head around and, using its black beak, snapped Hrul's dras shaft in two before refolding its wing over the splintered stub poking from its side.

Ahnkne launched his dras, embedding the head in the gryphon's haunch with enough force the muscled hindquarters stumbled sideways. Kif and Flewd launched theirs as well, one dras-head skewering the gryphon's front shoulder, the other penetrating its point of stifle. The silvery hindquarters flopped to the snow-covered ground with a muffled *thwup*.

The gryphon clacked its beak, then shrilled its secondary call —*KRUK KRUK KRUK KRUK*. The angry chucking noise accompanied the elliptic circling of its head, its front talons thrashing the snow muddy as it tried to pull its paralyzed backend forward.

After several moments of struggle, the gryphon folded its front legs into a squat and took a half-hearted swipe at the handle sticking from its breast, notching out two chunks before letting loose. The gryphon paused, its beak dropping open as it began to pant, its black tongue fluttering like a giant moth's wing. It gurgled another series of chucks—

kruk kruk kruk kruk—before dropping its head between its bent front legs onto the blood-stained snow, the fierce gleam in its azure eyes going dark as its forequarters collapsed.

Uhnkre ran to the beast—his axe held high above his head—and delivered a crunching blow to the gryphon's neck. The blade sank to the handle. He jerked the axe free then swung twice more, the last blow sending the gryphon's head skidding sideways.

Brynz watched the coordinated attack with a mixture of gratitude and horror. To see the cruel bite of the dras-head along with the speed with which the huge projectile could be thrown was sobering, and she understood more than ever why these northmen were feared. It was a wonder Garrod had survived, a wonder he had a foot at all when she realized a dras barb had stuck it to his horse. A chill ran through her as she envisioned him pulling a bloody spike out of what was left then stumping away from these giants who made no mistake with their aim. Her stomach churned.

As for the gryphon, the men were carving their dras-heads from its carcass using their sharpened blades, the blood of their quarry speckling their forearms and faces and the fronts of their shirts. Hrul held up his dras with a rueful shake of the head at its docked handle. He would have to repair it before the weapon would be useful again. Uhnkre's dras, though still usable, would also need repaired. She considered the other side of things. The loss of Hrul's dras, and the damage to Uhnkre's, made the group less safe should they encounter another gryphon or tusk-pig. That thought was sobering as well.

Uhnkre freed his dras from the gryphon's breast then wiped it down with a greasy-looking rag before loading it into the carrier. Each of the northmen did the same, Hrul's truncated dras disappearing down his carrier tube without a trace. He shook it once, then grimaced at its dull rattle.

A quick scrub with snow to get the blood off, and the northmen were ready to continue. After strapping their carriers onto their backs, they awaited the command.

"Kwulf lel," Unhnkre said, and the group set off, Brynz at their core.

Essiant had been tracking the Agya's progress with anticipation. Its minder, though naive to her true purpose, continued to progress toward the required end, despite the hardships wrought by the imbalances of the world. Her forest-hued wraithwolf, Kimbre, had guided her steps from afar, his guidance directed, in turn, by the express wishes of the Elect.

The tuskee, as was true of most sentient beings on Eolemar (the notable exception being marans), was sensitive to the increasing frequency of Eolemar's many vibrations, and though the matriarch didn't have a consciousness able to conceive of what they meant, its soul remained responsive to the mountain's whispered leadings. Whitemond's vibration had been increasing along with Therrania's. The monolith—buried under layers of dirt—now hummed its sacred song once more, drawing the minder's trusted matriarch ever closer to what had once been the center of Therran power.

Ten previous Uniters had also followed the parambek's call, only to have their sojourns cut short by failure. Each time Therrania's protector, the great good Grogauk, had begun the ascendancy vibrations to prepare the site and the megalith for resurrection, only to have to withdraw his hopeful Xha until another cycle was under way.

Essiant had gathered the other Voriens—Spectra, Embren, Ieeva, Ajai, Raya. Soon, they would howl Kimbre into their pack, once his night-ward joined Essiant's ward and her group. Until then, the Voriens applied their pack-mind to the success of Kimbre's endeavor, for his had been a hard, lonely path.

The loss of the grandmother, while foretold, had come earlier than expected, leaving Kimbre's night-ward without the benefit of the ancient deeta's wisdom. It was good the deeta had remained steadfast, always resisting the reviving forces of the Agya for all these many annums, urging her successor to do the same. Her span had been long by Eolemaran standards but not when compared to what it could have been had she misused the orb to maintain her youth. There was one who had long exploited the vivifying effects of the Infinite Eye of another great good Founder, and Eolemar and Oru Fen had suffered for it. Essiant had been hard pressed to keep his night-ward safe from the predations of that one who subverted the Eye's power for her own perverse gain.

It had been a calculated risk, allowing an Erynvor to grow to maturity while in the sphere of one whose every motive was at odds with the goals and purposes the Uniter had pledged to uphold, but, as with most things, there was a balance to be struck. Without that time spent learning the ways of vorik, his night-ward would not have been able to acquire the tangible skills needed to complete her pledge. That period was now past, and they could all move forward toward the goals the Elect had set before them.

There were challenges still to be met, and two wraithwolves yet to join, but Essiant could see the time for fulfilling promises was coming into sight. The Elect had preserved the Way, and with his help, his night-ward was learning more of those truths every day. Truths that would lift a parambek, a Protector, and a people, all at the same time.

CHAPTER THIRTY-SEVEN
A SUDDEN STOP

Thane had known the ways of water since he'd been founded. Felt its ebb and flow as it slipped through clay and sand and rock, heard its pulsebeat as it roamed over loams and peats and silts. He understood, too, the *tinka-tinka-tink* of its memory songs, those flutings that whispered where it was going and where it had been. But, most of all, he understood its differences. How the droplet squeezed from a blackened cloud differed from the frantic flow of a rapid as much as Wrynne's seven-toed cats differed from a mountain chassa—so different neither would see any similarity in the other.

Though he could sense water in all its forms, it was its memory songs that called to Thane most clearly. Within those delicate journey-tunes lay the key to coaxing water away from one place and into another. That's where many made their mistake, even so-called Aquillan wycches, assuming water must be overpowered, either through manual means or brute vorik, before it would respond. In fact, it was far better and easier to strike up a partnership in harmony with its trickling awareness. Once such a cooperation was established, all that remained were the tender convincements that persuaded the water to move where he wished it to go.

After discovering how to whisper water where he wanted, he knew he'd found a way to be acceptable to most of society, though never to his father. That was one maran who had never seen any good in Thane no matter how hard he tried. Then again, without his father's harsh rejections, he might never have found his way to the Rabboutiers, and in turn, discovered how valuable his water whispers could be, as evidenced by the bounty of brakken kelp and gilded pearls that had come of it. *Ah, well. No grit, no pearl, wasn't that the old saying?* Still, he wished the scars had remained on the inside. Having to wear one on his cheek seemed more than required.

Along with his ability to move water, he could also discern its hidden reserves beneath even the most barren-looking ground. Where it got tricky was persuading it to the surface if solid rock lay in between. For all his ability, he could not whisper water through stone in sufficient quantity and with enough force to be of much use.

He'd swapped horses for this jaunt, shunning the dullard for Rachmyn's chaser. They'd brought two ponies as well, emptying their pack saddles in anticipation of the waterskins' weight. To his mind, it was better to fill the waterskins now while he could, rather than wait and find out the ground's composition had become too difficult. It hadn't taken long to convince Elorah and the others, though their understanding of his limitations were lacking. All the better. He didn't like dwelling on his failings. He'd spent enough time doing that already.

Aikin and Haedyn rode behind, each trailing a pony. Aikin had made much of his ability to parse plant signatures to find his way back. With the plateau's monotony of rock and wind, Thane feared they could get turned around if they weren't careful. He hoped the tetchy blowhard wasn't spouting horse donk again. He seemed prone to it. Haedyn had come along to provide cover should they run into trouble. He'd done a job on the tusk-pigs and an extra set of hands never hurt.

Thane's mind fixed upon an underground river a league north. It was hard to say whether he'd have trouble coaxing the water to the surface, but its amiable burble made it seem as if he wouldn't.

Cold nipped his forehead, and he swiped at it then squinted at the thick, gray sky.

Just my luck. Another snowstorm. Fleek me, this weather leaves a lot to be desired.

He slapped his knee. What was he even doing here when he could be sitting in a warm alehouse playing cards and sipping sweetsweet with a handsome rogue—Rodric perhaps—who wouldn't say no to making a night of it? Instead, he was tracking across a forsaken barren in the company of two thickwits with no interest in him or each other, searching for water in a land drier than dust and filled with beasts—and men—intent on killing him. He couldn't have dreamed up a worse way to spend time if he'd tried. No auriels in it, either. He ground his teeth. *Fool! Softhead!*

The wind shifted, and both ponies lifted their heads, nostrils flaring, eyes rolling like white-rimmed marbles. The biter launched forward, breaking its halter. A duck of the head, and it was away. The other pony lunged into a series of herky-jerky bucks, a slashing front hoof severing its lead. It too raced away, tail flagging, chesty grunts accenting its flying hooves.

Aikin wheeled his horse around. Haedyn went after the bucker while Thane pointed his mount toward the biter then downed his heels when the horse burst forward.

A squalling roar shivered up from a nearby swale.

"Bravik!" Haedyn yelled.

Thane shot a panicked look over his shoulder. Haedyn had turned, his horse now galloping due east. *What's he doing?*

A beast taller and wider than Thane's horse came charging up out of the swale. Covered in shaggy gray, brown stripes marking its hindquarters and shoulders, the bravik had the long snout and legginess of a wolf coupled with the rounded ears and thickset body of a bear. Its black tongue lolled inside a dark mouth brimming with sharps and fangs. Thane's throat constricted and his hands went numb, his thoughts a mad scramble inside his head.

The bravik squalled again, the sound shaking Thane's internals into a frenzy of pounding and squeezing and letting go. Warm wet soaked the front of his leggings as he gigged his horse, all thought of catching the pony forgotten. The snow was picking up, and he squinted to see ahead, his mind screaming instructions—*Stop! Go! Turn! Run!*

The biter did not see the pit until it was too late. Its stiffened front legs and sat-down haunches were of no help, its momentum carrying it over the edge in a frenzy of thrashing legs. The pony bellowed a blood-freezing scream when it hit bottom, though Thane barely heard above the loud buzzing in his ears. He hauled back on the reins, his mouth screaming gibberish.

Another panicked look confirmed the bravik was a stride behind, its huge jaw hanging low, its curving fangs a dull white in the gray light. The massive creature launched, its front limbs clawing air, its gargantuan jaws widening in anticipation. With an agility born of stark terror, horse and rider juked left and left again a step before plunging into the pit.

One webbed front paw raked across the gelding's spinning hindquarters and Thane's leg before the bravik tumbled end over end into its tomb, a deafening squall and rollicking *THUNK* marking its sudden stop upon the wooden spikes at the pit's bottom.

The gelding belted away in a disunited canter, Thane catching the silhouette of another frantic escape from the corner of his eye. He pulled up and turned to see Aikin bent low over his galloping mount's neck, a second bravik close enough to snap a chunk from his horse's flying tail.

Thane's stomach fell as he pointed his mount toward Aikin's galloping horse and squeezed. The gelding broke into an off-balance canter before stumbling to a stop and holding up its hindleg. Only then did Thane notice the bleeding gash across the horse's hindquarter and the deep slice snaking up his own lower leg.

Another look saw Aikin changing course, the bravik circling around behind. He pressed forward in his stirrups as his horse galloped in the opposite direction.

He's seen the pit.

Large rocks flung up behind the galloping horse's heels, each smashing against the bravik's triangular head, the beast breaking stride with each strike. The diversion provided a mete of space between hunter and hunted. Aikin made the most of it, cutting his horse right, putting him on course for the pit. The bravik squalled as it swung round, its long claws slashing deep furrows into the snow-covered ground when it accelerated. The maneuver gained Aikin's horse another mete. Aikin yelled and stropped the horse's hindquarters with his reins. The gelding burst forward. More rocks flung up, striking the bravik's snout. It squalled and veered wide.

At the last moment, Aikin cut a hard left turn. The bravik attempted to follow, but its great bulk carried its hind feet past the pit's edge. Like a boulder bouncing down a mountain, its backend dropped, and it shoulder-slammed the ground. A shuddering spin and the forequarters went skyward, its light gray undercarriage flashing past as the beast fell from view. A thunderous squall and a sickening thump echoed up when the bravik hit bottom.

Thane dismounted and crumpled to the ground, his bleeding leg collapsing like a piece of string. He clutched his calf and gritted his teeth, the pain beginning to register. *Fleek me. Here's another scar to add to the list.* He let out a groan.

Aikin pulled up alongside and dismounted. He took one look and shook his head as he knelt. "By the Urslan, you're lucky you didn't lose your leg," he said, pressing his hands against the bleeding gap to staunch the flow.

Thane let out another groan as the pain kicked in full force. "I don't feel lucky," he moaned.

"I'm not a healer," Aikin apologized. "I only did the minimum to get through practicums." He leaned into his stout arms to increase the pressure. Thane shrieked as a hot split of pain raced to his brain and stabbed him between the eyes, clapping his eyelids shut and clamping his jaw hard enough he thought it might crack. A strange vibration, something like the buzzing of a fly rumbled into his ears. "You won't be riding back on that horse. I doubt we can even limp it back."

Aikin's words cut through the blackness in Thane's mind, and he opened his eyes, glancing at the sorry-looking gelding standing on three legs, its head hanging low. The rasping resumed and Thane realized with a start it was coming from Aikin. He was throat-singing some unknown tune.

Aikin bent forward then lifted his hands. The droning stopped. "It's quit bleeding," he said, inspecting the wound.

Thane grabbed onto Aikin's arm, a rush of gratitude closing his throat. *When a hand is given a heart is returned.* Something hard and bitter went soft inside as he looked into Aikin's brown eyes. Aikin looked away, his arm moving to his side as he got to his feet. Thane dropped his gaze, his cheeks going hot.

Aikin pointed toward his mount. "I'll put you on the horse and walk back." He rubbed his hand against his leggings before offering it. Thane grasped on, and Aikin heaved him to his feet. Or foot. He canted into a sideways hop favoring his useless right leg. He clutched Aikin's arm and limp-hopped to the gelding, swallowing a scream when his damaged foot struck the ground and another split of molten pain arrowed into his groin.

Getting on the horse was another excruciating ordeal of sweating and pulling and swearing before he was upright in the saddle, his mangled leg dangling because the pain of shoving his foot into a stirrup might have killed him.

Aikin gathered the chase horse and limped it through the snow to the other gelding.

Thane watched with a sinking heart. At that rate, they'd be a week or more getting back to camp. Longer if the snow didn't let up. "What about Haedyn?" he asked, remembering they'd started out as a threesome.

"He'll have to make his own way back."

"I doubt your intended will like that very much."

"Can't be helped. You and your horse aren't in any shape to wait around for faldings who take off at the first sign of trouble."

That seemed harsh, but Thane held his tongue. The painful pound in his leg made it easy to ignore the jibe. "As you say," he said, feeling woozy. He closed his eyes and braced as the horse started to move. The wind was picking up, driving icy bits into his balled-up face. He gritted his teeth.

This promised to be a long fleeking ride.

⁂

Haedyn had the pony in his sights. He dug in his heels and set the gelding's feet flying. They'd covered a league and were well away from where the bravik had swung up out of the swale. Had the others made it? He felt a pang of guilt that he'd run after the pony rather than staying to face the bravik with them. It felt cowardly, but in the moment of decision, he'd gone with his first instinct. He could still pull up and turn back, but the pony was close and losing speed with every stride. Wouldn't it be better to catch it first? He bent low and hoped so.

His bird was a lump in his vest pocket. Probably freezing, poor thing, Haedyn thought as snow stung his face.

The gelding's burst of speed did the trick. Haedyn reined the horse across the pony's path, and it swerved, slowing to a trot. Haedyn reined the gelding around in a blocking move, and the pony dodged sideways before stopping, its sides heaving.

Haedyn dismounted, taking care with his bow, and hurried over. He grabbed the pony's halter then realized he had another problem. There was no lead-line. How was he going to secure it to his horse? He looked at the reins. He would have to use one of them.

Keeping one hand on the halter, he unhooked the nearest rein, snapped it to the headpiece then tied the other to the saddle's pack ring. He unhooked the remaining rein, jig-knotted one end then threaded the other end around the horse's muzzle and through the open center of the knot to makeshift a hackamore. He tightened his cloak, brushed snow from the saddle, then jimmied aboard, his posture contorting to hold the shortened rein, his bow slung so far back it banged against his spine. He felt a faint shivering. Without vorik, the wemble was of little use to Fryk in the deepening cold. He blupped heat into his vest pocket as he got his bearings, wishing he'd paid better attention during the chase.

He was accustomed to Rachmyn navigating; it hadn't occurred to him until now that he was on his own. The snow wasn't helping, its white bulk rounding the landscape into a series of slumps and barrows. He squinted up at the pressing-down sky. No help there either. He sighed and took a last look around before pointing his horse in what he hoped was the right direction. A nudge from his heels and the gelding moved forward, the pony trudging alongside.

Elorah clutched her pendant as she watched Rachmyn follow Elgre to the far end of the boxytop brake, its sudden coldness providing little comfort. Her mouth went dry, unease puckering it like a sour fruit.

"Something's wrong. My insides feel wooshy." Mierrle agitated her hands in front of her midsection. Elorah understood. Her insides felt the same. Part of her wanted to jump onto a horse and ride until she found the missing three, but she knew that was the worst thing she could do when she had no idea where they'd gone. Waiting for their return felt equally bad.

First things first. They couldn't stay out in the open.

"We need to move," Elorah said, pointing toward the boxywood brake.

Mierrle reached out, and Elorah clasped her hand. Her friend's grip felt warm, despite the dipping temperature. Elorah squeezed before letting loose to gather up gear.

Soon, they were moved inside the brake, the purple undersides of the boxywood leaves like flattened plums blocking much of the snow.

"Now what do we do?" Mierrle asked.

"We wait," Elorah answered, staring up at the relentless white, her hand going again to her pendant, her staff still as stone upon her back.

CHAPTER THIRTY-EIGHT

SILENCE MOST GOLDEN

Haedyn stared through the gap between the gelding's ears at the inescapable snow, deep enough now that the pony sank to its knees, its chest and hindquarters straining to fling its snow-packed hooves high enough to clear the accumulation. The gelding was struggling too, its breath pluming white above its dogging head as it dragged everyone along. It was a lot to ask of the horse, pulling two extra creatures through this weather. Three, counting his bird. He gave his vest a pat, reassured when he felt the bump inside the pocket. He sent a blup of heat through his palm. At least Fryk was comfortable, unlike himself, bent forward in an awkward crick, face numb, feet two ice blocks attached to his ankles. If only he knew a way to blup heat onto those places the wemble cloak didn't reach, but the heat he made always flowed out. Never in.

He narrowed his eyes, trying to get a bead on his location. He wished he could do a peering, but that wasn't possible either. He'd tried to learn, many times, when he was young and surrounded by Shadowen, for whom it was easy, until Luchmyn took him aside and explained that because he was born of Fyrre in a land of sand and heat, he would never peer. He could still see the pity in Luchmyn's eyes, feel the empathy in his touch as he braced Haedyn's shoulders and told him he couldn't make himself into a Shadowen, no matter how hard he tried. He would always be Fyrre, the affinity of his birth. Of course, he'd suspected he was different, but to hear the bald words, that he was the odd amongst the many even, had still come as a blow. He would never belong in the way everyone around him belonged. He would always be *other*. Even now, the soft part inside longing for what he could not have squeezed tight at the thought.

Mustn't look back. Always look forward.

Without a compass, his only hope was for the storm to break soon. He now realized how little he could do on his own. He'd always considered himself an equal partner, but clearly he was not. Rachmyn would have easily found their way. True, there would have been chiding words, and that smile verging on a frown to endure. A cutting stare from those silvery eyes that missed nothing to squirm beneath. A small price to pay. As it was, he would be lucky if he made it out of this alive. The thought dropped like a stone into the hollow where his stomach used to be. At least he'd brought the cloak. If not for that, he'd have had no chance at all. There was no escaping it. He'd gotten into a right mess with no way to fix things.

A crust of ice was building along the ridge of the horse's neck, and Haedyn knew it wouldn't be long before they would have to stop. He'd only gone a league or two out of the way, surely, chasing the pony. How had he gotten so far off track? Unless....

Spunk.

He pulled the rein, and the gelding ground to a halt, the grateful pony stopping with a whickering snort. He'd gone the wrong way. That had to be it. He stared at the featureless white around him. Shifting stars. Why hadn't he at least tried to learn something about wayfinding? Maybe he *was* as foolish as Rachmyn thought.

He shook his head, then lodged the rein under the bridle behind the gelding's ears before straightening his spasming back, taking care with the crystalwood bow as he stretched. Tingling pain knifed through his shoulders, then down his back and into his hams, making him wish he hadn't bothered trying to unkink.

He surveyed the whited landscape, all peaks and swales, looking for somewhere to shelter. Up ahead, a dark-blue smudge caught his eye. A copse of silverneedle—two or three spiring bushes at most—standing tall against the snow. That seemed the best option.

He slung the bow onto his shoulder and bent forward to dislodge the rein, grimacing as his twinging muscles seized up.

The air around him stilled and the hairs on the back of his neck pricked up. A distant memory bubbled to the top. He'd felt this unquiet before, long ago, though whether it had been in a dream or when he was very young, he couldn't quite make out. The pains in his back disappeared as he took another look around. Nothing seemed amiss. He tucked his heels against the gelding and squeezed. The horse stepped ahead, its ears switching. The pony skyed its head and rolled its eyes before allowing itself to be pulled forward. Haedyn pointed the horse toward the silverneedle, his ears alive to the suffocating hush settling around him.

Brightness collected behind him, though when he turned to look, there was only falling white and thickening gray. His thoughts reached back, searching for a memory not quite there, nostalgia brimming warm inside. He decided his mind must be playing tricks on him. The snowy landscape lent itself to such imaginings, and he reminded himself not to entertain nonsense, Rachmyn's cautionary visage floating through his thoughts. He mustn't be fooled again. He might lack wisdom, but there was no need to keep proving it.

Rachmyn looked down at his body laid out in the shadowed depths of the boxytop brake, his cloak draped across his chest and upper thighs, the hood covering his face like a shroud.

He'd put the cloak on backward before he'd awayed and was grateful seeing the thin layer of snow fines clinging to the ridges where his nose and chin were. Elgre straddled his lower half then flattened, rug-like, onto his legs. The wolf proned his head, his muzzle near Rachmyn's feet. That should help, but Rachmyn knew he couldn't remain in Oru

Fen too long, or his mortal form would suffer. His hand went to his pocket for his shard. Yes, there it was.

Spectra nudged his leg, and he placed his free hand on her head. He fixed his thoughts upon the missing three and was surprised when two starshine pathways unfurled. One led east while the other took a northerly track. A choice was required. He looked into Spectra's all-knowing eyes, and she swung her head north.

He spun in a circle, creating a touchpoint, then was off, flying toward the top of the world, Spectra racing alongside. His concern turned to fear as the fury of the snowstorm increased around him. A moment later, he spotted his friend in a small clearing, huddled up against a desolate scrag of brush, his paled hands clutching his billowing wemble cloak tight to his neck. The gelding and the pack pony hunched nearby, two miserable statues pointing their heads toward the scrub and their tails to the wind. A hard truth smashed Rachmyn's heart as he comprehended the situation. It was because of him Haedyn had gotten lost. All their lives, Rachmyn had been the navigator, never once showing his friend the rudiments of setting a course. No wonder he'd strayed so far from where he should be. He hadn't even a compass to guide him. Too late, Rachmyn realized his folly. By doing everything, he'd crippled Haedyn, dooming his closest friend to a terrifying fate.

Rachmyn set another touchpoint, recrimination glooming through him, a vow to correct the situation on his lips as he stared down at his friend's miserable state.

It was only then he understood what he was seeing.

Haedyn hadn't found a clearing; he was creating one, the snow around him thawing as it fell. Rachmyn's heart lurched. His friend had to be spending vast amounts of vor to keep himself and the animals from being overrun. He'd likely already used a significant amount and Rachmyn knew Haedyn couldn't continue indefinitely without risking his internals. Fear turned to terror.

Don't spend yourself. I'm coming.

But Haedyn's mind was locked tighter than a moneyman's purse, his focus only on melting wide sweeps as the snow pelted down. Rachmyn fell to his knees, a feeling of tears in his eyes, though he had no way of shedding them in this inbetween realm. He shouted with all he had, trying to push his words through the invisible barrier separating those awake from those who walked. He'd done it before.

Listen to me. Listen To ME!

But it was no use. Haedyn wouldn't hear him.

Remember the others. Spectra's snarl was full of toothfang and claw.

He didn't want to remember; didn't care what happened to anyone else. Only Haedyn, his brother of the heart, mattered. Let the Wycche take the rest.

Spectra growled, her bared teeth scraping his ear as he knelt with his face near his knees. The gruff rebuke had its effect. Rachmyn swallowed twice to shift the strangling lump in his throat, then tightened his grip on his shard and got to his feet. Spectra shoved her muzzle under his opposite hand and pushed him toward a starshine pathway unfurling in a southwestern direction. It could only mean Thane and Aikin had gotten separated from Haedyn, and that Rachmyn must search for them elsewhere. It was the last thing he wanted to do.

Rachmyn cast a last look at Haedyn then tore himself away, his essence blowing fast as winter wind along the starry trail, the ground a glitter-white blur beneath his feet, Spectra a silvery wraith beside him. Soon he was upon the pair.

Though the snow was lighter here, their situation was bleaker than Haedyn's. Aikin was on foot, each hand hooked around the cheekpiece of a bridle as he led two horses back toward camp. One was limping from a gash across its hindquarter while Thane slumped atop the other, a nasty wound spiraling up his lower leg. Their progress was slow, and Rachmyn could see they were losing not only daylight but their will as they trudged forward.

Spectra bumped the back of his leg. *Northmen.*

Rachmyn pivoted and spotted a party of Drasgor working their way northward, forging through the snow as if it were nothing at all. They moved as one, a multi-legged beast, all muscle and fur with dangerous claws. The only exception was the one in the middle, who looked very different from the rest: a slimmer build, a softer face with no trace of beard. Not so much fast as steady, the northmen covered ground with practiced ease, impervious to the rough weather. It took Rachmyn a moment to realize they were on course to intercept Aikin and Thane, though whether that was their intent he couldn't say. Either way, the two were easy pickings as they limped along. If the Drasgor happened upon them, their ending would be swift and terrible.

With no time to lose, Rachmyn created another touchpoint then flew to the touchpoint where his body lay under a thin layer of snow. Elgre looked up, his eyes welcoming.

Rachmyn plummeted, letting out a cry as he slid inside his shell. His teeth began to chatter and his limbs to shiver, every part of him aching with cold. The wemble had done little while he was away, perhaps because his vor had been otherwise engaged. He hadn't accounted for that. It was only the wolf's body heat that had kept his form from freezing. His father had warned him to take care where he left his body while casting forth into the unseen, but he'd never before awakened to such misery. Elgre shifted positions, turning to place himself upon Rachmyn's chest. The wolf's weight made it hard to breathe, but his warmth was so wondrous Rachmyn hardly noticed.

He lay there for several minutes, the wemble hood warming his face, the wolf's heat sinking into his bones until his shivering subsided. Only then did the wolf move away and shake the snow from its double-layered coat.

Rachmyn got to his feet and made his way to the brake's other end where Elorah and Mierrle waited, his thoughts a stew of confusion. He wanted to rush to Haedyn first, but then again, his friend had more experience fending for himself. He could hold out longer than the other two who didn't know the imminent danger they were in. He could feel the abrasion of Spectra's teeth against his ear, reminding him he couldn't put his own interests first. Still, shouldn't he go where the odds were more favorable rather than spend precious energy on what looked like a lost cause? Then again, who was he to decide which causes were lost and which were not. His thoughts flew round and round until his head hurt.

In the end, he didn't make the decision; Elorah did. And though he wasn't happy about it, he was in agreement by the time they set out.

Thane groaned as another tide of throbbing rolled up his leg and into his groin. The whole leg was a pulsing, burning disaster, and he could think of nothing else. He'd had more than his fair share of cuts and stab wounds in his life, but he'd never felt this bad afterward. Perhaps the bravik's claws were poisonous. He felt poisoned.

Aikin threw him a backward look. "Can you make it?" he called. The snow had eased up, but a whistling wind remained.

Thane grunted. Aikin glanced at Thane's leg then went a shade paler before clenching his jaw and facing forward. Thane looked down. His leg had ballooned out below the knee, stretching his torn leggings apart enough that the puffy dimples of his purpling wound were visible. His gorge rose, and he shut his eyes, forcing it down. A heavy thud against his back reopened them. Aikin had vaulted aboard the horse behind him.

"Drasgor!" he yelled, jerking his thumb backward.

Thane swiveled, his gaze landing on a clot of gigantic men coming up fast behind them. A pair of muscular arms reached either side of Thane's waist to take the reins while Aikin's legs stretched forward to cue the horse. One dig into its ribs and the gelding broke into a series of stiff-legged bucks, dumping Thane to the ground in a quivering heap and throwing Aikin off its croup, one kicking hind foot striking the falling man in the forehead. Aikin slumped to the ground, as the horse skittered away.

Thane pulled himself over to where Aikin lay, a sickle-shaped lump jutting out above his left eye. "Aikin!" he shouted, shaking his shoulder. Aikin's head lolled sideways. Knocked out. Thane glanced toward the approaching Drasgor, close enough now he could distinguish scowling faces atop scragging beards.

Ahh, fleek me. We're dead. His pulse hammered as hard in his leg as his chest.

"KARK!"

The deep rumble of the northman's voice shredded what little courage Thane had left, and his mind cried to the water below, his only friend in times of trouble, beseeching it to come to his aid. The leg and Aikin became as nothing as his mind reached down through the rocky ground, until it found the cool, clear song of a meandering stream.

Coaxing the water away from its comfortable idleness would take every charming convincement he could muster, but so great was his desire, so fierce was his love, it could not resist. Upon his ardent summons, it strove upward, through layers of shale and sand, unstoppable in its journey to the one singing its memory song. His mind sang and sang, the water rushing closer and closer until he thought it would burst from the ground at any moment.

A metallic *swiff* scuttled into his ears. Thane opened his eyes in time to see a northman launch a dras toward him. Red-hot terror spiked, blistering his nerves. Time slowed as his eyes tracked the flight of the dras arcing toward his chest. It surprised him when his fear evaporated in the crystal-clear moment before certain death. But it was the water that surprised him more. Though he'd forgotten it, it had not forgotten him. A powerful stream shot skyward the moment the dras descended, knocking the hideous weapon aside and skewering it into the ice-crusted snow beside his leg with a crackling thud. The water settled to a pulsing spring, and Thane had to fight the urge to throw himself upon it in gratitude. Instead, he yanked the dras from the ground and hefted it onto his shoulder. The front-heavy weapon wanted to nose downward, and he had to concentrate to keep it steady. Aikin mumbled beside him. Thane hissed a warning sound as the Drasgor surrounded them, their drasheads forming a lethal ring.

"Kark."

One of the northmen stepped forward and pulled Aikin onto his feet as if he were a child's plaything. Aikin looked around, his unfocused eyes blinking, his forehead humping out, his legs wobbling as if newly made. Another northman came toward Thane, and he tightened his sweating hands around the weapon's wooden shaft. The northman started for him, and he lashed the weapon forward in an awkward swing. The rest of the northmen laughed as the near one caught the dras shaft and wrenched it from Thane's grip. With a flip of the wrist, the deadly end was pointing at Thane's chest. He braced for the inevitable.

"Don't kill them!" a female voice cried in Iellian.

"Foonk," the northman yelled mid-swing, jerking the dras skyward to avoid impaling Thane where he sat. The black-haired warrior swung the dras back around and leveled it at Thane's chest.

"Brynz!" the northman holding Aikin shouted.

"What have they done?" the female voice asked.

"Not Kelfuld," the northman holding Aikin replied.

"That one knows Iellia," the girl said, pointing at Aikin. She was tall, with fingerlings of dark hair fountaining away from her head. Besides the pelt wrapping her shoulders, she wore tattered clothing that looked familiar. Thane tried to place where he'd seen it.

The northman pulled Aikin into a lumbering half-circle. "This one? How?"

"I saw him at the festival. With the queen."

Ahh, yes. The festival.

The girl's pants and tunic were the same dark blue as the livery of the Iellian monarch. But how had she gotten in with these fearsome warriors? A happy accident, no doubt. Without her, he and Aikin would have already been dead. That was lucky. But it was also strange.

The northman took a half-step back, appraising Aikin before shaking his head, a clinking noise coming from the oversized teeth and claws braided into his dark-blonde hair and beard. From the size of them, they had to be bravik trophies. "Not Iellia. Dirt cutter."

Dirt cutter. That was one way of saying landed gentleman Thane supposed. Aikin was too addled to notice the slight.

"They die soon," the blond northman continued.

"Not if we help them," the tall girl countered.

"Why? They...." The northman spat at the ground.

The girl looked at Thane. "Tell him how you know the queen." She jerked her chin as if indignant, her gray-blue eyes flashing a different message. *Convince him and you might live.* Thane needed no more encouragement. If lying was required, he was happy to provide. He heaved himself to his feet, gritting his teeth to avoid screaming as the pressure increased in his leg, straightened as much as possible, and assumed what he hoped was an authoritative posture despite his leggings and feet being soaked. Already his lower half was going numb.

"Good sir, my friend and I are on assignment for Her Most Exalted, Queen Zephyrria Rennesseau. I can't confirm specifics, but I can assure you, we will be missed should we not make it back, with consequences commensurate for those responsible. It is quite urgent we make our return as soon as mayhap." He told the lie with all the fervor of a man begging for his life.

"Worth much alive. Nothing dead," the girl simplified. She leveled a stare at the leader, her expression a mixture of fear and defiance. The northman stroked his embellished beard.

A younger, blonder version of the leader poked his dras toward Thane. "Benk fler klek," he barked, his gaze as sharp as his dras.

"Kif, ank mek graw lel." The leader's eyes sparked hot, his tone the snappish growl of an alpha wolf. The younger man looked away, his lips bunching into a tight pucker.

"Now, see here," Aikin mumbled out of nowhere. The leader jerked his head round to direct a heated stare at his prisoner.

"There will be a handsome reward for our safe passage," Thane interrupted, adding under his breath, "Shut it. We're on the edge of a knife here."

Aikin frowned, his fingers going to his forehead to probe the angry wedge.

"Surely the queen will hear you if you take them," the girl said.

What was this? Thane's brow furrowed as he tried to understand the game being played.

The leader considered this for a moment. "They walk or they die," he said, giving Aikin's arm a vicious shake. Aikin's face stiffened into a scowl, his mouth opening to speak. Thane glared—*Shut it or we're dead* —and he closed it again.

"Can you walk?" the girl asked, her gaze taking in Thane's injured leg.

Thane nodded, unconvinced. She moved to place his arm across her shoulders.

"Alone!" the leader shouted.

The girl jumped and moved away, her eyes full of apologetic pity. Thane gave her a grim smile as his arm fell to his side. She rushed to a nearby bush and returned with a branch the thickness of Thane's wrist. She thrust it toward him, ignoring the leader's narrow-eyed stare. "Use this," she said before darting away as if avoiding a blow.

"Mawrg dras," the leader said. The northmen sheathed their weapons, the young, blond hothead doing so with hostile vigor.

"Darnk," the leader said, and the northmen formed up into a group around Aikin and Thane and the girl. Then, "Kwulf lel," and the group began to move.

Thane almost fainted when he tried the leg.

I should have let them kill me. Now I have to live with this.

But there was no time for wishing or weakness. Clenching his jaw, he managed to plant the branch and pull his mangled leg forward a half-step. The worst of the pain came in the fraction when he had to put his full weight on the foot. He'd felt many pains in his life, but this was by far the worst. It made him want to throw up and collapse and scream all at the same time. No other thought was possible when the pain seared into his brain, and in between, it wasn't relief but dread that replaced it, knowing the next half-step was coming, and it would be another explosion of pain blotting out all reason.

The northmen increased their speed, and Thane ramped into a shuffling judder, the good leg flinging forward, the bad leg limp-hopping behind, his mind locked in a torturous cycle of pain, dread, pain, dread. Soon he was sweating. The only thing he could hope was that the cold air upon his skin and wet leggings would numb him to the point the leg could be forgotten. A slim hope indeed.

"Where are they taking us?" Aikin croaked.

"Keep moving," Thane gasped as he shambled forward, tears shaming his eyes. *Stiffen up, young man.* The words of his father came flooding back. *Crying is for old women and fools.*

Then he felt it. A lifting of his bad leg, as if the air surrounding it were cradling it and moving it forward at the same time. He took another step. There it was again. The same sensation. The third time he didn't put the foot down at all, the strange air pressure providing all the support he needed. Without having to put weight on it, the pain eased. He looked around, trying to understand how this miracle was happening. He glanced sideways. The girl was staring at his skiffed leg whilst keeping pace with the northmen. The look of concentration on her face made him think she had something to do with the cradling air. All he knew was that whatever was happening, it was better than anything he'd ever felt before, which was saying quite a lot with the life he'd lived.

Haedyn was spent. The spark that had always burned inside, eager to jump from his fingers or chest had extinguished, used up in his bid to keep the snow from overrunning himself and his animals. His insides felt as dusted as an ash heap, the sad remains of a great fire that had once flamed high but burned no more. Now, he couldn't melt a single snowflake let alone the amount still coming down. He'd gambled and lost and would have to suffer for it.

He shivered and pulled his cloak tighter, but without his vor, the thin fabric was no better than cheap homespun for keeping him warm. His bird was even colder, and he huffed a few breaths into the vest pocket to help warm it. Fryk's half-closed eyes rolled up, two black accusations piercing Haedyn through. He'd let everyone down.

He'd already untied the gelding and the pony, rationalizing the two could find their way to safety if they weren't tethered, but they'd remained. He could only assume it was because the animals knew they couldn't find shelter elsewhere. At least they didn't seem bothered by the snow, stamping their feet and stoically enduring. It only made him feel slightly better.

The strange, hushed closeness from earlier returned, as if he were being watched by someone. Or something. Around him, the light took on the golden incandescence of a setting sun, brightening into a glow that forced his watering eyes shut.

Behind his eyelids, the golden light intensified, accompanied by an increasing warmth that wrapped around him. He let the feeling sink into his shivering limbs, basking in its pleasurable heat. Against his chest, his bird stirred, and his heart soared.

He opened his eyes and marveled at the complexion of yellows and reds twirling and spiking and rolling around him, as though he was at the center of a giant flame, looking out at a frozen world. Despite his affinity for fire, it was a startling view, and he wondered if he was going mad. And yet the beauty of it squeezed at his throat and expanded his chest in ways he'd never felt in all his twenty annums. If this was madness, let him be mad, if only for the delightful wonderment of this moment.

Even as he goggled at the beauty of the thermal plasma surrounding him, a creeping languor tugged at his eyelids, and though he fought it, he was soon within its blackened grasp. His eyelids drooped shut as his mind fell into that dark pocket of unknowing beyond the reasoning mind, his forgetting already begun.

WARNINGS OF A WRAITHWOLF (EXCERPT SEVEN)

The DREAMS that LINGER... gggrrr... past waking are OFT... gggrrrff... the profound MUSINGS... grrff... of a venerable SOUL... gggrrff... whether REMINDERS of PROMISES MADE... gggrrfff... or PORTENTS of THINGS to COME.

MARK THIS!

These GLIMPSES through half-lit WINDOWS... gggrr... are NOT the ERRATIC RAMBLINGS... gggrrff... of an UNQUIET MIND... Ggrrrff... Do not MISTAKE the SOUL'S ineffable DANCE ... ggrrf... for the EGO'S diverting PRANCE... Grrfff... One is AUTHENTIC... ggrrrfff... the other ARTIFICE... Ggrrfff... One PERCEPTION... gggrrfff... the other OBLIVION.

REMEMBER!

The perilous PATH of EXISTENCE... ggrrfff... hath TWO directions ALWAYS... Gggrrfff.... CHOOSE ye WELL... ggrrfff... for the JOURNEY of EVERY soul... gggrrfff... DEPENDS upon the WISDOM... ggrrfffff... or LACK thereof... ggrrff... of its ATTENTIVE MIND.

–Collected and Interpreted for the Most Exalted Monarch, Geldizian Rennesseau, by a scribe

CHAPTER THIRTY-NINE
THE ABSENCE OF GOOD

AH-BAH-BAH AH-BAH-BAH AH-BAH-BAH

The drums pounded out their warning beneath a moon as red and swollen as a ripened fruit.

Two moons had passed since Xyleea left her wasakagee. In all that time, the drums had remained silent, leaving the night to its rustles and sighs. But a blood moon had risen, provoking the warriors to smear blue dots and lines and circles onto their stringy brown bodies and hotfoot a path toward the grogakee's mountain, their heartbeats thumping in time with their drums.

Xyleea clambered up a waku tree when the first drumbeats sounded. She knew what a red moon meant. Kaambree knew it, too, and the matriarch disappeared into a stand of waxy-leaved killikell. Xyleea wondered what the tuskee thought as the bands of warriors trotted by, blue-marked shadows chasing fever dreams under the bloody stare of an angry moon. Her mind reached out, but the great mother had become invisible in every way.

The waku tree still held most of its leaves, though many were shed during her climb to its upper reaches, the blowpipe poking her hollowed-out midsection as she went. The chuulzu kereet made it difficult to thread her way through the tree's dense branches, and she'd stopped several times to adjust the headpiece after it got knocked askew. She checked it again, straightening it as she prayed to the ancestors to watch over her with the keen eyes of the hawk and the swift fury of the chassa. She reached into the kemeekemee for the daala, hoping for some huul waal as drumbeats flayed the night.

The bag was empty.

Her heart began to race. She scraped her fingers along the seam at the bottom, but the hard sphere was not there. She searched further up in the bag, her fingertips coming to a split large enough for the daala to slip through. The kemeekemee must have torn during her climb, its contents spilling as she went. A panicky fear took hold, squeezing her guts.

If the tear happened during her climb, the daala must be somewhere below. Her eyes searched the jagged shadows at the tree's base. What if the daala had been lost earlier on this trail running thick with Xetili warriors? How would she ever find it? She had a sudden urge to throw up, though there was nothing in her belly but air. She wanted to climb down—never mind it was still dark—get on her hands and knees and search. Her fingers would be her eyes until either the sphere was back in her grasp, or the sun had risen from its bed.

The sound of footsteps turned her attention to the trail. Another group of Xetili, eight this time, trotted by, heading in the same direction as the previous bands. *Where are they going?* Her thoughts worried back to the daala. Long moments passed, each stretched tight by churning fear. She had to do something. Before she knew it, she was shimmying down, the kereet tipping when she leaned her head back.

She was a man's span from the bottom when she heard the faint *woppa-woppa-wop* of running feet. She launched herself away from the tree, flying for a moment before falling onto hard ground. She landed awkwardly, the headdress pushing onto her brow, her right arm bending beneath her. Her knee struck something sharp, splitting open with a stinging gush as her blowpipe dug a chunk from her thigh. The knee got the worst of it, and even in the dark, she knew it was bleeding. She pulled the headpiece flat against her chest then lay still, trying to blend with the shadowy undergrowth, hoping her fall hadn't attracted attention. The keleekeluk was full of sounds she reasoned, as she forced her breaths through her nose. She was steps away from the trail, in a clearing stubbled with dead stems, the *woppa-woppa-wop* both a sound and a shaking as the warriors neared. She counted eleven this time, watching each pass from the corner of her eye.

She waited, her ears parsing every sound before she crammed the kereet onto her head then got onto her hands and knees to search. The split knee hurt but not as much as the throb inside her chest. She'd lost the only goodness she had left from her galeesha, the only goodness left in the whole world. Any moment, the ancestors would rain fire upon her for her carelessness. Around and around, over and through, she crawled, her desperation driving her onward even as her fingers shredded to bleeding stubs as they pushed through knife-sharp grass. Ants set upon her knee, biting at the raw of it, and she had to stop several times to brush them away when the searing pinch of their fierce attack became too much.

She only paused when a band of warriors went by, resuming as soon as they passed, her hands and arms and legs accumulating cuts and bruises as she went. But it was the knee that hurt the most, its gnashing rebuke constant as she continued to abrade it. Not until the sun had stolen every shred of red from the moon, did she think of it. The beeka mud. Maybe it would help with the pain.

She sat upon her haunches and retrieved the vessel. Mimicking what she'd seen, she tapped a dab onto her palm, worked her jaws then spit a glob into the blue, kneading with her pointer finger until the dust became mud.

She looked at the gash in her knee, crusted with dirt, and worked up another glop of spittle. It wet the cut enough she could wipe away the dirt with the heel of one palm before spackling blue mud across it with the other. The relief was instantaneous. Why had her people shunned this gift from the grogakee when it could have eased the suffering of so many? She didn't have to wait long for the answer, as a voice began speaking inside her head. Not her own voice but another, rich and powerful, in words of riddling rhyme. The voice of the grogakee.

Look for me where the white trees sleep, till she who frees, speaks the secret she keeps.

Over and over, the words lashed through her mind, more times than her own worried thoughts could remind her to look for the daala. Had she made herself beeka? She brushed at her blue-stained knee, spitting and scrubbing until blood wet her shin, all the while feeling nothing whatever. More than that, the gnawing hunger and raging thirst she'd lived with for over a moon had also gone, erased with the pain. She understood now the wisdom of her forebears. The mud was both a cure and a curse. Did the Xetili hear the grogakee in their heads when they wore the blue markings of war? She didn't want to believe it was so but could find no reason why it wouldn't be true. And if they did, what did the grogakee whisper between their ears when they attacked the Ushoku? Could a voice so reasoned and kind be filled with falsehood and blame? Or did the grogakee's words have different meanings in different minds? She couldn't be sure, the not knowing somehow worse than knowing would have been.

The drums had gone silent, though she hadn't noticed until now. Perhaps it meant the warriors had gone back to their beds. The wan moon, now thin and white, hung grimly in the western sky, though the sun shone bright above the grogakee's mountain. Xyleea's gaze moved up to the blue-shell sky. Another cloudless day. She couldn't recall the last time it had rained. The last time she could remember the sky weeping was when Cree Shee went back to the keleekeluk. She hadn't connected the two until now.

Colorful birds darted from branch to branch, singing their morning songs. Any other day, their chirps and whistles would have cheered Xyleea. But not today. Not with the daala missing. The grogakee's voice had gone from her head, and it was only her own voice reminding her of the ancestors' disappointment.

She resumed her search, going over the same ground. Now that the light was better, it all looked different as she crawled around. The ache was coming back into her knee as she searched, the beeka mud worn away.

A gust of wind racketed the leaves of the waku, and she heard the *thunk* of something falling to the ground. Xyleea jerked her head, her eyes going to a spot beneath the tree.

There it was, lying in a folded leaf as if it had always been there, though she knew it had not. The daala. She scrabbled over and picked it up, scarcely believing it was back in her hands. She pulled it close and closed her eyes, her mind sending her gratitude to the ancestors for answering her prayers. The great black bird of sorrow lifted from her chest, making her feel light. A snuffling snort followed by a low grumble pushed her mood still higher. Kaambree had emerged from the killekell and stood steps away in the dappled shade. She ran over and embraced the tuskee's hairy front leg.

"I'm so happy to see you, great mother," she murmured into the tuskee's brown fur, its musky smell filling her nose. Was there a better smell in all the world? Not to her. The tuskee flapped its broad ears and grumbled. Xyleea grumbled back, never happier than at this moment. She'd found the daala, and the tuskee had come back. Things were turning toward the bright, and she was turning with them.

That Aikin's horse had come back to camp was both a good and a worrisome thing. Good because it was needed for the search; worrisome because Aikin would never have given it up. Elorah searched for him with her Therran vorik, but without something for attunement, she couldn't distinguish his energy from the others pulsing through the rootweave. It was hard not to think the worst after Rachmyn related their predicament, and it took real effort to choose hope, rather than despair.

Haedyn's situation sounded equally bad. Caught out in a snowstorm without shelter, many leagues to the north. Rachmyn had insisted on going after him, but her instincts told her that wasn't the right choice. The pale-haired man had always doubted Therrania. It was understandable. He'd seen his friend perish in that time before and feared it happening again. She knew this, though she couldn't let on. All that remained from that long-ago tragedy was a deep skepticism toward sacrificing to a cause, along with an abiding fear that death lurked around every corner. If it hadn't been for Haedyn's persistence, Rachmyn would never have come on this trip, but his love for his friend was so deep and his need to protect him so strong, once his friend made up his mind, he'd had little choice. For that reason, she knew she should be the one to search for Haedyn while Rachmyn should put his efforts toward finding Thane and Aikin. There were also the Drasgor to consider. Rachmyn's ability with mindshields might prove crucial for Thane and Aikin's survival.

Once she'd convinced Rachmyn, there was the matter of Mierrle. Her friend had immediately assumed she would accompany Elorah, but was that the best idea? Elorah considered long before deciding it was. She'd gotten her friend into this, and she wasn't about to shift that responsibility.

Rachmyn took Aikin's gelding, while she and Mierrle took the other horse and pony. They chucked the rank ham, loading the pony with rucksacks, blankets, and the remaining wemblecloth. She'd also gotten a vial of speck from Rachmyn to use for attunement later. She wasn't sure it would work, but there was nothing else Rachmyn was willing to part with, so it would have to do. She did make him promise to keep his rucksack with him, in hopes that would be enough.

After assuring her Haedyn still had her grandfather's bow, Rachmyn gave her a general idea which direction to head. She would have to rely on the crystalwood staff finding its way to the crystalwood bow. After boosting Mierrle into the saddle then swinging up to ride double behind her, she'd taken the staff out of its case, held it up, and directed her intention into it. The staff responded, nearly leaping out of her hand when she pointed it in the direction Rachmyn had indicated. She placed it back in its case, satisfied.

They each set off, Rachmyn to the west, she and Mierrle to the north. It was another diversion from the path, another delay, but she couldn't think about that right now. As much as she wanted to get to Therrania, it was far more important her friends were found safe. All else faded in view of that.

Essiant threw back his head and howled long into the orusphere. Spectra and Embren, never far from each other, joined in followed by Ieeva, Raya, and Ajai, six voices blending into a greeting chorus that echoed throughout the realm. Their newest pack member had arrived.

Kelm, a powerful-looking wolf with eyes the amber-gold of a setting sun and fur the dusky tan of a sandstorm, stepped into the circle to take his place. It had been a hard journey thus far, with more dangers still to come, but at last, he and his night-ward were finding their place. He raised his muzzle and belted out a sonorous howl that counterpointed the higher-pitched howls around him. The stars brightened above their heads, the purple-gray forest solidifying as the seventh made his voice heard.

Essiant had long admired Kelm, a fearsome fighter with a glorious past. The other wolves in the pack had their strengths but fighting Malvisse wasn't one of them. Up until now, that burden had fallen to him, and though he would never complain or shirk a duty, he also didn't mind sharing that particular responsibility with a wolf as esteemed for his courage and fighting acumen as this one. The orusphere buzzed with rumors of the Malvisse and their plans, and Essiant was sure, no matter what else the Wycche attempted, another fight with her wraithwolf and his Malvisse cohort was inevitable.

Essiant was pleased with the progress the pack's seven night-wards had made thus far, though they'd yet to face the Wycche's full powers. He couldn't predict when or how the fierce adept would strike, but he could predict with certainty it would happen before the restoration of Therrania for that was the one thing the Wycche feared most. A rebalanced world would end her reign in Oru Fen forever. Essiant knew the Wycche was gathering every scrap of power the Arcana of Vorie Supin could provide, so that when the time came, she would possess all she needed to end this Erynvor's cycle.

Stealing etheriant was only one facet of the illicit Arcana's supreme wickedness. Inducing derangements of the mind including hallucinations, delusions, and nightmares were but a few ways the Arcana could be used. Diverting souls away from their noble purpose was another. All that was required to accomplish these corruptions was the turning of a wraithwolf from duty to decadence. That done, all could be achieved with a minimum of trouble. The turning of a wraithwolf whose night-ward had risen to prominence in the manifest sphere was the most coveted of victories, for those souls held many others in their sway. The bounty of etheriant harvested from such a coup could be enormous. Essiant knew that was where the Wycche would devote most of her efforts.

A few *Longesse*, as these wraithwolves were known, had already ceded their power to the Wycche in exchange for a rise in stature within the realm of dream and thought. Not enough yet to daunt his night-ward's destiny, but Essiant felt sure the Wycche was solidifying her position with these wolves of privilege either through deceitful promises or outright lies. He knew there was no limit to the Wycche's deviousness and sadly, no shortage of wraithwolves who thought it was they who decided the future, rather than their night-ward. It was a dangerous idea at odds with the All but one that had become more prevalent over the eryns.

Kelm stepped toward Essiant and bowed low, a show of respect for the white wolf and his night-ward. Essiant acknowledged the gesture with a nod. For such a warrior to bow was a measure of how esteemed Essiant's night-ward had become. Kelm's night-ward had not had the advantage of a school or a tutor to show her the dynamism she could wield. Yet, even with her lack of training, she had shown remarkable ability, and Essiant was encouraged for the future when that dynamism would be needed. Kelm bowed to each of the remaining five pack members, who reciprocated in kind.

Soon, their night-wards would enter their dreamspheres, and the wraithwolves would shepherd them through another dreamcycle. The Restoration was now of paramount importance, and the group would be crafting the intricacies required into their ward's dreams from tonight until it was accomplished. But for now, they stood united, committed to an ethos bigger and brighter than any of them individually. And it was good.

CHAPTER FORTY
BIRDS OF A FEATHER

Brynz's mind was alive with plans for these two captives as she contemplated how to find Zell. The red-haired one with the lump on his head was sullen and unfriendly, but the dark-haired one with the scar and the skiffed leg seemed open to an alliance, assuming she got the chance.

Uhnkre had the group moving west, their eyes squinting into the blinding brightness of sunlit snow. It was all she could do to keep the dark-haired man going using a microturbulence that wouldn't arouse suspicion. He seemed to know she was helping, judging by his grateful expression. She merely blinked back. She couldn't risk doing more. Besides, she wasn't doing it for him. She was doing it for Zell.

She recognized the red-haired man from the festival. Though he wasn't wearing shiny face dust or a costume, he had the same robust build and chiseled jaw. She'd seen his hostility toward the monarch—nobody could have missed it—which predisposed her to like him. He didn't recognize her, which was for the best. She doubted he would entertain her plan if he did.

The dark-haired man she did not recognize, but in him she saw an eager ally. He'd been only too happy to embellish upon her small lie in the most grandiose fashion possible. She wasn't sure what that said about his character, but it meant he wouldn't pose an obstacle and might be of help when the time came.

Kynflewn, the settlement to which they were headed, appeared as a dark smudge upon the horizon. And none too soon. Though the snow was no longer falling, it was deep enough to be a problem. Without proper boots, her feet were chilled, and the thought of a fire was a pleasure almost too delightful to contemplate. It had been moons since she'd sat next to a fire and warmed herself. One of the many little things she no longer took for granted.

The northmen's pace quickened as the village grew larger. Smoke, fulsome with the crackle and pop of countless blazes, drifted into Brynz's nose, and she lost her concentration. A low moan snapped her attention back. She'd forgotten the scarred man's leg in her preoccupation. She refocused.

Soon the group was entering the village proper. The baying of dogs greeted them, and within moments, a pack of huge, shaggy-haired hounds surrounded them. Uhnkre and the rest of the northmen paid them no mind, and Brynz followed their lead. She'd always liked dogs, and though these had tails strong enough to knock her down and heads massive enough to eat her, she didn't feel fear.

Dressed in their leathers and furs, the villagers looked as rough as old bark, each one scowling at the three captives as they passed by, their noses wrinkling as if they'd caught wind of something foul. The women were hardly distinguishable from the men, lacking only beards and great height, the children smaller versions of their elders. There was nothing of softness or grace or easy living here. Every villager looked as hard and sharp as the blades they carried.

The group huffed past several round stone buildings—their snow-covered roofs belching smoke—before arriving in front of a larger roundhouse holding forth like a giant amongst a gathering of smalls. But even it was not the tallest structure in the village. In front loomed a six-sided stone obelisk the purple black of night and stretching up to the sky. The towering pillar had been knapped from an even larger stone, its rounded top retaining its original roughness, its polished sides—the width of three spans—chiseled with cascading arcs and points and curves. The markings looked nothing like Iellian writing which marched from right to left and top to bottom in ordered lines. These were entirely different, and Brynz suspected the markings might form a pictograph. She didn't have long to ponder as she and the other two were shoved past and into the building.

Inside was a circle of men seated in rough-hewn chairs, each as murderous looking as the next, the stone wall behind them bulging with the bleached skulls of gigantic beasts, jaws hung agape to better display their enormous teeth. Each skull was twice as large as a gryphon's head with fangs longer than a gryphon's talons. This creature was no doubt the source of the teeth braided into the northmen's hair and beards.

Brynz couldn't imagine what these hulking warriors were thinking as they sat in their mammoth chairs, staring at three captives huddling near the blazing fire, trying to warm their marrows. No doubt they thought them pathetic. Proof that southerners were soft and weak.

The man seated opposite seemed an older version of Uhnkre, his bright-white beard and hair gleaming in the fire's glow. He had the same determined eyes, the same full lips creased hard. His blue eyes cut into her as if she were a carcass on a spit.

He leaned forward, the chunk of purple-black stone suspended from his thick neck catching the light amidst the low chatter of teeth and claws as his hair swept past the hills of his shoulders. He gestured toward her and rumbled something that sounded like a question. Uhnkre responded. The two exchanged words, the older man becoming more agitated, the younger man becoming more strident as the exchange continued. Beside her, the scarred man wobbled, and Brynz propped him up with a microturbulence. Meanwhile, the red-haired man glared at the northmen as if surveying an inferior breed. His disdainful stare hardly seemed helpful, and Brynz sent him a warning look, but he was beyond warnings. She reasoned the blow to his head must have fuddled his thinking.

Kif sallied forward and spoke to another of the seated northmen, this one with hair the color of mountain clay and eyes the green-brown of punked water. Hanging from a leather cord around the man's neck was a cumbersome ornament of three fangs, laced together so that the curved ends pointed away from the shape's center. The northman pursed his lips and frowned, considering what he'd heard. Ahnkne

442

grabbed Kif's arm and drug him backward, landing a cuff to his neck in the process. Kif's eyes flashed but he did not retaliate. Instead, his narrowed eyes landed on Brynz, a sneer lifting his lip.

Uhnkre spoke again, a long speech full of passion and vigor. Another northman, broad-faced with a bristling black beard and a snoutish nose, addressed the white-haired elder, whom he called Uhnlen, droning on for long moments.

Uhnlen's lips sucked in, revealing a sliver of dull gray teeth. A third voice rang out. Brynz whipped around. This northman, his brown hair shot through with silver, had a fox skull dangling from a thong around his neck. He spoke in a measured tone, his points punctuated by chopping hand motions. By the time he'd finished, over half the northmen were nodding their heads. Brynz braced herself. This wasn't going well. By her interpretation, most of the northmen wanted the captives dead.

Uhnkre's face reddened, and he slammed his fist into a stand made of antlers, sending a clutch of dras clanging onto the stone floor. Brynz startled, her heartbeat strong in her chest. Several of the elders leaped to their feet, their faces going red as they shouted. It was then she saw the blood dripping from Uhnkre's hand, though he wasn't bothered as he glared at the shouting men.

He stepped forward and grasped her arm, pulling her toward him. She motioned to the other two to follow, though she had no idea where they were going or what was about to happen as he marched her out of the roundhouse. She could hear the dark-haired man moaning as he limped along, and she gritted her teeth to keep from silencing him. Didn't he know weakness would get him killed? Get them all killed?

"Foonk!"

Uhnkre blatted the word several times as he dragged her along a path of beaten down snow. Ahnkne, Hrul, and Flewd had stormed out with him, and they now surrounded the captives, excited dogs circling and yodeling around them.

Uhnkre led them past several roundhouses before stopping in front of one at the western edge of the settlement.

Ahnkne opened the door, disappearing inside for a few moments before emerging and giving Uhnkre a nod.

Uhnkre pushed Brynz inside with all the gentleness of a keeper shoving an escaped pig into a sty. She fell onto the hard stone floor, pain shooting through her hands when she used them to brace. Flewd and Hrul manhandled the other two through the doorway, then shut the door, leaving them to sort out what had happened in the flickering light of a solitary candle lodged in a bone-colored wall sconce.

The red-haired man balled his fists, his jaw flexing as he stared at the closed door. The dark-haired one collapsed in a heap, his moan echoing in the windowless room. She flashed back to the bairns of her youth and felt a stab of pity for the poor animals forced to live in them. This room, despite its candle, felt like a tomb. The dark-haired man's moaning didn't help.

"Quiet," Brynz whispered. "Or you'll be killed. These northmen hate weakness."

The moaning subsided as the dark-haired man curled up like a wintering caterpillar.

She turned to the red-haired man. "I'm Brynz Alleu."

"Aikin Froigh dai Bairrtraigh." From the way he said it, there was no mistaking his high opinion of himself, but the name meant nothing to her.

She looked toward the dark-haired man. "And you?"

"Thane Arlot," he mumbled into his knees.

She leaned toward the leg. "What happened?"

"Bravik," Thane muttered through chattering teeth.

She retrieved a large gray and brown-striped fur from a bed near the wall, shook it out, then laid it across Thane's humped-up form. It didn't seem to help, and she suspected he was getting blood fever. She'd seen it in injured horses. Lancing along with scrubbing out had been the treatment of choice. She looked over at the red-haired man.

He was running his hands up and down the stacked stone of the wall, seemingly uninterested in Thane's plight.

"What are you doing?" she asked.

"Looking for weak points." His Iellian, while not flawless, was serviceable.

"Have you a knife?"

He turned, his eyes narrowing. "Why would you need a blade?"

"This wound needs lancing. And scrubbing. He's getting blood fever. If we don't do something, he'll be dead soon."

Thane picked up his head, his expression stricken.

"I don't have a blade," Aikin said, his gaze going to Thane. "Sorry."

Who travels without a knife?

Of course, she didn't have one either, but she hadn't planned her journey. Perhaps their travels hadn't been planned either despite Thane's elaborate tale. She looked around the spare room for something she could use. With only a chair, a bed frame, and a candle, there wasn't much to work with. Maybe if she spoke to Uhnkre. Explained what was needed. She went to the door and tried it. Locked.

"What are you doing?" Aikin asked.

"Looking for a way out." She stared at the smoke hole in the roof. Maybe she could fit through if she got up that high.

She dragged the chair over, lined it up then climbed onto the seat. She was still too low. She got down and went to the bed frame. She looked expectantly at Aikin then snapped, "I could use a hand."

They dragged the frame to the room's center before Brynz set the chair on the bed's platform then climbed onto the seat. She stretched high, her fingertips skimming the bottom edge of the opening, dirt fines sifting to the floor. She only needed another hand or two. She climbed back down. Aikin shook his head.

"I knew that wouldn't work."

"You'll have to boost me up." She tried to sound matter of fact, despite her doubts. His eyes went wide, and he cleared his throat. "Go on," she said, pointing toward the chair.

Aikin cleared his throat again, then hefted himself onto the chair. His gaze shifted to her, his expression full of trepidation. "Are you sure—"

"It's our only choice," she said, stepping up beside him, her body pressing tight to his as they balanced on the chair seat. He looked away, trying not to acknowledge the awkwardness of the situation.

"Either I climb you like a tree, or you make a handhold," she said, demonstrating by clasping her hands in front.

"Oh, right," he said, intertwining his hands. She placed her foot into the basket of his interlaced fingers then braced herself against his shoulder as he lifted. This time she went right up through the hole. She transferred her feet to his shoulders, almost losing her balance in the process.

"Hold my legs." She kept her voice low, but her tone was forceful. She felt his hands go round her knees, and her wobbling improved.

The view was better than expected with the setting sun casting a rose-gold sheen across the entire village. She could see past the large roundhouse to the eastern edge. A contingent of men was making its way south at a steady clip, their leader wearing a fox skull around his neck. Another contingent was making its way west, their leader wearing a fang cluster. They were close enough that Brynz could make out their faces. She crouched down, her bottom brushing the top of Aikin's head.

"What's happening?" he hissed, his shoulders starting to shake.

Brynz didn't reply. Instead, she slipped her feet forward, easing into a sitting position, her long legs draping either side of his neck.

"By the Urslan," Aikin spluttered.

Thane moaned from his spot on the floor.

She bent over to whisper in Aikin's ear. "Too many Drasgor."

He gave an involuntary shiver. "This is madness," he said, moving to hand her down. She tightened her legs, then threw her arms around his neck.

"Your friend is dying," she reminded him.

"He's not my..." Aikin paused then turned his head toward Thane, crimped up in a miserable-looking ball. "Fine." She unloosed her arms, and sat up, feeling self-conscious. She wished she could hear the northmen as they passed, but as ever, they were silent as clouds. All she heard was breathing and the creaking of wood as Aikin shifted positions.

She waited long moments before murmuring, "I'm going back up."

She jockeyed her feet, one at a time, onto his shoulders, then, using his head for balance, pushed herself through the hole. This time, Aikin grasped her legs without being prompted.

She brushed at the snow and realized the roof was a slab of moss-covered dirt. She braced her hands and swung her bottom up onto the frozen surface, ignoring the cold already numbing her hindparts. She leaned forward, straining to see if she could somehow scrabble down the snow-covered roof's steep pitch without sliding off and killing herself. Low voices drifted up. Ahnkne and Hrul. They were well-chosen to guard the door, their loyalty to Uhnkre beyond reproach. Movement caught her eye. A group of northmen armed with dras, stormed toward the roundhouse. A startling thought occurred. Uhnkre had put his trusted warrior-mates at the door as much for his prisoners' safety, as anything else. Without them, all three would have been at the mercy of these northmen who despised them.

A man in the group raised his head, and she plunked down the hole, her rear landing on Aikin's surprised face. The chair tipped sideways, spilling them both onto the floor as it clattered down, one chair leg breaking free and spinning across the floor.

Foonk.

The door rattled, and Brynz kicked her legs out, trying to move the bed frame. The last thing they needed was to be seen trying to escape. The floor heaved up and down, sending the bed and chair leg skittering against the wall as the door swung open. Hrul stuck his head in as the floor settled flat. Another moan sounded.

"Kilf rawn!" the northman brayed, his gaze landing on the broken chair.

POP

Hrul's eyes rolled toward the roof's struts. Another *POP*, followed by the *tickety-tickety-tick* of dirt peppering the floor. Brynz wondered if the whole roof was about to collapse. No time to worry about that. She rolled toward Aikin, her fist swinging round and punching his jaw. The look of shock on his face nearly undid her, but she managed to harden her expression.

"Don't try that again," she bellowed, punching his upper arm. Neither blow carried any sting, and she prayed he would go along with her ruse. She couldn't allow the northman to piece together his own version of why she and Aikin were sprawled on the floor next to a broken chair. A fight was the best she could do.

Aikin got to his feet, his eyes like ice, his upper lip quivering with barely suppressed rage. It was unfortunate, but she couldn't very well apologize with Hrul staring her down. Instead, she bulled ahead.

447

"Bring Uhnkre," she commanded as she scrambled upright. "I need to speak with him."

Hrul's gaze darted between her and Aikin. He grunted as he left, the door banging shut behind him. She turned.

"Sodding hell. What are you playing at?" Aikin's tone was low, but there was no mistaking his fury.

"Sorry. I didn't want him to think we were trying to escape."

"You *were* trying to escape."

"I need to talk to Uhnkre about Thane's leg."

"I thank you, maiss," Thane murmured in a voice laced with pain.

"And hitting me helped with that how?" Aikin whisper-shouted.

"If they think we've had a fight, they won't wonder about the broken chair." She shrugged. "It was the best I could do."

Aikin cleared his throat as he walked across the room, rolling his shoulders as he went. Brynz knew she'd come very close to getting hit. Good thing he was a man of honor. She straightened her clothing, making sure the gryphon feather was secured in her waist tether before he turned round. Another moan. Aikin's head swiveled. Thane's bundled-up form lay near the wall, shunted there when the floor moved.

Brynz undulated her hand toward Aikin. "Was that you?"

Aikin gave a grudging bob of the head.

Impressive.

The door rattled open. Uhnkre entered.

"What you speak?" Uhnkre demanded with a scowl. Hrul and Ahnkne filled the open doorway behind him, backed by the deepening gray of twilight.

Her heart went to her throat. She'd come this far. Might as well know her fate. She swallowed hard to force the tremble from her voice. "Do we die, or do we live?" Uhnkre's eyes, feral-looking in the low light, widened. "Do we die, or do we live?" she repeated, louder this time. "Because if we live, this man needs tending." She pointed at Thane. "If we die, I don't want it to be with this one." She jerked her thumb toward Aikin, ignoring the heat of his stare.

Time stretched tight before Uhnkre pronounced, "You live..." Another long moment. "...for now," the words dribbling out slow as cold syrup.

"We all live," Brynz clarified, jerking her thumb in a circular pattern to indicate all three captives. Uhnkre nodded. "Good. Then I need a knife, boiled clean, and hot water."

Uhnkre's gaze hardened into a glare that made her legs shake. She'd gone too far. Asked for too much. A peculiar tingling traced across her scalp, as if a sharp blade was separating it from her skull. "Umph," he grunted, then turned. Hrul and Ahnkne stepped aside as he walked out. Hrul shot a hot look at Brynz before pulling the door shut with a resounding thump. Brynz closed her eyes with relief.

"That was brave, maiss."

Brynz eyed Thane. *Brave you say. Foolish, more likely.*

"I'd rather have cracked his skull," Aikin muttered.

"And then what? Those two at the door would have had you dead a moment later." Why did men always want to solve their problems with their fists or their weapons? It was beyond understanding.

"He'll never bring a blade."

"If he doesn't, your friend won't live to see another sunset." Brynz knew how quickly blood fever brought down a horse, let alone an underfed man. Thane's pale face told her he hadn't long left unless something was done. Aikin flexed his jaw and stared at the wall behind her as if he could knock it down with his gaze alone. After seeing what he'd done with the floor, she wouldn't put it past him. But with what lay beyond that wall, she hoped he wouldn't try.

Rachmyn found his way to the touchpoint and, after a quick look, concluded that Thane and Aikin had been overtaken by the Drasgor.

Though he was good at reading sign, he didn't need to be to follow their tracks. The snow gave him all the information required. By his count there were six northmen, their footmarks twice as long as his own. Another set of tracks seemed the right size for Aikin with an additional set of smaller tracks. The final set showed a strong planting of the left foot and a dragging of the right. Thane limping. Rachmyn felt a pang of sympathy. A few paces further, the tracks organized into a pattern of nine personages in a diamond-shaped formation, their toe digs heading west. Rachmyn urged his horse along a parallel course.

He'd been following the trail for some time when a village appeared on the horizon. Elgre trotted a similar course, far enough north not to spook the horse. Rachmyn's stomach tightened. If spotted, the wolf could inflame the villagers and any dogs they harbored. He always worried when he and Elgre found themselves in a new place amongst unknown marans. As if reading his thoughts, the wolf veered north, his fluid gait carrying him out of sight.

Rachmyn considered his options. He couldn't very well ride into town; he'd be slaughtered. A mirrorshield would be difficult given the open terrain, and he didn't want to spend the vor if he could help it. A forgetting shield could work if he found a proper setting. There was no guarantee he could accomplish either.

He glanced at the sinking sun, his mind settling on a plan. He checked for his shard. Yes, there it was. His thumb stroked its familiar smoothness as he considered the fates. Haedyn's drawn face appeared in his mind, and his heart lurched. He'd placed his best friend's life into the hands of the unknown. It was a bitter root to chew as he considered his own future and the fight that lay ahead. Would he ever see Haedyn again? Could it be that neither of them would survive to see tomorrow? His throat constricted. He hadn't even said goodbye when Haedyn left with Thane and Aikin. Thinking of that mundane slipping away wrenched at his guts like a dull blade. Whatever came, he couldn't allow that to be their ending.

Elorah looked past Mierrle's head toward the snowy landscape in front of them. They'd traveled several leagues using the hum of her father's staff for guidance. When the staff had bonded with the crystalwood bow in her grandfather's cottage, she hadn't realized how vital that connection would turn out to be. That a life would depend upon that shared spark and glow.

The storm had moved on, but the going was still treacherous. She gave the gelding its head so it could pick its way through the drifts. Carrying two riders added to the horse's burden, and triangular sweat marks darkened its flanks. The pony labored harder, its short legs lifting higher and plunging deeper, and it snorted and blew in its exertion. The snow had prevented regular grazing, and Elorah knew both animals were losing condition. Working this hard would make that worse. She also knew the group needed provisions soon. The only upside was the snow meant a steady supply of water.

A yellowish glow on the northern horizon caught her attention. Their current course would take them right into whatever it was. If there'd been smoke, she would have thought it a large fire, but there was none.

"Do you think that's him?" Mierrle asked.

"Maybe..." Elorah paused, considering.

"It looks like a fire."

"I'm not so sure. There's no smoke."

Mierrle nodded, her hair blowing into Elorah's face. "What else could it be?"

"I don't know," Elorah said, remembering what Rachmyn had told her before they set out. *Haedyn's in a right mess. I think he's spent all his vor. I don't know how he'll stay warm until you find him.* Convincing Rachmyn she and Mierrle should be the ones to go after Haedyn hadn't been easy, and she'd seen the worry in his eyes when he relayed what he'd seen during the peering. Based on that, she hadn't expected Haedyn to have a fire, another reason she thought the glow must be something else.

A league later, the yellow light—clearly flame now that they were closer—was larger than a house. Curiously, it did not have the triangular shape of most fires. Instead, it was a fluid-looking oval, with a strange dollop on top.

"Do you see that?"

"It *is* a fire. A big one."

"But the shape... It isn't like most fires, is it?"

"I guess not..." Mierrle wrinkled her nose.

Elorah watched the dollop stretch up, lengthening into a thick column, a flare licking out at its apex. Still, there was no sign of smoke or smell of char. The gelding and pony plodded forward, unconcerned. A swishing noise filled the air as two flaming wings separated from the oval and spread across the sky. The dollop rotated into profile, a gapped beak and spiky crest becoming visible. There was no mistaking it now. She'd seen the pictures and read the tales. It had to be a fyrrefen—the flamebird paramvor of the Fyrre affinity. Like a bird-shaped sun, the fyrrefen imposed itself upon the sky, pushing back its wintry gray with undulating waves of red-gold light.

"What is *that*?" Mierrle asked, her voice struck through with awe.

"I've never seen one before, but I'm sure it's a fyrrefen."

"The paramvor of Fyrre? The instructors said they were a myth."

Elorah let the statement hang in the air as they both stared at the magnificent flamebird, its coronae head pointing skyward, its molten wings rising high, the entire landscape aflame with dancing reflections of glowing brightness. This was no myth or trick of the mind. Imaginative folly did not cast glittering jots of light across the snow.

Still, the gelding and pony remained unfazed by the giant flaming bird rapturing up from the cold breast of the horizon. Elorah wondered if the animals could even see it.

"Do you think it's come for Haedyn?" Mierrle asked.

"Better than that. I think it's pointing us to the spot where we'll find him."

CHAPTER FORTY-ONE
STEADFAST

Excitement coursed through the Wycche as her soul flumed away from the confines of her chamber into the otherworld of Oru Fen.

Venge stood waiting when she opened her eyes, his dark eyes glowing hot in the dim surroundings. Behind him were other wolves: Flaye and Mouk, Syba, Gnar, Tenze, Kruszk. These she recognized, but there were many more she did not. Venge assured her most of the new wolves were *Longesse* and possessed the far-reaching influence she desired.

The pack Venge had assembled brought a small smile to her face. That her liege had managed to turn the desires of so many wolves in such a short time told her that their cause was right, as she always knew it was. The Elect, for all their pontificating, were relics; their whims a burden no longer to be borne by those in the waking world or their wraithwolves in Oru Fen. Their time had passed, and the sooner their influence was nullified, the better.

At hand was the shaping of a better world, more wondrous than anything the Six Dragons had ever envisioned, a world where the individual fashioned their future free from the barriers imposed by the hated Founders, including living forever if one wished it to be. All that stood in their way now was the Erynvor and her white wolf.

One thought cut sharp. She'd already held the Erynvor within her grasp. In truth, she could have snuffed her out already, but the Wycche had learned from the past and knew killing an Eryvor only led to the advent of another. Hadn't she eliminated ten previous Uniters, only to have another come flinging into the realm on the behest of those interfering dragons who thought they ran the world? And so, she had come to a different idea, a more subtle approach. This time, she would perform a taming of sorts, a shaping of the will, whereby the Erynvor would be subsumed into the perpetual existence of a life without end. It was the perfect solution to the Uniter conundrum that had plagued the Wycche since she'd first discovered the Arcana of Vorie Supin and applied its principles to her own finitude that long ago day when the world was in tatters and her heart forever changed.

This time, she'd spent ten annums inculcating the idea that one soul, given enough resources and time, could change the world, knowing this was the desire of this latest Erynvor. It seemed a simple matter to bend that naive desire's trajectory enough to lead the Uniter to conclude that an indefinite life was the best outcome for all. The Wycche, of course, did not need convincing. She had come to that conclusion eryns ago when the horrors of the Great Destruction had torn her family apart, putting her father and uncle into their graves and sending her people scattering to the winds. The remnant of that peerless society that had once ruled the world was now forced to live in the shadows other marans feared. Someday, her people would return to their rightful place of honor and power, of this she was certain, but until then, it was up to her to ensure their pathway remained secure.

A ripple ran through the assembled wolves, a mixture of anticipation and greed. They hungered for what they had been promised and would not be satisfied until their desire was sated. The Wycche knew this hunger well. Indeed, it was the reason Astr Stell haunted her still, demanding she return that which he could not have. But it was best not to think of that now, with so many pairs of ravening eyes fixed upon her.

The wraithwolves had come hoping for etheriant, perhaps even counting on it, but that would be their reward. First, they must prove their worth. The white wolf's pack of Voriens must be put asunder before they gained even more strength. Another Vorien had joined, as Venge would have her understand, with more waiting on the fringes, their allegiance all but confirmed. The orucon crackled a warning with blistering speed—seize the now or lose the future.

Let us obliterate these, Venge's mindwords growled, his hackles spiking. *The wolf newly joined brings a warrior's mind and a warrior's experience. We must snuff out his influence before the risk becomes too great. If we miss our chance, we might never have another.*

The Wycche agreed with Venge's logic.

These wolves you command, they are equal to your proposition?

More than equal, great one. I've no doubt they will succeed at the task required.

The Wycche rubbed her hands together, calculating the risks. She could see no reason not to do as Venge suggested. *Your words persuade me. Lead on, king of shadow, and we shall soon celebrate a mighty victory.*

Venge's eyes brightened, his deadblack armor settling upon his lank frame.

The Wycche felt the tingling anticipation of impending battle, her raiment pulsing as she assessed her internals. Inside, vor surged, whetting her senses and inflaming her will, the result of relentless etheriant gathering over the past moon. She felt sure she now wielded enough to power this blooded pack.

A fierce wind struck up as the other wolves pulled deadblack from the ethers to gird themselves, dying away once their armoring was complete. The Wycche surveyed the Malvisse pack, a hundred warriors at least, each wearing the same fearless glower, the same slavering snarl. *Who could stand up to these?* the Wycche thought, delighted.

Lead on, my liege, for tonight your great glory awaits.

Essiant studied Kelm, gauging the warrior's reaction. To him there was no mistaking the poisonous intent stinging its way through the orucon. The sand-colored wolf cocked his head, his muzzle dropping as he stared at the murk beneath their paws. Essiant was sure Kelm felt the dark energies zinging through the collective thought underpinning the realm.

It has begun. The warrior's mindwords confirmed Essiant's conviction.

A sparkling cloud descended upon Kelm, forming into a set of stardust armor so full of shine, even Essiant was awed. The warrior wolf was taking no chances. Essiant pulled his own armor from the firmament, feeling it settle in place as the remaining Voriens donned their own protective sheathings. He surveyed the pack: seven magnificent fighters ready to take on any and all who would interfere with their night-wards' chosen paths.

They didn't wait long. The first of the Malvisse appeared to the west, their deadblack rendering them a malignant-looking pack of galloping feet, bobbing heads, and stringing tails, all bearing down upon the Voriens' position. The seven took up a circular fighting formation, their tails pressed together, their heads facing outward so that no approach was unseen. Essiant imagined they looked like a single, gleaming star, as they stood ready in their glittering armor.

A dark cloud hovered above the Malvisse as they pounded forward, a cumulus of black intent urging them on. Though Essiant could not see her malign face with its cruel eyes and crueler mouth, he knew who it was. The Wycche. He recognized her malefic energy signature from the many times he'd felt it in the past.

They'll surround us first. Stand tall and assert your strength. We cannot be overcome if we stick together. Place your mind upon the All. Think of nothing else, and the power of the realm will be ours.

Kelm's words girded the Voriens. Essiant could feel the crackling of their energies as they turned their minds to a singular thought.

All All All All All All All

Over and over, Essiant's mind intoned the word, until there was nothing else, each thought a brick set upon the next, building until they became a rampart higher than could be measured, his packmates doing the same.

The swiftest of the Malvisse crashed against the energy wall, sending a shudder through the group. Another assault, more wolves this time, smashing with a force beyond reckoning, intent on rupturing the breastwork the Voriens' mindwords were constructing.

The Voriens held fast.

ALL ALL ALL ALL ALL ALL ALL

Kelm's mind screamed the word, lest any lose their concentration. Essiant then heard Raya's stout voice—*ALL ALL ALL ALL*. Spectra and Embren took up the mantra, joined by Ajai and Ieeva and finally Essiant, whose cry came from the very depths of his soul. Another salvo of wolves crashed against the wall, more this time than before. Essiant refused to count the number, his concentration upon the Vorien's collective thought barrier.

All All All All All All All

Again and again, the Malvisse sought to break through the invisible wall separating the opposing forces. Again and again, the Voriens held strong, their minds focused on the only thought worth thinking. Soul-curdling screeches issued from the wycche-cloud circling above the Malvisse horde as bolt after bolt of frenzied hate-spikes rained down—some striking low, others hitting high—only to dissipate against the potent calculus of the Voriens' energy shield. Essiant felt each blow, hammerstrike after hammerstrike between his ears. Still, his mind did not sway. Nor did any of the other Voriens', their thought-rampart holding firm.

The collisions ceased.

The Voriens took a collective breath as the wycche-cloud pulled back, disappearing into the gathered gloom of a distant tree line.

Kelm's mindwords sounded again—***ALL ALL ALL ALL ALL ALL ALL***. The wizened warrior refused to let the pack drop their guard, even as the lull stretched on and on, until it seemed impossible the Malvisse hadn't retreated.

Essiant looked around. An eerie pall had settled. Trees that had started as scant smudges at the horizon now towered over the Voriens, their thorned branches glinting sharp. Essiant's gaze shifted, and the trees moved closer still. A rumble sounded through the orucon, and one of them fell, its spiked branches raking down the invisible wall and tattering the energy field. Too late, Essiant realized his attention had slipped.

It was the opportunity the Malvisse had been waiting for. More trees fell, each clawing rifts into the wall's energy field as they crashed onto the misty stratum—*boom boom Boom BOOM! kathunk kathunk*

Kathunk KATHUNK! The deadblack-clad pack burst forth from the shadows, a hurtling charge of terrifying fury.

BBBBOOOOOMMMM!

The collision was terrific, every wolf hitting the invisible energy wall at the same moment, their collective effort bolstered by an incalculable level of vor. The wall buckled from the strain, bending further, further, further until it seemed it would give way. Essiant wasn't the only one whose mind had slipped. He refocused, his mind screaming—*ALL ALL ALL*—his essence imbuing every shout with intentional will.

Kelm roared beside him, his mindwords lashing out like weapons— *ALL! ALL! ALL!*

The Malvisse ripped at the weakened wall with bone-gray teeth, their deadblack further depleting it. Two breaches opened, and Essiant felt Embren tense behind him. A loud snarling commenced, as the red wolf engaged with the interlopers.

TOGETHER! ALL! TOGETHER! ALL! Kelm shouted.

Essiant bared his teeth, his stardust armor fizzing against his fur. Two scragging wolves had made their way through. He clamped onto one, tearing into the bend where the head met the throat. Essiant jerked his head sideways, flipping the wolf onto its side, its deadblack beginning to fray. He let loose, and the wolf rolled onto its belly and crawled away, large patches of mildewed coat showing through its disintegrating armor.

A second wolf slashed forward, its mouth wide. Essiant met it toothfang against toothfang, a clattering that reverberated throughout his being. The Malvisse pulled back before ramming forward. Again, their teeth struck but this time, Essiant twisted mid-bite, gaining a grip on the attacking wolf's snout. He bit down hard, felt the nose and muzzle giving way. The wolf mewled, the sound going straight down Essiant's throat. With a fling of the head, he sent the wolf head-over-tail in a backward flip. Its deadblack winked out, and the grime-brown wolf skittered away, haunches digging deep into the substrate, ears pinned against its head.

Around him, Essiant could hear similar battles being fought as his packmates defended their positions. He returned his thoughts to the All. They had to rebuild the wall.

At first, he didn't hear the rumbling coming from beneath and above at the same time as he concentrated on the source word. But soon it gained strength, a deep grumble resonating until it seemed the orusphere was shaking apart. Like a tremendous explosion *ALLLLLLLLLL! ALLLLLLLLL! ALLLLLLLLLLL!* blasted up and out, hurling the Malvisse away from the wall and into the trees, their deadblack impaling upon the grove's stabbing thorns. High-pitched yowls issued from many as they retreated, their armor dissipating to nothing. Only Venge remained, his stare a malevolence Essiant could feel. But without his armor, the haggard wraithwolf posed little actual threat.

Essiant cast his eyes upward, looking for the Wycche. Unless her vor was also spent, she was still a danger.

A cold darkness hovered above the trees, drawing tighter until it formed into the shape of a cloaked figure. The wraith glissaded to the ground, a shadow resembling a hand extending toward the glowering wraithwolf. The moment the shadow-hand touched the wraithwolf's head the two streaked away, vanishing into the ethers. At the same moment, the spinose trees zoomed back, their forms diffusing until they were no more.

Essiant sighed as the pent atmosphere settled.

His relief was short-lived.

Ieeva is gone. Spectra's mindwords were worried. *She disappeared during the assault.*

Essiant sent a surge of vorik through the orucon, and then another, searching for the black wolf's signature, without result.

Embren stepped close. *Should we look for her?*

No, Essiant replied. He knew not where Ieeva had gone. Perhaps her night-ward had suffered some tragedy, and she had returned to Inverna with him. But the Malvisse would strike again, and when they did, the pack needed to be together. Although it was unbearable, their only alternative was to wait. *We should stay together and await her return.*

But what if she needs our help? Spectra's blue eyes pierced through him.

It was a question he was already asking himself. He looked off into the fog collected along the far margin, considering. His was not a journey of sentimentality. Always, he had relied upon his intellect when making decisions. He thought again of Ieeva, of all she'd been through and all that was yet to be. He thought of the vow every Vorien had made when coming into the realm. A realization dawned. Without the One, there could be no All. It was true they had pledged fealty to the All, but that vow had also been made to each other. They couldn't abandon one principle for the sake of another. Thinking of that made his decision.

You are right, he answered. *The All isn't a force outside of us. It is Us. And we cannot be Us without Ieeva.* Around him, the assembled Voriens nodded their agreement. They would search until they discovered their missing packmate, or her outcome. It was the only thing they could do and stay true to their purpose.

Essiant fixed his mind upon the search, waiting for a starshine pathway to reveal itself. When it did, he took the point, the rest falling in behind, Kelm assuming rearguard as they followed the shining trail before them.

CHAPTER FORTY-TWO
RETRIEVING THE LOST

The fyrrefen burst upward in a flaming thrust before spreading out, its shape suffusing into a red-gold light that filled the sky. Elorah's pendant warmed as she and Mierrle drew closer, the rosy glow only fading when they had Haedyn in their sights.

He was easy to spot: a wemble hump in a circle of damp, a bow lying nearby like a forgotten bone. Beyond lay snow, deep and white.

The staff's humming increased as it neared its pairmate until its song was the only thing Elorah could hear. She pulled up her horse, dismounted, and ran to him, her heart in her throat. Had they arrived too late? She shook his shoulder, and he toppled sideways, his hand poking out at the last moment to brace him up, his eyes startling wide.

"Haedyn! Can you hear me?"

His head wobbled as if coming unstuck. "...inside the fire..."

"Do you know where you are?"

"Has it gone?" He scrambled to his feet, his face tilting toward the clouds. "You saw it? It wasn't my imagination?"

"It was as big as the sky," Mierrle called, her arms sweeping up and out.

Haedyn embraced Elorah, his eyes going wet. "Shifting stars! I thought I was dead or mad or both!"

His touch sent a tingle through her, and she hugged him back, never more glad to see anyone in her life. Swept up, she nearly kissed him, only managing to swerve at the last moment, hot embarrassment pinking her cheeks. Where had that come from? The last time she'd kissed anyone was her first day at the Academie and then only a peck on her mother's cheek. This was something wholly different from that dutiful action. He seemed to feel it too, tightening his embrace until a loud *chirt-chirt-chirt* issued from his chest. He rocked onto his heels as his bird stuck its red-capped head out between the cloak's plackets.

"Look who it is, Fryk," he said, his finger stroking the grynt's crest. It directed a baleful glare at Elorah, and she averted her gaze. "Is Rachmyn with you?" He craned his neck.

"He went to find Thane and Aikin."

"What do you mean?"

"When none of you made it back, he did a peering and saw you'd become separated."

"They're alive? After the bravik..." He looked away, his expression taut, his palms slapping down onto his thighs.

"Thane and his horse were injured and the pony's gone." She watched Mierrle dismount before continuing. "There's something else. Rachmyn saw Drasgor heading for them."

Haedyn's eyes went wide. He sprang up, one hand forcing his bird into its pocket before thrusting out. "We have to go after them," he said, his voice rising as he pulled Elorah to her feet. He jammed the crystalwood bow up onto his shoulder, his gaze raking the landscape. "Have you seen my horse?"

"There," Mierrle said, pointing toward the gelding and pony huddling in the gap between two silverleafs.

Haedyn ran to the horse and jerked it forward several strides before Elorah grabbed his arm.

"Wait!"

"We don't have time to wait!" Haedyn shook her off and vaulted aboard.

"You can't–"

But he was already away, his horse plunging into the softening drifts, its thrashing legs going white with snow.

Why is he always so impetuous?

Elorah ran to her own horse, untied the pony, and thrust its lead toward Mierrle. "Mind the ponies," she said, indicating toward the one in the brake. Mierrle nodded, her eyes huge. Elorah sent her friend a surge of heart vorik then scrambled atop her mount, squeezing it into a canter. "You don't even know where you're going!" she shouted at Haedyn's retreating back.

Haedyn glanced behind—face flushed, lips drawn tight—then pulled up his mount.

"We need a plan, or we'll all end up dead!" She halted her struggling horse.

He looked toward the horizon. "What should we do?" he asked, his voice cracking.

"I'll do a peering," she said, ignoring the doubts shouting inside her head, concentrating instead on her warming pendant.

He pursed his lips, his golden eyes squinting at the unrelenting white.

"I'll do a peering," Elorah repeated. "Otherwise, we're lost already."

Haedyn nodded, his face grim. "It seems we don't have much choice."

Rachmyn watched the sun's last golden sliver slip below the rim of the world from the flat of a dry ravine-bed west of the northmen's village.

He'd used his reins to hobble his horse and tie up a drag-tail of boxytop limbs. The only thing left was to wait for dusk. He checked for his shard—yes, there it was—then thumbed it to settle his thoughts.

Once the shadows had faded into the purpling light, he started for the dark smear of the village, looking behind every few steps to check the drag-tail's obscuring scratch marks. It wasn't an ideal ruse in melting snow, but it would have to do.

The gathering darkness provided better cover. Though it wouldn't fool dogs, the low light and his unusual profile might fool the eyes of men who didn't yet know to watch for him. He hoped it would be enough to get him into the village. Beyond that, he had no plan.

He was near the roundhouses when the barking began. He'd suspected there'd be dogs—there always were—but his heart sank all the same. The barking increased, and Rachmyn drew his blade, his heart banging. He didn't want to take on a dog pack, but he would if he had to. A shape streaked past, and he swung toward it, his blade reflecting a stray lantern beam. Elgre's silhouette loped by, the village in his sights. The barking increased, and Rachmyn crouched down, blood roaring in his ears.

Come on, you scruffs. I'm ready for you.

He squinted into the dark, searching for some sign of the wolf.

Moments later, Elgre sprinted the other way, ears pinned back, lips flapping against jagged teeth. Behind thundered a pack of shaggy-haired hounds twice his size, their frantic baying an ear-splitting furor. The noise said they were dogs, but these were far bigger than any Rachmyn had ever seen. He held no fear for his companion. Elgre would lead them on a merry chase, with the dogs getting the worst of it but what of himself? What if the wolf's gambit hadn't lured away every hound? He set the thought aside. No sense worrying about that when there were more pressing concerns.

He ditched the drag-tail and crept into the village proper, his eyes taking in every detail. It occurred more than once that his friends might be dead, that he was on a fool's errand with a similar ending in store. Friends. The word caught in his throat like a piece of unchewed gristle. He hadn't thought of them as friends until this very moment. And though it felt odd, it also felt right. Why else would he risk everything, if not for friends?

The village was laid out like a wagon wheel, its muddy pathways forming spokes from a central hub. Rachmyn knew to avoid whatever was at the center, focusing instead on stalking the periphery, alert for any sign of Thane and Aikin.

He was on his second circuit when he spotted two bearded hulks worrying the doorstep of a roundhouse, their fur-clad bodies turned in the direction the dogs had disappeared. No mistake, the two were guarding the doorway and no mistake, they'd seen the hounds chasing the wolf. Rachmyn could think of only one reason for their presence.

His gaze went to a large pelt stretched onto an even larger frame standing next to the roundhouse opposite. He ducked behind it. The unfletched pelt stunk of rotten meat and urine, but its position afforded a good view. His blade clutched in one hand, Rachmyn leaned past the pelt's waggled edge.

The door opened, and a third northman emerged, this one blonder than the others. After a word, the blond man strode away, his hand stroking his beard, its ornaments clinking—*chikkety chikkety*—as he went.

None of the roundhouses had windows. The only way in was through the front door or the smoke-hole in the roof. Neither was easy, but the smoke-hole seemed the better option. Rachmyn plucked at the stringing attaching the pelt to the frame. Dried gut. He stepped up onto it and nodded when it held his weight. It just might work.

The next problem was moving the frame. He reckoned he could project a mirror shield without using too much vor, given the relative darkness, but that wouldn't make lugging the heavy frame any easier.

He shook the stretcher and, feeling a wiggle, ran his hand along its bottom edge, his fingers finding the lashing securing the frame to an anchoring beam.

He took off his cloak and rumpled it into the front of his leggings. Next, he cut most of the lashing, his free hand planted in the pelt's slimy center in case the contraption collapsed. He summoned his will, building a mirrorshield that painted himself and the frame in the essence of night. Two final slashes and the frame fell back, the rotten side splatting against his turned head. The stench was horrific, and he gagged as he stiffened his stance—knees knocked forward, arms cocked like wings—to keep from crumpling to the ground. He hadn't expected the spunking thing to weigh so much, and it took all his strength to straighten up then manipulate his way to the top before turning back-to-front and shouldering the upper bar. It was still sodding heavy, but at least it was manageable.

Hauling the frame was a tedious slog of drag-stop-listen, drag-stop-listen, the weight driving him into the ground with every step. By the time he reached the roundhouse, his back and legs were on fire, his shirt soaked with sweat.

He leaned the frame against the curved stone wall then cursed himself for a blistered idiot when it fell well short of the roofline. He grasped the nearest side-pole, shoved his foot into a gap then pushed himself up, the gut-string bowing under his weight, the entire frame quivering like jelly. He waited, expecting the string to give way or the frame to fall. When neither happened, he took a second handhold and pulled himself up another half-span. The stringing stretched long beneath his second foot, the frame shaking hard enough to rap at the stone. He stopped and waited for things to steady before reaching up again.

Three steps later, he'd reached the top. He planted one foot upon the upper crossbar, steadied himself, then planted the other. Using the wall as a brace, he straightened and rocked his head back. The roof was much closer now. He stretched up and placed his palm upon the roof's edge, poking his fingers through the snow to judge its makeup. Moss-covered dirt.

He pulled out his blade and, giving a mighty swing, stabbed it into the roof's snowy surface. The blade sunk to its hilt. He grasped on with both hands, gritted his teeth, and pulled, his feet scrabbling against the rock wall, his arms straining against their pinnings. A mighty heave and he belly-flopped onto the roof, his lower legs poking past the edge, his frontside stinging with cold. He wished he was wearing his cloak instead of laying on it.

He jammed his knees into the freezing roof, unstuck the knife, and swung again, embedding the blade further up. Another tremendous heave and the fronts of his boots found purchase. Four more stabs and he crested the slope. There was the smoke hole. Relief rushed through him, hot wind expelling from the furnace of his lungs.

He unstuck his knife and sheathed it then fumbled out his cloak and put it on. Its heat was immediate, and he closed his eyes with pleasure. He sat that way for long moments considering his next move. A rope would have helped, and he cursed himself for not thinking of it sooner. He peered down the hole into the dim interior.

He spotted Aikin right away, standing in the middle of the room, his shoulders jutting away from his thick neck like oaken beams. Another figure stood nearby, tall, with an angular build and dark twizzled hair. A girl, maybe, though it was hard to tell.

Rachmyn changed positions, his gaze drawn to a shape curled near the wall. The scar told him it was Thane. The Elequian looked in a bad way, his forehead chalk white, his eyes squeezed shut. Even if he'd had a rope, Rachmyn doubted whether it would do the stricken man much good. The figure with the knotted hair looked up, and Rachmyn pulled his head back, catching a glimpse of the face. Definitely a maiss. Perhaps this *was* the village thiefkeep. A grim chuckle escaped. After a lifetime spent avoiding it, he was about to put himself in the clink.

He swung his feet into the hole then eased down until he dangled at full stretch, his hands crabbed into the roof's glazed turf. He glanced past his feet. There was still a considerable drop to the floor.

"Great good night!" Aikin burst out as a strong wind gust rushed up through the smoke hole, nearly dislodging Rachmyn's hands.

His fingers dug deeper, dirt driving under his fingernails, his arms shaking. Below came the scritching sound of something being drug across the stone floor. Aikin and the girl were centering a bed platform beneath him.

"Let loose!" Aikin hissed.

Rachmyn relaxed his grip and closed his eyes, his arms embracing his knees a split before he hit the frame's stiff leather strapping. He struck and bounced once before landing on his side.

"By the Urslan, where'd you come from?"

Rachmyn opened his eyes to Aikin's staring face.

"Wyssfuss?" The girl's words blew past Rachmyn's ears.

Aikin straightened and turned to answer in kind, his words equally windy. The girl nodded, a pensive frown on her dirt-streaked face.

Rachmyn pointed at Thane. "Can he walk?" he asked, his mind already pondering how to get past the guards as he stood.

"He walked in, but I doubt he'll walk out," Aikin said. "He's got blood fever. Help me shift this."

Rachmyn helped Aikin trundle the bed frame to the wall, his mind elsewhere.

Shifting stars. How are we getting out of this disaster?

The girl spoke again, more words blowing past. Rachmyn looked to Aikin.

"She says if she had a clean knife, she could do something with Thane's leg. She's had experience with horses."

Rachmyn pulled his from its sheath, the blade shining as he laid it across his forearm. "It's far from clean–" The girl moved for it, and Rachmyn dodged back, pointing the sticking end at her chest. "I'll keep hold of my own blade, maiss," he warned.

The girl frowned, her hands dropping to her sides as she spat angry words Rachmyn didn't need translated. So be it. He'd be trussed before he'd let anyone get hold of his knife. He held the blade against the candle flame then swiped it against his leg. "Show me where to cut, and I'll do it," he said, his lip twitching up to expose the lower half of his front teeth. The thought of carving into Thane's leg made his stomach flop, and he swallowed hard.

Aikin whissed more words at the girl. She strode over and lifted the fur.

Thane was gripped into a ball of misery, his body shaking, his arms hugging his knees, his eyes two dark dimples in a white face marred by a whiter scar. The girl bent over his tattered pantling and gently loosened the black crust sticking the fabric to the swollen wound. Thane moaned, and Rachmyn drew a ragged breath, bile rising past his ability to swallow it away, its metallic burn all he could taste. The leg was much worse than he'd imagined.

The girl's blue-gray eyes bored into Rachmyn's as he came over and knelt. She laid a finger across his blade to indicate the depth of the cut before pointing at the spot where he should begin. She traced an imaginary line downward, her fingertip following the hooked shape of the gouge, stopping near Thane's ankle. She arced the finger upward, her eyes glaring—*wait*—then pointed at a broken chair leg and spoke to Aikin.

Aikin retrieved the leg, then, after putting Thane onto his back and straddling him, laid it across the stricken man's chest to immobilize him.

The girl used the fur to swaddle Thane's feet, taking care to leave the wound exposed, then laid the upper half of her body head-down upon his good leg, her long legs frogging out either side of his torso, her hands gripping the fur cocoon of his feet. She'd immobilized Thane with impressive speed; now it was up to Rachmyn to make a proper cut.

468

He wiped his sweating palms against his pants then gripped the knife handle and stared at the bulbous wound twining up the leg, his mind envisioning what his hands must do.

He plunged the blade in, and Thane shrieked, the sound blasting past Aikin's broad palm smashed against his lips, his torso straining upward against the pinioning chair leg. Meanwhile, the girl muscled his thrashing lower body into submission. Rachmyn kept his eyes on his task, steadily pulling the blade downward. Another shriek, followed by the muffled *thwap* of fist meeting face, once, twice, the leg shuddering with each impact before going still. Rachmyn's eyes darted toward the sound, his hands frozen on the knife handle. Aikin had knocked Thane unconscious.

The girl moved her keen gaze away from Rachmyn's knife to direct a hard stare into his eyes. *Get on with it.*

Rachmyn swallowed and pushed on, following the contour the girl had traced, pink-tinged froth spraying warm onto his hands and face. The smell was horrendous. He grimaced and continued cutting, closing his throat to keep from retching. When the blade neared the ankle, he looked at the girl. She jerked her thumb up, and he pulled the blade out, swiping it clean on the fur. He wasn't about to wipe the foulness onto his own leggings so he could wear it.

He stood and surveyed the deflating wound weeping corruption. The girl thumb-kneaded around the cut, driving more purulence from its depths. The pain brought Thane round, and Aikin had to lean harder against the chair leg to keep him still. The scarred man mewled like a newborn pup as the girl methodically forced gunge from the gash, his head thrashing, tears streaming from his clamped eyes, two reddened welts rising along his jawline where Aikin had chinned him.

The girl carefully inspected the wound and gave a curt nod before loosening the fur's hold. She pulled it away and got to her feet. Aikin rocked back then stood and tossed the chair leg aside.

Thane's eyes continued to stream, his mouth forming words with no sound, his body wracked by trembling spasms. Rachmyn felt his simmering enmity fade, replaced by an unexpected tenderness, the feeling coming upon him in that surprising way it had when he'd seen Haedyn's bawling, snot-caked face that long ago day. His mind leaped to his friend's plight—was he safe?—worry and uncertainty chewing at his stomach.

Aikin knelt and hovered his hands above Thane's wound. A baritone humming began, and it took Rachmyn a moment to realize the sound was coming from the kneeling man. The hum held steady, a droning noise something like a forest animal at dusk.

The door rattled. Rachmyn leapt up and scurried to the wall, flattening himself against it as he summoned up a mirrorshield. He sucked in a raw breath.

The door flung open, and the blond northman brawned in, the two dark-haired guards filling the open doorway behind him. The hulking blond spoke to the girl—whose face remained a studied blank—in flat syllables punctuated by long pauses. When he was done, she replied in measured beats, one hand indicating Thane's sprawled form.

The northman's gaze shifted to the moaning man. Though he'd ceased humming, Aikin continued to hover his hands above Thane's leg, his back to the commotion, trying to look as if he wasn't listening to the northman's every word. Rachmyn reckoned the smell alone should tell the blond giant all was not well.

The northman turned and barked a command. One of the guards disappeared, the other stepping over to fill in the gap. The blond northman turned to the girl, his eyes soft, his expression yielding. Whatever she'd asked for, he'd granted, not for the benefit of Thane but because she'd asked. That was an advantage Rachmyn hadn't counted on, but one he knew they could use. The northman braced the girl's shoulders, his beard ornaments clinking, and spoke again. The girl's chin dropped, and Aikin's head jerked round. Rachmyn had to remind himself to keep his shield up rather than try to work out what was happening.

Aikin's head swung back searching for Rachmyn, his expression an admixture of astonishment and consternation.

Rachmyn didn't dare let the shield fade as long as the northmen were in the room. *Steady*, he thought as Aikin got up and stepped in his direction, the Caeldish winding up for a real search. *Steady man!*

The floor humped beneath his feet, and Rachmyn stumbled sideways, the mirrorshield dropping as he regained his balance.

Spunk!

Aikin eased back, his face registering shocked comprehension. Rachmyn glanced toward the northman as he hastily reformed the shield, relieved to see the Drasgor's attention had remained on the girl. He gently tapped her shoulder before striding out, the door banging shut behind him.

Rachmyn sighed as he withdrew his vor, allowing the shield to dissipate.

The girl murmured, and Aikin let out a low whistle. He looked at Rachmyn, his eyebrows lifting toward his hairline. "That's some Shadowen trick you've got there." His tone held no admiration. "Did you hear any of that?"

"I heard, but I've no understanding," Rachmyn replied.

"You don't speak Iellian? The Most Exalted Tyrant will be most disappointed." Aikin smiled, pleased somehow, then came back to the point. "The savage has agreed we can leave." Aikin flipped his thumb to indicate Thane and himself. That was all Rachmyn needed to hear, and he moved toward the door. Aikin grabbed his arm. "Not so fast. There's conditions. He said we must wait until he clears the way. Otherwise, opposing etts will have us dead before we're a half-day gone."

"Etts?"

"That's the word he used. I don't have a translation for it." Aikin looked at the girl staring at the closed door, a fretful expression on her face and lowered his voice. "He means for the girl to stay."

"She's nothing to me," Rachmyn said with a shrug.

"Nor to me, only, she does have a peculiar precision with wind." Rachmyn jutted his chin, inviting Aikin to continue. "And if I'm not mistaken, that's the livery of the monarch's stables." Aikin gave a knowing nod then torqued his lips into a small frown at Rachmyn's blank stare. "Don't you see? She could do us much good in our bid to unseat the Most Exalted Pretender from our lands."

Rachmyn had no interest in Aikin's political ramblings. All he knew was that adding another maran would make it harder for any of them to escape. For that reason alone, he was happy to leave the girl behind.

The girl walked to Thane, looking first at his leg then at his face. She blew harried words at Aikin, and he hurried over, then stooped and placed two fingers against Thane's neck. He removed them and spoke to the girl, his expression grim.

"Is he alright?" Rachmyn asked.

"I doubt it. Getting out of here might mean leaving him behind."

Rachmyn puffed up, a surprising rancor taking hold. For some reason, he felt compelled to fight Thane's corner. "We're not leaving him behind, not while he still breathes."

"I never took him as any great friend of yours," Aikin remarked.

"And I never took you for a man without honor," Rachmyn shot back. The verbal blow had its effect.

"If it wasn't for me, he'd have been a meager meal for the bravik," Aikin ground out.

"Elbows for toes," Rachmyn said.

"Pardon?"

"Elbows for–" Rachmyn stopped, realizing Aikin had turned toward the girl. She was speaking again, her face determined, her finger jabbing first toward Aikin's chest, then whipping sideways toward Rachmyn. Aikin didn't bother translating her tirade or his terse reply. Clearly, she didn't intend to remain behind.

Rachmyn settled on the edge of the bed frame, his mind sifting possibilities. He checked his pocket for his shard. Yes, there it was. He was sure he had enough speck to overpower these huge men. With the girl's precision with wind, perhaps they could get the speck into the northmen without arousing suspicion. They'd have to take the girl with them, but they should be well away before the guards came round. As for the "etts", he was willing to take his chances even with the extra baggage of Thane and the girl. He was also willing to risk sending three northmen into Oru Fen without the benefit of their wolf guardians, knowing it was the only way they were getting out of this disaster alive.

Thane stood in a hazy mist, his eyes struggling to adjust. How had he gotten here? Where was he? He looked at his leg, expecting to see the terrible gash but no, the leg appeared unsullied. Likewise, the smashing pain had disappeared.

The mist thinned, and he could make out the gauzy outline of numerous trees. A forest then but a forest he'd never seen before. He swiveled to look behind, squinting into the gray-palled air. A rustle spun him forward, his legs bending, his arms lifting into a defensive posture.

A tall, black wolf sallied forth from the murky woods, slicing through the gloom with the ease of a rapier splitting fog. It walked with its ears pricked high upon its slim head, its intelligent green eyes lit with a silver glow. A crescent moon glinted upon the wolf's forehead when it turned its head.

Thane.

The melodious voice filled him with overwhelming joy, and he looked around, longing to find the one who had spoken to him.

Who calls my name?

It is I, Ieeva, your one true guardian and the keeper of your memories.

The wolf took another step forward, and he knew with startling clarity this beautiful creature was not only the voice inside his head but was also the better part of himself. She alone knew the way to that place he had tried to find so many times using strong drink and suspect charms. He felt something let go inside as his soul released its white-knuckle hold on the frail body he'd been dragging along, and he leaped high into the air. Such joy! Such peace! Such freedom! He would stay forever inside this overwhelming happiness, bask forever in this never-ending bliss.

You cannot. Ieeva's voice was firm. *But do not despair. Nothing will be as it was before.*

The mist formed into an impenetrable white wall before him.

What is this?

The question went unanswered as the first images appeared. A young boy—thin, sad, lonely—sitting in a cell-like room, starkly furnished. *My boyhood room!* he realized with a shock.

The boy's thoughts rushed into his mind—*Why can't I be someone else? Why must I always be me?*

My thoughts! his mind shouted. The anguished self-monologues cut as sharp now as they had then, the thoughts—*his* thoughts—like stropped razors ribboning his internals. How was this possible? He swiveled toward the wolf, thinking it was some trick meant to deceive him.

Still your mind, soothed the wolf. *Only then will you see true the beauty that is you.*

SWACK

With astounding speed, a belt struck the young boy's fear-stricken face, the buckle's prong ripping a bleeding gouge from his eye socket to his chin, splitting his cheek. Thane flinched, his hand reaching to his own cheek, his own scar, but his fingers found no indentation. He felt the other cheek, then the first again. Both were smooth as glass.

The boy cried out as he fell sideways, his hands smashing against his gaping cheek to keep his tongue from falling out. The image faded, though the sounds of the boy's sobbing continued on, growing louder until they became the crashing bellow of white-capped waves raking a shingle shore. Far off, two bright green eyes appeared above the heaving water, their mesmeric beauty irresistible.

Thane leaned forward and pointed. *Maarathia!*

No, the wraithwolf demurred. *Maarathia's helpmeet, sent to save you. The merequis to whom seafarers pay tribute in bread and wine.*

Always Thane had considered the Rabboutier ritual of casting bread and wine upon the waters before setting off to sea as so much nonsense, and it disquieted him to realize he might have been mistaken in this, too. He'd made so many mistakes.

The boy—older, thinner, sadder, lonelier—came into view, running into the surf, his skinny legs fighting the incoming tide for several steps before he hurled himself into the watery arms of forgetting. The boy sank, his chest burning hot despite the chill surrounding him, his limbs like stone. An unseen force shoved up against his aching, heavy body, only stopping when the boy's scarred face—*my face!*—thrust out of the water in the wide-mouthed arc of a leaping fish.

A horsey head sporting ribbed fins where the mane should be and iridescent scales where the coat should be, rose up in front, a broad back bumping against his legs until he wrapped them around the creature's scaly sides like seaweed. The merequis pommeled its way toward shore, though the boy knew little of it, for even now, it felt like a forgotten dream. Thane's waking recollections only began with the all-too-real pinch and scratch of shore rock against his back, and the wet, sucking sound of seawater in his ears, his eyes fluttering open to a ring of shadow-struck faces staring down.

But it was the Rabboutiers that saved me...

Yes, after a time. But it was the All that saved you first.

The words lingered in his mind. He'd known this and yet, for so long, he'd denied the existence of anything beyond the perception of his senses. The enormity of his blunder hit him full force as the memory played on.

Amongst the Rabboutiers stood a dark-brown youth, his wavy black hair flowing to his waist. Thane knew him instantly—*Rodric, so young and pretty.* The boy—*Me!*—grasped onto the youth's hand, and a thrilling shock spiked up his arm and into his heart.

Thane closed his eyes, regret crushing his chest. A nudge brought him round. Ieeva stared up at him, her eyes full of love.

You can yet restore that which was lost. Hope and belief always find a way.

The pressure in his chest eased, replaced by an incredible lightness that made him want to laugh and cry and sing and shout all at the same time. The wolf nudged his leg again, shepherding his giddy thoughts back to the fog-screen as another set of images appeared.

A different view this time—looking past curled chest hair into the black-brown thicket of a massive beard while strong arms bore him up and unseen legs stumped him forward.

Lemal Falla. The name carried a nostalgic pleasure when it popped into Thane's mind. Falla—his original captain—had been the first kind man he'd ever known, excepting Rodric, who was only a boy then too.

The view switched again, and Thane could see a boat anchored further up the way. Falla carried the boy—*Me!*—toward it, the cluster of Rabboutiers orbiting around him like stray sparks rounding a blacksmith's hammer. The dark-skinned youth—*Rodric!*—hovered nearby until the boy—*Me!*—was laid out on the rabbout's sea-silvered deck.

This he remembered as if it had happened yesterday, and yet, he'd forgotten so much. Why hadn't he remembered the merequis?

Nothing is ever forgotten nor lost. But not every memory serves. You had much to overcome before you were ready to know the whole of your truth.

I must be dead. It was the only explanation Thane could find for his circumstances.

You are not, the wolf responded. *Your healing is near at hand. From now you will remember these truths. Go forth and live accordingly.*

A new and different feeling came over him. An acceptance that his many flaws and mistakes were of no consequence in the grander scheme in which his life was viewed. They were all part and parcel of the maran he was becoming, and for that he was glad.

CHAPTER FORTY-THREE
WHAT IT SEEMS

The dreams started the night after the daala was lost and found.

Most were disjointed scenes of blue-skinned Xetili drumming and dancing and shouting atop the grogakee's shining mountain beneath an ash-gray sky weeping fat, happy tears. Twice, Xyleea had dreamed of her own people—the Ushoku—their nut-brown bodies painted blue, their pink-soled feet splashing water onto their bent knees and thick thighs as they jumped like young bajee into shining black puddles. Once, she'd dreamed of strangers, some with faces like pale moons, clapping and singing along with blue-marked Xetili and Ushoku, their flinging hands and upturned faces speckled with the dazzling glints from a skyful of sparkling leaves. She'd awakened afterward feeling there was some great truth lurking beyond the *beekabeeka* all dreams became once morning dawned.

Kaambree also seemed different since the daala's loss and return, its eyes often set upon the horizon for long spells, its supple trunk pointed into the wind to funnel out its secret scents. Xyleea tried reaching inside the tuskee's mind, hoping the old mother smelled water, but there was only the *dom-dom-dom* of its heart and the yearning of a mountain tugging at its feet.

Xyleea now carried the daala on top of her head, tucked beneath the chuulzu kereet. The first time she'd snugged the headpiece down, the daala had fitted up into the concave interior as if the two had been made for each other. Perhaps they had been. Had Cree Shee carried the daala there? If only she could ask her galeesha. The pain of Cree Shee's death tightened its grip on Xyleea's heart.

Carrying the daala on her head did something else. The yearning that pulled at the tuskee's feet had begun grasping her own thoughts, nudging her toward a future she couldn't make out, though she was as certain as Kaambree it lay on the grogakee's sparkling mountain. She now wondered whether the vivid dreams were her own, or images trickling down from the daala atop her head. The ancestors had never been so bold with their leadings—always confining themselves to inklings and coincidences—nor had her dreams ever felt so real.

Dreaming of the Xetili and their blue mud thrilled her sleeping mind but jumbled her waking thoughts into a confusion of empathy and fear. Always before, Xyleea had known her place in the world, as well as the place of her people, never questioning the rightness of her beliefs or traditions. But now, after seeing the Xetili's suffering and sharing their blue mud, after stomping and singing with them night after night, she wondered if the two tribes weren't more alike than different, their separateness more to do with ancestral warpaths than any real differences between them. In truth, without the scarring and the blue mud, the Xetili were as ordinary as the Ushoku, something she'd never imagined before venturing into the keleekeluk. That they revered the ooribos—the giant snake forever swallowing its tail—while her people venerated the grogakee—the great dragon formed from a mountain—seemed of little consequence when they were all facing certain destruction.

Perhaps the daala wished for both peoples to put aside their differences and cease their warring. Perhaps that was why an uncountable number of Xetili had been running toward the grogakee's home for as many days as she had fingers and toes. As soon as the thought struck, she knew it was right, in the same way she knew that she and the tuskee were being led to the mountain. But knowing something for oneself was far different than convincing others of an idea's truth. The losses on both sides had been severe. Her own galeesha had fallen to a Xetili dart—her parents too—as had the loved ones of many others in the wasakagee. To ask them to forget the losses they'd suffered and the cruelties they'd endured was akin to asking them to turn themselves inside out. The effort would be far greater than most could accept, with an outcome none could envision.

As Kaambree plodded forward, the idea prodded and poked, occupying Xyleea so thoroughly that long stretches passed without notice making it seem as though the sun had raced across the sky and into its red-streaked bed in the time it took a maandaba to hoot a warning.

Soon the dark would steal what light remained, and her eyes would turn again to the bright colors of her nighttime mind. She said a prayer to the ancestors and to the daala, asking both to bring forth the answers she sought as they wove together the dreams that would carry her through till morning.

Elorah, her staff in one hand, placed her other on Essiant's forehead. A starshine pathway unrolled like a glittering carpet, and the pair were away, streaking across snowy highlands at the speed of thought.

A settlement of round stone buildings with a six-sided pillar at its center came into view. Voriens howled her forward, urging her toward the western edge. Most she recognized, but there was one whose throaty voice was both known and unknown. How could both be true?

Your soul understands in ways your mind cannot, Essiant assured.

An elegant black wolf emerged from the fog, and Elorah felt her guardian's rising cheer.

Ieeva. The name came into Elorah's mind in a flash of understanding, bringing with it the knowledge that this was Thane's wraithwolf. The black wolf gave a bow then turned toward a roundhouse prominent before them, two huge men upon its doorstep like fur-wrapped statues.

With a thought she and Essiant were inside, slipping through the stone wall as easily as wind slips through trees. Elorah sensed four distinct presences. Aikin and Rachmyn, a girl who seemed familiar, and Thane, a seething darkness surrounding his prostrate form.

The darkness is his pain, the heat is his suffering.

The black wraithwolf bent low to peer into Thane's contorted face.

Elorah turned to her beloved guardian.

What can we do?

From here, very little. His physical form can only be healed using forces within the plane in which it exists.

Though disappointed, Elorah understood why Essiant's words must be so. The only thing to do was set a touchpoint and return, bringing with her the knowledge of how to find this roundhouse with all due speed. From what she'd seen, there wasn't a moment to lose.

Essiant, along with the other Voriens, rejoiced at the finding of Ieeva. The wolf had slipped away during the fray with the Malvisse, drawn to her night-ward for a battle of a different sort, a crisis of health crashing upon him. Ieeva had flown to his side to provide a steadying presence as he grappled with an acute infirmity that endangered his manifest form.

Though there was little the remaining pack could do for her ward's sufferance, they nonetheless sent their vorik to Ieeva as she ushered him through the memory renewal that would either prepare him for a return to Inverna or spark a rally of his physical state. The guardian had intuited her ward's need to unburden his mind of debilitating thoughtforms and had crafted a fever dream to restore his waking mind's recollection of events long suppressed. The plan had worked, her night-ward latching on to a deeper understanding of his path and a renewed sense of purpose. Essiant hoped it would be enough to see him through.

Coming back into her body was a terrific shock. Elorah hadn't realized what cold was until she found herself inside her frozen shell trying to force it awake. Her limbs hammered, and her teeth chattered, her eyelids sealing tight. Only the spot beneath Sylvi's pendant felt warm; the rest was some combination of numbness and shaking.

She was laid flat on a stack of blankets in the thick of a silverneedle brake, Haedyn and Mierrle sat on either side, and she could feel their worry beyond her body's shuddering and pain. She was wearing her grandfather's wemble, but it felt as if she'd been wearing nothing at all.

Haedyn pulled her shaking body against his own, fanning out his cloak to surround them both as he held her tight, her face mashed against his leather vest, her staff caught between them. Her chattering lessened as she listened to the stirrings of his bird, her mind conjuring up a memory of sitting in her family's witterang next to a crackling fire, her mother and grandmama discussing clan doings while the clock ticked away the night.

They stayed pressed together until her shaking ceased. Only then did she push herself away, her mind fixing upon what they must do, the twin suns of his eyes looking down at her upturned face with a softness that fluttered her stomach. The urge to kiss him struck again, and she scrabbled to her feet to keep from falling against him into oblivion.

"I thank you," she said as she cased her staff, a tremble in her voice.

Haedyn eyed her with a curious mixture of hopefulness and trepidation that quickened her pulse. Did he know what she was thinking? Her cheeks flushed as she looked at Mierrle.

Deep lines indented the space between her friend's eyebrows, her mouth forming a downward arc. Elorah smiled as she helped her friend to her feet.

"I know where they are."

"Where?" Mierrle and Haedyn asked in unison.

"Locked up in a Drasgor roundhouse." Mierrle gave an involuntary shiver, and she hugged herself. Elorah looked at Haedyn. "Rachmyn is fine," she said. His taut face went slack with relief. She turned to Mierrle, "As is Aikin."

Mierrle's face beamed before clouding again. "And Thane?"

"I'm afraid he's been injured." Elorah bit her lip to keep from saying more.

Mierrle's gaze dropped, the lines between her eyebrows deepening. "What if we don't find them?" she murmured.

"Worry steals hope," Elorah said, reciting one of Grandmama Vaytah's favorite sayings. "And hope steals fear. Keep worry far off and hope ever near."

Mierrle didn't look convinced. Elorah didn't blame her. An adage was one thing, real life something else. Perhaps another of her grandmama's sayings was more appropriate—every storm has its end, if one can endure until then.

Haedyn had the ponies cinched to his gelding, ready. They mounted up and set out, Mierrle riding double behind Elorah who picked up her reins and pointed the gelding west.

She forced herself not to think about the dangers between here and where they were going, concentrating instead on what they would do once they got there. That task would be difficult enough without worrying about things that might never happen.

The village was a day's ride away, but given the rundown state of the stock and the drag of snow melting to mud, it would likely take two. She said a prayer to the All to preserve Thane long enough for them to reach him. Though she wanted to go faster, she kept her mount's pace at a brisk walk, knowing she would be risking them all if they pushed too hard, admonishing Haedyn several times to slow down when he tried to forge ahead. She understood his urgency—she felt it herself—but she couldn't allow that to overtake her reason. The only concession she would make, as night began to fall, was to keep moving despite the dark and their own exhaustion. She hoped it would be enough.

⁂

The dark-haired man was dying. Brynz was sure of it. She'd seen blood fever too many times to think anything different. Even with the lancing and draining, the wound was full of corruption. Without flushing it thoroughly, its poison would soon overcome him. It was a pity; she'd been counting on him to help her find a way to Zell, but his prospects looked grim.

The pale-haired man dropping down from the smoke-hole had given her a terrible fright, an errant gust from her flapping hands nearly dislodging his clinging hands. Only Aikin's familiarity with the stranger had tamped her wind a blink before it blew the dangling man completely off his grip.

Her second shock had come when the pale-haired man disappeared then reappeared. Never had she seen such a wonderful trick, and she was desperate to learn how it was accomplished.

Uhnkre had provided her third shock, offering to escort Aikin and Thane to the border under his protection. He hadn't included her for reasons known only to him, but she did notice a softening of his manners and speech when he addressed her now, so she didn't think it was a cruelty on his part. She couldn't imagine what had changed, but she didn't mind not being shouted at with words that sounded like stone striking stone. Even the others didn't shout as much, except Kif who seemed to hate her more than ever. If he had his way, a dras through the chest would be her fate. He'd tried to get her killed when they'd stood before what Uhnkre called the Uhlk of the Etts. She had no experience with governance other than a singular monarch, so the idea of several leaders having equal power over the future was difficult for her to grasp. That Uhnkre had managed to influence proceedings enough to keep them from being killed was also hard to understand. It unsettled her head and made her stomach hurt, something like the tumult she'd felt when Garrod had plucked her from the orphan's home. With all she'd done since that fateful day, there were times she wished she hadn't been singled out for a better life. In her view, "better" only meant "different." It was hard to see her present life as preferable to a goatherd's on some remote mountainside. That quietude appealed far more than current circumstances.

Aikin and the pale-haired man sat on the bed frame, conversing in a language she didn't understand, their eyes darting toward her then away as if she were a curiosity. Being stared at and whispered about was familiar enough, but it still nettled. She sniffed and put her attention on Thane, determined not to let their low talk dent her. If they weren't careful, she'd blast them both against the stone wall and crack their heads open. Then, they'd have something worth talking about. She sniffed again, her will simmering up as the whispering continued. The air around her swirled as she surveyed Thane. He'd lain quiet for some time, and she had a sinking feeling they'd lost him.

Aikin jutted his chin and rose to his feet. She refocused, the air settling as he walked over, wariness in his eyes despite his thin-lipped smile. She cocked her head as he drew near.

He stood staring for a long moment, as if he didn't know how to begin.

"Yes?" she asked, one eyebrow raising.

"We were wondering whether you're happy staying behind once we leave?"

"No." She drew the word out as she shook her head.

He nodded as if he suspected as much. "My friend has something that can take down even the biggest men. A sleeping powder you might say. No lasting harm but a snootful in the right noses would give us time to get away with plenty of distance in between."

"Interesting," Brynz said. She gave the pale-haired man a cursory glance. "How does it work?"

"We'd have to be careful. Rachmyn is immune, but if you or I or..." he bobbed his head toward Thane, "...were to breathe it, we'd be out like..." he snapped his fingers, "...that."

"I see," Brynz said, not seeing at all.

"I've noticed you have some ability with wind. Very precise from what I've observed."

She was startled by his perception but managed to keep her gaze level as he pressed on.

"Between my friend's dust, and your excellent skill..." he wagged his thumb between himself and the pale-haired man, "...we could overcome the guards with no one being the wiser. Of course, you'd have to come with us. We don't have much to offer. Nothing at all except a chance at freedom, but if you want away as much as I think you do, this could be your chance."

Brynz crossed her arms and frowned then looked toward the pale-haired man. His silvery gaze was sharp. Could she trust these two? She glanced at Thane. "What about him?"

"We'll have to carry him. No way around that."

That they were willing to risk their own chances to save their friend helped bolster her trust. She nodded curtly.

Aikin turned. "Rachmyn, I think we've got a plan."

The pale-haired man—Rachmyn, she must remember to call him that—bobbed his head.

Elorah made another check of the map she carried in her head. The village, by her reckoning, should be coming into sighting distance.

They'd been traveling for long hours through the dark and, in an effort to keep fatigue from dragging down her eyelids, she plotted and replotted their course against the map she'd memorized and the intuition her peering had gained.

Mierrle slumped against Elorah's back, her slow breathing evidence she'd fallen asleep. After the first league, Haedyn had dropped back, keeping his mount a few steps behind as they traversed the changing landscape. The snow had reduced to white blodges scattered over stony ground painted silver-bright by moonlight. Soon the blush of dawn would chase the flattering shine away but for now, all about them was beauty and grace.

Ahead, an irregular series of lumps distinguished the village from the horizon.

"Smoke."

Haedyn's voice cut through her thoughts. Yes, she could smell it now. She'd been too busy inside her own head to be mindful, but now that she put her attention to it, the odor was unmistakable. They must be getting close.

She pulled up and signaled for Haedyn to draw alongside. With the darkness waning, she wanted a plan before they went further. She grasped her pendant as she coordinated her thinking mind with her intuitive self. She suspected their friends were in a roundhouse on the western edge of the village. That was where they should begin. The pendant warmed, its vibration tickling her palm. It was the confirmation she needed. She pointed. "There's the village," she whispered. "They're on the far side. We'll circle south and come in from the west. Once we're close, we'll decide how best to free them."

Haedyn studied the view. "A fire might help..." His face went somber. "...if I had some to spare."

Her lips lifted into a slight smile. "I might be able to help." His look of astonishment made her grin. "If need be."

CHASSABIRD

When chassabird crosses the sky,
And Ooribos swallows the moon,
White mountain will quake and tremble,
As the world turns from old to new.

Translator's note: Xetilian prophecy

Chuulzu Keleekeluk—(Spirit of the Forest)
Transcribed from witness statements collected and translated for the
Most Exalted Monarch, Geldizian Rennesseau, by a scribe

CHAPTER FORTY-FOUR
STONE AND WIND

Rachmyn opened the vial of speck with the greatest care, flaking off the wax seal with his fingernail so that not one grain was disturbed. He'd already struck a shim from the chair leg and wedged it into the doorframe three hands above his head. All that was left was to dribble speck onto the shim while the girl kept the air stilled around him. She stood next to Aikin near the back wall to avoid inhaling any of the wolfken.

He turned. The girl's gray-blue stare held steady while Aikin split his attention between Thane's balled-up form, the girl, and Rachmyn.

"Once she dusts them, how long before they fall?" Aikin asked.

"Not long. We'll need a ready escape." Rachmyn crossed to where the girl stood.

Aikin knelt. "I found a weak spot," he said, pointing near the floor. "There's a crack starting here..." His finger traced a stair-step crack up four runs. "...that goes to here. If I push these..." his finger outlined a triad of stones, "...everything between will fall away, leaving a hole here." He sketched an oblong shape onto the wall. "With any luck we can crawl through before the rest of the stones give way. Walls are hard to predict. We could bring the whole building down in one go. Curved walls are stronger than straights, which should go in our favor. Once the stones are down, we'll take Thane out." Thane moaned, and Aikin looked down. "It might not hurt if he got a snootful on the way." He turned to speak with the girl in her windy language, her gaze darting between him and the wall. She twirled a finger toward the door, and he nodded. He turned back to Rachmyn. "She'll come through last, once her wind has done its work."

"Speck has consequences beyond what you can see," Rachmyn said. "Involving forces you don't understand."

Aikin shifted his gaze, his expression hardening. "I don't need to understand any of that weirdness." He shook his head.

Rachmyn set his jaw. "I wouldn't expect someone like you to know the forces of which I speak, but make no mistake, they exist, and your ignorance of them does not change that."

Aikin shrugged. "I deal with the here and now. What I can see with these eyes..." His index finger pointed toward his narrowed eyes. "...and hear with these ears..." The finger jabbed toward first one then the other ear. "...and feel with these hands." He flung both splayed hands out, palm up. "That's enough for me."

"I've no doubt that's true," Rachmyn said. "One must know one's limits after all." Aikin's eyes flashed as he decided whether to be offended. Rachmyn gave him a rare smile. "But don't worry. You won't be called upon. There are others far more capable who are willing to step into the gap." He hoped, anyway. Oru Fen was tricky, far trickier than predicting a wall's subsidence. It was a risk they would have to take.

Aikin huffed and looked down at Thane. "We should make a backboard to carry him." He walked to the broken chair and examined it. The back was all of a piece, and a few stout kicks separated it from the seat and the remaining front leg. "This should work," he said, holding it up.

Rachmyn stuck an extra vial into his vest pocket before shouldering the rucksack. It never hurt to be prepared.

Aikin and Rachmyn were lowering Thane's crimped body onto the chairback when the doorhandle jiggled.

"Now!" Rachmyn shouted as the door swung wide, the cry getting swallowed by the rumble of falling stones. Aikin had preceded him, the wall shuddering. Three runs of stones tumbled inward, opening a large hole in the wall's center.

The blond northman stepped through the open doorway, his mouth gaping at the unexpected sight of the collapsing wall. He cried out, and two dark-haired guards rushed in, their faces craning over his shoulder.

A whoosh of air blew past Rachmyn's ears, driving the speck from the shim into the open mouths of all three northmen. The blond northman doubled over while the two behind leaned against their thighs, all three hacking and choking.

Rachmyn grabbed one end of the backboard and Aikin the other as they scuttled Thane over the strewn stones toward the wall's rough-edged opening. Rachmyn balanced the chairback on the rubble pile and climbed through before yanking it hard, inadvertently pulling it out of Aikin's grip. The chairback skittered through the hole then pitched sideways, dumping Thane onto the ground with a sickening thunk.

Spunk! I've killed him!

Aikin's shocked face glared through the hole a split before he clambered out.

Rachmyn bundled Thane onto the backboard, noting a lump rising on the scarred man's forehead to match the two lining his jaw.

"My head..." was all Thane could manage.

At least he's alive.

Rachmyn clamped his hand over Thane's mouth, his eyes roaming their perimeter. He needed to conjure a mirrorshield and quick. He stuck his hand into his pocket, his fingers curling around his shard as he summoned his will and projected what he was seeing.

"You fumbling fool!" Aikin whisper-shouted.

"Stop talking and start helping," Rachmyn gritted, his mindshield dropping then reforming.

"Where in blazes are you?"

"Here." Rachmyn dropped the shield until Aikin caught sight of him and slashed over.

The girl climbed back-first through the gap in the wall then looked around in confusion.

Aikin hissed words at her then blurted, "Show her!" Rachmyn

dropped the shield again, and the girl's face went wide with shock. He refocused while Aikin frantically pawed the air to get her moving. She hurtled forward, smashing against his bulk then bouncing off onto her hindparts. Aikin snaked out an arm and grappled her to her feet.

The blond northman poked his head out—eyes bleary, face shadowed—before wallowing his way through the hole. He shambled forward, his feet stumbling over rubbled stone. He stopped and turned as another ominous rumble sounded.

A second northman was halfway through the hole when the breached wall collapsed, engulfing his prostrated body in a massive pile of stone, a large section of frozen roof-dirt landing on top and breaking into uneven slabs.

The blond northman staggered backward, then forward, then backward before teetering down like a felled tree.

Aikin and Rachmyn sprang up—Thane stretchered between them —and scurried away, the girl grabbing Aikin's cloak to keep from being left behind.

The group bumbled toward the pathway in a herky-jerky caravan of Rachmyn pulling, Aikin pushing, Thane clinging on, and the girl stumbling behind, her grasping hand nearly tearing Aikin's cloak from his body.

Villagers ran toward the disaster, shouting words that sounded like hurled rocks. Rachmyn had to duck and dodge several times while projecting half-formed shadow-shapes to obscure the ragtag caravan humping an escape. It was exhausting, and he could feel his reserves draining with every step, his head throbbing from the effort of putting his attention on two things at once. He wanted to thumb his shard, but there was no way to stick his hand in his pocket and hold the backboard at the same time, so he settled for the feeling of it against his thigh as he progged forward.

They stuck close to the buildings until they were out of the village.

Rachmyn locked his eyes forward, trying not to imagine a swarm of armed hulks raging after them. Only when they neared the ravine did he slow, his eyes drawn to a familiar silhouette loping toward them.

Elgre.

The wolf looked no worse for wear from his recent foray with the village dogs. Neither was there any sign of the huge creatures, leaving Rachmyn to wonder what trick the crafty wolf had managed. He bent his knees and lowered the chairback to the ground, his screaming shoulders and stinging arms rejoicing at the relief.

"Thank the Urslan," Aikin said, setting down his end. "My arms are falling off."

Rachmyn checked his shard. Yes, there it was.

The girl stepped from behind Aikin and Rachmyn startled. He'd almost forgotten she was with them.

The wolf pricked his ears and stared into the distance before pelting away at top speed. Rachmyn wondered at that but turned his attention to Thane.

The scarred man pushed up onto one elbow. "I'm still here," he croaked.

The girl looked as shocked as Thane by his words.

No mistake, he wasn't out of danger, but hearing Thane speak gave Rachmyn hope. A man could do much for himself simply by believing he could. "You're all right," he said, grasping Thane's shoulder.

Thane looked up at him. "Thanks to you." His gaze went to Aikin, shifting his feet, and the girl a half-span beyond. "All of you."

"You would have done the same," Aikin muttered, his words overfull and raw.

"I wouldn't have thought so, but I hope you're right. It sits within me now, how uncharitable I can be, though I don't own it proudly. I've much to regret, I'm afraid."

"We've all regrets," Rachmyn said, clearing his throat. "This adventure for a start."

Thane coughed out a chuckle. "True enough," he said, chuckle-coughing again.

Rachmyn's eyes followed Elgre's run. The night had nearly gone, and they needed to move on. The Drasgor were likely already on their trail. But first, he needed his hobbled horse. "I'll be back," he said, setting off.

Aikin called after him. "Where do you think you're going?"

"To find my horse."

"And we're supposed to sit out here in the open until you get back?"

492

The Caeldish had a point. Rachmyn turned and strode to the chairback then waited for Aikin to take hold of the other end. They carried it to the ravine bed, setting Thane beside the overhang of an eroded escarpment. It wasn't a cave, but it would suit. The girl followed, her gaze flitting back the way they'd come.

Rachmyn set off again, the moon lighting his path. The gelding shouldn't be too far.

Elorah saw the wolf before Haedyn.

They'd been working their way toward the village when he appeared from the shadowy scrub, tongue lolling, teeth gleaming in the gray light, not three paces ahead.

"Elgre!" Elorah exclaimed, her horse shying sideways.

Mierrle's arms vised Elorah's waist. "Rachmyn's wolf?" She sounded groggy as her chin grazed Elorah's shoulder.

"He must be close," Haedyn said, pulling his skittering gelding alongside, his head swiveling to look for his friend. All the hoofed animals' heads riveted toward the wolf, their eyes rimming white, their nostrils flaring pink. One of the ponies blew a warning snort and stamped a front hoof.

The wolf took a step closer, his gaze intensifying.

"I think he wants us to follow him." Haedyn murmured.

Elorah nodded, her pendant vibrating against her breastbone. "I think you're right."

The wolf turned and loped away.

Haedyn gigged his horse into a chasing trot, snapping the reluctant ponies alongside as he followed the wolf. Elorah squeezed her gelding into a trot, her pendant urging her onward, Mierrle's hands bracing her waist.

WARNINGS OF A WRAITHWOLF (EXCERPT EIGHT)

The INFINITE EYE... ggrrff... known by many as the AGYA... ggrrff... YEARNS always for RETURN... ggrrff... to its SEAT of POWER... ggrfff... within the great good FOUNDER... gggrrfff... for whom it was CONFORMED.

HEAR THIS!

The END of SUFFERING... ggrrrff... BEGINS with the RETURN... ggrrff... of this VITAL SPARK... grrff... for IT ALONE... gggrrrfff... is the CONNECTOR... gggrrrfff... by which a FOUNDER'S... gggrrff... MANIFEST FORM may REUNITE... ggrrrff... with its SPIRITUAL CORPUS.

KNOW THIS!

ONLY when the INFINITE EYE... gggrrr... of EVERY FOUNDER... ggrrff... has been RESTORED... ggrrfff... will EVERY CREATION... gggrrrffff... within EVERY SPHERE... gggrrrfff... ACHIEVE the PERFECTION... gggrrfff... that is every SOUL'S DESIRE.

–Collected and Interpreted for the Most Exalted Monarch,
Geldizian Rennesseau, by a scribe

Eye Inside

I have an eye inside of me,
Revealing things I cannot see,
From veiled worlds where I cannot be,
When clouds of doubt lie in between.

I have an eye inside of me,
That takes me far past common dream,
To places fair where souls roam free,
In grace and ideality.

–Epigent Elorah Niav bai Calliaigh, aged 12
Volume 4579, Page 217
Essentia Libre, Academie Vorik

CHAPTER FORTY-FIVE
THE LAST AND THE FIRST

A sudden panic made it hard for Haedyn to breathe. Elgre had led them along a ravine of loose stone and eroded banksides until they'd come upon Aikin standing over Thane, the scarred man lying beneath an overhang, a tall girl with knotted hair crouched nearby. Haedyn took no notice, his eyes only looking for Rachmyn, but there was no sign of his friend. He watched Elgre lope north, his thoughts thick with fear.

Elorah crowded her horse next to him, her free hand taking hold of his arm, her eyes finding his. She gave him an encouraging smile, as if she could hear his quaking thoughts, and his terror began to fade.

"Don't worry," Mierrle said, her expression earnest.

Aikin hustled over as Mierrle and Elorah dismounted, then, taking hold of their reins, leaned forward to speak into Elorah's ear. Her face went serious as she rummaged her satchel from one of the pony packs and walked to Thane's prostrate form. Haedyn watched her go, a chilling fear for the scarred man taking hold.

Elorah put on a reassuring smile as she knelt and clasped Thane's hand. He opened his eyes. She murmured to him before easing off his leggings, exposing the full damage. Thane winced and groaned, his legs an alarming shade of pale except for the puffy, purpled wound. Haedyn's stomach lurched.

Mierrle hurried past, removing her cloak as she went. She fluttered it down onto Thane's chest. He blinked watery eyes, one tear tracing down his temple. Mierrle wiped it away, her own eyes welling.

Haedyn dismounted.

"He's lucky to be alive. No thanks to you," Aikin bit out.

Haedyn stiffened. "I'm sorry, what?"

Aikin sniffed. "Just like a falding to take off when trouble shows up. At least you salvaged the pony. I guess that's something."

Haedyn felt a stab of guilt. He hadn't meant to abandon Aikin and Thane, but things hadn't gone to plan. He rolled his head to crack his neck. "Where's Rachmyn?"

"Keep your voice down. He went to find his horse."

A dark blot appeared on the horizon. "Over here!" Haedyn shouted, waving his hand until Aikin chopped it down with a straight-armed swing.

"Shut it, you daft fool. You'll get us all killed," he hissed.

Haedyn's jaw tightened as he whipped round—one fist balling up, his shoulder lifting to throw a blow. A shiver raced down his spine. He turned to see Mierrle shiny-eyed, tears spilling onto her cheeks.

"Don't fight." She looked from Haedyn to Aikin. "Please." She unwound one arm from her waist to swipe her sleeve across her eyes and leaking nose. Without her cloak she was beginning to shiver.

Haedyn dropped his hand to his side while Aikin cleared his throat. "Yes, well. What's done is done," he muttered, thrusting the reins toward Haedyn before retrieving a blanket from one of the packs and stalking off.

Haedyn watched him go, anger pinching his eyebrows together. *Who does he think he is?* He led the horses and the ponies to a low-slung tree and tied them off with angry, looping yanks. It wasn't as if he'd known the damage the bravik would do. And anyway, he hadn't gotten off easy. He'd used every scrap of vor he possessed to save the horse and the pony. Where would they be if he hadn't? Even to his own mind, the excuse sounded hollow. Grief's teeth. Why was everything always so complicated?

Aikin wrapped the blanket around Mierrle's shoulders, and her tear-smudged face brightened as she tugged it close. He walked over to where Elorah was, leaving Mierrle to watch him go, her face falling.

Haedyn snorted as he put on his glove and nudged Fryk out of his pocket. He finger-upped the bird onto his shoulder, and Fryk's head swiveled, his glittery eyes homing in on Mierrle. She averted her gaze as Haedyn snugged the sock toe onto the bird's head.

Haedyn felt another set of eyes rake over him.

It was the knotty-haired girl. She cinched the fox pelt tighter as she watched him handle his bird. He hadn't credited how tall she was, taller than him by two hands. Taller than Rachmyn, even. She looked familiar, but he couldn't feature why. *Rachmyn will know. He always remembers faces.* He looked toward the horizon, the blot now taking on the proportions of his old friend.

Good.

His attention went to Thane. Elorah was bent over the damaged leg, one hand spiraling the shilk while she hummed in that way that made his insides feel buzzy. The tall girl shifted, her brow wrinkling, her hand flattening against her midriff as if she could also feel it.

Haedyn understood the tall girl's confusion, remembering well his first encounter with the sensations Elorah inspired. In the time since, his feelings had grown, his initial wonder turning into a delighted awe that, if he was being honest, occupied most of his thoughts. A part of him was embarrassed how often he replayed their moments together—Rachmyn would be appalled at the mental mush pot he'd become—but he couldn't make himself stop.

The wolf trotted by—ears pricked, tail stringing behind—unmindful of the stamping and whickering and pawing he caused as he passed by the horses and ponies.

The tall girl flattened against the bankside, her eyes going wide as the wolf glided past then cut a sharp angle up the embankment. A spindle of dirt roiled up, pushing at the wolf's heels as he crested the ravine bank and disappeared.

Haedyn had heard of wind wycches, but he'd never seen one. The girl paid him no mind, her attention on where the wolf had gone. He looked over at Elorah again.

She'd put away the shilk and had the needle-box out, its lid next to her knee. She reached in again and again, retrieving needles she hummed into bright threads then inserted into Thane's leg. Next, she retrieved the iridescent stone, bringing it to her lips and humming it bright.

Thane's face was blank as the stone sparked the needles together, binding the wound into a thin, pink line.

"She's wonderful, isn't she."

Mierrle was standing beside him. Haedyn smiled and nodded, wishing he could tell Elorah how she made him feel, though he knew he could never find the right words for the emotions inside. He looked again toward the horizon and saw a familiar figure—Rachmyn—the scowl as unmistakable as the two fist bumps. There was no sign of a horse.

Haedyn moved closer as Elorah put away her instruments and shook Thane's arm. He startled awake, then looked down, dread tightening his face until he saw his restored leg. "If this be a dream, don't bid me wake," he burst out, a disbelieving grin crinkling up his scar.

Haedyn recognized the line. Even he'd heard *The Hiegh Lad* enough times to know it.

Thane poked a finger at the tender-pink snakeline winding down his lower leg then shook his head and clambered to his feet. "Fleek me, I can't feel a thing!"

Elorah's smile wavered into a dismayed frown.

Thane laughed. "I mean it doesn't hurt!" He sprang forward and wrapped her in his arms, her gasp giving way to a giggle. Haedyn watched, the flame in his belly flaring into his throat, his head beginning to sweat. Thane set her down, and the inferno settled into its usual smolder.

"Best pull on those leggings and make ready," Aikin prompted as he walked by, the tall girl grabbing his arm to stop him. He leaned toward her as she spoke then nodded before finding a place to sit and check his boot.

Thane wriggled on his tattered leggings then pulled on his stockings and boots.

"What did she say?" Haedyn asked.

Elorah translated. "She's worried the Drasgor will find us. She says we need to be on our way." Elorah stowed her satchel in a pony pack and retrieved her staff.

"Who is she, anyway?" Haedyn asked.

"Brynz Alleu."

Haedyn whirled around. Rachmyn threw up a hand by way of a greeting, and the girl returned the gesture. "You know her?" Haedyn couldn't hide his surprise.

"I know her name," Rachmyn answered, waving away further questions. "The horse is gone," he added, walking over to where Thane leaned against the embankment. Rachmyn's gaze went to the leg. "Spunk. Didn't expect to see you standing."

"Nor did I," Thane said. He stepped forward with a little "ta-da" flourish.

"Your energy field is weak," Elorah interjected. "The shilk evened out what you have, but it's a thin veil you carry now. We'll put you on a gelding to preserve your forces."

She turned to Aikin, spraddle-legged on the ground, readjusting the twine around the leather pouch holding together his boot. "Do you think you can walk?"

"I can." He climbed to his feet, one hand spanking at his backside to clobber out the dust.

"Good." Her gaze turned south, her face taking on a soft radiance. Haedyn strained to see what was so captivating about wind-tangled brush and rocky ground.

"We're so close," she murmured. "A few sols more and we'll have the mountain in our sights and then..." She extended a hand toward the tall girl and spoke in a voice as soft as rain. Ahh, if only that voice was speaking his name. The thought sent a fiery bolt into Haedyn's chest. If he could speak the girl's language he might know what was being said, but no matter. It was enough to hear Elorah's soothing voice.

❦ ❦ ❦ ❦ ❦ ❦

The moment she clasped Brynz's hand, Elorah felt the wrenching emotion inside the tall girl's heart.

Though she hadn't known her name, Elorah recognized her from the festival. Judging by her ragged clothing and knife-sharp physique, she'd been on the run for some time, perhaps since that fateful day that now seemed a lifetime ago. Novah's devastated face floated into Elorah's mind, and her thoughts took a turn. How could she have left when all was chaos and strife? It made her feel a cruel monster for not staying to help her mother and grandmama piece their lives back together. Yet, how could they stitch together a meaningful Therran life when the center of their vorik power lay in ruins. Restoring Therrania was the only way her family and indeed every Caeldish clan could hope to thrive. The only way her people could live as the All intended.

"Welcome, Brynz," she said, using her Acadamie Iellian. "I am Elorah. It seems you are a long way from home." She loosed the girl's hand, then angled her chin, inviting a response.

"I have no home." Brynz said, her affect as flat as her stony eyes. "I have nothing." She stroked a large, silver feather poking from the tether tied round her waist.

"May I see that?" Elorah asked. She had a hunch the feather was important.

Brynz gripped the feather tighter, her gaze hardening.

"Is it from your beautiful gryphon?" Elorah persisted, a small smile creasing her lips.

Brynz startled as recognition lit her face. "You were there."

"Yes," Elorah confirmed.

"You saw what happened." Brynz paused, her expression softening. "You did something to Zell. Something that helped him fly."

"I only meant to mend his wounds," Elorah said. "I didn't realize–"

Brynz cut her off. "I'm glad you did it. I'm glad he's free. I only wish I knew where he was. I worry he's been recaptured, or..." She swallowed hard, her eyes going hot with emotion. "...worse."

Elorah reached toward the feather. "Sometimes, I can see what others cannot," she said in a low voice. "Perhaps I can see your gryphon."

After a moment of consideration, Brynz laid the feather across Elorah's open palm.

Elorah placed her other hand on top and closed her eyes,

summoning her Spyrrt vor then shining it through her palms onto the silver plume.

A vision leaped onto the screen of her mind. The gryphon, wearing bronze bands on its front legs, lounged upon an avobanc shelf jutting out from a larger mountain. Its piercing blue eyes stared at her with peculiar familiarity. Where before the gryphon's azurite gaze had made her fearful and weak, this time she felt invigorated, her heart leaping like a spring lamb, her cheeks flushing pink. Brynz loomed over Elorah in hopeful agony.

"Your gryphon is alive," Elorah confirmed, the vision fading. "And well, though he wears the leg bands." She paused before adding, "I believe he is content." It was an inadequate word for the gryphon's state of ease, but it was the best she could do with her limited Iellian.

Brynz's face cracked into a smile, and she straightened, looking toward the distant peaks. "Do you know where he is?" she squeaked.

"I can say he is on an avobank cliff." Elorah withdrew her vor and handed the feather back. "Wait here. I have something else." She fetched the hallett stone from her satchel then hurried back, feeling Aikin's consternation even as he pretended not to watch. No doubt he was appalled at her having a scrying stone, let alone using it. No matter. She held the thin disc out toward Brynz. "Touch it with the feather."

Elorah directed Spyrrt vor into the flat-black stone the moment Brynz touched it with the feather's rounded tip. Like a coming together of light and dream, the stone's depthless black suffused with a swirling, golden glow then flashed to life, stray sparks flying away from its surface as an image of the gryphon on its avobanc shelf came clear.

Brynz gasped, her hands dropping the feather as they flew up to cover her mouth.

The stone's light faded, and the image blurred into transparency before disappearing. Elorah picked the feather from the ground and handed it back.

"Thank you," Brynz said, eyes brimming as she reclaimed her prize.

"You have a home now," Elorah said, her voice thick. "With us."

Tears spilled from Brynz's eyes, and she gulped a ragged breath.

Elorah hugged the tall girl. Where before there had been sorrow and guilt, there was now relief and, if not happiness, at least its beginnings.

"To my heart you are family," Elorah murmured as Brynz leaned down to cry against her shoulder.

Elorah waited until everyone was asleep before retrieving her scrying stone once again.

After a fortnight, the distance between themselves and the Drasgor had increased enough to provide some comfort but sleep still proved elusive. With so much behind them and Whitemond looming on the horizon, excitement and fear took turns keeping her awake. Thoughts of home crept in as well, and she wished she knew how her mother and grandmama were doing.

Looking at Aikin, stretched out with his head cradled in one crooked arm, she wondered whether the Caeldish clans had capitulated to Her Most Exalted or if they were resisting Iellian rule. He wasn't wrong about the problems facing the clans. She knew this, even if they disagreed on how to solve them. She'd put her hope into raising Therrania, but now, as their moment neared, she wondered whether their efforts would have any real effect on the basin or its people.

She sighed as she stared down at the hallett stone in her hands. Perhaps she could find answers in its dark gaze. She gathered up her Spyrrt vor and pushed it through her palms, imbuing the artifact with a soft, golden glow.

A faint image of her mother appeared on the stone's surface. Elorah bent close, taking in the details. Novah's countenance looked grim, heavy lines denting the corners of her mouth and eyes, her forehead furrowed above pinched eyebrows. Her blond-and-silver hair was hidden beneath the weighty hood of her brown Council cape. Behind stood several similarly dressed figures. An official meeting, perhaps... Elorah concentrated. No, that wasn't it. These were all women, gathered in a forest under cover of darkness. A jangle of furtiveness ran through her. A secret meeting? As soon as she thought it, Elorah dismissed the idea. The images shifted, and she saw that many were holding crystalwood staffs.

How was it that so many still existed after the Council ban?

A shadowy figure handed out more of the rods from a wooden crate to the hooded figures without their own. Why would her mother need crystalwood? What were the emvors doing? Elorah bent closer.

The sound of a throat being cleared recoiled her vorik, the images disappearing as she jerked her head toward the sound.

"Have you always done such things?" Aikin's voice was low, though his gaze cut keen. He'd apparently awakened and come up behind without her knowing.

She sighed. It was no use denying this part of herself any longer.

"Yes," she answered.

He settled into a squat beside her, his gaze riveted on the stone.

"I've never believed in that," he said. "I'm not sure I believe in it even now."

"It isn't a matter of belief. It's a matter of whether such powers exist or not. It is no different than your Therran affinity."

"But you are also Therran. No one has more than one ability."

"There are many things we were never taught at the Academie," Elorah said. "And many truths that were hidden. That doesn't mean these powers don't exist. As you've seen, they do." She chose not to answer his larger question about how she could use both affinities. She hardly knew herself.

He pointed toward the scrying stone. "That seems like something no one should be able to do." His shoulders lifted as he shivered. He shifted his gaze, his eyes clouded with earnest confusion. She could see how hard he was trying to understand, and how much discomfort the effort was causing.

"I know this is all strange to you. It was to me too, when I first learned of it."

"How could you learn of such things if they are not taught or spoken of, or even contemplated by most marans? How is it you discovered these mysterious powers on your own and..." he lowered his voice further, "...how do you know it is safe for you to..." his hand twirled toward the scrying stone, "...use them on tools forbidden by our Council. They surely had reasons for outlawing divination stones and crystalwood."

"There are ways to misuse any form of vorik, as you know from your own efforts against the monarch."

"That was different."

"How so? When were you taught that using your ground-shifting skills to harm another was acceptable?"

Aikin lowered his head, an acknowledgement her words had hit their mark. "What you say has merit," he allowed. "It is something I have thought about, not without regret. But the cause behind my actions was just. *Is* just."

"Does belief in your rightness ameliorate your responsibility to your Academie oath to help all and harm none? Does that oath absent itself when another opposes your version of truth? When your personal aims override it?"

Aikin settled into a sitting position, then pulled up his knees and embraced them. "In truth, I don't know what I think anymore. I believed in the Urslan as a concept, but to see them rise from the ground as living things, that I would never have accepted had I not seen it for myself. Should I doubt my own eyes? I never doubted them before so how can I now? And if I cannot doubt them, how do I deny that the things I don't believe in do exist? I am pressed to face a hard truth, a truth I never wished to know. It gives rise to uneasy thoughts that my mind chews upon often in quiet times like this." He glanced at the scrying stone in her hand. "How did you come by such an arcane instrument?"

"It was a gift," Elorah replied, her mind reaching back to the day Silvi had offered it. Only now did it seem a strange thing for a seeing stone to have been in the rubbish pile of a gardener. Noticing Elorah's interest, Silvi had asked, "Would you like it, dear heart?" without saying what it was or where it had come from as she worked it free from the mound of jaggy pot shards, spent madder floss, and shriveled maycup corms.

"Who gave–" Aikin began.

Elorah interrupted him. "Here." She thrust the black disk toward him. "See for yourself."

Almost as a reflex, Aikin unwrapped one hand to push the stone away. Seizing her chance, Elorah rallied her Spyrrt vor and sent its glow through her palms.

At his touch, the faint imprint of another cloaked figure appeared on the stone's surface. Elorah recognized the imperious bearing and porcelain visage of Cassielle Froigh bai Bairrtraigh.

"What manner of wycchecraft is this?" Aikin blurted, his hand flinging backward as if he'd been burned. The light image blurred into a gold-tinged haze.

"Your desire to see your mother is strong enough to influence the stone," Elorah said. She pushed the instrument forward using one glowing palm while seizing his hand with the other. Caisselle's determined face reappeared in the haze. "As is her desire to see you. She must miss you terribly."

The imaged version of Cassielle raised her arm high, brandishing a crystalwood staff.

"My mother would never use a banned artifact!" Aikin spluttered.

"The stone is a mirror only. It has no ability to embellish," Elorah whispered, her eyes darting toward Thane as he mumbled and turned in his sleep. She waited before continuing. "If she does have a crystalwood staff, I'm sure your mother has a very good reason for it."

Mierrle awoke, one bent arm canting her shoulder upward, the other knuckling away sleep-sand from her eyes. "Is something wrong?" she croaked.

"All is well. Go back to sleep," Elorah soothed.

Mierrle nodded and lay back down, her face smoothing out as she closed her eyes.

Elorah turned to Aikin. "You've made such a sacrifice, leaving behind your loved ones and coming here. My gratitude could never equal what you've given. I should be better at telling you what it means to me to have you here."

Aikin's face softened as he looked at his hand still held in Elorah's grip. "You know, I wouldn't have come for anyone else. Even if Fyndd had asked, I'd have told him no." He gave her a meaningful look. "But now that I have done, I'm committed to giving my best effort."

"You always do," Elorah said. "If there's one thing I can count on, it's that."

"I have to confess, I didn't believe in this endeavor of yours, and my motivations weren't what they should have been. Even now, I can't say I understand more than I did when we set out. The only thing I'm certain of is I know far less about life than I ever imagined. I can't deny the things I've seen since we left the basin, and I can't deny how seeing those things has changed my viewpoint. I've even had dreams about what is to come, and I never thought I would say that." He mugged off a foolish smile, making Elorah laugh, then sobered again. "But if there is even a chance this plan of yours might restore the Caeldish to what they once were, without bloodshed, then I'm happy to be a part of it."

Elorah gripped his hand tighter. "There is a chance, Aikin. More than a chance. If we can work together, using our hearts and our minds, I know we can do much good, not only for the Caeldish, but for all the peoples of the world."

"All people? Even the Drasgor? That would take more than the raising of a parambek. That would take an intervention from the Urslan themselves."

"You never know. That just might happen." She smiled and gave his hand a final squeeze before releasing it. He sprang up.

"If anybody could arrange that, it's you," he said as he helped her to her feet.

THE SEASON FOR
WARNINGS...

...has passed, for that Restoration which was once augured as a distant hope or fanciful dream has, at last, begun. Seek ye now to attune to the quickening forces arising from the ruins of a sundering that has long blunted the vibrance of a wonderfully made world. Determine to be amongst those awakened to these higher energies, for the time has come that every soul may break free from the shackles of the past and dance again amongst the splendid stars.

Rejoice, as the bleak winter of deprivation gives way to the blossoming spring of renewal. No more must creations suffer the darkness and disunion wrought by self-aggrandizement and willful misapplication. No more must they stagnate in the moribund doldrums of imperfect awareness, decrying the spark of Creative Thought within whilst all about swirl the liberating ethers of transformation. Open your venerable soul to the expansive vibrations by which trees walk and serpents talk and stones fly, for they are the basis of all that is, and was, and ever will be. All else is illusion and errancy.

Soon, the anchoring forces of Therran shall resume their rightful place within the resonating energies of Eolemar in all their myriad forms, from the tremble of the invisible speck to the tremor of the insurmountable peak. So too shall these foundational forces stabilize energies long unbalanced *within the beings of the manifest world, and in so doing, help clear the path toward self-actualization, the so-called Way spoken of by the initiates of old. Know that this sacred pattern was writ upon your soul at inception, and there it remains, awaiting reawakening either by the application of the focused vibrations of a parambek, or by concentrated meditation upon same.*

By the hand of the Erynvor the first of the ancient gateways will resume its sacred charge, and a Noble Founder will be released from His long imprisonment. So too, individual souls will end their long toil under the yoke of spiritual blindness and ascend the golden steps of enlightenment leading to

Primeryn Vor, that great and glorious Maker of whom the poets write and the prophets dream.

We, The Elect, have spoken.

CHAPTER FORTY-SIX
UNDONE

The long-lost Therran Agya had resurfaced in the most unlikely of places—the wildlands west of the abhorrent mountain—after remaining hidden for uncounted eryns. Its keeper, a naif with little experience in either the waking or dreamtime worlds, had a wraithwolf as stout as ten and as wily as twenty. It was this fact that had allowed the orb-keeper to evade the Wycche's noose.

There had been no opportunity for subterfuge during the girl's waking time, as her only companion had been a pure-hearted beast. Opportunities had also been few in Oru Fen, the imminent threat to life and limb making the girl edgy and unable to sleep. Only lately had she begun to dream.

The moment the dreamspheres began appearing, the Wycche went on alert, the dreamer's cargo making her arrival in the realm conspicuous to those with an interest. And the Wycche certainly had an interest.

Once she'd identified the orb-keeper, the Wycche wasted no time, impressing upon her wraithwolf the importance of the Agya, as if he didn't already know it. In turn, Venge summoned twenty of the craftiest Malvisse, presenting them with a flourish.

Behold, my liege, these champions for the cause who await your bidding.

The Wycche surveyed the assembly, noting with satisfaction the black-hearted stares and aberrant sneers of the hardened etheriant thieves. With such a group under her direction, she felt sure the interference she had planned would force this latest Erynvor to either modify her rigid morality or retreat to Inverna.

But this wasn't the time for idle speculation; it was the time for swift results.

It was costly, each of the wolves requiring their etheriant reward up front as a condition of their service. Nothing would dissuade them from the bribe, not even promises of a doubled reward once the deed was done.

"Double of nothing is nothing," they all said, the canny chiselers, leaving her little choice. They fell for none of her ruses—the promise of delayed payment bringing higher reward, the attempt to bait and switch, the appeal to reason (they had little) or honor (they had none). Nothing worked, and so she bestowed the etheriant begrudgingly, with the promise of more in hopes the wolves wouldn't cut and run.

It worked for a time. The horde beset the orb-keeper's dreamsphere and its stardust-clad guardian with all due fury, but the wraithwolf was not one to be cajoled or bullied from its post. Nor was it easily drawn into a fight, leaving its night-ward vulnerable should it fail.

The Wycche soon lost all patience.

Overcome this deluded fool and make clear the door! she thundered, her dark raiment whipping into a malevolent twirl.

The deadblack-clad Malvisse attacked—toothfangs gnashing, curved claws slashing—their furious mindwords striking the guardian wolf's retorts like swords clouting a mighty wall.

Mouk and Flaye hit first, Mouk slashing at the guardian's chest armor and receiving a slashed cheek for his trouble, Flaye diving for the stardust on the guardian's back and losing the tip of an ear.

Kruszk, Tenz, plus seven more charged, five going for the wraithwolf's chest, two for the underbelly, and two for the hindquarters. Venge went for the throat, his gouging teeth embedding in the vertex where head met neck.

The guardian's armor breached as the Malvisse tore in, trails of stardust flowing out into the orusphere. The attackers' greedy deadblack sucked up the spilling energy, strengthening for a second attack.

The orb-keeper's wolf heaved back then lunged forward, its hindquarters kicking away from a set of snapping fangs. The move threw the Malvisse off but not for long. With terrible speed, three went in for the finish, two grabbing the underside of the Vorien's neck and dragging downward, a third biting behind the ears and jerking sideways. Stardust burst away, thread-thin rods of concentrated energy the Malvisse's deadblack consumed.

Like a thunderclap, the hated word—the one she dared not think, let alone speak—began to sound. She clapped her hands against her ears and wailed, her mind conjuring up a protection shield against the battering sound.

First one Malvisse and then another were hurled from the fray, their vorik unable to withstand the pressure of the hated word. They spun away in a flurry of yelping howls, their deadblack dulling before disappearing entirely. Without the benefit of armor, the two hied for the misty brume like hunted hares. A third wolf and then a fourth—their deadblack gone—scrambled toward the same gray margin.

Again and again the word assaulted the wolves still stout with stolen stardust, pushing them backward step by grudging step, its force pounding like a relentless hammer until they were clustered behind the Wycche's protection mindshield.

Move forward you worthless clods! she screamed, dropping her shield to summon her vor. Her mind stretched away, searching for the mucky fen of dark matter she knew lay beyond where most minds went, and finding it, plastered together a sticky fog she heaved at the orb-keeper's wolf.

The wolf staggered back, the word forgotten as it shook vigorously, trying to work free from the viscous cloud.

The Malvisse shot out from their huddle, barreling at the unnatural fog only to find they couldn't breach it either.

A shaft of starshine pierced its way out of the thick fog, its thin light beaming into the darkness. Another shaft emerged, and another, glistering pikes punching through the oppressive smog. Then, the brightening began, a steadily increasing glow as the wraithwolf's armor hefted away the pressing-down gray like a sun pushing away a stubborn cloud, clearing itself and its door.

It was the break the Malvisse and the Wycche were waiting for.

Now!

Sixteen wolves charged, hurtling past the guardian and ramming the dreamdoor, their combined force buckling it backward. A tiny crack opened along the edge, and the Wycche flew toward it, her form condensing to rapier thinness by the time she arrived.

The guardian wolf howled its night-ward's name a breath before the Wycche's bladed form inserted into the slivered opening, his call loud enough to blunt the Wycche's assault and awaken his sleeping charge.

The Wycche shrieked again as the dreamdoor, the wraithwolf, and the dreamsphere disintegrated, obviated by the sudden withdrawal of the orb-keeper's mind from the realm.

Anger burned through the Wycche. To have been so close to the Agya only to be outmaneuvered by a naive fool and her doddering wraithwolf was a crushing blow. Not only had she failed but she'd also been brought low before her constituency, their mocking derision clanging in her ears as the cruel wolves scattered, their deadblack subsuming into the ethers.

Laugh at yourselves miscreants, for this defeat was yours as well!

Her mindwords had as much effect as the howl of the wind.

Anger boiled again as she watched the wolves disappear. She had faced defeats before but never so many at a turn. Never after spending so much and gaining so little. Never without finding a way to prevail.

We go again.

Venge's mindwords cut through her rising despair.

We go again, my liege, for our cause is just and our will is strong.

The wraithwolf bristled, his ravaged coat a spiky darkness in the gloom. She laid a hand upon her wraithwolf's forehead. Ancient scenes played through her mind, scenes of destruction from that dismal time when the Elect had forced her and her people to suffer. A parade of loss and pain dredged up in staggering clarity from the depths of her ally's impeccable memory. Remembering that terrible time stoked the dwindling fire of her will. Venge had not given up and neither would she.

Yes, we will go again, my steadfast warrior. We must and we shall.

She would not give up fighting for her people's destiny. Not now. Not ever.

Chapter Forty-Seven
Shiny Bright

The howling echoed throughout Oru Fen. Kimbre—the last of the destined Voriens—had made his way to the pack after a journey fraught with peril, his night-ward—the orb-keeper—finally setting foot upon Whitemond.

Essiant's greeting was throaty and lush as he sang to the stars stabbing glittering javelins through the gloom. The rest of the pack joined in, welcoming the burnished-gold wolf with eyes the gray-green of winter grass.

Soon the Uniter and her helpmeets would join with Kimbre's night-ward and the much-fabled restoration could begin. Essiant's heart rejoiced at the thought. Long had he dreamed of this leap forward, as had every Vorien, only to end up disappointed when yet another Erynvor foundered upon the rocks of hubris and misapplication. He reminded himself the deed was not accomplished; there was still much to be done before Grogauk would be released.

Kimbre's mindwords made clear the reason for his early arrival.

The Wycche and her Malvisse horde came fast upon our trail, their desire fixed on the Agya. We barely managed to evade their terror trap.

Essiant understood. After being turned back by the Voriens, the Wycche had changed tactics, targeting the lone member still not joined.

It was a clever ploy. If she could waylay the Agya—the vital connector between the Founder's physical form and his spirit origins—the parambek could not be resurrected. It was a move Essiant should have seen coming. The moment the Wycche and her pack of reprobates were beaten back, they'd gone after the one wraithwolf not yet under the Vorien's protection.

You are right in your reasoning. It is crucial your night-ward completes her task, Essiant's mindwords assured. *From this moment, we stand with you against those seeking to deter your ward or the Agya she carries.*

Raya stepped out. *We will be ready and more than that, we will not be moved!* The dun wolf strode forward and touched a forepaw on Kimbre's as a pledge of her commitment.

Essiant nodded. He could always count on Raya's blunt courage.

The remaining pack members did likewise, Kimbre thanking each in turn.

Essiant felt the pack's courage rise as he touched his forepaw to Kimbre's and it heartened him, each guardian ready to sacrifice everything to a cause they had championed for as long as they and their night-wards had existed—enjoining their individual desires into a united All.

With the gathering complete, their true work could begin. The pact they'd made with the Elect upon choosing this path was coming to fruition. The Agya's return was the first step toward restoring a parambek long dormant and liberating Therran forces vital to Eolemar's balance. For eryns, the world had suffered deprivation and hardship, some places more than others, but a new dawn was rising, aided by the guidance and wisdom of these wolves who stood beside him, and Essiant couldn't imagine facing the undertaking ahead without them.

Xyleea couldn't explain the feeling she had, except that it was like coming home. Even her own wasaka had never given her the overpowering sense of familiarity and warmth now flooding into her heart when she looked at the shiny-bright slopes of the grogakee's mountain.

Her fear of the Xetili had faded, though she still watched for beeka-mud warriors who might think her an enemy.

The dreams played a large part in her newfound courage. After watching blue-painted men stamp and dance and sing their way through countless nights, their scarred faces had become as familiar to her as her own people's. Moreso, in her long absence away from her wasakagee. She thought of little else now.

She'd prayed to the ancestors many times to forgive her for the beekabeeka weaving its way into her fiber. She knew she should be ashamed and yet, she felt happier and more alive than ever, her insides brimming bright with hope for herself and her people. It defied all she'd learned about who she was and who she should be, and it was wonderful.

A few times she'd asked Cree Shee for forgiveness, but her silent prayers had been cut short by mandaaba hoots. It seemed the Watchmen of the Forest were keeping watch over her thoughts as well.

Of one thing she was sure. She had never been looking for water; she'd been searching for her wasakagee's future. Perhaps for the future of all the peoples of the keleekeluk. And now, it seemed, she'd found it.

The mountain was more dazzling than she'd ever imagined, covered in sun-catching trees casting multicolored sparklets upon the ground and cup-shaped flowers trinkling tunes when the wind tickled them with its invisible hand. Something about their happy songs made her feel lighter, as if she too were being tickled by a breeze until her heart laughed. If only her People could be here amongst the jingling flowers and rainbow-flecked trees. They could never be unhappy in a place such as this. What wouldn't she give for them to have this feeling, this joy of life that made everything possible?

She heard the mudpots before she saw them, their *blops* and *sloops* adding an odd syncopation to the warbling twitters and glottal clicks rounding through the underbrush from unseen birds. Kaambree seemed as curious as Xyleea about the sounds, the old tuskee weaving toward them in that way Xyleea had grown to love. She placed her hands atop the tuskee's silk-soft poll, her thoughts reaching out to the matriarch as it plodded forward.

The old mother knew what it was about, for the mental images came swift and sure of thumb-shaped pools of bright-blue mud, boiling with the thickened consistency of a goru-root stew. Xyleea wondered for the uncounted time how Kaambree knew about so many features of the keleekeluk when the tuskee had spent its entire lifetime either tethered to a post at the wasakagee's edge or performing drudging tasks under a keeper's watchful gaze. Xyleea could only surmise Kaambree had some connection with the greater whole that defied understanding.

The tuskee did not use the paths ground to dust by countless Xetili feet, preferring instead to bull through thickets of waxyleaf and cossiac —though never through the sparkling trees—making it sound as though a herd was on the move, rather than a single matriarch and its passenger, a trail of broken limbs and bone-dry leaves marking their passage.

It didn't take long, once the tuskee began its trailblazing, for Xyleea to perch her legs either side of the matriarch's topknot. It didn't entirely protect her from injury, but it was far better than leaving them dangling. Once, she'd pitched sideways, only avoiding a spectacular fall because Kaambree had stopped then canted its head to offset her imbalance, waiting until she'd reset before commencing forward.

They came out upon a white-rock shelf jutting from the larger mountain affording a wide view of the landscape. Below were the mudpots—liquid blue pools about the size of a wasaka—belching bubbles and steam into the warm air.

The beeka breath of the grogakee.

The spiderweb of pathways connecting the mudpots to the keleekeluk ran with a steady stream of brown figures fetching blue sludge in long-handled dippers before scudding back again. She tapped the tuskee then dismounted. Beneath her feet the rocky ground trembled, as if she'd stepped onto the shell of a massive beast.

Kaambree let out a snorting sigh, its river-green eyes tranquil, its pink-tipped trunk swaying, its drum-top ears flapping. It was the look of a weary traveler arriving at a long-awaited destination. Was this the place Xyleea was always meant to find? The place where her people could thrive? If so, it looked nothing like she'd imagined with its rainbow-shine trees and beeka mudpots and singing flowers. She'd grown up in the shadows of a green-limbed sky, grubbing for crumbs, her heart a shrunken knot of fear inside her chest. It was hard to imagine leaving that behind for a world full of light and song.

A silver glint caught Xyleea's eye. It was a feather, as long as her forearm, winking from the clutched branches of a scrubby bush. She knew most of the creatures of the keleekeluk, but she'd never seen a bird large enough to produce such a plume.

She worked the feather free, taking care not to fray its edges.

It was light for its size, its dark blue shaft nearly the color of beeka mud, its silver vane a complexion of iridescence and sky-blue. It seemed a good omen, and her immediate thought was to add it to the kereet.

She placed the feather on a flat stone then removed the headdress and the daala and laid them either side, making sure to fan out the kereet's deleemelee-feathered tail so as not to crush it. She stared at the three sacred objects, each a wonder on its own, and yet incomplete in their separateness. Only she could bring them together in the way they were always meant to be.

Inserting the large quill into the headdress proved difficult, and Xyleea's first attempts ended with the feather toppling out as soon she put the kereet onto her head. She pressed and flattened and pressed again until at last, she wedged the blue shaft behind the chassa paw, spiky black bajee horns jutting out either side. The silver plume towered above the headdress, sheening light onto the ground when Xyleea faced the sun.

She walked to Kaambree and, after scratching the tuskee's forehead, tapped the matriarch's neck. The tuskee knelt and Xyleea mounted, her attention going to the Xetili scurrying below.

She watched until night settled upon the keleekeluk. Still the Xetili worked, some carrying torches to light the way. To Xyleea, the frenetic activity meant only one thing: the Xetili were preparing for war, and not with one wasakagee. They were gearing up to fight a great many wasakagees, perhaps every one in the keleekeluk.

A creeping dread built into an unwanted knowing as Xyleea considered how she could prevent what would be a terrible tragedy. To see a disaster coming and not be able to stop it was a cruel blow to a deeta's heart. Even a deeta without a calling or a claim. A deeta like herself.

A decision formed. She'd started this journey believing the time for fear had passed. If she was to help her people, she must maintain her conviction, no matter how difficult that became.

With nothing before her and nothing behind, the time for beginnings was now.

Zell is free. Brynz repeated the words in her head, trying to make them seem real.

Despite everything, her vow had been fulfilled. Never again would her splendid charge be subjected to the whims of an unfeeling society that viewed it as a beast to be tamed rather than a being to be respected. The fact that Zell now lived high above it all, perhaps in the very peaks of its founding, where the sun shone brighter and the winds blew stronger, made every hardship she'd endured since his spectacular escape worth it.

The group had been traveling for weeks, and her fear of recapture had dwindled to occasional half-thoughts rather than a constant scream inside her head. The weather had also improved, warming enough that she didn't need the fox pelt except at night.

She stared into the campfire ignited by the golden-eyed man—Haedyn, she must remember to call him that—and marveled over the strange path her life had taken.

Her gaze shifted to the people she'd fallen in with, their faces ruddied by flamelight, their easy manners and ready charm a stark departure from the strict protocols of the Royal Stables. For the first time, she felt as if she belonged. That she was amongst friends. It was a feeling far deeper and more settled than the grasping appreciation she'd felt toward Garrod when he'd plucked her from the orphan's home. Then, she'd been blinded by the opportunities her unexpected luck had brought her, but she could see now it had been a life of loneliness and isolation. At the time, she'd accepted that her happiness should come second to the needs of her benefactors, an equitable trade-off for spending time with a living gift from the skygods (as all Iellians believed gryphons to be). Her capture by the Drasgor had given her time to reflect upon those youthful exuberances, her desires and dreams now seeming as derelict and shallow as the monarch she had served. Knowing she had anything in common with Her Most Exalted was a lashing sting to Brynz's conscience, but she must own her mistakes if she wished not to repeat them, and so, she cherished the sting as a useful reminder. These days, she knew better her place in the world. No longer did she wish to stifle the will of another creature for her own pleasure, nor did she wish to stifle her own joy in the name of useless propriety or false etiquette. All of that was in the past. With Zell's freedom confirmed, there was nothing tying her to that hollow existence.

The one who had revealed Zell's fate to her—Elorah, she must remember to call her that—sat across from her. She was gesturing to Haedyn on her left, one hand waving the roasted haunch of a cragdog like a tiny club. The dark-haired girl sitting to Elorah's right—Mierrle, she must remember to call her that—burst out laughing. Though Brynz didn't understand the words, she couldn't help laughing as well, the general merriment lightening her mood.

Thane leaned over to translate, a chuckle in his voice. "They're playing a game of Would You Rather. Haedyn has asked Elorah if she would rather fight a tusk-pig with no tusks or a bravik with no eyes."

"She already does not have tusks," Brynz said. "And why would she give up her eyes?"

Thane laughed. "I'm not explaining this right. The tusk-pig would not have *its* tusks nor the bravik *its* eyes." She blanched, and he added, "It's a rhetorical debate. A match-up of wits. A thinking contest for purposes of entertainment and humor."

"How is fighting ever humorous?"

"It isn't about an actual fight. It's about weighing the risk/reward ratio of an absurd situation and making a defensible choice."

Brynz furrowed her brow. "But both animals would suffer. Neither would win."

"You and she think alike, then. Her answer was that she would rather not face either, but if it were unavoidable, she would heal each of its pain and rely on its gratitude to spare her life."

The same as she's done for me, Brynz thought, her heart swelling.

"Of course, Aikin said it wasn't even a sensible question, and Rachmyn agreed, which might be a first for those two." He gave her a conspiratorial wink. She laughed, understanding full well the island Aikin always placed himself upon. Something about his manner reminded her of Kodston Tolleck, although he wasn't as prone to swearing and was more handsome despite the crescent-shaped scar on his forehead where the horse had kicked him. It was his air of better-than that nettled. He was good with the horses, which was a mark in his favor. And he'd helped her escape. Kodston would never have done that. She supposed she should be more tolerant of the copper-haired man's prideful temperament, given all he'd done for her.

It *was* surprising to see how well Thane was doing. She'd seen blood fever many times, and never once had its victims made a full recovery. To see Thane now—putting aside the state of his leggings—with his pinked cheeks and sparkling eyes and functioning limbs made her wonder if there was something more to this life, something unseen and unknown except to the clerics and the scribes who spent their lives studying such things. The ones she had come across were fond of rattling off pious homilies and pithy warnings to anyone who would listen, but she'd always assumed they were addled. Perhaps she should have paid better attention.

Elgre trotted into the flickering light of the fire, a marmouse dangling from his clamped jaws. She no longer feared the wolf, though she knew he wasn't a tamed creature and she should keep her distance. She envied the close bond he shared with Rachmyn. She missed almost nothing about her previous life except the inexplicable rapport that came from communing with a wild creature. Hadn't she spent every possible moment with Zell for that reason? Even Haedyn's bird, so disliked by everyone except its keeper, seemed an enviable companion by her standards. She'd handled enough winged predators to have developed a deep appreciation for their keen spirits and lack of artifice. The sharp-eyed little character perched atop the blond man's shoulder, wings pushed against its keel like loaded springs. In a thrice, the bird could be aloft if it so desired. As if reading her mind, Haedyn pulled a tattered sock-end from his pocket and slid it over the bird's head before smiling at Brynz. She realized she'd been nodding in unguarded approval of his actions, and she ducked her chin, putting her attention elsewhere.

Thane was using his thumbnail to pick at his teeth. "The taste is fair, but cragdog does make itself a nuisance afterward," he said, his hand dropping to his lap.

"It's not so bad if you don't cook it," Brynz replied.

Thane goggled. "You mean, eat it raw?" He shivered. "I'd rather die."

"You think that, but you can get used to it."

"Some things you should never have to get used to."

"True. But we don't always get to choose what we will and won't do."

"I suppose you wouldn't have chosen this, as an example." He made a vague hand gesture meant to encompass the wilds around them. "Coming, as you do, from a life of ease and elegance."

Brynz rubbed her palms against her faded blue leggings, now shot through with holes. "I've known nothing of ease or elegance during my time wearing this livery. If I had my way, I'd have it off here and now, except I've nothing to replace it with."

Thane's lips bent into a bemused frown as he looked down at his own sorry pantlings. He'd washed them out along the way, but the shredded leggings still bore the stains of his brush with the bravik. "At least you haven't this level of ruination as your only covering." He pointed toward the worst of the two legs.

She laughed. "That is true."

"Brynz, let us hear from you," Elorah called in Iellian. "Tell us two things, one true, one false, and let us discern one from the other."

They'd moved on to another game. A note of discomfort tumbled her stomach. She had little experience speaking of herself to others.

"Yes, Brynz! Tell us something we'd never guess!" Haedyn cried.

Thane translated then gave her an encouraging smile. "Go on. Talking about yourself only hurts for a moment." He laughed, his scar lifting toward his eyes.

She looked around then took a deep breath. "Two things... right." She thought for a moment. "I once trained a duck to ring a bell for its dinner." Thane translated for the non-Iellian speakers.

"And what's the second thing?" Aikin asked. She set her eyes upon him. "I can sing the Iellian national song backward." An obvious lie. She shifted her gaze to Thane as he translated. A buzz of murmured discussion went around the campfire.

"Those who think Brynz's first story is true, hold up one finger. Those who think her second story is true, hold up two," Elorah said, her gaze moving around the group.

Hands raised, half holding up one finger, the other half holding up two. An even split.

"Which of us has it right?" Elorah asked, her eyes sparkling.

"Iellia doesn't have a national song," Brynz replied with a small, smug smile.

Haedyn slapped his two-fingered guess against his thigh. "Spunk! I should have known that."

"How could you have known that?" Rachmyn asked, justifying his own two-fingered guess as much as his friend's.

"Well, I think they should have one," Mierrle said, her tone indignant.

"They have a motto." Brynz said. "Without Air, Nothing."

Aikin sniffed. "'Without Theirs, Nothing,' would be more accurate."

Mierrle burst out laughing, everyone else joining in. Even Rachmyn smiled, which was about as rare as hen's teeth. Brynz laughed, and it felt good. She never had to go back to the high-peaked land of deceit that had once been her home. And that felt even better.

CHAPTER FORTY-EIGHT
RECONCILING A SHATTERED WORLD

AH-BAH-BAH AH-BAH-BAH. AH-BAH-BAH

The drumming began as soon as the blood moon took its place in the clear night sky.

Xyleea swallowed hard and forced herself to continue on, the keleekeluk around her a dark fabric of sounds and smells and fears as she made her way toward the unrelenting beat.

The second blood moon in as many moons was a fearsome sign, and the Xetili drums were loud as they heralded the auspicious event. Xyleea couldn't imagine how many blue-painted warriors were running the paths toward Ushokan wasakagees.

After descending from the mountain, she'd walked the remaining distance alone, leaving Kaambree some ways back, though she knew from the snapping twigs and snuffling sighs behind her that the tuskee was following.

She went through her plan again and said a prayer to the ancestors for enough huul waal to see it through. Her hand drifted to the beeka vessel lodged between her weela bowl and her darts. It wasn't fear making her heart thump inside her head and her hands tremble like an old man's. It was thinking of all the trust her galeesha and her people had placed in her to do what was best. Was this beekabeeka in her mind the right thing to do? She would soon know.

The smell of smoke and gimchee was strong by the time she reached the encampment, her breath expelling at the number of dwellings spreading out in every direction. She couldn't begin to count how many Xetili were here. Every one of them by the look of it.

She proceeded, her bajee-clad feet silent as she picked her way around empty huts spilling hides and pots and pounding stones from their open fronts.

The crackle of fire and the beating of drums led her forward. There was another sound too, a persistent *fwap-fwap-fwap* that set her teeth on edge.

As she crept nearer, she realized it was the sound of dancing feet hitting dusty ground. Arm-in-arm, rings of Xetili gyrated in circles around five separate fires. All were painted with beeka mud, even the women and children, but there was something different about the markings this night. Rather than angry slashes and sharp hooks, the symbols were surprisingly similar to the gentle curves and placid dots she'd painted on her galeesha for the bone ceremony.

Xyleea hugged herself to steady her quaking arms, then walked forward, ignoring the loud buzzing inside her ears.

The drums stopped, but Xyleea did not, walking into the center of the nearest drumming circle. All around, hostile eyes watched, their ill thoughts burning hot on her skin.

Xyleea unwrapped her trembling arms and held them out, palms up, before raising them into the air. She stared straight ahead, her jaw clenched to keep her teeth from chattering.

Now or never.

She dropped one hand to her blowpipe, forcing herself to stare straight ahead as she curled her fingers around the weapon.

A screech of consternation went up followed by frantic motion as unarmed warriors made for their weapons. Xyleea noted the frenzied movement at the periphery of her vision while keeping her focus on a group of fierce-looking men staring back, their foreheads marked with a blue-mud dot centered above their eyebrows.

Xyleea pulled the blowpipe free and tossed it forward. It landed on the ground with a scuffing thud. Next, she untied her dart quiver, her shaking fingers fumbling to unknot the thongs holding it to her chest band. The quickest of the warriors were already back—their blowpipes against their lips—by the time she had the quiver undone. She ripped it free then tossed it forward, her gaze locked on the men's inscrutable faces.

She raised her hands then knelt, first onto one knee, then onto the other. A murmur went through the crowd, and the men moved aside, making way.

Her teeth began to chatter, despite her grimly set jaws, and the buzzing increased to a deafening roar. For a moment, she thought she might pass out.

A wizened woman, no taller than a half-grown child, toddled out, wearing an elaborate headdress. Her rheumy gaze fixed on Xyleea.

A deeta?

The headpiece, perched above a blue circle on the woman's creased forehead, was dominated by a carved browband depicting a dragon-headed snake swallowing its own tail. The remainder featured the iridescent black feathers of the mandaaba and the golden fur of the minkee.

The old woman's gaze swept toward the kereet, a puckery smile denting her face. She tottered forward until she was eye-to-eye with Xyleea, her smile widening into a crater with a single brown tooth. She brushed the tip of a knobbed finger against Xyleea's forehead.

The old woman spoke words—a question by the sound of it—that Xyleea did not understand.

She knew what she must do. She retrieved a pinch of beeka powder from the vessel attached to her chest band and, using her palm, mixed it with spit before daubing a mark onto her forehead. The old woman's smile broadened as she clapped her hands together. She spoke again.

"Welcome, daughter of Ooribos. We have seen your messenger and await your words."

This time Xyleea could understand the old woman despite her odd pronunciation and reed-thin voice. The elder gestured toward the kereet, her cloudy eyes reflecting the brightness of its silver feather.

The warriors lowered their blowpipes and shuffled backward, forming into a ring behind which the rest of the people began to gather.

Welcome, daughter of Ooribos Grogakee, of the Ushoku and Xetili.

Xyleea recognized the voice of the dragon inside her head. A thrill ran through her. It was wholly different from when she'd last heard the Ancient One.

Speak your words to these who have waited long to hear them.

My words? Xyleea could think of nothing other than questions and confusions.

Speak of what you have seen and what you now know.

Xyleea cleared her throat. "Four moons I have traveled through the keleekeluk looking for water for my people. High and low I have searched, walking the common paths of the Ushokan and the Xetili. In that time, I have come to see that all of us suffer under the same hardened sky. That we all are without enough to eat, enough to drink, enough to live in this keleekeluk we share. That is why I know we are not different. We are not two tribes in a single forest; we are a single people, divided by a foolish quarrel. A quarrel we no longer remember except as a tradition. A quarrel that has shed too much blood and ruined too many lives."

"Rise and say the rest." The old woman grasped Xyleea's shoulders and, with a feeble tug, urged her to her feet. Xyleea stood.

"I do not come as your enemy. I come as your forgotten daughter, your invisible sister, your long-lost family member. I come as one who wishes to see our unhappy family brought together as it was when the world was new. As it was when the voice of the dragon spoke and the whole of the keleekeluk listened and lived those words."

Xyleea looked at the men and women and children gathered around, their foreheads dotted with blue mud, their dancing and fires forgotten. No longer did their burning eyes scorch her skin. Instead, they lit a flame within her heart.

The old woman turned to face the crowd, one gnarled hand pointing upward. "Loved ones, we have all seen the shining chassabird fly across the heartmoon on wings of light, as the ancestors said it would. So too has the Keeper come to give back that which will raise Ooribos from his long slumber."

Without knowing how, Xyleea understood the old woman meant the daala. Xyleea looked up at the moon and was astounded to see it had changed. A shadow shape, not unlike the open-mouthed head of a dragon, appeared to be swallowing its reddened edge.

The old woman ululated as she lifted her arms toward the sky. "See the sign of Ooribos! Beat the drum and raise your voice! Sing! SING!"

The drummers rushed to their drums, the rest of the people widening into a circle encompassing the drummers and the five fires, with Xyleea and their deeta at its center.

AH-BAH-BAH AH-BAH-BAH. AH-BAH-BAH

The drums pounded out their cadence five times before the people began to sing.

"Ooribos, Ooribos, Lord of All, Lord of All, Ooribos, Ooribos, Now Arise, Now Arise..."

Xyleea's mind harked back to another song:

Grogakee, Grogakee. Come quickly, Grogakee, Grogakee, Chuulzu Palleea...

She chanted words from her Ushokan youth as the Xetili sang to their Ooribos while overhead a shadow-dragon swallowed a bloodheart moon.

The deeta turned, her extended finger reaching up. Xyleea bent toward her, and the elder pressed the blue mark above her eyebrows. Her head began to tingle.

"See true, daughter of Ooribos," the elder said, pointing at the kereet.

Xyleea straightened. *See true,* echoed the dragon's voice inside her mind. She closed her eyes, her heart settling into the drum's three-beat rhythm until she and it were one.

It is time for the daala to return to its rightful place.

Cree Shee's words tumbled out from their hiding place.

Show me, galeesha, where I must go. Guide me, oh ancestors, that I go where I must. Protect me, Ooribos Grogakee, that I return what you gave.

Xyleea sent the words flying up to Weeleekeela like mandaaba hoots, shouting them with her mind and her heart.

Listen, came the dragon's voice, *and you will hear your answer.*

The dreamdoors appeared in quick succession, each assembling from the ethers into fantastical mountings featuring elements drawn from Whitemond—white stone and chalumbra vines and crystalwood trees.

The Voriens had used their own memories to construct the dreamsphere gateways in the absence of conscious memory or experience on the part of their wards. Such a thing was not often done, for it could disrupt the tranquility of a ward's dream state. Precautions had been taken to reduce the shock of a foreign-seeming dreamdoor by draping wisps of familiar-feeling memory atop the underlying pith of foreshadowed fitments.

The Vorien pack stood in a radiating hub, each guardian facing their respective night-ward's door as they readied themselves for a shared experience that would leave them all forever changed.

Essiant's anticipation shone forth as a brighter sparkle from his gleaming white coat. He and the rest of the wraithwolves had already prepared for this most important of moments, a first for them all. A first perhaps in the timeless history of the realm. They would be attempting to join their individual minds into a singular vision that would both explain their night-wards' pasts while preparing them for the future they had pledged to create. Essiant and his night-ward had conceived the idea before she'd descended to assume the mantle of the Erynvor, both convinced the restoration of the parambeks could be accomplished in no other way.

Every previous Erynvor had attempted the restoration as an individual. Yes, they had had associates and mentors and friends, but never had they sublimated their individuality to the power available when one calls upon the greater All. In the case of Essiant's night-ward, the transformation should come easier, but it might prove a high hurdle for the rest, especially the two who had taken vorik-depleting injuries. Their ability to raise their vibrations might be affected by the energy deficits those mutilations had caused.

The High Gate had been the first attempt by his night-ward at what they'd determined would be the only way to overcome those entities working to oppose the realm's advancement into unity. The Elect, having no ability to overrule the inherent will of the manifest creations working for and against their overarching plan for harmonic alignment, had expressed their great good pleasure when their chosen Erynvor had posited the idea, avowing to throw their inimitable faculties behind the effort. It remained to be seen whether the novel approach would have the desired effect.

Essiant watched as each wolf parsed the orusphere, attuning to their night-wards' soulsongs. One by one, each howled, calling their wards into the realm.

Ajai's night-ward was the first to find her way into Oru Fen. Essiant watched the dark-haired girl greet her wraithwolf with the briefest of touches, their Saska bond flaring bright before she turned to face the dreamdoor created for her. She stumbled back in confusion, and Essiant sent a surge of heart vorik to Ajai to bolster his convincements. True to her trusting nature, she surrendered her key and entered her sphere. Ajai took up his accustomed place at her door, his alert ears swiveling, his taut body emanating the golden light of their Saska.

Next came Ieeva's ward, arriving amidst a crackle of charged energy. Though he had suffered a monstrous maiming, his soul had caught fire when the truth of his salvation at the behest of Maarathia had been drawn forth from his forgettings and rolled out before him. He thrust his key at his wolf and, flinging back the door, plunged into his dreamsphere. Essiant gave Ieeva a bow, a silent acknowledgement of her peerless tutelage. It remained to be seen how it would end, but the fact that her ward had been awakened to the truth of his past and now held an appropriate gratitude for it boded well.

Raya's and Kelm's wards arrived next, both surveying their dreamdoors with a suspicion that approached hostility. Raya's ward balked at the sight of entwining chalumbra flowers pulsing with light until Raya, blocking from behind, pushed him forward, forcing his ethereal form against the etheriant creating the door. Only then did her ward relax enough to hand his soulkey to his stalwart wraithwolf and place his hand upon the door. A crack opened, and he slooped inside. Essiant gave a nod to Raya as she took up her accustomed stance, her legs planting like four pillars, determination spiking away from her blocky frame.

Meanwhile, Kelm's ward had taken one look at her door and vanished. Essiant surmised the wraithwolf's charge had startled back into the waking world. He could feel Kelm's self-recrimination for the miscalculation, and he sent a surge of heart vorik. The warrior threw back his head and howled again, summoning his night-ward a second time. She reappeared, wide-eyed, but this time her guardian was prepared, projecting her beloved companion, the Cyrulian Blue gryphon, upon the door's brunnestone background. She calmed and approached; her apprehension replaced by a certainty of purpose. Kelm took charge of her key as she led her magnificent companion into the dreamsphere, her wraithwolf assuming his customary post.

Embren howled her night-ward into the realm, and he appeared in a rage of fiery light. The door to his sphere was equally fiery, a wall of flame surrounded by crystalwood spraying sparks, the belled chalumbra flowers formed of flames in a cauldron-like base. He flung his key and charged forward, barely waiting for their Saska vorik to fuse before the blazing door hurled wide then slammed shut. Embren gave a rueful head shake as she took a stance in front.

Spectra's howl floated through the orusphere as she united with her night-ward. His door was enormous, its grandeur drawn from his recent vision of Whitemond, rising high into the upper reaches. It was a fitting preamble to what lay ahead. After allowing their Saska bond to form, Spectra nudged her pale-haired ward and he produced his key, handing it over almost as an afterthought as he surveyed the mountainous door. Another nudge and he entered his dreamsphere, Spectra taking her place in front.

Essiant gathered himself, his ears straining to hear the soulsong he lived for. There it was, sweet and clear. He howled, and his night-ward appeared, the crystalwood staff in her hand. This time, she'd also brought through the Erynstone, and it quivered with energy from its place near her heart. Essiant cheered this unexpected achievement, astonished she had managed to bring the etheric versions of two physical items into the realm. Their Saska vorik conjoined, and he felt the exhilaration racing through his ward. She understood how remarkable her achievement was, and she was giddy with the thrill of it. It was an understandable reaction, but he moved to gain her attention. Dreamweaving seven different narratives into one shared vision was going to be difficult enough without the clouding influence of self-congratulation. It would take every ounce of Shadowen vorik she and Spectra's night-ward could muster, given the fact the remaining five were under no dream inducers whatsoever. Only because of the cooperation of their wraithwolves was the feat even possible.

Essiant ushered his night-ward to her dreamdoor, itself the most marvelous and vibrant of all with its sapphire panels and crystalwood groves and chalumbra vines in lifelike detail and dimension. Had Essiant not known better, he would have sworn he was looking at Grogauk's mountain. He felt the forces rising within his night-ward as she surveyed the grandiose visioneering her soul had constructed. He nudged her leg, and she turned toward him, her eyes luminous, the staff in her hand suffusing with an incandescence that defied the realm's graylight.

At last we begin.

Her mindwords echoed his own.

Essiant concentrated on the orucon beneath his paws, parsing its flow for any sign of the chaotic energy that marked out the Malvisse. He felt nothing. He expected another confrontation, but it seemed it would not happen this night. All the better. He and his night-ward had much to do without the interference of miscreant obtruders. Satisfied, Essiant prompted his night-ward.

Hold out your hand.

Her curiosity sharpened as she put forward her open palm.

One by one, her companions' wraithwolves approached, materializing the soulkey of their night-ward then dropping it onto her palm. Essiant could feel the tendrils of doubt shooting into his night-ward's thoughts as the keys to her companions' venerable souls were laid one upon another in her outstretched hand. She well knew the magnitude of trust required for a wraithwolf to surrender their night-ward's key; to hand over unfettered access to the mind of their beloved charge was to give her an unfathomable responsibility.

Essiant moved to counteract her understandable trepidation.

Never doubt, always trust, for you are mightier than the moon and more powerful than the stars. Just as you gave your pledge, so too have these, your companions, pledged their service to the All. Rise now and meet the destiny your combined intentions are creating.

His mindwords honed her focus, leaving no room for doubt or fear.

She brought forward her staff, her mind fixing upon it until it hovered in front of her when she reached for the topmost key. Like the completing piece to an intricate puzzle, she placed the key upon the glowing crystalwood. The compatible desire between the key and the staff created a bond that rendered them into a single wholeness while the unique vibrations of the key's soul rushed through his night-ward's ethereal body and through Essiant's. The staff's glow intensified, becoming more vibrant, its golden light brightening with the subtle color strands of the combining vorik energies. His night-ward repeated the process for each key so that when the last was placed, the staff's incandescence had intensified beyond measure, its prismatic shine bursting with reds and greens and blues and yellows, a brilliance that pushed the realm's shadows to its farthest margins.

It is good, Essiant confirmed as his night-ward surveyed the lighted area, the brightness stretching up and out in every direction. She placed her hand upon his crescent moon, drawing into herself the memories of that time long past when Therrania thrived and dragons spoke. The erynstone levitated from his night-ward's chest, coming level with her forehead then drawing tight against her Spyrrt eye, the unseen portal in the middle of the forehead that connects the waking self with its ethereal counterpart and, in the case of Spyrrt voricians, the ethereal self with its celestial corpus. It was exactly where the stone should be as she presented projections of the wondrous events to come.

Come forth, his night-ward called, the staff beaming the silvery light signature of the sphere's occupant onto the pale-haired Shadowen's dreamdoor. The door flung back, and he stepped out, his hand going to his pocket, his mindwords coming clear.

My shard. Yes, there it is.

The pale-haired man withdrew his hand.

A memory arose from Essiant's vast store—a luminous gray orb damaged beyond hope and bound to a dark pedestal—that he materialized between his ward and the Shadowen. It was a grotesquerie his night-ward had hoped never to see again, and she sagged back, a devastating rush of black emotion flooding through her and, by extension, through himself. For the wraithwolf, the emotional surge was nothing more than observable phenomena, but for his ward, it was a crushing cruelty that shook her to her core.

Essiant placed his forehead against his night-ward's leg to steady her. This was a hard truth she wished to avoid, but the time had come for her to understand the depravity of her opponents, and for the Shadowen to understand the enormity of the gift he carried in his pocket.

Spectra pushed her night-ward toward the orb until he was almost on top of it, staring down at the desecrated eye while Essiant's night-ward dwelt upon her memory so that both wards experienced the tragedy of the orb's mutilation together. Spectra's mindwords came to both Essiant and his charge by virtue of her night-ward's soul key attachment to the crystalwood staff.

Your shard is not yours alone.

The pale-haired man startled, his hand shoving into his pocket. *How is it not?*

You are only its keeper. It has come to you for a time, and times, but it is not yours. Soon, the Founder who has lent it will require its return.

The pale-haired man turned, the stubborn bulge of his fist around the shard visible.

It cannot stay with you forever. To this you agreed. Spectra nudged her ward again, and he produced the shard, crying out when it arced away from his hand and into the orb, its shape fitting perfectly into a black void.

Essiant's night-ward felt pity as the pale-haired man cried out again, his devastation almost unbearable.

Then Essiant's night-ward did something remarkable.

With a thought she was beside the grieving man, her staff hovering above them both and shining down a commingling of their vorik lights. Her ethereal body drew up until she was of equal height before leaning forward, the stone on her forehead connecting with his Spyrrt eye. Her memory of the orb's torture at the hands of the hooded assailants flowed from her mind into his. At the same moment, the brutal details of his parents' deaths came flooding into her consciousness. As the two recollections came together, with their attendant understandings, a new wisdom emerged, along with an elevation of purpose. Both tragedies had come at the hands of the same malevolent ideologues. Redemption would only come by combining their strengths. There was no other way.

Essiant felt a surge of power as the joint realization took hold, changing both night-wards forever. Where once there had been separateness, there was now a forged unity. A coming together enabling the rebuild of a once-glorious world to commence.

The weeping orb and its malignant pedestal devolved into infinitesimal expressions of vibrating matter, each a microcosmic duplicate of the whole from which it had formed. The tiny bits pulled apart, spreading farther and farther until only the shard remained, suspended where it had fitted itself.

The pale-haired man looked at his wraithwolf, his hand moving toward it.

May I?

The silver-black wolf nodded, and the Shadowen grabbed the floating shard and stuck it into his pocket, his relief its own chirring hum.

A wave of energy pulsed, charging the atmosphere.

Components tore away from the dreamdoors as a white mountain pushed up from the orucon, its flattened top rising high. Chalumbra vine and crystalwood trees unmoored then cleaved onto the mountain's assembling prominence while the staff's shine reflected their crystalline leaves, flashes of refracted light strobing across the mountain's face. In a moment it was done, an ethereal version of Whitemond towering mere steps from where Essiant, Spectra, and their open-mouthed night-wards looked on.

The remaining dreamdoors swung open, and the attendant wraithwolves retrieved their night-wards, escorting them to where they could view the proceedings.

A distinct three-beat reverberance began, gaining in volume as it shook its way up and down the mountainside, the strobing flash of crystalwood leaves syncing up with its rhythm.

Meanwhile, every dreamdoor disassembled, the remaining components decamping to the apparitional mountain.

Essiant's night-ward walked to each newcomer and, using the Erynstone, connected her Spyrrt eye with theirs, the staff's light changing to reflect their combined vorik signatures as she imparted the same message.

Remember this vibration, for it is the key to unlocking the mountain.

As the Erynstone forged the path to understanding, the crescent moon on the forehead of each wraithwolf took on a bright glow, signifying the transfer of thought forms to their memory-keeping. Each time, the impression made was the same, of the parambek as it once was, and how it was meant to be again, so that in the waking sphere, they could all hold the ideal in their minds.

When it was done, the ethereal Whitemond melted back into the orucon, taking with it all the accoutrements it had gathered from the dreamdoors, its reversion completing when Essiant's night-ward withdrew the Erynstone from the last of the five. The staff returned to her hand, its multi-hued glow dimming as first one key and then another removed itself and flew to the wraithwolf from whom it had originated.

The wraithwolves took charge of their night-wards, escorting each to the borderland before sending them back to their sleeping bodies. Essiant was the last to leave, allowing his night-ward a moment to savor the joy of her accomplishment. She would need that to hold on to when the impending storms of deceit came upon her.

Come, let us return, he said at last, leading her to her manifest form. His night-ward nodded, the light in her staff dimming down as she slipped into her slumbering shell.

CHAPTER FORTY-NINE
VOICE OF THE MOUNTAIN

Elorah awoke with a start, her mind grasping for the disturbance that had yanked her from her dream. Her companions were also awake and looking around in confusion.

ah-bah-bah   ah-bah-bah   ah-bah-bah

Elorah could make out a repeating thump coming from the direction of the mountain. She looked toward its flat-topped form, a huge blot of gray in the velvety dark.

ah-bah-bah   ah-bah-bah   ah-bah-bah

"Do you hear that?" She turned toward Rachmyn, sitting cross-legged near the sputtering fire, his wolf's head laid across his lap. He nodded, his eyes cutting toward the sound. The wolf raised his head to follow his master's gaze.

"It's like my dream." Mierrle pushed herself into a side-sit and adjusted her cloak.

"And mine," echoed Thane, climbing to his feet and stretching.

Haedyn and Aikin chorused, "Mine, too," each eyeing the other in surprise.

Elorah's gaze went to Brynz who was staring into the distance.

It seemed the vision of Therrania, still clear in her own mind, remained in her friends' minds as well. Elorah seized the crystalwood staff, got to her feet and held it out. "We have seen what we came to do. Now, all that's left is the doing of it. With this staff as our witness, let us pledge to use our combined forces against any and all that may try to sunder our alliance or betray our purpose." Elorah held out the golden-lit staff with both hands.

Thane was the first to step forward, one hand grasping above Elorah's grip. Five more hands placed themselves upon the crystalwood, forming a living sheath of determination. The staff brightened with the addition of each hand, as it had done in Oru Fen, her companions' red and blue and green and yellow energy threads intensifying its glow to a blinding white light.

"Remember what you've seen, for it was not a dream." She looked into the eyes of her companions to reinforce her words, each reflecting the brilliant shine of the staff.

"Never doubt, always trust, for you are mightier than the moon and more powerful than the stars." Her voice sounded strange to her ears. "Each of us is here to fulfill a promise made long ago. Hold Therrania in your mind as you saw it in your dream, and in ages past, that we might resurrect its manifest form this night." Elorah looked up as she spoke, her attention drawn to the reddened moon—the Dragon's Moon—asymmetrical now, its eastern curve an uneven darkness. An eclipse. A portent of this night's significance.

Elorah closed her eyes, the power within greater than it had ever been. She reached down, searching for a connection with the greater All, the distant throb pushing her forces further and faster than ever before.

bohhmmm bohhmmm bohhmmm

Eolemar's steady beat was synced with the sound coming from the mountain, each *ah-bah-bah* fitting atop the *bohhmmm bohhmmm bohhmmm* coming through her feet. She allowed the combining rhythms to fill her, clearing away all other thoughts and aligning her heartbeat. The energy threads of her companions within the staff were also aligning to the resonant beats. Only when the pulse beneath her feet, inside her heart, and through the staff became one did she open her eyes, her insides vibrating as if she were bursting through her skin.

"My body feels weird," Mierrle said, her eyes filling with tears despite her delighted smile. She swiped them away. "I don't know why

I'm crying." She sob-laughed, shaking her head in embarrassment. "I've never felt happier."

"I feel it, too," Thane said, pointing toward his own streaming eyes. "Look at these! Fleeking fountains!"

"It's the vibrations," Elorah said. "I'd say we're all feeling it in some way." She cast a sideways glance toward Aikin, his teeth gritted as if forcing down some unspeakable pain. "It's better to let the energy flow through you and out. Don't try to hold yourself apart from it." Aikin's tensed shoulders sagged as he huffed out a loud sigh.

Haedyn held up his bow. Elorah hadn't noticed it in his other hand. "My bow is on fire!" It was true. The bow had taken on a flamy red pulse. He cranked himself forward to look at his beltline and chortled, "Look, Rachmyn! The figures are dancing!" Elorah squinted to see the fluttery movement of golden jots on the black handle of his knife. "How long has it been?"

Rachmyn's hand shoved into his pocket as his silvery gaze shifted, his stoic expression broadening into a bemused smile. "It's been a while," he confirmed. Beside him, Brynz stared down at her feet in wide-eyed amazement. Elorah wondered if she too felt Eolemar's pulse.

The rhythm coming from the mountain was growing louder, more insistent.

"I think it's calling us." Mierrle looked toward Whitemond. "It wants us to come to it."

"If we hurry, we can get there before the moon completes its change." Elorah pointed toward the sky. Exclamations rounded the group as they disengaged from her staff.

"Maybe we should wait for first light—" Aikin began.

"We must go now." Elorah looked again at the moon, already smaller. "The time for waiting is over."

She stowed her staff, as the others struck camp. Haedyn tamped the fire, drawing its heat away with his hands. In a tick, the group was ready to move.

Elorah started forward, her see-true stone nudging her breastbone as she followed the voice of the mountain.

The rings of dancers broke apart as the Xetili made their way toward the mountain, stamping their feet, clapping their hands, and singing their songs as they went, the drummers hoisting up their instruments before falling into line.

Xyleea was hustled along as the people rushed forward. Overhead, the Ooribos had swallowed half of the bloodheart moon. Strong arms bore her up and she was aloft, the words to her galeesha's song tumbling out of the rough-faced men carrying her.

"Grogakee, grogakee, callaska hee..."

As she sang, the grogakee climbed into her mind, his huge sides and back, his long neck and legs, with wings above and a tail behind, all textured with mosses and shrubs, vines and trees, two crystalwood tree-horns reflecting light dazzles onto the grogakee's mossy head. But it was the grogakee's eyes, swirling with every color of the keleekeluk and shining the warm light of kindness, that captivated Xyleea most. She felt as she had when staring into the daala, the same overwhelming energy expanding her far beyond the limits of her tiny body.

The grogakee's head bent low to look at her, its infinite eyes staring into her soul as her mouth continued its singsong, the words gaining strength with every breath, the voices around her adding to every note. Over and over, Ushokan words rang out in the scar-shaped voices of the Xetili, a thronging shout echoing off the stark white cliffsides marking out the mountain from the brown foothills.

Two men held Xyleea up as the rest of the Xetili clasped hands and fanned out, forming into a circumference stretching around the white cliffs farther than Xyleea could see. Somehow, she could watch the Xetili stretch their ranks to surround the mountain, while also watching the grogakee's movements inside her mind.

The great head stretched toward the northern horizon, drawing her attention away from its breathtaking eyes and toward a young woman and her companions moving closer at the speed of wind. The woman held a shining staff in one hand, her forehead distinguished by a stone pressed against the spot where Xyleea had daubed her blue thumbprint.

Behold the Uniter, come to receive the daala.

The grogakee's tender voice melted through Xyleea, comforting her as nothing had ever done before. She basked in the exquisite feeling the way a lizard relishes a sun-heated rock after its winter sleep. Her voice sang louder still, louder than it had ever sung, her throat opening in some way she could not understand to allow the fullness of the vibrating words out as they rushed to prostrate themselves upon the mountain's white cliffsides.

The deeta had also been borne up by two strong men, her headpiece throwing its shadow upon the pale ground like a sacrifice. They were two deetas, side-by-side, facing the wondrous mountain and offering all they and their people had to give.

Even in the dark the trees shimmered, Xyleea marveling at the way their crystalline branches caught the moon's silvery gaze and made it brighter.

A series of long snorts sounded behind her. Without looking, Xyleea knew Kaambree was adding its tuskee voice to the shouting. She smiled, her love for the matriarch expanding her chest.

The ground shook, and the men stumbled, the grogakee inside Xyleea's head momentarily forgotten as she caromed sideways. She grabbed onto a shoulder, her other hand flying up to steady the kereet. The men shifted her as they regained their footing.

The mountain rumbled again, a seismic wave racing through the ground and stuttering her bearers' feet anew. She felt them give way, and her body stiffened for impact, but instead of hitting ground, she was thrusting upward again. It took her a moment to understand what had happened. She glanced down, astounded to see ten men clustered beyond the original two, their fierce faces concentrated on her, their outspread hands forming a living net to prevent her fall. She bobbed her head so as not to dislodge the kereet, unsure how else to acknowledge their actions.

The wizened deeta was also surrounded by a crowd of men, ensuring she remained aloft through the undulations. "Keep singing!" the deeta squeed at Xyleea. "Let Ooribos hear your voice!"

Xyleea launched into her song again, the voices around her joining in as the drummers thumped their drums. The mountain hurled the noise back, buffeting sound waves that penetrated Xyleea's body and made her quiver.

CRAAAAAACKKKKK

An ear-splitting breaking, followed by scudding and a monstrous thud shattered the air. A large section of cliffside had separated and spalled off, the Xetili nearest scrabbling for cover as the rock-slab sheeted down.

"Keep singing!" the deeta exhorted. "Ooribos has begun to rise! He needs your voices to lift him from the mountain!"

Atop Xyleea's head, the daala tingled, as did the thumbprint on her forehead, the two sensations making her feel as if her own head was splitting. She closed her eyes, bracing against the feeling and the strangeness in her throat as it continued to roar out words like a maddened chassa. What was happening to her? The whole of her was vibrating, and the more the Xetili sang and beat their drums, the stronger the vibrations became. She searched her mind for the grogakee, but the Dragon had left her. She alone had to integrate these dronings and hummings and tinglings or she would fly apart. She took a breath in the pause between two shouted song-words and forced herself to concentrate on the daala.

Another loud crack sounded, and she prayed to the ancestors that the men would keep her safe. The daala's tingling increased, as did the tingling on her forehead. Another thud reverberated as the mountain shed a second white-rock scale.

Grogakee, grogakee, callaska hee...

Xyleea closed her eyes and hooted the words like a giant mandaaba, loud enough for the disappearing moon to hear.

Elorah felt herself lifting from the ground, the roar of displacing air obliterating the thumping call of the mountain. She had to trust her companions were with her, the wind's noise making it impossible to hear them.

Between them, Elorah and Brynz were displacing enough air to lift the entire party above the ground and propel them forward. The tall Iellian was now at the rear, acting as a rudder for their airstream ride. The horses and ponies cantered like mad as the wind pushed them along, their thrashing hooves skimming above the ground.

In no time, they were at the mountain's base. Elorah withdrew her internal force by degrees to ease the group to ground, though the maneuver still had its challenges. The hoofed animals fared best, their galloping helping them as they hit the ground running. Mierrle and Thane had the hardest landings, both tumbling forward as their unprepared feet met terra firma. Aikin fared better, pinwheeling his arms and legs to keep upright. Rachmyn and Haedyn met ground with more agility, each lithing forward at impact and retaining their balance.

Brynz made for the horses and ponies, catching up their flying lead-lines before bringing herself to ground and halting them.

Thane helped Mierrle to her feet. "Are you sound?" he asked. When she nodded, he clapped his hands against his stick-thin legs to rid his leggings of dust. "It started well enough, but the ending left something to be desired." He smiled at Mierrle who giggled.

Aikin put in, "A bit like jumping down from a running horse."

"I wouldn't know," Thane said. "I make it a point to stop the animal first."

Aikin laughed. "Preferable but not always practical." He looked at Thane's flapping pantling, a teasing grin spreading across his face.

"Retrieve what you need from the packs," Elorah said. "We'll be leaving the stock here." She hooked her satchel onto her shoulder. As the rest made ready, she turned her attention to the mountain. She could hear people shouting along with the drumming.

An unsettling ripple moved through the ground.

"Whoa," Aikin said. "Did you feel that?" The ground wavered again, and he stared at his feet. "It's as if every root between here and that mountain is on fire."

Elorah sent her own Therran vorik out and felt a crackling heat, not unlike a fire, as roots sizzled and surged. Either the roots were pushing their energies at the mountain, or the mountain was pulling their energies toward itself, the friction heating the rootweave. The vorestone trembled against her chest.

"I feel it," she confirmed, nodding to the rest of the group. "We haven't a moment to lose. The great good Founder has awakened from his slumber and is beginning to rise." She looked up at the moon, a wheel of red cheese being gnawed down to its rind. Soon they would be without its light altogether. "We must get onto the mountain." Her staff suffused with golden light as she strode forward.

Rachmyn had grown up hearing stories about the hidden power of shadow-moons. He'd been a young boy the last time one had happened, too young to understand as older members of the Kalto band had pointed at the sky then hurried off with eager expressions. Only his parents had seemed unhappy, his father staring at the sky between black looks at Rachmyn's mother. The trembling in Rachmyn's pocket brought the memories back as he looked up at the vanishing moon. The shard had not been his then, only coming into his possession after his parents' deaths. It danced in his pocket now, becoming more animated the further the eclipse progressed.

Elgre was gone, having escaped the seizing wind when it swooped in and pushed the rest before it like dry leaves. Instead, the wolf had loped away on a southwesterly track.

"What about Fryk?" Haedyn's concerned face snatched Rachmyn from his thoughts.

"Hmmm?"

"Should I leave him or take him?"

Rachmyn detected the worry in his friend's voice. "We've no idea what we'll be facing. Best to leave the bird I'd say, without his hood or jesses. He's well able to fend for himself as he's proven." Rachmyn had no doubt the little eye-plucker would outlast them all.

"That seems sensible," Haedyn said, rousting the bird, untying its jesses and removing the sock toe. The grynt's eyes burned bright in the dim light. Haedyn straight-fingered the raptor onto his leather guard before bobbing his forearm upward. "Off now, Fryk."

The bird took to the air in a flurry of wingbeats, a loud *chirrt-chirrt-chirrt* trailing behind as it disappeared into the night.

"Well, that's that," Haedyn said, stiffening his chin.

"I'm sure he'll be fine. Come along, they're waiting."

"I've always wanted an adventure, but now that I'm about to have one, I'm not sure I want it after all."

Rachmyn clasped his friend's shoulders and gave them a shake. "That's the thing about adventures. We don't choose them. They choose us."

"Have you any idea what we'll be doing?" Haedyn asked.

"Not a clue," Rachmyn responded. He set his sights on the flat-topped mountain, trying to envision how it could transform into what he'd seen in Oru Fen.

Up ahead, Elorah was making her way forward, the staff lighting her way, the others stringing out behind as they started to climb.

Rachmyn and Haedyn looked at one another before bursting forward, racing each other until they'd caught up with the group.

The mountain had quaked as many times as Xyleea had fingers. Each time, the men had steadied her so that she remained above the crowd. Her gaze caught upon a dart-point of light working its way up the foothills. Her heart leapt.

The deeta twisted her head round, her eyes going wide. "Outsiders!" she screamed.

The nearest dancers stopped, their songs dying in their throats. The men bundled Xyleea and the deeta to the ground then clustered around them while strident voices rushed the news from mouth to ear around the dancing circle. It ground to a halt then broke apart, many seizing rocks and sticks before charging down the embankment toward the intruders.

"Noooo!" Xyleea roared, reaching toward the deeta, who scuttled away before turning toward the approaching light, the wrinkled corners of her eyes and mouth falling down.

"She is the Uniter! It is she who will return the daala to Ooribos! Tell them! TELL THEM!" Xyleea screamed, panic surging inside. She had to make them stop, or all was lost.

The deeta's head swiveled toward Xyleea, her down-turned mouth dropping open as black-and-green maandaba feathers lashed golden minkee fur. The men stepped back, and back again.

"TELL THEM!"

The deeta's eyes went wide, her open mouth gawping like a dying fish. The men encircled the old woman and moved her away from Xyleea, leaving her standing alone, one finger pointing at the deeta, the other pointing toward the attacking men.

TELL THEM!

The air quivered as the voice of the dragon thundered out, the weight of the words clapping down like falling rocks and sending the nearest Xetili diving for cover. The ones brave enough to look, stared up at Xyleea with white-rimmed eyes, their cheeks and chins pulled tight around their gaping mouths. Xyleea stared back, her throat burning as if she'd swallowed hot coals, the rest of her quaking like overheated stones from the sensations flowing down from the daala, inflaming her skull and backbone.

Xyleea heard a commotion, the thudding of blows, and a woman's pleas.

LEAVE HER!

Her throat burned hotter, her head and neck on fire as the words thundered out.

A strange wailing began, something like a chassa caught in a foot snare.

The men were now running back, their sticks and rocks forgotten as they raised their hands to shield their faces from Xyleea's blistering eyes. Several gave her appeasing smiles as they scurried past.

"What is happening?" she thought, staring at the cowering Xetili, their bulging eyes peeking at her from behind bushes and rocks and trees.

Only then did she realize the voice of the dragon had been coming from her.

CHAPTER FIFTY
MORE ALIKE THAN DIFFERENT

Elorah clutched the staff as it pulled her forward, her feet struggling to keep pace as she raced up the mountain. She didn't wait for her companions, her happiness overwhelming all thought now that she was at the place she'd dreamed of her entire life. All she could think about was running until she reached the top.

A thunderous voice rang out.

AFEE UULUK ONTA! AFEE DAALA AK OORIBOS!

Elorah stopped, her chin stretching up as she scanned the sky for the marvelous voice trembling her vorestone and brightening her staff. The whittled moon hung like a rusted sickle, low enough for the mountain to scythe a basketful of stars. A frisson burst through her as long-held yearning found its reward. She closed her eyes, her hand going to her vorestone, as she shouted, "I am here, Great One!"

The sound of approaching feet barely registered as she reveled in the accomplishment of arriving on Whitemond the very night she was needed.

Hot-breathed shouts and the thump of hard things hitting softer things pried her eyes open.

A confusion of scar-faced men with blue-blotched skin surrounded her, flinging rocks and swinging sticks.

"Peace! I come in peace!" she blurted, her startled words hardly making it past her lips before a blockish fist slammed into her chest.

APSEE AGEE!

"Uuuunnnggg," Elorah blubbed as she crashed to the ground, her staff skidding out of her hand. The man rushed forward, the rock in his fist a gray blur as he slammed it toward her head. She jerked sideways, then scrambled onto all fours, the rock swiffing past her ear. She reached for her staff, her fingers nearly there when a heavy blow jammed her face into the dirt. "I mean you no harm!" she spluttered, her arm snaking out and snatching the staff. She yanked it to her then folded around it as her head dove between her knees.

Another thunderclap of words fell from the sky.

ELLEE HROO

Elorah watched from beneath her armpit as the men sprinted away, their rocks and sticks falling from their hands as they pelted up the slope.

"Shifting stars!" Rachmyn bleated as he hauled her to her feet. "Are you hurt?"

Haedyn blasted past, bellowing like an angry bull, one arm holding his knife like a spear. Aikin came fast behind, his feet churning sprays of gravel as he charged up the embankment.

"Wait!" Elorah cried, breaking away from Rachmyn's grasp and running after them.

Aikin pulled up, but Haedyn charged on, his bellowing ratcheting into a war cry. Rachmyn ran after his friend, his long strides outpacing Elorah.

"Stop!" he yelled as Haedyn's form ducked out of sight.

Aikin ran past, his large frame blocking Elorah's view as he hustled after the two. Elorah redoubled her efforts, forcing her legs to go faster.

Rachmyn disappeared, and she thought her heart might give out before she made it to where they were. Behind, she could hear the pounding of feet as her own lifted away from the ground. Without realizing it, she'd summoned her Atmos vor, though she wanted to preserve what was left of her forces. She set her feet back to the task of running as she tamped down the internal flow that had gotten them flying.

She crested the ridge and found herself in a clearing. Haedyn stood nearby, his arms at his sides, staring about in disbelief. Rachmyn and Aikin were also staggered by the scene. She went to them, her chest heaving, her eyes taking in every detail.

Everywhere were people wearing woven-fiber skirts and shirts, their dark-brown limbs and faces splotched with blue markings. Most cowered behind rocks and bushes, their terror-struck eyes shifting between her group and a young woman wearing a tall headdress made of horns and hair with a golden feather tail and an enormous silver feather at the front.

The rest of Elorah's group straggled onto the ridge, Brynz staring dumbfounded at the young woman, her hand going to her waist tether.

"Fleek me," Thane panted. "My leg wasn't ready for that. Is it still attached?"

"I think I might be sick," Mierrle gasped, clamping her hand to her side and bending over. Elorah sent her friend a pulse of heart vorik before taking hold of Thane's arm and sending a pulse into him.

Mierrle straightened. "What's happened to your face?" she cried, reaching toward Elorah, her eyes filling with tears.

"I'm fine." Elorah caught Mierrle's hand in her own.

"Does it hurt?"

Aikin jabbed his elbow into Elorah's side. "She's coming this way," he whispered.

"Who?" Elorah asked, letting go of Mierrle.

"I've my knife," Haedyn blustered. "She'll not get past it."

"No." Elorah pulled Haedyn's arm down. "We're not here to fight. We're here to help."

The young woman's face beamed a smile, and she held out her hands as she continued forward. Elorah's vorestone thumped against her breastbone, the movement visible through her tunic. The young woman stopped, then spread her hands wide.

"Welcome, Uniter." The girl's mouth moved, but her voice's full, rich tone came from everywhere. "We have waited long for your return."

A tiny old woman sidled out from a scrag of brush, her back humped over like the top of a mushroom, a knurled brown hand clamping her headpiece onto her bowed head. She scuttled forward then kneeled at the young woman's feet, her headdress grazing the dirt as her skinny arms stretched forward in supplication.

Her see-true stone fluttered as Elorah watched the younger woman urge the elder to her feet then spoke to her in hushed tones.

"What manner of wycchery have we stumbled into?" Aikin breathed.

The young woman straightened and removed a small clay vessel from her chest strap. She handed it to the older woman already moving to stand beside her. The young woman beckoned Elorah forward, while the elder tapped blue powder from the vessel into her hand.

"For you..." The young woman's words shouted from everywhere as she removed her headpiece, revealing an object the size and shape of a large nut nestled in her golden-brown curls. After clamping the headdress beneath a crooked arm, the young woman plucked the brown sphere down and held it out in her hand. "I have brought the daala."

Though the words sounded different, Elorah could hear their message inside her head as if her own mind were speaking, understanding the object in the young woman's hand was a living part of the great good Founder. It seemed impossible, and yet, she knew it was true.

"What is she saying?" Mierrle whispered.

"No idea," Thane whispered back.

Elorah took a step forward. Aikin grabbed her arm. "What are you doing? These savages have already tried to kill you."

"They meant no harm," she murmured. She gazed down at his grasp, then into his constricted face. "We must go forward. We cannot go back."

He reluctantly let loose, his hand dropping away.

"He makes a good point," Thane lowed. "How can you be sure they won't attack?"

"One can never be sure until one tries," Elorah replied.

The old woman approached, the thumb of one hand grinding against a blue blob in her palm.

"Laa hee," the elder crooned, beckoning toward Elorah. She bent closer, and the old woman pressed her blued thumb against Elorah's forehead, a curious tingling marking the spot. The vorestone bounced wildly against her chest, and she drew back her neckline to have a closer look. The stone launched upward, its chain breaking as it flew to the thumbmark and sealed itself against the blue dot. Astonishment turned to excitement as memories of the vorestone's use in Oru Fen swept into her mind.

The younger woman waited as the elder thumb-marked each of Elorah's companions before holding out the brown sphere in her cupped palm. "I, Xyleea of the Ushoku and Xetili, by way of our ancestors and our peoples, present to you, the Uniter, this daala, and ask that you return it to our beloved Ooribos Grogakee, on behalf of his devoted caretakers." This time, the young woman's voice was soft inside Elorah's ears.

Elorah accepted the sphere and the elder ululated. "See the sign of Ooribos!" she cried, one hand pointing at the sky. "Beat the drum and raise your voice! Sing! SING!"

Elorah looked up. The moon had disappeared, replaced by a deeper-than-black disc-shaped shadow made darker still by the corona of orange-red light encircling it.

"The ring of fire," Haedyn marveled. "I never thought I'd see one."

Around them, Xetili crept out from their hiding places, more people than Elorah had ever imagined. The drums began to pound—*ah-bah-bah*—as the people formed a ring around the mountain.

Xyleea beckoned again. "Come Uniter. Help us raise Ooribos Grogakee from his long slumber." Her soft voice was compelling, and Elorah found herself moving with her.

"What is happening?" Thane asked, his voice rising.

"Come!" Elorah cried as she skip-walked toward the swaying ring of blue-marked people clasping hands and singing an ancient song.

Grogakee, Grogakee, Callaska Hee...

The blue-marked people widened their ring to allow Xyleea and the old woman to join, then widened it again for Elorah and her group. Hand-in-hand, they sang and banged their feet in time with the drummers' beat while Xyleea and the elder exhorted them to sing until the Ooribos Grogakee could resist their call no longer.

Essiant and the Voriens had made their way to Whitemond, their night-wards' voices ringing in their ears.

From their vantage point, they could see the splits and cracks in the mountain's base as the Founding Dragon worked his way free from the white-stone sarcophagus of his long confinement, his mouth releasing the tail he'd swallowed when first he'd wrapped round the sapphire heart of the mountain.

The wraithwolves positioned themselves in correspondence to where their night-wards stood singing the ancient song preserved by the parambek's caretakers. The wolves also had a song to sing. An ancient one from an ancient time.

"Birth!" Essiant howled into the purple-dusk firmament alight with twinkling stars.

"Birth!" the Voriens howled.

"Youth!" Essiant howled, his being coming alive with an energy unused for eryns.

"Youth!" The Voriens howled, their voices stronger.

"Vigor!" Essiant howled, his energy increasing.

"Vigor!" The Voriens howled, with limbering force.

"Wisdom!" Essiant howled with full-throated power.

"Wisdom!" The Voriens answered, with full vitality.

"Death!" Essiant howled with renewed purpose.

"Death!" The Voriens echoed, their voices unconquerable.

A descendant cycle was ending, an ascendant cycle taking its place. It was to this the wraithwolves howled. This and the imminent rise of a Founder from a mountain's stony grip.

It was a glorious reason to sing, and the wraithwolves made full use of it.

As the singing and drumming amplified, Elorah felt the ground tremble. She reached her mind down, finding Eolemar's pulse far quicker than ever before, though she took no notice. Instead, she concentrated on inserting herself into the inexhaustible energy flowing beneath her feet. With a thought, her vor enjoined with it, the light in her staff flaring to a startling white, the daala quivering against her palm. The immersion brought with it a sudden clarity.

She could now see that her mental faculties were the product of not one but four individual minds stacked one atop another like the layers of a cake. At the bottom sat her organic mind keeping track of her internal processes. Above lay her sensory mind registering feelings within and without her body. Next was her reasoning mind, collecting individual thought-sparks from her lower two minds and laying them out like gemstones upon the jeweler's bench of her overmind for stringing together into the thought-chains that went either into the halls of memory or the cellar of forgetting.

Her companions were swaying hand-in-hand with blue-painted people, belting out song-words strange to them, adding their individual voices—Thane's chime-clear tenor, Haedyn's fiery baritone, Rachmyn's gravelly growl, Mierrle's storm-dark alto, Aikin's tone-deaf bellow, Brynz's airy soprano—to the greater thrum trying to raise a Dragon.

"It is time," she murmured, her core now a resonant powerbeam as she attuned with the source of all vor.

Her overmind divided away, elevating into the secondary world of Oru Fen while her reasoning mind stayed behind to continue the busywork of managing her lower two minds. The shift took Elorah by surprise, disorienting her for a moment before she grasped her concurrent presence in both realms. Only by focusing on the idea of her companions could she perceive them with her split awareness.

She watched as Mierrle drew forth the packet of Wandering Silvi from her tunic pocket, folded back the silver-foil top then handed the pouch to Rachmyn, as Elorah had asked her to do. Rachmyn poured in a half-vial of speck and gave the packet a shake.

Then, a surprise. Thane produced a hoewler hidden from beneath his tunic and showed it to Rachmyn with a sly grin. The Shadowen arched an eyebrow as Thane balanced the dreamcrafting tool upon his palm before extending his arm forward, his head bobbing first at the hoewler then at the silver packet. A knowing smile flitted across Rachmyn's lips as he took the tool. He stood it on his own palm and tipped some of the packet's contents into it.

A familiar howl pulled at Elorah's overmind, and she willed herself to resist its persuasive tug.

Thane and Mierrle resumed their singing and foot stomping while Rachmyn, using the hoewler, began puffing speck into the group members' faces. When finished, he crammed the hoewler into his waistband, then slipped into the space Mierrle and Haedyn made for him.

With the greatest concentration, Elorah shuffled her manifest feet forward, coming to Thane first. "Bend forward," she said.

Thane complied, and Elorah placed her forehead against his, centering her vorestone upon his blue-thumbed mark, her overmind conjuring up the vision of the restored parambek and sending it through the stone as she urged him to *See True*. At the same moment, the speck began to take hold, and Elorah could feel Thane's shocked excitement as his consciousness divided and his overmind winged away to Oru Fen.

Elorah went to each of her companions and repeated the process, each separation sending a thrill through her own heightened perception as her companions' overminds zinged away from their bodies and into Oru Fen.

The Wycche flew up the starshine pathway into the realm that knew her best. Her grip on events was slipping, and it was all she could think about, even when awake, the crush of expectation and grief weighing her down as she watched the restoration of her once-noble family's rule move further and further away.

Erynvors! Bah! Toadies and moles for the hated Elect, every one of them. How she wished to see them all burn. Mindless devotees to an unjust cause and an unjust principle. How had it gone so far this time? Hot anger pushed up from her unsettled stomach, burning away all trace of malaise as she stepped into the purple-gray mist of her world. And it was her world. She brooked no doubt about that.

Venge stepped from the shadows, his eyes igniting a fire in her heart. He didn't suffer from these pangs that had begun to plague and muddle her thinking. He was never weak in the face of adversity. Nor should she be. Her weakness made her angrier still as her liege bowed before her. She signaled for him to stand, then placed her hand upon his rankly-made head.

The images flowed into her mind. The Erynvor was already here, and with her, a collection of ninnies under her spell. Then it came forth, the prick of luck she needed. The white wolf and his pack had yet to take the group under their care. They were unguarded. This was her moment. As soon as the thought struck, Malvisse melted out of the mist.

She lifted her hand and twirled herself into a cyclone of fury.

To the mountain! she cried, the touchpoint already in her mind. This Erynvor would not escape before the Wycche saw her defeated.

Rachmyn was the last to arrive, having waited until the others ascended. Upon his entry, a great howling erupted as the Voriens called their night-wards to them. Along with the howling came an uprush of energy, and for a moment, Elorah struggled to understand what she was seeing. Only when her soul connected with her wraithwolf did she realize what had happened.

Her staff was still in her hand, the orb in her other, her vorestone lodged against her Spyrrt eye. Somehow, Rachmyn had brought through Thane's hoewler as well as his own marvelous shard.

She shifted her focus to the manifest, shuffling her feet away from her companions—their mortal forms still dancing and singing even as their overminds were off in Oru Fen—to stand near Xyleea and the elder. Her companions' glazed eyes stared blankly as the vibrations of the grogakee's song permeated their physical forms. Her own manifest body looked on with the same glassy stare as her focus switched back to her overmind.

Welcome, Erynvor.

Essiant! her soul cried with delight.

Behold the mountain. Behold the ring of fire.

A purple-light version of Whitemond appeared out of the gloom.

Elorah scanned the realm's overhanging sky. Here too, a black disk obscured the moon while allowing its corona to shine. Beyond it lay stars as far as the mind could think.

Elorah looked at her guardian, surrounded by wraithwolves bearing the crescent-moon sigil of their pact. Each stepped to their ward, six soul-bonds forming and flaring golden light.

Whitemond gave a mighty heave, a sensation Elorah could feel in the manifest and in Oru Fen. Her companions looked about, unable to distinguish between the two as their ethereal arms went akimbo, their ethereal legs bent into semi-squats, mirroring their waking bodies' movements on the physical plane.

Essiant's head whipped round, his quivering ears pricked at high attention. His hackles rose, and he issued a low growl.

Prepare yourselves, his mindwords warned. *The Wycche has come into the realm.*

Though she knew she should keep her attention on the singing and dancing, Xyleea found her thoughts drawn to the Uniter and her enraptured companions as they swayed and sang. Such strange faces, so different from her own or the people she'd come to think of as hers. Some were pale as tuskee teeth, the rest the sandy brown of goru root. None were the deep brown of her and her people. And yet, something about their washed-out faces seemed familiar.

Then it came to her. They'd walked out of her dreams. At the time, she'd thought her mind too weary, her belly too empty, her heart too weak, to feed her dreamtime thoughts. But now, she realized, the daala had been working on her in far more ways than she'd known, showing her these people, more alike than different, so that when they appeared, she would not run or fight or fear their words, because they had already danced and sang together many times.

Like a stone falling on her head, it hit her how far she had traveled. When she'd begun, she'd had no idea what she was looking for, so to find herself here, a deeta in the midst of the greatest ceremony of her entire life—of any life—was beyond any beekabeeka she had ever dreamed as a child. If only her Ushokan people were here now, to live this with her. Oh, the stories they would tell; oh, the songs they would sing. Oh, the happiness they would feel, here on the grogakee's mountain.

The ground rocked beneath her feet, and she opened her throat wider in bellowing song, her deeta heart aflame with love.

CHAPTER FIFTY-ONE
AS ABOVE SO BELOW

A blink after Essiant joined with his night-ward, the horde of Malvisse were upon them, their blitzing attack overwhelming his ability to detect their approach.

The naives scrambled toward the base of the shadow Whitemond, an instinctive reaction as their terrified overminds struggled to cope with the nightmare around them. All five turned toward the snarling wolves, fear pulling their faces tight, courage rooting their feet to the orucon. Each pressed a hand against the sigil on their wraithwolf's forehead.

Do not fear these! Use your powers! Kelm's mindwords blared, the cry taken up by Raya and Embren then Ieeva and Ajai.

A streak of gold blazed past, blunting the Malvisse attack, deadblack-clad wolves veering aside like startled sheep. Kimbre had made a sortie run to slow the charge, his stardust armor shooting rays of condensed shine into the eyes of the frontmost attackers.

A sparkling quaver of energy hurtled toward the galloping wolf, exploding into a shower of light-splinters behind his streaming tail. A second quaver ripped in, striking the wolf behind the ears and bowling him tail-over-head into a disheveled heap. A large patch of stardust lifted away, its pulsing shine sucked into the deadblack of the nearest Malvisse.

Shaken, Kimbre got to his feet and hurtled forward again, a limp hindering his speed. Another quaver exploded against his back, knocking him to the ground. A low moan escaped as Kimbre struggled forward, his backend dragging like a broken tail, his tattered armor winking out when he crawled into a low fog bank.

Essiant set his stance, his searching vorik sweeping in the direction the quaver had originated.

It wasn't hard to see where it had come from. The Wycche, a malevolent twirl of nimbus, hovered above the Malvisse legion. She had come with a full bag of tricks this time, marshalling the realm's quarks and sprites while her horde's collective deadblack gobbled every spark of stray energy available. The sheer amount of deadblack created a palpable tow against Essiant's stardust, and it took more concentration than he wished to expend to keep his armor intact.

Co-opting quarks and sprites was a risky strategy. Essiant worried the disruption could destabilize the energy weave holding the realm together. He could not recall a single instance where it had been tried. Not until now.

The sprites, in particular, were troubling. Though a malleable form of light matter, easily manipulated into conglomerate forms, there were consequences. Plucking them from the weave reduced the realm's cogency. The orusphere was also thickening as unspent sprites collected, impairing thought impetus and coherence. Essiant could feel his own faculties straining as he surmised how the Wycche was managing this unheard-of malfeasance. She must be using the steady pull of the deadblack to harvest the sprites along with her own duplicitous vor to shape them into photonic bombs. The resultant explosions were damaging to stardust, but that didn't worry Essiant as much as the thought that the entire realm might implode from the Wycche's actions.

The main of the Malvisse advanced on the naives while a subset, led by the Wycche's dark wolf, made for Essiant and the Erynvor as well as Spectra and her ward.

Essiant howled into the gloom, exhorting the Voriens to fortify their shields, even as he sent another surge of vorik into the thick wall surrounding his night-ward. Above all else, the Erynvor must be protected and allowed to preserve her power. With the Agya, she held the future of Grogauk's sentience in her hands and until she ascended into Inverna and returned the mystical orb to the great good Founder, the restoration of Therrania could not progress. But before that could happen, the Wycche must be banished from Oru Fen, or the pathway to Inverna, now closed, would never open.

Essiant sent the whole of his thoughts to Spectra in the form of pictorial images, the fastest means of communicating a complicated idea, even as he obscured the strife from his night-ward's awareness by condensing the sphere of cloud surrounding her, knowing her first instinct would be to help her companions. This was not the time for heroics. It was far more important that the Erynvor protect the Founder's Infinite Eye and shield it from the Wycche's perception, though that was a difficult proposition. Its overwhelming energy pattern was not something easily hidden. The best Essiant could do was to obscure his ward and hope she kept the Agya inside its case.

Spectra's mind issued its own pictorial message, a projection of what she and her night-ward would attempt. It was a clever plan, and Essiant confirmed his approval before turning to the naives now locked into a stand-off with the Malvisse.

Their wraithwolves had co-opted their individual powers to build a whirling shield of icy wind and flaming bramblecane. It was an inelegant but effective solution.

Like a tentacled funnel cloud, the shield whipped round, forcing back the bulk of the Malvisse by perforating the wolves' brittle deadblack with its blistering firecanes. The boldest of the wolves heaved themselves into the construction's path, looking for a way through, but the shield's icy breath froze their damaged deadblack, the next lash of a fiery cane shattering it like glass.

Rachmyn had constructed his own disruption shield using his vor. His shard and its crackling energy kept the Wycche's wraithwolf and its cohorts at bay while the Shadowen pulled the hoewler from his waistband and placed its belled end against his lips. Had he wanted to conform the environment for dream sculpting, he would have blown through its mouthpiece to attune the ethers to his personal vibration, but that wasn't the aim. The aim was to attract the overcharges, freeing the environment of their debilitating pulses while simultaneously using their chaotic charge against the Wycche's nimbus.

The Shadowen sucked in through the upside-down instrument, much like sucking liquid through a straw on the manifest plane. Stray sprites gathered like fireflies around his head, and he'd collected a goodly number by the time the tears began to fall, a few at first, then more and more, droplets pummeling down from the dull gray firmament like rain. It was something Essiant had never felt before, a slippery viscosity atop the shine of his armor. He worried his stardust would not hold up, but a quick check reassured him his armor was undaunted. The deadblack, however, was not so impervious to the foreign-feeling thought-forms. A chorus of yodeling howls began, as thought-droplets were sucked in by the gluttonous deadblack in its continual grasp for energy.

Essiant searched for the source of this innovation. Ajai's mindwords made it clear.

My ward weeps for the pain of a broken world. Behold the tears of the wounded and lost.

Too late, the Malvisse began to construct their own shields to protect their greedy armor from contamination. But the damage had been done; most of the wolves scattering as their coverings began to dissolve. Only the shadow-dark wolf managed to avoid the plaguing tears by huddling beneath his night-ward's nimbus.

The Wycche, seeing the disarray, bellowed a rallying cry, a disharmonic gabbling that canceled the snarling and growling of the retreating horde. Her nimbus pulled upward, forming into a black column of immense size before crashing onto the orucon like a giant tree then sweeping in a wide arc, its tremendous girth marshalling the disoriented Malvisse. It changed shape yet again, pulling into a swirling ball before flattening into a canopy against the droplets raining down. Too late for the most grievously damaged, already dragging themselves away, their deadblack evaporating as they skulked into the misty brume.

The Wycche's actions could be construed as a form of benevolence toward the Malvisse, but Essiant knew better. It was a stalling tactic, nothing more. Sensory thought forms were rare in this realm, and the Wycche had not prepared for such a challenge.

It was the perfect moment to draw her away.

Spectra apprehended Essiant's thoughts, Rachmyn's enshielded form already rising toward the Wycche's canopy-shape like an escaping bubble. The pale-haired Shadowen had gathered enough sprites to conjure up his own illusion fed by his wraithwolf's memories. He reached into his pocket and pulled out his shard. He switched the hoewler's position with his other hand, blowing through the mouthpiece to clear away the Wycche's vibration and replace it with his own. As he did, the shard's shape rounded and darkened until it resembled the fantastical orb the Erynvor protected. The sprites gathered around the shard-orb, lending additional dynamism to the illusion, while the shard itself added its own depth of power as a lure. Spectra knew the Wycche desired the shard, but she desired the Agya above all and would go to the ends of the realm to chase it.

The canopy transformed into a beautiful woman. Rachmyn gaped, and it was only Spectra ramming her head against his thigh a jot before the woman's hand flashed forward that he kept from losing the shard.

He shot away, his wraithwolf beside him, both whizzing along an unfurling starshine pathway at the speed of thought. The raven-haired woman transformed again, her apparition twirling itself into the nimbus form the Wycche favored before giving chase, her own wolf taking the lead.

Essiant watched, aware that the entire Restoration was hanging in the balance. If the Shadowen was successful, his night-ward could ascend with the Infinite Eye. If he was not....

Essiant turned his thoughts away from that outcome, determined not to succumb to the trap of defeatist thinking. Instead, he scanned the opposition.

The leaderless Malvisse had separated into smaller groups. All the better. They would need to be nullified, and their lack of cohesion would only help with that.

I'm in a fleeking nightmare!

Thane tried to collect his thoughts as armored wolves charged toward him. He'd seen wolves like these once before in a horrible dreamcraft that had almost put him off the activity forever. At the time, he'd attributed the fiendish apparitions to adulterated speck so it came as a shock to realize he might have been wrong. Again. He knew he hadn't been poisoned this time, yet here were the same wolves he'd seen in that long ago dream-terror, wearing armor and slavering for blood. Or whatever passed for blood in this dream realm, because he was somehow aware this wasn't real in the way his awareness at the mountain was real, and yet it seemed real enough with the fiends coming at him, and his own wolf, Ieeva, standing by his side, urging him not to run but to use his powers.

It had all happened in a blink. One moment, he'd been chanting with blue-painted natives—a strange enough experience for any lifetime —in a language he didn't know and the next his mind was zinging off into the dream realm, his awareness in two places at once after Elorah placed her forehead stone against his brow.

It was almost more than he could comprehend, everything coming at him faster than a Bravik attack. But he had little time to dwell on it as Ieeva rammed his leg and put forward the thought of the icy northlands, urging him to actuate the memory. It seemed a simple enough concept, but he had no experience using his native vor in such a place.

Imagine how it would feel, and it will be so, Ieeva said. *Your mind will create it, and your vor will sustain it.*

The painful prickle of ice-laced wind against unclothed skin came to mind. He hugged himself against the cold.

Summon your vor to actuate your vision, Ieeva instructed.

He wasn't sure he knew what she meant, but as soon as he raised his vor, a version of the memory began spinning around him and his companions. The others were also putting forth vor-crafted imaginings that, in turn, created a whirling, slashing thought-form beyond the ken of any of them. The attacking wolves didn't stand a chance against their combined efforts. He wanted to shout, as the power of their shield shattered wolf after wolf, but Ieeva cut him short.

Think only of the illusion. Nothing else, she warned.

A tall order, but he set his mind to the task, knowing it meant everything.

567

Rachmyn felt the pound of his heart, Spectra's mindwords loud inside his head.

Everything begins and ends here.

It was the first place he thought of when his wraithwolf rammed his leg and bid him go. With a thought he was hovering above the spreading tail of Deadman's Peak, viewing a scene from a lifetime ago.

But there wasn't time to think about that, for a black cloud was bearing down hard upon him. He clutched his shard, intending to shove it into his pocket.

No, Spectra warned. *It serves better in your hand just now.*

But I cannot lose it…

Think again. Go!

The wraithwolf's head rammed his leg and another touchpoint popped into his mind.

Immediately, he was hovering above The Running Fox, the walls of the ramshackle inn shaking with bawdy songs and raucous laughter. A dissonant pang ran through him as he surveyed the merry scene.

Don't they even know?

They cannot know what they cannot see. Leave them to their cheer and be glad of it.

The black cloud had already found them, its dark shape obscuring the misty horizon.

Think again! Go!

Spectra's head rammed into his leg, and a third touchpoint occurred.

In an instant, he was at the mountain, watching himself and his companions hand-in-hand with a crowd of natives. They were stepping backward, moving away from the mountain as it shuddered and shook. He realized with a start he was viewing the action from two vantage points, one high enough that the mountain and its surroundings were made small, the other from the ground, his feet shaking, the mountain's cliff sides cracking apart like the shell of an enormous egg.

Behold the moon. Behold the ring of fire.

Spectra's words shifted his focus, and he looked up. The red had begun to push back the blackness. Soon, the blotting shadow and its power would be gone. He would never be stronger than he was now.

The moment the thought struck the black nimbus descended, its edges going gray as it dissipated into a filmy haze before reassembling into a golden-haired woman, her diaphanous garment eddying around her svelte figure.

It was his mother, Arwyn, come back from beyond to see him one last time. Her warm eyes locked onto his, and he was once again a little boy at her knee, so full of love that his swelling heart banged his ribs. Her milky-smooth hand reached toward his shard, and he wanted to give it to her. His concentration slipped, the illusion disappearing, as he opened his hand to her. The shapely hand snatched at the shard as a heavy thump against his leg stumbled him sideways. Sharp fear snapped Rachmyn's hand shut before he could give it back to his mother for it was hers, and he shouldn't have taken it.

I'm sorry, mother...

He opened his hand again, only to be bowled sideways by a tremendous shove. His hand clenched tight around the shard as he fell.

I mustn't drop it. I mustn't drop–

Give it to me, my sweet, crooned his mother's voice. *Give me back what is mine, and all will be well.*

This is not your mother! shouted another familiar voice.

That couldn't be right. It must be his mother. He would know her face anywhere. He would know her voice. She had come for the shard, and he wanted her to have it.

This is not your mother! howled the other voice.

He tightened his grip. Not my mother...

He stared hard into his mother's dark green eyes. Wait... That wasn't right... The eyes bloomed brightly blue, changing the instant doubt struck. He looked at the golden hair, blackened at the roots. *That isn't right either.* He white-knuckled the shard, his mind sweeping away the memories confusing themselves into his thoughts.

This is not my mother.

The apparition devolved into a faceless wraith as it lunged toward Rachmyn's hand.

It all begins and ends here.

Instantly, he was at the Deadman's Peak touchpoint. He checked for his shard. Yes, there it was in his hand.

Conjure a forgetting shield!

The reassuring presence of his wolf helped him focus as he blanked out every thought.

NOW!

Rachmyn squeezed together every scrap of vor inside as he placed the shard against the blue mark on his forehead. His internals compressed, his heart locking onto the boosting power of the darkened moon. A bolus of energy built inside, enough to shove the pernicious vacancy inside his mind out through the shard, the combination of vor and shard and darkened moon magnifying the shield beyond measure as the nimbus slammed into it.

He held his mind on the monotonous void, allowing no other thought to come in while pouring every bit of power he could muster into the erasing blankness smashing out of him.

The nimbus fought back, pulling and tearing at his ethereal form, his mother's voice screaming for him to let go. He perceived none of it, so focused was his mind on remaining blank. Over and over, conjured blankness blasted out through the shard and into the Wycche's nebulous shadowcast until there was nothing left for his vor to strike against.

It is done.

Spectra nudged his leg. The words floated by like smoke as he tried again to force his blankness onto the Wycche, his effort flinging away into the ethers.

It is done, the wolf repeated.

He exhaled, letting go of the concentrated nothingness that had been his focus and allowing his awareness of the realm to return. He opened his eyes, and scanned the gray-bowered sky, looking for any sign of the Wycche.

She is gone. Let us return to the others, for there is still much to do.

With a thought, he and Spectra were back at the mountain.

Elorah stared at the sphere in her hand, her staff hovering overhead like a welcoming sun inside the cocoon of cloud surrounding her. A deep peacefulness settled as she studied the strange gift.

What was it?

The beautiful young woman with the stunning headdress had handed it to her as if she should already know what to do with it, but she hadn't a clue. Her vorestone trembled against her forehead. Perhaps if she put the sphere against the stone, she would find the answer. She tried it, expecting a soul story to leap to life inside her mind, but there was nothing.

She brought the sphere down to the level of her eyes, staring at its construction. A thread-thin line bisected the brunnestone, and it occurred that the stone globe might be a case of some kind. She had an overwhelming urge to see what was inside despite her wraithwolf's warning to remain still.

Should she open it? She wanted to. Should she not? She thought again of Essiant's warning. He would be so disappointed in her. She traced her gaze round the stone sphere, rolling it to gain a better view of the faint indention where the halves fitted together.

She could tug it apart for a moment then put it together again.

Her hands set to it.

The upper half came away from the lower part with ease, revealing a luminous orb of mesmeric beauty. She was drawn into its limitless depths, until she was surrounded by its textures and hues. She stared at the splendid carnival, its stunning colors and malleable shapes combining and recombining into extravagant shadows that hinted at every form of sentience on Eolemar, an ever-changing celebration of creation in all its intricate disguises.

A voice boomed out.

Long have I waited for a Uniter to return that which once rested within me.

Like a candle snuffed out, the riotous conjure-show vanished, and she was once again staring at the orb. She brought it against her trembling vorestone, hoping to see as well as hear the dragon.

Instead, the cloud dome puffed away, and she was left standing upon a grand plain in the midst of chaos.

Snarling wolves in dark armor clustered in milling packs, their hot eyes locking onto her while her own attention was captured by a whirling convection of improbable design—ice and wind, bramblecane and fire—terrorizing the verge of a purple-shaded, etheric Whitemond.

She craned her neck. Where were her friends?

Her wraithwolf stepped near. *Do not fear for them for behold, they make their own way.*

She understood the churning funnel of icewind-firecane was a production of her companions' minds and abilities.

Rachmyn and his wraithwolf materialized from the gloom. The pale-haired man looked shattered, and Elorah's first instinct was to go to him. Essiant blocked her way.

The time has come to carry the Agya to the great, good Founder.

Elorah looked into Essiant's wonderful eyes. *How can I when my friends need me here?*

They have given much for you to make your ascension. Do not disappoint them now after all they have done.

She arrowed a look first at Rachmyn, then toward the mountain. The twisting icewind-firecane dervish was gone. In its place were Haedyn, Thane, Brynz, Mierrle, and Aikin standing in a tight circle with their wraithwolves, all facing outward, their right hands pressed against their wolf's forehead. They looked as worn as Rachmyn from their efforts and again she felt the urge to run to them. Haedyn caught sight of her and beamed a triumphant smile, one jubilant fist punching air.

Darkness-clad wolves turned toward the group, their attention sharpening. A few began a stealthy flanking move, their keen eyes shifting between their path and the Voriens with their night-wards.

Essiant howled the ancient rallying cry.

ALL   ALL   ALL   ALL   ALL

The Voriens took up the cry, their howls pushing back the purple mist.

The flanking wolves startled, then shrunk down. Each repetition of the word pushed them further back, their armor thinning. In pairs and threes and fives, the unclad wolves broke rank, tucking their tails and scuttling toward the mist-margins. Essiant watched as the rag-tag wolves skulked and stalked and scampered away, unable to maintain their defiance in the absence of their leader and her vor.

ALL   ALL   ALL   ALL   ALL

The mountain shook anew, its cliffsides cracking with every sirened howl.

Essiant broke away from the chant, his mindwords strong.

Come, there's no time to lose.

The white wraithwolf pointed his head toward a quaver of energy in front of his night-ward. Elorah followed his gaze and gasped.

A luminous pathway rolled away from the orucon, its leading edge moving toward the unseen above the flat purple top of Whitemond.

She looked at her wraithwolf, but already his head was against her thigh, bumping her forward. She reached up, and the staff nestled into her grip. In it she felt the strength of her companions. Her heart thumped as her gaze went to where the pathway disappeared. Her memory of the great good Founder filled her mind, her yearning to see him again a shaking she couldn't control.

She moved to the pathway, vaguely aware of her companions and their wolves gathering behind, her thoughts swinging between hope and fear and excitement.

Always trust. Never fear.

With her staff in one hand and the orb in the other, Elorah stepped onto the shimmering path, her intention focused on the golden light at the other end.

Chapter Fifty-Two

Shouting Up

Haedyn barely had time to think with armored wolves coming at him from all sides, urged onward by a roiling black cloud. He went for his knife.

Do not fear these! Use your powers!

The words flew past like leaves in the wind, and it wasn't until the red-gold wolf at his side made it clear—her voice somehow inside his head—that he must calm his panicked mind and join his vor with his companions that he managed to gain hold of his thoughts.

The other wolves must have spoken to his companions, because before he knew it, wind swirled, brambles formed, and ice gathered; he only had to add his fire to the spinning, funnel-shaped turbulence springing up from the combining ideas and vor of the others.

The creation spun and flamed and iced and lashed around the circled group and their wolves, increasing in size and power with each passing moment. The effort erased every other thought, blotting out the writhing blackness and the attacking wolves and the paralyzing dread.

He went on for longer than he imagined possible, or maybe it was only for a moment, pushing and pushing, until his wolf spoke again inside his mind.

It is done.

He had no concept of what had been accomplished when he tamped down his remaining sparks of vor, noticing his internal forces were running thin. His wolf nudged his leg, her head pointing his attention toward a clouded dome. Before he could make sense of what it was, it whisked away, revealing Elorah standing beside her starry-white wolf, the crystalwood staff hovering above her head as she stared down at her outstretched hands.

She looked over, her eyes reflecting the shine of her staff and his insides jigged, his face cracking into a wide smile as he punched the air.

He felt another nudge and realized the wolves had not disappeared; they had fallen back. He scanned above, looking for the furious cloud, but there was only misted gray. His gaze went back to the wolves, starting to gather, their eyes like embers in the gloom. A few broke away, trotting a circuitous route, their hot eyes flicking toward the group then away.

Haedyn startled as a shout began to sound.

ALL   ALL   ALL   ALL   ALL

As the words rained down, he could somehow feel them caged inside, struggling to be let out. He opened his mouth, letting the words fly free, his heart gladdening with every shout.

The wolves reacted, too. The deep black of their armor fading away, rendering them far less impressive once their scroungy coats and lank physiques were revealed. It wasn't long before the wolves turned tail and ran for the margins.

Haedyn watched them go, his heart rejoicing, though he didn't understand why he felt as he did.

The next thing he knew, he was moving toward a lighted pathway, angling up into the misty sky above the image of Whitemond. The others moved with him, though Rachmyn—where had he come from? —was already standing next to it with his silvery wolf. There were shadows and lines on his friend's face Haedyn had never noticed before, making him look older and more tired.

Haedyn bumped his fist twice, and Rachmyn returned the gesture. A moment later, he was standing across from his friend, the angling lightpath between them, Elorah stood at its end, her eyes focused on the spot where it disappeared into the clouds.

The time has come to shout the Erynvor up the mountain. It was his wolf again.

What does that mean?

A vision of him pushing fiery light into the path came into his mind, and he understood.

Gathering up his remaining vor, Haedyn veed his hands to funnel it into the path. A pulse of red began weaving into the luminous light, pushing its way up the incline, imbuing the path with his vor signature. Rachmyn's color pushed in next, a silver thread weaving around Haedyn's red on its way up to where the path disappeared. Thane's sea-green strand inserted between the first two on a steady progress upward followed by Mierrle's dark green, Brynz's deep blue and Aikin's vibrant yellow, each strand twining upward until the entire pathway was an intricate braid of their individual lights.

They began chanting *ALL ALL ALL,* their wraithwolves exhorting them to shout the Erynvor up the mountain.

A golden light strobed upward, and Elorah zipped behind it, disappearing into the clouds.

Haedyn started to cry out until a firm thump against his leg stole his voice.

The Erynvor has ascended. She needs your power now more than ever to return.

Haedyn refocused on his vor strand, determined not to let his attention slip again.

There's no ceiling, Elorah thought, looking up and seeing only blue sky.

She dropped her gaze, taking in the details around her. She was in a drawing room though it was so large she couldn't see any of the room's corners. Its avobanc walls were gilded with an interwoven design of luminae spirals that pulsed when her attention wasn't on them. The deep-purple floor was also fantastic, its glassy surface reflecting her canted form as if she were looking into a midnight lagoon.

The room was bathed in brilliant golden light, though there wasn't a candle or lantern or lamp to be seen. Dominating the room was a dimensional version of Whitemond formed from the nacre iridescence of pearl shine and rising from the purple floor into the blue-egg sky.

"Dear heart."

Elorah whirled toward the familiar voice, her heart lurching. "Silvi!"

"I am here," came the voice a moment before the gardener materialized. Gone were the wrinkles and gnarling, the stooped posture and wispy white hair. Instead, the face atop the long neck was flushed with the pink of youth and crowned by a mane of silvery waves cascading down her back. A pearlescent white garment fell from the tops of her well-formed shoulders, past her arms and her figure into a frothy pool at her feet.

Silvi's face lit with the familiar smile Elorah loved. "At last, you are here!" she cried, gathering Elorah into an embrace before stepping away. "Come. There is someone I want you to meet."

With a thought Elorah was beside her old friend near the shimmering mountain.

"See true," Silvi prompted, her hands spreading wide.

The vorestone vibrated against Elorah's forehead as she drew her Spyrrt vor into her head.

The mountain began to shrink, becoming smaller and smaller until it was no bigger than a footstool.

The air shimmied, and a brown-skinned man appeared, hovering cross-legged above the tiny mountain, his bald head bowed, his eyes closed, his hands in a prayer posture against his chest. His monk-like garb was a textured weave of greens and browns and grays dotted with pinpoint coruscations of purple and orange and red. The cloth reminded her of the woodlands around her family's witterang, and she felt a rush of nostalgic pleasure remembering the happy discoveries she'd made there.

She turned to share the memory, but Silvi was no longer beside her. Elorah twisted around. The gardener was standing behind her, a merry smile playing on her lips. She gestured for Elorah to move toward the hovering man, her mercurial eyes sparkling.

The orb urged her forward as well, its pull against her closed hand irresistible. With another thought she was within a finger's stretch of him. A peaceful exuberance came over her, her internals as jittery as the orb inside her hand.

The man modified his penitent posture, his praying hands arcing forward until his outstretched fingertips pointed toward the hand with the orb then, like the opening of a book, unfolding into a palm-up presentation.

The orb's ecstatic buzz became ungovernable, and Elorah opened her hand, astonished to see the orb launch into the man's cupped palms. Her heart soared as the orb settled there like a fledgling returning to its nest, a feeling of completion warming her bones.

The bald man opened his eyes, his gaze fastening onto the orb in his hands. It transformed into a glistering flower shaped something like a water lily. His gaze rolled up until his depthless eyes locked onto Elorah's.

She gasped, a shiver racing down her spine. She had seen his kindly, arboreal eyes once before, in her vision of the great good Founder, Grogauk. How could this man have the eyes of a dragon?

The bald man smiled, his sharply defined teeth whiter than bleached bone.

I thank you, oh Erynvor, for your journey and your gift.

Somehow, she understood the dragon's voice came from the man, though his lips never moved, and the sound was from everywhere.

The cross-legged man lifted his cupped hands to his forehead where, like water to a sponge, the flower-orb absorbed, leaving no trace. His kind eyes brightened into twin suns, and he floated up from the tiny footstool of Whitemond. Elorah rocked her head back, watching as he lifted higher and higher, becoming the merest speck in the wide-open blue.

Behold what is to come.

The enthralling voice filled Elorah with indescribable joy.

The speck exploded into a starburst of light before thrusting out then forming up into an immense dragon. From the flaring nostrils set above a wide mouth arrayed with well-fitted teeth, to the planed cheeks and large, intelligent eyes, it was the most exquisitely made head Elorah had ever seen. Even the two tree-shaped horns atop its poll were perfect. The whole of its body was textured with every manner of moss and vine and shrub, the long neck and powerful shoulders, the well-sprung ribs and strong haunches, the blocky legs with their five spiked talons on the front and four on the back to the girthy, tapered tail. But it was the great, arching wings that enthralled her most, when they unfolded in a billow of greenery across the sky.

She fell to her knees, her mouth dropping open, a single word repeating in her mind.

Grogauk...

The dragon dipped its head as Elorah sank onto her heels, overcome.

Silvi stepped in front, her warm smile beaming down on Elorah's upturned face. "Think of me, and I'll be near," she said inside Elorah's head. "I am the one called Astr Ven."

The older woman shot into the sky and, in a spectacle of alchemy and shapeshifting, transformed into a pearlescent dragon of unparalleled grace.

Elorah goggled, her nerves on fire, her mind screaming, *Silvi is a dragon! A Founding Dragon of the Realm!*

And what a dragon. Where Grogauk was power and might, Astr Ven was sleekness and grace. Her refined head was like a long-nosed steed, with delicate nostrils, a modest mouth and almond-shaped eyes set into a finely wrought backskull. A delicate fringe of shell-shaped scales began between her two antler-like horns and ran the length of her long neck—far longer than Grogauk's—before giving way to a set of lithe shoulders and slender front legs tipped by five thin crescents serving as nails. Her midsection was longer too, and far leaner, lending the perfect bridge between the svelte forequarters and the graceful hind with its rear limbs perfectly apportioned down to the four slim claws at the end. The tail was another marvel, a masterful confection of narrow scales and folding fins twice as long as Grogauk's taper. But the greatest marvel of all were Astr Ven's lacy wings, as airy as spiderwebs between the hyperlong phalanges.

Elorah might have spent the rest of her life staring at the two wondrous dragons if not for the shuffling of the footstool as it moved close to her feet.

She peered down in amazement. She was looking at the actual proceedings on Whitemond, from a distance far above.

There were scores of tiny figures encircling the mountain's base, dancing to the faint *thump-thump-thump* of their drums and singing the fainter *bzz-bzz-bzz* of their songs.

The base of the mountain shook, and Elorah saw the physical version of Grogauk emerge from the settling dust. His huge bulk comprised the entire base of Whitemond, the end of his tapered tail in the firm grip of his own mouth until he opened his eyes and spat it out. Then, after stretching out his stiffened limbs and wings, the dragon launched away from the mountain's center, flying past Elorah's face before swooping down to resettle near the mountain's foot.

The flybuzz song morphed into the rhythmic hum she had heard all her life—the Prayer Song of the Urslan. Elorah bent low. The sound was not coming from the mountain. It was coming from somewhere in the distance, somewhere she couldn't see from where she stood.

You should go back, dear heart. There are some who are already missing you.

Silvi's familiar words tolled like a bell within her as the drawing room walls drew back.

"The Erynvor has returned!"

Elorah blinked, trying to locate who was shouting at the same moment her mind struggled to orient into its changed surroundings. She felt an anchoring presence by her leg.

Essiant, his eyes luminous in the gloom. She looked for the pathway, but it had gone.

Essiant nudged her leg, and she turned toward the purple-shadow version of Whitemond, noting her companions and their wraithwolves were standing by the mountain already, shouting *ALL ALL ALL* again and again.

The drums seemed louder here, the singing stronger. Even the Caeldish humming was louder, much of it coming from Aikin. It made her happy to see the passion he put into the ancient tune, to see the belief he had in the ways of the Urslan.

Whitemond gave a giant heave, as it had done in her dream within a dream. It was a strange feeling, watching it happen again and knowing how it would all turn out.

It is time to return and usher in a new eryn of understanding, Essiant's mindwords urged.

Shouts of *ALL ALL ALL* in her ears, she joined hands with her companions, envisioning their return to the waking realm.

In a blink it was done. They were back inside their enraptured physical forms, shouting up the mountain for the return of a dragon.

CHAPTER FIFTY-THREE
BETTER THAN NEW

The weakness came upon her like a sudden storm, and for a moment, Xyleea thought she was dying. Her knees buckled and her chest went numb, a loud ringing inside her head. She wondered if she'd been hit by a dart, her hand slapping at her arms and legs for a quill.

The feeling only lasted a moment. She gulped in a breath and straightened the kereet, her gaze shifting sideways. The old deeta's hazed eyes never blinked, her concentration solely on chortling ancient vows of love to the mountain.

The people had moved far back from the mountain's base and its blupping mud pots once the tremors started. Now, instead of one continuous circle, there were segments of hand-holding devotees forming a broken ring. Overhead, the black disk was losing its grip on the bloodheart moon.

Xyleea looked at the faces of the Uniter and her people, now their own distinct group. They looked as her galeesha had looked when she was off in the nevernever, their eyes rolled upward, their expressions unyielding. She looked for the daala in the Uniter's hand, but it was gone. Her heart fell. Had she let down Cree Shee and the ancestors by giving away their most precious treasure to a stranger? The thought gnawed at her stomach as she stared at the Uniter's empty hand.

A mighty rumbling from the mountain interrupted her thoughts. Huge slabs of rock began sliding away, sending up a cloud dense with dust. The cracking away continued, and it was a wonder the people didn't run from the unfolding destruction. Perhaps it was the way the slabs disintegrated into gravel as they subsided that kept the people from panicking. Instead, they sang louder, and beat their drums with more fury.

OORIBOS!

The cry crescendoed as the huge form of a dragon with its tail in its mouth became visible in the red-tinged light beaming down from the half-sized moon.

All thought fled as Xyleea gawked at the sleeping grogakee.

"SING! SING!" The deeta exhorted, her eyes gone bright with purpose. "WELCOME THE GREAT OORIBOS!"

Xyleea glanced toward the Uniter and her group. They too were alive to the emerging dragon, their rigid faces having relaxed into wide-eyed, slack-jawed looks of astonishment.

The air shook, and for a moment, Xyleea thought the weakness had come back, but no, that wasn't it. She looked again at the sleeping dragon. Another crack appeared in the rock, different to the previous ones because it rolled upward, exposing a massive, liquid eye. Xyleea fell to her knees, as did every person around her.

The enormous eye moved back and forth, taking in the scene, before the stone-white lid shuttered down and up.

Another horizontal crack opened, this one half the length of the visible mountain, its edges jagged with sharp lamina. A deafening *POW* and the crack split open, its far end lifting at a giant angle, very like a mouth opening, while a tapering rock talus, very like the end of a huge tail, drew away.

Only then did the grogakee's form come to life, pushing up from the dust and the dirt onto four stout legs, taking with it waxyleaf and scrubthorn, crystalwood and chalumbra vine as it formed into a towering dragon made of every good thing upon the mountain, its mesmeric eyes shining brighter than the sun.

The kereet trembled atop Xyleea's head while deep inside, her heart expanded until her chest ached. A quickening ran up her spine as peace settled like a warm bajee pelt atop the shivering worry that had plagued her all her life.

The great head turned, and the large eye rolled downward, looking straight into her and she dissolved into tears, her throat going tight with gratitude and love, the rest of her vibrating so hard she thought she would explode with happiness.

The grogakee's moss-covered wings unfolded, refolded, then unfolded again before the magnificent dragon took a long step forward and launched into flight, calling out words as he ascended into the sky.

Honor the sisters. Honor the ways.

She mouthed the awkward sounds, wondering what they meant as the grogakee soared out of sight.

Movement at the corner of her eye turned her head toward another miracle: Xyree Muul's bugged eyes staring at the sky from behind a cossiac bush, a ragged line of men from her wasakagee behind him, their eyes white-rimmed, their chins on their chests.

Her overcome mind could only put forward a single word—how? —before turning its attention to a tickling noise inside her ears. It was coming from the Uniter and her people, a low, penetrative hum compelling Xyleea to try and gather her people together.

She paid no mind to the brown-gray wolf lurking nearby when she ran to Xyree. Instead, she took hold of his hands and dragged him toward the nearest Xetili, already forming a ring around what was left of the mountain. She heard the terror in her Ushokan brothers' footsteps as they stumble-ran behind her, felt their panic as they tried to understand.

"Come, Oomree, come, Benru," she cried, letting Xyree's hands go and grabbing the hands of the nearest two men before turning and running to the circle, dragging the reluctant men along, their free arms flapping like the wings of a deleemelee taking flight.

The humming increased as more Xetili flocked forward to join the circle and add their voice to the intentional sound. They had already raised a dragon from a mountain, a feat far beyond Xyleea's wildest imaginings, and yet, the people weren't through. They hummed to what was left of the mountain, and in due time, the remainder answered their call.

Elorah hummed the Prayer Song of the Urslan because Grogauk wanted it.

Honor the sisters. Honor the ways.

The prompting words had floated down like eiderdown when the great good Founder took to the sky.

As soon as she'd begun the song of return, Aikin had joined in. Within moments, Mierrle, Thane, and Haedyn were humming along, as were Brynz and Rachmyn. It felt good to hum the familiar song, memories of her mother and her grandmama and her people wrapping Elorah in a warm embrace.

Soon other voices chimed in, the sound growing louder, the air charging with vibration until the remainder of the mountain began to shake.

The people hummed louder still, as the shaking increased.

The golden-light apparitions of two huge bears lifted away from the top of the mountain and rose into the sky, taking a place either side of the emerging red moon.

"The Urslan twins!" Aikin cried in a voice overwhelmed by emotion.

But that was not an end; it was a beginning. More Urslan rose from the diminished mountain, their sides bulging with fecund loess and shining crystalwood, their heads pointing toward the eastern horizon. One after the other, the giant bear-shapes picked themselves up and set off in the direction of Valenvia, their cumbered bodies surprisingly agile as they gamboled away, the ground shaking from the pound of their rushing paws.

"They're returning to the basin," Aikin's strangled voice managed. "They're returning home."

Elorah turned toward him, her insides trembling with unbearable happiness. Tears streamed down his face as he watched the ancient legend he had known and trusted from his earliest memories coming to life before his astounded eyes.

"It was true," he breathed. "The stories were all true."

Another sight set her insides quaking—Therrania standing tall upon the rocky plain where a mountain had once been, its dust-covered walls intact, its mighty Urslan shape as magnificent as her visions had made it seem.

Instantly, she understood. After the great good Grogauk covered the Therran attunement center with loess, he'd encircled his glorious body around it to further protect it from a world turned upside down. She now understood how terrible the calamity of the Great Destruction must have been all those long eryns ago. In the times since, the Founder and the paramvors of Therra had waited while the world fell, and crawled, and fell, and crawled, and fell again, spiraling downward into a chasm of disharmony and unbelief, a cycle that might have gone on forever had the great good Founder not helped her see a different future.

That she had played a tiny part in the stupendous pageant of Therannia's restoration almost broke her, her feelings of joy and surprise and awe pealing out in waves of laughter.

Aikin started laughing too, gusty guffaws that rattled the dust-filled air. The effect was contagious, the rest of her group breaking into rounds of laughter.

Elorah swiped at her crying eyes, trying to gain control of herself. Whoever heard of a leader overcome by fits of laughter her mind scolded, as another airy chortle burst out.

Only the all-encompassing voice of Grogauk stifled her body's undignified reaction.

Behold!

Elorah's eyes went skyward, her laughter dying in her heaving chest.

Grogauk hovered above the Urslan-shaped monolith, his fantastic, mossed wings undulating to keep him aloft. His giant mouth opened to issue a mighty breath, the Xha of Creation blasting away the dust and grime on Therrania's walls, imbuing them with a deep-blue pulse that grew stronger and brighter with each passing moment until the entire edifice became like a giant sapphire heart, its brilliant blue walls beating with the pulse of a dragon.

Grogauk withdrew his wondrous Xha, his voice ringing out.

The Therrania of old is now better than new!

Wave after wave of vibration emanated from the beating heart of

Therran vor. Elorah could feel the change inside as her own vor aligned with the parambek's perfecting thrum.

Around her, people laughed and danced and embraced with abandon as their bodies absorbed the vitality-inducing waves.

The air shook again.

People of the Keleekeluk, hear my prayer. To you was given the spark of a Dragon, to vouch keep until the day of Restoration. You have served the generations well with your steadfast loyalty and unquestioning faith. To you that Founder now appeals with the greatest humility to do the same for his sacred gateway now resurrected from the dust. Keep it safe from those who wish to despoil or destroy it. For today is both a beginning and an end. A beginning for those who desire peace and an end for those who do not. Know that I am ever near, ready to bring the powers of the realm should they be required, but my presence is needed in many places and in many spheres. Will you accept this charge, as you have done in ages past, to caretake and protect the beating heart of Therrania for this present generation and the generations to come?

The two headdressed leaders, now standing together, threw their hands into the air, then joined one hand each into an exuberant fist-clasp toward the great Dragon. "HEE HUU!" The two women screamed, one old, one young. "HEE HUU! HEE HUU!"

Grogauk lifted away, his forest-clad bulk gliding across the face of the full moon—now a pink pastille nudging the horizon—before sliding past the twinkling star-outlines of twin bears and disappearing into the night.

Elorah looked once again at Therrania, no longer hidden beneath layers of dirt and rock, its pulsing sapphire walls and iridescent blue mud pots like something from a dream. Yet, here it was, right in front of her, better than any dream or imagining, because it was real in a way she could feel, its pulse aligning her forces as nothing had ever done before, not even the centering exercises she'd practiced at the Academie. Those were as nothing compared to the effortless tuning vibrations Therrania put forth.

She looked at Aikin as he basked in the emanating waves, his features peaceful. It was the first time she had ever seen him so relaxed. The other members of the group were celebrating as if they'd stumbled into a fantastic party, but for Aikin, she could see he was being changed into something more than he had been. He jerked his head toward her.

"We did it," he said. She nodded, and he turned his head back toward the parambek. "We actually did it."

Elorah felt herself being swept up into an embrace.

"This is the best day of my entire life!" Haedyn crowed as he whipped her around in a full circle before setting her feet on the ground. She looked into his golden eyes, her heart crashing against her ribs, so that when he bent toward her, she closed her eyes and melted, her mouth finding his. He clutched her close, his lips pressing against hers and setting her head on fire. Too soon, he pulled back and murmured, "Whoa," as he stared into her eyes, the sands of a sun-soaked desert swirling in his golden irises.

KEEEEAAAARRRRR

The distinctive cry shattered the pent atmosphere.

"Zell!" Brynz cried, her head turned toward the eastern sky.

"Chassa Delee!" cried the old woman, one skinny finger pointing upward, her cricked elbow poking into the younger leader's side.

A silver gryphon sailed overhead, completing two full circles above Therrania and sending the handful of people brave enough to have approached the megalith's pulsing walls scurrying back to the safety of the group.

The gryphon landed near the parambek, then bent its beaked head low to clip at one of the brass bands encircling its front legs.

Brynz charged toward the silver-plumed gryphon, before pulling up and curtseying. The gryphon's hindquarters plotzed to the ground like a giant dog as it lowered its head. The tall girl sprang forward and threw her arms around his feathered neck then stepped back and looked at the brass bands, her hands on her hips.

A red-capped dot came circling from the sky, amidst a loud series of calls—*chirrt-chirrt-chirrt.*

"Fryk!" cried Haedyn, breaking away from Elorah to thrust his guarded forearm into the air toward the descending bird.

The grynt ignored him, swooping away and landing near the gryphon before beginning to preen.

"You little monster," Haedyn murmured, hitching his thumb

toward the pocket raptor proudly sat on the ground beside the much larger gryphon as if they were equals in every way. "He's always thought much of himself."

Elorah giggled. "That is certainly true."

Haedyn ducked his chin and looked at her through his lashes. "I hope you know how much I think of you."

"And I of you," Elorah murmured, her hand entwining in his.

He broke into a goofy grin. "Shifting stars! This really is the best day of my life!"

An outburst of Iellian oaths turned both their heads. Brynz, beside one of the gryphon's front legs, pried at the brass band.

"I think Brynz needs help," Elorah said, starting forward.

Haedyn pulled her back. "I'll use my knife," he said, his hand going to his belt as he sprinted away. Brynz held up a hand and barked a command. He stopped then held up his knife, pointing first at the blade then at the band.

Brynz hesitated, her eyes flicking between his knife and Zell before she nodded. She held up a finger, and Haedyn waited as she approached. She took hold of his cloak near the collar, a question in her eyes. He nodded and unclasped the garment before handing it to her.

Her lips creased in grateful acknowledgement as she eased her way to the gryphon, the cloak behind her back, her voice low and soothing. She raised up on her tiptoes to speak into the gryphon's ear tuft, stroking the feathered jaw until its head dropped level with hers.

With adroit ease, she brought the cloak round and flared it atop the gryphon's head, obscuring its eyes before bending across it to keep the wemble in place. She jerked her head twice, signaling for Haedyn to approach.

He hustled forward and, using the tip, drew his red blade down from the top of the band. The gryphon's front leg flew forward, narrowly missing Haedyn's head, the brass band flinging away into the dirt.

Giving the gryphon's front legs a wide berth, Haedyn went round, making a sideward approach this time before sliding the knife tip down the second band. He jerked his head back a wink before the gryphon's leg flew forward, flinging off the second band. He retreated to where Elorah stood watching, the rest of the group clustered around her.

Brynz pulled away the cloak, gave the gryphon's neck a final pat then backed away.

The gryphon got to its feet and shook, plumping its feathers and fluffing its fur, its tail switching, the tufted end thwupping against its shining haunches. The silver wings unfolded, and the gryphon leaped into flight.

Haedyn whistled for Fryk, who had launched into flight a split ahead of the gryphon. After making a wide arc, the bird dove down to land on his upraised forearm.

He turned toward Rachmyn, a proud smile on his face, and fist bumped twice.

The pale-haired man grinned and fist-bumped back, his free hand drifting down to scratch Elgre between the ears, the wolf having emerged from the scrub.

Elorah smiled at her family as they stared at the sapphire parambek they had helped uncover. They stood in tattered clothing, their faces flecked with dirt, their bodies whittled down to gristle and bone, but that wasn't what she saw. Instead, she saw six pairs of eyes shining bright with accomplishment and purpose, six proud figures standing tall before a sight none had ever dreamed they'd see. Together, they'd done the impossible. Because of them the history books would need rewriting. The veneration tomes would need revising. The Valenvian Council would need restructuring. The Iellian monarchy would need rebuffing. Because of them, Therran voricians had a place of revival. Caeldish croplands had a means for renewal. Because of them, when the sun broke above the line of the horizon, its light would shine on a better place than the one it had left the night before. Because of them, the world was changed.

CHAPTER FIFTY-FOUR
A DIFFERENT HORIZON

Essiant howled into the misty dawn, relishing the resonant light of the starshine around him. It was one of the many changes wrought by the restoration of Therannia both here in Oru Fen and on Eolemar.

To see the return of the Urslan paramvors to their native environs, taking with them the fertile soils and rich minerals that had been missing for so long gave him much pleasure. To know that Caeldish emvors had guided their return using long-banned crystalwood staffs to connect with the crystalwood-clad Urslans gave him greater pleasure still.

The banishment of the Wycche had been another welcome development. It was temporary, to be sure, for a forgetting mindshield did not work forever, but for now, the realm was far less accessible to her and her wraithwolf than it had been for eryns. It would give the Erynvor and her group time to assess the grandness of what had been accomplished as well as the enormity of what remained to be done. So too it would give the Voriens time to recover from their recent expenditures.

Essiant gazed at his pack members—Embren, Spectra, Kelm, Ajai, Ieeva—as they kept watch over their night-wards. Only Kimbre had drifted away, his night-ward returning to her village to lead its people into the future she had made for them. The wraithwolf had thanked the Voriens for their many favors before trotting off toward a different horizon.

While Essiant kept his attention on his night-ward, and was glad for her success, he knew there were other challenges ahead. The restoration of one vibration, while a critical first step, did not prevent other imbalances from arising in response. Even now, forces were shifting, in both the constructs of societies and within Eolemar itself. Essiant could already see the effects of Therrania's restoration. Many things would become better, but some things would become worse. It was in the nature of things that this should happen until the remaining four parambeks were restored. But that was a worry for a different day. For now, it was enough to give thanks to Primeryn Vor for seeing them through the hard times and to the Elect for preserving the Way.

The orucon shifted beneath his paws, and he peered into the middle distance where the fiery Xha of another great Founder was opening a pathway to a different place. A knowing settled, quickening his internal forces.

The next step of the Restoration was already begun...

Glossary Of Terms

ACADEMIE VORIK — Renowned school for emvors located in the northwest region of the Valenvian basin.

AFFINITY — The strongest of the individual energy centers (params) in a particular soul. Allows a soul to access the powers of an elemental force (air, water, fire, earth, shadow, spirit).

AGYA — Third Eye of Guardian Dragons, currently in care of keepers away from the parambek for the five broken parambeks. Must be used when restoring a parambek to resurrect the dragon to its original state.

AMLYN — A silky overcoat issued to students at the Academie Vorik, color coded to reflect the level and affinity of study – light to dark green for Therran, light to dark red for Fyrre, light to dark blue for Atmos and light to dark turquoise for Aquilla, light to dark purple for instructors.

ANCIENTS — Eolemar's first inhabitants who lived before the Great Destruction, participated in the mythical battle between the forces for ALL and the forces for self.

APOGENT — 10th year student at the Academie Vorik.

AQUILLA — one of the six elemental affinities. Associated with forces of emotion.

AQUILLAN — A soul with the Aquilla affinity.

ARCANA — Ancient lorecraft used by the ancients. Neither good nor evil, but capable of being used by souls for either purpose.

AROCOL — Vorestone for Atmosians (air affinities). A bright, crystalline stone with prismatic qualities.

ASTR STELL — Founding Shadowe Dragon.

ASTR VEN — Founding Spyrrt Dragon.

ATMOS — One of the six elemental affinities. Associated with forces of vitality. The connector between the "lower" elemental forces (ground, fire, water) and the "higher" elemental forces (mind, spirit).

ATMOSIAN — A soul with the Atmos affinity.

AVOBANC — Soft white stone used extensively for stone shaping. A predominant feature of Whitemond.

BAIRTTRAIGH — A Founding clan of Valenvia.

BAJEE — Large mountain sheep with a reddish-brown fleece. Lives in the temperate rain forest.

BARBARIANS — Term used interchangeably with Drasgor. Indigenous peoples of the northern range of the Blackshale mountains and the northern tundras. Tribes are rumored to be fiercely warlike and brutal.

BASIN (THE) — Colloquial term for Valenvia.

BEEKA — Ushokan term for crazy; mentally unhinged.

BERRE — A bear-shaped fetish, formed of packed soil. After forming the berre, most families embellish it with other natural elements (rocks for eyes, moss or leaves for fur, etc.). Caeldish believe this fetish ensures a plentiful crop and prosperous year.

BLACKSHALE MOUNTAINS — Mountain range that borders the Basin along its eastern and northern borders.

BRAVIK — Fearsome beast of the northlands. The body of a large bear and the long legs of a large wolf with large teeth and poisonous claws.

BRUNNESTONE — Vorestone for Therrans.

BRUSHY-TAILED FOX — Native canid predator of the Blackshales and regions north.

CALLIAIGH — A clan of Valenvia, Not the most powerful, but a clan of seers and sages who still wield power and hold an honored seat on the Valenvian Council of Clans.

CHALUMBRA — A climbing vine with large, pearlescent-gold trumpet-shaped flowers. Native to Whitemond.

CHASSA — A predatory cat of temperate rain forests. Spends most of its time in the tree canopy. Mottled coats are patterned to resemble trees. Swift and silent, a master of camouflage, expert climber, nimble, with plush paws that make its footfalls undetectable even at a full sprint.

CHUULZU — Ushokan term for the spirit force.

CHUULZU DEETA — Spiritual leader of a Ushokan wasakagee.

CHUULZU KEREET — Ushokan term for the ceremonial headress of a Deeta.

CLANS OF VALENVIA — Bairttraigh, Calliaigh, Rairrsaigh, Fola, Thrast, Hiegh, Gorst

CRAGDOG — Ground dwelling rodent that lives in large underground communities. Easy to catch. A favored food of the Drasgor.

CRYSTALWOOD — A special tree renowned for its crystal-like wood which stores and amplifies vor along with intention. Grows most prolifically on Whitemond.

DAALA — Ushokan term for the highly esteemed orb of the grogakee.

DELEEMELEE — Carrion bird of the mountains, sporting a dark grey, nearly naked head, blue-green eyes and beautiful, golden feathers. Ushoku religious tradition hold this bird as a symbol of both the transience and duality of life.

DRASGOR — Brutish peoples of the northlands.

ELECT (THE) — Collective of Founding Dragons who, in cooperation with Primeryn Vor, co-created Eolemar, and its affinity-based power centers (parambeks). Composed of Astr Ven (Spyrrt), Astr Stell (Shadowen), Finnaila Brex (Atmos), Murathia (Aquilla), BeORNon (Fyrre), and Grogauk (Therra).

ELEQUIA (KINGDOM OF) — Northern kingdom to the east of Iellia.

EMVOR — Stock term for a sentient being with the ability to utilize and harness natural and universal laws in combination with their own vor to effect apparently supernatural changes.

EMVORITE — Student of Vorik at the Academie Vorik.

EPIGENT — Years 5-8 student at the Academie Vorik.

EOLEMAR — The Blue Planet, also known as the Blue-Eyed Sister. Purported to have been created along with the Amber Planet at the founding of the worlds in Caeldish mythology and religious tradition where each planet serves as the eye of a celestial Urslan twin.

ETHERIANT — subtle, soul-level energy. Provides the basis for vorik.

ETTS — Drasgorian term for clan groupings. These are loose associations that can shift depending upon political leanings etc. and are never considered a permanent designation.

ERYN — A cycle of time that starts with the entrance of an Erynvor and ends the moment before a new Erynvor incarnates.

FAKA — Ushokan for jungle plant with psychotropic properties, used to increase willpower.

FALDING — a clanless inhabitant of Valenvia, a person whose standing and protection are obtained through labor contracts.

FOLA — A Founding Clan of Valenvia.

FYRREFEN — The paramvor (spirit animal) of the Fyre affinity. A giant bird composed of flames.

FYRRE — One of the six elemental affinities. Associated with forces of the will. Also, the term for those with the Fyrre affinity.

GALEESHA — Ushokan term for a female grandparent; Also, a respectful term for a female elder.

GIMCHEE — Small- to medium-sized woody shrub native to temperate rainforests. Seeds are highly aromatic as well as flammable and prized in many cultures.

GOLDEN MINKEE — A primate native to broadleaf forests. Has short, brassy fur with cream-colored triangular tufts of hair where the ears are and cream-colored hair on the face with a fluffy tail twice as long as its hand-sized body. Large golden-brown eyes. Arboreal, eats small insects, fruit.

GORST — A Founding Clan of Valenvia

GORU ROOT — Starchy tuber consumed by indigenous peoples of the temperate jungle.

GREAT DESTRUCTION — The mythical battle between the forces for the All and the forces for Self that occurred in the time of the Ancients.

GROGAKEE — Ushokan term for "Dragon of the Mountain" (see GROGAUK).

GROGAUK — Founding Therra Dragon.

GRYNT — A black-eyed pocket falcon with deeply black plumage, a black beak, black legs, black talons, and a bright red head crest. Native to southland deserts.

GRYPHLING — Immature gryphon.

GRYPHON — Large raptor with the hindquarters and tail of a predatory cat and the head, front talons, and wings of a predatory raptor. Mature males are eight feet at the shoulder and mature females are 6 to 7 feet at the shoulder.

GRYPHONMARE — Female breeding gryphon.

HALLETT STONE — Deeply black crystalline stone, often used as a scrying stone.

HIEGH — A Founding Clan of Valenvia.

HIGH HELLS — Caeldish slang term for the High Iellian Guards, the fighting force of Iellia, the protectorate nation occupying Valenvia.

HOEWLER — A specialized whistle-like device used by Shadowen dreamcrafters to align the orusphere to their personal energy signature prior to dream manipulations.

HUUL WAAL — Ushokan term for inner fortitude.

IELLIA — Nation centered in the Blackshale mountain renowned for their scholarly endeavor and refined culture. Have served in the capacity of Protectorate Ruler of Valenvia for several annums at the invitation of a majority of the Valenvian clans.

INFINITE EYE — See AGYA

INVERNA — The unseen ethereal spirit realm, the home of Primeryn Vor-The One Above ALL.

INVERNA PASS — Ancient route through the Lawless Mountains leading to the Valenvian Basin.

IRLEMAR — The Amber Planet, also known as the Amber-Eyed Sister. Purported to have been created along with the Amber Planet at the founding of the worlds in Caeldish mythology and religious tradition where each planet serves as the eye of a celestial Urslan twin.

JARNY — A traveling food consisting of two slices of bread with meat and/or cheese between.

KELEEKELUK — Ushokan term for wilderness/forest/jungle.

KELFULD — Drasgorian term that roughly translated means "one of us".

KEMEEKEMEE — Ushokan term for sacred bag, usually leather, that holds a Deeta's auguries.

KRYCHLE — A docile species of tiny lizard that can fly despite the relatively small surface area of their translucent, folding wings in relation to their body length. Have a chirping song that is melodic and a good predictor of weather, as their high-pitched tone will lower when a storm is approaching. Native to the southland deserts, they are kept as pets by people from other areas for weather prediction and companionship.

LONGESSE — A subgroup of Malvisse wraithwolves whose nightwards are aristocrats and/or politically powerful.

MEREQUIS — Paramvor (spirit animal) for Aquillans. Has a form reminiscent of a horse, with front hooves of pearlescent gold, a strong fish-like tail, and a coat of scales composed of a myriad of colors and patterns. Their manes and tails echo the sea plants and corals of their home sea (can vary depending on climate and location.)

MOUNTAIN HARE — Rabbit species endemic to the mountainous regions.

NIGHT-WARD — The term used for soul bodies in the care of wraithwolf guardians in Oru Fen.

NIGHTJOLLY — Term for shadowen dreamcrafters, especially those with no real skill.

NOVICE — Years 1-4 students at the Academie Vorik.

OORIBOOS — Ushokan/Xetili term for Supreme Deity, symbolized by a huge snake swallowing its own tail.

ORU FEN — Secondary ethereal realm co-existent with the manifest realm of Eolemar. The realm of dreams and thought.

ORUCON — Mystical substrate in Oru Fen, conductor of vor energy.

ORUSPHERE — Vibrations in Oru Fen.

PARAM — One of six internal life energy focal points whereby a manifest body can connect to the elements (ground, fire, water, air, mind, spirit) of the wider world and access their powers. All manifest bodies contain six params with one being dominant (their affinity). In the case of an Erynvor, all six params are equally powerful, a condition that is known as the Original State.

PARAMBEK — An affinity attunement center created on Eolemar as a gift to the creations by the One Above All and the Founding Dragons for the purpose of purifying and strengthening an individual soul's natal affinity. Six parambeks were created during the time of the Ancients, one for each elemental affinity, to maintain the balance of individuals as well as the wider world of Eolemar.

PARAMVOR — A spirit-level guide and protector who appears in the form of a fantastical animal (a different form for each affinity). Cannot interfere with the free will of souls. Has limited ability to manipulate the environment.

PRIMERYN VOR — Originating Force; also known as the One Above All.

RABBOUT — A small, often make-shifted sailing vessel used by Rabboutiers. Can have sails and/or oars. Is usually too small for open sea travel.

RABBOUTIERS — Freebooters who spend most of their lives as rogue sailors, running less-than-lawful schemes to acquire high-value goods which they barter/sell using middlemen.

SAPPHIRE — Brunnestone that has been Xha-purified and appears as a vibrant, deeply blue stone. Main component of Therrania.

SASKA — The soul energy between a wraithwolf and its ward in the dreamtime realm of Oru Fen.

SHADOWE — One of the six elemental affinities. Associated with forces of the mind.

SHADOWEN — A soul with the Shadowe affinity. Often viewed with suspicion and disfavor by non-Shadowe affiliated souls.

SHILK — a short healing rod used to effectively channel vorik energy in a concentrated manner, often made of tenderwood.

SOLIMAR — Caeldish term for the sun.

SPYRRT — One of the six elemental affinities. Associated with forces of the spirit/soul. Also, the term for a soul with the Spyrrt affinity.

SWEETSWEET — Liquor made from fermented sweetcane stalks. Highly sought after.

TENDERWOOD — Shrub native to all temperate regions. Wood

highly prized by emvors for redirecting auric energies and the forces of vor.

THERRA — One of the six elemental affinities. Associated with the grounding of impulses.

THERRAN — A soul with the Therra affinity.

THERRANIA — Therran Parembek. A monolith of hewn brunnestone slabs arranged in a bear-shaped maze (atop Whitemond). When imbued with Xha, the brunnestone transforms into sapphire, a superconductor of magnetic forces that speed healing by rebalancing body polarity and electro-neural transmission.

THILLE — Consecrated soil used to form Urslan bear fetishes.

THRAST — A Founding Clan of Valenvia.

TUSKEE — A thick-skinned herbivorous pachyderm with sparse, dark brown fur marked by faint cream striping at the top of the legs; a topknot of silky brown hair; short ivory tusks; a mobile, one-fingered trunk; large, fan-shaped ears; intelligent brown eyes; and flat-bottomed round feet.

URSLAN — The majestic bear paramvor of the Therra affinity. Also features in the Eolemar creation story of the Caeldish peoples.

USHOKU — Native peoples indigenous to the dry upland forests surrounding Whitemond. Also known as "The People". Traditional rivals of the Xetili peoples.

VALENVIA — Alternatively known as "The Basin". The large fertile valley bordered by the Blackshale mountains to the east and part of the north, the Lawless Mountains to the west, the Dallovian Plains to the south and the Drasgorian tundra also to the north.

VERGRIZE — The personal lorebook of Therran Emvors; a collection of botanical notes, compounds, concoctions, and various healing methodologies.

VIEXHA — The raw and untamed divination of Vorik from supreme self-belief and perfect unity with the energy of the All. The life energy of Eolemar as a whole that can be accessed by highly evolved souls. Usually drawn in through the feet and up through the individual energy centers (params) located along the spine of physical creations to the Spyryt center located behind the third eye.

VOR — Soul energy, an internally produced component directly related to a soul's enlightenment. The more enlightened, the higher an individual's level of vor. This is not a measure of "purity" or "goodness" nor does its power correlate with those things. This is a measure of understanding of universal laws. Can be used for good or ill.

VORESTONE — Naturally occurring stones for each affinity used by envores to attune their vor in order to augment their vorik abilities.

VORICIAN — Practitioner/adept of Vor.

VORIE SUPIN — Arcana whereby vorik is involuntarily usurped from one soul to benefit another. The practice of stealing lifeforce energy from sleeping souls using deception, potions and Malvisse wraithwolves in the realm of Oru Fen.

VORIEN LEAGUE — Loose association of wraithwolves who work together to promote peace and understanding in Oru Fen. Their ultimate goal is the enlightenment of all souls within the Eolemaran realm and a permanent reunitement of all souls with Primeryn Vor.

VORIK — Manifestation of vor powers.

WANDERING SILVI — Ubiquitous, low-growing herb known for its healing powers.

WASAKA — Ushokan term for dwelling/abode/hut.

WASAKAGEE — Ushokan term for village/collection of wasakas

WEMBLE — A thermo-shifting fabric woven from Wemb silk.

WHITEMOND — Fabled standalone mountain peak located north and west of the Lawless Mountain range; home to a large Crystalwood forest.

WITTERANG — Traditional round structure of the Caeldish; usually has a thatched roof and natural elements as decoration/accoutrements.

WOLFKEN — The crystallized distillate of the Wolfshead orchid. Used by Shadowen to temporarily narcotize wraithwolfs in Oru Fen and facilitate dreamcrafting.

WOLFSHEAD ORCHID — A petite vining orchid with a wolf-head shaped, velvety flower. Black fading to dark purple around its pollinia, with a pair of yellow splotches that mimic the shape of wolf eyes on the petals. Skilled crafters use this orchid in the making of wolfken.

WRAITHWOLF —Paramvor of the Shadowe affinity. Serve as guardians and mentors in Oru Fen.

XETILI — Native peoples indigenous to the dry upland forests surrounding Whitemond. Traditional rivals of the Ushoku peoples. Also known as "People of the Blue Mud" due to their use of blue mud for ceremonial purposes as well as for warrior paint.

XHA — The purifying breath of the Elect, (The World Founding Affinity dragons). during the creation of the Parambeks.

PRONUNCIATION GUIDE

AHNKNE — AHNK-neh
AIKIN — AY-ken
AJAI — a-JI
AKTAL — AK-tal
ALLEU — ah-LOO
ALLIARI — ah-lee-AIR-ee
ANDYRRIA — an-DEER-ee-ah
AQUILLA — ah-QUIL-ah
ARLOT — AR-lut
ARWYN — AR-win
ASTR VEN — A-streh VEN
ASTR STELL — A-streh STEL
ATMOS — AT-mohs
BAI — Bi
BELEDAL —BEL-eh-dal
BENKRE — BEN-kruh
BAIRRTRAIGH — BAY-err-tray
BRYNZ — BRINZ
CAELDISH — KAYL-dish

CALLIAIGH — KAL-lee-ay
CASIELLE — ka-SHEL
CHALLYN — CHAL-lin
CHRYSOLAN — KRIS-uh-lan
CHUULZU — CHOOL-zoo
CREE SHEE — KREE SHEE
CYRULIAN — si-ROOL-ee-an
DAALA — DAY-lah
DAELL — di-EL
DAI — Di
DELEEMELEE — deh-LEE-meh-lee
DRASGOR —DRAZ-gor
DYSETHERIA — dis-eh-THEER-ee-ah
ECCTO — EK-to
ELEQUIA — eh-LEK-wee-ah
ELGRE — ELL-gruh
ELORAH — eh-LORE-ah
EMBREN— EM-bren
EOLEMAR — ee-OH-luh-mar
ERYN —AIR-en
ERYNVOR —AIR-en-vor
ESSIANT — ESS-ee-ant
FALLA — FAH-la
FLAYE — FLAY-eh
FOLA — FOH-lah
FROIGH — FRAHF
FRYK — FRIK
FYNND —FIHND
FYRRE —FI-er
GAEN — GI-en
GARROD — gah-ROD
GETABIT — GET-ah-bit
GHIELLE — gee-ELL
GNAR — NAR
GORSH — GORSH
GROGAKEE — GROH-gah-kee

GROGAUK — GRO-gok
GRYNT — GRINT
GRYSLIEK — GREEZH-lik
HAEDYN — HAY-din
HEBEDIAH — heb-e-DI-ah
HRUL — HROOL
HUUL WAAL — HOOL WALL
IELLIA — i-ELL-ee-ah
JAZH — ZHJAZH
JIMPKINS — JIMP-kins
KAAMBREE —KAYM-bree
KEARYN — kee-AR-en
KELEEKELUK — ke-LEE-ke-luk
KELM—KELM
KEMEEKEMEE — ke-MEE-ke-mee
KEREET — ke-REET
KHIN — KEEN
KIMBRE — KIM-bruh
KRUSZK —KROOSHK
LEMAL — lem-ALL
LONGESSE — lon-JES
LUCHMYN — LOOK-mun
LUMINAE — LOOM-en-ay
MAARATHIA — mah-ah-RAHTH-ee-ah
MALENVIE — mah-LEN-vee
MALVISSE —mal-VEES
MIERRLE — MI-eer-eh-luh
MOUK — MOWK
NOVAH — NOH-vah
OORIBOS — OH-rih-bos
ORU FEN - OH-roo FEN
PARAMBEK —PAIR-em-bek
PARAMVOR —PAIR-em-vohr
PERRENT — peh-RENT
PFOLAN — FO-lan
PRIMERYN VOR — Pri-MAIR-en VOHR

QUELP —KWELP
RABBOUT — rah-BOOT
RABBOUTIER — rah-boo-TEER
RACHMYN — ROCK-min
RAIRRSAIGH — RAYER-say
RAYA — RAY-uh
RENNESSEAU — REN-eh-soo
RODRIC — ROD-rik
RYLAN — RI-lan
SASKA — SAS-ka
SEBAZGH — se-BAZJ
SPECTRA — SPEK-trah
SYBA — SEE-bah
SPYRRT —SPEER-it
STULKO — STUL-koh
TENZE — TEN-zeh
THANE — THAYN
THERRA —THER-ah
THRAST — THRAST
UHNKRE — OON-kreh
UHNLEN — OON-len
UMBRAE — OOM-bri
URSLAN — UR-slan
USHOKU — you-SHOW-koo
VALENVIA - vah-LEN-vee-ah
VAYTAH —VAY-tah
VENGE — VENJ
VOR —VOHR
VORIEN — VOHR-ee-en
VORIE SUPIN —VOHR-ee SOO-pin
WHINDON WOOD — WIN-don WOOD
WRYNNE — RIN
WYCCHE — WICH
WYDDERHALLE —WI-der-hall
XETILI — zheh-TEE-lee
XHA — ZHAH

XYLEEA — zi-LEE-ah
ZELL — ZEL
ZENZ — ZENZ
ZENZAE — ZEN-zay
ZEPHYRRIA — ze-FEER-ee-ah

ACKNOWLEDGMENTS

We are incredibly grateful for the many people who supported us as we shaped our dreams into an actual book. First and foremost, to Greg (Dad), our paterfamilias who believed in us even when we didn't believe in ourselves—we love you beyond measure. Your unwavering enthusiasm pulled us through. To Chris and Jose, thank you for always understanding when we needed to take time away for yet another all-day book session. Your patience is so appreciated and we love you both in more ways than we can say.

To our beta readers, we can't thank you enough. For Jacob, your encouragement meant the world to us as we slogged our way through the sagging middle. For Merri Mike, your expert notes both humbled and inspired us. For Denise, we can't put into words how special your friendship has been to us over the years. And for our family and friends, we cherish each and every one of you.

To our teachers and mentors, we owe you so much. For our editor, George, thank you for your kindness and clarity. For our cover artist, Jeff, thank you for capturing our vision perfectly and for working us into your very busy schedule. And for our critique partners who shared their expertise and wisdom along the way, thank you for caring enough to make us better.

To our advanced readers who volunteered to read and review for us, thank you for the extraordinary gift of your time. Your generosity of spirit is truly appreciated.

And finally, to you, our reader, thank you. We couldn't do this without you.

—*Three Scribes*

Three Scribes are a mother/daughters writing team consisting of Sandra Mead Miller (Mama Scribe), Abigail Bender (Artsy Scribe), and Victoria Hungria (Extra Scribe).

Sandra, in addition to writing about dragons, is an avid supporter of Liverpool F.C., a keeper of hens, and a smiter of non-native flora in her two-acre wood.

Abigail and Victoria began building the secondary world of Eolemar in elementary school, a hobby they've continued for over two decades. Abigail is also a tea connoisseur, an artist, and an admirer of mycorrhiza. Victoria is a hometown festival goer and bookshop enthusiast for whom cozy isn't just a favorite genre, it's a lifestyle.

VISIT OUR WEBSITE FOR
EXCLUSIVE CONTENT AND RESOURCES

www.three-scribes.com